COCKTALES

THE COCKY COLLECTIVE

Print Edition
978-1-949202-01-4

FOREWORD

BY NANA MALONE

Tribes.

It's a word that has always fascinated me. I think it's because when I was a kid, my family moved around a lot and I never felt as if I had that group of folks who had the same shared experiences. I was always an outsider. A solo nomad.

In the last few weeks, that has all changed. Without much effort on my part, I found my tribe. I met a fabulous group of women—many of whom I honestly squealed about when I said their names aloud—who let me into their circle. I'm not sure how I got invited into this group (that's a lie, I totally know and THANK YOU—you know who you are) but I am so grateful.

And now, my tribe had grown by leaps and bounds, all because of one word: Cocky.

If you are reading this forward, it is very likely that you have heard about #cockygate and how a romance author trademarked a common word (cocky). For those of you just joining this little party, basically, if this trademark goes unchallenged, my understanding is that no author will be allowed to use the word "cocky" in a book title, retroactively from June 16, 2016 until forever.

You're probably wondering what this has to do with me, right? Well, I was messaged by this author a few weeks ago, just prior to the first book in my new series being published. My original series titles were perfect for the stories—which are about a swaggering, arrogant prince—and were perfect for my brand, which is sexy, smart romantic comedy.

The original titles were: *Cocky Prince, Cocky Royal,* and *Cocky King.* After years of writing and planning and working, I had the perfect titles, three amazing covers, and all the excitement I felt for this series.

I was ready to make this my breakout series.

I thought I'd done everything right—I'd even networked!

Shudder

(Seriously, I'm actually pretty shy.)

Five days before the reveal of the hottest covers I'd ever seen in my life, I got a notice from this author claiming I had copied her covers and her brand and that she was ready and willing to defend it to the "full extent" (i.e., take legal action).

How had this happened? I'd never heard of this author or her books before. Her message completely blindsided me. I have sixty-five books published, and not once . . . not ever, had anything like this happened before.

I did what any other author would do. I cried. There were tears. I howled. There may have been some screaming. I begged advice from this new band of women who, let me be clear, were shocked and flipping commiseration tables of frustration at my bad luck.

None of them had heard of anything like this happening either.

And then I got smart. I called a friend and said, "What is the name of your lawyer again? I need to make a call." Then I cried and bitched and complained to the lawyer.

Long story short, I was told that, while the claim was shaky, it was somewhat defensible, so unless I had a pile of money to burn, it was in my best interest to change my titles.

So, I bit the bullet and changed my covers two days before the reveal. No lie, that cover designer, AMY DAWS, is a saint. She made so many versions of that book cover it was unbelievable.

The next thing I did was get ahold of some other authors who had the word "cocky" in their titles. These were women I'd never met or talked to or shared a drink with at conferences, but I tried to warn them. Some I couldn't easily find, but those I did were appreciative, even though they hadn't had any trouble by that point.

So *Cheeky Prince*, *Cheeky Royal*, and *Cheeky King* were born. And you know what? Thanks to that newfound tribe, those books rocked! These women I barely knew shared and pimped me out like crazy. They put me in their newsletters and made blood pacts that my books would kill.

I moved on, occasionally grumbling to my poor husband, but I had let it go. I was mostly still mad about the funds I'd paid to my new lawyer just to find out this was a fight I couldn't win without tens of thousands of dollars to spend on legal fees.

And then, guess what?

A month later, all hell broke loose. One of the authors I'd warned weeks prior had been hit with a trademark infringement notice.

From Audible.

It seemed as if the Cocky ™ author had bypassed the fair warning cease and desist she'd sent me and started trying to take books down from vendors directly.

Some people said, "Don't change your title, she has no claim." Others said, "You don't have to do anything; it's bogus." But when someone is holding your livelihood for ransom, you'll do what you have to do to get it back, even if that means changing your original title. In my opinion, this Cocky ™ author knew that.

Overnight, several authors reported to the author community that takedown notices had been sent to Amazon for their books. Some had books removed, and some had their future revenue threatened. I guess that was the gong heard 'round the world.

Romancelandia came out swinging.

That group of women I told you about? My new tribe? They decided to let themselves be heard in the only way that mattered. They took action, have volunteered their time and words, and have reached out to others willing to do the same. They have brought you the cockiest of stories, *Cocktales*.

The goal for this anthology is for the proceeds to go where they will do the most good—helping the authors who have been impacted to fight back.

I must pause here and say thank you to Cassie Sharp for the eloquent and kind open letter she penned (if you haven't read it yet, read her blog about this issue), because it helped me find some compassion.

To these women who have taken action, I say thank you. Thank you for being my tribe. Thank you to the romance community. Thank you to RWA for your advocacy. Thank you to the readers. And thank you to those who have no skin in this game but see the terrifying precedent and have stood up to fight this fight.

Stay cocky, my friends.
Nana Malone

ABOUT THE COCKTALES ANTHOLOGY

'Cocktales' is a limited-release anthology (available *only* from May 26 – August 26, 2018) of original, never before published material, some of which is raw and unedited. Each story was specifically written for this anthology.

The goal of the Cocktales Anthology is to raise funds to fight against obstruction of creative expression. Specifically, what we believe are obstruction attempts through the trademarking of common (single) words for titicular use in books / or as a book series (eBooks, print, and audio).

ALL net profits will be donated to:

1. Authors already impacted by creative-obstruction, and
2. Advocacy for all authors of all genres against obstruction of creative expression.

COCKED AND LOADED

DYLAN ALLEN

Getting revenge on her childhood crush, turned tormentor, is has been Maria's dream for twenty years. But, when she finally gets her chance, will she be able to resist him long enough to see her plans through.

ONE

CockedandLoaded: Let's meet tonight.
LusciousCutiePie: Why the rush?
CockedandLoaded: It's been two weeks. Hardly a rush sweetheart. In fact, this is the longest I've ever talked to someone before I meet them.
LusciousCutiePie: Good things cum to those who wait.
CockedandLoaded: You're all talk. Meet me tonight. Or, I'm done.

I groan and glare at my phone. "You're such an asshole," I say through gritted teeth.

"Ummm, you know he can't see or hear you, right?" My roommate Tina drawls in disgust from the couch she's curled up on reading.

"Yes, I know," I say with more than a little annoyance and shoot her a dirty look.

"Don't scowl at me," she admonishes me "This plan of yours is ridiculous. I don't know why you think any of this is a good idea."

"I hate him," I say as I contemplate my phone. His message blinks up at me and I press the home button to clear it from my screen. "You don't understand," I whine and fling myself into one of the red plastic chairs that we use for our supposedly art nouveau dining table. It just looks like discarded tat from a family reunion in 1989.

"I understand *perfectly*. I just think it's a moronic idea. I also think you're going to be sorry. You should let it go and get on with your life."

"I've been waiting since I was thirteen years old for this," I say in exasperation. I hear how childish I sound.

"It's ridiculous that at the age of thirty-two, you're still carrying a grudge from middle school, Maria," she says without looking away from her book.

3

"Yeah, well, forgive me if I can't get over being called Maria Diarrhea from the age of eleven until I was thirteen." I don't care how petulant I sound, I feel justified in holding on to my anger.

She lets out a low whistle. "*Daaaaamn*. That shit stuck, huh?" She says and then drops her book down enough to reveal her eyes.

"No pun intended," she says. And even though I can't see her mouth, I know it's turned up in an unsympathetic mocking smirk.

"Laugh all you want. I'm going to finish this. Confront him and get it out of my system."

"Sure. Tell yourself that," she mutters disinterestedly, and turns the page of her book.

"What could go wrong. I'll go meet him, let him get all lathered up, tell him who I am and walk off." I say. The satisfaction I'm anticipating puts an easy smile on my face.

Tina puts her book down and shakes her head at me piteously.

"What?" I snap at her, making my eyes wide, "Just say it."

She narrows her eyes and stares at me thoughtfully. I'm just about to tell her to forget it when she says, "Has it ever occurred to you that he knows exactly who you are? You recognized him right away. What makes you think he didn't recognize you?"

I roll my eyes and bat this complete impossibility away.

"Well one, I don't have a mouth full of metal and eyes the size of silver dollars because of my coke bottle lenses anymore, acne and a head full of hair that looked like tumbleweed most of the time. And besides," I sigh in disgust, "I was probably just one of the hundreds of kids he tortured in his teens, I bet he doesn't even remember the stupid nickname he and his dumb friends called me."

"Okay, well then, why have you been putting off meeting him?"

"I'm not putting it off. I just want more time."

"Those are the same thing," she rolls her eyes in exaggerated impatience and covers her face with her book.

I cross my arms over my chest and pout in her direction. "You could be a little more sympathetic, you know. I'm *freaking out* here." I run an agitated hand through my hair. "I never thought I'd have a chance to pay him back for what he did. And now, I do. I'm not going to let your poopooing ruin this for me."

"By all means, ignore me. Walk into that burning building. I get all your shoes, though if you don't come back in one piece."

"Yeah, go ahead and laugh, I'm going to get this over with," I stand up and unlock my phone.

LusciousCutiePie: Fine, tonight. Text me where and I'll be there.
CockedandLoaded: You text me your address. I'm going to pick you up.
LusciousCutiePie: No. I've watched enough television to know better than to get into cars with strange men. Next thing I know, I'll be in some container crossing the border to be harvested for my kidneys. No thanks. I'm getting in the shower. When I get out, I'll check for the address. If you haven't sent it, date's off.
CockedandLoaded: Your imagination is pretty wild. Also, you're cute when you

think you're in charge. But, you're right. I'll let you have this one. Texting information in a minute. See you later.

"Maria, one. Chuck, zero," I say to myself as I turn the shower on to heat up. I strip in front of the mirror and look at myself with a critical eye. I see a woman who looks good for her age. Years of weight watchers and three times a week on my Pilates reformer have left me with excellent posture, a flat stomach, a tight ass and fantastic arms.

My hair's thick, lustrous texture is due to an army of vitamins, regular visits to my very expensive hairdresser for a ruthless color and cut that keeps my naturally nondescript light brown hair a vibrant, shimmering copper.

No way he'd recognize the girl whose heart he'd shattered with a few cruel, careless words.

I haven't shared that part with Tina. It's not just the nickname. It's what I overheard him say to a room full of his friends about me.

I had a crush on him. A *big* one. He was the cutest boy in our class and we'd been paired together for our first science project of sixth grade. He had been nice to me. We walked home together a few times after the project was over. I thought we were friends.

Every day, he and a group of his friends huddled in one of the stairwells in the north wing of our huge school. They skipped study hall every day to practice their dance moves instead. I went to watch. They never knew I was there and it was one of my favorite things. Watching Chuck moonwalk, pop and lock, and sometimes, they would even rap rhymes they'd made up.

Then, one day, someone asked him if he was ready for our big history test the next day. He mentioned that we were studying that evening. I felt the familiar squeeze in my chest that came every time I remembered how I'd been crushed by his betrayal. I rub my chest absently and drift back to that awful day.

"Why do you go to that girl's house every night? She's fugly," one of the boys says in a jockeying voice. Its jovial tone is in such sharp contrast to the wicked words he's speaking that it takes a second for them to register. My hand flies to my mouth and covers it just in time to stifle the gasp that a swift rush of hurt forces out of my chest.

But nothing prepares me for the way it feels to hear Chuck say, in an equally jovial voice, "She's too ugly to eat lunch with, so I have to wait until the sun sets before we can study together."

A sledgehammer collides with my heart and shatters it into a million pieces. I feel lightheaded. I don't have to cover my mouth, there's no air in my lungs to propel any words or sounds. When my vision blurs, I close my eyes and try to clear it. Tears, hot and unwelcome, roll out of the corner of my eyes and trail down my cheeks. Their laughter sounds like a horrible echo and I'm not sure if they're still laughing or if the sound is trapped in my head.

I'm overwhelmed by the sudden need to leave. I force myself up on shaky legs and cling to the rail as I climb up the stairs toward the fourth floor.

"Man, thank God. I was worried you were kissing Maria Diarrhea after school." I stop. I can't take another step. The fragments of my heart feel like they are disintegrating in my chest and my stomach lurches violently.

I have to swallow back the saliva that fills my mouth from the nausea that rolls over me. Is that what they call me? They burst out laughing and I can hear Chuck's voice loud and clear. That laugh, that I've loved and treasured now sounds as sinister as the cocking of a gun's hammer.

The sound makes something inside of me snap. In the blink of an eye, my pain disappears. The betrayal I was feeling just minutes ago, withers and is replaced with cold fury. I'm not the one who has anything to be ashamed of. Why am I running? My daddy didn't raise me to run from anything. I'm not going to let him turn me into a coward. He's stolen enough.

I turn slowly, carefully on the small heel of the pretty, delicate champagne pink Sam and Libby ballet flats. I wore them in hopes that it would soften my distinctly indelicate, unpretty appearance. What a joke. It takes all of my strength to hold my head high and walk down the stairs. Each step took careful concentration. But I did it. I knew when they became aware of me.

Their laughter died off in a trickle, like dominos falling as the one next to it collapsed. Only when I stepped onto the landing where they were gathered do I take my eyes off the step. I don't even acknowledge the other boys. I just stare at Chuck. His big hazel eyes, with impossibly thick, curling lashes that would have made him pretty, if the rest of his features weren't so strong. Those eyes that normally smiled at me, were staring at me in what can only be described as horror.

"Maria," Chuck says, his voice cracking on the last syllable of my name.

"Diarrhea?" I snarl and surprise myself with how strong my voice is.

He winces, but I don't miss the self-conscience flick of his gaze toward his friends. Even now, he cares what they think. "Listen—"

"No, I've heard enough. It's fine," I say my voice still holding strong.

"It's not."

"Yes, it is. Now I know you're a terrible person," this time he flinches like I splashed water into his eyes. I scoff and feel my rage starting to lose some of its cool. "Yeah, I forgot. You think I'm too hard to look at in broad daylight."

One of his friends snickers and Chuck shoots him a dark glance before he looks back at me. "Listen, that was just—"

"That was how you really feel," I say quietly and I feel the first prick of tears in the back of my eyes. "Stay away from me. Don't come to my house. I never want to talk to you again."

His face pales and his mouth drops open. I step around him and walk down the stairs. I don't look back, but there's a part of me that's hoping he will call my name. Run after me and tell me he's sorry. But he doesn't.

I step out of the shower and check my texts. I see his message with the address of a restaurant that's in my neighborhood. I'm not surprised. The Heights is the new cool kids hang out in Houston. Lots of new restaurants opening up and old ones remodeling and reinventing themselves to fit the hipster, eclectic vibe of this neighborhood.

I take my time and arrive almost thirty minutes later than we agreed. He texted a few minutes ago to say he had ordered us drinks. I sit in my car gathering my composure. I scream when there's a knock at my window. I smile apologetically and hold up my finger to ask the valet to give me a minute.

I barely register him slipping the claim ticket into my hand. I feel like I'm floating as I walk into the restaurant. Here goes nothing.

TWO

CHUCK

When Maria walks in, I have a quick flash of doubt. Will this work? Will she be able to keep up her little charade long enough for me to apologize properly? The memory of that day always sparked a current of shame that I felt in every single pore of my body. I will never forget the look on her face when she had called me a terrible person. She had been right.

When I moved back to Houston last month, I was determined to find her. When I googled her, I found her Facebook profile right away and I remember staring dumbstruck at how beautiful she had become.

I stand up as she and the hostess approach our table. I force a smile even though my heart is racing. I hate not being in control. I hate not knowing what's coming next. But, I have no choice. "Luscious Cutie Pie?" I ask before I lean forward and brush a kiss across her soft, lightly fragrant cheek.

She's smiling wryly when I pull away, but it doesn't reach her eyes. Her entire face is bracketed by tension.

"It sounds awful when you say it aloud, doesn't it, CockedandLoaded?"

I grimace at my own awful screen name. "Call me Nicholas," I use my full name and hide my smile when I see the spark of recognition in her eyes. She was one of the only people who knew it. "Nice to meet you," I step around her to pull out her chair.

"I was worried that maybe you weren't coming," I say honestly. Our waitress appears with two margaritas and sets them down in front of us and slips away.

"Well, you sort of left me no choice. And you can call me Anna," she picks up her drink and takes a delicate sip. Her lips are the color of dark plums, the lower one has a prominent seam down the middle and when she puts the glass down, her lipstick has left an impression of her mouth on the side of the glass.

"Okay, Anna. You had a choice. We could have stopped talking instead," I say

7

with a raised eyebrow. She acknowledges the truth of my statement with a small shrug but, doesn't respond. She reaches for one of the salty tortilla chips that someone dropped off right before she got here and busies herself with piling it with salsa. I watch her hands. They're still the same. Long fingers, with big broad palms. Her nails are longer and painted the same burgundy as her lips. She's wearing a dark blue sapphire ring on her right ring finger, but otherwise, her hands are bare.

"I'm glad you're here. You're beautiful," I tell her and her head snaps up. Those eyes, the color of my favorite bottle of brandy, transport me back to the time when we met.

"Thank you," she says with a tight smile before she turns her attention back to her chips.

"So, here we are," I say and try to break some of the tension.

"Yeah, here we are."

"I have to say that I was pleasantly surprised when you wrote. I thought to myself, now that's the prettiest girl I've seen on this app the whole time I've been using it. But damn..." I drawl and wait for her to look up again before I continue.

"That picture didn't do you any justice." I have to bite my lip to fight the grin that wants to show itself when she blushes and runs and hand absently down the side of her neck. She did that when we were kids, too. When she was nervous or excited. I don't know which one of those inspired the gesture, but it's comforting and encouraging to see.

"What's your biggest regret?" She asks suddenly.

"That's a heavy question for a first date," I chuckle nervously.

This time, it's her cool eyes that are direct and mine that want to hide. I'm prepared for this question. Just, not yet. I thought she was going to try to keep up the same act she'd been playing since we connected two weeks ago. I had planned on being CockedandLoaded until I could see I'd gotten her guard down.

"This is hardly our first date. We've been talking online for two weeks," she says, her gaze not wavering.

"Yeah, you're right. Well, it's actually not that hard of a question to answer," I start slowly and try to make sure I say exactly what I intend.

"Really? Lots of regrets, or none?" she asks.

"Only one," I say with an expression that I hope is meaningful.

Her eyes widen slightly, and she glances around the restaurant as if to make sure no one can hear her before she leans across the table toward me. Her long red hair spills over her shoulders and the tips brush the top of her hands. I want to reach out and touch it. It's the most fundamental change in her drastically changed appearance. It used to be dark brown, curly and cut short.

"Well, what is it?" she asks, her voice slightly breathless.

I take a deep breath and go for broke, "Well, I had a friend. A girl. I did something stupid, hurt her feelings and never apologized," I say and watch her eyes start to soften before she collects herself and turns them into flinty chips of amber again.

"Well, what stopped you from apologizing?"

"My pride. I was a cocky little shit," I say with a dry, self-deprecating laugh.

8

She gives me a withering glance and raises her dark eyebrows in blatant skepticism. "And you're not anymore? Mr. *Cocked* and Loaded?"

I laugh nervously, "Yeah, I guess the name is a little dumb, it was my dad's call name in the Air Force and after he died—"

Her sharp inhale of breath stops me speaking.

"What's wrong?"

"Your father died? When?" Her expression is stricken. I've forgotten that she'd known my dad. Only a little, because I'd gone over to her house more than she'd ever come to mine.

"It's been nearly seven months, he was an adrenaline junkie to the very end and died doing what he loved," I smile at the memory of the last time I saw him. He was so fucking happy. "He was flying, hit a really bad thunderstorm and it blew his plane apart. Even for an accomplished Naval test pilot, there was nothing he could do." I shrug and take another sip of my drink. I miss my dad, he was the only person I told about what I did to Maria all of those years ago. And he always encouraged me to find the balls to apologize.

"I'm sorry,Cole," she says softly. She used my real name. She doesn't catch her slip up and I don't let it register on my face that I did. I loved hearing it on her lips again.

"Thanks. What about you? Your folks alive?" I ask.

"Yeah, they've moved to Guatemala. Bought a place down there and only come here twice a year. I miss them, but it's fun to go and visit."

"Nice," I say and then bring us back on topic. "We were talking about regrets. That was mine. Messing up that friendship. Not apologizing sooner."

She stares at me in surprise for the briefest of moments before she shakes her head.

"Do you have any?" I ask.

"Nope," she says glibly and then picks up her margarita and chugs it. I watch as some dribbles out of the corner of her mouth.

"Let's get out of here," she says and slams the drink down. She wipes her mouth with the back of her hand.

"Uh, okay," I say and lift a finger to call our server. I signal that I'd like our check and take one sip of my drink.

"Where are we going?" I ask.

"Your place." She says easily.

I can't hide my shocked expression. "I thought you were worried I was going to kidnap you and hand you over to some Mexican cartel," I joke. But I'm not amused. I didn't expect this. I mean, I'd love to take her home. But I have the distinct feeling that her request to go to my place is more of a "Plan B" than a spur of the moment whim.

Something about what I said was unexpected and threw her off.

"I'm sure you're not a murderer," she says as she grabs her purse and stands up in one fluid motion." She stands in front of me, her stance closer to that of someone who is preparing for battle instead of sex.

"You called me all talk, today. I'm ready for action," and without another word, she spins on her heel and marches through the restaurant. I watch her walk away, marveling at how gorgeous the view is from the rear. Oh yeah, I can't wait to have that ass in my hands tonight. I stand up and follow her out.

THREE

MARIA

Oh, my God. I rush out of the restaurant, my thoughts jumbled. This isn't what I expected. In every conversation we've had by text, he'd been exactly who I had expected that boy in the stairwell to be. Confident to a fault, unrepentantly sexual, someone who believed his own hype.

Why is he not an asshole anymore?

Why is he even more beautiful now than he was when he was a boy?

Why the fuck did he apologize?

I hand the valet my ticket and just as he's walking away, Chuck appears at my side, slips a hand around my waist and calls out to him. "Hey, give me that ticket, we'll come back for the car before you close tonight."

I jerk my head back in surprise and gawk at him.

"You can't do that," I say indignantly.

"You drank that margarita really fast, and there's no harm in me driving us over," he reasons. The traitorous valet walks back and hands the ticket to Chuck, as if I'm not the one who gave it to him.

"Excuse me," I say and he pauses. His nervous gaze darts between Chuck and I, but I don't feel sorry for him.

"Do you normally ignore the women whose cars you park when their men tell you to?" I demand and fix him with an imperious stare.

"Uh no," he stammers.

"Good, then, please go get my car," I say.

"No, don't go get her car. But, please get mine," Chuck says to him. The poor young man starts to look distressed. I glare up at Chuck. "Look what you've done. Maybe you should try asking instead of demanding next time."

I look at the valet driver and decide to show him some mercy. It's not his fault Chuck thinks he's the master of the universe.

"That's fine. I'll come back for my car later." I say a little embarrassed at conceding, but also deciding that this is one battle I'm prepared to lose if it means that I can get on with my plan.

Chuck squeezes my waist slightly and a shudder runs through me. Then he dips his head and whispers in my ear, "Save that attitude for when we get back to my place, where I can spank your ass for it."

I erupt into gooseflesh. "As if—" to my horror, my voice comes out in a breathy whisper. I clear my throat before I continue. "As if I'd let you," I dismiss him. Even though the thought alone is melting my insides.

"Oh, you will. You'll beg me for it," he says gently but with a tense edge in his voice that excites me in a way I can't remember being excited before.

"You wish," I say feebly and step out of his grasp when I see the valet driving back in a big black Range Rover. Of *course*, he would drive a flashy car.

I open the passenger door as soon as he stops in front of us and almost laugh at the surprise on his face before he hops out.

"I'm in a hurry, too," Chuck says when he climbs in behind the steering wheel. When he grips it, I notice how big his hands are, and think about the sting they would make if he were to spank me. I hate how much that turns me on.

I think about what else those hands and fingers could do and I start making some revisions to my plans.

I'm still going to leave him hanging, but what harm would there be in letting myself have a little fun first. Just a little and then, I'll confront him and leave.

We pull out of the parking lot and onto San Felipe. This is one of Houston's most congested streets. And tonight is no exception. As we crawl up toward the 610 Loop, a comfortable silence descends and I let my mind wonder.

. Half of me is filled with anticipation. I wonder what it will be like to kiss him. I feel the attraction between us, but it's at a simmer. He's bantered in sometimes outrageously sexy ways over text, but he's been subdued in person. The rest of me is dreading this. How will he respond when I tell him I've been playing him all along?

How will I feel when I walk away from him? Will I be able to? Because, I have to admit that being with him is easy. I've spent the last twenty years loathing him. Yet, since we started talking weeks ago, that's diminished some. Because, the thing about him that drew me when were kids is still there. Even more so now that we are adults. He's funny, and his confidence is actually attractive. I have a strong personality. Most of my relationships have ended because the men I was dating didn't like that I wanted to take the lead sometimes. Or they liked it too much and left me feeling dissatisfied in bed and in general.

Chuck isn't intimidated by me. He seems to like my stubborn streak.

"We're here," he says and my eyes focus. We've pulled up into a covered driveway of the Houstonian Residences. A man in a dark red bellhop's uniform is hurrying out of the revolving glass doors of the building.

"*This* is where you live?" I ask gawking. I've never been here before. It's one of the most exclusive and expensive addresses in the entire city of Houston.

"Impressive, right?" One of his big hands lands onto the suddenly super sensitive skin of my thigh and I jump. His touch sends a heated jolt of awareness through me.

I lift my eyes to his and nearly melt in my seat. Whatever doubt or worry had clouded his expression and mood in the restaurant is gone. In its place is a very blatant sexual desire. His eyes are hooded. As they roam over me, they linger on the spot of my neck where my pulse is thrumming and my heart starts to beat even faster. They sweep over the expanse of skin my light pink camisole leaves bare and leave a trail of tingling, prickles of heat all over. His gaze is heavy and I feel it as surely as if his hands were on me instead.

Oh, my God. I *want* to have sex with him. I don't want to give him, or myself blue balls.

Fuck.

I clench my thighs, my body instinctively seeking relief from the throb that has started between my legs. The string of need that had been drawn taut between us all night has been plucked.

Now, it's vibrating.

By the time our gazes meet, I am helpless to hide the need that I know my eyes are conveying. His hand slides up my thigh and the tips of his fingers disappear under my skirt.

"Co—" my passenger door opens suddenly. I turn my head to find the uniformed man holding the door open and beaming at Chuck before turning back to him, "Good evening Mr. Moore."

He slips his hand down my thigh and holds my gaze for a few heated seconds before he looks at the man and smiles placidly, as if his eyes hadn't just leveled me to nothing.

"Evening, D, how's it going?" he asks jovially as he unbuckles his seat belt and climbs out without bothering to cut the engine.

"Can't complain, the missus is happy, so I'm enjoying the quiet." The man's round cheeks are covered in a very nicely trimmed grey beard. When he laughs at his joke, he looks like a better-groomed version of Santa Claus. He offers me a hand as I climb down. "Happy wife, happy life, eh?" he says with a wink before he shuts the door behind me.

Chuck immediately puts his hand on the small of my back. It's a light touch, but with only the thin silk of my top between us, I can feel the heat of his hand on my skin. God, I wish I was naked.

When we step into the lobby, I can't help but let my eyes take in the opulently decorated space. It's dotted with plush armchairs and sofas in rich jewel tones that lend it a decadence usually reserved for luxury hotels.

"Should I park her for the night or you going back out, sir?" D asks as he walks in behind us and ushers us down a wide corridor, to a bank of elevators. He presses the call button and one of the doors pops open immediately.

"Yeah, go ahead, I won't need her again until morning," he says and cups my elbow and pulls me ono the elevator without missing a beat.

By the time his words register, the elevator door is starting to close. "Night, D," he says with a tip of his invisible hat.

"What do you mean? I have to get my car back tonight," I demand.

He turns to face me fully and the full weight of that gaze is back on me. I inhale sharply, take a step back and find my back pressed to the cool glass wall of the elevator. He takes one long step and puts us toe to toe. I feel...trapped and I like it.

"What are you doing?" I ask breathlessly, hopefully.

His slow, sensual smile is predatory as he places a hand on either side of my head. My heart racing, my nipples pulsing as if they're being tweaked. His expression is that of an unrepentant sinner. He leans down slowly, his head falling slowly, his dark hair brushing my cheek as he puts his mouth to my ear.

"You're staying here tonight, Maria."

My stomach plummets to my toes. I pull back and don't even register the thud of my head hitting the glass. My wild panicked gaze meets his triumphant, cocky one and I can feel the blood draining from my face as the truth registers.

"You knew?" I whisper in utter dismay.

"Of course," he says quietly, his expression completely unreadable.

"For how long?" I ask, dreading the answer.

"From the moment I saw your profile picture," he says and I want to disappear. I can't believe this. "So, all this time, you knew who I was. Knew my name wasn't Anna and you didn't say a word?" I ask in disbelief.

"I wanted to see what your end game was. Well, at least that's what I wanted in the beginning," he says. His smile is a full-on gloat as he leaves the rest of his thought dangling like a cube of cheese in front of a mouse. My pride should stop me from doing what he wants, but it's too late for pride. He's been playing me all along. I thought I was the one in charge of this little game. But he's been two steps ahead of me all along. He won this game before I even messaged him.

I concede defeat and ask, "And now? What do you want now?"

"I thought you'd never ask," he puts each of his massive hands on either side of my head and lowers his face to mine. The tips of our noses are touching and our lips are only a hairsbreadth away from being locked together.

His eyes are too close for me to focus on them, but I don't need to see when I can *feel* everything. His intent pours out of every single cell in his body. I know before he says in a low, deep voice, *"You."*

He drops one hand to snake it around my waist and yank me flush against him and holds me there. His lips brush mine softly. Yet, it's a profound touch, and I feel it in every fiber of my being. "I plan on taking you up to my place and I plan on fucking you all night," he bites my lip but doesn't try to soothe it. Instead, he tugs it into his mouth and sucks it so hard it stings. I love it and I groan.

He lets go and his hazel eyes glitter with possessive need as he searches my face. Whatever he sees there makes him nod with satisfaction.

"Yes… you like that," he says with a slow smile.

"I do. Yes," I nod eagerly and wish he'd do it again.

"You want more?" he asks and then dots a fleeting peck on my lips. I lick them to try and get a taste of him.

"Yes," I say.

"Good, then let's talk. Because when I fuck you tonight, I don't want anything between us."

The elevator's doors pop open as if on cue and he cups my elbow and leads me, like a lamb to the slaughter, down the hall to his apartment.

FOUR

CHUCK

"So, you were going to get my cock hard and then leave?" I ask with a begrudgingly impressed smile. "That's pretty unrealistic, Maria," I say. Just to fuck with her because when she's annoyed, she's fucking cute.

She scoffs, "Why, you think I wouldn't have been able to get your cock hard?" she says derisively.

I put my drink down and walk over to stand in front of her. I put a hand over the denim covering the hard erection in my jeans and adjust myself. Her greedy fucking eyes laser in on my hand and follow it's up and down motion. She licks her lips.

"No, princess. You already did that. It's unrealistic to think you'd be able to leave once you'd had my cock in your hand." I take advantage of her slightly parted lips and slip my thumb into her hot, wet mouth. She sucks on it and I groan low in my throat. With more reluctance than I've ever experienced, I pull my thumb out and step back.

"You were right to be so pissed off. I was a stupid twelve-year-old boy trying to look cool in front of some equally stupid boys. If I could take it back, I would. I never thought you were ugly," I tell her.

She rolls her eyes and tucks her hair behind her ears. "Yes, you did. Because I was. You're just saying that because you want to fuck me now. Because I look like this." She sweeps her hand over her frame in a careless gesture.

I'm lost for words. Not that it matters, I don't think she'd believe anything I said now, anyway. I go back to that day, the way she'd looked at me in that stairwell. I'd felt like the worst person in the world. And yet, I knew what I'd done wasn't forgivable. How could it be? I thought no way I'd forgive her if it had been me. So, I'd let her walk away. What a mistake that had been. I'm not saying that at twelve I knew I'd grow up and fall in love with the woman she'd become.

15

Too late, I realized what I should have realized then. That she was a better person than me. Not only would she never have talked about me like that, she would have forgiven me if I'd had the courage to go after her. I sit down next to her, take her hands in mine and turn her to face me.

I stare at her, into those smoky cognac-colored eyes that are currently full of confusion and smoldering with lust. I'm going to take care of both of those. I can't wait to be done with confusion so I can get to lust.

"You want to know how I knew?" I ask and cock my head to the side to watch her. "That it was you on that website?"

She nods, and I can see her throat working to push down whatever she's feeling and trying to mute.

"Your eyes," I tell her. Those same eyes widen.

"My...eyes?" she asks with surprise.

"Yes, they haven't changed. They were kind, open, interesting then. And they still are. I would know you anywhere. And when I sold my company and moved back from Dubai, I moved to Houston because I knew you were here. You think you found me? I found you. I own that dating website," I let the bomb drop and watch her jaw fall along with it.

"Yup," I say and nod. "It took my dad dying for me to get the nerve to come back and face you, Maria. What I did was fucking terrible. It would have been terrible no matter who I'd done it to. But the fact that it was to you, made me feel like a monster."

A tear rolls down her cheek and I use my thumb to wipe it away before she even notices.

"I'm sorry, Maria. I hope you can forgive me I really do. Because, in the last two weeks, I've gone from wanting your forgiveness, to wanting your screams when you come on my tongue," I say.

"You're still that smart, stubborn girl who was cockier than I was even in her headgear." She blushes and giggles.

"And now you're also old enough that I can touch you and *I'm* old enough to know how to touch you. And the frosting on the whole cake is that you're hot as fuck."

She worries her plump lower lip with her teeth and looks up at me through her lashes. A slow smile spreads across her face and she says, "Yeah, I know."

Fuck, that shit is so hot. I stand up and face her.

"Spread your legs," I command. She grins, it's an excited and very naughty grin, and then spreads her thighs.

"Good, now put your fingers between your legs and tell me if you're wet."

"Oh, I'm wet," she says as she slides her hand up under her skirt anyway.

"Oops," she says and widens her eyes in mock innocence. "I forgot to put on my panties," she croons and then sighs in pleasure as her hand starts to move under her skirt.

My mouth waters.

"Does that feel good, princess?" I start to unbutton my jeans and pull my cock out. I stroke it from root to tip and my thumb slides through the bead of moisture that's already there.

"Fuck, can I get in you?" I groan and take another step toward her.

"I thought you'd never ask," she says and in a flurry of movements my lust-

16

addled brain can't keep up with, she stands up, grabs me by the biceps, spins me so that my back is to the couch and pushes me down. I land with an oomph. She unzips her white pencil skirt and it slides down her hips to land in a puddle at her feet. Her bare pussy is at my eye level and I lean forward to try and lick it.

"Ah, ah," she tsks and dances out of my reach. "Later, for now, I want that cock inside me so badly." She spreads her legs so that she's standing with one on either side of my legs. The stance means I can see the slick flesh of her pussy and I groan.

"If you want to fuck me, you better do it right now. Cause in about thirty seconds, I'm going to stop restraining myself and pull that juicy pussy of yours to my face and eat it."

"Oh, no, not yet. After we fuck. You got a condom in that wallet, right?"

I nod and reach into my pocket to fish it out. I toss my wallet onto the floor and have the condom open and on in less than twenty seconds.

She grabs the base of my cock and starts to lower herself to me. I fist my hand in the thick fall of hair at the back of her head and give it a yank.

She hisses and grunts softly. "Yes!" She huffs out.

I hold her gaze and slip my free hand between her thighs. "Jesus. You're soaking," I say and then put my fingers to my mouth and suck them clean. Then I kiss her. She whimpers when I tighten my grip in her hair and I slip my tongue into the warm welcoming recess of her mouth.

We kiss hungrily, our tongues sliding against each other like they were trying to become one.

She continues to lower herself onto me. The first soft, warm touch of her pussy on the head of my cock pulls a moan out of my throat that spills into her mouth and mingles with her own sounds of pleasure as she sinks all the way down, taking all of me. I let go of her hair and clutch her ass and start to move her up and down on my cock until she takes over. She rides me with her eyes closed in concentration. She is as determined and fierce in the pursuit of her orgasm as she was in her pursuit of me.

Fuck man, I could get used to this. My own orgasm takes me by surprise. I don't see it coming and it barrels through me like a freight train.

"Oh my god, Chuck," she moans my name and hastens her rhythm, just I start to lose mine. She collapses in a trembling pile on me, her thighs quivering as her orgasm rocks through at the same time as mine rockets out of me.

We stay like that, trying to catch our breath. I don't know how long we're there. It could have been two hours or ten minutes. I'm so caught up in the woman that is in my arms, that everything else fades away.

"I have an idea," her voice, husky with fatigue and satisfaction, breaks our prolonged silence.

"What's that?" I ask. I trail my fingers lightly down the silky expanse of her back and slip it under her top to touch her skin. She lays her head on my shoulder and her exhaled breath tickles the fine hairs on the back of my neck.

There's something so sensual about having her lying on me, breathing me.

I want her again. I rock my semi-hard cock up into her. Her pussy tightens around me and I feel all the blood rushing into my cock and in seconds, I'm as hard as I was when the night began.

"Since no one else in the world can handle our bad ass cockiness *and* given the fact that I just had a mind-blowing orgasm with zero foreplay, I think we should maybe give dating for real, a try."

I laugh, press a kiss to her neck and cup her ass and thrust upwards. I'm about to tell her that she's damn right we are. But, I decide to let her have the last word.

THE END.

ABOUT THE AUTHOR

Dylan Allen is a Texas girl with a serious case of wanderlust.

A self-proclaimed happily ever junkie, she loves creating stories where her characters chase their own happy endings.

When she isn't writing or reading, eating or cooking, she and her family are planning their next adventure.

---

http://www.authordylanallen.com

Book+ Main: https://www.bookandmainbites.com/dylanallen
Twitter: @dylanallentwrit1
Instagram: @peddlerofpassion
Facebook: https://www.facebook.com/dylanallenwrites
Bookbub: https://www.bookbub.com/authors/dylan-allen
Amazon: http://amzn.to/2tpN6TF

ALSO BY DYLAN ALLEN

Rise

Remember

Release

Thicker Than Water

Leap

Envy

DOUBLE COCKED

JANA ASTON

This is super short, super dirty, and the heroine is a real bitch. You've been warned.

ONE

Sam nips my nipple with his teeth as I pull his head closer and buck my hips against his thigh, trying to get pressure on my clit.

"Jenny, we need to talk," he says, then wraps his mouth around my breast.

God help me. His mouth is so warm, wet, and perfect.

"Okay, babe," I say, guiding his head to my other breast. We do need to talk, I just hope it's about the same thing. I want to talk about my tag-teaming fantasy and find out where he stands on the idea. Fuck, I'm getting wetter just thinking about two men at once. I grab Sam's head and push him toward my pussy. He takes the hint like a champ and slides his arms under my thighs while kissing his way down my torso.

"So, we're talking?" he prods, dropping my ankles over his shoulders.

"Yeah, baby. What do you want to talk about?" I wrap my fingers in his dark hair and press myself closer. I don't mind if he talks while he's eating.

His tongue slips into my belly button, and I sigh in contentment.

"I want us to be exclusive."

What?

I pop up on my elbows and look at him between my thighs. "You know I'm seeing Greg too," I remind him. Tonight, actually. I need to finish this up with Sam in the next hour if I'm going to shower between them.

"I know." He skips over my pussy to rim my asshole with his tongue. "But I'm ready to take our relationship to the next level."

Fuck.

TWO

I tell Sam I'll think about it, then give him the blow job of his life to soften the blow. Pun intended.

Sam is perfect. He's rich, virile, smart, and beautiful. He's a doctor. Well, a dentist, but it still counts. He's thirty-five with the stamina of a twenty-five-year-old, and he's an all-around gold medalist in fucking. My ass, my mouth, my pussy—hell, he even makes sure I come while fucking my tits.

And he's in love with me.

The problem is, Greg's in love with me too. Greg is twenty-four and a bartender at a family friendly chain restaurant. You're judging me, aren't you? But Greg is hung. Like, urban legend hung. I honestly didn't think it was possible for a white guy to pass the eight-inch mark. It is. He does.

That fucker hurts—in the best possible way. I get wet just thinking about it... the way the first few thrusts hurt every time—and did I mention his girth? Yum.

I took pictures once, with his cock buried inside me. I made him lean back so I could snap a picture of my pussy stretched around him. I shudder a bit when I look at it...my skin pulled so taut, it looks like it should tear. Then I masturbate with an average sized dildo. I love Greg's penis, and they make Greg sized dildos, but who's capable of impaling themselves on that? A cock that big needs to be forced into me while I pant and sweat and scream a little. No way I could inflict it on myself.

I know what you're thinking. Do I have a picture of Greg's erect cock next to a soda can for reference and can you see it?

Of course I do. I'd share, but I'm a bitch. Plus, I don't have your email, and you know I can't post that shit on Facebook. Fucking Zuckerberg. *"Someone reported your photo for displaying nudity."* It's like a breeding ground for tattletales.

I bet Eduardo would have voted to let us post penis pictures. Too bad Zuck kicked him out. That reminds me, I need to call my best friend and thank her for lending me her stylist for the wedding last weekend.

The wedding. I'd suspected Sam was growing a vagina while witnessing his friends commit to a lifetime of monogamy. I'd suspected, but I'd buried those suspicions under a few gin & tonics and focused on planting the idea of a three-some in Sam's head. With Greg to be clear. What the possible fuck would be in it for me if Sam and I had a threesome with another woman? Splitting one penis between two vaginas? I don't think so.

So, I'd gotten Sam a bit drunk at the reception and asked him if he'd ever experimented in college. He'd looked at me strangely, said no, and then fucked me missionary.

My work was cut out for me.

THREE

I pull up to The Ivy and hand my car off to the valet. I'm meeting my bestie Darlene for a two-hour lunch on a weekday.

Do you hate me yet?

I'm rich too, you might as well know. I've done nothing to earn it either. My father is an aging gay pop star. You know the one. Did you feel sorry for me when I was born? Did you read the spread in People magazine, a picture of my fifty-year-old father cradling me on the cover, and wonder what kind of life I'd have? Did you go to one of his concerts and nudge your date and mutter, "*He'll be sixty-eight by the time his daughter graduates from high school!*"

Or were you more concerned I was being raised by a gay man? Did you post something bitchy on Facebook about a little girl needing a mother? You weren't alone. Lots of people passed judgement and made nasty comments.

Guess what? If you have enough money, the court of public opinion doesn't matter.

Thanks to money, a fifty-year-old gay man can give the middle finger to the world, buy an egg, hire a surrogate, and nine months later, be blessed with the miracle of me.

My childhood was fan-fucking-tastic, in case you're wondering.

I was, and still am, the apple of Daddy's eye. Imagine being raised by someone who thought every silly finger painting you did was artistic genius worthy of museum-quality framing. Someone who showed up to watch every dance class and sat front row during your recitals, then greeted you after with a bouquet more appropriate of a Broadway performance.

You know those machines indulgent California parents rent so their privileged offspring can experience snow? I never got one. When I mentioned wanting to see snow as Daddy tucked me in with a bedtime story, he'd have the private jet fueled, and an hour later, we'd be Vail bound. I'd slept on the plane and woke to a winter wonderland.

Any maternal needs I had were covered by my nanny, Martha. I had the same one my entire life, and she was always there for me when I needed a female shoulder to cry on or help with girl stuff. She's retired now, since I don't need a nanny at my age, obviously, but she's still on payroll, just in case, and she's at every holiday, just like family.

So, my childhood might not have been what society thought it should be, but it was perfect.

As an adult, I live on a healthy trust allowance, but I'm not a total deadbeat. I do work, designing purses. By designing, I mean I draw an occasional sketch and select materials while a team of people run the company with my name on the door. People may think I have it easy, but it's a lot of work building a brand. A lot. It doesn't happen overnight. In fact, I've been working hard at this for eighteen months. Eighteen! Then, just last week, the child of a washed-up actress launched her own line of handbags. Puh-lease. Everyone knows I'm the celebrity child handbag designer, and she's riding my coattails. She can try, but she won't succeed. People buy the handbags because of me—because they want to be me. I asked my lawyer to send her a cease and desist. She can design a line of sneakers if she wants. The handbag market is mine.

In addition to working four to eight hours a week, I maintain a vigorous beauty and exercise routine. You've got to be red carpet ready in Los Angeles at all times. Just last month, I escorted Daddy to the Grammy's where he was honored with a lifetime achievement award.

I'm blessed.

I'm a bit of golden girl on the celebrity child circuit. Twenty-five years old, and I haven't had a single arrest or stint in rehab. Plus, the handbag thing. Maybe I'm not doing the grunt work there, but I tell everyone I am, and life is all about perception.

I'm practically perfect in every way.

I stride into The Ivy, and the hostess leads me to a table where my best friend is already waiting. Darlene is the daughter of a supermodel and an Oscar-winning Hollywood director.

She lost her virginity at fifteen to the twenty-nine-year-old leading man of her father's latest film.

I cried for a week. It was the first time she'd gotten something before me, and it was offensive to my soul. It had taken me a week to work out a solution. After I dried my tears, I fucked her father. Oh, don't look at me like that. Her parents had long since been divorced, and I never told her how I lost my hymen. I'm not a monster.

"Hey, doll," I greet as I settle into the chair being held for me by the Maître d'. "Sorry I'm late."

"No worries, Jenny," she replies. She means it too. She really is that sweet.

"Tragic news," I sigh after we place drink orders and put our menus aside.

"What's wrong? Is your Dad okay?" Darlene's perfect brow wrinkles in concern.

"Dad's as fit as ever. It's Sam. He wants us to be exclusive."

"That's wonderful!" Darlene beams. She just got engaged to an entertainment lawyer. I'm sure visions of sugar plums and joint wedding planning excursions are dancing in her head.

"I'm not ready to give up Greg."

"There is no future in Greg. Sam is a catch."

I shrug. "I like them both."

Darlene groans. "You can't have everything, Jenny."

The waitress places our drinks on the table as I ponder Darlene's words. Why can't I have it all? I deserve it all.

"Why can't I have them both? I want them both."

"Both?" Darlene raises her eyebrows in disbelief.

"Yes." I'm firm. "Sam is the smartest, most successful man I've ever dated. He's the perfect date for public events."

"And Greg?" she prods.

"Greg's just..." I sigh. "Greg makes me feel like I'm the smartest, most successful person he's ever dated."

"Because you are the smartest, most successful person he's ever dated," Darlene points out with a shake of her head. "So, you're proposing you continue to date them both indefinitely?"

"Together."

"Together?"

"Yes, together."

"You want a relationship with the three of you?" She looks dubious. I'm surprised. She's normally very supportive of my goals.

"Sure. Why not?" I ask.

"Sam and Greg aren't gay, for starters."

"No, no," I interrupt. "I don't want them to fuck each other. I want them both fucking me."

"Oh," Darlene responds, finally getting it. "At the same time?"

I nod.

She looks skeptical again.

"Well, good luck with that," she says, then raises her glass to toast.

I laugh and clink my glass against hers.

FOUR

The following week, Greg arrives at my door with a six-pack of beer and a hard on. We take the beers outside and open a couple while watching the sunset.

Greg tells me about his lunch shift at wherever the fuck he works, and I tell him about my day of approving designs for the launch of my spring line.

He rubs my feet while we talk, and his touch makes me tingle all over. I can't give him up. I scoot over on the outdoor chaise we're snuggled on and throw one leg over his so I'm straddling his lap. I unbuckle his pants and pull his cock out with one hand while wrapping my other behind his neck.

"I missed you," I tell him, then suck his earlobe between my teeth.

"You just saw me," he replies as he wraps his hand over mine on his cock.

He's right. I did. And we normally only see each other a few times a month, but Sam asking for exclusivity has made me realize how much I'd miss Greg if I had to give him up.

"Are you seeing anyone else right now?" I ask.

"No one serious," he replies. "Are you still with Sam?" He looks curious.

"I am," I say, keeping a firm grip on his cock. I rotate my wrist a little as I slide it up and down, his hand still lightly covering mine.

"Why are you asking?" Greg brushes his thumb along my bottom lip, and I suck it into my mouth before responding.

"I was thinking we could try something new."

He smiles, a dimple appearing on his cheek. "You want to try anal?"

"No. Not with you, big guy." I give his cock an extra firm tug and laugh. "I was thinking the three of us could experiment." I hold my breath, awaiting his response.

"You let Sam fuck your ass?"

That's the detail he wants to focus on?

33

Greg's hands slip under the hem of my dress and grip my lace-covered ass while I choose my response.

"Baby, you're too big for anal." I decide on flattery as I sit up far enough to slip my panties off.

"What exactly are you asking for, Jennifer? You want to invite Sam over to watch us fuck?"

Greg slides his palms across my ass cheeks and spreads them roughly, then shoves a fingertip inside me.

I love a finger in my ass, but I never encourage backdoor activity with Greg. It's a slippery slope back there, ladies. Admitting you enjoy their finger in your ass quickly escalates to their cocks prodding for entry.

Which, I enjoy, to be clear. As long as the penis isn't super-sized.

But Greg's words excite me, so I slide deeper on his finger as I replay what he said. The idea of fucking them individually while the other watches is downright enticing.

This threesome idea has even more possibilities than I'd even imagined.

"I want to take you both at the same time," I tell him, moving up and down on his finger. I rest my forehead against his and grip his jaw with my hand. "But the idea of Sam watching us fuck sounds fun too."

Greg fists himself and slaps my pussy with his cock. "So, I'd get your pussy and Sam would get your ass?"

I nod. Fuck, I think I'm going to come just from talking about this.

"It would be an awfully tight fit, don't you think?"

"Yes."

"You think you could fit two men inside you, baby? You think you can take us both without tearing you in half?"

"I could try," I manage to respond. I'm having trouble focusing. The pressure between my legs is volcanic.

Greg taps my thigh, indicating I should raise up and allow him access. He guides the head of his cock to my slick opening, and I bob up and down on the tip, teasing us both.

"I love fucking you from this angle. I can see my cock splitting you open."

I whimper, loving his filthy mouth. I place my hands on his shoulders, balancing myself as he uses his thumbs to spread my lips open so he can watch himself slide into me. It's a little humiliating to be treated like his fuck toy, but it makes me wet all the same.

"Fuck, Jennifer. Just talking about fucking two men at once is making you a soaking wet little slut."

I whimper and bite my lip as Greg wraps his hands around my waist and thrusts into me. I mewl as he buries himself to the hilt.

He's deep. Too deep. I need to move, to alleviate the pain of his cock shoved against my cervix, but he's holding me tight. My thighs burn from trying to lift myself while he holds me down.

"Greg, let me move."

"Not yet."

He slides his hands lower, circling my asshole with his fingertip.

I can't do anything but squirm as sweat trickles from my neck, running between my breasts.

He pushes his finger roughly into my ass.

"You want this, baby? You want both holes filled?"

I nod.

He eases his hold on me, and I grin while sliding myself up and down his cock.

Our tongues battle while his hands are everywhere: pinching my nipples, gripping my ass, wrapping around my neck until I'm lightheaded.

He slams me down on his cock and pinches my ass so hard, I know I'll bruise, but that small bite of pain pushes me over the edge. I come, and Greg follows, muttering a stream of obscenities as he floods me with his cum.

"That was great." I'm lying on his chest, nuzzling his neck and basking in postcoital bliss.

Greg grunts non-committedly and sits forward, lowering my back to the chaise.

His feet hit the concrete floor of the patio as soon as his dick slides out of me. I feel his cum on its way south as he drops to his elbows and covers me with his mouth.

Holy yes. He's never done this before. It's been on my fantasy list for some time, but I've never found the words to ask him to clean up his own mess.

"Fuck, baby. That feels good."

I weave my hands in his hair, encouraging him to continue.

His tongue sweeps inside me, and my toes curl from the pressure of his mouth. He slides over me, our chests pressed together, still clothed.

I sigh, and he covers my mouth with his own, depositing our combined cum into my mouth.

I was not expecting that.

Greg places a finger under my jaw, and a soft kiss on my lips.

"Swallow."

I do. I don't have a choice.

Greg grins as the muscles in my throat constrict.

I smile back and lick my lips. Might as well be a good sport.

Greg stands and tucks his dick into his pants as he zips up.

"Set it up with Sam. I'll do it."

One down, one to go.

FIVE

ater that week, I pull into the driveway of my father's Bel Air estate still triumphant over my success in convincing Greg to join me in bed with Sam. I still have to convince Sam, but life usually goes my way, so I'm not too worried.

I find my father by the pool sipping iced tea with a man about my age.

"Jennifer, sweetheart, you remember Philip?" Daddy asks, waving his hand at the young man. He looks familiar as I glance at him a moment before realization hits.

"Philip?" I ask, unnecessarily. Philip is a friend of mine from high school. I haven't seen him since the summer after graduation. Wow. I can't believe he tracked me down through my dad. I always knew he had a thing for me in high school. Everyone did.

"Jennifer!" Philip is out of his chair and hugging me before I can process it. "So nice to see you again."

"You too! How sweet of you to come out to Daddy's estate just to see me."

Philip smiles and averts his eyes, and my father coughs.

"Actually, princess, Philip lives here."

Oh. My. God. How embarrassing. Philip is on Daddy's staff? I could have sworn he went to an Ivy League. How in the hell did he end up on my dad's household staff? Sad. I plaster a smile on my face and take a seat. Rosa places a cold glass of iced tea on the table in front of me.

"That's great, Philip." I take a sip as Daddy smiles reassuringly at Philip. So sweet, my daddy. "What do you do here?"

"Do?" Philip looks confused as he glances between us. Daddy reaches over and places a hand over Philip's as he turns to me.

"Philip doesn't work for me, princess. He's my lover."

Holy. Fuck.

I manage to plaster a smile on my face before speaking, but what the hell? There's a fifty-year age difference between Philip and Daddy.

"Daddy, Philip is my age."

"So? We make each other happy. If it's okay for Hugh Hefner, it's okay for the gays, darling."

I open and close my mouth, unsure of how to respond to that.

"Listen, Jenny. I called you over for lunch to let you know we're going to miss your birthday this year."

What?

They're a "we" now? And Daddy is missing my birthday? He's never missed my birthday. Ever.

"I'm taking Philip to Italy. He's never been. Can you believe it?"

"Tragic," I say, though I could not care less. How dare Daddy miss my birthday? This is unheard of treachery. I make a mental note to ask my lawyer if we should request a mental competency check before this gets even more out of hand.

SIX

Sam hands me a glass of wine as I drop onto his couch and toe off my heels. He sinks into the spot beside me and rubs the back of my neck as I let out a groan.

"Rough week, babe?" Sam asks.

"Like you wouldn't believe."

"I've had some tough patients this week myself."

I try not to roll my eyes. I mean, he's a dentist. That's hardly a comparison to the week I've had.

"My father has a new lover!" I blurt out, needing to get the conversation back where it belongs: on me.

Sam pauses at my outburst, his hand stilling on the back of my neck before he drops it and picks up his drink.

"You must be so excited for him," Sam suggests, eyeing me over his glass.

"I want to be happy for him. I do, but..." I pause to think for a moment. "I'm worried he's being taken advantage of." There. That sounds better than saying I'm annoyed my father is fucking someone I don't approve of, right?

Sam stares at me a moment longer before averting his eyes to the view of the Pacific Ocean from his living room.

"Your dad has a very strong personality, Jenny. I highly doubt he's being taken advantage of."

"I don't think you understand how serious this is." I mean, how could he? His parents are schoolteachers from the Valley. He has no idea what it's like to be me. "He's taking his new lover to Italy—on MY birthday! He's obviously being manipulated."

"You're turning twenty-six."

I don't care for his tone or the insinuation that at twenty-six my father's priorities should not revolve around me.

"Excuse me?" I raise a perfectly manicured brow meant to convey my displea-

39

sure. I know it's a perfectly manicured brow because I pay a specialist from Brazil three hundred dollars a week to keep them flawless. No one wants to buy a luxury handbag from an unkempt hobo.

Sam looks like he's about to say something, then pauses. "I'm sorry this has you so upset, babe," he finally says as he goes back to rubbing the back of my neck in reassuring circles. "How can I help?"

See? That's why I keep Sam around. He understands that I'm always right. I went out with an actor once who suggested I was selfish. I dumped him immediately, because how dare he? Everyone knows actors are narcissists. I only bothered dating him in the first place because he was an Oscar winner and I thought being associated with him would help build my brand. It did, because when I broke up with him, my PR team made sure to let everyone know how wronged I was, and my position as the "sweetheart of celebrity children" was locked in place.

I put my drink down and slip my hand into Sam's pants. He's earned a hand job. Also, he just unknowingly opened the door to the conversation I really want to have.

"I want you in my ass tonight," I purr into his ear as I grip his dick hard enough to make a lesser man uneasy. Then I rake my fingernails lightly over his length as he hisses in pleasure.

Sam palms the back of my head and pulls me in for a kiss while I continue to masturbate his cock until he's thick and hard and ready to serve me. Then I stand and drop the scrap of pricey lace I wear as panties before kneeling over him on the couch.

"Get it wet," I instruct. He knows exactly what I mean and slides two fingers into my cunt. I'm already soaked, and he uses it to lube his dick, never taking his eyes off me.

"I love you, Jenny."

Of course he does.

I bend my knees until my asshole is aligned with the tip of his cock. Once it's in place, I sink down farther. The head forcing its way past the first ring of muscle burns, but I like the pain. I drop lower and lower still, until my ass cheeks rest on his thighs and his cock is buried to the hilt. We both groan in pleasure, not moving, just enjoying the moment. After a beat, I raise up, slowly letting his cock drag free from my ass until just the tip is still inside, then drop back down in one solid motion.

"Fuck, Jenny."

"It's so tight, isn't it?" I pant into his ear.

"God yes. You feel so good, baby." Sam wraps his hands around my hips, assisting my rise and fall onto his cock, his hips moving below to meet each thrust.

"You're so big and hard, filling me up like this."

"Yes, yes." Sam's head falls back against the couch, the word *fuck* falling from his mouth in little whispers.

"You know what would make it even tighter?"

"Hmmm?" he replies in a non-committal hum.

"What if I had a cock in my pussy too? Can you imagine how much tighter my ass would feel then?"

Sam raises his head, paying attention now. "You want me to fuck your pussy with a dildo while I'm buried in your ass?"

"Maybe." I nip his earlobe. Not quite what I had in mind, but he's headed in the right direction, so I'll encourage it. "Maybe that could be a thing we do," I offer. "But the first time I'm filled like that should be special, don't you agree?"

"Special how?"

I tighten my asshole around his cock until he grunts. "Two dicks," I whisper. "One of you in each hole."

"With who? Greg?" His voice is strained, and I know he's close to blowing his load straight into my colon.

"It'd really help make my birthday special," I murmur. And then he unloads.

EPILOGUE

I got dumped on my birthday. Twice.

Greg said he was tired of being treated like he isn't smart. When I pointed out he isn't smart, he said I was only proving his point.

Sam said I'm a narcissist with a borderline personality disorder. He said he tried to love me despite it, but there was no fixing crazy.

I told him there was no fixing being a dentist either.

Then I fucked my plastic surgeon, which everyone knows is the highest level of doctor on the dating chain.

Last I heard, Sam and Greg are living together—with some girl named Sierra. After I put in all the work to set that up, that bitch rode my coattails onto two perfect dicks. I wish them nothing but light and love because everyone knows that's the kind of person I am.

Besides, I've already moved on to better, more important cock. Cock I've worked hard to get and cock I deserve to have.

Light, love and cock. That's my motto.

ABOUT THE AUTHOR

Jana Aston likes cats, big coffee cups and books about billionaires who deflower virgins. She wrote her debut novel while fielding customer service calls about electrical bills, and she's ever grateful for the fictional gynecologist in Wrong that readers embraced so much she was able to make working in her pajamas a reality. Jana's novels have appeared on the NYT, USA Today and Wall Street Journal bestseller lists, some multiple times. She likes multiples.

Facebook: http://bit.ly/FBJanaAston
Reader Group: http://bit.ly/GrindMeCafe
Amazon: http://bit.ly/AmazonJanaAston
Bookbub :http://bit.ly/BBJanaAston
Goodreads: http://bit.ly/GRJanaAston
Instagram: http://bit.ly/IGJanaAston

COCKSURE GRIN

WHITNEY BARBETTI

Millie thinks all she needs are her chicken pajama pants and sad microwaved nachos until she meets Ben, a man with a grin who is more than just the stranger she thinks he is.

COCKSURE GRIN

"You are going to become a crazy cat lady if you never leave your house, Millie."

I groaned and shoveled another microwaved nacho into my face. "I can't. I'm allergic to cats."

"Well, I already know that's a lie."

"I'm allergic to fun then," I said. Which wasn't entirely a lie.

"Come onnnn," my best friend Elizabeth said, the whine in her voice like nails on a chalkboard. "All you do is sit at home and watch mysteries on the Investigation Discovery channel, in your fleece pajamas, with a sad plate of microwaved food in your hands."

Mid-chew, I glanced down at my 'lounge pants'—because that's what they were called when you were *lounging*. Just because they had dancing chickens on them did not make them pajama pants. Though, I supposed the same couldn't be said for my bunny slippers.

But I couldn't deny she was right about the damned nachos, which were more chewy than crispy so, as far as nachos went, they were pretty damn sad. "But going out means pants, and I don't want to wear pants that aren't made of elastic."

"Going out means skirts," she told me. "Or, at the very least, a really tight pair of solid-colored leggings. Preferably ones not made from pajama material, if you even have ones that aren't. Come on, Millie. Your life is sooo boring."

"I think you're trying to insult me," I said, shoving another miserable chip in my mouth. I picked a sharp corner from between my teeth and looked down at my paper plate and the hole in my pants that stretched one chicken's face wide enough to show my pale white leg. I sighed. "And it's working, just a little."

"Good." I could practically hear her beaming. "I'll be there in fifteen minutes."

"Fifteen minutes?" I said, pulling my phone away and catching my unkempt reflection on my phone's screen as I checked the time. "Might want to push it to twenty."

"One-five. Fifteen. That's it. Be ready, or I'm dragging you out of your cave, clothes or not."

Luckily, because I often slept past my alarm clock, I was pro at getting ready in such a short amount of time. Not like, NFL pro level. But like Wednesday night bowling league—at the sketchy bowling alley behind the abandoned motel—pro.

By the time Elizabeth had shown up, I'd transformed from my baggy chicken lounge pants to black leggings that I practically had to grease my limbs just to fit into and a top that covered my microwaved nacho bloat. I gave myself one last look in the mirror as I shoved in the hoops I found under my nightstand in my earlobes. I cleaned up okay, for a Wednesday night after a shit show day at my job.

Elizabeth, though a bit harsh, wasn't wrong. My life *was* boring. I guess I kind of owed it to her to try to liven things up. She was one of the few friends I had that actually cared that I subsisted off of terrible instant food and no fun.

"From Amelia to Millie, in fifteen minutes," she said, giving me a high five when I got into the car. "Proud of you, kiddo."

I rolled my eyes at her use of my full name and flipped the visor down. While I'd managed to slide my body into constrictive clothing and pull my shoulder-length bob into a messy half up-do, my face still needed a bit of work.

"Don't put too much on; you don't need it."

"I don't need it?" I asked, lipstick coating my bottom lip. "I thought we were going out?"

"Well..." She drummed her fingers on the steering wheel at the stoplight. "Technically, you are going out, because you left your house." She gave me one of those bared teeth nervous emoji smiles, and I just knew that she'd conned me right out of my poultry pajama pants.

"Where are we going, Elizabeth?" My tone was less than amused, but a grin curled her lips.

"Just a small get-together. At Finn's house." Finn, her boyfriend of the month, who put together dinner parties like he was Martha Fucking Stewart.

"Greaaat," I said, not feeling great at all about the prospect of subjecting myself to Finn's antics. "Don't tell me he invited the guy who spent the last dinner party, begging everyone to fund his start-up."

"No, not this time."

Small mercies. "How many other people will be there?"

"You...me...Finn, of course." She gave me a wide grin. "And Finn's friend from college."

I winced. "Oh god. Is this like a double date or something?"

"No, no."

Her tone was less than convincing and at my *give-it-to-me-straight* face, she winced and continued.

"But Finn figured Ben could use some new friends." At my answering groan, she hurried on. "He just got a new job here."

"Greaaat," I said again. I applied the littlest bit of mascara, planning on getting toasted, since Elizabeth was driving me. She always did this—setting me up with her boyfriend's friends. Just because *she* was actively dating didn't mean *I* needed to be too. I had a busy and terribly boring job and relished my time watching murder mysteries with shitty-tasting nachos. I didn't need anyone coming into my life, interrupting the flow. Least of all, one of Finn's likely weird friends. He, like Finn, probably tucked his sweaters into his pants and bragged at least three times every hour about how many miles he could get on a tank of gas in his hybrid.

But I would eat my words, because the moment we pulled into Finn's driveway, the Columbine Blue convertible parked there made my jaw drop. "Did Finn get a new car?" I asked, even though I knew sensible Finn would've never shelled out the kind of dough this car had to have cost.

I hopped out of the car faster than if my ass had been on fire. I couldn't resist touching it, running my fingers over the glossy paint. Even the inside had been lovingly restored to its original factory state. I had to resist pressing my face to it to see if it was real.

"I normally charge for that kind of touching," a warm, low voice said from the open garage.

I shielded a hand over my eyes to block out the setting sun, watching the figure approaching me. He was tall and, to my surprise, the light gray sweater he wore wasn't tucked into his pants. My eyes climbed higher, up to his face. The panty-dropping smile made my stomach do a little somersault, but it was the killer baby blue eyes that did me in. "Whatever you charge, I'll pay."

He raised one eyebrow—Jesus, why was even *that* so fucking hot? It was just a stupid eyebrow. But coupled with the raise of his eyebrow and the hand he ran through his lush dark hair, I was a goner. I wondered, could an eyebrow be fuckable?

"Really?" he asked, stepping closer still. "Whatever I charge, you'll pay?"

"Yes," I said, and leaned up against the baby blue car of my dreams. "Anything."

My *anything* probably meant I could badly microwave some nachos for him, while his *anything* very likely meant something sexy and out of my element. But elements and inhibitions be damned—this guy was something else.

"Ben?" I asked, grazing my hand lovingly over the shiny rearview mirror.

"The one and only. Amelia?"

I couldn't help the gut reaction to scowl at the name my mother had given me. "Millie."

"Millie," he repeated, the double L sounding absolutely delectable rolling off his tongue. Could a word sound delicious, I wondered? Maybe only words that came from those full lips, coupled with that ridiculously gorgeous eye-fuck he was giving me.

Listen. I was no prude. Maybe I was just ... deprived. My sex life was in desperate need of ending its unintentional year-long sabbatical. After a string of one long term relationship after another, I could use a good romp to dust off the cobwebs, maybe get me back out there in the dating world—so I could enjoy real nachos and not the crusty shit I'd been subjecting my mouth too.

As Ben and I exchanged looks hot enough to melt the paint off his car, Elizabeth trilled, "Who's ready for a margarita?"

"I am. Don't be stingy with the booze on mine," I called out, never taking my eyes off Ben and his fuckable eyebrow and his cocksure grin. On any other man, that kind of arrogant, self-assurance would be a huge turnoff. But on him? It was like tossing gasoline onto an already well-lit fire. It just set his appeal ablaze in a way that made me want to rub my palms all over his chest.

An itch I hadn't felt in a long, long time crawled up my spine. It was that sex itch, the one that I hadn't given into for so long that I was mildly concerned I couldn't remember how to do it. I mean, I knew the mechanics of basic straight sex: one peen plus one vageen. But the rest of it? Did I even have sexy moves in my arsenal still?

Or even more pressing: why was I even worried about it when all he'd done was *look* at me? There wasn't an offer of sex on the table or anything.

But maybe I could get one.

"So, you love mustangs, huh?" he asked, coming closer to me when Finn and Elizabeth had made themselves scarce.

"Who doesn't? But this one." I let out a low whistle, moving to the front of the car and practically laying my whole body on the warm hood. "1966 High Country Special Mustang, right? In Columbine Blue?" What were the odds that this guy would have the car of my dreams? And what were the odds further still, that he'd be this attractive? It was as rare as an alignment of all the planets in our solar system.

Unlike the start-up obsessed Finn Friend of the last dinner party, this was one I couldn't slip through my fingers.

He raised that eyebrow again. Damn, he really had to stop doing that. "You know your cars."

"Correction: I know *this* car. This beautiful, shiny, rare little gem." When I turned my head, he was close. So close that our breath mixed, and his eyes held mine. For just a moment, my toes curled and my stomach flipped. With his dark eyebrows, bright blue eyes, and that wide, beautiful smile, he looked like the actor from the Star Trek reboot, but with his own kind of intense masculinity.

Why was I thinking about planetary alignment and Star Trek when a beautiful man was looking at me like he wanted to spread my legs and explore *me*?

I wasn't the kind of girl who fell face first into deep lust. Maybe the car was affecting my inhibitions. Maybe my starved sex drive was driving my movements.

Or maybe it was him, and the way his tongue snaked out of his mouth to lick his lower lip for just a second before his lips spread in that grin—like he knew exactly what I was thinking about. He leaned in closer still, and smelled like sandalwood and cinnamon, spicy and earthy and I had the thought to just kiss him—to get the tension over with once and for all.

"Want to go for a ride?" he asked, breaking my focus on his mouth. When I looked up at him, I was so dazed by those blue eyes that I wasn't sure if he meant the car or himself.

I toyed with saying no—to both, even if only one option was on the table. But I thought of my sad microwaved chips and holey poultry pajama pants and realized that I'd probably never see Ben again anyway, so what was the big problem with planting one on this guy, right in the middle of this driveway?

"What are you thinking?" he asked me.

"I don't think you want to know." I sounded wanton and tried not to let the embarrassment of it flood over me.

"Do you remember what I first said to you?"

When he looked at me like that, like he wanted to peel my leggings off with his teeth, it was hard to remember a damned thing he'd said. "Uh..."

"Well, you see," he said, leaning in and effectively pinning me to the car. I held my breath as he leaned over me. "You're all over my car right now."

I swallowed the lump of lust that clogged my throat. "I'm guessing I owe you?" I asked, breathy and eager. I didn't want to question it anymore. Not when the tension was drowning us both, not when my body was coming to life in a way it hadn't since ... well, I couldn't remember how long.

"I won't take unless you give." His breath was hot, washing over my ear and doing the most delicious thing to my chest. I knew, if he pulled back, he'd see my nipples standing at attention. But I didn't want him to pull away, so I did the only thing I could think of.

I grabbed the front of his sweater and yanked him down, sealing his mouth to mine as I laid on his car. And even though I'd been the one to initiate, he quickly took over.

One hand came around my neck while the other dove in my hair. He sucked my lower lip into his mouth and bit, gently enough that a moan escaped my throat before I could stop it.

The itch had turned into a full-blown forest fire and my lips were starving for oxygen, starving for him. I pulled him closer still, even as he bruised my mouth with his sucking and biting, so close that the only thing that separated us was our clothing.

His fist in my hair tugged and another moan came from my throat. I'd never been so wanton, so desperate for more. And, when we pulled away a second later, I'd never been more brazen than when I told him, "You're coming home with me after dinner." I tapped the hood. "And you're bringing this car." But almost as soon as it left my lips, I regretted it. Not because I didn't mean it, but because I worried if we walked away from this moment, the sexual tension would fade, or we'd—meaning me—would be too shy to continue it.

"Or," he said, "we can skip dinner and," he pushed my hair over my ear, his voice like an alarm clock that just woke up my libido, "move right to dessert."

He read my fucking mind. Shiiiiiit. Was I really about to do this? Bail on my best friend for some guy I'd just met at her dinner party? Before we'd even had dinner?

That fuckable eyebrow lifted and the riot of butterflies in my belly did a dip and I forgot the question I'd just asked myself. "Say yes, Millie."

Jesus Christ on a cracker, even the way his tongue dipped between his teeth to enunciate the double L in my nickname was sexy. There was no fucking way I was backing out of this.

In answer, I straightened and ran my hands down my leggings as if it was a skirt I'd taken pains in selecting and not the only clean pair of leggings I owned at the moment. I grabbed the passenger door handle and gave him an expectant look. "Let's go."

The beautiful blue interior welcomed my body as I sunk into the seat. I had the forethought to shoot Elizabeth a "sorry, but I just got propositioned and I don't know what's come over me, but my inner sex demon needs to get laid," text as Ben revved the engine and I listened to that beautiful motor purr. "Jesus," I said.

"Actually," he said, backing out of the driveway, "it's Ben."

I laughed, but as soon as the laugh left me, and I'd given him directions to my place, nerves flew through me, chasing away the butterflies. The sexual tension was still there, so *there* that I rolled the window down to see if we could get a little breathing room.

"So, what do you do for a living, Ben?" I made a mental note to make sure I filled out my address correctly to receive my World's Worst Small Talk award and promptly forgot to actually pay attention to his answer. I was mesmerized by the car, by the human who drove it, and by the way he'd directly affected the sleeping bear that was my libido, with that one insanely hot kiss on his car's hood.

He asked me, and I told him that I was a writer for a small press, which wasn't entirely a lie … just, mostly. Yes, I did writing. But the things I wrote were often numbers about debits and credits. And it wasn't so much a small press as it was a failing press—small because we'd had so many layoffs. But "writer" sounded sexier than "accountant" and "small press" sounded more respectable than "failing business model badly in need of an overhaul."

After exhausting the most basic small talk, we arrived at my house and I looked at its black door with laser eyes, trying to remember if I'd even cleaned up the place recently. I was almost positive that my nachos were still on the coffee table, and my chicken pajamas were flung somewhere on the floor.

Sex pad, it did not scream. Sad but comfortable, it did.

"Millie?"

"Yeah?" I asked, turning to him.

He put his hand on my knee and even through the legging material, I could feel its warmth. "It's okay," he said. "I don't usually do this, either."

My chest deflated because the pressure was suddenly gone. "You could tell?"

"Oh yeah. It was only so obvious because I'm nervous too." He squeezed my knee. "We don't have to do this. Like I said before, I won't take unless you give."

"Ugh." I tracked my hands over my face. "I guess I should've asked if you have a girlfriend or something. Man, I'm so bad at this."

"I don't." He squeezed my knee. "I'm assuming you're single too?"

"Oh, so single that I practically define 'single.' In Elizabeth's words, my life is so boring."

As if on cue, Elizabeth replied to my text and I tilted my head to read my phone's screen: *oh, thank god. Let that sex demon loose!*

It wasn't until I heard his warm laugh and felt it reverberate down his arm, to the hand that held my knee, that I realized he could read it, too.

"Sex demon, huh?" he asked.

"I mean …" How was I supposed to reply to that? "I guess I wouldn't say sex demon as much as just 'thirsty demon.'"

"Uh huh," he said, blue eyes twinkling in the glow from my front porch light. He looked at my door and looked at me. "How thirsty?"

Bless him for not making me feel even more embarrassed than I already felt.

54

"She's parched." I pursed my lips, nodding. "And, I think I owe it to Elizabeth, you know, you make sure I take care of that."

His answering grin was so full of charm that I was surprised I wasn't already undressing in the car and throwing my clothes at him in a furious haste.

By the time we made it inside my house, though, the charm pushed me right over the edge and off came the clothes, his *and* mine in a furious rush, mingling on the floor as I pushed him onto my couch. I wished I wasn't so impatient, because from what I could see, his body deserved an A+. But my nerves and my need mingled and translated into a frenetic energy that he matched.

His erection strained against his pants and we both stared at it before our eyes met. He laughed, and then I did too. This was probably the most comfortable I'd been having sex with anyone—even long-term boyfriends. There were no games spurning us forward, just our equal and honest desire. And since he'd given me an out in the car, I felt like all the pressure was off completely. We'd scratch our mutual itches and then go our separate ways.

He unsnapped the button on his jeans and then, time slowed way, way down. Or at least, that's how it felt. He pulled down the zipper painfully slow and then rolled them down his legs even slower. It could've been the ache building within me, that painful, eager ache, waiting to be satisfied that made time move at a snail's pace, but suddenly, he couldn't cover my body soon enough.

"Come here," he said, with a flick of his finger, so I did. He brushed the hair from my shoulders and placed his warm palm on my chest, down and down in a punishingly slow pace until he'd grazed over just the tips of my nipples and then moved further down until his hand was between my legs.

I had to actually force my body to still, not to push against him like we were two magnets drawn together. He grazed his knuckle over my center and it seemed as if my entire body opened to him with a satisfied sigh, my back curving off the couch and my head tilting back to open everything up to him.

While still holding my gaze, he dipped his finger inside. My stomach clenched, and my hands held him as if I needed balance, needed to hold onto him as he rocked my world with just that one finger. Over and over, he teased me, his mouth moving to my neck and down my stomach until I couldn't take it anymore. I gripped his cock and ran my thumb over the tip—again and again until he yanked my hand away with a tortured groan.

"I hope you brought a condom," I told him, both a request for one and a request for him to finally—blessedly—slide inside me. I pulled him back to the couch, deciding the ten further steps to my bedroom was too damn many.

"I did." I watched in amazement as he slid it over his erection, but he didn't make a move to bring it between my legs when it was encased in latex. Instead, he leaned down over me on the couch and licked up my jaw, biting the sensitive skin behind my tear and then he blazed his tongue down my neck; licking and sucking the entire way down.

"Jesus," I said, surprised by the way that lit tiny little fires inside me and had me squeezing my thighs together, desperate for even a tiny bit of contact action.

"My name's Ben," he said again and as I laughed at his joke, he slid inside so quickly that I gasped from the instant pressure and the simultaneously instant relief.

Ben was a giving lover, I learned. He met me stroke for stroke, and even

55

though I knew he came way before me—which I took as a compliment—he still rode me hard until the climax hit me with the force of a semi-truck, sending me sprawling off the couch and to the floor.

Wave after wave poured over me, so powerfully that I wasn't entirely sure that he hadn't somehow broken me. Was sex always like that? I couldn't do a mental inventory of all my sexscapades, not when my leg twitched, and my chest heaved with each breath. He was breathing heavily too, but not so winded that he couldn't pick me up off the ground with a laugh and heave me up onto the couch beside him.

"That was fast," I said in between deep breaths, my arms deadweight at my sides.

"Uh, yeah," he said with a pained laugh. "Sorry about that."

"Oh!" I put my hand on his thigh—still naked, still hot—and shook my head. "No, that's not what I meant. I just meant that I met you, what, an hour ago?" I swallowed and couldn't help but laugh. "But yes, *that* was fast too."

"I know." He dragged a hand over his face. His lips were wet and if I'd had the energy I would've straddled him to suck on them. But alas, all I did was make what likely resembled blowfish lips at him, imagining it. "I'm sure Finn is less than impressed."

"He's probably grateful that you got that monster vehicle out of his driveway, lest he ruin his street cred."

Ben laughed, and I decided that I wanted to bottle up the sound and bring it out to listen to on special occasions. Like when I went back into sex hibernation.

"You're funny, Millie." He dropped his head against the couch cushion and looked at me in a way that made me feel all tingly. "I needed this before I start my new job tomorrow."

Realizing that I didn't even know what that job was, I nodded like I knew exactly what he was talking about. Post-coital wasn't the best time for me to ask him what he did for a living, not when I couldn't be bothered to worry about the fact that we were inches away from my paper plate of half-eaten nachos. "Are you trying to thank me for the sex?" I asked.

"Well, not in such frank terms. More like I was going to thank you for giving me a night to reflect on when I'm stuck in meeting after meeting tomorrow."

"In that case," I said, leaning against him a little bit. "You're welcome." I tried not to nuzzle him too much. What was the protocol after great stranger sex? "I mean, you satisfied my thirsty sex demon, so I guess we're square."

"Is she satisfied?" he asked with a wicked little lift of his lips. "Because, like you said, we don't want to disappoint Elizabeth."

I grinned back at him. "She's satiated. For now."

He moved and immediately, I jerked back. Was he trying to tell me to give him space, so he could be on his merry way? But he merely grabbed his phone from his pants and pulled it out.

Oh, even worse. Was he going to ask me for my number only to never call? I didn't need an obligatory phone number exchange. But instead, he pulled up his web browser and typed in pizza delivery.

"I hate to be presumptuous," he said. "But I don't think I can show my face to Finn right now. How do you feel about eating?"

"I feel like that's the very least we should do, don't you think? Eat something? Elizabeth would be *so* disappointed if we skipped her dinner and then didn't even eat."

"You're right. We mustn't disappoint Elizabeth." He thumbed through his phone. "How do you feel about pizza?"

"Oh." I pressed a hand to my chest. "I have a deep and abiding love for dough and cheese and marinara."

"It just so happens that I do, too. Would you object to splitting a pizza?" His face was so earnest, like he wanted an invite without having to ask for one in a way that put either of us in an embarrassing situation.

He *wasn't* running. Not yet, at least.

"I mean, I guess I can be persuaded," I said. "I had such big plans, though."

"Oh." He nodded, playing along, and motioned to the stupid paper plate on the coffee table. "I don't want to interrupt your gourmet meal."

"Yeahhh." I stood and grabbed the paper plate. "I was kind of hoping you wouldn't see that." I stepped behind the couch and shoved it and the tiny bit of dignity I had before he'd seen it down as far as I could reach.

"The pajamas are something else, too."

I wanted to shove my face down into the trashcan too. "Oh, yeah?" I asked, acting totally cool and not at all like the evidence of my sad little singledom was at the feet of this gorgeous man. "You have a thing for chickens?"

"Do *you* have a thing for cocks?"

"Wh-what?" I snapped up the offending pajama pants and tugged them on.

He wagged a finger at my pants. "The cocks."

"Chickens," I corrected.

"Roosters. Roosters are cocks."

I looked down at the pants, yep, there were indeed a few roosters sprinkled among the many shades of white and brown chickens. "Then yes, I have a thing for cocks. And chickens." I tried not to look right at his lap as I said it and snatched up my t-shirt, tugging it over my head. This was it. Me in all my pajama-clothed glory. And somehow, he still grinned at me like it was somehow charming.

When the pizza came, we pigged out on equal shares, with Investigation Discovery playing on in the background. "How'd you know what kind of car that was anyway?" he asked me, just as a string of cheese slapped my chin.

As delicately as I could, I pushed the cheese into my mouth. "My dad was super into old cars like that. Making them purr. He didn't have a ton of money to do so, though, so he took me to a lot of car shows. The fact that you have that car kind of blows my mind. I wish he could see it." Wistfully, I picked at a piece of pepperoni. I didn't want to talk about my dad and the dreams he'd never achieve. I handed Ben a napkin when cheese attached itself to his chin. "It's my dream."

He stretched his arm behind my head and I snuggled against him, feeling more comfortable than I'd expected to feel in the presence of a man who was still a stranger. A stranger I'd seen naked, sure. But stranger nonetheless. He brushed a piece of hair away from my face and I inhaled his scent deeply, wanting to retain this moment in my memory long after he was gone.

It was getting late and I was tiring fast. I knew I was two yawns away from a deep sleep when his voice rumbled, "Any time you want a ride, just say so."

Unlike the first time he'd said it, this time his voice was free of sexual innuendos. He was genuine, as far as I could tell, but I just couldn't imagine that I'd see him again after a night like tonight.

A thought which was confirmed when I suddenly awoke, alone on my couch, with a piece of notepaper on top of the empty box of pizza.

Thanks for the laughs. - Ben

My resigned sigh was followed with the immediate reminder that I had to get ready for work, pronto. I pulled on the leggings I'd worn for all of twenty minutes the night before and grabbed a shirt from the dryer that wasn't entirely dry yet and ran, like a mad woman, out of the house to work.

It was meeting day. Every Thursday, the owner—George—filled out conference room with bagels and coffee and donuts. People filed in to fill the chairs around the obnoxiously large table—larger now that half of our employees had been laid-off—and since I was late and not wanting to get on George's radar so early, I snuck in and slid between Joanne from marketing and Patsy from human resources and acted as if I was terribly interested in their conversation about new management and saving the company. Secretly, I was gearing up for a second interview with another firm, hoping they would see my potential and snap me up faster than I'd propositioned a stranger the night before.

After grabbing a cup of now-cold coffee and making sure I avoided sitting next to the office gossip, Felicia, I slid into one of the last remaining seats like this was a game of musical chairs I desperately needed to win.

Luckily for me, it was right in front of the bagels. I grabbed a poppy seed one and started mowing down on it.

Unluckily for me, the seat I'd chosen was directly in front of the lone empty seat.

The door to the conference room opened and the room quieted as George escorted my new fucking boss to the seat directly across from me. He gave me a surprised and sure smile for a minute before giving lesser smiles to everyone else around us.

I wanted to slide right under the table.

When a man was deep inside of you for the first time, his face contorted in that sexy mix of pleasure and determination, one could argue that it's decidedly not the best time to ask important questions, such as:

- Are you single?
- Are you a serial killer?
- And, most significantly in that moment: what did you say you did for a living?

If only I'd asked that third question, I could have saved myself a lot of awkward.

Because seated across from me was Ben, who happened to be my new fucking boss.

Pun not intended on the 'fucking' part.

Like the excellent and professional employee I was, I barely listened to George make his speech about restructuring and eliminating the constant pace we'd maintained with downsizing. All the while, I was fishing stupid poppy seeds out of my teeth and studiously avoiding making eye contact with the man whose face I had practically tried to swallow the night before. Felicia, the 'subtle one' of the office, made advance after advance in Ben's direction, since she was seated directly to his right, but he was deflecting them with an ease I was impressed with.

Not that I was looking at him. Oh, no. I most certainly was not.

When George announced private meetings to discuss our positions for the company, with Ben, I choked on my bagel, which had become rock-hard in my mouth, and gagged down some cold coffee, before ducking out of the room entirely and into the hallway.

Oh, I could tell Ben all about my fucking positions. Literally. But I wouldn't have to, *because he already knew.*

Every swear word I'd ever said or thought or read flew from my mouth as I paced the hall outside the conference room.

I was going to fucking throw up.

I was going to die.

I was going to die with a giant bite of bagel still in my gullet and poppy seeds all over my teeth, in a pile of my vomit.

I'd barely made it to the bathroom when I heard the meeting disperse and people greeting Ben with limp fish handshakes and half-hearted messages of welcome.

I waited a full five minutes before exiting the bathroom, hoping to sneak by without that little one-on-one meeting, but I'd barely made it past his door before he was calling me in.

If there was a God who'd have listened, I would have sent him/her/them every prayer request I'd ever withheld, just to not be alone, with Ben my boss.

"Hey," he said casually, like this wasn't a Big Fucking Deal—proper style like that. "Have a seat." He closed the door behind me and I sat unceremoniously into the chair across from his wide and empty desk. I wanted the chair to dissolve under my ass, and then under my feet, so I could just fall straight through the floor and not be here.

"So…" I began, clasping my hands in my lap and rocking back and forth. "You're my new boss."

"Yeah," he said on a laugh and wrapped his hand behind his neck, rubbing the tension that had to be there away. "I guess this is awkward, right?"

No, I thought. *You dusted off my vagina a mere twelve hours ago and now you're my boss. Totally normal, bro.* "Just a little."

"I'm just going to get this out of the way—if I'd known…"

"I know," I interrupted, wringing my hands together, wanting to say what he was going to, before he had the chance to. "Last night was a mistake."

Silence fell over us, the ticking of the clock and the beating of my heart in my ears the only sounds I heard, until he asked, "Was it though?"

I lifted my head. "Are you seriously asking?"

"Yes. I am."

He pinned me with those baby blues and I wanted to groan when that stupidly perfect eyebrow rose. It was like he *knew* what that did to me. I'd thought banging him would get him out of my system, but seeing him, in a suit and in the daylight was blowing a lid off the cap of my libido.

"This..." I waved between us. "Complicates things."

"It doesn't have to."

"What does that mean?"

"It means that I don't think last night was a mistake." He came around the desk and instinct had me pushing in the chair—thinking it was a wheely one, but instead I just wobbled and nearly fell over. My dignity was still at the bottom of my trash, along with my microwaved nachos. "It means that while we're in a delicate situation here..." He paused for effect and it worked because I raised my head, so I met his eyes. "We don't have to pretend that last night never happened."

"But don't we? This makes you unbiased, especially if you're examining our individual positions in this company."

The side of his mouth curled. "Positions..."

I hated and loved the way that word hissed from his mouth. "See? Oh, shit. You cannot possibly be unbiased."

"You're wearing the leggings you wore last night." He was eyeing them the same way he had then, like he wanted to remove then with his mouth. I crossed my legs.

"Oh no." I laughed. "See? This will never work. Now, you're my *boss* and you have to decide if I'm worth keeping around here or not and you can't very well make a clearheaded decision about that considering the fact that we boned on my couch last night and now you're looking at my legs like you want to nibble on them."

"I do, you're right." At my tortured groan, he laughed and stepped even closer to me. "So, whether we continue what happened last night or not—it makes no difference, right? Because it's already happened, so—in your mind—I'm already biased."

I slouched in my seat for a moment, forgetting where I was. "Then what do we do?"

"We." He smiled at my use of a plural pronoun. "I simply disclose my inability to be biased when it comes to you, which means that George or someone else will take over in interviewing you for your position." He said this matter-of-factly, like it was *so* obvious. "And then we figure out *us* together."

We and us, when the night before the only we I'd known had been me and my chicken pajamas. "And that's it?"

"That's it." He leaned against the front of his desk, so close that our knees brushed and neither of us pulled back. "I like you. And I'm willing to bet you like me at least a little. You need fun and so do I. So, if you're up for it, I am too."

I chewed on my lip for a moment, studying his stupidly perfect, handsome face. He made it sound so simple. I mean, my job was still on the chopping block if the downsizing continued, but the night before I'd been lamenting about my boring life and now I had a man-sized snack asking me to figure shit out with him.

"Was it the pajamas that sold you?" I asked.

"The cocky pajamas? Yeah, pretty much sealed the deal for me."

I nodded. "I figured." What was I waiting for? Chicken pajamas and sad nachos were yesterday. A baby blue convertible and a man named Ben were today. "I guess we owe it to Elizabeth to find out what this is," I said and was rewarded with that cocksure grin.

"Like I told you before, I won't take unless you give."

I crossed my legs at my knees, remembering how much he had taken and given the night before. "Oh, I'm counting on it."

The End

ABOUT THE AUTHOR

Whitney Barbetti writes character-driven contemporary and new adult romance novels, heavy on the emotional connection. She lives in Idaho, where potatoes are abundant and delicious.

http://www.whitneybarbetti.com/

Facebook Page: https://www.facebook.com/whitney.barbetti/
Facebook Group: https://www.facebook.com/groups/barbettisbabes/
Instagram: https://www.instagram.com/barbetti/
Newsletter: http://bit.ly/WhitneyBarbettiNL
Amazon Author Page: http://author.to/WhitneyBarbetti

ALSO BY WHITNEY BARNETTI

All are on Amazon: http://author.to/WhitneyBarbetti

--- STANDALONES ---

The Sounds of Secrets

The Weight of Life

Hooked

Ten Below Zero

--- DUETS ---

The Mad Love Duet

Six Feet Under (Book One)

Pieces of Eight (Book Two)

The Bleeding Hearts Duet

Into the Tomorrows (Book One)

Back to Yesterday (Book Two)

The He Found Me Duet

He Found Me (Book One)

He Saved Me (Book Two)

A WICKED, COCKY PLAN: A PREQUEL TO WICKED FORCE

SAWYER BENNETT

Short story prequel to Wicked Force, featuring Kynan McGrath from the Wicked Horse Vegas series. Kynan will be spinning off a new series called Jameson Force Security in March, 2019.

KYNAN

I normally wouldn't answer my phone while a gorgeous redhead was performing a strip tease for me in my bedroom, but it's Rachel calling, and my second in charge at Jameson Force Security wouldn't bother me if it weren't important. Besides, I'm just cocky enough to take on a business call while receiving personal pleasure.

"This better be good, Hart," I say curtly after connecting. My gaze drifts ever so briefly down to the almost empty glass of scotch in my hand before going back to the woman who is dry humping one of my bedposts to some rock song I don't recognize. She watches me through heavy-lidded eyes, knowing that I'll reward her with spectacular orgasms and the pleasure of my cock.

"I don't know if 'good' is the word," she drawls. "There's a lot of money involved, but you aren't going to like who it's from."

"If it's that bloody congressman who hired us to babysit his duffer son, the answer is no." I learned from that job there are some things money can't buy.

"What the hell is a duffer?" Rachel asks.

"Someone who's useless," I tell her distractedly as the woman peels off her bra, exposing a pair of gloriously perky tits.

"You Brits have a funny way of talking," she replies. "Why couldn't you just have said 'useless'?"

My lips curve up into an amused smile, but she'll never know that. My tone is one of impatience when I tell her, "Just tell me what the job is, and I'll approve or deny it."

"It's Jocelyn Meyers."

My blood pressure spikes, and my fingers tighten so hard around my glass, it wouldn't surprise me if it were to shatter. It's difficult not to yell into the phone, but there's no mistaking the force of my words. "Not only no, but hell no. What-ever she needs, the answer is a bloody fucking no."

"I think you should listen—"

"I said no," I bark into the phone. "Now, is there anything else we need to discuss that doesn't have to do with Jocelyn Meyers, or can I get back to what I was doing before you tried to ruin my night?"

"She's in serious trouble," Rachel snaps at me.

"Don't care," I snarl back.

"Her life is in danger."

Every muscle in my body goes rigid, and a slight sweat breaks out on my forehead that has nothing to do with the woman who is currently shimming out of her panties. I give a hard shake of my head, wondering why Jocelyn still has the power to do that to me after all these years. Still, I manage to grit out between my teeth, "Don't. Care."

"That's what you want me to tell her?" Rachel asks calmly into the phone.

"I don't give a shit what you tell her as long as the word 'no' is somewhere in your sentence." I push away every bit of concern for Jocelyn that's starting to rear its ugly head. "Refer her over to Miller's agency. They do protection detail just fine."

There's a long moment of silence as Rachel digests what I'm saying. She's well aware of my enmity toward the world-famous Jocelyn Meyers, and I can't understand why she wants to fight me on this. I let my eyes roam all over the now fully naked woman—who is indeed a natural redhead—and hope she will distract me from this distasteful conversation.

"Fine," Rachel says with a sigh. I choose to ignore the fact that I'm also strangely unsettled that nothing is actually really resolved. Not for Jocelyn anyway. "I understand and respect your decision. But you can tell her yourself."

What Rachel says hasn't quite penetrated before Jocelyn's soft voice comes over the line. "Kynan," she says hesitantly.

I bolt upright in my chair, my spine stiff and unrelenting as I set my glass onto the table beside me.

"Kynan," Jocelyn says again, and her voice quavers with emotion. "I could really use your help."

Fuck.

I scrub a hand over my face and blink stupidly at the woman as her hand works between her legs and she moans softly.

My jaw locks hard for a moment as I tell myself to stay strong. "We aren't taking on celebrity detail anymore. We can refer you to a good agency to better suited for your needs."

Not the truth, but she doesn't need to know that.

There is no one better than us.

Jameson Force Security has expanded greatly since I bought it from Jerico Jameson two years ago in a cool, seven million dollar deal. The first thing I did was change the name from The Jameson Group to Jameson Force Security. I thought it brought a bit of pizazz and made us more marketable to the civilian population who might be in need of protection. While our most lucrative contracts had come from the U.S. government or various foreign allies for special forces work, as my business grew, I took on more mainstream and run-of-the-mill security jobs.

Like protecting celebrities and installing top-of-the-line security systems for them. It was work that was below my expertise level, but I hired the best of the best to handle this stuff. I personally vet every single member of my company and I'd trust them all with my life.

"If it's a matter of money—"

I cut her off. "It isn't."

"Please, Kynan," she implores, and I can hear the watery tears in her voice.

Thankfully, I'm momentarily distracted as the redhead crawls on her hands and knees toward me. Blue eyes flashing with heat and her tits swaying provocatively. I sit silently and with a little bit of satisfaction that this woman before me is exactly what I want and need, and the woman on the other line, probably sitting in her multi million dollar Malibu mansion, is not.

The woman's hands come to my thighs, slide up, and work at my belt. My cock finally decides to get into the game and thickens at the prospect. I settle back into the chair, lifting my hips briefly so she can reach inside my pants to pull me free.

I suppress a groan as her hand circles me tight and starts to stroke. I cup her breast, relishing the weight of it before giving her nipple a pinch. Her lush lips peel back into a wicked smile and then her mouth is on me.

Fuck yeah. That's exactly what I need.

My hand goes to her hair, fingers gripping tight. I help her bob up and down, starting to get lost in the sensation.

"He almost killed me last night," Jocelyn says, and for a moment, her words don't register.

When they do, I pull the redhead off my cock. She looks at me in surprise, but I give her a small shake of my head as I sit straight in my chair again.

"What?" I manage to rasp out.

"A stalker," she whispers. "He's been harassing me for a really long time, but he managed to break into my house last night. I couldn't get to my panic room in time."

The air in my lungs freezes.

Everything around me seems to freeze for that matter as my ears ring with her revelation.

"He heard the sirens approaching before he could . . ." Her words trail off and bile rises in my throat. She takes in a breath and lets it out before finishing softly. "He ran off, and they didn't catch him."

I clear my throat from the thick emotion that's built up. "Where are you? Is someone with you now?"

Jocelyn gives a mirthless laugh. "I'm in your office. Over on Clarke Avenue."

She's here?

In Vegas?

"Put Rachel back on the phone," I instruct her, my words clipped and impersonal.

There's an indistinct murmuring between the women as the phone gets passed. Rachel's voice comes through brisk and professional. "What do you want me to do?"

I look longingly at the redhead, who has since moved to lounge in a sexy pose on my bed. I want to get lost in that and forget everything else.

There's no holding back the long sigh of resignation that escapes me. "We're taking the case. Starting now. Bring her to my house."

"Your house?" Rachel asks with surprise.

"For safety's sake, she stays with me until I can figure out who to assign this case to."

Rachel is silent for a moment and then says in an ultra low voice. "But you aren't alone."

"True," I reply as I push up out of the chair, assuming Rachel must have heard the music and moaning. My pants barely cling to the edges of my hips and I've lost my hard-on, a matter that needs to be rectified immediately. I walk around the bed and stare at the beautiful, luscious creature lying there. "But that's none of Jocelyn's concern. We're nothing to each other but business."

"Gotcha, boss," she says, and I can hear the amusement in her voice. Rachel's known me for years, and we were fuck buddies for a time. She caught me on the tail end of my and Jocelyn's breakup, and I got easily lost between her legs as we traveled the world, seeking adventure and thrills.

But Rachel and I aren't like that anymore. We became colleagues at Jameson over a decade ago, and it's been purely professional since. After Jerico sold the company to me, Rachel took the spot as my most trusted peer in this business. She's also non judgmental and won't hold it against me if my treatment of Jocelyn is less than civilized.

The redhead comes to her knees and scoots toward me. Her fingers work at the buttons of my shirt, and she leans in to place a kiss on the center of my chest once it's bared to her.

My cock comes back to life, and I disconnect the call.

Jocelyn is forgotten.

For the time being.

JOCELYN

"Kynan's done well for himself," I murmur to Rachel as we pull into the driveway of a monstrous Spanish Colonial-style mansion. It's bigger than my house, and mine sits at just over seven thousand square feet of space that I never use.

"That he has," she replies as she puts her Maserati Quattroporte in park and cuts the engine.

I don't make any move to open the door and neither does Rachel. My heart is pounding at the prospect of seeing Kynan again after all these years, but this isn't as scary as what happened in my house last night. Unconsciously, my fingers come to my throat where they skim the purple bruises there.

"How old is your kid?" I ask Rachel as I turn slightly to look at her. She blinks at me in surprise, but I throw a thumb over my shoulder to the child safety seat in the back.

"He'll be six months old on the twenty-third."

I smile as I do a quick calculation in my head. "He was almost a Christmas baby then."

"Yup," she says with a laugh. "My husband Bodie insisted his middle name be Kris in honor of the holidays."

Kris Kringle. Cute. "What's his first name?"

"Anthony, but we call him Tony," she replies.

Traditional sounding. "Family name?"

She shakes her head with a laugh. "No. We named him after Tony Stark."

"You're kidding me?"

"I never kid about the Avengers." She grins for a moment before her expression turns reassuring. "Ready to get this over with?"

I nod back at her, but what I really want to do is tell her to just start the car again, take me to the nearest airport, and let me take a flight somewhere that no

73

one will know about. I can melt away into obscurity, and the psychopath who is after me will be left far behind.

Except . . . he's managed to find me time and time again over the last few years. I've moved four times, purchasing my homes under fake aliases, but always, he still finds me. Threatening notes followed by long, flowing love letters. Bouquets of flowers at the gated entry to my house or decapitated squirrels, depending on his mood. It was sporadic enough that I'd sometimes get a false sense of security that he'd gotten bored and moved on, but then something else would happen.

But he had never come into my home before.

And I knew it was him.

My stalker.

He managed to cut the power, which alerted me that something might be wrong. When I heard glass break near the back patio, I dialed 9-1-1 and raced toward the panic room. Even though he cut the power, my security system had a battery backup, and I knew a silent alarm would be ringing somewhere, hopefully notifying the police.

It was a good thing too, because the man took me down in the hallway just mere feet from the door to the panic room and before 9-1-1 could even answer my call. My only saving grace was the security company alerting the police and a cruiser just blocks from my house. The wailing sirens as they pulled up in front of my house caused him to run. Which was good, because I was very close to losing consciousness from his hands locked around my throat.

My fingers drop away from the bruising, but Rachel's gaze lingers on it, surveying the marks he left behind. When she looks back at me, her eyes harden. "Kynan will protect you. We'll figure out who this shit head is, and he won't bother you anymore when we're done with him."

I manage a tremulous smile. "That's the most reassuring thing I've heard in a long time. The police haven't been able to do much with what they've had over the last few years."

Her eyes go soft and almost apologetic. "I don't know the details of what happened between you and Kynan, but I know the general gist of things."

Heat flushes through me, and I drop my gaze to my lap. "He hates me."

"I have no clue as to that," she remarks simply. "But don't expect him to be nice. If you want him for this job, just be ready to deal with that."

I nod in acknowledgment of something I was pretty sure she didn't need to explain. Kynan and I split ways twelve years ago, and it wasn't pretty at all. It's one of my greatest regrets in life, but that doesn't make things any better for either of us.

My gaze rises and locks with Rachel's. "I know exactly how Kynan feels about me, and yet, I'm still here. He's the one for this job."

"Why?" she asks with a head tilt. "There are a lot of other great security firms out there."

She's right, and I researched them back when the stalking started. I've even used some of them for personal security services and could easily use the same ones again, but something tells me they wouldn't be enough.

My lips curve into a sardonic smile. "No matter his feelings toward me,

Kynan is a man of integrity. And I know he'll take this far more serious than anyone else would. I trust him."

"All right then," she says as she grabs the handle to her door and opens it up. "Let's go on in."

I follow Rachel up the walkway, which is lined with cacti and tropical-looking plants. Even though it's June in Vegas, I pull the sides of my zip hoodie around me for protection. I'm not looking my best, that's for sure. After I refused an ambulance to the hospital, I gladly accepted a police officer's ride straight to the airport. I'd thrown on some yoga pants, a tank top, and grabbed my hoodie from the closet. I didn't bring anything else other than my purse. I have no makeup on, my hair is a rat's nest, and I don't even have a brush because I don't keep one in my purse. No, I wouldn't do something as common sense as that. I had to have the huge cosmetic/vanity bag in addition to my purse, which held all the essentials I needed to stay looking glamorous at all times. I never even thought to bring that with me because my only thought was getting out of Los Angeles and getting to Kynan for help.

There was never any doubt of where I'd go once I approached the ticketing agent at the airport. The police officer kindly came in with me and stayed by my side until I made it to the security line. Still, I didn't stop looking over my shoulder until I was on the plane to Vegas and every last passenger had boarded. My life is now one that is led by fear and survival instinct, and I know I can't survive it alone.

We get to Kynan's front door, and to my surprise, Rachel punches in a security code and walks in without knocking.

The splendor of his house is lost on me, not because I'm immune to opulence but because it isn't important to me. Over the years, many things I thought were important have become trivial.

Crossing my arms over my chest, I look around with minimal curiosity and mostly nervousness over seeing the man that I once loved and who now hates me.

Rachel shuts the door and walks into the open living room that has wide, glass doors that look out over a spacious veranda. It's filled with potted plants, a huge grill, and high-end furniture, but I barely take it in.

I hear a door open from above and my gaze sweeps up the massive, curved staircase that sits between the foyer and living area. There's laughter—both male and female—and then Kynan walks down the staircase with a ravishingly beautiful woman wearing nothing but one of his t-shirts. He has his arm around her and is whispering something in her ear that causes her to giggle again. Kynan wearing a pair of track pants and a T-shirt. His dark blond hair is mussy, and it's clear they just spent some time in bed together.

My face flushes with embarrassment over being in Kynan's home unannounced and clearly ruining an evening with his girlfriend.

When he reaches the bottom of the stairs, his eyes come to me, but linger only briefly and without a flicker of emotion. Then they slide to Rachel. "I don't need anything else tonight, Rach. Get home to Bodie and Tony."

Rachel inclines her head and gives me a last reassuring smile that misses the mark with me. "See you later, Jocelyn."

"Bye," I whisper, my throat feeling extremely parched from nerves and still raw from last night's attack.

When the door closes behind her, Kynan's hand drops to the woman's ass and he squeezes it. "Be a love and get me a club soda from the bar."

"Not another scotch?" she purrs with her hand to his chest as she leans into him.

He shakes his head and looks at me. "Want something to drink?"

"I'm good."

Kynan's eyes drop briefly to my throat, but I don't see so much as see a facial tick from him. His expression is as bland as unbuttered grits.

The red-headed woman sashays off without an introduction to me. I watch her swaying hips briefly as she walks over to a recessed wet bar built into one wall before turning to Kynan. I swallow to wet my throat and say, "I'm sorry. I shouldn't be barging in like this and interrupting time with you and your girl-friend. I can go to a hotel, and we can meet in your office tomorrow."

Both Kynan and the woman give simultaneous snorts of amusement, but she's the one who responds to me. "Oh, I'm not his girlfriend."

My eyes move back and forth between the two.

Kynan just shrugs. "We just met this afternoon."

"Oh," I say softly, the implication hitting me. I mean, I'm not shocked because there's nothing wrong with one-night stands or anything like that, but why in the world did he have Rachel bring me here if he was in the middle of one?

"We met at The Wicked Horse," the woman adds on conversationally. "I was getting flogged in the stocks, and Kynan rescued me. Whisked me off to this luxurious mansion for an evening of fun."

I blink stupidly, trying to process. "I'm sorry. The Wicked Horse?"

"It's a sex club I belong to," Kynan replies and walks over to a sumptuous-looking armchair. He drops down with elegant grace and motions with his hand toward the couch, indicating I should take a seat.

Now I'm shocked. So much so that I'm rooted to the spot. "Sex club?"

"Oh, don't sound so boorish, Jocelyn," Kynan chastises me in that sexy British accent. "You should give kink a try sometime. You would have no shortage of movie stars and rock gods lining up for you."

I can feel the heat creeping up my neck as the woman walks over to Kynan with a glass of club soda in her hand. She settles down right onto his lap, and I'm stunned when his hand goes between her legs.

Not to squeeze her thigh or give her a caress.

Goes right to her core, and while the hem of her robe covers what he does to her, I know it must feel good because her eyes roll into the back of her head, which then lolls on his shoulder. Her legs start to fall open to give him better access, and I get just a glimpse of a smirk on Kynan's face as he watches me closely for a reaction.

I spin away, mortified and equally pissed off. I start for the door, unwilling to stand for whatever it is he's trying to prove here.

"Stay," he commands, and for a heartbeat, I almost obey him. That voice of his . . . all cultured sounding but incredibly arrogant and demanding *almost* ensnares me. I used to obey him a lot when it came to sex, but I chalk that up to the fact I was just oh so young when we were together.

I'm not young and naïve anymore, so I keep walking.

I make it to the foyer before he calls out again, "Walk out that door, Jocelyn, and you know your life is in danger. Your psychopath could be out there right now."

They are the right words.

I freeze in place, feeling my shoulders slump in resignation.

I'm pretty much in a no win situation, and I had known when I walked through his door that Kynan's help would cost me more than just money. It's clear that as a means to repent for what I did to him, he's going to humiliate me first by making me stay while he gets the woman in his lap off.

But to my surprise, I hear him say, "We're going to need to call it a night, love. Go get your clothes on and call yourself a cab. I've got some money in my wallet on the dresser to pay for it."

"Sure thing," I hear her reply and then there's nothing but the sound of kissing, some moaning, and a deep groan from Kynan. I can only imagine what she's doing to him, but I refuse to turn around and look.

Only when I hear the woman's soft steps on the staircase do I give my attention to Kynan again.

KYNAN

I t's another punch to my gut when Jocelyn turns to face me. Surprisingly, she's even more beautiful now than she was twelve years ago at the age of twenty. She's filled out in all the right places, and despite the haunted look in her blue eyes, her face is a work of art any man would be hard pressed to ignore. Her hair is more of a platinum blonde than when we were together, and I find the pale color looks even better on her. Though, it does make the bruising on her neck stand out in stark contrast against it.

Those marks, clearly from a man's hands around her throat, were the first thing I noticed when I laid eyes on her. I was battling a rage so intense that I almost stumbled down the last two steps of the staircase.

I've seen Jocelyn a lot over the years.

Usually on entertainment shows, giving interviews and such.

Accepting awards and signing autographs.

She's come a long way from her early days as the opening act for a Vegas singing legend.

It took one savvy talent scout to catch her crooning an Alannis Morrisette song, and her life changed in an instant.

So did mine, and not for the better.

"Take a seat," I tell her with a nod at the couch.

She listens, but her walk is slow, her steps measured. There's a slight limp there, and I'm guessing more bruising lurks somewhere under those clothes from whatever happened last night.

I try to ignore the cold chill that races up my spine as I realize that Jocelyn could have died last night and I would have heard about in on the news.

I can imagine the headlines now. *Reigning Queen of Pop Murdered in Her House by Stalker.*

Jocelyn sits stiffly and awkwardly with her hands clenched tight on her lap and her gaze focused there.

"Tell me everything," I say.

Her eyes come to me slowly. She licks her lips, and just that little action right there causes more of an erotic sense of pleasure within me than any of the dirty things that were just done to me less than twenty minutes ago. I hate that she can get a physical reaction from me when she isn't even trying.

"A little over two years ago, I got a letter in the mail that was definitely different from the crazy sort of fan mail one can expect . . ."

I let her talk for almost a half hour, interrupting her sparingly with questions. In that time period, the redhead comes down the stairs as unobtrusively as she can and slips out the front door with a wink at me before it closes. I don't acknowledge her in any way and Jocelyn keeps talking.

When she's finished, I've heard enough to know that she's got one seriously twisted, but incredibly smart, psycho after her. The fact he's been able to track her down to new homes purchased through aliases tells me he's a hacker of some sort. If he's as good as I'm afraid to believe, I wouldn't be surprised if he knows she's in Vegas.

Possibly even at my house.

Not likely, but not impossible either. Just because someone is a nut job doesn't mean they're short on smarts, and all indications tell me that this guy is intelligent. I'll know more once I can get my hands on the mail he's been sending her that the police have. Jocelyn tells me she's saved it all and it's in police custody right now.

When she quiets and I know she's told me all she's capable of recounting at this point, I push up from my chair and set my empty glass on the coffee table. Without a word, I head to the wet bar and pour her a glass of cabernet. She was a white wine drinker twelve years ago, but she's matured since then. I peg her liking red now.

She blinks at me in surprise when I'm standing in front of her, holding the glass out. We stare at each other a moment before she takes the wine and whispers, "Thank you."

I return to my chair but don't sink into a relaxing position. Instead, I perch on the edge with my elbows to my knees and wait for her to give me her undivided attention.

"He isn't going to go away," I tell her with surety. I've dealt with a variety of stalkers over the years, and I know someone who has gone to the lengths he has is not going to rest until she's dead. There's a psychological component there that can't be overcome. He'll keep coming and coming at her until he satisfies his fantasy or gets arrested. Those are the only two outcomes.

Well, not the *only* two.

I could kill him.

"I know," she murmurs before taking another sip. "It's why I need your help."

"Why me?"

Her expression is shrewd and defiant. It's the first I've seen of her fiery spirit since she walked in here. "Because I trust you."

"That's an awful big gamble," I point out to her. "Especially how things ended between us."

"Kynan," she murmurs in a pained voice. "You know how sorry—"

"Don't," I cut her off with a palm raised toward her. "It's not relevant to this

80

discussion. You're a potential client now, and I take my job seriously. It's enough to know you trust me."

"Potential client?" she asks with mild alarm in her expression.

"You haven't heard my price," I drawl.

"I'll pay whatever. You know money's not an option."

I nod. "I know that. But I have a plan, and you might not like it."

"What is it?" she asks curiously.

"We're going to bait him to come after you," I tell her and then brace for her reaction.

She stares at me a for very long moment before she tips the wine glass to her mouth. She chugs the remainder in four long swallows and then gasps, "You want him to come after me?"

"He won't get near you."

"Can you guarantee that?" she rasps.

"Yes. I promise you." I'm sure that won't be the only lie I tell Jocelyn in the days to come, but I need her calm and assured right now. She's had enough fear to last her for a while.

I can't promise her one hundred percent safety. I can't do that with anyone. But I believe the best chance of taking this guy down and preserving her life is to do it on my terms and not his. I want to see him coming, so I need to open a pathway to her. I'm confident I can keep her safe while we wait for him.

Jocelyn stands and moves to refill her glass before taking her seat again. When she does, she kicks her tennis shoes off, curls her legs underneath herself, and leans against the armrest. After contemplating the color and legs of the red liquid she swirls around in the glass, she lifts her eyes to me. "What would that look like? How would you accomplish this?"

"We're going to put on a show for him, and he won't be able to resist coming after you." At least that's my initial thought. I'll run this by my team for additional input, but I feel confident in the idea. "We'll get your publicist on it. Announce that you and I are a couple. We'll do a few photo ops. I'm going to brag about how you're absolutely protected now under my watch and this loser isn't going to get anywhere near you. His ego won't be able to handle it. His psychosis will demand he prove me wrong. Then you and I are going to take a little trip somewhere for an 'extended vacation,' and we're going to reverse hack him. We're going to leave a trail of bread crumbs, and then we're going to watch as he picks them up. Hopefully, we can identify the bastard before he even gets near you."

Jocelyn takes another healthy slug of the wine before asking, "And you think this is the best way?"

"I do," I tell her with that cocky assurance I'm known for in my line of work. Without the ego I have, I'd be dead by now.

Her gaze drops to her glass, and her words come out so softly I can barely hear them. "And you're . . . okay with helping me?"

I tamp down the anger that has been bubbling low in my belly since she walked through my door, but I don't keep the chill from my voice. "You're a client, Jocelyn. The amount of money I'm going to charge you makes it more than okay for me to work for you. But don't think you're anything more than a good-paying job that will make my stock portfolio look a lot nicer by the end of the year. I'll protect you, keep you safe, and take this psychopath down. Then I won't think about you again after it's over."

Jocelyn cringes, and the corners of her mouth draw downward. Still, she nods in acknowledgment of the boundaries I just set.

Of the rules by which we will both abide.

I'm surprised when she looks back up to me, her face impassively blank. "And just where are we going to go on this 'extended vacation'?"

I give her an amused smile. "You're going home, Jocelyn. I'm taking you back to Cunningham Falls."

<<<>>>

The conclusion to this prequel, Wicked Force, releases in March, 2019.
You can pre-order at:
Amazon: https://amzn.to/2Ianb9T
iBooks: https://apple.co/2KhO7Rx
Goodreads: https://bit.ly/2rJKKeL

If you want to check out The Wicked Horse Vegas series, you can find the books at:
http://sawyerbennett.com/bookstore/the-wicked-horse-vegas-series/

If you want to check out the original Wicked Horse series, you can find the books at:
http://sawyerbennett.com/bookstore/wicked-horse-series/

For all of Sawyer Bennett's other books, you can visit her Book Shop at:
https://sawyerbennett.com/bookshop/

ABOUT THE AUTHOR

Since the release of her debut contemporary romance novel, Off Sides, in January 2013, Sawyer Bennett has released multiple books, many of which have appeared on the New York Times, USA Today and Wall Street Journal bestseller lists.

A reformed trial lawyer from North Carolina, Sawyer uses real life experience to create relatable, sexy stories that appeal to a wide array of readers. From new adult to erotic contemporary romance, Sawyer writes something for just about everyone.

Facebook: http://www.facebook.com/bennettbooks

For all of Sawyer Bennett's other books, you can visit her Book Shop at:
https://sawyerbennett.com/bookshop/

MAGICAL COCK
AND BULL

K.F. BREENE

A bonus short story set in the Fire and Ice and Magical Mayhem worlds featuring Moss, Darius's right-hand-man.

This is raw, original material written just for this anthology. Due to constraints and the immediacy of the timeline, this story has not been edited.

ONE

"I wouldn't go in there if I were you, vampire."

Moss slowed in his approach to the mansion hugging the side of the cliff, overlooking the Pacific Ocean. Lights illuminated the large picture windows, showing elegantly clad people standing within, drinks in their hands and smiles on their faces. By his estimation, they would be nearly ready for the transformation that would secure his boss a new generation of revenue earners.

He turned slightly, spotting a woman sitting on the hood of a nineteen sixty-nine Corvette in mint condition. Stretchy black material covered her toned body, ending in black boots with one scuffed toe splattered in deep crimson. A leather band circled her trim thigh, supporting a large blade that had likely found its way into more than one poor sod's rib cage.

He hadn't noticed her sitting there, blanketed in moonlight. He couldn't even smell her, though the breeze should've carried her scent right to him. She had effectively hidden from him in plain sight, a rare feat with a vampire of his age.

"And why is that?" Moss asked.

Her shrug was minimal. She slowly shifted her gaze to the large house not far away. "Call it a hunch."

His phone vibrated in his pocket, awakening the watch at his wrist. They were ready for him.

He paused in starting forward, her loose posture and easy confidence tickling his predisposition for caution. "What do you know?"

A smile drifted up her lovely face. A vein gently pulsed along the side of her neck. His hunger gnawed at his gut, he having foregone feeding in anticipation of the Turning to come.

"Oh nothing," she said in a teasing tone. "Just that a bunch of furry men and women are waiting a mile or so away for when the vampires—you—are the most vulnerable. Same old, same old with one of these things, isn't it?"

Moss couldn't help the rigidity in his body. She meant shifters. If they caught vampires feeding on humans, and especially attempting to turn them from human to vampire, they'd enforce the supernatural laws and kill on sight. They loved this part of their job. Got off on it.

But his maker and boss, Darius, had personally overseen the planning of this Turning. He'd received written consent from each human, and had homes and wills properly laid out for afterward. They'd all been monitored for secrecy. If they'd told anyone of what would become of them, Darius's people would've known.

Which begged the question, how had this woman found out about the Turning?

"This is Darius's show, is it not?" she said before he could ask, her velvety voice sliding over his skin. Heat kindled in his core. "A friend of mine helped a woman under Darius's protection. The Natural Witch, they call her. Do you know her?"

She meant Penny, a powerhouse of a magic worker that had been integral to taking down the Mages' Guild not long ago. Which meant, this woman's friend must've been the warrior druid that had been paid to stay by Penny's side.

He barely kept his mouth from dropping open.

"Not much of a talker, huh?" she said, and slid off of the hood of the car. Shadows reached for her body, momentarily wrapping her up and confusing his mind. A moment later they were gone and she was striding toward him, her hips swaying erotically. His cock started to pound and hunger pinched his gut. His fangs elongated, desperate to be buried in her neck.

"You're a druid," he murmured.

"A warrior druid, yes." She laughed, a low, husky sound. "It took you a while to realize it. I have a kill order for someone in that house. A human—soon a vampire. He's wanted dead or alive. I prefer to take them in dead. There's less unnecessary begging." She reached him and ran one sharp, manicured nail down the side of his neck. "My friend respects Darius. He would've wanted me to warn you about the danger."

"What about the others in the house? Did you warn them?"

"No. They are pee-ons, yes? Expendable. But you..." She stopped in front of him, and finally her scent reached him. Earthy and rich, it crawled into his consciousness and lay there, delighting his senses. "You are in charge here. You're also strong, and fierce. And hungry." Her hand glided over his chest and on down, over his stomach. Down further still. "I can feel the hunger in you. The aching lust. You want to fuck me. To bite me."

He clenched his jaw as his phone rang yet again. He was late now. He had to get inside. He had to cure this insatiable hunger.

"I've never had a vampire," she purred. "Stopping you from going into that house would save you, and give me something I've been meaning to try. What do you say?"

"And the kill order?"

"Why waste effort killing him myself when the shifters will do it for me? I just have to go in after and bag the pieces." She shrugged as her hand wrapped around his hard bulge.

"You called the shifters."

Her smile was dazzling. "Maybe."

"Why?"

Her hand stroked slowly. "The contract wasn't officiated until after this party was underway and trying to kill vampires is tedious. I'd rather work smarter, not harder. Apologize to Darius for me. Tell him it's business. He'll understand."

Moss pushed her out of his way and stalked forward, bringing the phone up from his pocket. "Odd way of showing your respect."

"Okay, okay," she called after him. "You got me. Stopping you was selfish. Can you blame me? You're handsome, made more so by the power of your magic. I long to experience it."

Moss gritted his teeth as he reached the door and pulled it open. His cock throbbed and his hunger was like a live thing, scrambling his thoughts and slowing his movements. All he wanted to do was thrust into a warm body while sucking in hot, thick blood. Only now, this new development put everything in jeopardy.

"Sir, there you are." Carmen, a slight female in her twenties with a doll-like face rushed forward, her pupils dilated and her fangs dropping from her gums. As a lower middle-tier vampire, she didn't have nearly the control he did. Her intense hunger showed in every line on her face. "The subjects are ready. They are in the kitchen."

"They've consumed the serum?" he said, bringing up his phone app.

"Yes. The transformation is starting to happen. I can barely keep the others at bay. Blood lust is setting in."

Moss bit back a swear as he tapped Darius's name. "We have to move. The shifters have been notified of this Turning."

The blood left her face. She shook her head. "We can't fight like this. We're all starving."

Darius answered on the second ring. "Yes?"

"We've got a problem, sir." He explained quickly as he reached the kitchen.

"Get them out. Now," Darius barked through the phone. "I'll send you arrangements."

"It's not that easy, sir. I'm the only one who can withstand the bloodlust, and I'm fighting it hard."

Carmen grabbed one of the humans leaning against the edge of the kitchen table, a tall man with thick cords of muscle. A sheen of sweat covered his face and his erection tented his pants. Before she could lift him to standing, trying to get him moving, he slid his hands up her body before cupping her breasts.

She froze and her eyes drifted closed. Her fangs finished their descent and her body trembled. Before Moss could command her to move, she yanked the man closer and swung her face down, digging her fangs into the side of his neck.

The man moaned and fell back, dragging her with him onto the table. Her hands pulled at the buttons on his pants and he ripped her shirt open in the front. Buttons scattered across the table.

Another vampire grabbed a female human before unceremoniously biting the inside of her wrist. His hand felt up her inner thigh before massaging her apex. She writhed under his touch before pushing on the top of his head, clearly wanting his mouth to replace his hand.

"Fuck," Moss swore. "I'm losing them."

"Get Felicia Draven and get out," Darius yelled. "Call me with your location.

I'll send someone to get you. And kill that druid. It's business. She'll understand."

Moss gritted his teeth, drowning in desire and hunger. Trying to get his thoughts back on track.

He'd barely be able to get out of the house, let alone kill a trained assassin purposely bred for the role. Darius had clearly forgotten Moss wasn't an elder. Some things were beyond his reach.

Without delay, he shoved a younger vampire out of the way and reached for a beautiful human, her eyes dizzied with lust. The telltale sheen of sweat covered her forehead, and she was panting. She needed blood to continue the change.

He threw her over his shoulder, and then groaned as her hands explored down his back. The second he could get her to a secure location, he'd be all too happy to give her what she craved.

A loud crash tore through the house, coming from the back. Another out the side. Glass shattered as a huge wolf body crashed through the sliding glass door on the other side of the shifters.

That damn druid had sped up the shifters, he'd bet his life on it. And if he didn't get out of there fast, his life would be exactly what he was betting.

TWO

Moss dodged a lunging wolf, its jaws snapping and a line of spit flinging past him. The stench of shifter permeated the space as shapes darted in. Carmen jumped off of the writing human and into a crouch, blood dripping down her face. Her body exploded into her other form, with leathery skin, long claws, and increased reflexes. It was the vampire fighting form, similar to a shifter changing into an animal.

Canine snarls preceded a vampire screeching. A human screamed.

Moss didn't wait around to see how it worked out.

He sped off toward the interior of the house, a direction the glorified dogs wouldn't expect. He climbed the stairs in twos, desperately trying to ignore the firm touch of the woman on his back. At the landing, he barely caught a glimpse of a four-legged shape running in his direction.

He turned right and raced down the hall, all his focus on getting out in one piece. These wolves were clearly organized, which meant they were higher up in the shifter hierarchy. The situation had Roger, the head alpha, written all over it. That druid had gone all the way to the top.

He bit back a swear and kicked open a door before sprinting to the windows and looking down. No roof. It was a straight drop. He turned as a furry shape surged into the room after him.

Moss dropped the woman—Felicia—onto the bed before lengthening his claws. Strength and power filled every inch of his frame as the wolf attacked. He grabbed the head and whipped the body around, smashing it into the wall. One wolf was no match for a vampire of his advanced age.

The wolf rose, but Moss was there, grabbing it by the throat with his fangs and ripping out the jugular. Hot blood rolled over his tongue, heady and delicious. His senses exploded and his stomach clenched, everything in him wanting to lap it up. To give up the plight and indulge in the much needed substance.

That was a sure way to die.

With everything in him, he turned away. The door was clear, for now. He grabbed the woman and darted out of the room, giving a quick glance to make sure no one else had followed him up. They were shifters, though. They'd smell his trail. They wouldn't be long.

He ran into the last room and found what he was after: a window leading out onto the roof. He took a moment to open it before climbing out. A moment later, a wolf loped through the door.

Moss yanked down the window and gave the doggy a wink. Wolves didn't have thumbs, and breaking through this glass would mean it couldn't stop in time before plunging off the roof. Sucked to have a four-legged animal for a second form.

He threw the woman over his shoulder again before jogging along the roof to the side of the house. Away from the cliff, the manicured lawn ran into coastal trees, the land quickly becoming wild. Further along and a wooden fence with a flat top closed in the backyard. He hopped onto it, jostling the woman but landing easily. With effort, he ran along the top, ignoring the snarls from around the corner of the house. The vampires were still putting up the good fight, but Moss doubted they'd make it out. Not if Roger had been in charge. Darius would lose a good few minions he'd be loath to part with.

Off the fence now, at the back corner of the property, branches reached out to cover his progress. His feet crashed through the underbrush, stealth impossible in his current state. His stomach felt like it was turning inside out, famine making his movements stiff and clumsy.

The cars waited off to the left, and if he could get inside one, he'd be fine. He'd get out of there by the time a shifter could change and break the glass. But the odds of the shifters leaving an obvious getaway unattended were small.

The scent of Felicia's skin teased him. Her body grew heavier by the moment. Her hands more exploratory.

Laboring, he weaved in and out of the trees, putting distance between himself and the house. Soon he'd tug out his phone and see what Darius had organized in the way of pickup.

A howl drifted from behind him, near the house. Another sounded away to his left. One more, in front of him.

The wolves were on the hunt.

He changed direction and put on a burst of speed, fighting his body's downward spiral into blood lust. His breath came in hard pants. The woman tried to hook her foot under his cock, but only succeeded in jamming up the churning of his legs.

"Hungry," she said in a breathy whisper, her firm touch sliding down his back. "Horny."

The sound of light feet interrupted the *thrushing* of the distant waves. The stench of shifter announced the wolves' presence right before two burst through the bushes. More footfall indicated two more on the way.

They'd brought a large host to take this party down.

For the first time in decades, a thread of fear wormed through Moss's middle.

He slowed, then stopped, turning to face the closest wolf. Running was futile. He'd have to stay and fight.

The woman mewed in protest when he set her on the ground. He couldn't fight with her on his shoulder.

The closest wolf chuffed. The other lowered its heads and moved forward, its lips lifted in a silent snarl. Two more joined the semi-circle.

Moss felt the surge to change form, but without the resources of blood, it would drain precious energy. He cracked his neck.

"Well?" he asked, staying loose. He put up his hands in a *come on* gesture. "Are you waiting for an invitation?"

The first wolf took three fast steps before launching through the air. The next, then another, ran a moment later. He caught the first wolf body before ripping his claws down the wolf's side and flinging it away. The next wolf nearly hit his middle, trying to knock him back. He grabbed it as the third made contact, forcing him to the side. If they got him off his feet, he was in trouble.

He punched claws into the wolf in his grasp before swiping down with the other hand, catching not much more than fur. Paws hit the center of his back before teeth tore into the back of his neck. He hadn't heard the rear attack coming.

Easily ignoring the pain, he swung around, ripping out with his claws and opening his mouth wide so the fangs could fully descend. Canine teeth bit into his upper thigh. Another body slammed into his side.

He staggered again and this time, his feet caught on the rugged earth. His momentum carried him off-balance. More teeth, ripping at his chest. Another body, helping him fall.

Snarling, he lashed out in a frenzy. He'd go down, but he'd take as many with him as he could.

A mouth of white, sharp teeth opened, the animal standing above him. It moved in, aiming for his jugular.

THREE

S hadows moved. Coalesced. Moss's mind dizzied, watching that mouth dip to his throat. He tried to pull up his hands to protect himself. To lash out. But dull teeth bit into his wrists. Heavy bodies held him down.

Part of the wolf head disappeared into grays and blacks. Air swirled around them, thick and earthy. A knife came out of nowhere. It slashed down, without a hand attached. The blade pierced the wolf in the neck, sinking in deep.

The beast cried out and spun, snapping its jaws at the unseen attacker. A foot swung out of the unnatural mist, catching the newly dying wolf in the side and propelling it out of the fight.

A woman stepped out of the shadow, decked in tight black clothes and with a new splatter of blood on her heavy black boots.

"Six against one is not a fair fight," she said in a feminine hum with a smile on her beautiful face. "I think the vampire needs fresh blood in this battle." She winked at him, her version of humor.

She bent, the knife striking out, her movements lithe and graceful. Oh so lethal. Her knife dug into a furry body before she yanked sideways cutting off the howl of pain. Her face showed no emotion as she moved to the next, diving away from snapping jaws, rolling, and popping up without so much as a grunt. A bow came out of nowhere, an arrow nocked in a moment, before loosing at a wolf running into the scene. A fletching blossomed red in gray fur before the wolf staggered and died where it stood, the shot perfect.

Without skipping a beat, she slashed her knife to the side, opening a throat, then switched stance and kicked out, dislodging a jaw.

Moss blinked in utter confusion, not having seen many non-vampires fight with the ruthlessness of this woman, and never seeing such a beautiful, graceful dance when they did.

"You like when your women do all the work, yes?" The woman gave him a smile before she stowed the bow out of sight and slipped her knife back into the sheath, the movements fast, practiced and elegant, easily disguised from prying eyes with her magic. She grabbed the wolf chewing into his side and threw it. It landed on its back before scrambling to its feet.

The woman uncoiled to standing, a grin on her face, murder in her eyes.

Three wolves waited in the clearing with their heads lowered and lips pulled back from their teeth. They stared at her from wary, yellow eyes. Bloody bodies law strewn around the dirt, Moss's being one of them. He was the only downed creature still alive.

The woman whistled, like she was calling a pet. "Here Fido. Heeere Fido. Mommy has a treat for you." She whistled again and put out her hand like she was offering that treat. "Here boy."

Despite the situation, and his severe lack of energy, Moss couldn't help but smile. He liked her style.

One of the wolves took a step forward and its body braced. Moss rose to sitting, fatigue dragging at his muscles and hunger churning his stomach.

The wolf paused, its head swinging his direction. The others started backing up.

"Even nearly dead, you give them pause," the druid said, approval in her voice.

"I am fully dead," Moss said, struggling to standing. "Which is why I heal quickly."

The wolf furthest away turned and loped off into the trees. A moment later, the rest followed.

"They'll get reinforcements." Moss staggered and reached for his pocket, needing to call Darius.

"Wait here. I'll be back," the druid said. Shadow formed, clouding his mind and draping across her body. A moment later, she was gone—her body, her smell, her sound, everything.

He blinked at the empty space. He'd seen the effect before, but every time, it left him befuddled.

Or maybe he just needed to feed.

"Hungry," he heard in a weak mew.

Legs protesting, body strung out, Moss moved to the untouched human-in-transition, knowing the shifters had intended to bring him down before moving on to her. They wouldn't have let her live. She couldn't be salvaged at this point. Either she got the necessary blood and became a vampire, or she withered away into nothing. She was an easy kill for the shifters—entirely vulnerable. She'd be dead now if it wasn't for the druid. They both would.

Of course, she'd be well on her way to becoming a vampire if it wasn't for the Druid, too...

Claws morphing back into badly shaking hands, he crouched by the woman while tapping Darius's name on his screen. The sweet scent of her body called to him, driving him to his knees. The world tilted as she reached forward and ran a firm hand up the inside of his thigh.

"Please," she whispered. "Hungry..."

The world spun, his answering hunger blotting out thought. The phone fell from his hand and he pitched forward, fangs once again filling his mouth. He slid his body along hers, moaning when she dropped her knees wide to accept him. He grazed his lips along her neck, sucking in the scent of her. The exquisite desire.

"Oops. Probably a bad idea just now..."

That soft, sultry voice of the druid rolled heat through him. He wanted them both, at the same time.

The druid stood beside him with his phone to her ear and a nondescript plastic bag held in her other fist.

"I've mostly disguised your trail," she said, "but shifters have a great sense of smell. I can't hide yours and the girl's like I can hide my own. So we need to get out of here, I'm afraid." She turned her attention to the phone. "Yes, hello— vampire call center? I'd like to order a pick-up."

Soft lips created a trail of heat along Moss's neck. A blue vein pulsed under the human-in-transition's creamy skin, inviting him.

A long howl drifted behind the druid speaking on the phone, giving coordinates. Another answered it, the wolves re-organizing.

"Who's up for a jog?" the woman asked.

A hand fisted against his back before his body was yanked from the human-in-transition. He hit the dirt and rolled, rising with a hiss.

"Wow. You're beastly. I've never seen a vampire as old as you reduced to this untamed sort of creature. You guys are usually so...glossy. Refined. I rather like this change. " The druid grinned at him as she picked up the mewling human-in-transition. "I wonder if you'll rip into your victim's skin? Because that could be interesting. I do love violent sex. It's thrilling. Just don't change into your other form before I fuck you. It's hideous. It'll be a deal breaker. Come on." She jerked her head before throwing Felicia over her shoulder. "Let's get moving. We need to get you out of here before you lose the plot entirely."

She turned and started to jog.

"What a fun experience," he heard her mutter. "I had no idea what I'd land in when I started this contract. Pure stroke of luck."

The druid was right, he was far gone. Hungry beyond rational thought. He needed to be closed away from society until he'd properly fed and fucked his way back to level.

He barely remembered the jog to the small coastal road, and definitely didn't remember the car ride where the human had been unceremoniously dumped in the back of the vehicle and he'd sat in the middle seat alone, doing everything in his power not to rush one of the two viable blood sources in the car.

They landed back at a moderately sized house on the outskirts of the small coastal town, a place of refuge on the route between San Francisco to Los Angeles. Besides the generic remodel done a few years prior, it had largely been left as is, nothing more than a daytime sanctuary and place to safely feed.

"Instead of dining in, you took your food to go?" Marie, a middle-level vampire Moss had worked with a lot lately, said as she pulled into the barren garage. She hit the button to lower the door. "And you got one for me? How thoughtful. Which is mine, Moss? The desperate human, or the silky woman with dangerous eyes?"

"If you don't have a dong, you do not belong, love," the druid said with a laugh, exiting the vehicle. "I want the male lost to blood lust."

"That just makes me want you more." Marie slid out of the SUV, her gaze following the druid through the windows.

"Maybe we'll team up one day, who's to say?" The druid opened Moss's door with a flurry of her scent, raw and earthy, rich and complex. "I've gotten to the age where mundane sex bores me. Maybe I'll strap on a...well, strap on. Why not. We can play at sword fighting."

"Something is...amiss with you," Marie said slowly.

The druid laughed, putting out her hand. Moss stared at it in a dumb-stupor, coherent thought laborious. Movement stiff and unpracticed. Her eyes sparkled and she withdrew her hand slowly before bringing up her other hand and sticking out a glittery blue nail with a sharp tip. The skin in her wrist dented with the pressure, and she drew that glittery blue across lightly tan skin. Crimson welled up in its wake.

The fresh scent of blood blasted through his awareness, firing all his nerve endings and surging electricity through him. He lunged for her, grabbing her wrist and yanking her toward him. She twisted and jerked her arm to the side, breaking his hold.

A lusty smile curled her full lips. "Shall I lead the way?"

Without a word she turned and stalked to the door at the side of the garage. He followed behind her like a starving dog sensing a meal. Through the door and she stopped at the kitchen, eyeing the fringe of curtains hanging half over the window. Her gaze took in the few ornaments along the window sill, large and colorful roosters with large plumage. They matched the brown and red roosters decorating the curtains, and that etched on the sugar and flower canisters.

"My, my. Someone really loves cock." The druid's eyes sparkled with humor. "It's a different sort of cock than I am into, but to each their own."

"It's a farm theme," he managed, summoning all his strength to attempt some sort of decorum.

"It's some kinda theme." She turned for the hall as Marie strolled through the garage door with the human-in-transition cradled in her arms like a baby. A smear of blood marked Felicia's neck and a red trickle dribbled down Marie's chin.

Moss's legs lost feeling, and he sank down to his knees.

"Uh oh. Here we go." The druid picked him up under the arms and hoisted him to his feet.

There went decorum. It had been a good effort.

Marie tsked. "Moss, this will be very embarrassing for you tomorrow."

Didn't he know it. But there was nothing he could do about it now.

The druid helped him into the last bedroom, the cock theme carried through in the curtains and on the bedspread. A wooden rooster adorned the dresser.

"Cocks everywhere," the druid said as she directed him to the bed before shutting the door and throwing the lock. She huffed. "Stupid me. Vampire magic can unlock doors." She shrugged, leaving it.

Her gaze snagged on Moss, laying on the bed, doing everything in his power to maintain control. She pulled her hands up her middle before reaching behind her. A bow and quiver drifted away to the side, her ability to keep them hidden amazing. Her knife came away a moment later, dropped to the ground.

"Ordinarily I'd just go for it, but I have a feeling you'll rip through my clothes," she said. "I need these for tomorrow."

"Just say when," Moss ground out, his voice rough and thick with strain. He dropped his head back onto the bed, desire pumping through his body. Hunger throbbing. "Just say when."

"I'm going to fight you. Just so you know. I want to see if you can overcome me."

"Stop fucking talking and fucking say when."

"Hmm," he heard, her voice silky. "Very cocky. Maybe this house was fashioned after you, only, you don't get the joke."

He didn't give a shit about jokes. He needed to sink his fangs into soft flesh, and his dick into her warmth.

"Ready."

That one single word flipped the switch. One minute he was focusing everything he had on control, and the next he'd given himself over to bloodlust entirely.

She said she'd fight. He'd seen her skill and ability. She thought she could handle it.

He'd let her try.

FOUR

He surged up, his age and vampirism lending him super human speeds, and his blood lust giving him a boost. He hit his feet in a frenzy, his fangs down and his cock aching.

She was ready for him, her nude body gleaming in the soft light from the window. Her hands waited at her sides and delirious anticipation spread across her face. One shapely hip was cocked sensually to the side.

He ran straight at her, seeing her hands dart up at the last moment. She struck him in the sternum with one hand and batted away his reach with the other. He pushed through it, hitting her body with his and ramming her against the wall.

She head butted him, hitting his nose and breaking it. He jerked back. Her hands grabbed his side, and then he was flying across the room, her strength incredible.

He fell to the ground, hearing her feet thumping across the floor to him. He waited a moment, strategy flitting through his mind. His goal programming his movements: blood.

She reached him, planted one of her feet, and pulled back the other, readying a kick. He grabbed her ankle and yanked, pulling her weight out from under her. She fell on him, her elbow out, cracking him in the ribs.

Blood dripped from his nose. Pain blossomed. His desire and hunger rose exponentially. Excitement vibrated through his body.

Invigorated, he rolled and took her leg with him, knocking her off kilter. She tried to bring her elbow down again, but he was ready. He flipped and caught her, pulling her down on top of him. He rolled quickly, using his heavier weight to pin her under him.

She shot up with her upper body, aiming for another head butt. He dodged to the side and grabbed her wrists, forcing them above her head.

She groaned in desire, her legs spreading.

"Take me," she said with a breathy whisper.

He released one of his hands, holding her wrists with the other, before running his palm down her chest and over her budded nipple. He let his fingers slid over her smooth stomach and pulled off of her a little so he could reach between her spread thighs.

She ripped her hands out from his grasp, but he didn't give her a chance to pummel him. He struck down with his fangs, digging them into her yielding flesh and releasing his vampire serum.

Her moan preceded her hands speeding across his back before rubbing down to his butt.

"Holy fuck," she said, tilting her head away so he had better access. "Holy—"

If he could speak, he'd mirror her sentiments.

Her blood exploded across his senses, soaking into him and clouding his mind. Sweet and savory, the elixir was one he'd never tasted before, delighting him. Entrancing him.

He sucked, swallowing her nectar. Unable to fight just now. Not wanting to.

He slowly ground his hard cock against her, feeling her eager gyrating to match his movements. He released her neck and licked her wound before pushing himself up, allowing his dizzied mind to settle before continuing.

Her sparkling gaze tracked him, and she ran her palms down her nude chest, watching as he unbuttoned his shirt.

"That feeling is incredible," she mewed, approval in her voice.

"We're predators. We stun with pleasure before claiming our victims."

"Yes. I like being your prey."

Lust washed through him, and he quickened his movements. He shrugged out of his shirt before drifting his hands down to his fly.

"Let me." She sat up, pushing him back as she did so. Her hot mouth fastened on one of his nipples before she ripped his fly open, sending shivers of anticipation through him. Her lips slid down his stomach, and her teeth nipped his fevered flesh.

He groaned and closed his eyes as his pants were pulled down. His boxers followed a moment later, released his hard length.

"Hmm," she said in appreciation. "This will be a treat."

A hot mouth took in his girth before a hard shove forced him off balance. He fell to the ground, stopping himself from rolling and rising, a natural response to aggression. He was rewarded for his self-control.

She pulled his pants off of his legs before running her palms up his inner thighs. Her breasts slid against his skin as she got into position. Her pink tongue flicked across his tip before swirling around it. Her lips widened before she looked up at him, her blue eyes dancing wickedly. He watched his cock disappear into her greedy mouth, all the way until his blunt head bumped the back of her throat. Her chin hit his balls and his eyes rolled with the suction.

He put a hand to the back of her head, feeling her rise off of him, before plunging down a second time. Without thinking, he fisted his hand, clutching her hair.

"Hmm," she said, resisting his direction just enough to make him push harder. "Mmm," she moaned again.

A predator could sense the demands of the prey. Could feel what it would take to overcome, with fear, with pain, or with pleasure.

He was the ultimate predator.

He yanked her up by her hair, dragging her head off of him. Without warning, he sat up and grabbed her shoulders before throwing her. The springs screamed in protest as she hit the bed. The wood of the frame cracked under the duress.

He ripped off his unbuttoned shirt, nude now, like her. Her gaze raked down his body, appreciation in her eyes. She needed a different kind of pounding, one she would strain toward, and not away from.

He pushed one of her muscular thighs up before bending between her spread legs. He licked up her center before circling her clit. She gasped, her body stiffening. He sucked in that small nub, working his tongue around it while threading his fingers into her wetness.

"Mmm," she said, gyrating up toward his mouth.

He started a fast pace, working her with his mouth and fingers. Making her writhe and moan with pleasure. Her muscles flared as he worked her higher, keeping her straining for more.

"Yes," she said, arching back. "Mmm yes..."

He pulled off of her, keeping his fingers thrusting into her, and sank his fangs into her exposed thigh.

"Oh!" He pumped in as much serum as he could, flooding her body to offset the pain. To heighten the pleasure. "Oh fuck. Holy...fuck. Oh *fuck!*"

She stiffened, shaking under him. Her nails dug into his shoulders, ripping skin.

He sucked in a few mouthfuls of her blood, feeling the magic pulse through his veins. Feeling his energy ramp up. One drop of her blood was worth a swallow of a humans. She was intensely powerful and deliciously mighty. He'd gladly take Darius's punishment for this experience.

Slowing now, letting her soak up the moment, he kissed up her skin and sucked in a nipple, twirling it in his mouth languidly. He switched to the other, hearing her breathing increase again. Her chest rise and fall with mounting desire.

He continued up, settling his weight over her. Her greedy mouth met him and her arms curled around his neck, the fight gone, pure pleasure taking over.

"You've won, vampire," she said languidly. "Claim your prize."

He smiled against her lips. "Your wish is my command." He gave her a teasing kiss before pulling back his hips, dragging his tip against her wetness. It snagged on her opening and he stopped before applying pressure, pushing against her.

Her breath caught and held.

He pulled back a little and let his tip slide by, disappointing her. Increasing the anticipation.

A shaky laugh disturbed the silence. "You play women like a violin."

"Yes."

"I like it."

He took her lips again, plunging in his tongue. Her blood called to him, but he couldn't take too much at one time. It would decrease the time she would last, and he wanted her for as long as he could have her.

His tip slid along her again, her wetness dizzying his mind. Desire clouding his thoughts. Like her magic. Like her.

Her palms roamed his back and she moaned into his mouth. His tip snagged, and this time he trust, hard. His shaft dug into her tight depths until he was fully sheathed, hugged by her warmth.

"Fuuuck." The word road her long sigh. "Mmm yes," she said.

He let his lips skim her chin while he pulled out and then thrust, keeping his movement coarse. Firm and rough. Her eyes fluttered and her legs tightened around him.

"Bite me again," she begged, her voice wispy. "Please."

He trailed his fangs across the hollow of her neck before increasing the pressure when he reached that throbbing vein. Her breath caught again, and like before, held.

He wouldn't disappoint her this time.

He pulled back his hips before ramming into her as he bit down on her fragile skin. His fangs tore through and blood once again rolled over his tongue.

He sucked and thrust, over and over. Keeping a fast, hard pace. She groaned before her volume increased. Her nails scratched down his back. He rammed into her, releasing the vampire serum. Pumping into her body.

"Yes. Oh yes. *Oh yes*," she said, loudly. Out of control.

He lost himself to the blood. To her body. To the moment.

Pleasure washed through him. Around him. Her essence invigorated him, made him strive harder. Pump faster.

He hit a plain and released her neck, thrusting low over her. Rubbing her budded nipples with his hard chest. Her words were nothing more than sounds now, wild. Animalistic.

He kissed her, sucking in her tongue and letting her taste the sweetness of her blood, which sent her to new heights in their passion. They hit the edge of the cliff, stalling.

He slammed into her body.

"Oh!" She screamed with release, her body shaking.

He succumbed a moment later, feeling an orgasm tighten his balls and explode through him. It filled up every inch, out through his limbs and heating his middle. He shook over her, sweaty and satisfied.

"Wow," she said as they came down, hugging him close. "That was…"

He let silence linger for a moment, letting the final stages of the orgaism tingle his body. A moment later he said, "That was…just getting started."

He chuckled darkly, giving her another moment to relish in the euphoria, before starting again.

FIVE

Moss opened his eyes as soft murmurs drifted through the closed door. He lay on his back in the king sized bed, the sheets twisted around his body, and the space next to him empty.

He let his head fall to the side, looking at the empty pillow where the druid —she'd never given her name—had slept. Her scent still clung to the sheets, and to his body. Sitting up, he saw that her clothes and weapons were gone from the floor. She'd banged him, then taken off.

He couldn't help a smile. He would expect it of a woman like that. She was wild. Not one to be tamed. Not one to stick around after she'd gotten what she wanted. He respected her more for it. She'd been a damn good lay. Exactly what he'd needed after the night he'd had. A night she had created.

At least now he wouldn't have to kill her. Darius wouldn't ask him to hunt her down. The situation had worked itself out, in a way. He'd take the punishment without a problem.

He pulled the sheets from around his legs before swinging them over the edge of the bed. The murmuring outside rose and fell, a conversation going on between more than one person. He knew better than to think the druid was out there making nice with Marie. So then, who was?

He checked the closets, but didn't find any satisfactory clothing. No one had kept up with stocking those types of things for the vampires passing through. He'd have to rectify that situation.

After stepping into his pants and securing them around his waist, he made his way out of the room, leaving his shirt on the floor. Wearing soiled clothes didn't interest him. He would've gone nude if he didn't think Marie would take that as an invitation.

At the edge of the hallway, he caught a glimpse of who awaited him in the kitchen.

He froze. Then started to backpedal. He hadn't expected the absolute worst

105

case scenario. He was on a nice little high from the day before with the druid, he didn't need that tarnished.

"Well, well, well," the she-devil said, pushing back from the table.

Reagan Somerset. The bane of his existence, and the absolute best asset Darius had in his arsenal.

"I never thought I'd see you doing the walk of shame." She gave him a shit-eating grin as Darius stepped into view. "Not even a shirt. Don't get me wrong, it's not like you have glitter all over you or anything but, I mean, you have sex hair, Moss. Sex hair and dirty jeans. Who *are* you right now?"

"Is there a reason you're here?" Moss asked her, forcing himself to continue forward. He hadn't even put on shoes. She'd never forget this. She'd taunt him about it for the rest of eternity.

She clasped her hands in her lap demurely, but her delighted smile said she wasn't even close to being done. "You got used and abused. She hit it and quit it. Loved ya, and left ya. That's gotta sting."

Moss paused next to the wall at the edge of the kitchen. Marie stood by the counter, presentable in front of their boss. She'd brought a change of clothes.

"I couldn't dispose of her like you'd asked," Moss said to Darius. "At the Turning site, I was too weak. She kept me from an eternal death. Then back here…" He let his voice trail away. He didn't have an excuse, and so he wouldn't bother making one up.

"You saved the key target," Darius said, thankfully ignoring his bond mate and her taunting. Trying to quiet her would just make her more violent, and Moss wasn't in the mood. "And you entertained one of Cahal's favorite people."

Cahal was the very old warrior druid that had helped them take down the Mages' Guild. While the woman he'd…entertained had been incredibly skilled and excellent under pressure, Cahal was in a league of his own. He was the best their was, and his help had been invaluable.

"Had any harm come to Abarrane, he would've attempted to kill us all," Darius went on. "Even knowing he'd likely die trying, he would set out to avenge her."

"Let's hope he's not jealous, eh Moss?" Reagan flapped her eyebrows at him. "You'll have your hands full. Stiffed by the girl, beat up by the guy… A real shitty situation, that."

Moss wasn't sure what he'd done in a past life to deserve this woman hanging around, but whatever it was, he was sorry for it.

"As it stands," Darius went on, "Cahal feels he owes us, since she unraveled my plans in order to get her mark. I can only be thankful her mark was different than my target."

"I'm going to be honest, what she did was genius." Reagan leaned against the table. "She just pitted one magical species against the other and sat back. She's good at her trade."

"She is lucky she has the protection of Cahal," Darius said, his voice flat. The small hairs rose along Moss's body. She was very lucky. People didn't get in Darius's way if they hoped to live.

"She didn't just save the damsel—I mean, Moss—because she wanted to bang him." Reagan rose from her chair and went to the fridge. "She probably knew that saving him would alleviate some of your anger, Darius. Everyone you lost was replaceable. You know it, and she likely knew it. She warned Moss not to go into that house. He did anyway. She followed him when he got out. Then stepped in when things were dire. She would've played this whole situation easily if it hadn't been for protecting your right-hand-man." Reagan nodded and took out a water. "She knew the score, and she put herself on the line to protect your asset." She eyed Darius. "Her allegiance is to you over the shifters. And we get Cahal for sure, now. We're in a good spot. This worked out well."

A slow smile drifted up Darius's face as he looked on his bond-mate. "I'll teach you strategy yet."

Reagan rolled her eyes. "Ew. No thanks. You do the thinking, and I'll do the killing."

"There's no point in teaching a blunt instrument how to think," Moss murmured.

Her face turned slowly and she laughed. "Sticks and stones, Moss. Stick and stones."

Moss shook his head and turned back for the bedroom to retrieve his clothes, his mind drifting back to the druid. He wondered if he'd ever get a second chance with her, and if he did, if he'd want her to stay.

ABOUT THE AUTHOR

KF Breene is a USA Today Bestselling author of paranormal romance, urban fantasy, and fantasy novels with over two million books sold.

---

www.kfbreene.com
Facebook: https://www.facebook.com/AuthorKF/

ALSO BY K.F. BREENE

DON'T GET COCKY

RUTH CLAMPETT

The artists at the Sketch Republic animation studio are in an uproar thanks to their noble leader wanting to do a series featuring a politically incorrect rooster character named, Sir Cocky Doodle Doo. Love struck Nathan and his dream girl Brooke (from Animate Me) hatch a plan to sabotage the Cocky show, and all the artists get behind them in an uprising of animated proportions.

DON'T GET COCKY

This story features Nathan and Brooke from Animate Me, and takes place around a third into the original story, where they have become close friends ... with additional *benefits*. Meanwhile Sketch Republic is in an uproar thanks to their noble leader wanting to do a series featuring a politically incorrect rooster character named, Sir Cocky Doodle Doo.

In all of my years in the animation world, I've never seen anything like it. Arnauld, the ever-annoying head of our animation company, Sketch Republic, has called for a "very special story meeting," and hasn't just called forth the writers and directors from each team, but instead a strange mish-mash of people throughout our company's staff. It's as if Arnauld had his assistant randomly pick twenty names out of a hat for this momentous occasion.

Sure, two of the team's directors and a few of their writers are sitting around the large conference table or the chairs scattered along the meeting room wall, but there are also animation in-betweeners, digital colorists and even Chester, the IT guy attending—all people who have nothing to do with story development.

Dani, a background illustrator on my team, catches my attention from across the table and gives me a dramatic eye roll after scanning the room, and I shrug back. Who knows what that twat Arnauld (or as I like to call him, *Arnold*) is up to? He has no idea of our production process, so if he's deciding to get involved now, he has a long way to go before any of us take him seriously. I'm pretty sure I never will.

A few moments later the double door swings open and Arnold, President of Sketch Republic, steps gallantly inside with two people right behind him. I half expect to hear an orchestral fanfare playing to match this flamboyant entrance.

I'm distracted for another long moment observing my coworker's startled looks just to see this man in one of our story meetings, but then someone catches my eye and a warmth sizzles through me like a sparkler on a dark night. It's my dream girl, Brooke, and she flashes me a smile as soon as our gazes connect. Knowing that Brooke is head of Development under Arnold, I was hoping she would be here, and now knowing that she is makes all of this pomp and circumstance tolerable.

The atmosphere of team story meetings at Sketch Republic is usually boisterous; with rude character drawings eventually covering the dry erase boards, sporadic games of desktop football, and random offerings of Red Vines and Pringles being passed around. But as management comes in and claims their seats it's as quiet and composed as a church service.

Our noble leader, 'Arnauld,' who we privately refer to as *Arnold Lord-King of BooFoo or Mojo Jojo*, is rambling on that this next season is especially competitive with Netflix and Amazon getting in the cartoon market and how we have to up our game. So he's here today to make sure we are at our creative best.

Do we resent him implying that we are lacking creatively and that somehow he's going to inspire us to do better? Oh, King Boo-Foo, you have no idea. I can imagine the cartoony slingshots aimed at the buffoon, and huge anvils about to drop over his head, being conjured by the creatives in the room. The reality is that it actually feels like a soggy towel has just been thrown over us and the most productive thing he could do for this meeting is to return to his office as soon as possible.

Everyone turns and gives Brooke, our creative advocate and friend, a pleading look. Unfortunately she doesn't take the bait and instead encourages him on. "So Arnauld, tell us about your new series idea based on the unique character you've developed."

"Which is?" I boldly ask. This blowhard can't be doing character and story development now or we are surely doomed. It's as if I've signed up for a cruise on the Titanic.

Arnold stands and flips the protective flap over a drawing on matte board and then proceeds to hold it up for us to see. The image is of a cartoony, psychotic-looking black rooster with the orange thing on his head looking like floppy feathers slicked back. To make matters worse, he's got dark Rayban sunglasses and a heavy gold chain around his neck. "Team, let me introduce to you our next star...Sir Cocky! His full name is Sir Cocky Doodle Do."

Everyone is silent for several long beats until someone breaks the silence with a loud laugh. "Ha! Cocky ... Cocky Doodle Do?" Kevin, our group wildman wearing the Beavis and Butthead shirt, spits out. "Oh man, you really had me going for a minute. I thought you were serious."

Arnold's eyes narrow as he glares at him. "I'm perfectly serious, Mr...." he turns to look at Brooke.

"Hughes," she responds.

"You *are* serious?" my team director Joel asks, looking concerned.

The rest of the room sits stunned because for one, they assumed Arnold never watched our cartoons, let alone wanted to be involved in development, and two, it's the stupidest, most offensive idea they've ever heard.

"I'm dead serious and you better be too. Because Sir Cocky Doodle Do, the rapping rooster is going to lift us out of our ratings rut. And he's quite the ladies man, which all the moms watching with their kids will appreciate, right Brooke?" Arnauld turns to her waiting for her endorsement.

I look over at Brooke, who is biting her lip like she's fighting back a laugh or a grimace—I can't be sure. She finally nods at him, "Clearly you were inspired when you came up with that character, Arnauld."

For a panicked moment I think that my dream-girl Brooke has gone over to the dark side, agreeing with this idiot just to make him happy, and I feel gutted. Brooke has always had integrity and outstanding taste in her cartoons and comics, so this leaves me wondering if she fell and hit her head since we last spoke. How can I love a woman so completely when she supports such low level ideas in this medium that I love so much?

Thankfully, my spirits are lifted when I glance up at her and she winks at me. I let out the breath I've been holding and tip my head at her with a concerned look. She mouths at me "it's okay" and I have to believe in her. Anything less would just break my heart.

Our IT guy Chester, who is black, speaks up. "So this black Cock with a gold chain that dogs on women is a rapper?" He looks completely offended by the social misappropriation.

"He is! Isn't that awesome Chester?" Arnauld says proudly. "Our big Cock lady's-dude and bad ass rapper is hot stuff for our moms out there, and Sir Cocky Doodle Do is a big personality for the kids!"

Chester does not appear happy with his explanation and folds his arms over his chest. "Damn," he hisses.

"And what exactly do you mean by cocky?" One of the girls asks with an arched eyebrow.

Arnauld shrugs. "You know, confident—he knows he's hot stuff and a catch for any little chickadee out there, and he can charm their feathers off. He's like that lover-boy skunk that was in those old cartoons."

"Are you talking about Warner Bros.' Pepe le Pew who was always going after Kitty?" Dani pipes in.

"Yeah that's the one," Arnauld agrees, apparently happy with the comparison.

"I don't know about that," Genna points out. "He was way too aggressive. That behavior won't fly with the #MeToo generation."

Arnauld makes a face like he can't be bothered. "We can't have a small minority define our initiatives."

Small minority? He hears gasps and then eye daggers being thrown Arnauld's way from every female attending – and most of the men too.

Brooke squeezes her eyes shut and pinches her fingers on the sides of her temples like she suddenly has a migraine, but Arnauld keeps rambling on.

"The show will take place on an urban farm right in the center of a big city like New York."

"So it's like if Central Park is a farm with this cocky rooster?" Dani asks in her most sarcastic tone.

King Boo-Foo's eyes light up like he just hit the jackpot in Vegas. "Great idea! The farm will be deep in Central Park! Good work ... what's your name?" he asks Dani.

"Dani," she says weakly.

He turns to Brooke, "Make note that I want her working on the pilot script."

"But I'm a background artist," Dani points out, giving me a panicked look.

He waves his hand in the air. "No matter! Great ideas can come from anyone."

Dani's face is rapidly losing color as she looks over at me with a wide-eyed look of panic. I shake my head in disbelief.

"Sir Cocky's object of affection will be Chicky Chica, the smart-mouthed hottie from the hen house."

"So how exactly is this a kid's show?" Genna asks.

"Funny animals, cute songs and bright colors ... all the things kids love!"

"As if that ogre has any idea what kids love," Bruce mumbles next to me just loud enough for me to hear.

My stomach is churning at this point, and I can't even look up when he reveals the Chicky Chica art. But when I glance over at Nick, our head writer, he looks like his head is going to explode. He pipes in: "Are there any Asians in this show? Because as long as we are offending entire ethnic groups we shouldn't leave anyone out." He leans back in his chair with a scowl and Arnold scowls back at him. "Watch your attitude. We aren't offending anyone. "We're celebrating their cultures."

"Sure you are," responds Chester, shaking his head.

The whole room is the most somber I've ever seen it because it's becoming clear that Arnold is not going to back down from this disaster of a concept.

"I read recently that cartoons perform best when they are written on two levels - one for adults and for kids. I'm so sure of Sir Cocky's appeal that I've already trademarked, secured copyrights and had my lawyer send out some cease and desist letters to people who have used that name."

"Someone else did a cartoon with a character called Cocky Doodle Doo?" Bruce, the other animation director in the room, asks, his voice laced with disbelief.

"Actually, it was a series of gay pornos that came out a few years ago, but we're shutting them down."

"Nice," Kevin sarcastically mumbles with a frown.

Dani looks over at him dismayed since Kevin seems to be agreeing with the cease and desists.

"That series was one of my favs. Why do the creatives always end up getting screwed by greedy narcissists?" Kevin laments and Dani nods in agreement.

"Hey wait a minute," Joel says. "You said you came up with this character so the writing would play to both adults and kids. Our show *Bucky and the Beaver Patrol* does that in spades, and without offending women and people of color."

"I'm not here to argue with the staff. We're here to launch a new initiative and I need everyone on board if they still want their jobs here."

Joel wilts back in his seat. He just bought a new house and he can't afford to be out of work right now, so he gets quiet and resigned to the new reality.

My disgust is so overwhelming that the rest of the meeting is a murky blur. The only command that stands out is his direction that our team and Bruce's team will be working on the pilot together, and naturally it's a rush job since he has to present it to the corporate mothership before they sign off on the series.

It's a good thing that Arnold has to rush off to a big-wig meeting, since that allows everyone to vent all the way back to our cubicles.

"I'm not working on this misogynistic, racially insensitive, ludicrous concept," Dani insists. "I wish Billie was in that meeting, she would've kicked his ass."

I picture that very idea with a smile on my face. Billie, the owner of our favorite comic book store and all around badass, takes no prisoners. She would have Arnold quaking in his Armani shoes after his proclamation.

"And who does he think he is, having his lawyers send cease and desist demands to existing users of the title when we haven't even made a cartoon yet?" Bruce comments.

"I'm calling the union," Genna states. "I'm not working on that garbage, and neither is the rest of my team if we can figure a way out of it."

We're almost back to our work area when I quietly take a detour and head to Brooke's office. Her assistant isn't at her desk, so I step into her doorway and wait for Brooke to get off the phone. As soon as she sees me, she wraps the call up and waves me in, telling me to shut the door behind me.

She gestures to the couch, but I remain standing with my hands shoved into my jean's pockets. "What was that all about?" I'm surprised that I have the courage to be so direct with her, but Arnold pushed me over the line. Besides, I can't hide my disappointment in her encouraging his craziness.

Is her resulting fallen expression guilt? She purses her lips together and looks down at the papers on her desk. "I tried, Nathan … you have no idea how hard I tried to talk him out of this. He just wouldn't listen to me."

"You should hear them downstairs. We're a few grumbles away from a walk out."

"I know, I know," she says with a sigh.

"But I thought that we were better than this, Brooke. I mean, not all of our shows are great, but none of them are sensational just to get the wrong kind of attention. We won't just hurt many of our viewers … we'll be the laughing stock of the industry."

She leans her elbows on her desktop and rests her face into her open hands before groaning.

I clear my throat. "I'm not going to get behind this and have my name attached to such an offensive idea." I silently wonder how she could have ever started dating such an ass as Arnold and then agree to their "open" relationship. Maybe this fiasco will be the final straw that breaks up what is already a relationship for show at best. Then I'll be right there to show her how much better a devoted boyfriend like me could be.

She lifts her head up and gazes at me with hope in her eyes. "There's got to be a way to stop him. I'd really appreciate it if you helped me figure out how."

I think about all the time we've spent together the last few weeks outside of work, our special friendship starting with me helping her transfer her data from one computer to another and then evolving into so much more. If you would have told me just a few months ago that after divulging my geeky social awkwardness to Brooke, that she would be spending quality time with me and teaching me how to not just charm a girl, but how to be a great kisser, I would have thought you were nuts. But now look at us. Just remembering how our last time together felt makes my face feel hot. I hope I'm not beet red.

"Okay, I'll help you, Brooke," I respond to her plea. "But you know that means we're going to have to be super heroes. So I hope your Wonder Woman tiara and silver cuffs are easily accessible."

She sits up taller and grins. "They are. And will my Clark Kent be ready to transform into Superman? Dealing with Arnauld will be a piece of cake for you compared to stopping a speeding bullet."

"Indeed," I agree, pushing my glasses up my nose. "He'll regret ever challenging the likes of us!" Holding my arms open to beckon her, I command, "Come here Wonder Woman."

She quickly gets up and steps around her desk until she is close enough to fall into my arms. "Oh, thank you Nathan!"

I wrap my arms tightly around her and rub my hand up and down her back to calm her. I feel guilty that all of my anger about what Arnold has planned is fading away, replaced with the sheer perfection of having Brooke pressed up against me. The longer I hold her the more she seems to relax, and when she finally looks up at me, I am overcome with desire to kiss her again. And this wouldn't be one of our kissing lessons, but something far more spontaneous.

She seems to have the same idea as she reaches up and cups her hand around my neck to draw me nearer. Next thing I know our lips are pressed together, with each kiss becoming deeper until I'm wondering how this will possibly stop - since I'm pretty sure I could kiss Brooke forever.

It's the blasted knock on her office door that finally snaps us back to reality.

"One minute," Brooke calls out to her snarky assistant.

"He's calling you into that meeting, and he says to hurry," Morgan warns through the crack in the door.

"Okay, okay," Brooke calls out. She smoothes her hair and pulls her shirt down over her slacks. "Is my lipstick all over my face?" she asks me.

I lovingly wipe off the bits that look suspect on her flawless skin, and then grin at her before dragging the back of my hand across my lips. "What about me?"

"I think you got it all," she says with a smile. "I'll call you later," she whispers as she turns and rushes out the door.

Brooke messages me later that she wants me to come over tonight and help brainstorm a plan with her. She already told Arnold that her stomach is bothering her, so they will have to put his "celebration dinner" off for another night.

I show up at her condo in the Hollywood hills with two six packs of Stella beer and a box of Krispy Kreme doughnuts for dessert. Meanwhile, Brooke picked us up French dipped beef sandwiches at Greenblatt's deli. We eat outside on her balcony. With the warm breeze, the terrific view of the glittering L.A. skyline, and Brooke right next to me, I'm by far the happiest I've been all day.

"How are you doing?" I ask, "You're kind of quiet tonight."

She frowns and pushes her plate away. "I just never thought my career would end up being so ridiculous. All I wanted was to work with talented people, and put out quality, imaginative animation. But I'm left with my bogus, sham-of-a-boyfriend-slash-boss humiliating our studio with his unmanageable ego and idiotic ideas. What is my life, Nathan?"

I reach out and take her hand. "Don't be so hard on yourself, Brooke. After all, what is a dynamic career if you don't have at least one or two idiots for bosses? That should fuel your ambition when you realize you are so much smarter than they are."

"Aww, you're trying to make me feel better. Thank you, but what about our immediate problem? He's not backing down from his bird-brained concept."

"The beauty of filmmaking is that there are always reshoots and editing. If there is a clear vision and goal, anything can happen," I say cryptically. "Hey, I brought my remastered Looney Tunes DVD's. What do you say we watch some?"

She gives me a soft smile. "Well, between curling up with you, those cartoons and this," she holds up her second bottle of beer that I just opened for her, "I should be feeling much more optimistic very soon."

"Good!" I say with a smile.

Over an hour later I'm feeling quite content with Brooke snuggled up next to me as we watch some of my all-time favorite cartoons. As a kid I never caught some of the political comments, pop culture references, or racy gags because they were all delivered by a stuttering pig, wacky duck or smart-aleck rabbit. You don't have to hit viewers over the head with such subjects. You just let them appreciate the subtle things they catch while watching, their kids not aware of anything but the funny story. This Sir Cocky the rapping rooster nonsense is destined to be heavy-handed and offensive—so what can be done?

And just then, an image lights up in my mind like those old comics where there's a big light bulb over Felix the Cat's head. What if we make the cartoon so bad and offensive that Arnold's bosses trash the project? Given the already inappropriate idea behind the show, it wouldn't be hard to take it down several notches. I toss the idea and potential problems around in my head until I feel certain this is an idea worth considering.

"Brooke!" I turn and realize she's half asleep against me, so I gently rock her awake. "Brooke, I have an idea for our problem!"

She blinks her sleepy eyes open. "Really?"

"Yes! Are you awake enough to talk about it?"

She rubs her face briskly and sits up straight. "I am now!" Her expression is so bright and hopeful that I really don't want to let her down.

"So I was thinking, I remember reading an interview with one of the original Looney Tunes directors and he said that they had a special technique of dealing with their network censor's constraints on adult humor."

"Yes, and what was that?"

"This director said he would add extra footage throughout the cartoons with more obvious inappropriate humor. Nine times out of ten the censors would reject all the added racy stuff and leave the marginal stuff, which looked tame in comparison. So all that was needed was a quick re-edit and they were good to go!"

"And that actually worked?" she asks a skeptical look on her face.

"Well, most of the time. The funny thing is that there were a few times when the censors missed the real obvious stuff that was meant to be edited out, and it's still in the cartoons today."

"Wow!" she laughs, a big smile on her face. But her smile suddenly fades as quickly as it appeared. "But there is no way we can get away with that. Arnauld will be seeing early cuts before any censors do. He swears he is going to be hands-on with this whole project since it's 'his baby'."

"But there will be a formal presentation for the corporate peeps, yes?"

She nods. "He's already talked about that. They were already coming in May so it'll be then."

"That explains the crazy tight deadline. But I'm talking about loading up the extra content to be seen by the execs first before the network sees it. That way they will certainly pan the series idea and we'll never get as far as the network censors seeing it. It will already be dead in the water."

"Oh," she replies, her eyes light up at the sheer idea of it.

"See, if we plan it out like a bank heist and are very clever, we can do a last minute switcheroo before the digital projection for the execs. And doesn't Arnold always show those test group results at these presentations? I assume he'll be doing that too."

Brooke's eyes grow wide with disbelief. "And you'd show the test group the extra-racy version too?"

"Of course! Again, we'd have to time everything with extreme precision so that the results are presented mid-meeting."

She gasps and slaps her hand over her mouth. "He will lose his mind. I don't know, Nathan. This could backfire and we could all be looking for new jobs."

I shrug. "Let him try. When word gets out about all the offensive material he was developing, the whole story will bite him in the ass. This is a media sensitive time in the world."

"It is," she agrees before letting out a deep breath and curling back against me. "You are so amazing, Super-Nathan. You give me hope that we can rise above this, and continue to do cartoons we are proud of."

I kiss her on her forehead and pull her tight against me. "And we will," I whisper.

After a few more cartoons Brooke is sound asleep against me and I'm dozing off too. In my sleepy daze, I feel her shift in her sleep and her hand ends up pressed against my chest. Her holding me only makes me relax more - but right on the edge of sleep, I feel her hand shift down until it's resting against my crotch. You would think this sensation would wake me up. Instead, my overactive imagination leads me into dream land, where all my pervy dreams can come true.

My dreams tend to be highly cinematic, but this one is looking IMAX Theater-worthy. I'm up on a mountain but my view is obscured with the sun in my eyes. When I hold my hand over my brow to shade my vision from the glare, I see my curvy Wonder Woman on the edge of a cliff, her long hair gently waving in the wind. I take a step toward her just as she turns back to look at me. Her smile is warm as she reaches her hand out inviting me closer.

"I've been waiting for you," she says as I approach her and pull her into my arms. Considering our super hero strength, we are gentle with each other as she pushes my stray curl off my forehead, and I stroke her cheek. With the next breeze my cape wraps around us and I pull her into a deep kiss. It's a superhero-worthy kiss, and she sighs happily. When we finally pull apart, her hand remains below my waist where it had slide down just before we fell asleep, and her eyes blaze with passion.

That's all the reassurance I need as I nod toward the valley below. "Are you ready?" I ask.

She takes my hand and we gracefully lift off in flight, soon soaring over clouds and the lush green fields. We pass waterfalls and forests dense with trees until I find the perfect spot for us to lie together. Moments later we are standing on a soft bed of grass with a tree shading us. She begins to slowly remove her Wonder Woman uniform and I watch eagerly as every inch of skin, every gorgeous curve, is revealed. Impatience kicks in though, and we begin to help each other, more anxiously. Once Wonder Woman has my tights pulled down I love how she grabs my ass and moans roughly. I'm pretty sure this is going to be a wild ride.

She's gloriously naked when I lift her up into my arms and she wraps her strong legs around me. We can't be bothered to remove her tiara and magic silver cuffs as I lower us to the ground. All I want is to fill her again, and watch my goddess come undone.

But before I do I tend to every part of her, devouring her mouth as she grinds against me, then kissing her neck, down to her perfect breasts where she cries out as I gently bite her nipples. When I spread her legs open even further and taste her between her legs, she winds her fingers into my hair like she'll never let me go.

"Fuck me Superman," she finally growls. And so I do. Each thrust pushes us into the earth. She rakes her fingers across my back, and bites my neck while thrusting her hips up just as hard as I'm thrusting my pelvis down. We are so amped up, I'm sure I could make love to her into the next millennium, but I desperately need the high of us coming together both spiritually and physically.

I sense she sees the desperation in my face, so when I start to groan, "I need…" she nods with a complete understanding because she needs it too. Her legs tighten against me and we desperately kiss as I thrust deeply into her. I sense the moment she starts to soar.

A flush burns across her skin like a wildfire and she cries out, "Yes! Yes!" And I'm calling out too because I'm soaring with her. I'm no longer awkward, bumbling Clark Kent, but her man of steel, and she's my wondrous Wonder Woman.

After we come down, I hold her tightly as I roll onto by back, pulling her with me. We continue to lie heart to heart. She is gloriously stretched over me as we let our breathing settle. That's the final moment I remember before I wake to the sensation of Brooke's hand tightening over me, where I'm fully hard.

It takes everything I have to carefully peel her hand off of me instead of encouraging her to do more. I can't afford to lose what is building between us. I'm confident that if I do right by her, one day we will end up together.

Just a minute later she stirs and slowly wakes up. "What time is it?" she mumbles.

"Almost one. I'm going to head home." I slowly lift myself off the couch, thankful that my erection has subsided.

"I'll walk you out."

I grab my DVD and head to the front door with her. Right before I open it she wraps her arms around me. "Thank you for everything Nathan."

I smile at her and she reaches up to kiss my cheek. She pauses there, and kisses me again.

"What?" I ask.

"I had this superhero dream..." Her face gets pink.

I feel my cheeks getting hot too. Could she have had the same dream? I don't really want to know so I can always believe that she did. "Was it a good dream?" I ask.

"Mmm," she purrs. "So so good."

I grin. "See you tomorrow?"

"Indeed, see you Superman," she says.

My heart thunders joyfully all the way to my car. Whatever that meant, a guy can dream, can't he?

Everything happens very quickly the following week. Arnold's batshit crazy treatment is turned into a lame pilot script and Dani, our background painter who was thrown into the writing process, sneaks an early script to us. The scenes are divvied up between the two animation teams and Joel and Bruce, our harried directors, stay focused on getting the main storyline and gags done with their animators. Meanwhile, we gather in groups after work in various people's apartments and houses to spend our late nights working on all the "extras" that we hope will blow this show's chance of getting picked up right out of the water.

I tend to go wherever our team slob and deviant Kevin goes, because he sets the tone for the evening by always coming up with the most outrageous stuff. He conjures up Banging Betty, the chicken that will lewdly rub up against any one or anything that holds still long enough. The plan is to always have her in the background going to town, so it's not an immediate read but when you catch her thrusting up against the fence posts or whatever, she serves up quite a wollop.

Sometimes the jokes are in the backgrounds. Like there's the small sign over what we assume is a doghouse with the words "Huff and Puff" printed in block letters above a neon green cross. Nothing should get the bigwigs riled up more than a marijuana dispensary in one of their kiddie cartoons.

The dog that lives in that house is usually stoned and smoking behind the doghouse so all we see is the end of his tail peeking out, and the continual puffs of smoke rising.

Sex- obsessed Kevin has Cocky's right hand guy, a sarcastic Duck named Quackers, wander through the barnyard quacking out, "Calling all booties!"

Genna suggests a sign near the henhouse that says "Line up for Harem Inspections Here." And Dani proposes that a calico cat character wanders into the frame and Sir Cocky calls out, "Hey, can someone grab that pussy for me?"

As our ideas get bigger and our time grows shorter, we finally realize that we are going to pick and choose among the inappropriate bevy of gags we've all come up with. Once that is decided, with the directors having the final say, it's time for the animators and background artists to jump on the extra work. The good thing is that everyone is so motivated that it doesn't feel like work. We are united in a cause we all believe in and know is worth fighting for.

Our team of editors are our champions in the technical process, as they have to take their original final cut for our pilot and switch out many scenes with the "new added material" scenes. This is no small task with sound syncs also changing, but they rise to the occasion and do a fantastic job working right up to the wire.

Meanwhile, Arnold has not ventured down to our area to actually see our progress despite his early assurances that he was going to be very 'hands on' during the production process. This is probably thanks to Joel and Bruce, who loaded key scenes on Arnold's private drive hoping he'd never actually wander down to our area. The directors also shared with us that Arnold a.k.a. King Boo-Foo reported back that he was pleased as punch with what he had seen in the comfort of his own office.

We still have two main hurdles to get over if we're going to be successful. First, the marketing angle with the test screening is pivotal. Luckily this challenge is being managed by Brooke since she's perfect for it. We knew it was too risky to have her involved in any way with the animation part of the coup, but Brooke has a good relationship with Anne, the marketing head, who happens to detest Arnauld, so we're optimistic we'll get her support.

Brooke explains to Anne that this new pilot concept is very controversial and we are all very concerned. When Anne hears the details she is horrified and agrees to show the X-rated pilot to the testing group as long as she is assured that the little kids won't get the dirty references. She also agrees to delay the testing and revealing the results until the big-wigs are already in their meeting. Brooke will rush the result in and apologize for the delay due to program errors.

Finally, our silent soldier Chester has the most important job of all. He will make the last minute digital switch of the X-rated pilot with the original right before the big-wigs watch it. I have a mild panic attack at the bravery required to make this switch less than thirty feet away from the execs, but if anyone can keep his cool under fire, it's Chester.

The night before our big reveal, everyone on this project except Brooke, the editors, and Chester meet up at the Smokehouse bar. It feels so good to cut loose and forget about the potential that we all may be jobless by tomorrow night. Every time I have a second thought about our coup, I push it out of my mind. It's too late to change my mind now anyway. We are heading down a steep hill with no breaks, and my anxiety level teeters somewhere between a heart-attack and just the sheer thrill of it.

The next morning most of us show up a little late since we're hungover, and we were told the afternoon before that Arnold had a breakfast meeting with the execs at their hotel before they head to our studio. He's really pulled out all the stops to make this a successful presentation.

Brooke summons me just minutes after I've set down my workbag and turned on my drafting table lamp.

"What's up?" I ask after I step into her office and shut the door behind me.

My concern is amped when I notice that her hands are trembling. "Everything okay?"

She picks up a folder and waves it at me. "This is the test audience result for the pilot." Her eyes look like they're going to pop out of her head.

"It's that bad?" I ask, trying not to grin since she looks so freaked out.

"Bad is an understatement," she grimaces. "The kids thought it was stupid and don't like roosters, and the moms were horrified."

"Awesome!" I say gleefully. "That's the kind of response we were hoping for!"

"But I'm worried we went overboard! He's going to lose his shit!"

I shrug. "Well, it's better that we get our desired result by going overboard than being tame and losing."

"He's going to kill me. He'll know I was behind all this."

"He won't if you act pissed off with us."

"But I started this. I can't act like that now with him. It wouldn't be right."

I sit down across from her and pull my chair as close as I can, than reach over and take her hand. "Brooke, even if I didn't care about you, which I really, really do, I'd never want to hang you out to dry when you stood up and made the choice to do the right thing. You've stuck your neck out and risked a lot by giving us the information we needed to pull this off. We care about our viewers and have pride in our work, and if we pull this off today, our dignity will be preserved. Jerks like Arnold will do anything for money, even if it's being sensational at the expense of innocent kids. If he wants to do edgy controversial cartoons, he needs to do deals with adult-centric channels like Adult Swim."

Brooke silently nods in agreement, and then takes a deep breath. "Okay, so you'll be there for me when he kicks me to the curb and I'm jobless?"

"You're so respected in this field that you'll never be jobless, but yes, I will totally be there for you."

Morgan knocks sharply on the door and then opens it before Brooke can reply, but we've already released our handhold. "It's time," she barks.

Brooke nods and we both stand. I give her a final hug, and whisper in her ear, "Now go wave your magic lasso and do your thing, Wonder Woman."

She winks at me and walks with a confident gait right out the door. As I exit, Morgan gives me a puzzled look and I smile at her. "I think I need some Starbucks, Morgan. Can I get you something?" And just like that her suspicious look melts into a smile.

"Thanks Nathan. A grande mocha with whipped cream."

"Got it." I reply and head toward the elevators.

For the next forty minutes the building is quiet as a tomb. After I've returned from Starbucks it occurs to me that everyone must be holding their collective breaths. I hope no one is second-guessing their involvement with all of this, but I'm confident with this group that everyone is still convinced we've done the right thing.

We have a group What'sApp chat set up and suddenly it's buzzing with posts.

Chester: Nadia at the front desk said the group of top execs just stormed out the front door.

Katie: Morgan just told me that there's lot of yelling coming out of Arnauld's office.
Nathan: Does Morgan know if Brooke's all right?
Katie: Morgan said it doesn't sound like he's yelling at Brooke, just yelling about firing assholes or something.
Chester: Nancy in HR said there's going to be a company wide meeting.
Joel: Oh hell no!
Chester: It's not sounding good. Do the animation teams that weren't on the project know what happened?
Joel: Yes, and they support us with what we did.
Nathan: At least there's that. Look no matter what happens, we know we did the right thing.
Dani: No regrets!
Bruce: I liked working here—the staff was cool, but yes. No regrets!

And then my phone pings over and over as everyone shares the same sympathy that quickly becomes a hashtag: #noregrets.

It's agony waiting until three p.m for the company wide meeting. Not a single bit of work is done. When we finally file in, no one dares to sit in the first few rows. Everyone is somber and wondering where they should send their resumes as soon as they're updated.

We sit there awkwardly until Arnold finally graces us with his presence, marching on stage like a general. His level of rage is quite evident, with a scowl so fierce his eyebrows have met in the center of his forehead. Brooke and Nancy walk in behind him and take seats facing the audience to Arnold's right. No one in this auditorium, including them, looks okay with being here.

"So I'm sure by now you've all heard about the unbelievable abomination some of your teams executed to destroy our fine studio. Our executive group was not pleased at all by this lack of respect for our company, and the blatant disregard for the quality of our cartoons. We will not stand for such outrageous behavior and those involved will be immediately terminated."

Sonia, a Hispanic digital colorist, boldly stands up and challenges him. "What about your lack of regard for respecting women and people of color in our cartoons? The content of that pilot was offensive and a disgrace, and you had no regard for that fact."

Arnold angrily points his finger at her. "You will be taken to HR when this meeting is over." He turns to look at Nancy. "Make note of her."

Sonia waves her hand at him disregarding his motion for her to sit back down. "I'll head up there now so I don't have to listen to any more of this garbage."

I get an adrenaline rush so strong that I feel like I should drop my head between my knees, but I don't want to miss anything. I turn to watch badass Sonia throw the auditorium door open and sashay right out. "Wow," I whisper.

I look up to the stage and Brooke and I lock gazes. She looks stoic and I'm glad for it. She's going to need to be strong for what is coming up ahead.

"So you all need to know that we won't stand for traitors among us. Each of you that participated in this fiasco will not just lose your job, but all your respect in the industry. I'll make sure of that. So right now I want you to stand up if you were a part of what happened today."

There's a long silence where not one person stands or says a word. Arnold barks a laugh. "So no one will own up to what they did to our company? None of the traitors will stand up?"

Dani suddenly rises and crosses her arms over her chest, and Chester is right behind her. I follow next, and then people are standing up in groups of twos and threes until it looks like our entire group is standing.

Arnold nods his head with an ugly sneer. "Okay, you losers will follow Nancy upstairs to HR when we're done here, and the rest of you are welcome to stay as long as you don't support these rebels.

Josh from Ricky's team stands up. "I support them." I want to hug the guy, I'm so proud of him.

"Then you can get in line with them," Arnold commands.

And just like that, this amazing energy suddenly fills the cavernous room as one by one, and two by two, people stand to join us in solidarity, until there isn't a single seated person left. Quietly everyone moves to the center aisle and starts to line up for the march to HR. It looks like there won't be any creative staff left at Sketch Republic by the end of the day, and Arnold looks like he's been hit by a truck.

As we slowly move forward the tone is somber but powerful as people hug and thank the supporters for the stand they are willing to take on our behalf. I can only hope I'd be that brave for them. When I'm near the door I look back at Brooke and see her dabbing her eyes with Kleenex while Arnold storms back and forth across the stage muttering curses. Nancy from HR has apparently already headed upstairs. She sure has a long night ahead of her. The whole thing feels like a dream.

Over an hour passes, and people stop standing in line and just start sitting on the floor wherever there's room. Groups make vending machine runs until there's no junk food left to buy, so everyone shares what they have. Some people are scrolling through job boards on their cell phones but most are just hanging loose and chatting since it's been a day like no other.

It's almost five when Nancy finally comes out to tell us about the final decision about our fate. We move to the open atrium near the elevators, and Nancy climbs to the top of a small step ladder so we can all see while she addresses our crowd.

"As you know, Arnauld was perfectly willing to terminate our work agreements with all of you involved in today's fiasco. But when the entire creative staff joined in in the spirit of solidarity, it obviously wasn't in the best interest of the company to fire our entire creative team today. As you well know, we have shows in active production and have not prepared at all for a massive hiring effort. So here is what we are offering: if everyone agrees to stay on at Sketch Republic, the perpetrators of today's fiasco will be formally written up and will lose one week's pay and be on a trial period for the next three months. Any further sabotage will be cause for immediate dismissal. So for anyone who wants to stay employed here, if you aren't on the following list now being posted next to every elevator bank, you are free to go and return back to work by nine AM tomorrow morning. If you are on the list, please get in line so you can review the following agreement and sign it to continue your employment."

The group spreads out and I don't bother to look at the list, I just get into the line forming near Nancy's office. Ultimately I'm glad I'll still be working here at Sketch Republic, because I like the people I work with and we have fun with our show. And of course as long as Brooke is here, I want to be here too.

It's almost surreal when I walk out the front doors at six PM., ironically the official end of our workday. I think about the copies of my newly signed and stamped work agreement that are shoved into my messenger bag as I trudge toward the parking lot. *What a crazy ass day this has been.*

Some of the team is talking about meeting at the Smokehouse again tonight, but all I really want is to be with Brooke and make sure she's okay. Once in my car I call her and the phone only rings once before she picks up.

"Oh God, Nathan, I've been worried sick waiting to hear what happened to you. My understanding is they are letting you guys stay with provisions. Did you agree to that deal?

"I did," I smile to myself. I'm so happy that she genuinely cares about what was happening to me. "Hey, would it be okay if I came over?"

"Of course," she says quietly.

"I'm on my way."

My heart is racing the whole way up the hill to her place. What am I going to say to Brooke? On the one hand it feels like everything has changed, but the reality is that nothing really has. She's still sweetly helping me woo a girlfriend – all just a guise to get more of her time. I'm still wildly in love with her while she's still involved with our cocky boss. *Oh, the agony!*

After I park, she buzzes me into her patio gate and waits for me at the front door. I almost trip and land in her open arms, but I steady myself by grabbing the doorjamb so I don't knock her to the ground.

She looks alarmed as she pulls me inside. "Are you okay? It's been one hell of a day, hasn't it?"

"I'll say," I agree as my eyes grow wide. "Hey, can we sit out on the balcony? I bet the view is great tonight."

"Sure. Let me just grab us a couple of beers."

Once we're settled, I gaze out at the vast view just as the city lights are starting to flicker on and shimmer in the purple dusk between day and night. I'm having so many feelings as I think about how we all live with hopes and dreams, and I wonder if it takes sheer magic to really make our most desired dreams come true.

She leans over and gazes up at me. "What's going on in that head of yours? Are you all right?"

"I'm okay. Actually... a lot happened today that made me rethink everything, and just now I was thinking about you."

"Oh, that's sweet," she replies.

I clear my throat. "You see, Brooke, I like you."

"I like you too, Nathan."

I nod and try to sort my thoughts. I'm not sure this is going the way it should. "I mean I really, really like you. And I know you have a sort of boyfriend, and you want me to hook up with Dani, but do you think...?" I swallow hard, not sure if I have the courage to continue.

"Do I think what?" she patiently asks.

"That maybe one day, when I've had more experience and you're completely over being told that you aren't good enough by Arnold, which really pisses me off by the way..."

"I know it does," she says with a sad smile. "You know if I didn't love my job so much, and he wasn't my boss, we would have been over long ago. I'm working on it, believe me."

"Do you think that if that happens one day, you would consider being my girlfriend? You can't even imagine how good I would treat you ... you'd be my queen. And I know I'm not a big executive yet, but I'm ambitious Brooke, and a really hard worker. One day I'm really going to make something of myself. Do you believe me?" I ask nervously.

"Yes, I'm already sure that you will make something of yourself. Nathan, you told me once that you are self-publishing your own comic book. So in my mind, you are well on your way."

"Thank you. I'm very proud of my comic book." She hasn't replied to the rest of my question, and my eye starts twitching I'm so nervous.

Brooke reaches over and takes my hand in hers. "As for the rest, Nathan ... I think you're amazing. Do you believe dreams do come true?"

I nod. "Yes ... yes I do."

"So do I. And we seemed destined to have met, so why don't we take this one day at a time and see where things go. Alright?"

"So that's not a yes or a no. Am I right?"

"Yes, you're correct. It's a maybe."

At first I'm a little disappointed, but then I give my self a mini-Wayne Dyer talk and decide I can live with that. "Okay, maybe is good."

She's about to respond when something swoops over our heads, and we look up to see that a large owl has landed on the edge of her roof. He gazes down at us while we sit stunned, silently gazing back up at him. It's both breathtaking and eerie at the same time. One long minute later, the owl spreads his majestic wings and takes off again into the night sky.

"Wow," I say as I let out the breath I was holding.

Brooke squeezes my hand. "Did you know that's a good omen for us?"

"I didn't, but I'll take it," I say with a grin.

"I love owls," she says with a sigh.

"I do too," I agree. "And they're so much better than cocky roosters. Don't you agree?"

She laughs and leans over so that we're almost face-to-face. Then right before she kisses me, she whispers: "They are so much better in every way."

When our lips finally meet, it hits me that all that happened these last few weeks - and the drama of today - has been worth it. Because at this very moment I've got a maybe in my pocket, with big dreams for our future ... and to top it all, Brooke is kissing me on her balcony under the stars and that's better than anything.

The End.

~A NOTE FROM THE AUTHOR~

I love our indie romance readers and writers, and being in this community has brought so many wonderful people and experiences into my life. I'm honored to be part of this collection which is driven by writers who are refusing to be bullied, and we're determined to protect our creative rights. A huge thanks to our noble leader, Penny Reid, and to Fiona Fischer, CD Reiss and the others who have pulled this project together.

Thank you dear reader for your support by purchasing this anthology!

ABOUT THE AUTHOR

Ruth Clampett is a 21st century woman aspiring to be Wonder Woman…now if she could only find her cape and magic lasso. Meanwhile she's juggling motherhood, a full-time job running her own art business, and writing romance late at night. Travel is her second obsession after writing, and it's enabled her to meet reader and writer friends all over the world. She's happily frazzled, and wouldn't change a thing about her crazy life.

Ruth has published nine books: Animate Me, Mr. 365, the Work of Art Trilogy, WET, BURN, Unforgiven and Encore. She grew up and still happily resides in Los Angeles.

Newsletter Sign-Up: http://bit.ly/2fR0ZV3
Facebook: https://www.facebook.com/RuthClampettWrites/
Instrgram: https://www.instagram.com/ruth_clampett/
Twitter: https://twitter.com/Ruthywrites

ALSO BY RUTH CLAMPETT

Animate Me

Unforgiven

Encore

Burn

Wet

Mr. 365

Work of Art~Book 1 The Inspiration

Work of Art~Book 2 The Unveiling

Work of Art~Book 3 The Masterpiece

Work of Art~The Collection

ILLUSIONIST SEEKS NEANDERTHAL

L.H. COSWAY

Have you ever wondered what would happen when two characters from completely different book worlds collide? Well, wonder no more. Illusionist Seeks Neanderthal is a short story featuring Jay Fields (Six of Hearts) and Janie Morris (Neanderthal Seeks Human).

ONE

SOME TIME AGO, BEFORE THERE WAS EVER A
QUINN OR A MATILDA, TWO CURIOUS SOULS
CROSSED PATHS...

Jay

This prick isn't gonna see shit.

He's all up in my grill, bald head a shining, beady little hawk eyes following my every move. They always have the same idea, thinking if they keep their focus on my hands they'll catch me off guard. Figure out the trick.

Wrong.

It's the ones who stand back, outside the gathered crowd, only vaguely interested, that you've got to watch for. You ever been hanging out, waiting for a bus, or I dunno, standing outside a store waiting for your girl to try shit on, your eyes disinterestedly scanning the street, when all of a sudden you randomly spot some motherfucker slipping his hand inside a purse and stealing someone's wallet? The same rules apply to illusion. You're far more likely to see what I'm really up to if you're not actually looking.

I was in Chicago, one of my favorite cities. I had a couple night club shows lined up but today I'd taken to the streets, mainly because I needed some extra cash to pay for my hotel. I never really made a whole lot from my gigs, a couple hundred dollars at most, but I figured if I just kept performing, kept on hustling, maybe one day I'd make it to Vegas. That was where you earned the big money.

"You've got a card hidden inside your shirt sleeve, don't ya?" said Baldy, perspiration collecting on his forehead he was concentrating so hard. A decent crowd had gathered but this dude was killing my buzz. I didn't get why some people couldn't just enjoy the show, they wanted to know how you were pulling it off. And they were always disappointed when you gave them the truth. That's why I never did. I hated the look of disillusionment in their eyes, much preferred the glittering excitement of mystification.

Shuffling the deck, I slid it back in my pocket and stepped away from him. "That'd be telling, buddy." His lips firmed in annoyance but I decided to ignore

139

him and move onto another trick. "Okay, I need a volunteer for this next one, anyone interested?"

"Me! I'll do it," said Baldy but I pretended I didn't hear him, eyes scanning the crowd.

"I'd like to volunteer," a tall, pretty red head who was waving her hand eagerly in the air enthused.

I smiled and gave her a quick sweep up and down, a silent interview if you will. Right off the bat I knew she wasn't gonna work. I had to admit though, she was smokin'. Intelligent eyes, too. She had that whole sexy librarian thing going on. From what I could see under her dark green sweater, she had a fantastic rack, legs that went on for miles and a face that made fools out of men. I'd certainly have some fun unbuttoning all that prim and proper.

"Sorry, darlin', but I don't think you're right for this one," I said, my tone apologetic. "Someone else." I moved my attention over the crowd and found a short guy with his hand up. Unlike the red head, this dude was perfect. I was just about to call him forward when prim and proper spoke up.

"Why not?" Her brow was furrowed and she looked disappointed, like a kid who'd just been told she was too short to ride the rollercoaster.

I gave her another once over and reconsidered. There was something about her that made me feel bad, something that made me want to give her what she wanted.

"What do you do for a living?" I asked.

Maybe this could work. *Maybe.* I already had a fair idea of her profession, the top three possibilities being a statistician, an economist or an accountant.

What told me this, you ask? Well, a number of things, but we won't get into those now.

"I'm an accountant."

Booyah. Unfortunately, though, my first guess was correct. This trick just wouldn't work with her.

"I'm sorry. I gotta go with this dude," I said, nodding over to the other guy who'd volunteered.

She appraised me curiously. "Why?"

"Just the way the cookie crumbles."

"I'd really like to know," she persisted.

"Stick around and maybe we'll talk," I told her, then moved toward the man. I had no idea why I'd said that. People asked me questions all the time, but I never offered explanations. This woman, though, I liked the look in her eyes, if that made sense. Nevertheless, she didn't seem too happy with my brush off, folding her arms over her chest. I didn't *really* intend to reveal anything to her, but I did want to talk to her some more. Maybe she'd be open to joining me for a drink in one of the many bars that lined the street.

Pulling a pen and a piece of paper from my pocket, I handed them to the guy. "What's your name?"

"Ben," he answered, seeming a small bit nervous now that everybody's attention was on him. It was perfect.

"Okay, Ben, think of an object. Any object. Picture it in your head. You got one?"

"Yeah."

I watched him intently. "All right, not that one. Change it. Now change it again. One more time. Right, now you can safely say there's no way I could know what it is, right? In fact, go ahead and pick a different one. This is the last time, I promise. You all set?"

He nodded. "Now, I want you to draw it for me. I'm gonna go stand over there with my back turned so there's no possible way I could see."

I walked away and he immediately started drawing. Turning, I counted to twenty in my head. "You done, Ben?" I called over my shoulder.

"Yeah," he replied.

"All right, now I want you to fold that bad boy up and put it in your pocket, somewhere I ain't gonna get my hands on it." Once he'd tucked the paper safely inside the back pocket of his jeans, I pulled a five-dollar bill from my wallet and handed it to the red head.

"Do me a favor and go grab me a paper from the newsstand, would ya, gorgeous?" I asked and a small blush colored her cheeks.

She looked away and I could see that something I'd said caught her off guard; her response a squeaky, "Okay."

I enjoyed watching her walk away, my eyes roaming that shapely behind. When she returned she handed me the paper, neatly folded in half. Her pretty eyes were alight with interest and I could tell she was getting a real kick out of all this. She might not have been a good candidate to volunteer, but she was the ideal spectator. I could tell she was bursting with questions but was holding them all back. Sometimes the human desire to be surprised trumped the need for knowledge, even in a woman as curious as this one.

I shook out the news rag then very carefully opened it to reveal a folded piece of paper inside the middle page. Some interested mutterings sounded from the onlookers while Ben swore under his breath, "What the hell?"

Removing it, I handed the rag back to the red head then unfolded the paper so everybody could see. A drawing of a pineapple was revealed and Ben swore some more.

"Check your pocket, buddy," I said, a grin tugging at the edges of my mouth. I fucking loved this part. Ben slid his hand in his pocket, coming up empty. "It's gone," he breathed.

I held up the drawing. "Is this what you drew?"

He nodded fervently. "It's not just what I drew, that's *my* drawing...how the hell did you..."

I shot him a wink then raised my hands in the air. "I give you the beauty of illusion, ladies and gents." They all started clapping and whistling, while a bunch of people came forward to drop some cash in my hat. They had no clue how much I needed it.

After a minute the crowd dispersed and I picked up my hat, folding it in half and shoving it in my backpack. When I glanced up only one person remained and a grin tugged at my mouth.

"You wanna go grab a drink with me?" I asked, eyeing her.

She checked her watch. "I'm on my lunch break. I have to be back at the office in forty minutes."

"I'll make sure you're back in thirty-five."

"I'm involved. With a person. Who is my boyfriend . . ." she went on, then cringed. It came out awkward, like she was trying to convince herself that spending time with me was a bad idea. "Not that I'm implying that you're inferring anything, I just like to be honest about statuses."

I wasn't an idiot. I knew what people saw when they looked at me. Tattoos, baggy jeans, scuffed boots and the premature grey patches under my eyes that spoke of living rough and too little sleep. By contrast, this chick was nothing like me. Maybe that's why I liked her.

"I'm not asking to get hitched. Just one drink," I cajoled. "What's the worst that could happen?"

I saw her lips twitch and knew she wanted to smile. Yeah, she was charmed. How could she not be? I was a charming bastard when the mood took me, even if I did look like a street thug.

"Okay, fine," she relented. "No need to invoke Dr Pepper. Just one drink though."

"Just one drink," I said and held my arm out. She hesitated a long moment then carefully took it. "Now I'm in the mood for some cola. Did I just subconsciously suggest that to myself or did you?"

She smiled and let out a small giggle. "You do know Dr Pepper isn't technically a cola, right?"

"I did not," I grinned.

"Well, legally speaking, it isn't," she went on, her face animated. "Up until the 1960's the drink was confined to the South and Southwest, because Coca-Cola and Pepsi had already built their respective networks of independent bottlers, and those bottlers held the exclusive contracts to turn the syrups into colas and distribute nationwide. In order to get around this, there was a federal court ruling in 1963 that declared Dr Pepper's unique flavor marked it as not *actually* a cola product, hence allowing nationwide distribution. Much to Coke and Pepsi's dismay, obviously."

"Obviously," I echoed.

Seriously, where had this chick come from? Who got this jazzed up about the definition of cola? I was in love already.

A moment of quiet passed between us as I led her to a decent looking cocktail bar and opened the door. She stepped through, casting her gaze to me over her shoulder as I followed her inside.

"You're not going to tell me why you wouldn't pick me to volunteer for your trick, are you?"

I pulled out a stool by the bar and gestured for her to sit. "Why do you want to know?"

She chewed on her lip. "I don't really like not knowing things."

I glanced at her mouth then back up to her eyes. "Yeah, I got that."

"Is it because of my job?"

"Your job?"

"You asked me what I did for a living, and after I answered you seemed to decide definitively that you didn't want me for the trick," she explained.

I rubbed at my jaw. "Tricks like the one I did today work on suggestibility, and some people are more suggestible than others. There isn't one simple answer as to how I determine a person's suggestiveness. It's more a collection of factors."

"Such as?"

I chuckled. "You're not letting this go, are ya?"

She smiled and shook her head. It was cute. I let out a deliberating breath and leisurely let my eyes run over her. She really was nice to look at, and the sexiest part was she didn't even know it. "Well, in your case it was a matter of not being nervous enough. Usually, when I single people out, particularly in an environment where they have to come up on stage, they get nervous. It makes them a whole helluva lot more suggestible than a calm person. You were too calm for me to suggest anything to you, because you were far too absorbed with curiosity about my tricks to be nervous about being put on the spot. It's also the reason why sociopaths don't make for good volunteers. They don't get nervous," I joked and she paled.

"I'm not a sociopath," she said fervently.

Christ, now I'd offended her. "I know that. That wasn't what I was saying. I've had my fair share of experience with head cases to know you're not one of them," I told her, my voice unexpectedly sincere.

She studied me a moment, and it wasn't often I felt like someone was really seeing me, but right then it felt like she did. Her expression turned a little sad. "Yeah, tell me about it."

I eyed her. "Your sister or your mom?" A pause as I took in her expression. "No, wait, your old man?"

She sucked in a breath. "How did you..."

I tapped the side of my head. "I see more than most people, Janie."

Now she gasped. "I never told you my name."

Reaching forward, I picked up the lanyard that hung around her neck and flipped it over. "Pretty easy to figure out when it's right in front of me," I smiled, allowing my knuckles to skim her be-sweatered chest ever so slightly. I thought I saw the tiniest tremble go through her.

She put her hand to her forehead and rolled her eyes at herself. "Duh. I'm an idiot."

I shot her a perceptive look. "We both know that's not true."

For the second time she blushed at me. I liked it. Turning to grab the barman's attention, I ordered a beer then looked to Janie. She fiddled with the hem of her sweater, glancing overhead at the cocktail menu. I knew she'd made her choice when she sat up straighter. "I'll have a margarita."

I smiled. "Letting loose, huh?"

"If you think one margarita is letting loose, you should come to my knitting group sometime," she replied.

"Oh yeah? You like to get tipsy while making mittens and shit?"

She shook her head. "Well, I don't actually knit, but anyway, that's a whole other story. The point is, I'm tall. It takes a lot more than this to get me drunk," she said as the barman got to work on our drinks. I leaned my elbow on the counter and studied her. I had to admit, she had me intrigued. There was this mixture of innocence and worldliness about her that appealed to me. When the barman set her cocktail down in front of her, I watched as she took a sip, bringing the salted rim to her lips. She tipped her tongue to it ever so slightly and my balls stiffened.

Quit looking at her mouth, ya perv.

143

I cleared my throat. "So, you like being an accountant?"

She shrugged and set her glass down. "I know what you're going to say, it's unusual for a woman to pursue a math based career."

I frowned at her sudden defensiveness. "That's not what I was gonna say at all. In fact, the whole 'girls don't do well at math' thing is a form of cognitive bias." She wore an interested expression so I explained further. "If you tell someone that the majority of people fail a certain subject, then that person is already more likely to fail because the idea has been planted in their noggin. It's what they call a stereotype threat. There's this study I read about once, where they took two groups of men and women and gave them a math test. The first group was told that men usually outperform women in the test, and the second was told that both genders typically performed equally well. You wanna guess what the outcome was?"

Janie's eyes lit up. "The women performed worse in the first group and better in the second. I've read that paper. "Stereotype Threat and Women's Math Performance" by Spencer, Steele and Quinn, 1998."

She paused then, looking embarrassed that she knew all the specifics. I thought it was awesome. Shooting her a wide smile, I clinked my glass to hers, "See, I knew there was a reason I liked you."

She glanced at the bar top. "I read. A lot. I read a lot of things."

"Yeah? Me, too."

For a second we just smiled at one another. Then Janie asked a question. Actually, she whispered it, first glancing from left to right as though someone might be listening in. "Are you a member of The Magic Circle?"

This surprised a laugh out of me. "You've heard of The Magic Circle?"

"Of course," she answered like it was obvious. "I thought you must be a member since you won't tell me all the reasons why I'm not suggestible enough for your tricks. Each member of the organization undertakes an oath not to reveal their magical secrets to anybody except for other members under pain of expulsion from the circle."

"Where'd you hear that?" I grinned.

"I read it on Wikipedia," she answered simply. "It all sounds very exciting, in my opinion, like Harry Potter or something. You should apply to join."

"Nah, too much like a cult for my liking. Besides, I'm too cool for that shit. The circle is full of stuffy Brits."

Janie giggled, a wide smile on her face. She was too fucking cute when she smiled like that. I leaned a little closer and elbowed her in the arm. "Hey, I know I said I wasn't asking to get hitched, but you ever picture yourself marrying a guy from Boston?"

I know, I was a shameless flirt.

Janie inhaled a sharp breath and grew flustered as she straightened in her seat. "Um...I...I don't think so."

I lifted my beer and took a swig. "No?"

She shook her head, her gaze focused intently on her margarita now.

"Well, maybe it won't be to me, but I can definitely see that for you. There's a big, manly Bostonian in your future, Janie Morris, you mark my words." I was teasing her now, but it was fun. I liked seeing her blush.

She shifted a little. "So, um, what's your favorite cognitive bias?" she asked and I chuckled loudly.

"That your way of changing the subject, sweetheart?"

She didn't answer my question, instead she kept on talking. "I think mine has to be the Dunning-Kruger effect."

"Oh yeah?"

Janie nodded. "It relates to how the less we know about a certain topic or skill, the better we think we are at it. The more we learn about things, the more we realize just how little our knowledge base actually is. I find it fascinating. Like, you get all these teenagers playing video games set in warzones, and the games teach little to nothing about actual combat, yet you'll get all these gamers going around thinking they could be real snipers, or dispose of bombs, or take down a terrorist organization. I remember when I used to spend the weekends playing *Street Fighter* when I was growing up. I actually felt a little like I could kick someone's ass at the end. In reality all I was adept at was tapping buttons at an alarmingly speedy rate," she finished.

"So, illusory superiority, right?"

"Right!" Janie exclaimed, a grin taking shape. "Now tell me yours."

I rubbed at my chin, thinking about it. Seriously, I know I joked about it earlier, but what exactly would it take to get this woman to hitch a ride to Vegas with me and get married? *What's your favorite cognitive bias* had to be the best conversation starter I'd come across in a while.

"You ever heard of the Just World Hypothesis?" I asked and Janie shook her head. "It's like in the movies, where everyone always gets what they deserve in the end. People think that the world is ultimately just, so that when something bad happens we can say that person deserved it. That their previous actions were the cause and therefore they only got what was coming to them. In real life, though? Well, we're all just a bunch of monkeys flinging our shit around and there's no moral to the story. A lot of the time bad stuff happens for absolutely no reason at all."

Suddenly I was staring glumly into my beer, realizing I'd just depressed the fuck out of myself, and probably Janie, too.

"Sorry. Now I'm making your fun margarita hour into dreary Tuesday."

"No, no," Janie was quick to reassure me. "I actually find you incredibly fascinating and engaging." Right after she said it she clamped her hand over her mouth as though embarrassed. "Oh my God. I didn't mean to say that out loud."

I winked at her. "I thought you were too tall to get tipsy off one cocktail?"

"I'm not too big to admit I was wrong," she responded with a self-deprecating smile.

"Will do you something for me?"

She eyed me curiously. "What?"

"Come see my show tonight."

Janie glanced away and started rifling through her purse for something. "Uh, well, I have plans tonight. With the person," she mumbled.

"The person?"

"With which I am involved. The boyfriend."

"That's cool. Bring him with you."

"I don't think..."

"Give me your number and I'll text you the address," I cut her off before she could finish.

"I don't own a cell phone."

"Why not?"

She stuck out her chin. "I don't believe in them."

God, this woman, could she be any cuter? "You know what, I'm gonna use that one sometime. I don't own a car. Maybe if I go around telling everyone it's because I don't believe in them they'll think I'm enlightened instead of broke as fuck."

Janie barked a loud laugh and she slid a bill onto the counter. "I really do have to get back to work now," she said, wiping tears from her eyes as I picked up the money and placed it carefully back her in hand. She jumped a little when my fingers brushed hers.

"Drink's on me," I told her.

We shared a look and then she withdrew her hand. "It was a pleasure to meet you...oh crappers, I just realized I don't even know your name," she said in horror, like she'd been incredibly rude not to ask.

I gave her a warm look. "My name's Jay Fields, and it was a pleasure to meet you, too, Janie Morris."

Her gaze drifted over my face, and for once I couldn't tell what someone else was thinking. Maybe I'd been too distracted by all that gorgeous, curly red hair. It was twisted up in a bun and I was struck with the urge to see it down.

"You should wear your hair down. It's too pretty to be up like that."

The compliment made her blush again but she didn't say anything, just ducked her head, gave me a final wave and made to leave. I'd moved fast, so she'd already gotten to the door by the time her bun unraveled. She paused midstride, glanced at the hair that had fallen around her shoulders and muttered to herself as she turned back to me, laughing. Sleight of hand could be useful for more than just magic sometimes.

I grinned and held up the hair tie for her to see. She shook her head again, shot me a parting smile, and went on her way.

TWO

Janie

"So, he's a magician?"

I nodded, glancing between the street map and the building's address.

"Janie, if you had a phone you could just Google the address. Why don't you just Google the address?"

"There is no accepted definition of the word 'Google' other than as an American multinational technology company specializing in Internet-related services and products. You want me to '*American technology company*' an address? That makes no sense."

"You know what I mean, smartass. I want you to do a search on the magical internets, on your cellphone—"

"I don't have a cellphone, but you knew that. And there is no such thing as magic."

"And yet, here we are. On our way to a magic show." Marie shivered as a gust of wind had us stopping and bracing. We waited for it to pass before continuing.

"I don't understand. The building should be right here."

After I'd left Jay at the bar earlier today, I'd belated realized he never gave me the address for his show. Disappointment filled me. But then, later on, as I rummaged through my purse for a napkin, I found a neatly folded piece of paper that turned out to be a flyer for the club where he was performing. Again, he'd bamboozled me. I had no clue how he'd managed to slide it into my bag without me seeing.

"Do you want me to *American technology company* the address or not?" Marie whipped out her phone.

"Not. People located addresses for centuries prior to the advent of Google."

"Or, they died in a tragic mugging on the streets of Chicago and were

147

mourned by their cats. Forgive me if I'd prefer to use a little cell phone magic instead."

There is no such thing as magic, I repeated in my head.

Sleight of hand, meticulously planned scenarios and outcomes, subliminal influencing and cold reading. That's all it was. And yet, there was something mysterious about Jay Fields. Something truly...well, magical. I'd spent less than an hour in his company and already I was eager to see him again, eager for him to marvel and astound me. He was captivating, and just like a magnet, he pulled me in.

The main reason I wanted to see his show, however, was because today was the first time in a long time that I'd actually felt excited. Lately, a lot of things had been bringing me down; my job, my relationship, so I just wanted to spend tonight being entertained. Let Jay tap into my imagination and sense of wonder like he'd done with every person standing on that street today.

"So, Jon had to work late?" Marie questioned, tugging up the collar of her coat to defend against the cold.

"Yes, we were supposed to have a date, but you know him, he's a workaholic."

Marie studied me in a way that made me self-conscious. "How's everything been going with you two?"

"It's been fine," I replied, not really wanting to talk about the man in my life.

My main squeeze.

My significant other.

My other half.

These days he certainly didn't feel like the other half of me, or in any way significant. In fact, he merely felt like the person with whom I shared a bed, a bathroom and kitchen/lounge facilities.

I loved him but, well, something was missing. Maybe it was never there to begin with. Or maybe I just needed to accept that it was a real-life relationship. Real-life relationships were nothing like relationships in movies starring Kate Hudson.

Marie arched a brow. "Just fine?"

"Fine is good. Fine is better than not fine. Fine is better than very many things."

"Janie, the fact that you're using the word 'fine' so much makes me suspect things aren't fine."

"We've been together a long time," I said. "And when you're with someone a long time, things are no longer exciting, passionate, electric or a whole host of other adjectives. When you've been with someone a long time, things are usually fine, and so, that is what they are between Jon and I."

"You're talking in circles," Marie griped just as the door opened to a building we passed. It was a black door, non-descript, and didn't appear to lead to a business. However, when it opened, a loud round of cheers and clapping rang out, before a familiar Bostonian accent said, "And that's why I don't buy microwaves from gypsies no more." Laughter ensued.

"Weird punchline," Marie muttered as I grabbed her elbow and pulled her inside.

"This is the place," I said as we stepped into the dark club. It was one of those bars that people only knew about through word of mouth. Pretentious, yes, but obviously a good marketing tactic since the place was packed. When people thought something was exclusive, they tended to want it more. It was psychological. Like, if someone told me there were only five hot dogs left in a hot dog stand, I'd automatically want a hotdog more than I did a minute ago.

Actually, now I did sort of want a hot dog.

"This is it?" Marie asked, not sounding very enthusiastic about being pulled into an unmarked building.

"Yes, look! There he is," I replied in a hushed voice and pointed to the stage where Jay stood doing a card trick for a woman in the front row. He wore the same jeans from earlier and a black tank top. Now I could see the extensive tattoos that covered his arms, and though I'd never been particularly attracted to that sort of look, I had to admit they suited him.

Marie looked from the stage and then to me. "Okay, not what I expected."

"What did you expect?"

"I don't know. Some guy in a dickey bow pulling a rabbit out of a hat."

"I guess that is what we imagine when we picture a magician."

"He's a bad boy," Marie said, pointing her finger at the stage. "I never knew you were into bad boys, Janie."

"I'm not. I have a boyfriend. Jon, remember?"

"And he's cocky," Marie went on, ignoring my statement. "Look at that smirk and those dimples. The poor woman might as well hand over her panties right now."

The woman she referred to was the one Jay had roped into volunteering for his trick. I briefly wondered what *she* did for a living, still unsure if I was disgruntled or flattered that I wasn't suitable as a volunteer. I liked to imagine it was because I was just too darn smart.

"He's not cocky," I replied. "He's confident. Cockiness implies arrogance."

"Well, too much confidence can lead to cockiness," Marie said. "It's a fine line."

"Ladies, there's an $8 entry fee, but I'll let you in for $5 since you've missed a lot of the show," said a man in a black blazer. Neither of us had noticed him sitting by the door.

"Yes, sorry, we got a little lost. You don't make this place easy to find," I said, keeping my voice low so as not to interrupt the show. I rummaged in my purse for some money and handed him a rumpled ten. He gave us two ticket stubs and Marie and I quietly made our way to some empty seats at the back.

We brought our attentions to the stage when Jay spoke. "For my next trick, I'll need another volunteer," he said and scanned the audience.

Marie nudged me with her elbow. "You should do it."

I shook my head. "I don't make a good volunteer, apparently."

She frowned. "What? Why?"

Before I could respond, Jay said, "You, the red head at the back, you had your hand up, right?"

I blinked. Jay was staring right at me, confident smile in place. How had he even seen me back here? And I definitely hadn't had my hand up. The slight twitch of his lips told me he knew well and good that I hadn't.

"I think you're mistaking me for someone else," I called out.

"Aw, don't chicken out now," Jay teased and people started turning their attention to me, whispering and speculating.

I straightened. "Somebody once told me that I don't make a very good volunteer for magic tricks."

"This isn't your typical magic trick. You'll be more of a spectator than a volunteer," Jay pushed, undeterred.

"Go on," Marie whispered giddily and nudged me out of my seat, "get your butt up there."

Disgruntled, I stood and wiped my sweaty palms on my skirt, suddenly nervous. I tried to recall if I'd ever been on an actual stage before. Maybe in a childhood school play.

I walked up the rows until I reached the stage, but there were no steps leading up. Jay reached down and took my hand, his magnetic eyes meeting mine. They dazzled me, made feel like a kid stepping into a funfair. A jolt went through me at the feel of his palm. When was the last time Jon had held my hand? I honestly couldn't remember. A second later Jay led me to the center of the stage where there was a narrow bench. It was the only set piece, the rest of the area being empty.

Jay gestured for me to sit then pulled a newspaper out of his back pocket. They seemed to be a favored prop of his. He sat next to me, his thigh resting against mine and I wondered if it was intentional. Soft piano music started to play. Carefully, he unfolded the paper, first taking one sheet and spreading it out on my lap, then taking another and spreading it out on his. He continued in this vain, speaking as he worked his way through the paper.

"The Victorian art critic John Ruskin once said that a little thought and a little kindness are often worth more than a great deal of money. When I was a young kid, I didn't have a home. I slept on the streets and in abandoned buildings, and sometimes the only thing that kept me from freezing to death was a bit of old newspaper that I used to cover my body."

Both our laps were covered in newspaper. Something in my stomach unfurled at his unexpected, yet casually spoken words. He'd been homeless? A sense of sadness filled me up just to think it.

Still talking, Jay continued spreading the newspaper out over our laps until he used every sheet. Then, he began to carefully fold it, starting at the outer corners and working his way in.

"Someone might've left their newspaper on a park bench, not realizing that later I would find it and use it to survive another night. Maybe you could call that unconscious kindness. They had no clue they were helping me by leaving that paper behind. Then you have conscious kindness. One day I was performing magic tricks on the street, and a smartly dressed woman dropped a hundred-dollar bill into my hat. That hundred might've been a drop in the bucket for her, but to me it meant I could go buy myself a sleeping bag and food to last the next two weeks. It meant survival. The sleeping bag was cheap, sure, but it might as well have been a four-poster bed at the *Four Seasons* compared to what I was used to. Her kindness that day was like seeing a flower bloom when you've been traipsing through an arid desert, because you know that means water is near."

I was captivated by his tale of hope, the soft piano music tinkering at my heart strings. I was so transfixed that I only now realized he'd folded the sheets of newspaper in a way to look like a bunch of flowers. He held them out to me, but before I could take them there was a rustle and a beautiful white dove emerged from the paper. I gasped. It flew out and landed on Jay's hand. My pulse thrummed, it was so unexpected.

"Her kindness was a miracle. It was a white dove flying out of a bit of tatty old newspaper. People don't need much. Sometimes we just need someone to be kind to us. One act of kindness can transform our lives. Often, our inclination is to hoard what we have, keep it all for ourselves, going to no use, when there's someone out there whose entire world could be changed if we gave them just a tiny portion of what's ours. Tupac Shakur said this world is a *gimme, gimme, gimme, everybody back off place*. He asked how one person could have $32 million dollars and another person could have nothing," he swiped his hands around his dove and it disappeared. *Wow.* "And yet the person with 32 million can still sleep at night. I guess what I'm trying to say is, the only way the world will ever get better is if we're kinder, if we share a little of what we've got but don't need, with the next person who hasn't got it and does need it. After that day when the lady gave me that money, things started to slowly get better for me. It was the starting point to me getting off the streets. So, there's your proof."

As he spoke, Jay tore the newspaper flowers strip by strip. Pieces of paper fell to the floor like so much confetti, until only one folded and torn piece was left. "Kindness worked for me, and maybe it can work for you, too," he finished, then unfolded the paper. There was an audible gasp, because somehow, he'd managed to tear it in a way to form the words "Be Kind". He threw the paper into the audience, took a bow, then walked off the stage.

I sat there, enthralled, as the audience gave their applause. I couldn't move, was still absorbing his speech and the beauty of the act, the meaning of his words and the simple truth of them. This was the first time I'd felt true wonder since I was a kid. When I realized I was still sitting there, slack jawed, I got up, and instead of climbing off the stage I walked in the direction Jay had gone.

I found him backstage, placing his dove in a cage before taking a swig from a bottle of water.

"That was beautiful," I breathed, snagging his attention. His smile lit up his face, and there was an energy about him, a kinetic field that shimmered and pulsed.

"Glad you liked it, Janie."

"Why did you ask me up on stage?"

He gave a little grin and lifted a shoulder. "Felt like you needed a thrill."

Hmmm, maybe I did. I certainly felt…I don't know, more alive somehow. But still, I sensed that wasn't the reason. "I don't believe you."

"Maybe I just wanted an excuse to charm you. See if you'll take me home with you tonight. My hotel's been feeling a little lonely."

My mouth fell open. I closed it. "I told you, I have a boyfriend, and we live together, so—"

"But if you didn't live together…" Jay arched a suggestive brow. Perhaps Marie was right about him being cocky after all. He threw his hands up. "Relax, I'm joking. I'm just happy you decided to come. I was a little disappointed when you didn't show."

"I was late because this place is so ridiculously difficult to find."

"Why didn't you just Google it?"

"I..." I trailed off, not wanting to get into the whole Google thing again. "I don't have a cell phone, remember? Anyway, I just wanted to say that I think you're very talented, and I wouldn't be surprised if you make it big one of these days. I only caught the end of your performance tonight and it gave me serious chills. Good chills. The kind you get when you're reminded of a fond memory, not the kind a cat gets when it's frightened. Did you know that we inherited goosebumps from our animal ancestors? When cats are scared, they get goose-bumps and their hair stands on end to make them look bigger, and therefore more threatening to the predator that's frightening them. Anyway, I'm getting off topic. What I mean is, your act is incredible, and I want to make sure you know it. Plus, your message really struck a chord with me, and with a lot of people in the audience I'm sure. You're not just doing magic tricks, you're making people think. And making people think is important. People don't think enough these days, if you ask me."

"Janie." Jay's voice was seductive whisper.

"Yes?"

"Shut up for a second." His eyes glittered as he took a step forward, placed his hands on either side of my face, and kissed me right on the lips. With tongue. My heart stuttered, and I wobbled on my feet. I was dumbstruck and tingling all over. One hand left my face so that he could wrap his arm around my waist, probably to keep me from toppling over, which I was thankful for. I'd taken my fair share of swan dives in my time and they weren't pretty.

What was pretty was Jay's warmth, and the soft, sure pressure of his lips on my lips, the wet slide of his tongue on my tongue. I closed my eyes and surprised myself with a girlish moan. I rarely moaned, and certainly not girlishly.

He smelled good, too. Like cloves and manliness. Unwittingly, I reached up and wrapped my arms around his neck, pulling him to me, wanting to prolong the kiss. When Jon kissed me, it didn't feel like this. When Jon kissed me, I felt a surprising amount of nothingness. Right now, I felt a surprising amount of everything-ness.

Jay was alive in a way I'd never experienced before.

Wait a second, Jon!

In a rush, I pushed away from Jay and wiped my hand across my mouth as though that might erase the amazing kiss we'd just shared. As though it might eradicate the guilt that started to niggle at me.

I wasn't a cheater. I would never cheat, but...

Hell. I got swept up in the moment, and getting swept up in moments was the downfall of many a lady.

"I think I have a crush on you," Jay purred with that mischievous grin I was coming to recognize.

I wagged my finger at him, feeling breathless "That was...that was..."

"Phenomenal, I know."

"Oh, my goodness, you *are* cocky," I blurted, flustered.

"I prefer the term unquietly confident, or loudly self-assured, but cocky works, too," he said, stepping toward me again. I took a step back. He kept coming at me and I kept moving away until my back hit a wall.

"Hey, I get it. You're taken, but I couldn't help myself. You're a very tempting woman, Janie Morris."

I laughed then, because no one had ever described me as tempting before. Cute, yes. Chatty, sure. Clever, of course. But never tempting. I was flattered, I couldn't help it. I liked the way he saw me. He saw me in a way most people didn't, and it was a tiny bit intoxicating. Okay, a lot intoxicating.

I needed to get a hold of myself, go home to my boyfriend and forget about this mesmerizing man, this magician who had very much cast a spell over me.

And I didn't even believe in magic.

"You know, it's too bad I gotta leave and go back to Boston tomorrow. If I was sticking around this boyfriend of yours would have himself some serious competition."

I giggled, unable to help being charmed. I folded my arms across my chest, probably to keep from grabbing him and kissing him again. It was wrong. I knew that. But Gloria Estefan was right, the bad boys made you feel so good. "I'm sure he would. If I ever come to Boston, I'll be sure to look you up."

"And if I ever come back to Chicago, you better believe I'll be darkening your door, Janie Morris. Your door will be so fucking darkened you won't know where to turn. Or look."

That didn't even make any sense, but I was still laughing. Jay had wacky sense of humor and a funny way with words. He came forward, pressed a soft kiss to my cheek before whispering, "I guess I'll see you around. Promise you won't forget about me?"

He was gone before I had a chance to reply. I didn't see which way he went, but I was suddenly aware of my hair around my shoulders. I reached up, unable to find my hair tie. Why that little...

He'd let my hair down again, and I hadn't even seen or felt him doing it. His sleight of hand really was up to scratch. That was two hair ties he'd stolen from me now. I was going to have to start keeping a tab.

I definitely didn't need to make the promise though, because there was no way I'd forget him any time soon.

"There you are," Marie exclaimed. "It took me forever to convince them to let me come back here and look for you."

"I was talking to Jay," I replied, still a little flustered from his kiss and sudden departure – and hair accessory theft.

"Oh, where'd he go? I was hoping to ask him to come for drinks with us. I want to pick his mind about the trick he did with the dove."

"He's gone. I'm not sure we'll be seeing him again, not for a long time anyway."

Marie seemed disappointed. "Well, that's too bad."

"Yeah, it is."

I had a feeling Jay was one of those people who never settled anywhere. He flittered into your life, left a big impression, and then was gone almost as quickly as he came. Like a fairy god-mother, or a genie in a lamp. Only I never got my three wishes. Just a kiss I'd be dreaming about for many nights to come.

Marie slid her arm through mine. "Come on, let's go to the bar. The first two lemon drops are on me."

As she led me through the club, something on the floor caught my eye. It

153

was a piece of torn up newspaper, but when I bent down and picked it up I realized it wasn't just any old bit of paper. It was the same one Jay had thrown from the stage, the one the was shaped into the words "Be Kind". Without thinking, I folded it up and put it in my pocket.

He had my hair ties, it was only fair I got to keep a memento of this most unforgettable and magical night, too.

End.

ABOUT THE AUTHOR

L.H. Cosway lives in Dublin, Ireland. Her inspiration to write comes from music. She thinks that imperfect people are the most interesting kind. They tell the best stories.

www.lhcoswayauthor.com
Facebook: http://www.facebook.com/LHCosway
Twitter: http://www.twitter.com/LHCosway
Instagram: http://www.instagram.com/l.h.cosway

ALSO BY L.H. COSWAY

Contemporary Romance

Painted Faces

Killer Queen

The Nature of Cruelty

Still Life with Strings

Showmance

Fauxmance (coming Autumn 2018)

The Hearts Series

Six of Hearts (#1)

Hearts of Fire (#2)

King of Hearts (#3)

Hearts of Blue (#4)

Thief of Hearts (#5)

Cross My Heart (#5.75)

Hearts on Air (#6)

The Rugby Series with Penny Reid

The Hooker & the Hermit (#1)

The Player & the Pixie (#2)

The Cad & the Co-ed (#3)

The Varlet & the Voyeur (#4)

Urban Fantasy

Tegan's Blood (The Ultimate Power Series #1)

Tegan's Return (The Ultimate Power Series #2)

Tegan's Magic (The Ultimate Power Series #3)

Tegan's Power (The Ultimate Power Series #4)

COCK AND BALLS

A BRITISH SPORTS ROMANCE

AMY DAWS

Only Camden Harris is cocky enough to think he can elope to Scotland with his fiancé, Dr. Indie Porter, and not tick off at least one of his brothers.

ONE

COCKY TEAMMATES

Camden

"Specs!" I shout as I jog across the grass toward my fiancée. She's in the middle of the Tower Park pitch surrounded by a sea of balls and has her hands all over my brother Booker.

Normally, my woman's hands on another bloke would send me into a jealous rage. But Specs—aka Dr. Indie Porter—is the assistant team doctor for Bethnal Green F.C., so I kind of have to deal with it.

Bethnal is the football club—or soccer team, as Americans call it—my dad, Vaughn Harris, manages in London. It's where my younger brother, Booker, and my twin brother, Tanner, play. Last year, I was right beside them until I signed on with Arsenal. Our older brother, Gareth, plays defence for Manchester United. We're a family of footballers through and through. And even though our sister, Vi, doesn't play, she's the loudest fan you'll hear in the stands at any of our matches.

Needless to say, we all eat, sleep, and breathe football.

That's why I thought my life was over when I tore my ACL last year. I was caked in mud from a rainy match when they wheeled me into The Royal London Hospital on a stretcher. With my football career at risk, I was feeling the lowest I'd ever felt.

Then a stunning, curly-haired redhead with cheetah-print glasses and a sexy smart mouth waltzed into the exam room, claiming to be a doctor. I thought she was way too young and gorgeous to be a doctor, but it turned out she was my surgeon and a brilliant one at that.

She is way too good for me, which is exactly why I put a ring on her finger several months ago.

"Oi! Get your hands off my brother, you slapper!" I crow as I kick a few stray balls out of the way and reach Indie, who's hunched over as she stretches out

Booker's hamstring. I rear back my hand and slap my fiancée's arse with a satisfying crack.

"Ouch, Camden!" Indie squeals. Her hands immediately drop Booker's leg and fly back to rub her rear end. She turns wide, angry eyes at me that are framed by a pair of red glasses today. "What on earth are you doing? This is my place of work! You can't come in here and do that!"

I roll my eyes at her overreaction. I grew up on this pitch. This is where I learned the game of football. There's absolutely nothing I could do here that would shock anyone.

I wrap my arm around Indie and pull her to my side. "Relax, Specs. When your dad manages the team, no one blinks an eye at you." I release my hold on her to bend over and pick up one of the many footballs spread out all around us. Moving away, I begin bouncing it on my knees and head nod to Booker, who's still lying on the grass. "Hey, Book."

"Cam," Booker replies, pulling his knee to his chest to stretch himself like he was perfectly capable of doing all along. The cheeky wanker.

I glance over at my beautiful fiancée, who is currently shooting daggers at me. Her brown eyes are stunning as ever, but they do not look soothed by my words. "I'm serious, Cam. You can't come around the pitch to see me whenever you feel like it."

I stop bouncing the ball and clutch it to my hip. "Why not?"

"Because it's unprofessional."

"Stuff that! You've broken the rules for me before," I reply with a wink. Memories of Indie playing hot doctor and me being the naughty patient will be the highlight of my life when my balls are old and saggy. Forbidden romances always do taste the sweetest.

"Well, no more," she retorts firmly. "I don't need anyone else talking crap about me because I'm engaged to the manager's son." She closes her eyes and grimaces like she didn't mean to say the last part.

I drop the ball and turn to my brother. "Who is talking crap?"

Booker rises up to a sitting position and props his arms on his knees. "Tanner and I put them straight. Don't worry about it, Cam."

"Tell me," I nearly growl and kick the football high, toward the goal that's over half a football field away. It bounces off the top bar and misses.

Out of nowhere, Tanner leaps up onto my tensed back. His beard tickles the side of my face as he bellows, "Hey, broseph! What are you doing here? Did the Gunners fire you already?"

He tries to pull me in a headlock, but I shove him off and kick another football in frustration. "No...I'm already done for the day. What's this shit I'm hearing about the team trash-talking Indie?"

"Camden!" Indie exclaims, attempting to grab my arm and pull me toward her. "Just leave it. I've got it handled."

Tanner's eyes narrow as he crosses his arms and stares back at me. It's hard to take him seriously with his man bun and Dumbledore beard. However, he's lost all humour on his face, so I know this isn't a laughing matter.

"I've had words with them," he states with a grim tone that's very unlike him.

"Words with who?" I ask through clenched teeth. I rear back to kick another football. This one makes it in the net easily. "What are they saying?"

Out of the corner of my eye, I see Booker shake his head at Tanner.

My blood pressure spikes. "What are you guys not telling me? I want to hear it all."

Tanner exhales heavily. "We have to tell him, Book."

Booker winces and yanks off his goalie gloves before hopping up to his feet. "I overheard some of the guys saying that you only put a ring on Indie's finger as a publicity stunt for your new team."

"What?" I roar, my hands raking through my hair. I clench the locks tightly in my fists because I'd rather be punching their faces. A lot of the guys used to be my teammates. Who the fuck would say that?

"Guys, stop!" Indie exclaims, trying to stand between the three of us to halt our conversation, but we've essentially boxed her out. This is a brother moment that can't be interrupted. If Gareth were here, he'd be initiating a Harris Shakedown.

Tanner looks straight at me and replies, "They were saying you don't have any intention of marrying her. They were even saying the ring is a fake."

"My fists of fury are going to fucking fly!" My face heats with rage as I spin on my heel and boot four balls in a row. Three of the four hit the goal. The last one buzzes way over the top bar because I scooped under it too much.

My eyes dart all over the pitch to where the rest of the players are making their way toward the changing room on the opposite side. I begin walking. "Time for me to have words with some of my former teammates."

"We handled it, broseph," Tanner barks, grabbing hold of my arms and yanking me backward. "Trust me. Booker and I both got fined for *handling* it."

Indie rushes up in front of me and pushes my chest. "Camden, you're only going to make it worse!"

Her voice breaks on the end with barely contained emotion. It's then that my rage is tempered. Snuffed out. Crushed by the woman I'm in love with. I look down into Indie's glossy eyes and it fucking guts me.

"Indie, they are saying I don't want to marry you because we haven't set a date," I grind out through clenched teeth though I hardly need to spell it out for her. She's the smartest person I know. "There are two ways we can fix this. Either you set the date already, or I punch their fucking lights out."

Indie's face crumples in worry as she nervously gnaws on her lower lip. Her anxiety kills me because she has all the power here. I wanted to get married right away, but she was the one dragging her bloody feet.

My jaw is tight when I plead with her one more time. "Specs, just set a bloody date already."

She turns away from me and begins hurriedly picking up stray footballs. Months. It's been months that my brilliant fiancée has avoided this conversation with me and I'm tired of it.

With a heavy sigh, I turn back to Booker and Tanner. "Tell me what your fines were so I can pay you back. You guys don't have to fight my battles for me."

"Fuck off," Tanner growls while tightening his hair-band. "We're Harris Brothers and Indie is our friend. This is as much our fight as it is yours."

Booker nods in agreement and they both cross their arms over their chests, clearly setting their decision in stone. After a moment of staring at them, I finally nod a silent thanks and they give me a hearty pat on the back before making their way off the pitch.

Indie is still completely focused on placing the stray balls into the sack, clearly trying to avoid talking to me.

I stride over and bend to grab a ball. "Is this a typical job for the team doctor?"

"No," she snaps quickly, then adjusts her glasses as they slip down her nose.

"Specs." I state her nickname softly and walk toward her as she bends to pick up another ball. "Specs," I repeat as she fumbles to drop the ball inside with only one hand.

The bag falls to the ground, several footballs spilling out around our feet. I reach up and grasp her cheeks in my hands to force her to look at me. Her eyes swerve nervously all around as she checks for people who may be watching us.

"Camden, please," she croaks, her voice thick with emotion as she tries to pull out of my embrace.

"No," I reply, moving my hands from her face and wrapping them around her waist to hug her to me.

Indie has never been huge on affection, but she's changed with me. When we're together at our house in Notting Hill, she's completely open. Right now, she's reminding me of the closed off surgeon who was raised by cold, unfeeling parents who left her alone in boarding schools for most of her life.

"Indie, I love you. Fucking marry me so we can put this stupid gossip to bed."

Her eyes fly wide. "I'm not going to marry you because a couple of guys don't know how to keep their mouths shut in the changing room!" she snaps.

"Then marry me because I asked you to. Marry me because I want to take the next step with you!"

"And who will attend this wedding?" she asks, stepping out of my arms and swiping under her glasses as errant tears fall from her eyes. "Your entire family and my one and only friend, Belle? Not to mention the fact that Belle is married to Tanner, so she's technically your family!"

"So what! Who cares who we invite? Everyone loves you."

"My parents don't even send me birthday cards anymore. You think they're going to attend their only daughter's wedding? Highly doubtful."

My heart plummets when the truth comes out at last. Indie has been pushing off on setting a wedding date because of her horrid parents.

"We don't need your parents there," I reply through clenched teeth. "Truth be told, I don't even want them there."

"Who will walk me down the aisle?" she sobs, and the pain on her face cuts right through me. In a flash, I kick all the balls out of my way and pull her into my arms.

She presses her face into my chest as her body trembles against me. I haven't seen her get emotional about her parents in a long time. I'm such a prat for not realising this is what has been bothering her.

"Any of my brothers would love to walk you down the aisle. You can take your pick." I run my hand down the back of her neck and she sags into me a bit.

"I know my dad would be honoured, Specs. Hell, I'll walk you down the aisle myself if you'll let me."

"I'm sorry, Camden," she mumbles against my shirt before looking up at me, her brown eyes full of pain and embarrassment. "This is so stupid. I shouldn't care about this, but I do. I don't want to be the bride everyone feels sorry for because there's only one friend on her side of the church."

"So let's get married alone!" I reply, my voice rising in pitch.

She scoffs and shoves me in the chest. "Be serious. Your family would murder you."

"I don't give a toss!" I tilt her chin up so she looks me in the eyes and sees how serious I am. "I care about you and me. My family will get over it. Most of them at least. Tanner will probably weep for a few weeks, but he'll be fine."

Indie smiles at the image and shakes her head from side-to-side. "We can't possibly elope, can we?" she asks, her voice sounding mildly hopeful.

"We can do whatever we want!" I exclaim, tossing my hands out wide. "Let's do it this weekend. We're both off, which basically never happens in the world of football. It's a sign, Specs. It's meant to be."

Indie bites her lip and adjusts her glasses, clearly thinking through all the details like the sexy nerdling she is. "Are you completely sure you're okay with it just being us? I don't want you to do this because of what the players are saying, and I don't want you to have regrets."

"I'm one hundred percent sure I want to marry you this weekend...Just us," I add, stepping in and hugging her to me again. I press my forehead to hers and whisper, "Let's go make those cocky bastards shut their arrogant mouths."

TWO

COCKY BAGPIPER

Indie

"The piper's ready for ye!" the wedding planner states in a thick Scottish accent as I stare at myself in the mirror of the hotel lobby in Gretna Green, Scotland.

I'm wearing a simple pleated, strapless wedding dress. The ivory colour compliments my fair skin, and the skirt is just full enough to make it feel like a wedding dress. The sweetheart neckline gives it a sexier feel while the row of buttons up the back adds a touch of elegance. No accessories and definitely no glasses. I can't wait for Camden to see me.

We only had three days to prepare everything, and doing it all without his family finding out was incredibly difficult. Those five Harris siblings are balls-deep in each other's lives. His sister called three times when we were on the train yesterday. Even my best friend, Belle, nearly figured things out when she caught me shopping in our old neighbourhood in East London a couple days ago. It's been a whirlwind!

But Cam has always loved a *challenge*.

Now we're here, at the Gardens Hotel in Gretna Green—a village in southern Scotland, over the border of England. It's famous for runaway weddings, dating back to the 1800s. Young lovers would cross the border to defy their families and get married in secret, which is perfect for what Cam and I are doing.

The Harris family is going to flip when they find out what we've done, but I couldn't be happier right now. From the exciting train ride, to arriving at the station, to a limo escort, everything has clicked into place. The wedding planner took care of all the details, including separate hotel rooms for the night before. It was important to me to have some traditional aspects in our elopement. I didn't want to lose all the elements of a normal wedding just because it was a spur-of-the-moment decision.

At our romantic dinner the night before, I swear you couldn't wipe the smiles off our faces because we knew what we were about to do. Not even rain on my wedding day will bring me down.

I move through the lobby to the rear exit that leads to a stunning garden filled with perfectly manicured hedges and a giant Japanese red maple tree. Drops of rain glisten on the petals of purple heather blooms that head toward a small pond where Camden awaits.

"Whenever yer ready," the wedding planner says, handing me an open umbrella. "Good luck."

She moves back as I tuck myself underneath and step out into the light mist. An elderly man strides up from behind her, wearing a traditional Scottish kilt and carrying enormous bagpipes in his arms.

He smiles a crooked-tooth smile and says in his thick accent, "They say rain on yer wedding day means good luck for fertility." He shoots me a lewd wink and I can't help but laugh.

"That's good to know."

"Are ye ready, lass?" he asks, putting the reed of his instrument in his mouth.

I clutch my bouquet of pink roses and give him a quick nod. "Completely ready."

And just like that, I'm walking through a beautiful—albeit wet—Scottish garden with a traditional Scottish bagpiper leading me down the aisle.

When I carefully cross over a stunning, red-railing arched bridge, I finally see my future husband standing tall and proud under the rustic pagoda.

Camden is, of course, kitted out in a kilt himself. It was a bit of a shock when he said he wanted to wear one. But when the wedding planner showed him the tartan for the Harris name and he nearly wept with joy, I couldn't say no.

God, he actually looks sexy. The knee-high socks are exactly like the ones he wears on the football pitch, and the suit jacket is tailored to his build perfectly. What can I say? I like my man in a skirt!

My focus on him is diverted when the bagpiper in front of me trips over a stone. He belts out a cringe-worthy, nasally note as he tumbles to the ground, landing hard on his elbow. Without pause, I rush over to him and drop my umbrella on the ground.

"Are you all right?" I ask, squinting through the rain and placing my free hand on his ankle.

The Scotsman's eyes go wide. "Yer hair, lass. Yer dress!" He nearly drops the bagpipes as he grabs the umbrella to hold over my head from his position on the ground.

"It's fine," I state, pushing my long red hair back behind my shoulders. The hairdresser spent hours taming my mane into perfectly smooth tendrils, but I knew it would never last as soon as I saw the rain. *Curly hair problems.* "Are you hurt, though? It looked like you might have twisted your ankle. Stay still while I have a look."

His eyes are nearly hidden amongst the crinkles that take over his entire face. "Aye, I'm right as rain. Just an old geezer who cannae watch where he's walking." He wipes away the mud on his knee and smiles apologetically.

I smile and shake my head. "It must be difficult with that thing strapped to your front."

He nods and hands the umbrella back to me so he can stand. With great effort, he pushes up off the ground and readjusts the bagpipes over his chest. "Let's get ye married, aye? Or perhaps ye want tae ditch this wee lad and run away with me instead? I promise, I'm more agile than I look."

I erupt into laughter as the cocky bagpiper waggles his brows at me suggestively.

"Everyone okay?" Camden's voice pulls my attention away as I look over and see him approaching. He's left his position under the dry alter where we'll exchange our vows. Rain beads off his wool suit jacket and down his arms, but something about his blue eyes in the grey daylight is dreamy.

"We're fine," I reply with a laugh. "Although, it's good you've come. I think our proud piper here was just about to whisk me away to the Highlands."

Camden frowns at the old man, who doesn't look the least bit intimidated as he places the reed in his mouth and begins playing again with an extra flourish and more eyebrow waggles.

Cam turns back to me in confusion. "I think I should walk you the rest of the way. I don't trust the twinkle in that bloke's eyes."

With a huge smile, I reach out and grab his hand, pulling him under the umbrella with me. "Sounds perfect."

He smiles down at my rain-drizzled face, his own just as damp as his smoothed back hair. When his body presses up against mine, I instantly wish we were done with the wedding part and in our honeymoon cottage.

"It's strange to see you without your glasses, Specs," Camden murmurs softly, a wicked glint in his eyes.

"It's strange to see you wearing a skirt, Camden," I retort, glancing down and taking in his suit jacket, vest, and red tartan tie that matches his kilt.

"It's called a kilt. It's very manly," he corrects with a tight jaw. "And just wait 'til you see what's underneath. That's definitely manly."

I can't help but giggle and roll my eyes—a very familiar response when it comes to my future husband. He drops a kiss on my forehead, then pulls back to look at my full body.

"If I were smarter, I would have let you struggle a bit longer in the rain."

"Why is that?" I ask, my brows knitting together as I look down at my dress that has a good inch of mud on the hemline.

"Because your dress is white." He waggles his brows and glances down at my chest with a lascivious smirk.

"You're cockier than the bagpiper I think," I murmur under my breath and jab him in the ribs with my bouquet.

"And you're the most beautiful woman I've ever laid eyes on," he replies quickly, his face losing all humour as he stares straight into my soul.

My kneejerk reaction is to complain about my ruined hair or my runny makeup, or maybe whine about how I didn't have time to get my dress hemmed and now it's ruined by the rain. But I'm too happy to let all those thoughts cloud my mind. Today I'm marrying Camden Harris and nothing is going to get me down.

As we follow the bagpiper down the aisle, Camden holds the umbrella over us and leans down to whisper in my ear. "Hey, Specs, why does Snoop Dog need an umbrella?"

I look up at him curiously. "Why?"

"For drizzle."

Camden's pun causes a laugh to burst unexpectedly from my belly, and I think it caught the bagpiper off guard because he let one of those high notes slip again. Thankfully, he didn't trip.

We finally make our way up to the safety of the pagoda in one soggy piece. Our earlier teasing is forgotten when the registrar begins the service. Camden and I face each other, holding hands beneath the hanging glass lanterns that twinkle yellow lights all around us. A portable heater warms my bare arms and shoulders as I adjust my strapless dress. I wipe at some mud splatters on my skirt that only end up smearing, and I'm instantly transported back to the first time I met Camden.

He was covered in mud and laid out on a stretcher, playing the part of a cocky football player. But he wasn't only an athlete womaniser looking to have sex with his surgeon. He was a Harris Brother, which meant more than I ever could have ever realised on my own.

The registrar indicates it's time for us to say our vows to each other, and Camden is the one to go first.

"Indie Porter, I promise to love you more than cheesy puns, more than James Patterson novels, and more than football. I promise to pour you coffee every morning and let you spoon me every night without talking about it the next day. I promise to be understanding when you'd rather read a boring textbook than watch telly with me. And I promise to be fully supportive of your career in sports medicine, no matter how many blokes you have to put your hands on.

"You made me want more out of life, Specs. You saw so much more in me than just my family and football. You helped me see a life outside of my own little world. Because of that, for the rest of my life, everything I have is *thine*. All my possessions, my wisdom, my humour, my hopelessness and hope, my passion and, above all, my love is thine, as thou art mine."

Tears slide down my cheeks as he repeats the mantra that has become my most treasured words out of his mouth. He said them to me the first time we made love. Every time I hear them now, I remember exactly what made me fall in love with him.

The registrar gestures for me to begin, so I take a deep breath and steel myself to speak from the heart, which has never been as easy for me as it has been for Camden.

"Camden Harris, I had a list of qualities for the kind of man I wanted to marry. A description. A type. I had everything planned out. Then you happened." I pause and fail to wipe the smile off my face as I have flashbacks of Camden and his brothers barrelling into my hospital. "I had this person's character traits listed out in great detail, but the one thing that was never on my list was love. Love was a foreign concept to me because of how I grew up. That's why I appreciated my charts and checklists. They gave me a sense of purpose. But you were someone I never could have planned on because you don't belong on a list, Camden. You belong with me. You were meant for me, and I'm so grateful to take the Harris name today. I'm ready to be a part of a real, genuine family...with you. You are my family, Camden. You've shown me what love feels like. Because of that, I will be thine forever and always. Thank you so much for being inappropriate and kissing me in the hospital when you were my patient."

Camden laughs, his glossy eyes spilling tears down his face. "I believe it was you who kissed me in the surgical theatre later on."

I giggle. "We are full of inappropriate moments."

He nods proudly. "And now we'll have a lifetime to make more."

The registrar says a few more things I don't hear. But when he says we can kiss, he has my full attention.

Camden leans in, cups my face in his hands, and presses his lips to mine in the most tender, soul-affirming kiss of my entire life. It isn't a kiss of passion or lust, sex or attraction. It's a kiss that feels like home and a lifetime of promises to be there for each other, no matter what.

THREE

COCK AND BALLS

Camden

It's dark out when I carry Indie through the rain, up to the entryway of the secluded stonewall honeymoon cottage that's been prepared for us. The building is tiny and located on the grounds of the majestic Caerlaverock Castle. It's apparently where the groundskeeper lived back in the 1800s, but the wedding planner said it is the most romantic place you can find near Gretna Green.

I finagle the door open and carry my giggling bride across the threshold into a stunning one-room cottage, covered in pink flower petals and illuminated by the fireplace and dozens of votive candles. The cottage looks like it was plucked straight out of some historic Scottish Highlands magazine. Indie slips out of my arms and gasps as she takes in the untainted character of a cottage that's easily two hundred years old. The original stone walls and cedar-plank flooring coupled with the roaring fire, plush rugs, and cosy furniture transform this piece of ancient history into a hideaway you never want to leave.

"Will this work okay for you, Mrs. Harris?" I ask, loosening my tie and following her as she makes her way over to the fire crackling in the stone hearth.

She smiles at my reference to her new last name. "It's a dream, Mr. Harris," she replies, her eyes trailing from the exposed beams on the ceiling to the giant four-post bed in the middle of the room. "This entire trip has been a dream. I'm so happy, I could burst."

Her curvy silhouette is outlined by the golden flames of the fire, and I can't help but think how fucking lucky I am to call her my wife. She's not just beautiful. She's intelligent, and quirky, and fun. She's everything. And the image of having little ginger-haired babies with her cleverness makes my chest ache with a desire that's stronger than I've ever felt before.

"I'm happy, too," I reply, draping my damp jacket over the sofa and stepping up behind her. I rest my chin on her shoulder and wrap my arms around her waist as we both gaze into the fire. "And I'm so glad that it was just the two of us today."

"Are you really?" she asks, her tone hesitant. "Are you sure you're not disappointed your family wasn't here? I mean, this wedding was kind of a mess with the rain and everything. Maybe something in London with your family would have been a bit more proper."

"Indie," I chastise softly and drop a kiss on her bare shoulder. "This wedding was us. Nothing about our relationship has ever been proper. Bloody hell, we started off under the guidance of a penis list for fuck's sake."

She giggles and covers her face with her hands. "Don't remind me."

With a proud grin, I turn her around to face me, my hands tightening around her waist as I pull her flush against my body. "I love my family, but I love us even more. Today was everything I hoped for."

Indie smiles and exhales heavily as she wraps her hands around my neck. Her brown eyes look thoughtfully up at me. "Very well then. But now that I'm a Harris, I intend to behave like one, which means I'll start inserting myself into everyone's business."

My chest vibrates with a silent laugh. "Is that how you see my family?"

She nods stoically. "Pretty much. Overbearing and over-caring. But I can survive it, especially since your brother married my best friend. Belle and I have great plans for you Harris twins."

"Oh?" I ask, arching a brow and squeezing her to me. Impatience rolls through my body as I realise we're both wearing way too many clothes in this honeymoon cottage. "Are you going to let me and Tanner in on our future plans that you have so clearly mapped out already?"

She shrugs and begins fiddling with the buttons on my shirt. "Well, obviously we're going go on holidays together."

"Obviously," I state, biting my lip and watching her focus intently on the task of removing my shirt.

"And eventually we'll want to move out of London to get away from the noise and the traffic. Something a bit quieter, possibly near your dad."

"Is that right?" I ask, my hands roaming up and down her ribcage as she yanks the tails of my shirt out from under my kilt.

"Of course we'll be neighbours with Belle and Tanner because we don't just want Harris Sunday dinners, but Friday Tequila Sunrise nights and Saturday morning English breakfasts while our kids play in the garden as well."

"Kids?" I ask with a laugh, completely captivated by this rant Indie is on and never wanting it to stop.

Indie frowns petulantly and pushes the shirt off my shoulders. She licks her lips and runs her hands down my bare chest and abs. I groan from the feeling of my cock growing hard beneath the tartan pleats.

"Of course," Indie replies, looking up at me and combing her fingers through my damp hair. "Our children will be best friends with Tanner and Belle's kids, and we'll want to live near the rest of your family so the cousins can remain close."

"Naturally," I add, biting my lip and reaching around to her back. My fingers find the long row of buttons down her spine, and I quickly begin sliding them through the loops. I lean in and murmur into her ear, "And how many children do you see for us, Mrs. Harris?"

"Oh, at least four."

I can hear her smiling. "Really? Just four?"

"Mmhmm. I'll still want to work, but I won't be travelling with a football team once I start having children. I imagine I'll open up my own athletic training centre that specialises in injury prevention. It will be revolutionary, of course."

"Of course," I murmur as her dress slides down her breasts. I push it over her hips, and it pools on the floor around her feet. She steps out of it, kicking the fabric off to the side so she stands before me in nothing but her white heels, her white strapless bra, and white knickers. My virgin bride.

Not quite, but she is one hundred percent mine, and there's a carnal part of me that loves the fact that she's never felt another man inside of her. I was her first. My seed is the only seed to have entered her body, and the thought of making babies with her has me hard as stone beneath my kilt.

My fingers reach back for her bra clasp. "What are your plans for me?" I whisper, kissing her earlobe and nuzzling into her scent.

She sucks in a sharp breath when her bra tumbles to the floor. I pull back to gaze down at her pale pink nipples, hard and pointing straight at me. I lean down and drop soft kisses on the mounds of her breasts.

"You'll retire eventually." She lets out a soft cry when I pull her tiny bud into my mouth. "And have loads of investments, so you won't have to work if you don't want to."

"That's good to hear," I reply, smiling as I suckle her other nipple and pull it hard and long between my lips.

"Oh God, but you'll bore easily," she moans. "You'll most likely start coaching our kids' football teams or helping out at Bethnal Green."

"That's very logical." I reach out to grab her hand and place it on my groin to show her the effect her words have on me. She bites her lip and wraps her fingers around me, letting out a tiny sigh of appreciation.

"You never asked me what I was wearing under my kilt, Specs," I murmur in a deep, wicked tone.

"I can already guess," she husks, swallowing and slowly slipping her hand up under the fabric. She grabs my bare shaft and smiles with glee. "Just as I suspected. Cock and balls."

I laugh at her cheekiness, and it takes everything I have not to rip her knickers off and fuck her senseless. This is our wedding night. It needs to be about more than uncontrolled lust.

I clear my throat and concentrate on the words I want to say next. "Are there any other plans you want to inform me about?" I ask as I slide my hand down the front of her knickers and gently tease the crease of her pussy.

She whimpers when I find her clit and apply delectable pressure. Her whimper changes to a full-on moan when I plunge a finger deep into her tight, wet centre. "We can alternate hosting Christmas and other holidays," she cries.

I grin and continue plunging into her. "You know, for a bird who likes her space, you sure have concocted quite a plan to keep everyone close."

She opens her brown eyes to me. They are filled with something meaningful and important. Something that I want to remember forever. "It's because I'm madly in love with you, Camden, and you've completely changed me."

My chest soars with pride from her words. In a flash, I lose the battle to take this slow and yank her knickers off, along with the rest of my getup. I lay her down on the plush fur rug in front of the fire and gaze down at our naked bodies as her legs wrap around my waist.

The head of my cock teases her opening and she pumps her greedy hips up toward me. "I love you, too, Indie," I reply, pushing her hair back from her face and staring deep into her eyes.

With one meaningful look, I thrust deeply into her. As deep as I can reach. As deep as she can take me. I let my weight sink down on top of her so my body consumes her. So I can feel every breath she takes and every moan she utters.

My jaw is tight as I pull back and stroke my cock inside of her, building speed with each and every pump. The fire heats my skin and the rug sticks to my palms, but the silkiness of Indie's skin against mine is perfection.

Her hands run over my face, my shoulders, my arms, and my back. Her moaning grows louder and more frenzied as she reaches around to grab my arse. She pulls me tight against her, holding me inside her as she tenses. I hold my breath and watch in wonder as her orgasm detonates through her entire body, vibrating in her chest, then her stomach, through her thighs, and finally clamping down on my cock inside of her.

I feel it all. Her orgasm. Her desire. Her passion. Her love.

When her eyes open and look up at me, I can see it all. Our future. Our plans. Our family. Our life.

Once her climax descends and her body relaxes, she lifts her head and grabs my face to kiss me. Her tongue dives hot and wet into my mouth, and it's all the touch I need to fall over the edge as well.

Our mouths break apart, but I'm still inside of her, pulsing and groaning as I empty everything I have into my wife.

My life.

My Indie.

FOUR

COCKY HOMECOMING

Camden

W e're back in London just in time for the weekly Harris Sunday dinner. Indie and I can't stop smiling the entire drive out to Dad's house. As far as weddings go, there is no way any couple in the whole world could have enjoyed themselves more than we did in Scotland.

When we walk in through the kitchen, I see my family out back in the garden. Tanner, Booker, and Gareth are doting over our niece, Rocky, who's playing with a football in the grass while Booker's pregnant girlfriend, Poppy, sits at the nearby picnic table with Dad, Belle, Vi, and Vi's fiancé, Hayden. Everyone is here. Everyone is always here. Harris Sunday dinners are sacred. They are the one constant we all have regardless of how busy we are or how much our family is changing. And seeing the huge changes that have been happening as of late, I'm certain that our news won't be that big of a surprise.

Vi sees us come out back and gives us a jovial wave. "Hiya, guys."

Everyone looks at us expectantly, as if they instinctually know we have something to share.

"You're pregnant," Tanner bellows, shaking his head knowingly.

"I'm not pregnant," I reply, rolling my eyes at him.

He rolls his eyes right back at me. "I mean Indie's pregnant."

"She's not pregnant," I retort, quietly adding, "Yet."

"What?" Vi asks, her brows furrowed in confusion.

I inhale a deep breath. "Well, first comes love...Then comes marriage."

"You got married?" Vi squeals, shooting up from the table.

I nod. "We eloped this weekend. I'd like to introduce you all to the new Mrs. Indie Harris."

My family erupts into cheers and they all rush over and sweep us into one big hug. Even my brother Gareth, who has been a moody sod for months now,

177

seems genuinely happy for us. I look around and wonder why Tanner hasn't lifted me over his shoulders like the mental patient he is. It's then that I see him standing on the outside of our hug, his arms crossed over his chest with a pouty scowl on his face.

Booker rolls his eyes and attempts to yank Tanner into the group, but Tanner resists. I move past Indie, but Tanner turns his back on me when he sees me approaching and loudly says, "Booker, would you tell Camden that I'm not speaking to him?"

Booker frowns at me and replies, "He's standing right here and can clearly hear you, so no, I'm not telling him that."

Tanner narrows his eyes at our youngest brother and shoves him hard in the shoulder. He re-crosses his arms and juts his chin up into the air. "Would you tell him that he had a lot of nerve getting engaged without telling me first, but to go off and get married without me by his side is total bollocks and completely unforgivable."

Tanner's voice breaks on the last word, and I have to cover my mouth to stop myself from bursting into laughter. Indie winces at his reaction, but I place a reassuring hand on her arms to soothe her.

"Tanner, come on now. It was an important decision for us." I move to grab his shoulder, but he recoils away from me.

"Tell my former twin brother that I won't speak to him for the rest of my life." Tanner's voice wobbles as he crosses his arms and turns his back on me again.

"Tanner!" I shout his name in frustration. "We had our reasons."

"I don't care!" he bellows and Belle strides over shaking her head at him.

She hits him with a dark, warning stare. "You're being ridiculous."

"Wife!" Tanner exclaims, dropping his arms and stomping his foot like a petulant child. "You're supposed to be on my side."

"No," she retorts. "You're being obnoxious. Our best friends just got married. We should be happy for them or at least fake it until our egos recover."

With a heavy sigh, Tanner turns and looks at me, shaking his head gloomily. I move in and wrap my arms around his shoulders, squeezing him tight to me. "I only married Indie so quickly because now we can have our babies together, bro."

His eyes fly wide. "What?" he exclaims. "What are you talking about?"

"Ask Belle what she and Indie have planned for our futures and tell me it doesn't sound brilliant. We can start our families together, Tan."

Tanner looks at Belle with childlike excitement spread all over his face. "Our kids can be best mates and learn how to play with balls together like we did!"

I nod knowingly. "And play football together."

"This changes everything!" Tanner bellows, clapping his hands together in anticipation.

Belle shakes her head. "You are aware that medically there's a high proba- bility that Indie and I won't conceive in the exact same month. Who knows what our fertility cycles are like. Not to mention, I'm a bit older than Indie, so my egg quality is slightly lower."

"Oh, Wife," Tanner cuts her off with a hearty slap on her arse. "Would you stop being a doctor for one minute and just dream with us?"

"Yeah," I add, pulling my bride under my arm. "Besides, Harris Brothers have super sperm. If we will them, they will come."

Tanner hoots with laughter and high-fives me. "Classic pun, bro!"

"And not at all cocky," Indie says with a great big smile meant just for me.

The End

Check out Camden and Indie's full-length story *Challenge*
http://www.amydawsauthor.com/challenge

And sign up for my newsletter to be notified of my latest book news.
www.AmyDawsAuthor.com

ABOUT THE AUTHOR

Amy Daws is an Amazon Top 25 bestselling author of sexy contemporary romance that take place in America and across the pond. She's most known for her footy-playing Harris Brothers and writing the majority of her words in a tire shop waiting room. For more of Amy's work, visit:

http://www.amydawsauthor.com

Facebook: http://www.facebook.com/amydawsauthor
Instagram: http://www.instagram.com/amydawsauthor
Twitter: http://www.twitter.com/amydawsauthor
Book + Main: https://bookandmainbites.com/amydaws

ALSO BY AMY DAWS

The Harris Brothers Series:

British Sports Romance

Challenge: Camden's Story

Endurance: Tanner's Story

Keeper: Booker's Story

Surrender & Dominate: Gareth's Duet, Coming Soon

Wait With Me: Romantic Comedy Standalone

The London Lovers Series:

Becoming Us: Finley's Story Part 1

A Broken Us: Finley's Story Part 2

London Bound: Leslie's Story

Not The One: Reyna's Story

That One Moment: Hayden & Vi's Story

One Wild Night: Julie's Story, Coming Soon

Pointe of Breaking

Chasing Hope

For all retailer purchase links, visit:

www.amydawsauthor.com

LANDMINES

MARIAH DIETZ

A short story featuring Ace and Max from the His Series.

This is raw, original material written just for this anthology. Due to constraints and the immediacy of the timeline, this story has not been edited.

LANDMINES

There are certain obsessions best left alone. After having lived in Alaska for the past couple of years, I should know this better than most. I had chased my obsession with tracking down my father who'd up and left my two older brothers, mom, and me when I was nine, only to learn that being a commercial fisherman is comparable to the seventh circle of hell, and that my Southwestern roots didn't prepare me for the often cold and rainy months up north.

I've been back home to Southern California for six weeks, but it only took the first minute for my neighbor Ace Bosse, to take full residency in my thoughts. I knew my curiosity and interest in her was a stone best left unturned. After all, I'm living with my mom for the summer, and I didn't come alone. Landon and Jameson—two of my best friends who I met while living in Alaska—followed me down to The Golden State. I'd wanted to get a place of our own in San Diego, near campus where I'm enrolled to begin my junior year of college. My comfort level for digressing and going from independent-living to sleeping in my childhood bedroom was less than enticing, but when my uncle said he had a rental we could use for half the price and twice the size of anything we could find, I swallowed my pride and we moved in with my mom who also happens to be best friends with Ace's mom, Muriel.

That's just one of the many landmines presented when it comes to my blonde-haired, brown-eyed neighbor. The first issue—maybe what should be considered the biggest issue—is that she has a boyfriend. I loathed the guy before I knew of his existence, and then even more once I met the ass-wipe. He's a douche dressed in khakis and polo shirts.

"I'd tell you that I'm sorry I can't go with you today, but that would be a lie," Jameson says as he slides on a pair of flip-flops.

I place my cereal bowl in the dishwasher so my hands are free to flip him off. Jameson laughs.

"It was fate," he continues. "I told you I'd never go on a commercial fishing boat or a building site again. Done. Finito. And apparently, college agrees with me, because they said today was the last day to go sign things. But ... I'm sure you're going to be a valuable asset to the team." He pats my shoulder just to lay insult to injury.

"You've known you had to go in for weeks, you lazy bastard. This was just a convenient excuse."

He grins. "How long is your shift?"

"Eight hours."

Jameson winces. The weather has been hot and dry, two norms for summers here, but it doesn't make going out in the required jeans and long-sleeved shirt any more appealing. "The good news is you're definitely going to be scoring some brownie points. I mean, you're volunteering to help build a house for a family in need. Mention what you're doing when you see Ace. This is the kind of stuff that melts panties."

I can't help but chuckle. Jameson talks like he's a player, but he's not. Not even remotely. And he has set his sights on Ace's older sister Kendall. "If it's such a panty-melter, why aren't you coming out this afternoon?"

"Believe me, I was considering it. I almost called my counselor and told him I had the flu, but then I opted to forego using manual labor to impress Kendall and ordered her flowers."

"Nice. So, material shit in place of selflessness. I dig it."

He frowns. "Don't give me a guilt trip."

"That wasn't a guilt trip. Did it sound like a guilt trip?"

It was a total guilt trip.

"I'm going to finalize everything so I'm able to attend college in the fall, so I can get my degree and contribute to society."

"You've got to stop quoting the brochures," I tell him. "You sound like a putz."

Jameson laughs. "I actually liked that one. It has an edge of sincerity to it. But really, you need to mention this to Ace."

"So she can give me a high five?" My tone is sarcastic, bordering on annoyed. He's been working to convince me of spending more time with my neighbor. Since I'm already warring with myself over the same desire, I don't need his added influence.

"I'm telling you, man, she's interested in you."

"If she were, she wouldn't still be dating that clown." I have to tell him this again, because I need to hear the words myself.

"Trust me. Just, trust me."

I shake my head. "You say that like you know something."

"Maybe I do."

I stare at him. Jameson is one of the most loyal and trustworthy people I've ever known. He very well might know something, then again, he's also overtly confident about some of the most ridiculous things. He proved this time and time again while we worked on a commercial fishing vessel together—never learning when to stop challenging some of the senior crew members to dares and bets and card games that often left him nursing a hangover.

"I have to get going, or I'm going to be late."

"Have fun. And if I see Ace, I'll do you a solid and mention what you're doing so you don't risk sounding like a cocky asshole." He grins. "You do that well enough on your own."

"You're such a dick." I grab my metal water bottle and head outside to my Jeep. I'm not sure how exactly I got involved in this project. Ace's mom, Muriel, is on the board and had mentioned it while she and my mom were asking me questions one afternoon about what sort of construction Jameson and I had done while living in Alaska. I'm not sure if I volunteered willingly or they coerced me into signing up, but a few days later, my mom had a schedule that Muriel had dropped by.

Initially, I dreaded the idea of participating in building a house. Like Jameson, I'd been anxious to have a summer off—even if it meant living with my mom. But in California, the homeless population is shockingly apparent. The nice weather and high cost of living create a dangerous concoction that leaves too many on the streets. The construction we'd done in Alaska was elaborate and extravagant—vacation homes for the wealthy. It seemed almost right to use the knowledge I'd earned there to give back to those who really needed it. Now, I'm actually anxious about getting outside and doing something familiar that will help others.

The drive to the build site isn't long enough for me to block out Jameson's suggestion to tell Ace about this. After spending most of my life not caring what others think of me, I've begun caring entirely too much about what *she* thinks of me. I want to impress her. I want her to imagine wrapping her legs around my waist half as often as I think of it.

I want her to break up with her damn boyfriend.

I have to park a block down from the build site because dumpsters and cars are lining the sidewalks around the beginning construction. I grab my leather builder gloves and tool belt, and head toward the skeleton of the house. They've already laid the foundation and done much of the framing. I look over the initial construction, noting details they've done well, and others that could use improvement.

"You here to volunteer?" I turn and face a man with a large beer gut, covered in a plaid shirt. He's wearing an orange hard hat and is holding a clipboard. His nails are too clean, his hands free of blisters and cuts. I'm guessing he's on the board with Muriel, because he's certainly not here for construction.

I nod. "Yeah, I'm Max Miller."

The man peruses his list, searching for my name. When his pencil stops over it, his face lights with a smile. "I see you have experience in construction."

Again, I nod.

"Great. Let's get you a hard hat, and get you started..."

His words fade as I see her.

Ace is standing in front of a large miter saw, intently listening to a man give her a brief summary of the power tool. Her rounded eyes make it apparent she's intimidated by whatever task they've assigned her, but she works to hide that as she nods and smiles at her instructor.

"...we're finishing with the framing today and tomorrow, and then we'll start installing the windows and doors." The man beside me continues.

"How many volunteers do you have? I ask, interrupting him.

The man frowns. "It varies. This week has been so hot, less are coming out.

Plus, it's summer. We have many more volunteers during the school year when kids are trying to pad their college applications. Companies also seem to remind their employees to volunteer around the holidays, so it's a bit scarce today." He wipes a bead of sweat that falls from his temple. "You ready for a quick tour?" He takes several steps forward.

I take another look at Ace, finding her watching as the instructor uses the miter saw in demonstration.

This is going to be a disaster. There's no way I'm going to be able to focus on anything with her here, especially not when they've tasked her with a power tool that could easily cause so much damage to her.

"Do the volunteers need to have experience with some of these tools before they use them?" I ask, still not moving.

He shrugs. "It's best if they do, but many who have experience want to be compensated if they're going to be doing this kind of work. You're what my wife would call a unicorn. We try and do the best with prepping all volunteers, and everyone signs release forms, so we…"

The moment Ace's instructor leaves and she lifts a board, my attention veers solely to her. I don't even recall making the decision to move, and yet as she slides the board forward to make her first cut, I'm there beside her. I place my hand on top of her gloved one that's preparing to squeeze the saw to life. She gasps with surprise, and instantly releases the saw before looking up. Recognition has her smiling. I know this expression well—hell, I've memorized it. The tiny dimple, the straight rows of her teeth, how her chin dips when it's genuine and rises when it's not. I know the curve of her lips, and how she closes her eyes when her smile turns into a laugh. I know it all.

Weeks ago, it was easier not to return the same smile, but it continues to be more difficult. Currently, it's not. I saw her boyfriend over just yesterday, and being here was my opportunity to do something that would get me out of the house and away from my persistent thoughts of her. "You can't cross your arms while using this thing. You'll cut your arm off." My voice is gruff and unforgiving.

Her smile falls and her big brown eyes grow wide. "But he said I need to anchor it so the shorter piece doesn't hit me."

"Use your left hand to guide the saw."

"But I'm right-handed."

I stare at her blankly.

Ace drops her chin and rolls her eyes. "I see your dark and broody side is back." She raises her eyebrows, and repositions her hands on the saw and piece of wood she's holding. "You can go. I've got this. Tom's already shown me how to do this."

"Clearly he hadn't shown you very well. You were about to—"

"Cut off my arm. I know. You already mentioned it." She moves her gaze to the saw, dismissing me.

I should take this opportunity and go. Get the tour from the volunteer who checked me in, and find a task that will have me working on the opposite side of the yard. But Ace has become an itch I need to scratch. *Have* to scratch. I circle the table so I'm standing beside her. The scent of her coconut shampoo fills my nose, then I get the sweetness of her perfume, and I take a step closer to her.

Ace turns her head, glancing at me. She doesn't say anything. She doesn't have to. I can tell by the way her body gently sways closer to me, and how her shoulders round that she's affected by my presence.

I'm so tempted to reach my hand down and cup her ass—to pull her toward me and kiss her until logic and reason are silenced by how badly I want her. However, the landmines associated with her practically glow on her forehead, reminding me of all the reasons doing so would only cause things to blow up in my face.

I need contact with her. Something. Anything. I reach forward and rest my hand on her lower back. "I'll hold it. That way it will be more comfortable for you."

She looks at me, her familiar smile absent. Perhaps she's working just as hard as I am to understand my motives. "You really don't have to babysit me."

"I thought we decided we were friends. Friends help each other, right?" I was the moron who'd slapped that label on us. I've never had any interest in being her friend. I spent eight years living beside her and dutifully ignoring her as an endless train of guys from school worked to impress her and vied for her time. I swore I wouldn't be one of them. Wouldn't jump through hoops in an attempt to gain her attention. Yet, since I've been back it seems like she's everywhere.

Skepticism is apparent in her slanted eyes, but Ace shakes her head, and the edges of her lips tease into a smile that's even more distracting than the last. Then she leans into me even further, and my hand on her back constricts. We're silent and still for a moment, and though it's too warm to be standing this close while dressed as we are, neither of us attempts to move.

"Why don't you cut this piece? It makes me more nervous to have you holding it."

"You can use your right hand this way."

"I realize that, but I'm worried I'll accidentally hurt you."

I stare at her, listening to her words play on repeat in my head as they slowly sink past comprehension.

What if I accidentally hurt her?

What if I mess this up and she hates me?

I shake my head. "You won't hurt me. Grip the saw with your right hand, and just slowly lower the blade. If you bring it down too fast, the wood will splinter and it won't be a clean cut."

Ace pulls in a deep breath and reaches for the saw again, creating a small cushion of space between us that I close by stepping closer to her, my chest against her shoulder as I hold the end piece she'll be slicing off. She purses her lips with determination, and grips the handle of the saw. When it comes to life, she glances at me once, then focuses on lowering the blade directly over the pencil line. She should be wearing safety goggles and ear protection, but those details are far in the recesses of my mind as I watch her complete her first cut and slowly raise the blade back up and turn it off.

Ace doesn't smile with triumph or completion, instead, she inspects the edge like the perfectionist she is, running her gloved-thumb over the clean edge.

"Like a pro," I tell her.

Before she begins any practice cuts, we go in search of goggles and ear protection, and then we find some scraps. She's a quick study and within no time, looks like she's skilled at using the power tool. I enjoy the time, not ready to tell her she's more than ready to begin, because I'm enjoying the excuse to remain so close to her.

"Want to help me with a couple of these?" she asks. I doubt she realizes that when she lowers her lashes and looks up at me like she is, that it's nearly impossible for me to focus on what she's saying.

Ace reaches for my waist, and for a second I consider what would happen if she were the one to make the first move. If she kissed me right now, would it deactivate all the risks associated with her?

She unclips my measuring tape from my tool belt and smirks, like she knows I'd stopped breathing. She makes quick work of measuring a piece of wood, and then proceeds to cut it.

The volunteer wearing plaid approaches us as Ace is measuring another piece of wood. I'm fairly certain I'm only standing here for my own sanity at this point —she hasn't asked me for help or even direction since we went over the steps together and she repeated them back to me for clarification.

"You ready to get started?" he asks.

I'm reluctant to leave, but realize this is one of many instances where this isn't my place. As her neighbor and friend, I should have walked away a while ago. Slowly, I nod, and turn to go.

"Max?" Ace calls my name. I stop, and immediately head back to where she's finished another cut. I'm surveying the space, ensuring all ten of her fingers are there, that there isn't any blood, that the saw is turning off. "Thanks for helping me. I really appreciate it." She presses her lips together and glances past me, exposing her shyness. I had never considered Ace shy. Though I hadn't known her well, she always had friends and boys hanging around her. It wasn't until this summer when I began spending time with her, that I realized she strayed more toward being an introvert and preferred being around her closest friends and family.

"You're a natural," I tell her.

"I'll come find you for lunch." Her tone rises, making her statement sound more like a question.

"Yeah, and if you get done here, come by and find me."

Once again, she smiles, and once again I forget all the reasons I should be avoiding her.

If distraction were a noun, it would be Ace.

I haven't managed to accomplish nearly the amount of work I should this morning, because my attention continues navigating to where she's currently using a nail gun to secure the base of the floor.

After she'd completed her task with the miter saw, the plaid-wearing volunteer had led her over to the house, opposite of where I was helping to complete the framing. She had the same overwhelmed look on her face when someone presented her with a nail gun, but this time, she asked more questions.

My phone buzzes for a third time as a guy secures the side I've been holding into place. I wipe my brow before reaching for it. It's hotter than hell today, and there isn't a single inch of shade on this piece of property.

Jameson: ...Kendall says Ace is volunteering at the building site, too.

192

Me: Yeah, no need to tell her where I'm at.
Jameson: Now's your chance to impress her.
Jameson: This is the perfect setting. You can even turn up your cockiness without looking like a bastard ;)

I don't bother replying to him. Instead, I pocket my phone and follow two others who have been working with me to get this side of the frame up, to take a water break.

"Things are looking really good!" A woman with bright red nails and a clean, white T-shirt smiles as she hands us each a water bottle. "This place is going to be done in no time." Her sentiment reminds me of the crap Jameson's been spewing from the college brochures: promises that often sound far easier and faster to accomplish than they really are.

"Hungry?" Ace appears beside me, her sleeves pushed up to her elbows.

It's too hot to be hungry, but I nod.

"Great idea!" The man in the plaid shirt appears as well, standing too close to Ace. "We'll all take a break for lunch. Cool down."

Ace grips the crook of my arm, and reason and logic transform. No longer am I considering all the reasons I shouldn't be with her, but every reason that I should.

Continue the journey with Ace and Max, and begin Becoming His, today:
myBook.to/BecomingHis1

ABOUT THE AUTHOR

Mariah Dietz lives with her husband and three sons, who are the axis of her crazy and wonderful world in North Carolina.

Mariah grew up in a tiny town outside of Portland, Oregon, where she spent most of her time immersed in the pages of books that she both read and created.

She has a love for all things that include her family, good coffee, books, traveling, and dark chocolate. She's also obsessed with Christmas ornaments and all things Disney.

Website: http://www.mariahdietz.com
Amazon: http://amazon.com/author/mariahdietz
Facebook: https://www.facebook.com/AuthorMariahDietz/
Bookbub: https://bit.ly/2I487tz
Goodreads: https://bit.ly/29IMA7X

ALSO BY MARIAH DIETZ

Becoming His

Losing Her

Finding Me

The Weight of Rain

The Effects of Falling

CURVEBALL

EXCEPTION

A Thousand Reasons, a new novel releasing June 21st, 2018

COCKY BB: TWO BOYS, ONE PROM

BB EASTON

Cocky BB: Two Boys, One Prom is a work of creative nonfiction based on characters introduced in BB Easton's bestselling memoir, *44 Chapters About 4 Men*. While the settings and most of the situations portrayed in this book are true to life, the names and identifying characteristics of all characters have been altered to protect the identities of everyone involved.

AUTHOR'S NOTE

For those of you who aren't familiar with me, I write stories about my own life. About the actual, questionable, choices I made and the actual, regrettable men I dated.[1] These stories are usually funny, definitely self-deprecating, shockingly sexy, and for some reason, oddly unifying.

I've been moved by the unity our little indie romance community has demonstrated as of late, so I'd like to contribute to this movement with one of my most sacred stories. One I have never told any of you. One that will live on in infamy. It is the story of the time I took my two ex-boyfriends—sworn mortal enemies—to the same prom. I call it...*Cocky BB*.

Enjoy!

[1] **Dated** (verb, past tense)—to risk contracting venereal diseases, tetanus, and jail time with a man in exchange for attention, free piercings and the occasional meal at Waffle House.

INTRODUCTION

Let me set the scene for you. It was April of 1998. I was a junior at Peach State High School—a huge, working-class public school in the suburbs of Atlanta. On paper, I looked like the model student: four-point-oh grade point average, on track to graduate early with honors, no disciplinary file, aside from a few tardiness-related detentions. However, in person, I looked like a drug-addicted gutter punk. My once-shaved head had grown into an inch-long helmet of hair that I'd bleached platinum blonde and tried to tame with hair gel and bobby pins. I wore too much black liquid eyeliner and not enough of anything else. And my steel-toe combat boots practically weighed as much as my emaciated ninety-five-pound body.

You've probably heard the term "high-functioning alcoholic" used to describe someone who suffers from an addiction yet manages to excel in at least one area of their life. That was me. I was a high-functioning bad-boy-aholic. At any given moment you could find me chilling on the Dean's List while some sexy, broken, tattooed, miscreant with washboard abs and a killer smile was completely ravaging the rest of my life.

Or in this case, two.

Ronald "Knight" McKnight had been my first love, if you could call it that. A professional would have called it Stockholm Syndrome. Knight was a friendless, joyless, vicious sadist whom everyone at Peach State High School had learned to steer clear of. He looked like a skinhead, lifted weights with the football players, and physically assaulted anyone who so much as spoke to me. By tenth grade, Knight had completely isolated me from my friends and made himself my only option for rides home, for friendship, for *everything*.

Naturally, like the dumb attention-starved fifteen-year-old that I was, I grew to love the psycho. But when his violent tendencies became more than he could control, Knight joined the Marines and shipped off to Iraq. He exited my life the same way that he'd entered it: before I was ready and without my permission.

Leaving the door wide open for Harley James to waltz through.

I had just turned sixteen. I had just gotten my first car. And I had just gone through my first real break up. What better time to hook up with a sexy, care-free, blue-eyed, blond-pompadoured, tattooed mechanic? Harley was fun and flirty and bad to the bone. He organized illegal street races, sold illegal street drugs, had a cache of illegal firearms, and had been in and out of jail more times than Lindsay Lohan.

To a girl with a bad boy problem, Harley was perfect.

His tattoos, on the other hand...not so much.

Harley had the worst tattoos I've ever seen on a real person. Sure, we've all seen bad tattoos on the internet. We've even shared them with our friends and had a good laugh. Well, some of those tattoos are Harley's. I know because I'm the one who submitted them to badtattoos.com in the first place.

I was able to overlook a lot when it came to Harley James—his lack of intellect and formal education, his criminal record, his trunk full of sawed-off shotguns—but the one thing I was never able to see past were those horrible fucking tattoos. In fact, they were the cause of our first breakup.

Or maybe our third? I can't remember. We broke up a lot.

Harley had been telling me for weeks that he wanted to get a huge tattoo of *me*, right on his bicep. He had me draw dozens of mock-ups for him: sad clown BB, sugar skull BB, Bettie Paige BB, bionic angel BB, anime BB, hell, even pirate wench BB. So, when I got the call that Harley was at the tattoo shop and needed a ride home, my heart and my Mustang practically defied gravity as I sped over to see which design he'd chosen.

I lurched my car into the first parking space I could find and bounced through the front door, ready to see myself immortalized in ink. Harley gave me a smug, sleepy-eyed grin from his tattoo chair, where a hulking beast of a man was putting the finishing touches on his upper arm. With a skip and a hop, I landed right next to Harley, where I stared in horror at a gray cartoon donkey with a pink bow on its ass.

Eeyore.

My boyfriend had gotten Eeyore, the depressed jackass from *Winnie the Pooh,* tattooed on his arm. Forever.

Make that my *ex*-boyfriend. I high-tailed it out of there and vowed to never be caught in the same room as that fucking tattoo ever again. I was done. I had dignity, goddamn it. I...

Still needed a prom date.

Shit.

After pouting and screening Harley's calls for a week, I finally answered and told him that if he scrounged up a tuxedo and took me to prom I'd *consider* taking him back.

Harley wasn't real excited about my proposition, considering the fact that he was a) a grown-ass man, and b) had been expelled from Peach State High School, but he said he'd see what he could do. Which I knew was code for, *I'm going to get high and forget we had this conversation in five...four...three...*

ONE

"Eyore?" Juliet's cackles flooded out of the dressing room she was thrashing around in, causing everyone in the quiet dress shop to turn and scowl in our direction.

"You have got to be fucking kidding me," Goth Girl deadpanned from the purple tufted ottoman she had commandeered in the seating area. Of course, she'd already found her dress. She'd simply walked in, grabbed the first floor-length black thing in her size, and parked her Wednesday Addams-looking ass down to wait in annoyance while Juliet tried on every other dress in the building.

Juliet tossed the curtain back dramatically. She had on a shimmery, midnight blue strapless thing that looked like it was meant to be worn in front of a wind machine.

"So what did you do?" Her almost black irises twinkled as she beamed over my misfortune. Juliet had *real* problems—like, an eleven-month-old at home and a baby daddy in prison kind of problems—so Harley's little Eeyore tattoo was the highlight of her week. That and getting her mom to babysit so that she could go dress shopping.

"I just left." I shrugged.

Juliet laughed and slapped her hand on the side of the fitting room. "You just left him there?"

That pulled a grin out of me. "Yeah, and I didn't answer his calls for a week."

"So, is he coming or what?" Goth Girl asked, lazily looking over the top of a Bridal magazine. I was kind of surprised something that girlie hadn't spontaneously burst into flames in her hands.

My shoulders slumped. "I don't know. He said he'd try, but...it's fucking Harley. You know how he is."

My friends both nodded in morose silence.

"You know what will make you feel better?" Juliet asked, her usually bitchy voice more cheerful than ever. I turned and looked at her skeptically. "Trying on this dress!"

"You're not gonna get it?" I asked, admiring her again. She was standing in front of a full-length mirror outside of the fitting room, holding her long black braids up with one hand. I had to admit, as much as I loved the dress, it wasn't right on her. Juliet had dark skin thanks to her African-American mother; dark, almond-shaped eyes, thanks to her Japanese father; and killer curves, thanks to motherhood, but that dress did little to accentuate any of it. She needed something bright. Something form-fitting. Something low-cut.

She needed to remember what it felt like to be a slutty teenager again.

I, on the other hand, had zero curves, green eyes, freckled skin, and couldn't wait to grow the fuck up.

"Yeah, okay. Fine." I sighed.

I grabbed the smallest size they had, pulled it on over my head in the fitting room without even bothering to take off my skin-tight jeans or combat boots, and tossed open the curtain.

Juliet's mouth fell open, and Goth Girl's drawn-on eyebrows lifted almost to her hairline.

"You have to get it. You have to." Juliet whispered. I glanced at Goth Girl, who gave me an apathetic nod of agreement.

"Dude, it's like," I lifted my arm to peek at the price tag, "two-hundred dollars. And I don't even have a date."

"You have Harley!" Juliet beamed. She was wearing a sequin-encrusted body-hugging, halter-top number with a slit all the way up one thigh. It was red. It was slutty. And with some matching lipstick, it would be perfect.

"If he bails you can always just go stag," Goth Girl drawled, not even glancing up that time. "Or I can break up with Steven, and we can go together. I hate that asshole anyway."

I snorted out a laugh as excitement bloomed in my belly. Glancing back and forth between my two best friends, I smiled and said, "Fuck it. I'm going to prom."

TWO

A few minutes later I came skipping out of the store two-hundred dollars lighter, plus tax, but with my signature cockeyed optimism fully restored. I hugged my friends goodbye and strutted over to my little black Mustang hatchback with my head held high, squinting into the warm, spring sunlight.

I don't need no man.

I smiled, hitting the unlock button on my key fob.

I'm an independent woman.

I pulled open the driver's side door and laid my garment bag across the backseat.

I can go to prom all by myself.

I sat behind the wheel and tossed my purse onto the passenger seat.

In fact, maybe I will. Maybe I'll just call Harley up and tell him to go fuck—

My inner pep-talk was interrupted by the sound of my cell phone ringing.

Oh, shit! Maybe that's him!

I sprang into action, afraid that I'd pussy out if I waited too long to talk to him. Yanking my slouchy, fuzzy, tiger-striped shoulder bag into my lap, I dug through the contents until I found the source of the noise. Jamming my thumb into the TALK button, I lifted the phone to my ear on the second ring.

"Hello?"

"…You answered."

Most people have a fight or flight response to fear. I have a freeze response. Like a stupid fucking deer. With those two clipped words, all of my bodily functions seized up completely. My blood turned to ice. My feet to lead. And my lungs to deflated balloons as I exhaled his name.

"Knight."

Swallow, BB.

I swallowed.

Blink, BB.

I blinked.

My eyes darted around the parking lot. "Where...are you?" I managed to ask.

"At the shop."

The Shop was Terminus City Tattoo, Knight's home away from home. Before he'd enlisted in the Marines, Knight had been a tattoo artist, body piercer, and sometimes-resident there when things got bad at his Step-Dad's house.

Which was always.

"You're home?"

Knight exhaled through his nose. I pictured him smoking a cigarette out on the Terminus City fire escape, the smoke disappearing as it floated in front of his almost colorless, ghostlike blue eyes.

"If you call crashing on a couch in the fucking break room *home*."

I did. That couch and Bobbi, the woman who'd hired him and let him stay there, were more of a home to him than he'd ever known.

"Are you..." I had to consciously tell myself to breathe just to have enough oxygen to finish my thought. "...doing okay?"

Knight had been in either boot camp or Iraq since last May. He'd written me a few letters, but we'd had very little contact since he left. His departure hadn't exactly been under the best circumstances.

"When the fuck have I ever been okay?"

When you were with me.

Part of me wanted to go to him. Pretend like the past didn't exist. Run away together and live in that faraway land called Denial. But the other part of me couldn't forget all those nights. Those horrible, horrible nights. Nights where I'd been physically restrained and screamed at, hog-tied with seatbelts or hand-cuffed to bedposts. Nights where my boyfriend had picked fights with perfect strangers in public. Nights where he'd destroyed everything he could get his hands on and left me to pick up the pieces.

Nights that, when triggered, still had me breaking out in a cold sweat and gasping for air.

"How long have you been home?" I choked out around the swelling lump in my throat.

"Not long enough to know how the fuck to do this."

Knight was broken when he found me and broken when he left me, but now? I could hear it.

He was shattered.

"Hey..." I cooed, as if speaking to a skittish bird. "Do you...want some company?"

He remained silent as I cringed, kicking myself for the offer.

"Punk..."

"Yeah?"

"You know what's gonna happen if you come here."

Bad things. Wonderful things. Bloody things. Tears.

"Then we'll go get coffee," I said, shifting my car into reverse.

Coffee. That sounds grown-up. Just a couple of exes grabbing a friendly cup of that shit I hate to drink on a Sunday afternoon. What could possibly go wrong?

"Coffee," Knight echoed. "Fine."

THREE

I sped into Atlanta with a bowling ball in my gut, a cigarette between my fingertips, and the wind rustling the nylon garment bag in my backseat.

Knight was home.

As much fun as I'd had with Harley, as much as I appreciated him for making me feel good again, for distracting me from my pain, I didn't love him. I simply wasn't able. Knight had taken my heart with him when he left for Iraq, leaving me with nothing to offer Harley but my time and my body.

And my Mustang, of course, which he'd tricked out in order to win more money at the track. If he ever found out I'd used all that extra horsepower to go see his mortal enemy, Ronald McKnight, Harley would probably rip out every aftermarket intake and valve he put in.

With his bare hands.

But I didn't want to think about Harley. And I damn sure didn't want to ruminate over the colossal mistake I was making by going to see Knight. So, I turned on my car stereo, cranked the volume knob to the right, and let Local H distract me with their own hard-hitting, three-chord tales of woe instead.

By the time I pulled into the crumbling parking lot behind Terminus City, I had almost convinced myself that everything was going to be fine. That Knight and I would walk to the corner coffee shop, catch up like a couple of old friends, then go our separate ways with a hug and an empty promise to stay in touch.

I rolled up my windows and turned off my car on muscle memory, my mind hard at work trying to trick the rest of my body into staying calm. Fabricating lies. Taking deep breaths. Reciting positive affirmations. With every shaky step I took toward the fire escape entrance, my self-talk grew louder, trying to drown out the rumble of excitement and panic building inside of me.

I was a few feet away from the concrete stairs I'd spent countless nights smoking and laughing and crying on when the thick metal back door at the top flew open and a ghost from my past came stomping out.

I froze, a fawn in the presence of a hunter, every muscle tensed, every sense on high alert, every brain cell cocked and ready to fire.

One second ticked by before Knight saw me, but in that second, I saw *him*. His white-blond buzzcut looked the same. My fingers twitched, remembering how velvety it felt beneath them. His sharp features were still scowling. His almost colorless eyelashes, eyebrows, and irises were just as striking as they'd been the first time I saw him. His body was still armored with muscles on top of muscles. His shoulders still tensed from holding up the weight of the world. His feet were still adorned with black combat boots. But his wardrobe of rolled-up Levi's, skinny suspenders, and band T-shirts had been replaced with military-issued camouflage cargo pants and a tight black T-shirt.

I watched in suspended animation as Knight pulled a pack of Camel Lights, my brand, from his pocket, his movements as familiar as my own. I knew exactly how he would shift his weight as he reached for his lighter, how he'd hold the unlit cigarette between his teeth before sparking the flint. In that second my trauma, my fear, and all my good sense dissipated.

I was just a girl, staring at a boy, trapped inside of a trained killer.

Knight bit the end of his cigarette just like I knew he would, but before he could light it, his eyes landed on me.

I stared as Knight's hardened expression softened. To anyone else, the change would have been imperceptible, but I saw it. I saw the way his pale eyebrows lifted and pulled together slightly, the way his angular mouth turned down at the corners. I realized in that moment that I was looking at a man who probably hadn't been hugged since the night he told me he was leaving...eleven months ago.

That look trumped my desire for safety and self-preservation. Without thinking and without a word spoken between us, I marched straight up the stairs, wrapped my arms around Knight's waist, and buried my face in the curve of his thick, corded neck.

He smelled like home. An uninhabitable, condemned, broken home with a gas leak that could explode at any minute, but home nonetheless.

"Punk..." Knight's strained voice begged, his hands hovering inches above my body. It was a warning.

"It's okay," I whispered against warm skin, my lips grazing a rapidly pulsing artery. "It's okay."

Knight's arms circled my upper body, coiling around me like a Boa Constrictor. My breaths became labored from the crushing force of his embrace. I felt his remorse and pain. I felt his Adam's apple slide up and down against my cheek as he swallowed.

And I felt his erection swell against my waifish body.

Desire flooded my bloodstream, clouding my judgment. It caused me to do stupid things, like place a kiss on Knight's thumping jugular.

Then another one, a little lower.

One second, I was being crushed against Knight's hard chest, the next I was being crushed between his hard chest and the graffiti-covered back alley wall of Terminus City Tattoo. Abrasive bricks clawed at my skin while Knight devoured my mouth and took his frustrations out on my clothing. As he bit and sucked and stole the breath from my lips, Knight fisted the low neck of my thin white wifebeater with both hands and ripped it completely in half. Shoving my padded Wonderbra up over my breasts, Knight broke our kiss just long enough to glance down at his handiwork. Two silver hearts encircled my nipples, held in place by barbells shaped like arrows.

Knight pressed his forehead to mine as he palmed my tiny A-cups. "Fuck, Punk."

I looked down too, but mostly to admire the massive bulge that extended up the front of his camo pants and into his tight black T-shirt. I ran my hand up his length over his clothing and felt his hips thrust into my palm involuntarily.

The sound of a car door slamming shut in the parking lot caused Knight's head to snap to attention. "Inside. Now," he growled, yanking open the fire escape door and all but throwing me inside.

Before the exit had even clicked shut Knight was on me again, pressing me against the wall in the narrow door-lined hallway and shoving my tight ripped jeans down to my knees. He slid a scarred, callused hand between my legs and smiled against my lips.

Knight never smiled.

"You still have that one too," he rasped, teasing the silver barbell in my clit. The one he'd put there before I was even old enough to drive.

"Mmhmm," I moaned as a thick finger pushed inside of me.

Suddenly Knight's smiling mouth was gone, nipping and biting its way down my sternum, teeth grazing my protruding ribs, canines catching on my jutting hipbones, until his warmth was where I needed it most.

With his middle finger buried in me to the last knuckle, Knight ravaged my slippery flesh the same way he'd attacked my mouth. Licking and sucking and taking no prisoners. My legs shook. My knees, tethered to one another by my jeans, threatened to buckle. And my hands finally found an excuse to rub Knight's fuzzy, velvety-soft buzzcut again. I knew I wouldn't last long, but when Knight caught my barbell between his lips and flicked his tongue back and forth across the oversensitized flesh I was a goner.

I contracted around his thick finger and clamped my thighs together around his hand and writhed against his merciless mouth as fireworks exploded behind my eyes and the sparkly embers coursed through my veins.

I sank to the floor where Knight was still kneeling and kissed his slippery, self-satisfied lips as he unbuttoned his pants. Tugging his black Terminus City T-shirt over his head, I marveled at the new United States Marine Corps tattoo on his left pectoral muscle. A lot had changed since I'd seen him last, but for now, we were going to focus on the things that had stayed the same.

Like the way our bodies and pulses and pupils responded to one another regardless of what our brains were screaming. Like the undeniable black depths of our connection. Like the way Knight always figured out a way to fuck me with my boots and jeans still on because he was too impatient to deal with taking them off.

As my eyes roamed down, past Knight's new tattoo and over the ripples of his stomach, they stopped and stared at the sight of his cock, free and thick and dripping with precum. I reached for it, saliva pooling in my mouth, but Knight caught my wrist and spun me so that I was facing away from him.

Pressing his length against my ass, Knight draped his chest over my back and snaked an arm around my waist, bending me over until I was on all fours. "I've waited too long to come in your fucking hand," he growled, sliding the head of his cock between my legs as he kneaded my ass with his free hand. "I thought about you every fucking second, Punk." He gripped my ass harder and pressed against my entrance. "Fuck, I missed you."

Tears pricked my eyes as I nodded against his cheek. Lifting one hand off the floor, I gripped his hard forearm where it was locked around my waist and whispered, "I missed you, too."

With a surge of emotion, Knight reared back, pulling my torso vertical as he filled me to the hilt. The hand that had been on my ass wrapped around my jaw pulling my face to the side as far as it would go. Knight kissed me with his serpentine tongue as his arms coiled around me in another soul-crushing embrace. With every thrust, I felt his apology, and with every tear, he tasted my acceptance.

FOUR

I woke up, sore and sated, on the cold tile floor of Terminus City Tattoo. The hallway was now dark, save for the red light from the EXIT sign overhead. My jeans and panties were around my knees. My bra was shoved up under my armpits. My tank top had been ripped down the front. And a sleeping Marine was molded to my back, his cock already hard again where it had come to rest between my sticky thighs.

So much for coffee.

"Knight," I whispered, propping myself up on one elbow. "Knight, wake up."

"Come back to bed," he mumbled, pulling me back against his chest.

"We're not in a bed," I chuckled, elbowing him in the side. "We're on the dirty-ass floor, and it's dark out. Get. Up."

Knight's stomach growled in agreement.

"See? You need to eat," I insisted, sitting back up and shimmying my bra into place.

"No. *You* need to fucking eat." Knight's eyelids snapped open, pinning me with his laser-scope stare. He reached out and jammed a thick finger into one of the valleys between my ribs.

"Ow!" I hissed, swatting his hand away. Knight was the only one who knew about my...*issues* with food. He'd watched me enough at school to realize that I was hiding it during lunch. Throwing it away in my napkin. He used to confront me about it and threaten to force feed me if I didn't take at least a few bites.

I guess I'd fallen off the wagon since he'd been gone.

"Does he even give a shit?" Knight barked, sitting up abruptly. His zombie eyes narrowed, his face bathed in dim red light. "Does he not think it's weird that he's fucking a skeleton?"

I felt as if I'd been punched in the gut. My mouth fell open and my eyes welled with tears. There he was. The motherfucker who'd pushed me away time and time again. The one who humiliated me when we were together and stalked

213

me when we were apart. The one who flew into violent rages at the drop of a hat.

The boy I'd just slept with was Ronald.

This motherfucker was Knight.

Feeling ugly and exposed under his disapproving sneer, I pulled my ripped wifebeater closed with one hand. "You didn't seem to mind this afternoon." I wanted to sound bold and bitchy, but the words came out weak and wounded instead.

If I could have run away I would have, but I was covered in cum and in desperate need of a new shirt. Schooling my emotions, I crawled away instead, in the direction of the restroom.

"Oh, I fucking mind," Knight's voice called out from the hallway as I sat on the toilet. I had just begun to pee when he pushed open the door and flipped on the light. He'd tucked himself back into his camouflage pants but hadn't bothered to put on his shirt.

"I *mind* that while I was off getting shot at in Iraq, you were back here fucking some piece of shit dropout who doesn't give two fucks whether you live or die."

"He didn't drop out, he got expelled," I corrected, trying to stay calm as I wiped at the mess between my legs in vain.

"Will you hand me a wet paper towel?" I sighed, extending my open hand.

Knight did as I asked, his jaw clenched and nostrils flared. I could almost see the anger radiating off of him in waves as he wrung the white square out in the sink.

I snatched the cloth out of his hand and stood to clean myself up. I could feel the humiliation staining my cheeks pink, which only upset me more. I was trying so hard to act unoffended, but I knew my stupid fucking face was giving me away. "You did this," I snapped, turning my back on him as I wiped the evidence of our blissful reunion away. "If you don't like what you see," my voice broke, revealing a glimmer of the insecure teenager I tried so hard to hide, "then maybe you shouldn't have left in the first place."

I threw the paper towel into the wastebasket, followed by my decimated wifebeater, and pulled my panties and jeans up over my ass.

"Better yet," I pushed past him without making eye contact, "maybe you shouldn't have come back."

"Punk." Knight grabbed my wrist, but I twisted it free and continued down the hallway. In the year that we'd spent together, I'd learned how to get out of all kinds of restraints.

I'd had to.

I stomped into the main tattoo parlor with Knight right on my heels. Black leather tattoo chairs lined both sides of the darkened room, and beyond that, a cash register sat atop of a long glass case filled with merchandise. Squatting down behind it, I began digging through stacks of Terminus City T-shirts. The only light in the room was the glow from the streetlights and headlights outside.

"Punk, I'm sorry." Knight's black combat boots stopped mere inches away from mine.

"Good." I finally found an extra-small on the bottom shelf.

"I just...hate to see you like this."

"Fuck you," I spat, unfolding a smaller version of the T-shirt Knight had been wearing earlier.

Knight's arm shot out and cleared the top of the glass case in one fell swoop. I ducked and covered my head as stacks of flash art notebooks and tattoo magazines crashed to the ground.

"Fuck me? Fuck me?"

Shit. Time to go.

I turned and marched back in the direction of the fire escape door, pulling the T-shirt on over my head as I walked.

"What did I say when I left, Punk? Huh? What the fuck did I say?" Knight matched me stride for stride. "I told you I loved you. I told you I was doing this for *you*. I told you to find somebody fucking *better*! And what did you do? I wasn't even out of basic training yet and you were already off getting high and fucking that piece of shit, Harley!"

I snatched my purse up off the floor and pulled open the fire escape door. Night had fallen, but there were still plenty of cars on the road and people milling about downtown. Thank God. Whenever Knight got like this it was best to have witnesses.

Ignoring him and fighting back tears, I dug my keys out of my purse and hit the button to unlock my doors. Jerking my driver's side door open, I turned to face Knight. I was about to say something catty and unfair before speeding off dramatically into the night, when Knight cut me off.

"What's that?" he asked, his eyes trained on the white fabric filling my backseat.

I followed his gaze. "It's a fucking garment bag."

"What's in it?" His tone was accusing.

I threw my hands up. "Oh my God! It's not good enough that you have to know where I am and who I'm fucking at all times, but now you want to know what's in my backseat too? It's a dead body, okay? I better go before it starts to smell."

Knight pinned me with a murderous stare, his pupils pulling the truth from my lips like twin black holes.

"It's a fucking prom dress, okay?"

"When?" Knight hissed through gritted teeth.

"Saturday. Listen, before you give me the third degree about going with Harley—"

"Oh, you're not going with fucking Harley," Knight sneered. "You're going with *me*."

FIVE

I nch-long pixie cuts don't exactly lend themselves to up-dos. Juliet and I tried spikes, tiny curls, lots of little barrettes, one giant flower barrette, and even a few stupid headbands before I finally just parted it on one side and slicked it all down with hair gel.

Fuck it.

With our hair finally done, Juliet and I stood side-by-side at her bathroom sink, caking on the eyeliner—mine liquid, hers kohl.

"So, no word from Harley, huh?" Juliet tried to sound casual, but I could tell she'd been dying to ask me all day.

"Nope," I replied, emphasizing the *p*.

"Wow. What…a fucking…asshole."

I shrugged, reaching for my mascara. "Whatever. I didn't want him to come anyway. He'd probably just get fucked up and do something to get us thrown out, and then I'd have to wait with him in the parking lot until the limo came back while he tried to stick his hands up my dress."

Juliet snorted out a laugh. "Girl, that's exactly what would happen. You're better off with no date than fucking Harley. Or a gay one, like mine."

Juliet beamed. She was going with JayShawn Butler, her buddy from school. It was too damn bad he wasn't into girls because the two of them together looked like Will and Jada Pinkett Smith. Until he wagged his head and snapped his fingers in a sassy little arc, that is.

"I have a date," I said barely above a whisper, swiping on another coat.

"You what?" Juliet's head snapped in my direction, causing her freshly curled braids to bounce around her shoulders.

I swallowed, staring straight ahead into the mirror.

"You're not gonna like it."

"If you say Knight, I swear to God…"

My eyes flicked to hers in the mirror as my face contorted into a guilty grimace.

"No! BB, what the fuck?" Juliet screeched. She hated Knight for the obvious best friend reasons, but also because he kinda sorta beat the ever-loving shit out of her baby daddy one time and carved *BB IS WITH KNIGHT MOTHERFUCKER* into the hood of his car.

"Oh my God, you're such a fucking idiot." She shook her head.

"It's not my fault!" I whined. "I couldn't tell him no, Jules. You know how he is. He's fucking crazy!"

"Oh, I know." Juliet nodded in sarcastic agreement. "I also know that that asshole is *not* riding in the limo with us."

"I wouldn't do that. I didn't even invite him to dinner, I swear." I held my hands up. "I told him where the dance was, and he said he'd be there. That's it."

Juliet gave me a nasty side-eye, then suddenly burst out laughing.

"What?" I asked as she gasped for air and blotted the corners of her eyes.

"I was just wondering what kind of tux Knight would wear…" She cackled. "And then I realized…it'll probably be made from the skin of his victims!"

"Ha, ha." I rolled my eyes. "Very funny. He's a psychopath, not a cannibal."

"Hey!" Juliet shouted in a defensive tone. "Cannibals are psychopaths too."

Now I was the one laughing my eyeliner off. "Oh my God," I snorted. "I fucking hate you."

Goth Girl and Steven, her Lord Licorice-looking boyfriend, showed up at Juliet's house around five, giggling and falling all over each other like they'd smoked a pound of weed on the way over. They were in head-to-toe black, per their usual, but happily, Steven had left his black lipstick and fishnet shirt at home.

JayShawn showed up right after them, wearing a perfectly tailored tuxedo with a crisp white shirt, black bow tie, and a shimmery black and gold paisley jacket. I tried to talk him into trading outfits with me—I was already way over the whole high heels/strapless bra thing—but he said blue wasn't a good color on him.

Juliet's little brother watched the baby while Juliet's mom took pictures of us in the front yard. She had us stand in front of a cluster of overgrown azalea bushes with the sun in our faces, then yelled at us to stop squinting.

This was a stupid idea, I thought, turning my head from left to right on command. *My first date stood me up, and according to Juliet, my second date might possibly kill and eat me.*

"BB! Smile like you mean it!"

Damn, woman. I cranked my phony smile up wider. *My cheeks hurt. My feet hurt. And this stupid dress cost two hundred—*

"Ho…ly…shit." Juliet muttered through her forced smile. "Look who decided to show up."

I heard the low, throaty rumble before I even turned my head. God, I loved that car. It was a '69 Mustang fastback, fully restored, Boss 429 engine, matte black paint job, matte black wheels, and the sexiest loser driving it you've ever seen.

As long as his tattoos were covered up, that is.

Harley parked in the cul-de-sac in front of Juliet's house and stepped out of the car. At first glance, he looked amazing. Blond pompadour messily pushed back. Black suit. White shirt. Skinny black tie. Chain wallet. Simple. Masculine. Badass.

But the closer he got the more comical his outfit became. The sleeves of his suit jacket stopped at least three inches above his wrists. The button looked like it was going to pop off at any second and put someone's eye out. Harley's tie had literally been tied in a knot like a pair of shoelaces. And speaking of shoes, he was wearing his ratty old black combat boots, which helped to hide the fact that his pant legs were also at least three inches too short.

"What the fuck is he doing here?" Juliet whispered through her teeth like a ventriloquist.

"What the fuck are you doing here?" I whispered through my teeth as he approached.

"I'm takin' you to prom, lady." Harley flashed me that panty-melting, baby-faced, bad boy smile, and all four females, plus JayShawn, sighed in unison.

Standing next to me, Harley wrapped his arm around my shoulders, kissed me on the side of my head, and posed for the camera.

Fuck. Me.

SIX

"So...Harley," Juliet smiled awkwardly as she took the seat to my left in the back of our white stretch Lincoln Town Car. "Glad you could make it."

I reached over and discretely pinched the shit out of her thigh.

Harley was kicked back on my right with an arm around my shoulders and an ankle resting on his knee. He gazed down at me with genuine affection in his pretty blue eyes and gave me a little squeeze. "If my woman wants to dance, I'ma take her to a fuckin' dance."

Not rolling my eyes was physically painful. *His woman.* He hadn't even called me in over a week.

"You look good, man." Goth Girl deadpanned. She was sitting between JayShawn and Steven on the sideways bench seat, facing the wet bar. "Where'd you get that suit?"

I looked around as all three girls, plus JayShawn, bit our lips and tried not to laugh at Harley's shrunken, wrinkled excuse for formal wear.

Steven was oblivious.

"Thanks. I borrowed it from my brother." Harley smiled at Goth Girl as if there was absolutely nothing to be embarrassed about. "He bought this for a court date a while back." Harley admired the fit. "It's a little snug, but fuck it, right?"

"Honey, do you mind if I..." JayShawn gestured toward Harley's tragic tie situation with a look of pity on his beautiful face.

"Fuck yeah, man. Do that shit," Harley leaned forward so that JayShawn could fix his tie. "Just don't make it into one of those little bows...No offense."

I laughed through my nose and turned my head to glare at Juliet, who was also about to burst. Shaking my head slightly, I mouthed, *What the fuck do I do?*

She simply smiled with her big red lips and shimmered in her bright red gown and shrugged in amusement over my impending doom. "Drink?"

By the time we got to the Ruth's Chris Steakhouse in downtown Atlanta, the six of us were higher than the Bank of America building. Goth Girl had a brick of weed in her clutch bag. The limo driver had "accidentally" left a few bottles of champagne out, probably hoping for a fat tip. Steven had a silver vial of coke hanging around his neck under his shirt. And Harley had a flask full of tequila in his breast pocket.

Or he did, before we got ahold of it. Now he had an empty flask, and we all had a bad case of the giggles.

Our server, a middle-aged fellow who looked like he probably taught chemistry to little shits like us during the day, took full advantage of our inability to comprehend what was on the menu by bringing each of us the surf and turf, a side salad, a dessert, and a bill for five million dollars.

That sobered us up real quick.

We rode to the Fox Theater in quiet contemplation of our life choices.

Me especially. I was minutes away from what had the potential to be World War motherfucking III. A jealous, rage-fueled, psychopathic Marine with a hair-trigger temper and unresolved childhood trauma was waiting for me, and I was going to walk up to him arm-in-arm with a scrappy, impulsive drug-slash-gun dealer who probably still carried a shiv as a memento from his days in the clink.

My hands trembled, my armpits began to sweat, and "Someone's Gonna Die Tonight" by a grimy little punk band called Blitz played on repeat in my mind like elevator music from hell.

When the limo pulled to a stop underneath the twinkling white lights of the Fox Theater's marquee, my stomach lurched, threatening to spew tequila-soaked chunks of lobster and filet mignon all over the off-white carpet.

Someone's gonna die tonight! Oi oi oi! Blitz cheered in my head, taunting me, as I stepped out of the Town Car. When fists didn't immediately start flying, I stood up, a little wobbly on my stilettos, and looked around. The sidewalks of Peachtree Street were lined with smiling, sharply-dressed teens. Sequins and satin glittered under the marquee as they filed into the historical, Moroccan-themed theater.

No one was screaming.

No one was being murdered.

In fact, there was no sight of Knight at all.

I exhaled a deep, shaky sigh and glanced at Juliet. Her face contorted into a cringe that was anything but reassuring, and we shrugged at each other in mutual confusion and hesitant relief. Taking my elbow, Juliet ushered me into the building before Harley could offer to be my escort, just in case a certain pair of zombie eyes were watching.

Once inside we had to check in at a table manned by four Peach State High School teachers. They wanted to see a student ID from at least one member of each couple, and every student had to sign in and provide the name of their date. I scrawled our information with trembling hands, looking over my shoulder every few seconds.

Student Name: Brooke Bradley
Accompanied by: Harley *motherfucking James*

Tucking my ID back into my shimmery silver clutch bag and praying Coach Johnson couldn't smell the alcohol on my breath, I followed Juliet and JayShawn across the lobby to the photographer's booth. Harley was right on my heels, but Goth Girl and Steven were already gone, probably making out in a corner somewhere.

"Let's get our pictures taken while our hair and makeup still look good," Juliet suggested, staring at me as if she were trying to communicate something telepathically.

"Um, don't you think it would be better if we danced first and waited for the line to die down?" I replied with my mouth, but what I said with my eyes was, *What the fuck are you doing? I can't be standing here with Harley when Knight shows up!*

"Nah. If we do it now we can see what everybody's wearing as they arrive. It's good people-watching." Juliet replied, cocking her head to one side and glaring at me.

People-watching. She wanted to watch for Knight so we'd know when he got there.

I nodded, my senses on high alert as I glanced at the front doors.

"I can't believe they let you in," JayShawn laughed, clapping Harley on the shoulder. "Didn't you get expelled a few years ago for punching the principal or something?"

My cheeks reddened, but per his usual, Harley just laughed as if there was absolutely nothing to be embarrassed about. He was so fucking cool it drove me crazy. I hated to admit it, but seeing him in that borrowed suit with his combat boots and chain wallet, looking effortlessly badass in a sea of stuffy rented tuxedos, had me questioning why we broke up in the first place.

Then an image of a plush donkey with a pink bow on its ass popped into my mind.

Harley chuckled. "Nah. Principal Jenner actually punched *me*. Clocked me right in the jaw, that motherfucker."

Juliet and JayShawn gasped.

"And you didn't sue his ass?" Juliet snarled.

"He had it coming." I smirked up at Harley, all too familiar with the story. "You shoulda heard what he said about Principal Jenner's mom."

Harley shrugged and smiled back with those full lips and mischievous blue eyes. "Saying somebody gives a good rim job is a compliment in my book."

Harley distracted us from our impending doom as we slowly made our way to the front of the line. When it was our turn to have our picture taken underneath the arch of black and silver star-shaped balloons, Harley stood behind me with his hands around my waist and gave the camera a lazy grin. I, on the other hand, stood stick-straight, held my breath, and smiled through clenched teeth. I didn't even look at the camera. I couldn't. Because just beyond it, walking through the front doors wearing a scowl, was my worst fucking nightmare.

Or should I say, Knightmare?

SEVEN

"Smile!"

Before my eyes had a chance to recover from the flash, Juliet was hauling me away by the arm, telling the guys we had to pee and would meet them inside.

"I'm gonna drag Harley to the back of the dance floor," she whispered in the hallway outside the ladies' room. "You go talk to Knight, and for the love of God try not to get eaten."

I nodded aggressively, psyching myself up to face him.

Spinning around, Juliet and I walked back into the lobby. With a shove, Juliet thrust me toward the sign-in table, where I stood, stilettos rooted to the ground, and gaped. Knight didn't look like a tattooed skinhead psychopath. He looked like a...knight. He was wearing his U.S.M.C. dress blues—royal-blue slacks, a navy-blue blazer fastened with a white belt and brass buttons all the way to the neck, and a white hat with a black brim shadowing his eyes. He looked regal and handsome and nothing like the savage asshole I'd come to know and sometimes love.

Coach Johnson leaped to his feet to shake Knight's hand...right next to the sign-in sheet where I had already written *Harley motherfucking James* as my plus one.

Ohhhhh shit.

I won't be able to get him in.

He's gonna see Harley's name on the sheet.

We're all gonna die!

I was about to turn and run, grab my two best friends and head for the hills, when Coach Johnson and Knight let out a guttural, "Oohrah!" in unison.

The coach slapped his fellow serviceman on the shoulder and gestured toward the lobby with an outstretched arm. Knight stepped past him with a nod, locking eyes with me immediately.

I searched his features, frantically trying to gauge his mood, but that damn hat shielded his face. Had he seen Harley's name? Had Coach Johnson just let him in, no questions asked? More importantly, did he think I looked pretty?

Forcing a smile, I swallowed my fear and held my ground as Knight approached. "Hey," I said, my voice rising an octave at the end for no reason. "You look so handsome in your uniform. I almost didn't recognize you. Not that you don't normally look handsome, just..."

I had to lift my head slightly to maintain eye contact as Knight walked toward me. He stopped a foot away from my face, close enough for me to see the corner of his mouth twitch upward.

I was safe.

"This is the closest thing to a fucking tux I can stand." His words were sharp, but his eyes were soft. "You look good, Punk."

I glanced down at my flowing, floor-length, dark blue dress and smiled. "Hey, we match."

As my eyes roamed back up, I noticed for the first time that Knight had something in his hand.

Lifting the clear plastic container, he offered it to me with a grunt.

"Knight..." My breath caught when I saw what was inside. A single white rose framed with black tulle and silver ribbon. A colorless corsage from my colorless boy.

"Figured your punk ass would be wearing black." He shrugged. "I like the blue though."

I blushed, using the corsage as an excuse not to look at him. I slipped it onto my bony wrist using the elastic band attached to the back. Lifting it to my nose, I inhaled the sweet fragrance and smiled. "It's perfect. Thank you."

I turned away, seeking a trash can for the plastic container, and noticed a familiar pompadoured figure standing at the top of the central staircase.

Fuck.

Harley had his back to us and appeared to be talking to a group of goth kids, but the sighting definitely got my ass in gear. I backed up against the wall beside the staircase, which just so happened to be the end of the line for pictures, and waved Knight over.

"Hey!" I chirped as he approached with suspicion in his icy eyes. "We, ah... should get our picture taken, since we match and all."

Standing that close to Knight without being able to rip his clothes off was physically uncomfortable. As much as I hated him, as many times as he'd hurt me, as desperately as my head and heart tried to convince me to stay away, my body was simply too weak to resist the pull. We didn't just have chemistry, we had magnetism. A negative charge and a positive charge so strong that the only thing to ever successfully keep us apart was an ocean. And now here he was, on the wrong side of the sea, wearing that damn uniform and making me forget that the tears I'd cried over him could fill an ocean of their own.

When the bulb flashed and our awkward smiles fell, I glanced back at the top of the stairs. The space was empty.

"I'm...ah...I'm gonna run to the restroom real quick. Be right back!" I blurted, darting away before Knight could protest or try to follow me. I sprinted to a hallway on the far-right side of the lobby that not only had restrooms, but an elevator. Ducking inside, I hit the door close button and exhaled in relief when it shut without Knight's arm shooting out to block it.

I got off on the second floor and followed the sound of thumping bass into the Egyptian Ballroom.

Inside the house lights were off, sconces illuminated the hieroglyphs carved into the massive columns lining each wall, and horny teenagers dry humped each other on the scarab-themed carpet. I knew that unlike Harley, Knight would give me about thirty seconds before he came looking for me, so I tore through the room, scanning the crowd for a baby-faced blond. Instead, I found Juliet and Goth Girl pouting with their arms folded across their chests over by the DJ booth.

"Hey!" I panted. "Where are the guys? Where's Harley? He's not looking for me, is he?"

"Fuck the guys," Goth Girl slurred, taking a drink from a beverage I knew with one-hundred percent certainty was spiked.

Juliet leveled me with an annoyed, albeit glassy-eyed gaze. "What she said."

"What happened?" I yelled as Outkast rapped about hushing that fuss and moving to the back of the bus.

"JayShawn is off dancing with some asshole in a pink tux." Goth Girl hissed.

"And Steven left with some bitch who said she could score him an eight ball," Juliet added.

"Wait. He just...left?" I cried. "What the fuck? He just left you at prom?!" Glancing back and forth between my scorned friends, I asked, "What about Harley?"

Juliet shrugged and flicked her chin in the direction of a shadowy corner beside the DJ booth. "He's over there, talking to the Phish-heads."

Phish-head was what we called the stoner hippie kids at our school. The ones who played hacky sack and wore moccasins and said *dude* every other word. I looked in the direction of Juliet's gaze and saw them, huddled in a circle, a familiar mop of blond hair sticking up out of the middle.

I should have turned around. I should have been satisfied that he wasn't looking for me, and I should have hightailed it back to Knight. But something about that hippie cluster didn't sit right with me. Harley was a friendly guy, but not *that* friendly.

Tip-toeing over to the congregation, I peeked in between two scraggly-haired losers in tuxedos just in time to see Harley taking twenty-dollar bills from five anxious palms, replacing each one with a little white pill.

"Oh my God," I groaned.

All of their faces snapped up in shock, then the group scattered, leaving me alone with my douchebag ex.

"This is why you fucking came tonight, isn't it?" I placed my hands on my narrow hips and glared at him as he discretely pocketed a fistful of cash. "I thought it was weird that you didn't call me for a week and then showed up in a borrowed suit acting like we were BFFs, but it makes perfect sense now." I swept an arm out in front of me, gesturing to where the congregation of hippies had been. "You just used me to get in here so you could find some new customers."

"Lady..." Harley smiled, his voice dripping with condescension.

"Punk."

Harley's panty-melting grin morphed into the hardened glare of an outlaw as his eyes shot contraband bullets over my shoulder.

I spun around and held my hands up, as if that could possibly shield Harley from the wrath of Ronald McKnight. Knight's hand shot past me and grabbed Harley by the tie. Yanking him forward, I found myself crushed in a Knight-Harley sandwich as the two men bared their teeth at each other over my shoulder.

Couples slow-danced around us as Steven Tyler sang about not wanting to miss a thing.

"Guys," I warned. "Do not *fucking* fight here. Do you hear me? Knight, you could go to *military* jail, and Harley..." I swiveled my head backward to make eye contact with him. "You've got a pocket full of ecstasy, dumbass."

Knight's eyes and nostrils flared as he began taking slow steps backward toward the door, dragging our two bodies with him. "Fine," he hissed in my ear through his clenched teeth. "We won't fight *here*."

Harley began pushing against my back, urging us to walk faster. "Let's go, motherfucker," He turned his head and spat on the dancefloor. "Anywhere you want."

I should have done more to stop them, but the sensation of Knight's chest against my chest and Harley's crotch against my ass caused my hormones to mutiny and take over the whole damn ship. I wasn't thinking about how to prevent bloodshed. I was too focused on the way their breath felt against my skin and their strong hands felt gripping my hips and arms.

We shuffled, locked in a three-person stalemate, out of the Egyptian Ballroom and into the hallway overlooking the two-story lobby below. As soon as we were out of sight, Knight wrapped his free hand around Harley's neck and body-slammed him into the wall, not giving two shits that my body was in between their bodies.

"What the *fuck* are you doing here?" Knight seethed.

Harley's hands released me and wrapped around Knight's neck in return.

Unable to speak, both men choked and glared at each other as I thrashed in between, squealing and grunting, cursing and shoving, kneeing and elbowing, until I heard a woman scream at the end of the hall. All three of us turned our heads at once to see my Spanish teacher, Mrs. Santos, clutching her chest in horror before running off to get help.

"She's gonna call the fucking cops!" I screamed. "Stop it!"

I saw Harley's fingers relax and fall away from Knight's thick, corded neck just before I felt his body slide down the wall behind me and slump to the floor.

"Harley!" I turned and knelt beside his unconscious body, palming his cheek and feeling for a pulse. He was breathing, thank God, but he had deep, purple, finger-shaped welts on his neck and his beautiful baby face was flushed and red.

"Harley..." I slapped his cheek lightly with my hand. "Harley, wake up."

I turned to scream at Knight, but the insults and accusations turned to ash in my mouth the moment I realized that no one was there.

Knight had vanished like a ghost.

Just then, I heard Coach Johnson's voice boom through the lobby below. "Yes, officer. Right up the stairs there."

Shit!

"Harley," I whispered, more frantically. "Harley, the cops are here! Wake up!"

His eyes fluttered, but he made no effort to move.

Glancing back and forth between my unconscious ex and the staircase where the heavy footfalls of the law were approaching, I suddenly knew what I had to do.

And I had to do it fast.

EIGHT

Six people arrived at the Fox Theater in that white stretch Lincoln, but only three of us made it back out.

Goth Girl, Juliet, and I sat side by side on the ride home, guzzling champagne and giggling over our prom pictures, which Juliet had insisted that we pick up before sprinting out the front door.

"Steven is so fucking ugly," Goth Girl hiccupped. "What the hell was I thinking? He looks like—"

"Lord Licorice from Candy Land?" I interrupted, causing Juliet to spit a mouthful of Korbel onto the off-white carpet.

"Oh my God, you're right!" she cackled.

"Not that I'm one to talk," I giggled. "Who the fuck brings two dates to the same prom?" I held up both eight by ten photos, fanned out in one hand.

"No shit!" Juliet snorted, nudging me with her shoulder. "You cocky as hell, girl!"

"Not as cocky as that motherfucker, Harley. I can't believe he just used me to sell drugs at fucking prom." I rolled my eyes and took another sip of champagne.

"So, what's gonna happen to him?" Goth Girl asked. "I know he's a dick, but I still feel kinda bad about leaving him there to get arrested."

"Oh, he won't get arrested," I smirked, handing Juliet my champagne flute so that I could unclasp my silver clutch bag. Reaching in, I pulled out a fat wad of twenties, Harley's flask, and a baggie full of pills stamped with little lightning bolts. "They don't have any evidence."

Juliet and Goth Girl squealed in delight as our chariot delivered us home.

Prom might not have turned out to be the magical night I'd envisioned, but I still managed to leave with two people I loved.

And call me cocky, but I made one hell of a profit too.

ABOUT THE AUTHOR

BB Easton lives in the suburbs of Atlanta, Georgia, with her long-suffering husband, Ken, and two adorable children. She recently quit her job as a school psychologist to write stories about her punk rock past and deviant sexual history full-time. Ken is suuuper excited about it.

If that sounds like the kind of person you want to go around being friends with, then by all means, feel free to drop her a line. Just don't be surprised if you get a reply at four a.m. with an inexplicable Shia LaBeouf meme or a text that was clearly meant for someone else. BB is what doctors call chronically sleep-deprived—or, as Ken pronounces it, depraved.

You can find her:
On email: authorbbeaston@gmail.com
On her website: www.authorbbeaston.com
On Facebook: www.facebook.com/bbeaston
On Instagram: www.instagram.com/author.bb.easton
On Twitter: www.twitter.com/bb_easton
On Pinterest: www.pinterest.com/artbyeaston
On Goodreads: https://goo.gl/4hiwiR
On Spotify: https://open.spotify.com/user/bbeaston

Selling signed books and original art on Etsy: www.etsy.com/shop/artbyeaston

Giving stuff away in her #TeamBB Facebook group:
www.facebook.com/groups/BBEaston

And giving away a free e-book from one of her author friends each month in her newsletter: http://eepurl.com/c4OCOH

ALSO BY BB EASTON

44 Chapters About 4 Men: A Memoir

The 44 Chapers Spin-off Series:
SKIN (Knight, Book 1)
SPEED (Harley, Book 2)
STAR (Hans, Book 3)
SUIT (Ken, Book 4, Coming Fall 2018)

THE COCKIER THE DRAGON, THE HARDER THEY FALL

JAYMIN EVE

Short story featuring Jessa and Braxton from the Supernatural Prison series.

The Cockier the Dragon, the Harder they Fall.
A Supernatural Prison Short Story.

Eve, Jaymin
The Cockier the Dragon, the Harder they Fall.

1st edition

ONE

A fiery heat trailed down my spine, the firm hand sliding around to cup my hip. Waking up to Braxton's touch was pretty much what my dreams were made of. I was tired, but the moment he brushed the slightly calloused skin of his palm over my body, my senses fired up.

"Think the twins will give us twenty minutes?" The grumble of his voice in my ear sent goose bumps across my skin.

I'd been lying in his arms, my back pressed against his front. But I needed to see him. Flipping over, I pressed both hands to the thick muscles of his chest. "Honestly, ten minutes would do me right now."

His hand glided a little lower.

"Even five," I said breathlessly.

At this point, with one of the twins waking up almost every single time we had a spare second together, I would take anything. His eyes were dark, a true midnight blue as they lazily assessed me. Yellow flashed in them for a brief instant, and I shivered at the sight of his dragon peeking out. He curled his arm under me and dragged me on top of him. Our naked skin slipped together and need roared inside me. It was need for my mate. To touch, taste, and feel every inch of him.

Leaning down, I licked a trail across his chest and over one nipple before continuing to move higher, giving in to my need to taste him. His body rumbled under me, and as always, he struggled to let me take the lead. We often fought for dominance, alpha shifters were like that, but it was even worse for him—he was a dragon. After I'd lost my dragon and had gone back to being a regular wolf shifter, everything inside me had calmed down. But I remembered the feeling.

He was working on it, though, and that meant everything to me.

My mouth had just reached the base of his neck when he couldn't take it any longer, flipping me onto my back, his huge body completely dwarfed me. "I need you, mate. This is going to be hard and fast."

239

No apologies. Because I sure as fuck didn't need them. Braxton and I made love plenty; this morning I was all for the more brutal side of his personality.

"Bring it, mate." My wolf howled inside me, some of her animalistic nature leaking out.

Yellow flared in his irises again, and his body seemed to swell in size. I hooked my arms around his neck, and he lowered his body to mine. I loved having his strength against me. His hardness. His fingers brushed across my center, and when he assured himself of my readiness, he sheathed his length inside in one smooth movement.

I groaned, and he waited a beat for me to adjust. I might be ready, but with Braxton's size, a girl needed a moment. When he moved, it was just as he promised. Hard and fast. He used one hand to hold himself up, and the other went under my ass to lift me so he had a better angle to slam into me.

The sensations built at a steady crescendo. I wanted to fight against them, because I knew it was going to be over too fast—I almost came the second he was inside me—but there was no stopping. Not today.

"I got you, baby," he growled, voice much more guttural than normal.

"Fuck, Brax." I gasped. "Don't you dare stop."

His grin, those fucking dimples, it was too much for me, and I lost control as my body detonated into a million pieces. I cried out, more than once, and Braxton let out a final groan, finishing just after me. He rocked against me a few more times, drawing out the pleasure for as long as possible. When I reached the point of it being almost too much to handle, I threw my head back and let out a strangled chuckle. "Dude, you're literally going to kill me one of these days."

He dropped the hand out from under my ass, placing it on the other side of my head, so his arms framed me as he stared down. Still inside me. Still as hard as hell. My body was already starting to respond again. Before the twins, we often had sex over and over in a single night, but since the little boob monsters were born, it had been harder to find alone time. I missed my mate. But neither of us would wish for anything different.

Our babies had stolen our hearts.

As though they'd heard me, a low cry sounded through the wall between our room and theirs. Braxton had built a small nursery just off the side of us, so they were close, but there was a door we could shut for sexy times. Not that they were old enough to care, but it was nice to have the illusion of privacy.

He leaned down and kissed me hard, his tongue brushing against mine, and I realized that we hadn't kissed once during the sex. It had been all about the eye contact. Damn, he was as sexy as hell.

"I'll get him," Braxton murmured, against my mouth.

He pulled out slowly before sliding back into me again, as if he just couldn't leave so abruptly. "Really fucking cold out here without you, Jessa babe," he said with a wink.

I just shook my head. "Get off, I have to clean up."

With a snort of laughter, he finally rolled off me. "Such a romantic."

I shrugged, because I really wasn't and he loved me anyway. I escaped into our bathroom to clean myself up and pull on some clothes. I paused just as I was about to step out, my eyes going across to the bed. Braxton was laid back, head propped up against the pillows across the headboard. Our son, Jack, was in his lap staring up at him.

"Hey, little man." Braxton's voice always got this special low tone to it when he talked to the babies. I propped myself against the door so I could watch without disturbing them.

There was nothing in this world that could tear me apart faster than watching Braxton handle our babies. He fucking adored them. My heart was so full in that moment; one hand pressed to my chest as if I could ease the ache there. This was worth all the sleepless nights and stress in our world. We were taking these perfect moments. They were ours, Goddammit.

Braxton's head shot up, our eyes clashing together. There was no way for me to sneak up on them, not even if I could somehow magic myself invisible.

You look beautiful.

He was much more romantic when he used our special mate bond to communicate.

I love you.

I guess that I was too.

Jackson started cooing and waving his arms when he saw me, and I hurried over to gather him into my arms. The second I held the chubby little guy, everything inside me calmed. My wolf relaxed, her rumble almost a purr as I snuggled against Braxton's side and I put Jackson on the boob. We had this routine down, and I loved that Braxton supported me in whatever way he could. I might have to do all the hours and hours and hours of feeding—my kids were hungry little supes, let me tell you—but Braxton was there for everything else.

"Tomorrow we're meeting with the council from Canada," he said, voice low as his fingers played in the lengths of my long, dark hair. "They want to negotiate some more prisoner exchanges."

"Will you meet them at Vangaurd?" I asked.

Braxton, and his brothers were the leaders of the American Supernatural Council, which meant they had a shit-ton of responsibilities. One of the largest was making sure that the prison near our home in Stratford, which housed some of the worst supernatural criminals in the world, remained safe and ran smoothly. There was a network of these prisons around the globe, and since local criminals were usually moved away from familiar territory, the boys were often negotiating prisoner exchanges.

"Yeah, they want to see our facilities for mermaids. Apparently, theirs is a real bitch. I assured them we have the perfect isolation tank for her, but you know how this bullshit works."

He sounded pissed, and I didn't blame him. Braxton was a powerful dragon shifter, smart and capable, but he couldn't stand politics. Because he was strong and feared, he'd gotten the position of council leader for shifters. But he really didn't want it.

Evie cried then, and Braxton was up and in the nursery in a flash. Jackson was finished, so it was easy to transfer him to his daddy so I could feed my little girl. After that was done, it was time to start the day. Clothes, nappies, kids, toys . . .

My life sure as shit had changed, and I was happier than I'd ever been. As we travelled downstairs, the sound of laughter hit me. We shared this house with our pack, and just like my babies, this closeness never failed to bring me joy. It had been Jessa and the Compass quads for a long time, but it had become so much more.

Mischa, my twin, was mated to Maximus, who was the vampire part of the Compass quads. Grace was a true mate to Tyson, who was the magic part of the quads. And Jacob, the fey of the quads, remained happily single. We were all taking bets about when he was going to be taken down by whatever woman was destined for him.

After so many years of mate bonds being scarce, fate was finally bringing them back, but Jacob was determined to skip out on all the "true love bullshit."

"Hey, Jess." Maximus wrapped his arms around me, and I returned the hug with force. Braxton held the twins, which meant I could really enjoy the hug from my favorite vampire.

"Where's Misch?" I asked, looking around for my twin. We were almost identical, only our eye color and a few freckles differentiated us.

"Lily had a little accident," he told me, eyes searching up the stairs. Ah, that was why he'd been standing near the base, he'd been waiting for them to return.

"What sort of accident?" Braxton asked, sounding amused rather than concerned. If it had been anything serious, Maximus would not be down here with us.

"She crapped all the way up her back, it was in her damn hair!" Jacob yelled from the kitchen. "If there was ever a need to enforce birth control with supes, they'd just have to show a video of that."

My chuckle burst out before I could stop it, and Maximus shook his head. "I'm probably going to kill Jacob by lunchtime. I hope you aren't too attached to him."

I was very attached to him—to all of my pack—and I would rip the head off anyone who hurt them, but since Maximus was mostly joking, I shrugged. "We could probably replace him easily enough. I mean . . . plenty of fey to go around, right?"

"Hey!" Jacob shouted again before he poked his head around the corner of the kitchen. "You would be devasted without me. I am irreplaceable."

"Who's irreplaceable?" Grace asked, stepping in from the back porch. She looked happy and windswept. She and Tyson were spending an awful lot of time in the forest, which bordered the back of our large cabin home, and if the amount of twigs in her hair was any indication, they were not just hiking.

"Just deciding who we're going to replace Jacob with in the pack," I told her, and she laughed before hurrying over to Braxton. She relieved him of Evie, snuggling the baby close to her.

"How's my baby girl today?" she cooed.

Tyson walked in then, his eyes shooting straight to his mate and the baby she held. They darkened, and I recognized that look. Ten to one, we were adding some more babies to our pack in the next few years.

"Breakfast is ready," Jacob yelled and then added, "you ungrateful assholes!"

All of us laughed, and then we trooped through into the large dining room. I used to think Braxton's huge-ass table was over the top, but not anymore. We definitely needed the space. Since Jackson and Evie were too young for food, Braxton and Grace put them on their tummies in the specially designed area we had in the corner. I leaned down and ran my hands across their blond hair, needing to touch them.

As I stood, Mischa hurried into the room, her arms full of a sparkling clean Lily. The babies mop of dark curls was getting long already, and they'd have to tie it up soon to get it out of her eyes. She went in with the twins, the three of them started doing their communication thing. I would swear they all talked in little coos and grunts and hand waves.

Jacob dropped the first plate of food down, and as Maximus went to sit at that spot, I kicked him in the side, knocking him four feet back.

"No!" I said, pointing at finger at him. "When you're breastfeeding two hungry babies for half the night, then you get the first food. Until then . . ." I trailed off, eyeing him as he held both hands up and backed away slowly.

Mischa stood next to me, and I caught her amused look from the corner of my eye. "You think he'd have learned by now."

"Yeah, it's only been twenty years," I said, sticking my tongue out at him.

I kept an eye on Maximus while I took my seat, and he just chuckled before ruffling my hair. "Don't ever change, Jess."

I would have flipped him off, but I was too busy reaching for food. I'd save the extra insults for later. I might have gotten in first, but the pastries, eggs, toast, and bacon disappeared so fast. We all had big appetites, being growing supernaturals and all that.

Mischa was the only one to still eat like she was human or something. Her food didn't even spill out over the side of her plate when she took her share. Some days, I wondered if we were actually related. When I was finished, I eyed the empty platter with sadness. I'd really wanted another chocolate croissant, but I hadn't wanted to be completely greedy.

Really regretting that choice.

"Here you go, babe."

Braxton slid his slice of the chocolate deliciousness closer to me, and I had to physically stop myself from just reaching out and snatching it up. With a sigh, I shook my head. "No, seriously. You have it."

Snickering laughter started up around the room, and I narrowed my eyes before swinging around to give them all a death stare. "Shut up, I'm trying to be nice."

Braxton wrapped his arms around me, half pulling me out of my chair so he could kiss me. I forgot all about food and chocolate as another hunger flared to life within me. This morning had *not* been enough. It would never be enough.

He set me back down gently, and I was rocked for a moment as I tried to remember what year it was. There was a soft scraping sound as he slid his plate closer. "It's yours, Jess. Always."

Don't cry. Don't cry.

"Still the only supe I know to cry over food," Braxton smirked before he leaned forward and pressed his lips to the corner of mine. That kiss, it almost sent the emotions I was feeling into overdrive. A single tear escaped, and he brushed it away.

Lily screamed then, and that distracted everyone long enough for me to pull myself together. And eat my pastry. Because I sure as hell was not letting any of these bastards get their hands on it. Not that they would. Braxton's dragon shared food with me and no one else. He was likely to get very pissed if anyone touched his offering.

Mine.

The dragon and the food.

TWO

I decided to go with the quads the next day to the prison. Mischa and Grace were watching the babies, and I should have at least three hours before one of mine decided they were starving to death. My parents were also stopping by, because they couldn't go more than half a day without seeing their grandbabies. The Compass grandparents were just as bad.

"Remember all the months we spent looking for this prison?" Jacob chuckled, as we walked through the forest. "I never thought we were going to find it."

I shook my head, looking around at the familiar flora. "Literally feels like that was a hundred years ago. I can barely remember my life before the dragon mark."

We all fell quiet, no doubt thinking about the crazy events that had happened during the time of the dragon marked and the dragon king. He'd been a megalomaniac sort of dude—not one you wanted to stop by your city. But we'd gotten rid of him in the end, and the dragon marked were finally free to go and live their lives. I still bore the huge dragon shaped tattoo on my body, and I looked at it with reminiscing sort of happiness. My Josephine. My dragon. She was living in the Faerie lands, ruling them like the badass dragon she was.

I missed her so much, but it was nice knowing I could visit her again. She was always there.

"Does the doorway still move all the time?" I asked when the boys led me into a deep, dark section of the woods.

Maximus nodded. "Yep, we have to send out coordinates for the new spot every few days. Make sure the location is not repeated within a year period."

There were so many things they took care of now that I didn't even know about. I'd been in a real sleep-deprived haze for the last few months. "If you four ever need help, you know you only have to ask, right?"

I was used to being the only chick in the group. Having four overprotective guys as best friends meant they took care of most things while I hang around,

245

causing trouble and eating food. It was a dynamic that worked for us. And they knew I loved them . . . I just wasn't always the most helpful supernatural around.

"You grew some babies, now you continue to grow them, Jessa babe." Tyson wrapped an arm around me. "You're doing like ten times the work we are. We're all so damn proud of you."

The five of us slowed, almost in sync, which was just like the old days. I realized then that it had been a long time since it was just the five of us together. So much had changed, but at the core, we were still the same. Family.

"I love you all," I said, randomly needing to say the words.

I got a ton of hugs and ribbing in return, and it felt even more like old times.

"Come on," Braxton finally said, opening the door that would lead us into the underground. "We're going to be late."

When we were in the underground area, we strolled across to the front gate. The guards lowered their heads and greeted their council leaders as we passed. Being the leaders here was a big deal, and no one fucked with the Compass quads. But it was nice that they also seemed to respect and like them. My boys had done well. Really well.

"Are the Canadians here yet?" Maximus asked the troll in the first guard booth. Demi-fey were very good at keeping the prisoners under control, and they held a lot of the main guard positions here.

The troll nodded, his barky skin shining in the fluorescent lighting of this section. "The sorcerer dropped them off about ten minutes ago. They're in the front waiting room."

He handed us our medallions, and we looped them around our necks before setting off. The prison's security went far beyond just the guards and solid walls, there were magical elements woven throughout that countered the natural strengths of the five supernatural races. Shifter, vampire, fey, demi-fey and magic user. Hence the need for the medallions to counteract the silver and blood magic. I'd been here once as a prisoner, it was much nicer entering this way.

The Canadian group consisted of two vampires and two shifters. Bear, if my nose was correct. My senses were definitely duller inside these spelled walls, even with the medallions.

"Welcome to Vanguard, Dineal," Braxton said, shaking hands with the first shifter. He was a huge burly man, with a closely shaved head and eyes the color of rich cinnamon. Age was difficult to tell in supernaturals, but I thought he looked like someone with experience about him. Probably around eighty.

I wasn't overly fond of bear shifters, had too many bad experiences with their growly asses to ever trust one, but I also really shouldn't cause any political turmoil for my guys. So, when it was my turn to be introduced, I just shook hands with Dineal and kept my mouth shut.

"You really don't need an introduction," he said, holding my hand for a beat too long. "Everyone knows the dragon marked who took down the king."

Braxton only made one noise, barely even a scary one, and Dineal dropped my hand and backed up a few steps. I narrowed my eyes at my mate, because I sure as shit did not need him to scare off the men. I could do that all on my own.

The others didn't come near me after that, and I knew Jacob was laughing at me. His eyes were practically sparkling. Dicking fey. Once the introductions were over, it was time to enter the prison. There was about thirty minutes until lunchtime, so it was pretty quiet in the large communal area that all five races shared at certain periods of the day. We walked straight past the cafeteria tables and the gym, making our way to the tanks that held the mermaids and selkies.

Mermaids were nothing like the cartoons humans watched. They were scary, with claws and fangs and dirty, sea-colored hair and skin. Their eyes bothered me, empty depths of darkness. Oh, and there was also that thing about them liking to lure people to their deaths just for shits and giggles. That bothered me the most.

"We have three mermaids in at the moment, but the one in this tank is due for release next week," Tyson explained, as we closed in on one of the giant glass structures. "Her tank is designed specifically for the difficult cases. She's a head banger."

I took a step closer. The water was so clear that I was sure crazy mermaid had already escaped. Then, she appeared on the other side of the glass so quickly that I *almost* took a step back. I had no idea how they hid themselves in the water that way but if they stayed very still no one could see them. It was as if they could reflect their surroundings.

She stared at me. Black orbs. No white at all in them. Her tail was a khaki-green, and her hair, which was almost the full length of her body as it trailed out around her, was a few shades lighter in color than her tail.

When the mermaid smiled, her pointed teeth flashed ivory in my direction. It was not a nice smile, it was a I-enjoy-snacking-on-shifters sort of grin.

"Are you sure this bitch should be back in the ocean?" I asked Maximus, who stood next to me. "She looks like she's a few fish short of a full load."

Braxton pressed in close to my back then, and I immediately rubbed myself across him. Because why the hell not. I was nothing if not inappropriate. His hand slid across my ass and down it, so quickly I almost missed it.

Goddamn him. I was horny . . . again.

"She's done her time," Maximus said, shaking his head at me. "She gets a second chance." He didn't sound any happier about it than I was.

I'd been advocating for the death penalty to be brought in. Doesn't matter how horrific a supernatural's crime is, if they surrender peacefully, they get to keep their miserable lives. That was fine, until criminals started escaping and killing again. Or even doing their time and getting out to hurt innocents again.

It had to stop. Two strikes and you were dead was my new motto.

The Canadians spent about twenty minutes examining the cage. The entire time they walked around it, testing strength and magical barriers, the mermaid followed their movements. Wherever they were, she was on the other side, and the hunger on her face was fucking disturbing.

Finally, they seemed satisfied, and the paperwork was brought out to sign. This was just as the lunch rush started, and when we left, we found ourselves surrounded by criminals. Guards closed in to where we were standing, but Braxton just waved them away. Only a fucking moron would take on the Compasses. We were in no danger here.

"You assholes are going to die!" A loud voice broke out across the racket of lunch noise. "I know what's coming for you, and I can't wait to stand over your corpses and laugh."

Okay, apparently we had some fucking morons in here after all.

A vampire broke away from a group near the buffet. He kept shouting as he got closer to us, hands waving around while he drew attention. "Warren Chalms." I heard Jacob mutter. "He's just come out of solitary for threatening those women."

Oh, he was definitely a moron. Before anyone could stop me, I stalked across toward him, ready to meet him face to face. Threatening women was not okay with me.

I heard some groans and laughter from behind, but I didn't wait around for more. He swung at me as soon as I was within reaching distance, but I'd been fighting for most of my life, and it was second nature to simply side-step his fist. Swinging myself around, I kicked him straight in the face hard enough that I heard his teeth rattle. Warren went down, smacking his head on a table that was nearby. He got up just as fast, vampires were strong and quick, and he was going to be ready to kill me.

Fangs out, he lunged forward and grabbed a handful of my hair while he tried to wrench my throat back to bite me. My elbow crashed into his nose, splintering it and sending blood spurting everywhere. Dammit, I hated when I got blood on my clothes. That meant I had to go shopping again to replace this top. I hated shopping as much as bloody clothes.

Before he could recover, I ripped my hair free and kicked him hard in the gut. When he was on the ground, I dropped both of my knees into his face. My wolf surged forward and I let her strength infuse me. My next punch knocked him out cold, his ugly head lolling to the side.

Rising slowly, I wiggled my shoulders and stretched myself out. It had been a while since I'd had a good old-fashioned fight. A few more vampire closed in on me.

"Don't even think about it." Braxton's words sounded almost lazy, but there was an immediate six feet of space around me.

"Cocky dragon." I grinned at him, showing all of my teeth. "I had it handled."

His eyes did that midnight blue thing again, followed by gold, and then all I could think about was this morning. His body over mine.

Fuck.

This was out of control, what sort of pheromones did dragons have? Neither of us moved, both waiting for the other to make the first move. I was all amped up from the fight and from my hormones, so that gave me an extra slice of attitude. And I was already pretty headstrong.

I wasn't about to break the eye contact, but I did notice Jacob shove Maximus forward. "Move her or we'll be here all day," he muttered.

Maximus bared his fangs at his brother "Fuck, no. Are you kidding me?" He shot back. "No one touches Jessa babe when she's like this."

I had taught them well.

"How about a compromise?" Braxton had all of my attention. I crossed my arms and tilted my head to the side.

"Listening . . ."

"We meet in the middle."

A grin was trying to break out across my pursed lips, and I fought against it, but I couldn't stop. "Fine, I can agree to those terms."

He took the first step, which I knew cost him dearly, but he did it for me. That was how I knew Braxton loved me more than anything—he could literally fight instinct for me. And I would do the same for him.

I ran then because . . . screw meeting in the middle.

His arms wrapped around me as I leapt at him, and my legs closed around his waist as our bodies slammed together. His lips were on mine in the same heartbeat, and then I forgot about the rest of the world.

It was true what they said: the cockier the dragon, the harder they fall. It was the same for wolves. Guess we could just be cocky bastards together.

I was pretty okay with that.

ABOUT THE AUTHOR

Jaymin Eve is the USA Today bestseller of over 25 fantasy and romance novels. She lives in Australia with her husband, two daughters, and a couple of crazy pets.

Stay in touch with Jaymin:
Facebook: www.facebook.com/JayminEve.Author
Website: www.jaymineve.com

ALSO BY JAYMIN EVE

Secret Keepers Series
Book One: House of Darken
Book Two: House of Imperial (1st July 2018)
Book Three: House of Leights (1st August 2018)
Book Four: House of Royale (1st September 2018)

Curse of the Gods Series (Reverse Harem Fantasy)
Book One: Trickery
Book Two: Persuasion
Book Three: Seduction
Book Four: Strength (2018)

NYC Mecca Series (Complete - UF series)
Book One: Queen Heir
Book Two: Queen Alpha
Book Three: Queen Fae
Book Four: Queen Mecca
A Walker Saga (Complete - YA Fantasy)
Book One: First World
Book Two: Spurn
Book Three: Crais
Book Four: Regali
Book Five: Nephilius
Book Six: Dronish
Book Seven: Earth

Supernatural Prison Trilogy (Complete - UF series)
Book One: Dragon Marked
Book Two: Dragon Mystics
Book Three: Dragon Mated
Supernatural Prison Stories
Broken Compass
Magical Compass
Louis (2018)

Hive Trilogy (Complete UF/PNR series)

Book One: Ash

Book Two: Anarchy

Book Three: Annihilate

Sinclair Stories (Standalone Contemporary Romance)

Songbird

TRICKY BOND

A HOLLY WOODS FILES SHORT

EMMA HART

A short story featuring Noelle and Drake from the Holly Woods Files - and a missing parrot.

ONE

"Noella!" The scream of my name accompanies the sharp slam of my front door. "Noella! I need-a you!"

Oh, God.

Nothing good ever came of those words from Nonna.

"What do you want?" I ask, stirring the cake mixture.

My third attempt. After all this time, I should really know that I cannot bake, and I really should have taken my mom up on her offer of making the twins' first birthday cake.

At this rate, my poor babies weren't going to have a cake.

Not that they deserve one. I wasn't over the poop party my darling son threw this morning.

Nonna stills in the doorway. "Noella? Are-a you-a baking?"

"No, Nonna. I'm stirring thin air."

"Your-a attitude-a stinks."

"So does you running into my house. How did you get a key?"

Nonna sniffs, but otherwise declines to answer as she shuffles across to the table where I'm working. The chair screeches against the floor as she pulls it out and takes a seat. "I am-a in-a crisis. I do-a not-a need a key."

I don't like the sound of that. And it doesn't answer the question of how she got the key—something Drake and I have been fighting for the last six months.

"All right, Nonna. I'll bite." I put the bowl and spoon down and wipe my hands on my apron.

That's right. I'm wearing an apron.

I'm a real adult now, don't you know?

"What's your crisis?" I ask her, leaning against the table.

Her lower lip juts out, and oh, God—she's going to cry. "It-a is-a Gio."

Has the little rat died?

Is that cruel?

257

Maybe a bit. Damn, but I hate that bird.

"What did he do now? Drake already told you we won't talk to him about stealing underwear when he's let out of his cage." I fold my arms over my chest. "I mean it. I did it once behind his back, but I won't do it again."

"Nooooo!" She covers her face with her hands. "He is-a missing!"

I raised an eyebrow. "He's missing? Did you check the attic?"

"Noella! I am-a serious! Gio is-a gone!" She waggled one wrinkled finger at me. "Start-a being serious!"

You couldn't pay me to be serious about that damn parrot.

"How do you know he's gone?" I can try to care, I suppose. "Have you checked the house? And Dad's new shed?"

"*Si, si, si,*" she wails, clutching dramatically at her chest.

Give me strength. Someone. Anyone.

"He is-a gone!" She continues, whipping a handkerchief out of her sleeve and dabbing at her eyes.

If I didn't know better, I'd say she was laying this on thick. Really, really thick.

So, I ask the most logical question. "Well, where is he then?"

She sobers up quicker than you can snap your fingers. "I do not-a know! If-a I knew, do-a you not-a think-a I would-a have him?"

Makes sense.

"How did he escape?"

She looks around as if we're being spied on, then leans forward, conspiratorially narrowing her eyes. "I think-a some-a-one stole him."

The laugh snorts out of me before I can stop it.

"You-a laugh at-a me?"

"No, I just—" I pause, sighing. "Nonna, the notion that someone stole Gio is, well, ridiculous."

She gasps, hand to her chest once more. "He is-a lovely bird! Anyone would-a be lucky to-a have-a him!"

I respectfully disagree, but whatever.

"Nonna, nobody stole Gio." I cross my arms and lean against the counter. "I'm sorry. Nobody in this town is crazy enough to want that damn bird."

She wails. Long and high and oh, God, make it stop. I'm pretty sure she's so high-pitched that dogs are the only ones who can hear her.

"What the hell is that noise?" Drake demands, stepping into the kitchen with a twin on each of his hips.

I swear. If I didn't have to clean poo off my walls at five-thirty this morning, looking at him right now might make me want another.

"Gio is-a missing!" Nonna exclaims.

Drake looks at me. "What?"

"Someone stole him," I say wryly, taking Alessia from him.

"They're tired," he says. "And I'm never taking two one-year-olds to the park on my own again. I don't need to go to the gym this week. I already got my work-out in."

I chuckle and stroke Antonio's little dark head. "I'll put them to bed." Then, lowering my voice, I say, "Please explain to her that nobody would steal that damn bird."

He rolls his eyes, but slides Antonio over onto my other hip. I carry the twins upstairs to the sound of Drake asking Nonna what she's talking about.

"Mama," Antonio babbles. "Mama, bed."

"Mama's putting you to bed, okay?" I kiss the side of his head and bump the door open with my hip. Their cribs are on opposite sides of the room for obvious reasons, and with the skill I've mastered over the last several months, put Antonio in his crib before moving an already sleeping Alessia into hers.

I kiss and tuck them both in, leaving Antonio babbling at the stuffed turtle in his crib. That boy could talk Nonna to death and he can only say five words.

Mama, Dada, no, juice, and poop.

I walk into the kitchen. Nonna is nursing a cup of hot tea, and Drake is looking anywhere but at me.

"Noella! Good-a news! Drake said you-a will-a find-a Gio!" Nonna exclaims, smiling cheerfully.

"He said what now?" I ask, shooting daggers at him. "I assume by "you," he means the both of us?"

Drake jerks his head around and opens his mouth to reply, but Nonna beats him to it.

"Oh! That is-a good-a idea!" She claps her hands together. "I will-a watch-a the twins, and you will-a find-a Gio!"

"But, I—" Drake starts.

"Will gladly help me," I finish through gritted teeth. "Won't you, *honey*?"

He forced a smile and looked at Nonna. "Of course, I'll help."

TWO

"I cannot believe you," I say, slamming the car door. "We'll find the parrot? Are you insane? This is the best thing that's ever happened since that parrot came into our lives."

Drake sighs, locking the car. "What could I do? She was crying."

"They were crocodile tears! Your daughter is already an expert at it!"

"She gets that from her mother," he mutters.

"Heard that, asshole."

He laughs, pulling me toward him. "I said we'd look for him until the twins wake up, then she has to call your brothers. That's all. It's only an hour."

"I don't care. I don't want to find that parrot."

"The bonus is that you don't have to make the twins' cake now. Think of it like that," he says brightly.

I stop in the middle of the street and look at him. "You sound a little too happy about that."

"Well, sweetheart—"

"Think very carefully what you're about to say, Mr. Nash."

He bites the inside of his cheek. "Your first one was so burned it looked like a chocolate cake, and the second... Well, I don't know what the fuck you did to that."

"I followed the recipe!"

"For what? A mud pie?"

"Ugh." I fold my arms and glare at him. "Fine. I'm happy that Mom is doing the cake so I don't have to," I admit. "But that's not the point. I don't want to chase the devil bird around town."

"Neither do I." He holds out his hands and steps toward me, cupping my face in his hands. "But, she is your nonna, and she loves the bird, so at the very least, we have to look."

261

I stare up at him. I'm not happy, but he's right, and there's no way I won't not look for the damn creature.

"Okay, I'll look, but we're splitting up to cover more ground."

"Done. We'll meet back here in thirty minutes?"

"S'pose," I mutter.

Drake laughs, dipping his head to kiss me. "What do we do if we find Gio?"

"You won't find Gio. You can't find your socks in your sock drawer, and you think you can find a parrot in Holly Woods?" I snort, stepping back. "I'll call you when I find him."

"That's awfully cocky for someone who doesn't want to find him." He quirks a brow, lips tugging to one side.

"I don't want to find him, but I know you won't, so therefore, logic dictates that I will find him." I cross my arms. "I know you hate losing, but you'll have to deal with it."

"I hate losing? Right. You threatened to burn the Monopoly board last week, Noelle."

"That game is stupid, and you cheated!"

He laughed and backed up. "All right, all right. Fine. I'll wait for your call for when you find Gio."

"You better be looking! You're not allowed to bail on me! You got us into this situation!" I yell as he leaves the office parking lot and walks down the street.

Drake puts one hand up in goodbye, and I "psh" in his direction.

Why did I marry him again?

Oh, that's right. Because I fell in love with the fool.

Sigh.

"What are you yelling about?" Bek asks, stepping out into the sunshine. "If someone died—"

I laugh. "Nobody died." After a spate of murders over two or so years, we are finally murder-free again in Holly Woods. "Gio is missing, and Nonna enlisted me and Drake to find the stupid bird instead of me baking like I'm supposed to be."

She tucked her red hair behind her ear and wrinkled up her face. "Why would you find Gio? You hate him."

"It wasn't by choice. Drake agreed for me, so I roped him into it, too."

"So why are you shouting?"

"Because he reminded me of last week's ill-fated Monopoly game and it made me mad," I mutter. "How are you feeling?"

"Well, my breakfast stayed down this morning, so..." She gives me a weak smile and crosses her fingers.

I grimace in solidarity. "I don't miss morning sickness. Did you call your doctor for some meds yet?"

She sighs. "I'm gonna have to. Brody is hovering over me like a fly around shit, and next time, I think I'll just vomit on him to make him go away."

"Sound plan."

"Do you want some company? I could use the fresh air. Literally everyone is in the office today and there are clients in and out every fifteen minutes. It's giving me a headache."

"Are you going to vomit on me?"

She shakes her head. "No. But if I stay here much longer, I will."

"Sure. Come with me. I have to find Gio first, anyway."

She pauses. "Why?"

"Pride." I shrug. "Besides. I can't lose to a man who can't find a pair of matching socks on a morning, can I?"

Bek raises an eyebrow. "A matching pair? I'm lucky if Brody can find any at all."

"Yeah, well, if I didn't do laundry, Drake wouldn't either."

"Okay, where do we start?" Bek flattens our awkwardly hand-drawn map of Holly Woods out on the coffee shop table.

I put my iced coffee down and uncap my red marker. "This is my parents' house." I circle it. "So, he started there, and he definitely made his way into town. This is the only route he knows, and while I don't like Gio, he's stupid."

"Do parrots have a sense of direction? I mean, they don't migrate for the winter, do they?"

I tap the pen against my lips. "I don't know. We know he isn't at the vet and that she hasn't seen him since we called, but she is keeping an eye out for him. So, we'll go to the obvious place."

"The park. The trees."

I nod. "I don't know if there's anywhere else he'd be."

"I agree. It's pretty logical. Birds like trees, so..."

"Even if Gio isn't a normal bird," I add. "Why do I feel like we'll find him somewhere super random like the bank?"

"Because Gio is an asshole," Bek says matter-of-factly. "Hey, if you and Drake are on a wild parrot chase, where are the twins?"

"Napping. With Nonna. Thankfully."

"Thankfully that they're with her?" Her eyes bug.

"No. Don't be stupid. Thankful they're napping while they're with her," I correct her. "All right. Let's go to the park and hope we find a parrot."

"Sounds good to me." She grabs her take-out cup of ice water and stands up. "Noelle? Question."

"Mm?" I fold up the map and grab my own drink.

"What the hell do we do with Gio once we find him?"

I open my mouth, and then—crap.

"That," I say slowly, "Is a very good question."

"So, we're praying for a miracle."

"Pretty much."

THREE

It isn't going well.

How the hell do you find a parrot in the middle of a town? I don't even know what I'm doing. Neither does Bek. We're basically wandering around like hapless, headless chickens, waiting for Gio to do something useful for once and fly in front of our faces.

That will never happen, because as Bek said, Gio is an asshole, but hey. I'm a dreamer.

Actually, I'm a complete realist, but dreamer sounds better.

"How did Gio get out?" Bek asks. "Did she check the attic?"

"That's what I asked her," I reply. "But yes, she said she did, and I don't know how he got out. She likely forgot to close the window before she opened his cage, then walked out, and off he went." I shrug. "She's insistent that he was stolen."

Bek chokes, thumping her chest with her fist. "What? Why the hell would anyone steal Gio? You couldn't give the creature away, never mind anyone stealing him."

"That's what we tried to say to her, but you know what she's like. You'd have better luck getting a conversation out of a stone." I sigh and look around the park. "I don't think we're going to find him here."

"Do you think we'll find him at all?"

"Hopefully not," I mutter.

She snorts.

"I don't know. On one hand, I want to find him for Nonna, but damn, this is a lot of space for a parrot to disappear in. I mean, I can find cheating spouses and murderers by putting myself in their headspace, but how the hell do I do that with a glorified chicken that speaks pirate?"

"Not to mention you left your children with the town's crazy lady."

I groan. I don't need that reminder. The last time she was alone with them,

265

she spoke almost exclusively in Italian in the hopes they'd be more fluent than me and my brothers.

They were nine months old. They pooped, crawled, cried, and threw spaghetti at me.

They weren't ready for Italian lessons.

My phone vibrates in my pocket, so I reach in and pull it out. It's a text from Drake asking if I'm having any luck.

Me: *None. This is ridiculous.*
Drake: *And there's two of you.*

"Uh-oh," I say. "He knows you're with me."

Bek shrugs. "He's still not going to find the parrot. Nobody can find the parrot. This isn't a zoo."

Ah. It's so nice to see her pregnancy hormones setting in.

I open the text thread and hit reply.

Me: *She needed fresh air and I was going to fresh air. Would you deny a pregnant lady?*
Drake: *You're not using that again. That's why I once spent sixty dollars on ice-cream when you were pregnant. The guilt trip sucks.*
Me: *You did that because you love me.*
Drake: *Mmmmph.*

I laugh to myself and look up.

And see a flash of green.

"Did you see that?" Bek shouts, grabbing hold of my arm.

"The green?"

"Uh-huh."

"Will you vomit if you run?"

"No, but Nonna owes me fifty billion pans of lasagna."

"Done." I clutch my phone tight and run in that direction. Bek is hot on my heels as we run across the park after a flash of green.

That may or may not even be Gio.

Two years ago, I was chasing murderers in my Louboutins. Now, I'm chasing a parrot in sneakers that were vomited on last week.

Mom life for the win.

We manage to reach the snack kiosk before we both have to stop. I push my way to the front of the line to the teen girl behind it. "Did you see a parrot fly past here? Just now?"

Her eyes widen and she looks at me like I'm crazy.

It's okay, kid. I know I'm crazy. You have to be to survive the Bond family.

She shakes her head slowly, and I groan, thanking her before I turn around.

"Damn it," Bek mutters. "What if he flies close to Drake? Then we lose."

"And I have to live with it," I moan.

"Ma'am?"

I turn, ready to cut the person calling me ma'am. I'm not a ma'am, damn it!

Unfortunately, he's the cutest, spottiest teenager who looks positively terrified at speaking to me. "Yes?"

"Is the parrot y'all are looking for green?"

I nod once.

"I saw him. He went that way." He pointed toward the main road leading out of the park.

Bek gasps. "Let's go!"

"Thank you!" I shout as she drags me away and in the direction of the parrot.

Run. Run. Run. We run like hell after the green blur that we can't even see anymore.

"Bek. This is ridiculous." I stop and grab hold of a post, bending over to catch my breath. "We don't know where he went."

"Uhhh." She clutches my hand. "Noelle, I'm gonna be sick."

Oh no.

Oh no, no, no.

She bends over, and I instinctively reach out to her. I scoop back her hair and hold it as she vomits into a bush behind me.

"It's okay," I say softly. "You're fine. I've got you."

She grips hold of the fence behind the bush and takes a deep breath. "Damn it. Does this stop soon?"

"Yes. When you visit your doctor," I remind her, releasing her hair as she stands up. I shrug off my sweater and use the sleeve to wipe her mouth.

"Noelle," she says flatly. "Seriously?"

"Instinct. Sorry. I see vomit and I have to clean it up."

"That's gross."

"No. Gross is wiping shit from your walls at five-thirty in the morning. Vomit is lovely compared to that." I give her a wry smile. "Do you need to go home?"

"She doesn't have a choice." Brody's voice interrupts whatever she was going to say.

"Aw, shit," she whispers.

I have to fight back laughter, but that quickly disappears when I see Drake right behind him.

"Noelle!" Brody points at me. "Why the hell do you have her running around after Nonna's fucking parrot?"

"Excuse me? She wanted fresh air. Don't put this on me!" I point right back at him.

"She can't even pee in the morning without vomiting."

"Say it a little louder, Brody. I want everyone to know that information," Bek snaps.

He—wisely—ignores her. "You can't have her go running everywhere!"

I hit my little brother with a death glare that makes even Drake take a step back. "Brody, believe it or not, I don't control her. I didn't want her here. Sit your ass down and shut up, idiot."

He opens his mouth, but he's shut up by Bek.

"Brody, she's right. I wanted to come alone. Neither of knew we'd end up chasing a parrot through the park only for him to disappear," she says wearily. "But I think going home is the smartest choice."

"What about your car?" he asks.

"I can drive it back to y'all's place," I reassure them. "Go home and get into bed. We've got this."

"Will you text me if you find the wayward bird?" she asks, tucking herself into Brody's side. "I want to know."

"I swear I will," I promise. "Now go relax."

Still slightly white-faced, she nods, and Brody guides her off toward wherever it is his car is.

Instantly, I reach out and smack Drake's arm. "Why'd you tell him, huh?"

"Whoa, crazy." He grabs my hands and pulls me toward him. "I didn't tell him a thing. I was on my way over here because someone said that they'd seen a parrot flying in the park. I bumped into him, and he said he'd help me look to get in Nonna's good books. Just so happens that Bek threw up when we showed up."

"Of course, she did. Damn it. Okay, what did you find out about the parrot?"

"Not a lot," my husband admits. "I know he's been spotted here, but that's it."

"We saw him," I say, moving away from Bek's vomit bush. "He darted past us, and we chased him, but he's gone. I don't know where the hell we're supposed to go from here, and I'm starting to feel light-headed."

Drake pauses. "In other words, you've exhausted your internal sugar reserve, and I need to go and buy you a cupcake."

I grin. "Yes."

"You do realize that as long as we're running around getting you cupcakes, we won't find Gio?"

"Do you actually think we're going to find him? He'll probably return home soon enough. Don't they do that?"

"I think that's dogs," he says slowly. "Then again, I'm not sure I've ever heard of a parrot running away from home."

"That's because he was stolen," I remind him wryly. "There's a bird thief on the loose."

"Honestly, if he'd been stolen, all we'd have to do is sit at home and wait for the thief to return him." He pauses, lacing his fingers through mine. "I wouldn't even arrest them for it."

"You'd have to arrest them for bringing him back," I mutter. "So...where did we stand on the cupcake?"

FOUR

"It's been an hour and a half," I say, stopping in the middle of the street. "Are we seriously supposed to keep looking for Gio? The twins will be awake and—"

"I already texted your mom." Drake shoots me a glance.

"You did? When?"

"When you were frosting-deep in your cupcake. I knew they'd wake up soon, and as great as Nonna is, your mom will stop another Italian lesson from happening."

"I would pay to stop that happening." I sigh and looked around. "Seriously. Why are we doing this? We need to just go home and tell her that we couldn't find him. I have so much stuff to do for the twins' party, never mind the fact there's an actual stack of paperwork in my office I need to handle."

"And breathe." Drake chuckles, resting his hands on my upper arms. "Fifteen more minutes, and if we don't see him, that's exactly what we'll do, okay? Maybe we can print flyers and pin them up around town just in case he's flown in somewhere and gotten stuck."

I groan, but I don't have a choice. I know I need to do this for a little longer, if only because Nonna can't complain if we've put in two solid hours of searching.

But. Ugh. I'm getting tired, my feet hurt, and I really do have a ton of stuff to do. Motherhood and owning a business aren't conductive to leading a parrot hunt.

Drake grabs my wrist. "Don't move."

"Why? Did I step in dog shit?" I glance down at my feet.

"No. Gio. He's over there."

I jerk my head up and look in the direction he's pointing. Holy shit, he's right. Gio is sitting on a little round table outside the café like he owns it.

"Oh my God," I whisper. "How do we get him?"

Drake opens his mouth and stills. "Shit. We didn't think this through, did we?"

I shake my head. "But, he's right there. How do we get him back to Nonna?"

"Chase him?"

"And let him fly off? It's not like we can put a leash on him."

"Yeah, well, if we ever get the little fucker home, I'm going to make Nonna chain him to the damn cage," Drake mutters. "Hold on. Let me call your mom."

I sigh and lean against the wall while he takes a few steps away to call her. This is turning into the nightmare I knew it would be. Seriously—how do you catch a parrot? I'm not a birdkeeper. I have no idea what I'm doing.

"Well, that didn't help at all," Drake says, coming back. He grimaces at his phone. "She thinks we need to try to corner him and catch him."

"Oh, gee. We never thought of that." I slap my hand against my leg.

He snorts.

"This whole thing is so fucking stupid. It's not like he's going to fly to my finger and stay there."

"I don't know, Noelle. He does have that weird crush on you."

I glare at Drake. "Yes, but I deliberately shot him with a water gun last summer and now he doesn't like me quite as much."

Drake sighs. "I forgot about that. All right, what do we do? Maybe he'll come to me?"

"God, it's like herding cats," I whine.

"Except the cats have wings and swear in pirate."

"This couldn't get any worse."

"I'm going to try to get him. He likes me. I feed him." He shrugs and checks the road is clear before crossing it.

I take it back. I can already see this getting worse.

I cover my mouth with my hand and watch my husband approach Gio. His steps are slow and calculated, and he hunches over as he gets close to the table.

Gio turns his head and, with a squawk of, "Fuck no!" flaps his wings and flies off.

I move my hand up to cover my eyes and groan. Great. More running.

Drake is already chasing after him as I check the road. It's clear, so I cross it and run after him.

I swear. I'm going to have an entire pizza to myself tonight after all this running. And a bottle of wine. Drake can wake up in the middle of the night for the babies as punishment for roping me into this.

Within minutes, I'm wheezing, and I have the worst damn pain in my side. I am going to kill my husband and force my grandmother to cook for me every day for the next month.

Not to mention that I'm not designed to chase a parrot. I'm not a parrot. I don't have wings. I can't fly. This is the stupidest thing I've ever done, and I've done a lot of stupid things.

"Ohhhh," I moan, catching up with Drake. I grab his arm and lean into him, trying my best to catch my breath. I'm dying. I know it. I'm so dying. "Where did he go?"

"Over there." Drake points to a new store.

A pet store.

"Holly Woods has a pet store? Since when?"

He shrugs. "Not sure. Mom would probably know. But Gio flew over there and around the back."

I frown. "Why would he go there?"

"There's food there? I don't know, babe. But we have to go in and see what's going on."

"He's probably there for the food," I mutter, crossing the street once more. "How many trays of lasagna do you think I can get away with asking Nonna to make us?"

"At least one a week for the next year." Drake pushes open the door to the pet store. A tiny bell above our heads jingles, and we step into what is, quite literally, an animal wonderland.

Birds, hamsters, rabbits—you name it, and it's here. A massive caged area stands in the middle of the room, sectioned into four. Three hold rabbits and the fourth a slew of guinea pigs. Fish tanks line the wall to the left of us, filled with a whole selection of different kinds of fish.

Note to self: bring Antonio here.

"Can I help you?" A man with a deep Southern drawl appears from behind a high shelving unit.

"I sure hope so," Drake replies, holding out his hand. "Detective Drake Nash with the Holly Woods PD. This is my wife, Noelle. She owns Bond P.I."

The man shakes both our hands. "Calvin Royce. What can I do for you, Detective?"

"Please, call me Drake. I'm not here officially." He smiles. "You wouldn't happen to have seen a green parrot, would you?"

"Well, sure. Got two of 'em in the back." Calvin stuffs his hands in his pockets.

"Not yours," Drake says. "Noelle's grandmother is the dubiously proud owner of a green parrot with a potty mouth, and he's escaped."

Calvin tilts his head, smiling slightly. "Does this parrot speak like a pirate?"

"Yes!" I say a little too loud. "Have you seen him?"

"Sure have. He's out the back. Got here just before y'all did. Follow me." He nods toward the back, and we follow him. "It's the third time he's been here this week. Reckon he's taken a liking to my lady back here."

"The third time?" Drake questions.

"Sure. He was here two days ago, and again at the weekend." Calvin nods. "He flies in through this here back window, stays a while, then goes off. I wondered what he was doing, and I tried to get him in a cage, but he wouldn't let me."

"That sounds like Gio," I mutter.

"He's a lively one."

"He's something all right."

Calvin chuckles. "There he is, right next to my lady, Dora."

Dora? What kind of a name is that for a parrot?

"Gio!" I scold him. "What are you doing here?"

He squawks. "Filthy wench! Off with yer head!"

Well, that's new.

"Are we British royalty now, Gio?" Drake asks.

271

Calvin moves to shut the window, laughing quietly.

"King Gio!" Another squawk.

Why...Where the hell did he hear that?

"Come on. You're coming home. Nonna is going crazy."

He bristles, flapping his wings. He flies up and perches on a cage with Dora in.

Calvin grimaces. "I don't think he'll leave without her."

Drake looks at me.

I step back and shake my head. "No. No. Fuck no, absolutely not. She does not need another parrot!"

"But he loves her," Drake reasons.

"No. He's a parrot. They don't fall in love. Absolutely not, Drake."

Gio whistles, moving swiftly into an off-key rendition of what is, in all probability, a commercial tune. It's freaking miserable, and I cannot believe I'm standing in the back room of a pet store I never knew existed, arguing over whether or not Gio is in love.

The bell rings, and Calvin excuses himself to go back to the front of the store.

"Come on, Noelle." Drake positions himself in front of me. "We have Gio. It sounds like he's been sneaking out of the house—"

"Yeah, how exactly?"

"I don't know, but I'll be talking to Nonna about security," he says. "Still, it sounds like he's going to keep on coming back to see Dora."

"Which is a stupid name for a bird."

"Completely agree. I can't help but picture that stupid little cartoon explorer Less won't take her eyes off." He runs his hand through his hair. "It's Nonna's birthday in a month. It can be her early birthday present. Let's just buy Dora and take Gio home, okay?"

"No, it's not okay." I pout, crossing my arms. "But I don't suppose I have much of a choice."

"Good answer." He kisses my forehead and moves to the door.

"But when Mom freaks out about it, I'm blaming it on you entirely."

Drake sighs and pushes the door open. "I'll take it."

FIVE

"I'm going to kill you," Mom says, staring Drake in the eye. "Slowly, painfully, and thoroughly."

He looks at me. "That's where you get it from."

I pick up Alessia and shrug. "I warned you. I didn't want to bring one bird back, let alone two."

"I cannot believe you would do this to me," Mom goes on. "After all I've done for you. I was on your side when you were dating, and Noelle was being unreasonable—"

"Hey!" I reach down and stroke Antonio's head as he grabs at my leg. "I was not unreasonable!"

Drake shoots me a withering look.

"And all the other things in between, and you bring the crazy woman another goddamn parrot!" Mom finishes.

"Okay, in my defense—"

"You do not have a defense! This is indefensible!" Mom wiggles her finger at him. "In. De. Fen. Si. Bull!"

Drake takes a step back. "Point taken. I understand. I'm a terrible son-in-law. Expect flowers tomorrow."

I laugh, sitting on the sofa so Antonio can climb up onto me, too.

Mom crosses her arms. "I also accept wine and chocolate as bribes."

"Duly noted." Drake nods.

"Ah, she is-a perfect, no?" Nonna says, ambling into the living room, carrying both Gio and Dora's little cages. "No-a wonder he-a loves her. She is-a *bella*. They will-a make-a *bella* babies."

Mom's eyes widen into saucers. Total deer-in-headlights look.

Drake leans into her and whispers, "How does a day at the spa sound?"

Mom turns her head to him. "Make it two and I won't poison you at dinner on Friday."

"Done."

Drake props his head up on his hand and looks down at me. "Do you think Gio can still have babies? Isn't he old now?"

"I don't know. How long do parrots live?" I ask, adjusting the covers over me. "I guess that constitutes whether or not he's old."

"I don't know, and quite honestly, I've fucking had it with parrots. Not only did I manage to double them in the family, but it's costing me around three hundred bucks."

"I told you. You're paying the price of pissing off Mom. Even you should know better than that by now." I tap his nose.

"Whatever. It's made better knowing that I won."

"Won? What did you win?"

"Finding Gio."

I sit up and stare at him. "How did you win?"

"I saw him first. On the table outside the café. I found him. Therefore, I win." He grins smugly.

"Well, if you wanna use that logic, me and Bek found him first."

"But you didn't, did you, honey? You saw a green flash that may or may not have been Gio, and you couldn't find him once you saw him."

I roll my eyes. "Whatever. We didn't shake on it."

"Oh, but if you'd found him, you would have totally won."

"Well, yeah. I make the rules."

Drake sweeps one arm around me and pins me down to the bed. He leans over me, eyes piercing into me. "I won, and you just have to deal with it."

"I refuse to accept the result."

"How about I make it up to you?"

"And how do you think you're going to do that?"

He dips his head and kisses the side of my neck. "Like this." He kisses down my neck and over my collarbone. "And this..."

Down.

Down.

Down.

His mouth moves further down until his lips are ghosting over the curve of my breasts.

Okay. I can take this kind of making up.

I wind my fingers in his hair and pull him up, bringing his mouth to mine. He kisses me slowly, teasing me by tugging my bottom lip between his teeth. Shivers shoot down my spine, and—

Crying.

Drake drops his forehead on the pillow next to me with a heavy sigh, whereas all I can do is laugh.

"I'm on it," he groans. He gets out of bed and adjusts his boxers over his cock, and that only makes me laugh a little harder. "Don't laugh. I'll be back to finish that," he says, right as the sound of a second cry joining the first sounds. "Ah, shit."

I sigh and get up, too. "See? You just had to get cocky, didn't you?"

Pre-order FOUR DAY FLING now! An epically awkward romantic comedy coming July 24th. Visit www.emmahart.org/four-day-fling for all retailer links!

ABOUT THE AUTHOR

Emma Hart is the New York Times and USA Today bestselling author of over thirty novels and has been translated into several different languages.

She is a mother, wife, lover of wine, Pink Goddess, and valiant rescuer of wild baby hedgehogs.

Emma prides herself on her realistic, snarky smut, with comebacks that would make a PMS-ing teenage girl proud.

Yes, really. She's that sarcastic.

Website: http://www.emmahart.org
Facebook: http://www.facebook.com/emmahartbooks
Instagram: http://www.instagram.com/emmahartauthor

ALSO BY EMMA HART

COCKAMAMIE

STACI HART

Short story featuring Rin and Court from Piece of Work.

This is raw, original material written just for this anthology. Due to constraints and the immediacy of the timeline, this story has not been edited.

COCKAMAMIE

Rin

You *can do this. Just walk in there and be a boss bitch—don't let him scare you.*
I smoothed a hand down my pencil skirt, which, to the naked eye, might have looked like I was righting the material. In truth, my palms were a swampy, clammy nightmare. Must have been where the moisture in my mouth had gone—it was dry as the Sahara at high noon.

Drawing myself up with the aid of a fortifying breath, I stepped into Dr. Lyons' office and put on my best smile.

He looked up from his desk, and I was struck dumb and senseless for a moment, just as I had been every time I'd been in his presence since I'd started my internship at the museum last week.

My God, he was gorgeous. So gorgeous that I forgot just *how* gorgeous, and the shock of seeing him hit me like a lightning bolt whenever we shared air. The long, stunned moment would always be spent cataloging every line and angle of his body—the hard cut of his jaw, this chiseled bow and curve of his lips, always resting in a discerning line, the ridge of his dark brow over stormy, gray eyes, the shock of thick, dark hair casually tossed, as if he'd combed it first with a comb, then with his fingers. The thought of his big hand running through that dark mane was enough to send a shiver spiraling down my spine.

"Good morning, Rin," he said, breaking the silence.

I took the steps required to get me to the chair across from him, my mouth answering automatically. "Good morning, Dr. Lyons. What can I do for you today?"

His eyes flickered with something I couldn't place before it was gone. "We have a last minute addition to the exhibition—a pearl pendant from the Medici treasury. Add that piece to your research today."

I scrambled for my notebook in my bag. "Of course."

He watched me fumbling, and one side of his lips lifted slightly in what I'd come to learn was his version of a smile. "I emailed you the information on it."

My cheeks warmed just as my fingers closed over my notebook. "Thank you. I was wondering—"

"Morning, Court," a cheery, sensual voice said from behind me, and we looked to the sound to find Bianca, his assistant and the bane of my existence, standing in the doorway. Her smile slipped when she saw me, everything about her flattening with discontent. "Sorry, I didn't realize you were in a...*meeting.*"

I fought the urge to look away, curl into myself, try to disappear—which was a really, really difficult thing to achieve when you're six feet tall—and instead I kept a smile on my face and hoped I didn't look terrified.

All I'd wanted was to come into this internship and learn, to do well, to impress my superiors. I could land a permanent position at The Met if I worked hard, if I did a good job, earned their respect. Or so I thought. Neither of them had been impressed with me, although I thought I might be winning Dr. Lyons over. Bianca was hopeless—I had a better chance of winning the New York City Marathon, and I hadn't run since I'd donned matching yellow gym clothes under duress in high school.

Bianca eyed me for a split second before looking back to Court. "I'll swing back by later. I wanted to go over our itinerary for Florence."

I shifted in my seat, feigning interest in my notebook so I could sneak a glance at him—his expression was closed and unamused. "I'm working on my Medici publication, thanks to Rin's help. And thanks to you sparing her a little time to work on it."

"Oh, it's no problem," Bianca said, and I wondered if he caught the hint of aggravation in her voice.

Because it was no skin off her nose. Last week, she'd permanently banished me to the library to work on my dissertation, stripped me of all my responsibilities. Which was almost worse than being fired.

"Let's talk about it over lunch then," she insisted.

Somehow, he closed off even more. "Just email me what you need, Bianca. Thank you," he said, dismissing her.

By some miracle, she left the room. I was a little surprised she didn't pull up a chair so she could have a clear shot at exploding me with her eyes.

I jotted in my notebooks. "I'll make the pendant a priority today, Dr. Lyons. Is there anything else you'd like me to focus on for your publication?"

"No, thank you, Rin."

I nodded at my hands, smiling genuinely this time. "You're welcome."

"I mean it," he said, and something in his voice made me look up to meet his eyes, eyes so demanding, they held me still. "I've found your research...inspiring. I wouldn't have had the idea for the publication if it weren't for you. So keep it up."

My cheeks warmed again. "Thank you." I slipped my notebook back into my bag and stood, hoping I looked collected and cool at the compliment. And in my fluster, I didn't realize my heel was caught on the strap of my bag, which had somehow wrapped around the leg of the chair.

No, I didn't realize it at all, not until the office tilted, and I flew into the desk and practically into his lap with an unladylike *oof.*

He was close enough to smell—the clean, crisp scent of soap and spice—so close I could see the stitching on his lapels and feel his breath on my face. I was bent over his desk, ass out, frozen still and stupid as I looked up to meet his eyes. But his were down. And I realized too late that my cleavage was on display like a rack of meat.

His eyes flicked up to mine as he realized the same thing, and he stood, reaching for my arms to help me up.

My cheeks were so hot, if I'd cried like I probably could have in the moment, the tears would have sizzled.

"Oh my God," I mumbled, bringing myself to stand with his help. "I-I'm so sorry. I'm *so* clumsy—I shouldn't even be allowed in public."

He chuckled—a deep rumbling in his chest. "Are you all right?"

"Yes," I said, reaching for my bag, hiding behind my long, dark hair. "Yes, I'm fine. Let me know if you need anything else today." I hurried toward the door, not looking back. "See you this afternoon."

A pause. "Have a good day, Rin."

"Thank you," I said automatically for the hundredth time that morning and rushed out and toward the elevator that would take me to the library where I could properly hide.

It wasn't until I was settled in that my heart finally quit chugging like a freight train. And, once my pulse was back in a normal range, I opened my laptop and read through his email.

The newly acquired piece was a beautiful baroque pearl rooster, set in gold and gems, including a large ruby in his scabbard belt and diamonds in his tail feathers, and clutched in his claws was a bejeweled caduceus—a symbol of trade that shared with the medical field.

Finding out about the piece wasn't easy—there was precious little on the internet about it—but there were a few Medici books in the library I thought might have what I needed, so I wandered through the bookcases, finding them by memory.

I cracked open the books and got to work, skimming the indexes for clues. And within a few minutes I was lost in work, happily researching. It's weird, I know. Who has two thumbs and loves citations and bibliographies? This girl. And when I was digging in the indexes, my heart skipped when I saw *rooster*.

I flipped to the page and began to read, and the more I read, the harder it was not to laugh.

See, the Medicis were the most powerful family in Italy, and were largely regarded as the harbingers of the Renaissance through their investment in the arts, education, founded colleges, ran a very, *very* successful bank. The Medicis had this rival—the Pazzis— who were constantly trying to assassinate them, and succeeded a few times.

Now, Guiliano Medici was a renowned party hound who would throw a rager at the drop of a hat, so the Pazzis had someone suggest a party in a village, and Guiliano was, of course, down. The plan was this—wait until everyone was tanked, then sneak the assassins in to pull a Game of Thrones style Red Wedding on the Medicis.

Except to get to Guiliano, the assassins had to cross a yard of roosters. The birds went ballistic crowing and cawing, and everyone woke up at the ruckus, thus busting the assassins and leading them to the chopping block. Guiliano was so grateful, he had ceramic rooster wine pitchers made for everyone in the village as thanks, a symbol to bring them luck and protect them from danger.

Saved by the cock.

A laugh slipped out of me, imagining it as the title for an article. And my brain skipped away, writing cock citations, forming a parody piece that was too loud. So loud, I couldn't think about the *actual* work I needed to do. So, I typed it out in an effort to get it out of my head, snickering and smiling and all too amused with myself.

Medici's pearl-encrusted cock is well known for its stately, erect appearance. This cock is as brave as he is handsome—note the shine on the cock, the gleam on its tip, the way he holds his head up high and the stiffness of his neck. It's an Italian tradition to give cocks to friends and family—everyone loves a good cock, especially when wine is involved. Even today, people have cocks all around their homes as a ward against evil and for good luck. Because cocks are loud, proud, and cannot be ignored.

I paused for a small fit of giggling.

And so the cock became the symbol of the Medicis, a symbol of power. A symbol of good fortune. A symbol of strength and vitality. Guiliano Medici would tell you that cocks can save lives, if placed just right. The assassins were caught off guard by all those cocks, and it led to their deaths. So remember—respect the cock, or the cock will ruin you.

I swiped at an errant tear that had fallen in my hysteria and blew out a breath before typing up an email to my roommates, not wanting to be the only one to experience it in all its glory.

And with that done, I got to work on the *actual* piece I was supposed to be working on, interrupted intermittently by my phone with texts from my roommates.

Amelia: That cock is regal AF.
Val: Seriously, it deserves a crown. Or a medal. Or a pearl necklace.
Katherine: A cock would give a pearl necklace, not wear one.
Val: Killjoy.
Katherine: Cocks really do save lives though. They fill a void on farms. Who else would fertilize all those eggs?
Amelia: BWAHAHA
Val: And I mean, who doesn't want to get woken up by some cock?
Me: Some aggressive cock.
Katherine: Aggressive cock—sounds like a garage band.
Val: I would go see that show.
Katherine: Free gonorrhea with every ticket!
Amelia: Cock saves lives! I want that on a T-shirt.
Val: I'm on it.

And with imaginings of what Val would put on a T-shirt—because if I knew her at all, she absolutely would—I muted my phone so I could actually get some work done.

A few hours later, I'd actually written and cited enough information for Dr. Lyons, so I opened my email and popped off the message with the attachment, my mind already on my dissertation, which was the only thing I had left to do today.

Thirty seconds. Thirty seconds of blissful ignorance before my email pinged with a message from him.

I need to see you in my office in five minutes, Ms. Van de Meer.

Adrenaline zinged through me, my fingers instantly freezing as I looked down the email, realizing with absolute terror that I hadn't sent him my research.

I'd sent him Medici's cock.

Panic swept over me, and I picked up my phone with shaking hands.

Me: OH MY GOD I SENT IT TO MY BOSS BY ACCIDENT

Messages popped up like fireworks.

Amelia: NO.
Val: YOU ARE KIDDING. PLEASE SAY YOU'RE KIDDING.
Amelia: NO. NO, NO, NO.
Katherine: Okay, don't panic. Maybe he'll think it's funny.
Amelia: NOOOOOOO!!!
Val: Oh my God. OH MY GOD, RIN. Are you freaking out?
Me: Of course I'm fucking freaking out!! It's like I'm trying to get fired. Maybe the universe is trying to tell me something. This job has been on disaster after another since I walked through the door. I should just clean out my desk. I AM NOT MEANT FOR THIS WORLD.
Katherine: Send him the right file and be super ambiguous when you email him back.
Me: He wants me to come to his office. Like, RIGHT NOW.
Katherine: Fuck. Fuck!!
Amelia: What are you going to do?!

I swallowed so hard, my throat clicked, and resignation washed over me.

Me: I have to go up there. I have to face the music. Be home in an hour lol.

Val: Don't say that. It's gonna be okay, Rin. Just smile and try to make a joke out of it.

My face flattened.

Me: It's like you've never met me.

Val: Seriously. It was just a joke. He's not going to fire you.

Katherine: I mean, he might fire you but it's unlikely.

Val: UGH, KILLJOY.

Katherine: Seriously, he'll probably just dress you down, but he's not going to fire you for a joke.

I groaned. *Me: I have to go. He's expecting me.*

Val: Face the head of the cock. Look him in the eye. Show him who's boss.

Amelia: Please text us as soon as it's over. I can't handle this. I think I might have a heart attack.

Katherine: He's not going to fire you.

Katherine: But maybe send him the new piece, just in case.

I did, firing off a quick email that explained I'd sent the wrong thing with the *correct* attachment, checked three times, just to be sure. I shoved my phone and laptop into my bag, hurrying to straighten up the library as my mind fired a dozen scenarios like a horror reel. And a few minutes later, I was in the elevator, trying not to hyperventilate.

By the time I was walking up to his office, I thought my heart might actually be trying to hammer through my sternum. And when I stepped in, I found him sitting on the edge of his desk, dark and brooding, hard and sharp in an impeccable suit, his hand resting in his pocket as if he were relaxed.

He was most definitely *not* relaxed.

"Y-you wanted to see me?" I asked stupidly, unable to bear the silence.

"I thought you took this job seriously, Miss Van de Meer," he said with disappointment thick in his voice.

To my credit, I kept my spine straight and my eyes up. "I do, sir."

He reached for a paper on his desk and began to read. "*Medici's pearl-encrusted cock is well known for its stately, erect posture. This cock is as brave as he is handsome.* Should I go on?"

"Oh my God," I said under my breath, simultaneously mortified and turned on by the word cock from his lips. "Dr. Lyons, I am so sorry. I just…I read the story about the roosters saving Guiliano from assassins and I just…I couldn't stop laughing, so I wrote that as a joke but sent it to my friends—did you get my research? My real research?"

He nodded, frowning, his face tight. "This department, this job, is not a joke for you to make with your friends. This cockup cannot go unaddressed."

I watched him, trying to determine if he'd made a cock joke or if he was unaware.

Surely he couldn't be unaware.

Could he?

"Really, you should be cocksure when you compile your work," he continued, his face still as stony and still as it ever was, though I caught a gleam of laughter in his eyes. "This job is hard, *so* hard, and if you're not careful, you'll get cold-cocked by reality. It's a cockfight out there, Rin, and you've got to be prepared. And if you ever want to curate, you should *always* take your research seriously. Especially when it comes to cocks."

A small, shocked laugh burst out of me, and I said without thinking, "I wrote that cockamamie piece to make my friends laugh. We always laugh when faced with cocks. It's why none of us have boyfriends."

That broke him—his face bent into a smile that displayed the most gorgeous, toothpaste commercial teeth I'd ever seen in real life, and his laugh filled the room.

He shook his head, smiling down at the paper in his hand. "Man, it was so hard to keep a straight face, especially when you thought you were in trouble."

"Not gonna lie—I was scared to death. I thought you were going to fire me."

Something passed behind his eyes, something dark and hot and welcoming. "No, you're not getting fired, Rin. Not as long as I'm here."

I sighed my relief. "Well, good. I was all cockeyed about it."

A laugh. "We definitely don't want you *acock*. Do we?"

Yes, yes we do. Acock you, maybe.

Ugh, he's your boss, Rin! Get it together!

I was trying to come up with another cock reference when he said, "I went over your actual research. Once again, you've impressed me. And just when I think I can't be surprised, you prove me wrong. And I'm not often wrong."

He said it with a touch of wonder in his voice, almost overpowered by the command in his tone and inflection. But I heard it loud and clear.

"Thank you, sir," I said quietly. "If you didn't have anything else for me, I should get back to work."

This was a lie. All of a sudden, I didn't want to leave that office.

He watched me for a moment, and I got the sense he wanted to say something. But instead, he nodded, pushing off his desk. "Glad you're in the cockpit with me, Rin."

And I smiled. "Nowhere else I'd rather be."

ABOUT THE AUTHOR

Writer, music lover, art lover, gamer, graphic designer, mom, ex-waitress

———

Website: http://stacihartnovels.com
Facebook: https://www.facebook.com/stacihartnovels/
Instagram: https://www.instagram.com/quirkybird/
Bookbub: https://www.bookbub.com/authors/staci-hart

ALSO BY STACI HART

Piece of Work

Romantic Comedies

With A Twist

Chaser

Last Call

Wasted Words

Tonic

Bad Penny

Contemporary Romance

A Thousand Letters

Living Out Loud

A Little Too Late

COCKY COUTURE

A YOURS TO BARE DELETED SCENE

JESSICA HAWKINS

An equally sexy and cocky deleted scene from Yours to Bare, an Amazon Top 10 bestseller from Jessica Hawkins.

Editing by AW Editing

COCKY COUTURE: A YOURS TO BARE DELETED SCENE

Through my camera's lens, I watch my girlfriend stretch her arms up until her fingertips graze the top of the living room doorway. Halston's black lace teddy doesn't cover as much as I'd like it to, and her nipples are hard—they always are when my camera's aimed at her. Before I can mention it, she repositions her long, blonde hair, fanning it over her breasts to make sure she's fully covered.

She knows I'll never publish these otherwise.

"How's that?" Halston asks.

I check her over. I promised myself I'd be all business today, but that doesn't mean I'm not tempted to put the camera down and peel that thing off her, strap by strap. I don't really understand how a one-piece can be as sexy her next-to-nothing lingerie, but the way Halston wears it, my pants are getting tight.

I take her picture—the first of many we'll get for today's job—and check the screen to make sure I didn't capture her face or any identifying details. "Good."

"Just good?"

"Better than good, babe. You know that."

"No I don't," she says. "I can't see."

I glance up at her. She *doesn't* know. Every time I realize that, it surprises me all over again. We've only been together two months, but already, she's my sun. Somehow, she manages to forget now and then how she lights up my world.

"You look good enough to eat," I assure her. "And if we didn't have a job to do, I *would* eat you. Right now, in that doorway."

She blushes. I'm man enough to admit that since meeting Halston, the shade of pink that blooms over her cheeks has become my favorite color. I lift my camera and make sure to capture it for myself.

This Valentine's Day photo shoot is sponsored by Butter Boutique, a lingerie and wellness company. After agreeing to it, we found out that a portion of the profits from their current line, Cocky Couture, will benefit the prevention of cruelty against farm animals while also raising awareness—and cocks, apparently—around the nation. Per our arrangement, I'll post the best shots on our social media account with the purpose of driving our followers to Butter. I just hope anyone—male, female, or poultry—who sees that color warming the exposed skin of Halston's chest and neck understands it was the man behind the camera who made her feel that way. *Me. Her* proud cock.

"Finn?" she asks.

I look up. "Hmm?"

"If the pictures are so good, why aren't you taking more?"

Because I'm busy being in love with you, I want to say. It's still new, though. I only just confessed how deeply my feelings run for her. I don't want to spook her by saying it too often. "I'm just adjusting the settings," I say instead.

Once the leotard has been thoroughly photographed, Halston leaves to change into another outfit meant to titillate and tease a lover. I open a window and check the lighting. When she returns to the living room, I gesture to the sofa. "Lie down."

As she passes me, my eyes nearly pop out of my head. Her ass is on full display. "What the fuck is that?"

She looks back. "What?"

Even though I specifically gave Butter Boutique guidelines as to what we would and wouldn't photograph, they sent a thong. "It's too revealing."

"Then don't photograph the back," she says.

They'll know. People will look at my girlfriend and know there's a string up her ass. "No."

"But the photographs don't even show my face. The whole point of this is that I'm anonymous."

It's true. Some of our success online is thanks to the mystery around Halston's identity. The photos, artfully sensual, stand on their own, but our followers are also curious about her. I shake my head. "You promised, Hals. You agreed that if we did this promotion, I'd get to call the shots."

After a moment, she nods. I have to draw the line somewhere. Last month, when Butter Boutique reached out to us, my original answer to having my girlfriend pose half-nude in *cocky* lingerie had been a resounding *hell no*. But Halston had forced me to see this was a joint decision. It's her business too. It took some convincing to get me to agree, and the five-grand they offered us didn't hurt, but my one condition was that I'd have final say over the pictures.

As she passes on her way back to the bedroom, I take her upper arm. "Hey."

She looks up at me, her big, gray eyes open. Loving. "I understand," she says. "Don't worry."

I bend a little to kiss her but stop. If we start down that path, I won't be able to pull myself back. "I'm trying."

"I know you are." She rises onto the tips of her toes, angling her mouth toward mine, but I draw back. "What's wrong?" she asks.

"We have to keep this business until we're done, or I'll go and fuck everything up. Your hair, makeup, this . . ." I trail my finger along the waistband of her thong. "Put it aside for when the camera's off."

She arches an eyebrow at me. "So you *do* like it?"

"Can't you see that I'm hard right now?"

"Oh, yes. I can see that you're very *cocky*." Her eyes sparkle. "It's going to be hours before I can do anything about it, though."

"That'll only make it sweeter when we get there."

Halston changes into a red, Kimono-style silk robe. Still sexy but not as revealing. I've photographed her fully dressed and made her impossible to resist, so I'm not worried it's too modest. She nails the fantasy. Butter Boutique recognizes that.

Halston wears rooster-red lipstick to match the robe. Paired with her blonde hair, she's a verified seductress. My instincts war inside me, even with poultry on the brain. My heart races seeing her this way. One of the reasons I love her is her ability to strip herself bare for me. To open up and show me—and the camera—her wants and needs, her insecurities and vulnerabilities. I want to claim her, remind her she's mine. At the same time, the purpose of this photo shoot is to share her with others. To post the pictures, advertise Butter Boutique, and get publicity for our account and the cause. Halston has been so focused on building our following lately. The more followers we get, the more she wants. It makes her happy.

She pulls the sleek collar of the robe up around her neck, and I take the photo, making sure to get only her red lips and blonde hair in the frame. Next, she turns around and looks back over her shoulder at me. I brush strands of hair from her face, but they fall back against the corner of her mouth. This close, you can see the faint, butterfly-and-blossom print of the robe. It's perfect. Butter will love the shot. Everyone else will love Halston.

We work all afternoon. She models ruffled bra and panty sets, a dusty rose-colored babydoll dress, a nude negligee that ghosts over her nipples. If I squint, she looks naked in that one, so I try not to squint. In editing, I'll make sure she's covered.

Over a hundred photos later, the winter sun hides behind the New York City skyline. "That was nine outfits, right?" I ask, eager to finish. My hard-on's getting painful. "There's one more?"

"I saved it for last," she says. "It might take me a few minutes to change."

"Need some help getting into it?"

One corner of her mouth lifts. "Better if you stay here. Otherwise, we'll never get around to finishing the shoot."

Considering she's just paraded around like a waking wet dream, I can't imagine this getting better. Truthfully, I'm not sure I can handle anything more. If I hadn't committed to photographing ten different outfits, I'd call it a day. I need to be inside her. "Just make it quick."

I go into the kitchen to make us each a drink because I'm happy this is almost over, and five thousand dollars is definitely worth a toast. Halston gets looser when she's buzzed, but I don't want her drunk. We've both been frustrated for hours, and I anticipate a long night of de-frustrating ahead.

I get two tumblers and a bottle of bourbon from a cabinet and set them on the counter next to Halston's journals. *Journals*—plural. I still can't believe there's more of the sexy poetry I found months ago in a coffee shop. Page by page, I'd gorged on her before I'd even met her. I'd drunk her in, made myself sick on her. And then she'd revealed there were other journals.

Can I handle more? After fate had given me just a taste of Halston, I'd done everything in my power to find her. I love that journal—it led me to right to her. I want more of it. I also recognize the sometimes dangerous power her words have over me.

I don't want to torture myself any more tonight, but temptation gets the better of me, and I pick up the journal Hals called "dark." With her approval, I've read parts of it, but only when she isn't around because she's self-conscious about it. I was interrupted mid-passage last night when she came home from work, so now, I open to that same page. She describes the cinch of a silk tie around her wrists. Being fastened to a bed, made helpless. How the cold hardens her nipples, but she has no way of covering herself. All that turns me on. Hals and I have experimented with tying her up, but we never get very far before we give in and fuck. But it's the next part of her entry that nearly has me coming in my pants.

Spread out
I lie still as death
While you move just the ends of me,
Post to post.
Helplessly bared
My ankles in your possession,
You unfold me—

"Finn?" Halston calls from the other room.

I put the journal down—interrupted again and hard as fuck. The image of her ankles spread on the bed is fresh in my mind as I pick up our drinks. *Mine.* Completely mine to do with what I want.

I walk through the doorway, and Halston's standing tall in high heels by the couch. A pink satin corset with little black bows flattens out her tummy and boosts her tits nearly up to her chin. The ends of her blonde, curled hair quiver with each breath, brushing the neckline. As if that weren't sexy enough, the outfit comes with matching garters and thigh-highs.

She glances at the drinks and starts across the room. "Is that for me?"

"Stop."

"What?" She freezes, then smiles shyly when she notices my hungry expression. "You like it?"

This is no time to play coy. I can practically feel my erection tearing through the fabric of my jeans. "Let's do this one in the bedroom."

"I thought our bed was off limits?"

It'd been another one of my stipulations for agreeing to this. Our bed was too personal to shoot images for money. Now, though, I can't think of a better place for this one. "Bedroom," I order. *"Now."*

She turns and struts down the hallway, her half-covered ass cheeks bobbing with each step. I follow with the drinks and my camera. Sadly, my bedframe lacks posts, so there's nothing to which I can tie her. I obviously wasn't thinking ahead when I bought it.

I hand Halston her drink. She sniffs it as I step into her, sipping my own bourbon. I tuck some of her hair behind her ear and kiss her forehead, her cheek. "How do you want it?" I asked. "Soft? Hard? Want to be made love to tonight, or something else?"

"I want whatever you want," she breathes.

"That wasn't what I asked. Tell me now, because I'll be completely lost in you soon. Too lost to make coherent decisions. I want to make you happy."

She flattens her hand on my chest and tilts her head back to look up at me. "I don't have to tell you how I like it best. You always seem to know."

I drop a gentle, light kiss on her lips. "Sit. Take your drink with you."

She backs up and perches on the edge of the bed. Without instruction, she holds the glass of amber liquid between her legs. I take a picture. She dips her finger in the alcohol and draws a wet heart on the curve of her breast. *Snap*. She lies down, arching her breasts toward the ceiling, and I capture the curved space between her lower back and the white comforter.

"I want to see you," I say from the foot of the bed.

Something flashes through her eyes. Fear? Anticipation? She knows I'd never photograph her this way for anyone other than myself . . . doesn't she? She unclips her stockings, removes them with the garters, then lifts her hips off the bed to strip her underwear off. I graze my thumb over the arch of her foot and take her panties, tossing them aside before I set my camera on the armoire behind me.

She watches my every move, her chest rising and falling faster. I lift her bare ankle to my mouth to kiss her skin where it's thinnest. Stepping sideways, I place her foot at one corner of the bed then do the same with her other one. She's spread out, her warm, pink pussy open to me.

"What are you going to do to me?" she asks breathlessly.

"Arms above your head." She raises them. I move each of her hands to the top edge of the mattress. "Hold on to that. Don't move. At all. Even if it feels impossible."

"Impossible?"

I admire the long, white line of her inner forearms, tracing a fingertip down to her face as goose bumps light up her skin. I lift her chin, thumbing the bow of her plump lips. She quivers but doesn't move. I trail my fingers down her neck to the tops of her breasts. I'd bet all our earnings her nipples are hard as pebbles under that bustier. I'm tempted to open it, to free her tits for my hands and mouth, but I'm turned on enough as it is.

Halston manages to keep still until I caress the sliver of skin between the bottom of the corset and her mound. She bucks her hips and I press down on them, stilling her. She follows me with her eyes. Once her body is quiet again, I reach between her legs. I keep my eyes on hers as I slip one finger between her folds.

Her face crumbles. "Please," she begs, even though I've barely touched her.

"You won't move, will you?"

She starts to shake her head but stops. "No."

I push the sleeve of my sweater up to my forearm and run my fingers around her clit a few times. She looks pained as she tries not to move. I explore her warmth, but my own patience is thin. Once she's wet enough, I slide two fingers into her, appreciating the way she groans.

"Will you come this way for me, Hals?"

"Yes." She sighs. "Yes, Finn. Please."

I pump my fingers in and out of her, getting even more turned on by the fact that I'm fully dressed while she's naked from the waist down and at my mercy. All I can see from my vantage point is her face and my hand cupped between her legs, my fingers disappearing inside her. I make her climax like that so she'll be nice and loose for me to fuck.

After coming on my hand, she calms as I stroke her thigh. She blinks at me a few times. "May I move now?"

"Depends where you want to go."

Hesitantly, she removes a hand from above her head, sits up, and reaches for the fly of my pants. Our eyes lock as she pops the button open. My hand is still on her leg, and when she takes me out, I inadvertently squeeze her thigh. My cock is thick and heavy in her hand, nearly purple with the need for release. Halston's slender fingers feather up and down my shaft. She traces her nail along the rim of my head.

"If you keep that up, I'm going to come all over that precious corset of yours."

She grins at me. "Good thing we don't have to return it."

Seeing her smile, her good humor, I just want to be close to her. I take her hand off me and kiss her palm. Eye level with my cock, she puts her mouth around me without prompting. It isn't what I had in mind, but I thread my hand into the hair at the back of her head and growl up at the ceiling. She's more confident than she was the first time she blew me, more in tune with how I like it. Which, to be honest, is however she gives it. Slow, fast, deep, shallow. I resist fucking her mouth because I know I'll come sooner than I want to. I reach over to the nightstand and get a condom. "Put this on me, babe."

She pulls back, panting a little, and opens the packet without questioning me. As much as I want to feel her skin to skin, to fuck her raw and trust the birth control, I can't. She knows I won't. I made that mistake before with my ex and paid the price.

I still have one hand in Halston's hair, unwilling to let her go as she rolls on the condom. "I wonder if Butter Boutique knew this is where we'd end up."

"Anything to benefit the barnyard," she says.

"*Cock-a-doodle-doo*," I agree, and then promptly lose my train of thought as she pushes my jeans down around my ankles. I step out of them as Halston stands and wraps her arms around my neck. "What do you want?" I ask.

"Lift me." I pick her up and she wraps her legs around me. She nuzzles her nose against my neck. "Now sit."

I do as I'm told and turn with her in my arms to sit on the edge of the bed. Halston pulls herself closer to me, lifting up. I catch on quickly, lining up my cock for her. She sinks down, gasping for breath. Like every time, I fill her fully, completely, but especially in this position. If it takes her time to adjust, I don't know it, because she seats herself all the way down until I'm buried in her.

I grab her hips and rock her against me, forward and backward, as she keeps a firm hold around my neck. With her head tossed back, her soft, blonde hair, cascades around her. "You're so beautiful," I tell her. "And you're all mine . . . my pink Valentine."

I kiss her, opening her up. Our tongues meet, wet and eager. She's warm

302

everywhere—her pussy yielding to me like the inside of her mouth did. Her gyrations become less controlled, more fervent. I bring her down onto me harder and harder. I won't last much longer. I dip her backward to deepen the angle and to give my mouth access to the swell of her tits. Consuming each other, consumed *by* each other, we fuck. Her fingers dig into my hair and pull. I suck her neck. I manage to keep my orgasm at bay until she writhes, her cries growing louder and less breathy. Once I feel her pussy clamping around me, pulling me deeper, I lie back on the bed and bounce her up and down my cock until I can't hold back another second. I squeeze her waist and erupt for what feels like minutes. Even after I've finished, I pump my hips a few times, bobbing her forward so she has to flatten her hands on my chest to keep herself upright.

I slide my hands from her waist up to her shoulders, hugging her to bring her close. She folds in against my chest. This is just one of the many ways I love to have her—exhausted by me, vulnerable, quivering, close to my heart.

I can't believe how big my love feels after relatively little time with her.

"Halston?" I ask after a while.

She must've fallen asleep, because she starts. She shifts just her head to look up at me. Her gray eyes are closer to blue tonight, sated and sleepy. "Hmm?"

"Will you be mine?"

"I already am."

"I mean for Valentine's Day."

She wrinkles her nose up at me. "Don't you know? I'm yours every day of the year. The date doesn't matter."

I smooth her hair from her forehead. Of course I know, because when a cocky bastard like myself catches a break from fate, he makes sure to appreciate it.

I know something good when I see it.

And Halston might be the best *something* to ever happen to me.

Read Finn and Halston's complete story in *Yours to Bare* by Jessica Hawkins. Also available as an audiobook narrated by Sebastian York and Andi Arndt.

ABOUT THE AUTHOR

Jessica Hawkins is a *USA TODAY* bestselling author known for her "emotionally gripping" and "off-the-charts hot" romance. Dubbed "queen of angst" by both peers and readers for her smart and provocative work, she's garnered a cult-like following of fans who love to be torn apart...and put back together.

She writes romance both at home in New York City and around the world, a coffee shop traveler who bounces from café to café with just a laptop, headphones, and coffee cup. She loves to keep in close touch with her readers, mostly via Facebook, Instagram, and her mailing list.

Facebook: http://www.facebook.com/groups/jessicahawkins
Instagram: http://www.instagram.com/jessica_hawkins
Mailing List: http://www.jessicahawkins.net/mailing-list

ALSO BY JESSICA HAWKINS

SOMETHING IN THE WAY SERIES
Something in the Way is an epic saga of forbidden love and a USA TODAY bestselling series.

It was a hot summer day when I met him on the construction site next to my parents' house. Under the sweat and dirt, Manning Sutter was as handsome as the sun was bright. He was older, darker, experienced. I wore a smiley-face t-shirt and had never even been kissed. Yet we saw something in each other that would link us in ways that couldn't be broken...no matter how hard we tried.

I loved Manning before I knew the meaning of the word. I was too young, he said. I would wait. Through all the carefully chosen words hiding what we knew to be true, his struggle to keep me innocent, and infinitely starry nights—I would wait. But I'd learn that no matter what you achieve in life, it means nothing if you suffer the heartbreak that comes with falling for someone you can never have. Because even though I saw Manning first, that didn't matter. My older sister saw him next.

Available on all retailers, including Audible.

EXPLICITLY YOURS SERIES
"*Pretty Woman* meets *Indecent Proposal* in *Explicitly Yours,* a seductive series that'll leave your heart racing."—Louise Bay, *USA Today* Bestselling Author

Lola Winters doesn't think she can escape her life as a waitress— until she receives a shocking proposition from a sexy stranger. Wealthy businessman Beau Olivier wants Lola for a night, and in order to get her, he's willing to make her dreams come true.

But what if one night isn't enough, and Beau isn't ready to say goodbye in the morning?

Available on all retailers and coming to audio this summer.

SLIP OF THE TONGUE SERIES
Slip of the Tongue (#1)´

"Addictive. Painful. Captivating. Tumultuous. Juicy. Sexy. *Slip of the Tongue* is an authentic, raw, and emotionally gripping must read that I just loved. A highly recommended favorite of mine."—Angie's Dreamy Reads

Her husband doesn't want her anymore. The man next door would give up everything to have her.
Sadie Hunt isn't perfect—but her husband is. Until Sadie finds herself in the last place she ever expected to be: lonely in her marriage. When rugged and sexy Finn Cohen moves into the apartment across the hall, he and Sadie share an immediate spark. And while Sadie's marriage runs colder by the day, she and Finn burn hotter.

Slip of the Tongue is a **forbidden romance** that can be read as a standalone or as book 1 in the *Slip of the Tongue* series.

THE FIRST TASTE (#2)
"*The First Taste* is a delicious read that will have you craving seconds. I promise!"—Kim Karr, *New York Times* Bestselling Author

Andrew Beckwith has already devoted his life to one girl—his daughter, Bell. As far as he's concerned, she's all he needs. Amelia Van Ecken is an independent, smart, and savvy businesswoman who doesn't have time for sex, much less love. Andrew and Amelia are complete opposites, but on one thing they agree—relationships are overrated. But that doesn't mean they can't be rated X. Because when sharp-tongued Amelia and stubborn Andrew cross paths, sparks fly—and burn.

The First Taste is a **sexy, single dad romance** that can be read as a standalone or as book two of the *Slip of the Tongue* series.

YOURS TO BARE (#3)
"Sensual, evocative, and spellbinding."—K.L. Kreig, *USA Today* Bestselling Author
Halston Fox's journal is the one place she can be herself—as long as she can tie it up and put it away when she's finished. But when a stranger in a coffee shop undoes the bow, he pulls strings that could unravel both of them.
Yours to Bare is an **artist-muse story** can be read as a standalone or as book 3 in the *Slip of the Tongue* series.

CULINARY COCK-UP

A COCKY COLLECTIVE SHORT

JULIE JOHNSON

When two cocky chefs at rival New York City restaurants clash over a famous chicken dish, sparks fly and sexual tension simmers. Can their relationship take the heat? Or will they go down in flames?

❦

CULINARY COCK-UP

Ask any tourist on the street about the busiest spot in New York City, they'll tell you the same thing: *Times Square*. They're wrong, though. Anyone who actually lives in this cockamamie city knows there's no place more chaotic or crowded than the chef's kitchen at a five-star restaurant in Midtown Manhattan on a Friday night.

Especially if I, Emmeline Pryce, am the one in command.

"Izzie, I said *mince* the garlic, not crush it," I yell to the girl working the veggie-station, rolling my eyes as I move down the line. "And you'll need to redo those tomatoes entirely. By *coarse chop* I was not referring to whatever you've allowed your hairstylist to do to your bangs."

"Yes, Chef. Sorry."

The knife in her hands trembles as her tempo increases, resulting in a mess of lopsided garlic chunks. It takes every bit of my self control to resist the urge to go over there and do the task myself. But that would only reinforce the reputation I've built for being, quote-unquote, *intolerable to work for* and, on the rare occasion, *making the employees cry in the broom closet halfway through their first shift*.

Spare me.

It's called a French Brigade kitchen for a reason.

Male chefs frequently get away with being tyrants — I'm looking at you, Shmordon Shmamsey— and no one makes a peep about it. Meanwhile, we females are expected to coddle and comfort our way to the top, soothing our staff into basic competence instead of scolding them for lacking it entirely. Thankfully, expectations matter about as much to me as the nutritional merits of a Taco Bell burrito.

I don't care about the words coming *out* of people's mouths; I'm far more concerned with the taste of the food they put *into* them when they visit my restaurant.

Don't give me that aghast look.

I challenge you to find a single head chef on the planet who *isn't* a total control freak — at least, when it comes to the operation of their kitchen. Cockiness is part of the job. And I'm not talking about my frequent handling of raw poultry.

"Next on deck?" I call to the new guy running the pass, impatience creeping into my tone as I watch him flip through incoming order tickets. He's greener than the parsley that garnishes my critically-acclaimed duck confit.

"Um, we—" He looks up at me, cheeks stained red, and swallows hard. "We—"

"*We* don't have all day." My eyes narrow. "Spit it out or start sending applications to restaurants where it's acceptable to serve food forty minutes after the order comes in."

"Yes, ma'am."

My brows lift all the way to the edge of my tall white hat. "Did you just call me *ma'am?*"

"Yes, Chef. I mean, *no*, Chef. Never again, Chef."

His babbles taper off as I stalk over and grab the stack of orders from his grasp. "I'll handle the tickets. You—" I eye him speculatively. He's in his mid-twenties, only a year or so younger than me, but he looks like he's never stepped foot in a kitchen before this moment. "Go garnish the plates. Help Izzie with the veggies, if you can stop shaking long enough to hold a knife. Perhaps between the two of you, someone will manage to correctly chop a clove of garlic."

"Thank you, Chef. I appreciate the opportunity, Chef. I won't let you down, Chef. I—"

"Enough." I hold up a hand. "Flattery will get you nowhere, nor will sucking up. Hard work, however, may convince me to keep you on my staff. So, *go*. Show me you can take the heat. Otherwise…"

Get out of my kitchen.

He scurries away as my eyes drop to scan through the tickets. I rattle off a series of sharp commands — meat ragout, ratatouille, bouillabaisse, steak tartare — and everyone jolts into motion.

For the next few hours, my world is a whirl of carefully controlled chaos. Every burner on my custom gas range is occupied, spitting fire like a demon through the wrought-iron gates of hell as we simmer, season, and stir raw ingredients into culinary perfection. Plates vanish like clockwork off the pass, servers rushing back and forth as tables turn over and the night wanes on. All eight members of my kitchen staff, from the salad prepper to the sauté chef, somehow manage to maintain the breakneck pace — even the new guy, whose name I haven't yet bothered to learn. (There's little point; he'll probably quit before his second shift rolls around.)

I'm everywhere at once, a five-foot-three blur in a starched white chef's jacket, moving too fast for camera frames to catch me in focus: my hands in every dish, my tongue unleashing a razor-sharp torrent of critique.

Steve, this marinade tastes like your personality: utterly flavorless.

Izzie, for god's sake, it's a paring knife, not a machete.

Kevin, you're a saint, keep doing exactly what you're doing.

Cooking is art. A dance, perfectly choreographed. There's a rhythm to each sweep of my spatula, a cadence to each dip of my ladle. I lose myself in the music of every dish, reveling in the freedom I only ever feel when I'm totally in control of all variables.

I'm checking the progress of the mussels steaming in a massive pot on the front burner when a throat clears at my back. I turn to find a blonde server standing there, shifting nervously from foot to foot. My eyes scan from her squeamish expression down to the plate gripped in her white-knuckled fingers. A portion of my world-famous *coq au vin* — tender chicken braised in a white wine sauce with provincial mushrooms —sits untouched at the center.

"What are you doing here?" I ask, frowning.

"The gentleman who ordered this..." She looks down, as if she's afraid to hold my stare. "He sent it back."

There's a collective intake of air from everyone in the kitchen.

No one — *no one* — sends back my *coq au vin*. It simply does not happen.

"Did he say why?" I ask, feeling my pulse kick up a notch.

She squirms again.

"Tell me."

Her eyes flash to mine, full of apprehension. "He said it was bland and..."

"And?"

"Unimaginative," she murmurs with a grimace. Her voice is no louder than a whisper, but it rings through the kitchen like a gunshot.

My coq — my award-winning coq — unimaginative?!

Impossible.

I shove my ego down as deep as I can manage, trying not to let the anger creep into my voice or onto my face. Everyone seems to hold their breath as I step forward and remove the plate from the server's hands.

"I see," I say carefully, trying to slow my racing pulse. "Please tell the gentleman in question I will endeavor to put more *imagination* into my next attempt."

And I do.

I braise and season with meticulous precision. I take painstaking care with every step, going so far as to chop the damn carrots myself. When I finally pull the cast iron skillet from the oven, fragrant and still bubbling, a contented smile crosses my face as I examine the utter perfection that is my *coq*.

"If he doesn't like this, there's something seriously wrong with his taste buds," I tell the server as I pass the warm dish into her trembling hands.

She nods and disappears into the ornate dining room.

Crisis averted, I return my attention to more important matters — micromanaging my staff until they meet the exacting standards I demand. The night is winding down, less than an hour left before closing time, but our pace only seems to pick up speed as a steady stream of patrons filter through the front doors. They are faceless strangers, distinguishable only by the orders they place.

Foie gras with poached pears.

Escargot with garlic-butter.

Gratin dauphinois with crème fraiche and gruyere.

I am a constant flurry of motion, a ceaseless storm of activity... until the sound of a familiar feminine throat clearing brings me to a standstill.

"Um. Chef Pryce?"

My jaw locks. My hand clenches around my whisk.

No.

Not again.

Passing off the roux to my sous chef, I turn stiffly to face the server. She's hovering there with another goddamned dish in her hands. My dish. My perfect dish. The *coq au vin* looks totally undisturbed, as though he — whoever the hell *he* is — couldn't be bothered to try more than the smallest of bites before sending it back.

For the second time.

I swallow down a scream.

"I'm sorry." The waitress winces. "He told me to return this one as well."

"What is it this time?" I practically growl, striding forward and snatching the plate away. "Let me guess — *too* imaginative?"

Her lips press into a line. She looks like she might cry.

"Just tell me," I prompt impatiently.

"He said..."

My brows arch.

She swallows hard. "He said he's tasted better chicken at KFC."

Izzie's gasp is audible from across the kitchen. Kevin drops the whisk to the floor with a clatter. Even the new guy, who knows me only by reputation, seems stunned by this grave revelation.

"He said *what?*" I hiss.

"That he's tasted better—"

"I heard you the first time!" I set the plate down on a stainless prep table with a bang. "Who the hell *is* this guy?"

"Just a normal guy, as far as I can tell. Sandy hair. Blue eyes. Expensive suit. Sort of familiar looking, but I can't quite place him. And he's dining alone, which is a little weird... but otherwise he seems super nice." Her cheeks flush. "I mean, besides him sending back the dish."

"*Twice,*" I mutter.

"Right. Twice." She blows out a breath. "What do you want me to tell him, Chef?"

Tell him to go stuff himself.

My teeth grit to contain the less-than-prudent words. "Give me fifteen minutes. I'm going to remake the damn dish. *Again.* And by the time I'm done, come hell or high water, it's going to be the best damn *coq* he's ever put in his mouth."

A strangled sound of amusement comes from Kevin's direction.

I turn my gaze to him. "What was that?"

"Nothing, Chef." His lips are twitching. "I wouldn't dare laugh about your *coq.*"

Rolling my eyes, I turn away and get to work.

I have a job to do.

Namely: making Mr. KFC eat his words along with every godforsaken bite I serve him.

Thirty minutes later, we're putting finishing touches on the last round of orders before closing. I'm smiling as I call out commands, finally feeling like myself again. That rattled sensation I experienced earlier has all but faded... until it happens.

A door, swinging.

A throat, clearing.

A server, shifting.

The very world stops turning beneath my feet as I spin around to meet her apologetic stare. I don't even bother looking down at the plate in her hands. I already know what I'll see there: an untouched helping of my most-beloved recipe. The same recipe I slaved over for years in culinary school. The one I perfected in every spare moment I had, while working my way up the hierarchy of kitchen after kitchen as my twenties slipped away. The one that finally landed me this coveted position at Mistral at age twenty-eight, the youngest head chef in the city — at least, at any restaurant that merits a visit.

My coq au vin.

The French may've done it first, but I do it better.

It's my *brand.*

My signature.

I should trademark the damn recipe — it's that good.

I'm that good.

And yet...

The server looks like she would rather be anywhere on the planet except standing in front of me. I recognize her expression easily — it's the same one my last three dates have worn when they dropped me off on my front doorstep without so much as a kiss goodbye or a promise to call.

That's what happens when you spend the entire evening critiquing the meal instead of making conversation, Emmeline.

I hold my breath until she speaks.

"He said—"

"You know what?" I cut her off. "Invite Mr. KFC back here. Let him tell me himself."

She blinks slowly, stunned by the proposition. In the year I've spent running this kitchen, I've never once invited a patron into my domain.

A general doesn't allow civilians into a war-zone.

Then again, I've *also* never had anyone send back an exquisite dish *three times* in a single night.

Desperate times, desperate measures.

He's in no rush, that much is clear. He makes me wait nearly twenty minutes before he deigns to appear. My pulse pounds a bit faster with each passing moment. I try to focus on my orderly checklist of closing tasks, but my mind whirls in a maelstrom of untempered indignation and wounded pride.

Bland.

Unimaginative.

KFC.

By the time the kitchen doors finally swing wide, announcing his presence, the burners are off, the ovens are cooling, and my staff has switched modes from *stir-simmer-serve* to *scrub-scour-sanitize*. Bracing myself, I set down my inventory clipboard and turn to meet the arrogant ass who's made my night a living hell...

And promptly suck in a sharp breath.

Cock-a-doodle-do-not-lose-your-shit-Emmeline.

I'm not sure what I was expecting. Someone significantly older, maybe. Someone significantly less attractive, *definitely*. The man standing there is a certified stunner with a crop of thick blond hair and a set of piercing blue eyes. His tailored suit drapes his chiseled frame like it was made for him.

Normally, just the sight of a man like this would be enough to make my mouth water. Normally, seeing such a fine specimen of manhood, when it's been eighteen months, two weeks, six days, and five hours — give or take a few minutes — since I last had sex with someone other than myself, would be enough to make me strip out of my chef's jacket and hurl myself at him like a heat-seeking missile.

Normally.

But not tonight. Because, in addition to the fact that I hate this man on principle for insulting my cooking... I already hate him for an entirely different set of reasons. Namely, because I *know* him. I've known him for ten years, since I was no more than an eighteen-year-old kid enrolled in her first-ever cooking class, who thought *bouillabaisse* was something you might find in The Kama Sutra, not the Joy of Cooking.

Emmett Fox.

Former culinary school nemesis at Le Cordon Bleu, current rival executive chef at La Folie — our biggest competitor in the city. I haven't seen or spoken to him for eight years, but as soon as our eyes lock, I feel a long-simmering rage begin to bubble to the surface.

"Emmeline," he purrs, lush lips twisting into a smirk. "It's been too long."

"*You.*" I nearly spit out the word. "I should've known."

"Oh, come on. Is that any way to greet an old friend?"

My scowl intensifies. "We aren't friends."

"You're right, Ems. Back in school, you were always far too focused to make time for friendship." His eyes gleam with amusement. "Guess some things never change."

"Don't pretend you know me," I snap. "And *don't* call me Ems."

"Touchy, touchy."

"You are aware there are several lethally sharp blades within my reach? Test me at your own peril, Fox."

He grins as if he finds my rage utterly adorable. "Aren't you even a little glad to see me?"

"*No.*"

"So bitter." He pauses. "Rather like your homemade tomato sauce, if memory serves."

A squawk of anger flies from my mouth. "My sauce is not bitter!"

"If you'd loosen up those apron strings a bit, it might help — with your demeanor, not the sauce." He waggles his brows. "A pinch of sugar should do, for that."

"Forgive me if I don't take cooking advice from a guy whose ass I whipped all the way through culinary school."

He snorts. "If that's how you need to remember it, it's your choice. And by *choice* I mean delusion."

"I see your ego hasn't diminished since the last time I saw you."

"And I see your insane need to win every argument is as intact as ever," he volleys back. "Tell me, Ems, did you ever wonder what things might've been like between us, if you'd set aside your competitive drive for one damn minute? Whether it might've been... different?"

"Hmmm." I pretend to think about it for a second. "*Nope.* I was too busy beating you."

He shakes his head, grinning. "Amazing."

My brows arch in question.

"So much piss and vinegar in such a petite little package."

"Get out of my kitchen, Fox."

"You invited me."

I scoff. "Consider your invitation rescinded!"

He doesn't move a single muscle. He just stands there, that infuriating smirk still twisting his lips, cockier than the chicken dish he so rudely rejected. *Thrice.* His muscular arms are crossed casually over his chest in a way that tells me he's not the least bit apologetic for his actions tonight. If anything, he's rather pleased with himself.

I wish that smug self-confidence was enough to mitigate the effects of his chiseled features on every woman in the room. Izzie is shamelessly stealing glances at him as she wipes down her station. Mary is restocking the fridge a bit too slowly, eavesdropping on our every word. Even Tina, who I know for a fact is happily married with four children, looks like she's about to start drooling on the freshly-washed dishes.

I heave a deep sigh. "Seriously, what are you doing here, Fox? Besides driving me to drink?"

"Call it... competitive curiosity." His mouth curls in a smile as his eyes sweep around the kitchen. "I couldn't resist a chance to check out the infamous dragon's lair."

Dragon?!

I clench my teeth so hard I worry I'll snap a crown.

Emmett catches Izzie's eyes across the kitchen and winks at her. "Tell me, is it true she breathes fire when you displease her?"

Izzie ducks her head to hide a smile but — wisely — chooses not to respond.

"And the true mystery..." His gaze swings back to mine then slides down my frame, taking in my every detail. "How do you fit those scaly wings under such a tight uniform?"

"More insults." My eyes roll. "How very predictable."

"I don't recall insulting you."

I narrow my eyes at him. "*Fire-breathing dragon.*"

"That was a compliment." He laughs and his whole stupidly handsome face lights up in the process. "Mostly."

Izzie's shoulders shake in silent amusement.

Kevin thinly veils a chortle with a coughing fit.

My scowl returns. "Go away, Fox. It's been a long night, and I don't have the energy to play this little game with you."

"I wasn't aware we were playing a game."

"You sent my *coq au vin* back three times! You had me running around my kitchen like a maniac!"

"Sorry to break it to you, babe — guess I'm just not into *coq*."

Several of my staff members giggle helplessly. I'd glare at them, but I'm too busy directing all my rage at the man standing before me.

"Well, that's just fine, because I won't be cooking it for you ever again."

"Even if I beg?"

"Even if you show up on my doorstep dying of scurvy and malnutrition."

"Scurvy *and* malnutrition?" His head tilts to the side. "Isn't that a little redundant, as threats go?"

My hands curl into fists at my sides. "Just go away."

"Why?"

"Because I hate you."

"Liar." His eyes hold mine, so blue I can't look away. "You feel something for me — but it's definitely not hate. We both know that, Emmeline."

"You're delusional." My heart pounds a bit faster when he says my full name. "And rude. Intolerable. Irredeemable."

"That all?"

"That's not *enough*?"

"Really, what have I done that's so terrible?" he asks lowly. Heat saturates his stare, overtaking all traces of amusement. "Besides fail to ask you out, ten years ago — which I see now was a terrible oversight on my part."

I ignore him — and the butterflies that burst to life in my stomach at his words. When I speak, my tone is as arctic as my glare. "Three letters, asshole."

His sandy brows lift.

"*K.*"

I take a menacing step in his direction.

"*F.*"

Another step.

"*C.*"

And one more, so I'm right up in his face.

Actually... he's about a foot taller than me. So I'm not exactly *in* his face. But I'm *close* to his face. In the general *proximity* of his face. Which totally conveys the same threatening effect.

Right?

Shit.

Emmett's lips twitch as he looks down at me. I fear my lethal glare isn't quite as intimidating as I thought it would be.

"Don't you dare laugh," I growl under my breath, hoping no one else can hear.

"I wouldn't dream of it." A dimple pops out in his right cheek and more butterflies burst into flight. "You know... you're pretty fucking cute when you're angry. No wonder your kitchen staff puts up with your tirades."

The butterflies die instantly, incinerated by a fresh wave of anger. "I do not have *tirades*."

"Fine." He pauses. "Diatribes?"

I hear several telltale snorts from behind me and swivel my head around.

318

Sure enough, every single one of my underlings is staring avidly in our direction, fascinated by the sight of two premiere New York City chefs mere inches away from strangling the life out of each other.

Or... maybe, doing something entirely different to each other. Something I refuse to let my brain contemplate.

"Everyone is dismissed," I bark gruffly, making them all flinch. "I'll finish the clean-up. See you tomorrow night. *On time.* That means you, Steve."

With a murmured chorus of *"Yes, Chef"*, they slip out of the kitchen without a word of protest. The door bangs shut with finality. Steeling myself for another round of battle, I glance back at Emmett and find his smirk is more pronounced than ever.

"Tell me again how you *don't* have tirades rivaling that of a small, tyrannical dictator?"

"You know, when I ordered everyone out, that applied to you as well." I look pointedly toward the door. "Shoo."

"Did you just *shoo* me? Like a dog?" He laughs again. The sound pools in my stomach like a warm shot of whisky.

"If the fleas fit," I say sweetly, turning my back to him. I cross to the closest stainless prep table and grab the bottle of disinfectant spray. There are still plenty of counters to clean and utensils to store, thanks to my early staff dismissal. I'm glad for the distraction.

He won't leave?

Fine.

I'll ignore him.

I set to work, misting the surface and wiping it down with rhythmic strokes. Usually, this kind of monotonous task would be enough to calm me. However, tonight, with Emmett standing five feet away watching my every move, I find myself more keyed-up than ever. Nervous energy zips along my nerve endings.

"Ignoring me now?" His voice is wry and warm.

I scrub harder.

"That's fine, Ems. We don't have to talk."

I hear footsteps heading my direction, but I don't look up — not even when he comes to a stop next to me. He's standing so close, I can feel the heat off his skin, can hear the soft, steady breaths escaping his lips. Shifting so much as an inch would bring our bodies into direct contact... and I'd be lying if I said, just for an instant, I'm not reckless enough to consider the repercussions.

What would happen if I closed that gap?

If, just this once, I let my unparalleled self-control lapse?

I push the voice away, cursing myself for even considering such madness. No matter what he looks like in that suit... I hate Emmett Fox, and I always will.

Even if he's hotter than the blow-torch I use to caramelize my creme brûlée.

Holding myself perfectly still, I hardly dare to draw a breath as I wait for him to say something that will shatter the heady tension filling up the narrow sliver of air left between us... but he doesn't say a single word.

My heart begins to pound faster.

My fingers clench the rag harder.

After a moment, a large, calloused hand reaches into my line of sight and grabs the disinfectant spray. To my everlasting relief — and, admittedly, a tiny shred of disappointment — Emmett steps out of my space. My lungs resume functioning. Keeping my eyes locked on the cleaning cloth in my hand, I listen as he rounds the kitchen island and takes up a position directly across from me.

With the stainless table planted firmly between us, I feel safe enough to steal a small glance at him. Just one, tiny peek won't hurt...

Right?

Wrong.

My heart stutters a beat as I take in the sight of Emmett shrugging out of his expensive jacket and tossing it onto a nearby shelf. There's something almost erotic about the way he rolls up the sleeves of his crisp white button-down, those dexterous fingers folding back the fabric to reveal a set of sun-bronzed forearms. My mouth feels suddenly dry as I watch his muscles flex beneath the cotton fabric of his shirt when he sprays down the stainless surface and begins to wipe it clean with practiced motions.

"Wh-wha—" I swallow hard. "What are you doing?"

"Playing basketball," he deadpans, not looking up.

I sigh. "Why are you helping me clean?"

"Contrary to what you might think, I'm actually a nice guy."

"Not from what I remember. In fact, *nice* wouldn't even make the top fifty adjectives I'd use to describe you, Fox."

"Fifty adjectives, huh?" He whistles. "Guess that means you think about me a lot."

"Try *never.*"

"You're breaking my heart, Ems."

"Wasn't aware you had a heart."

He glances up, catching my gaze immediately. There's a lighthearted look on his face, but his eyes are more serious than I can ever recall seeing them. "You're certainly determined to carry on this feud, aren't you?"

"*Me?*" I snort. "Refresh my memory — was it *me* who went to *your* restaurant, sent back *your* signature dish three times, then came into *your* kitchen to troll you in front of *your* staff?" I pause. "No! That was *you.*"

"Come on, Ems. Where's your sense of humor?"

"Somewhere in the garbage, along with the three uneaten batches of *coq au vin* I made tonight."

"I'm sorry, okay?" He sets down his rag and braces his hands against the table. "Yes, it was a dick move... but it was also my *only* move. If I'd asked to come back here to see your kitchen — to see *you* — would you have rolled out the welcome mat for me? Or would you have sent that waitress straight back to my table with a message to get the hell out of your restaurant and out of your life?"

I jerk my chin in lieu of an answer.

"Yeah," he mutters. "Thought so."

"In case you're forgetting — it's not like you deserve a red carpet reception, Fox. Not after all the shit you put me through back in culinary school."

"Such as?"

"How about the time you slid skewers inside all my baguettes, so I couldn't slice them?"

"You mean, *after* you'd removed all of mine from the cooling rack without permission, to make room for your own?"

I have no rebuttal for that.

Emmett snorts. "Cooking with you was like a military coup d'état — no compromise, no communication. Just a seizure of control without any concern for anyone else."

"Nice," I drawl sarcastically.

"True," he counters softly. "You may blame me for starting this rivalry, but of the two of us, you're the one who made everything such a damn competition. I was just... rising to the challenge."

"Oh, spare me. Not all your pranks were so justifiable." I narrow my eyes at him. "What about the time you dyed my chef's hat bright green with food coloring? I walked around all week looking like a damn leprechaun."

"It was Saint Patrick's Day! I was being festive. And you dyed my soufflés blue in retaliation," he reminds me, smiling. "Or am I not permitted to mention *your* offenses, prosecutor?"

"Fine." I cross my arms over my chest. "Maybe I did that. But *I* wasn't the one who carved *my* initials into *your* final dessert evaluation. When I pulled my perfect cheesecake out of the fridge to present to our instructor, you'd completely defiled it!"

"It needed a little embellishment. Pretty sure my efforts only helped your grade point average." He shrugs. "Plus, in return, *you* changed FOX to FOXY in the student record system. I don't even know how you managed that one, but every single piece of paper from that point on was affected. Attendance sheets, grade reports, permanent files. I'm surprised my damn diploma didn't read EMMETT FOXY."

I can't help cracking a grin. "That was some of my best work."

"Honestly, I'm still curious how you made it happen."

"I'll never reveal my sources." I pause. "However, I will say, it always pays to befriend the school secretary."

He shakes his head sternly. "Devious. Truly."

We both grin and, for a moment, it's easy to forget he's my arch-rival.

"See?" His smile falters a bit. "It wasn't all bad."

"It wasn't exactly good, though." I sigh. "I'm surprised we didn't kill each other. Probably best we haven't crossed paths, since we graduated."

"I don't know if I'd say that." His Adam's apple bobs as he swallows roughly. "It's nice to see you. It always is. Even when you're glaring at me or threatening to carve me into bits with your rather impressive knife collection."

I blink slowly, startled by his words.

"Look..." He runs a hand through his hair and blows out a sharp breath. "I can't apologize for all the shit that went down ten years ago, 'cause the truth is, I'm not sorry. Sparring with you was damn entertaining. Some of those pranks we played on each other were the best times of my life. You may be a tyrant with a spatula... but you're a hell of a lot of fun, Ems."

My mouth gapes.

Did my nemesis... just... compliment me?

"That said... I'm not the same guy I was back then. I've changed."

"Yeah?" I put on a bitchy tone, hoping it might drown out the pounding of my pulse. "Is that why you spent the evening insulting me in every way possible?"

"I insulted your cooking," he corrects, eyes narrowed. "Not you."

"Same thing!"

"Is it, though?" His tone drops to a low, intent murmur. "Are you really so defined by this job, you don't know who you are outside this kitchen?"

I don't answer.

"When was the last time you got out of that chef's hat, Emmeline? Let your hair down? Got a bit wild?" He leans in, across the table, eyes never shifting from mine. "When was the last time you did anything at all just for fun?"

Truthfully?

Back in culinary school. With him. Playing stupid pranks.

Since then, my life has been one long string of late nights and endless work. I've been so caught up improving my craft, pushing myself to succeed... I can hardly recall the last time I did something just because it made me happy.

"Emmeline."

My eyes fly up to his and I realize I've gone nearly a minute without responding. I search my mind for a convincing lie, coming up short as I get lost in his too-blue stare.

"I... I..." I fumble and, without any other options, blurt out the truth. "I don't have time for a life. Not yet. Not when I've worked so hard to get to this place." I gesture around at the empty kitchen. My small empire. My entire reason for existence, contained within one room. "Not when I've sacrificed so much to land here."

Emmett shakes his head. "Don't you see, though? You can't wait to start living. If you do that, you'll end up on your death bed, lamenting all the shit you should've done. Life isn't about work."

"But work *is* my life."

"Bullshit."

"It's not bullshit!" I snap back. "You should understand better than anyone — what this world is like, how hard it is to get to the top, let alone stay there. Don't act like you'd walk away from La Folie after everything you did to score that gig."

His grip tightens on the table. "I never said I'd walk away. And I do get it — trust me, I do. Why the hell else do you think I'm here?"

"Frankly, I have no idea!"

"I came to see you, Emmeline," he growls. "I had to see you."

My breath catches. "*What?*"

"I know it doesn't make sense — not after all this time. The truth is, I don't even understand it myself. But... for months, since I first heard you got the job here... Hell, long before that, since the fucking day we left school... I've been thinking about you. Wondering about you. Wanting to see you. And I can't stop." His voice drops so low, it's almost inaudible. "I don't want to stop."

My mind is spinning. My eyes are wide as saucers.

He stares at me for a moment — one, two, three thudding heartbeats — before he pushes off from the table and starts walking. Every step of his designer shoes against the tile floor rings out like a gunshot as he comes around to my side. He stops a foot away, so close I have to crane my neck to keep my eyes on his.

"Here's the thing..." His voice is no more than a murmur. "You drive me fucking crazy. You're the most cocky, competitive, crazy-ass woman I've ever met in my life. I don't see you for eight years and yet, after eight seconds with you, you're right back under my skin."

My brows lift. "Is there a point to this deeply complimentary speech? Or am I just supposed to stand here as you list all my less-than-attractive qualities?"

His eyes darken as he leans down, invading my space. I'm breathing too fast as his gaze drops to my mouth, lingering there for what feels like an eternity.

"My point?" he whispers, so close I can feel the words against my lips. *"This is my point, Emmeline."*

Before I can respond, before I can move, before I can breathe... his arms wind around my back and he hauls me up against his chest. Our bodies collide the same second his mouth crashes against mine in a hard, unapologetic kiss. I can barely wrap my head around the fact that I'm kissing the very man I swore to hate for all eternity because...

Holy. Mother-Effing. Shit.

Passion explodes between us like two opposing storm fronts. I taste lightning on his tongue as a hurricane of emotion churns through my veins, spinning me out of control within the circle of his arms.

We are a wild tempest. A cyclone of arrogance. A squall of indignation.

He touches me, and a whole decade of hate and lust lashes me like warm rain. He pulls me closer and ten years of need and torment claw at me like gusts of wind.

In the span of a heartbeat, I've abandoned my ability to breathe or think or do much of anything, except hang on for dear life while Emmett Fox singlehandedly ruins me. His hands fist in the fabric of my chef's jacket as he deepens the kiss, his tongue spearing into my mouth as though he's staking a claim over my body.

My memories.

My mind.

My heart.

His lips are somehow hard and soft, playful and passionate. A steel blade and the softest caress. I can't quite suppress the small moan that emanates from my throat. I'd be embarrassed he's managed to elicit such a sound in so short a time, if I could summon a single thought except *holy-shit-holy-shit-holy-shit* as his lips move over mine.

We're both panting hard when we finally break apart, breathless and dazed from the force of this strange new attraction tugging us together. His forehead comes down to rest against mine. Our ragged breaths mingle in the gap between our faces. And, for once...

We are entirely out of words. I can conjure no insults, can fathom no quippy retorts. I simply stare at him, dumbfounded by his kiss even as the desire it ignited continues to pump through my system like a drug.

I hate Emmett Fox.

Hate him.

Hate.

Him.

Except…

What if I didn't?

My lips twitch in the beginnings of a smile as I look up into the eyes of a man I've loathed and cursed and taunted. A man I've wanted and hated and tortured. A man I've never been able to get out of my head, whether it's obsessing over ways to destroy him or dreaming of what it might feel like to take a peek under his chef's jacket.

"Emmett," I whisper finally, shattering the silence. "You do realize this is going to make our feud a bit more complicated, right?"

"Oh, Emmeline," he murmurs, smirking back at me as his hands squeeze my waist tighter. "On the contrary — I think this just made our rivalry a hell of a lot more interesting…"

THE END

ABOUT THE AUTHOR

JULIE JOHNSON is a twenty-something Boston native suffering from an extreme case of Peter Pan Syndrome. When she's not writing, Julie can most often be found adding stamps to her passport, drinking too much coffee, striving to conquer her Netflix queue, and Instagramming pictures of her dog. (Follow her: @author_julie)

She published her debut novel LIKE GRAVITY in August 2013, just before her senior year of college, and she's never looked back. Since, she has published eight more novels, including the bestselling BOSTON LOVE STORY series and THE GIRL DUET. Her books have appeared on Kindle and iTunes Bestseller lists around the world, as well as in AdWeek, Publishers Weekly, and USA Today.

You can find Julie on Facebook or contact her on her website www.juliejohnsonbooks.com. Sometimes, when she can figure out how Twitter works, she tweets from @AuthorJulie.

For major book news and updates, subscribe to Julie's newsletter: http://eepurl.com/bnWtHH

Instagram: https://www.instagram.com/author_julie/
Twitter: https://twitter.com/AuthorJulie
Facebook: https://www.facebook.com/juliejohnsonbooks/

ALSO BY JULIE JOHNSON

STANDALONE NOVELS:

LIKE GRAVITY

SAY THE WORD

FAITHLESS

THE BOSTON LOVE STORIES:

NOT YOU IT'S ME

CROSS THE LINE

ONE GOOD REASON

TAKE YOUR TIME

THE GIRL DUET:

THE MONDAY GIRL

THE SOMEDAY GIRL

UNCHARTED

THE FADED DUET:

FADED

UNFADED

CRIMSON COCKTAIL

KARPOV KINRADE

When Ember White wakes up married to a stranger, she thinks it can't get much worse, until she finds out he's a vampire and has turned her into one too--and someone's trying to kill them both. Just another day in the life of a librarian.

A standalone novella from the USA Today bestselling Vampire Girl world.

This is raw, original material written just for this anthology. Due to constraints and the immediacy of the timeline, this story has not been edited.

CRIMSON COCKTAIL

A thirst like I've never before experienced wakes me from a deep sleep full of vaguely haunting dreams. When I peel my eyes open enough to take stock of where I am, I realize three things at once. First, I'm in a bed not my own. This one is far too comfortable. Too luxurious with silky soft sheets and thick padding that seems to conform to my body. Second, there's a stranger's arm draped over my chest... and we both appear to be naked. I study the arm in a detached kind of way, like a scientist studying a strange animal. His muscles are well-defined, and his skin is a shade lighter than mine, which is saying something given my pale complexion. His hand—and presumably both hands—are manicured with long tapering fingers that I imagine are perfect for playing piano. It's an attractive arm, but one completely unfamiliar to me. And that's the third thing I realize: I can't remember a single thing from the last night.

Nothing. Not a whiff of a memory floats inside my confused brain.

The last thing I can recall before this moment is my best friend dragging me to a club on the strip after work to "blow off steam". As if working as librarians in Nevada is so stress-inducing.

An ache at the base of my throat reminds me of my thirst... or maybe it's hunger. I can't actually tell, which is odd in itself. I just know I won't be able to focus on anything else until I drink or eat something. I carefully extricate myself from the strange man's arm and scoot to the edge of the bed to sit up.

It's then that I realize a fourth thing.

I'm wearing a wedding ring.

And not just some cheap gold band, either.

I'm wearing a rock to rival all rocks. A glittering diamond the size of a small egg tucked between sapphires on either side. It's antique-looking. Art Deco maybe. I gawk at it, confused. Surely it's not real. But damn if it doesn't look real.

I suck in my breath, and all thoughts are lost as the scent of something delicious overtakes me. My eyes land on the crimson cocktail sitting on the nightstand, and my mouth literally waters. With drool. It's not a good look, and I have to wipe my chin with the back of my hand to keep from dribbling on the expensive sheets.

I reach for the cocktail, not even bothering to question why I'm craving liquor first thing in the morning, and I sniff. I can't place the smell, but it's tantalizing and setting all of my senses on fire. I take a tentative sip, expecting something with blood orange, or maybe a Bloody Mary, but it's nothing like that. It's viscous and coats my throat in a way that eases all worry and care. I drain the cocktail without pause and have to force myself not to lick the glass clean.

Who am I kidding? I totally licked the glass clean. You know us librarians... wild to the core.

Whatever was in that drink, I feel the effects pretty instantly. My whole body pulses with energy and adrenaline surges through me. My senses are heightened. It was unnaturally silent in this room thanks to a private suite in a fancy Vegas hotel. But now, I can hear all the little things that keep the room functioning. The buzz from the lights. The currents of electricity surging through the wires in the walls to power the television. I can even hear guests on other floors; their sounds of chewing or early morning lovemaking. And that's when I begin to worry about what was in the drink. Am I hallucinating?

Maybe the stranger in bed drugged me last night, and that's why I can't remember anything.

And now I've just voluntarily drugged myself.

I rush to the bathroom without bothering to dress first. As soon as I get to the toilet, I do my best to induce vomiting. If that drink was drugged, maybe I can get most of it out before it's absorbed. My mind whirls, planning as I lean over the porcelain rim.

First, get dressed and find my phone—or any phone for that matter.

Second, get out of the room and call Molly. Find out what the hell happened last night and make sure she's okay.

Then, head to the ER and have them do a rape kit, just in case. I'll also need STD testing and a morning-after pill. This has never happened to me before. I've never had a one-night stand. I've never been overtly sexually assaulted. But I live in Las Vegas, so of course I've heard stories. And naturally, I have a contingency plan. What woman doesn't?

Oh, and before I escape this hotel suite I need to find the identity of the man in bed. In case he did do something to me.

When my stomach is emptied, and red bile floats in the water, I flush and stand up, then lean against the sink. I splash water over my face, wash out my mouth, and then stare at my reflection in the mirror. I look more pale than normal, which isn't surprising given a night of drinking and god knows what else.

What *is* shocking is that I actually look effing amazing. And I don't mean pretty-good-all-thing-considered amazing. I mean photoshopped glam pic amazing. My skin is flawless. The permanent line in my brow—what Molly calls my librarian line—is gone. A pimple that had just started to form by my nose has disappeared. Dryness. Sun damage. All those little imperfections we get used to... all of it gone! My eyes, normally a dullish blue, now sparkle and look like they've been run through a filter. Even my cheekbones seem more pronounced. Sexier. My mousy brown hair looks shiny and rich, like chocolate. And everything else is... perkier, let's just say.

"What the hell happened to me last night?" I whisper to myself.

I'm not prepared for a deep British voice to reply. "Do you remember nothing, then?"

I turn, shocked, to see the man attached to the arm standing in the bathroom door. He's as naked as I, but this doesn't actually bother me. Believe it or not, I have a relatively low modesty scale and am perfectly comfortable in my own skin. Even Molly is shocked by this. So I don't attempt to cover up when he stares at me, and I don't avert my eyes from him either.

For the record, this man's body is a specimen of god-like perfection, and I do not make that claim lightly. He's tall. At least 6'4", with washboard abs, a face chiseled from marble, piercing blue eyes and dark hair that looks purposefully disheveled, though I know for a fact he just got out of bed. I've had my share of lovers. Never one-night-stands, as I said, but I've been around the block a time or two. And never have I ever seen a...

"I see you drank your cocktail?"

I pull my thoughts back to the matter at hand, which is most definitely not his... man-bits.

"It was drugged," I accuse, trying to seem imposing and likely failing.

He smirks. Smirks! As if this wasn't deadly serious. "I can see how you would think so, and you likely have a lot of questions—"

"So you admit you drugged me?" I ask. My fear is pulsing at the surface of my mind, but I shove it down. I can give into that later, once I'm safe. For now, I must stay strong. Focused.

"I did not drug you," he says, his voice so deep, so smooth, that I nearly melt into it.

"Then what's wrong with me? Why don't I remember anything?" I hold up my left hand and point to the enormous rock. "And what's this? Did we get married?"

I think I will die of embarrassment if he says yes. What kind of person gets drunk and marries a stranger in Vegas, then forgets it? And I live here! I'm no random tourist. People will find out. I can only imagine Mildred's face when she hears about this. She'll never let me live it down, and she may be pushing eighty, but that old bat has no plans to retire. I'll never hear the end of it.

"We did get married. Though that wasn't part of the plan. And that's not actually the most significant thing that happened to you last night."

I look down at his hand, and he's also wearing a wedding ring. It's similar in style to mine but more masculine. They seemed to have been made for each other.

"What's your name?" I ask, though I can barely get the words out from the mortifying shame of it.

His lips curl as if amused by my distress. Cocky one, isn't he? "Sebastian Kingston, at your service," he says, giving a little mock bow.

While still naked, in case anyone forgot that not-so-tiny detail.

"Do you know *my* name?" I ask, the challenge clear in my voice.

He raises an eyebrow. "Ember Elaine White. You're a twenty-nine-year-old librarian who lives alone and is considering getting a cat but hasn't found the right one. You fancied becoming an English teacher at one point, but discovered a deep love of the library and thus chose library sciences when it came time to declare your focus for your Master's program. But you didn't stop there. You went on for a Ph.D. and then spent a year traveling the world exploring all the great libraries before settling into a position in Las Vegas. You like chocolate, but never with fruit. You hate lemons but love the smell. And when you get really excited your face scrunches up in the most adorable manner."

I exhale deeply and lean against the sink, suddenly exhausted. I don't think anyone but Molly knows that much about me. Maybe not even her. I'm a private person. I'm not on social media. I prefer books to gadgets. I don't share every little detail of my life everywhere. I've often thought I was born in the wrong era, but I do relish my independence, despite lingering social sexism, and would not want to live in a time where I would be considered property.

"Did the drugs make me say all that?" I ask, my voice a whisper. I'm no longer attempting any bravado. Now I'm just confused and scared.

He steps forward and raises a hand to gently brush a strand of hair out of my face. "Ember, there were never any drugs. At least not while you were with me. This is possibly a side effect of being turned."

"What are you talking about?"

"Watch my face and try not to panic."

That kind of language isn't helping matters any, but I steel myself for what's about to come.

His lips part, and the shift happens so fast I almost don't notice. But there they are. His canines have elongated into sharp daggers.

Adrenaline surges in me and I attempt to move away from him but he grabs my arms and forces me to face my reflection. "Look, Ember. Look at *your* mouth."

My curiosity overrides my fear and I face the mirror as he stands behind me. He's a full head taller than me, and I should be able to see him in the mirror, but I can't. He's invisible.

But I'm still visible, and I look at my own teeth, now elongated in my mouth.

"I'm... I'm a vampire?"

I need clothes for the discussion that will follow. And I need him to be wearing something as well. Unfortunately, all I have to wear is a slinky silver dress Molly insisted I wear. It's better than nothing, I suppose. Though that could be debated considering wearing nothing is infinitely more comfortable.

Once we are both reasonably dressed we sit in the living room facing each other. Sebastian called for room service, though I questioned why. Do they serve blood?

Yes, it finally hit me that the crimson cocktail I guzzled down this morning wasn't blood oranges or a Bloody Mary. It was just blood.

But Sebastian said I will still need food for a bit as my body completes the transformation. Until that time, I'm more vulnerable than I was even as a human. But soon my strength and stamina will increase, and I will find myself capable of things I never before imagined.

"You're not fully a vampire yet," he says. "That's why you could see yourself in the mirror this morning. That will fade until you no longer have a reflection."

"How did this happen?" I ask. I should be more scared. Or angry. Or something. But I find myself mostly curious. An otherworldly event occurred last night, and I need to understand it.

"For reasons I'm still trying to piece together, you were targeted by a group of rogue vampires who are wanted for a series of murders throughout the world and most recently here in Las Vegas. You would have been their next victim, had I not found you in time. I had to turn you or let you die. I chose to save you."

A knock at the door interrupts us—room service has arrived—and I use the extra moments to compose my thoughts. I nearly died last night? And what of Molly? Where did she end up? Is she dead? Also, as a completely vain aside, how will I ever apply makeup properly if I can't see my own reflection?

I visually search the room for my cell phone and see it peeking out from under the bar. I stand and am about to get it when the door crashes open and the room service cart goes flying, sending orange juice, pancakes, muffins and fruit everywhere.

Sebastian growls in a primal kind of way. "Ember, to the bathroom."

His command is an odd one, but given he appears to be fighting three very large men, I don't argue.

Once in the bathroom, I close and lock the door, and sink to the floor as I look for something with which to defend myself. The only thing I can find is a curling iron, so I plug it in and hope it's the kind that heats fast.

My hands are shaking as I clutch it and wait, listening as a battle ensues on the other side of this door.

I feel as if I've walked into one of my books. Vampires? Great battles in a hotel suite? Drinking blood for breakfast?

I'd pinch myself to see if I'm dreaming, but I know I'm awake. I know this is all somehow real. And I know I can't let it derail my focus right now. Not if I want to survive the day.

After a moment, the sound of fighting subsides. I hold my breath and wait to see who comes to the door.

The curling iron is hot now.

I'm as ready as I'll ever be.

My impulse is to get as far away from the door as possible, but I don't want to back myself into a wall or trap myself in a corner. I try to recall the few loosely held self-defense lessons I took when the library did our safety week. Unfortunately, none of them involved fighting vampires... and I'm fresh out of wooden sticks. Where's Buffy when you need her?

Still, I position myself in a fighting stance, hot iron at the ready.

There's a knock at the door and my heart nearly stops, until I hear his voice.

"Ember, open up. It's safe, for now."

I put the curling iron down and dash to the door. When it swings open I throw myself into his arms without thought. His arms wrap around me and he comforts me as I shake.

"It's all right, love. You're in shock. You need blood, food and rest. But first, we have to get out of here."

I pull away enough to see around him. To see the bodies littering the expensive wood floors.

"They're... dead?"

I look up into his eyes, but they register no remorse, just steely determination. "It was them or us. Would you rather I let them have us?"

My perspective shifts and I glare at the bodies of the monsters who attacked us. "I hope you didn't leave a tip!"

Sebastian laughs, and the sound is startling, even to him, judging by his expression. "I knew last night you were special. No one has ever made me laugh the way you do. You have such a unique way of looking at the world, Ember, and that's saying something given how long I've been around."

I frown. His words are sincere, but... "I wish I could remember. You're a stranger to me, though I feel... something... between us."

"Your body remembers what your mind does not. But your memories will return in time, as the transition completes. Be patient."

He cups my face and looks as if he's about to kiss me, and I can feel a stirring in my belly that means I'll likely let him. But then his head jerks up. "We have to go. Now. More are on the way."

I make a move to leave the bathroom but he stops me. "We can't go that way. They're already here. We need a safe house, and I know just the place. But I need you to trust me. Can you do that?"

"Do I have a choice?"

He smiles. "You always have a choice."

I raise a skeptical eyebrow.

"Well, aside from last night, but those were extenuating circumstances. Would you rather be dead right now?"

Touché. "No. No, I wouldn't. If what you've said is true, then thank you for saving my life."

He cocks his head. "Okay then. Take my hand and hold on." He smiles at me. "There's a reason vampires can't see themselves in mirrors. For us they are portals. All mirrors connect to each other like doors, and if you know where you're going, you can travel via them. Like we're going to do right now."

He reaches out for the mirror and places his hand on it. I try not to tense my muscles, as I assume this is like getting into a car crash. The more relaxed you are the less injurious it is.

A tingling energy flows over my body, like being walked on by thousands of ants, and I shudder as the feeling begins to penetrate my skin. My vision darkens until all I can see is black, and then I feel as if I'm being sucked into a vortex of time and space, my very being undone by the physics of it all. Everything around me is spinning, or I'm spinning within everything. I clutch at Sebastian's hand and feel relief that he is still here, with me.

After some unfathomable amount of time my body recovers its own mass and thuds heavily against Sebastian. He catches me in strong arms and helps me regain my balance. We are in a hallway, I realize, as my eyesight returns. It's dark. The walls are draped with red silk embroidered in exotic patterns, and the only light source are candles perched in iron candelabras that have left a coating of wax along the marble floor.

On one end of the hall is a large mirror, the one we presumably came out of, and on the other end is a door that's reminiscent of Rodin's Gates of Hell, with writhing bodies in perpetual states of torture.

In the center of the door is a sculptured eye that appears to be watching us. I shiver and stand a bit closer to the large vampire next to me, clutching his hand more tightly. I haven't quite made up my mind about him, but at the very least he's proven he doesn't want me dead just yet. Which is, admittedly, a remarkably low standard, but it's the best I've got at the moment.

A booming voice coming from the door nearly gives me heart palpitations as we approach.

"Who dares enter The Black Lotus?"

Sebastian sounds resigned as he answers. "Tell your master Sebastian Kingston is here to ask a favor."

The eye on the door closes and it goes silent. I shift closer to Sebastian. "So... I assume that door is magic?"

He looks down at me, then puts his arm around my shoulders and pulls me closer to him. Despite my troubled mind, my body relishes the contact, craving the closeness even as I question my sanity in all this. But there's no denying the pull that exists between us. I'm attuned to his moods, to the movement of his body, to his very orbit, and he seems to be responding the same way to me. It's nothing I've ever felt or experienced before and I'm a bit mind-blown by it all.

"You're about to see more than you can possibly imagine," he says. "All the stories and fairytales and legends? They're all based in truth. There's so much more to life than what humans believe to be true. There are creatures of myths, magicks that defy understanding, and other worlds. Vampires are only the beginning."

"Other worlds?" I ask, a new kind of excitement bubbling up in me. After all, I am a librarian. I spend my days surrounded by portals to other worlds. In my most secret of hearts I always imagined someday finding the wardrobe to Narnia or—yes, I will admit it—getting my letter to Hogwarts. Some part of my brain is trying to tell me I need to panic. That real life isn't supposed to work this way. That I've already almost died even if I can't remember it. But I can't find it within me to be that scared. I'm too excited. Too amazed at the possibilities that exist now that I'm becoming something more than human. Now that I'm being ushered into the secrets of other worlds.

"Legends say there are nine worlds created by the dragons long ago, but I've only been to three. I've met others who have been to a few more, but some are said to be uninhabitable." He says this so matter-of-factly, like dragons are just a real thing he throws around in conversation willy-nilly like, and it's easy to see the many years he's lived despite his youthful appearance. What marvels must exist in his mind. What wonders he must have seen. What books he must have read! I've got to give myself some credit for randomly picking quite a catch for an impromptu husband.

I look at the door again in wonder. "Are we... is this another world?"

He chuckles. "It will definitely feel like it, but no. This is its own place entirely. This is... "

"The Black Lotus!" says a man who is now standing where the door stood just moments ago. He is draped dramatically in robes the color of gemstones and has an aristocratic face with an equine nose, bushy eyebrows and black hair slicked back to showcase a prominent widow's peak.

He glances at both of us, then dips into a sweeping bow. "Allow me to introduce myself. I am Sly Devil, proprietor of The Black Lotus, safe house for all manner of paranormal and fantastical beings."

He gestures us to follow him, and as we enter, the door that seemed to have disappeared now slams closed behind us. It's an ominous sound that rattles my bones. We are in darkness as we walk nearly blind until we reach a great hall that is lit with dripping candles everywhere. I shudder to imagine the safety violations present here, but I must admit the effect is startling. In the corner a piano unaccompanied by any kind of musician plays a beautiful concerto in a minor chord. One wall is taken over entirely by an underwater tank, like the kind you might see at a zoo. Only instead of fish or sharks, this tank features a mermaid. She is beautiful in a vicious sort of way, with green and blue hair flowing behind her that matches her fins, and skin a sheen of pale blue. Her teeth are spiked like a shark's and her eyes narrow in on us with a predatory gaze.

Sly notices my attention on the creature and smiles. "That's Marasphyr. She's a regular visitor to this establishment. Don't concern yourself with her threatening demeanor. All guests here are safe on pain of death."

We continue through the hall to a smaller room that is no less impressive. It's lined wall to wall with books and I nearly die when I see them. Ignoring the dramatic couches in the center of the room and the table laden with mouthwatering food... and what looks suspiciously like goblets of blood, I head to the books and run my palm along the spines, my mind whirling with all the wonders contained within such ancient tomes.

Sly watches with something like affection on his face. "You appreciate literature," he says.

"Quite so," I say. "I am a librarian by trade."

He nods. "I sensed a kindred spirit in you. Have your pick, my dear. My library is yours."

I won't lie, I nearly swoon right then and there. I know that's not very modern of me, but I have never in my life seen such books, and I've been in some of the finest libraries in the world.

I let my hand wander until it chooses a book at random. I pull it out and take it with me to the couch, where I sit next to Sebastian as Sly sits across from us.

Sebastian looks tense and I can feel an edginess coming off of him. He reaches for a goblet of blood and hands it to me. "You will need to feed on my blood soon, but this will suffice for now. You should also eat some human food."

My stomach turns now that I know what I'm consuming, but the smell is intoxicating. I hold the goblet and look to Sly before drinking. "I don't mean to be rude, but was this blood... humanely sourced?"

Sly laughs. "You're a charming creature," he says. "The blood was donated by willing humans who were more than fairly compensated. None were harmed in any way."

That's good enough for me. I drink it down in one long gulp, my body soaking up the life force. It takes an edge off I didn't know I had and frees my attention to nibble on freshly baked bread spread with a soft cheese and fruit puree.

Sebastian sips his blood more slowly and turns his attention to Sly. "I need your help," he says plainly.

"Yes, I see that. But I do seem to recall you vowed never to return here again." Sly flicks his hand and a scene from the past, built of smoke and light, appears. It's Sebastian, Sly, and another man with pointed ears. He and Sebastian are arguing. Sebastian punches the man in the face and storms out of the room, vowing never to return.

The smoke dissipates and Sly waits for Sebastian to respond.

"I have stayed away for over 100 years," he says.

I nearly choke on my bread. It's one thing to know your new husband is an ancient vampire. It's another thing entirely to hear that 100 years is just a fraction of his life.

"But things have changed. The Rendali brothers are back. They nearly killed Ember last night."

"Well, well. And so you chose to turn her to save her?"

Sebastian's eyes harden. "Yes."

"I assume without permission from the council?"

"You know very well it was without permission. There was hardly time for that. She would have died!"

I have so many questions, but these men are clearly locked in some kind of battle of wills and I'm loathe to interrupt.

"Is that why you married her? To circumvent the rules?"

He glances at me, then back at Sly. "The why is irrelevant. We are married, and therefore immune to any consequence from the council, as per their own bylaws."

"You always did know how to find the loopholes. You should have stayed, Sebastian. You would have gone far in the council."

Sebastian guffaws. "I have no interest in being part of that charade. But I do need their help in stopping this latest threat. To save Ember, I had to kill Billy Rendali. Now Steven is after us."

Sly whistles. "For a man who has vowed to stay out of it, you sure have stepped in quite spectacularly. This is indeed a complicated mess you've made, but I may have a piece to your puzzle. We captured a woman last night who has knowledge of what transpired." He looks to me with a nod of sympathy. "I believe you may know her."

He stands and we stand to follow him, but instead he turns with a flourish and pulls out a wand. "Before we venture further into this dramedy you two have created, I must fix these dreadful clothing choices."

He looks at me first, his expression thoughtful. "Normally, I'd pull out the finest gown for one as lovely as yourself, but you strike me as a more practical dresser." He flicks his wand and fairy lights take over my vision as they work my body over. It all happens in a flash, and I find myself standing in the most unusual outfit. I'm wearing a white V-neck blouse with a black vest laced in leather and a kind of skirt pant in black with black boots. I feel like quite the badass, I must admit.

Sly nods. "Perfect." Then he turns his attention to Sebastian, and with a flick of his wand replaces his benign jeans and polo shirt with an outfit similar to mine, but more masculine. We look made for each other.

Once our wardrobe is to his liking, we follow Sly into the bowels of this mysterious place. Through corridors and stone halls and down winding stone stairways until we reach what can only be described as a medieval dungeon with magical influence.

It smells of sulfur, urine, excrement and body odor.

I gag as we walk through rows of imprisoned criminals, of which only a few look vaguely humanoid, until we reach our destination. It's dark inside, and I can see only the edges of a human foot, soiled and bleeding.

Sly grips the bar of the door and calls to the prisoner. "You have a visitor, my dear."

The person within crawls forward, and it's only when their face is pressed against the bars that I can see who it is.

"Molly?"

To say I'm stunned would be an understatement. Vampires. Magic doors. Mermaids. Other worlds. No problem. Seeing my best friend shackled and imprisoned in a dungeon? I'm officially freaking out. I drop to my knees and face her, reaching for her hands through the bars, but she pulls away and spits at me.

"Molly? What's going on?" I look up at Sebastian, but he just shrugs, clearly in the dark about this. So I look to Sly for answers. "Why's she in here? Release her immediately."

"I'm afraid I cannot do that, my dear. She has violated our laws and must pay."

"What laws did she violate?" I look back to her. She's red-eyed, her skin sallow, her hair a jumbled mess of tangles and dirt, turning her golden locks to a mud brown. "How did you get here?" I ask her.

She glares at me. "You're supposed to be dead! If you'd died like you were meant to, I wouldn't be here at all. I'd be a god by now."

I fall back onto my heels, my hand dropping to my side. This isn't the woman I've known for three years. The woman I've worked side by side with day in and day out. The woman I've shared meals and books with. The woman who helps me pick outfits for dates and who understands my obscure literary references.

"Molly, it's me. Ember. I'm here to help."

She reaches through the bars and grabs my hair, pulling me toward her, my head thumping against the metal painfully.

Sebastian growls and lunges for me. Sly just flicks his wrist and Molly howls in pain and lurches away, releasing me in the process.

Sebastian pulls me away from the cell and holds me while I try to compose myself. "Are you injured?"

I shake my head. "No, just… confused. What's wrong with her?"

Molly crawls forward again, her body still shuddering from whatever Sly's magicks did to her. "What's wrong with me? The same thing that's wrong with you. We are pathetic. Two nearly middle-aged women with no romantic prospects. We're librarians for crying out loud. Maybe you're content with that boring life of drudgery and mediocre pay, but I wanted more. And then... I met a man. But he wasn't just a man, he was a god. And he promised to make me his goddess. We would rule mankind together for eternity, and I would bathe in blood and diamonds. That's what he promised me, in exchange for one thing."

My stomach sinks as a flash of memory whiplashes through my mind. I squeeze my eyes shut as the past overtakes the present and I am back at my house. Molly has just arrived for our evening plans.

I've got wine and cheese set out, and I'm in a comfortable cardigan and loafers when she shows up dressed to the nines and not carrying the book we were meant to discuss that night. "What's all this?" I ask.

She hands me a bag with a slinky silver dress in it. "Put this on. We're going out. No more librarian brain tonight. We're going to drink and get laid."

"Um... " I try to protest, but she pushes into my house and leads me by the hand to my bedroom. Within twenty minutes I have been transformed from mousy bookworm to a woman on a mission. My hair is fashioned in a tasteful updo that highlights my cheekbones, and the dress hugs my figure in ways that are, frankly, difficult to walk in. As I've said before, I'm not modest by nature, but I will admit to being a creature of comfort, and that dress was as far from comfort as one could imagine. Particularly when paired with matching high heels.

But Molly is a hard person to say no to, and her enthusiasm carried me out, into the sparkling night of the Las Vegas strip. We bar hopped for the first hour before landing at a place I've never been. She insisted we give it a try, saying we needed to expand our horizons.

I reluctantly agreed, though I definitely felt a sense of foreboding.

I should have listened to myself, but I had Molly's voice in my ear urging me forward.

This particular bar, in defiance of local laws, allowed smoking indoors. A point I made to Molly in favor of finding somewhere more suitable for a night of well-considered debauchery. But again, she insisted this was the place where our dreams would come true.

We weren't there more than five minutes when two gentlemen approached us and offered to buy us drinks. Molly, already cozying up to one of the men, agreed for both of us. I had to use the restroom and asked Molly to watch my drink like a hawk. I didn't trust these men, and generally do not trust strangers at bars.

I assumed she did, so I had no hesitation in drinking the fruity cocktail when I returned.

That's when things get muddy.

I remember the world spinning.

My stomach quivering.

Being led outside for "fresh air."

Molly laughing and twirling around like a fairy child.

More men arrived, and all looked ominous. Their faces shifted and morphed in my drug-addled mind.

And then pain.

So much pain.

I scream in my memory, and Sebastian clutches me against his chest as my screams carry to the present.

I open my eyes and stare at the woman caged before me.

"What did you do?" I ask, my voice hoarse, my heart broken.

"I traded you for immortality. But like the selfish bitch you are, you didn't fulfill your end of the bargain. And now he's dead. My love. My life. He's dead because of you."

Sebastian moves to face her. "He's dead because of me. Ember had nothing to do with that since your boyfriend and his pals drained her of blood. And he would have done the same to you if a hunter hadn't captured you first and dragged your sorry ass here. Be grateful you get to live at all. That vampire you hooked up with is a serial killer with a particular taste for women."

Her face pales and she bares her teeth at him like an animal. "I was different. He loved me. We were going to rule the world forever."

"Do you know where his brother is?" Sebastian asks.

She answers by spitting in his face.

Sly cringes at the display and hands him a handkerchief, which he uses to clean up the saliva. He then stands and helps me to my feet. "We're not going to get any more from her." Sebastian gives Sly a look, then the three of us leave the dungeon, as cries of despair follow us out.

When we reach Sly's library, I sink into the couch and pull my legs to my chest. I feel weak. Tired. And so very sad.

"Allow me to give you both some privacy while I check on other matters of concern. I'll see what the hunters have dug up about the remaining Rendali brother and what his plans might be, and I'll have a room prepared for the two of you. You might be here awhile."

Sly leaves and I stand and pace the room, thinking. "Are there phones here? I need to call work and let them know I'll be taking an unexpected vacation."

"No phones. Tech isn't very reliable in The Black Lotus, and you can't leave. It's the only place you're safe with Steven Rendali gunning for you."

I nod. "Fair enough. I'll figure out a way to explain my absence upon my return. Perhaps some forged medical documents showing I was in a temporary coma?"

Sebastian raises an eyebrow and smirks. "I expected there to be more tears and less planning."

"My tears will come. Right now, the rage I feel is turning them to fire." I stop and face him, feeling utterly vulnerable and alone. "I trusted her, and I don't trust easily. How could she do this to me?"

He stands and comes to stand close to me, his hands reaching for mine. "There are no limits to what people will do for the chance to live forever. And the Rendali brothers are very cunning."

I square my jaw at him and frown. "I would never have succumbed to such an immoral plan."

A grin plays at his lips. "I have no doubt you would always make the right choice, Ember."

Another wave of memory washes over me and I stumble into his arms as the past crashes into my brain.

Teeth sinking into my neck. So many men feeding on me at once, draining me.

Pain. Anger. Fear.

I feel violated.

And I hear her. Molly. Laughing. Flirting.

Then I see her, licking one of the open wounds on my body, tasting my blood, rubbing it on her face.

Then it all goes blank and when next my eyes open, they look upon the face of a dark angel. Sebastian, with his ocean eyes, black hair flopping in his face.

When I come back to the present, he is holding me, his eyes tender. "You're regaining your memory?"

"Some," I say. "It was... horrible. She's a monster."

My eyes prickle with tears and my throat clogs with emotion. "The pain. I can't describe the pain."

"You're shaking. You need more of my blood to help complete the transformation." He holds his wrist to his own mouth and bites. Blood pools on his pale skin and he holds it to my mouth.

We are inches apart. His blood drips onto the floor as he waits for me to feed. The scent of blood, of *his* blood, overwhelms everything. My teeth elongate and I sink into his wrist and drink.

His other arm wraps around me, holding me against him as I feed on him. I feel what he feels, sense what he senses. There is affection. Worry. Fear, which he is not used to feeling.

When I am done, I release him and step back. My emotions bubble to the surface and I feel myself losing control of them. I crave him like I've never craved anything or anyone. I need him. Want him. But...

I haven't forgotten what he and Sly said about our marriage, and I step back and pull the huge ring off my finger, holding it out to him as I steel my heart against the desire and—dare I say it? Love— that is growing there.

He frowns. "What's this?"

"I know you only married me to avoid whatever punitive punishment this council might effect. I release you from that vow. Thank you for saving my life. You owe me nothing further."

I can't read his face as he stares at the ring, but I just need him to take it. I will never be able to move on from him, but I must try. I certainly won't hold him to a vow he made to save me, just because my ridiculous emotions are making a hormonal teenager of me.

"Ember... this isn't—"

A blaring sound fills the room and Sly appears behind us as if from air. "We have something of a situation," he says.

"What's happened?" Sebastian asks, turning away from me. I slip the ring back on for the moment and face Sly.

"Molly is dead."

It's a gruesome sight, what's left of Molly Lambert. Her hair is torn out by the roots and left in clumps around her cell. Her eyes have been plucked out and left

343

to rot by the pissing pot. Her skin has been scratched and bitten until there's almost nothing left identifying her as human. But none of that killed her. No, it's her torn out throat that did the deed.

I squat over her remains, as something niggles my brain. I've read enough cozy mysteries to dissect a crime scene in my sleep. I point to her hands. "She did this to herself," I say in a low voice.

Sly leans over to look at what I'm pointing to.

"Notice her nails? She tore out her hair, plucked out her eyes and scratched up her skin. Even pulled out her throat."

"That would make more sense than someone else being able to kill her here," Sly says. "I would know if anyone attempted to harm someone under my care."

"Why would she do this?" Sebastian asks.

Sly shrugs. "Madness inspires mad acts. But worry not, you're safe here."

Except I'm not just worried about my safety anymore. "Maybe Molly was always insane, and I'm just now seeing it, but I can't help but blame these brothers. How many women have they killed?" I ask, as my mind inadvertently flashes to that night.

To the teeth.

The bites.

The pain.

"They've been around awhile," Sebastian says. "So... a lot. In the thousands, likely. Or more."

My stomach drops. Thousands? Or more? That's not a serial killer. That's mass murder. That's... insane. "The women on the news recently? The ones missing?"

"Not missing, I'm afraid," says Sly. "We've had our Council of Hunters searching for them, but this is the first lead we've had. They're good at covering their tracks."

"And he wants me dead because he blames me for his brother dying?" I ask.

Sebastian nods. "That's my fault. He should be coming after me, not you."

Sly smirks. "Rest assured, dear boy, he's coming for you too. She's just easier prey."

An idea that's been knocking around in my brain finally lands. "Then let him find me," I say.

Sebastian frowns. Sly looks intrigued.

"Use me as bait. If he wants me so bad, then use that to catch him."

"No way," Sebastian says. "Not going to happen. He's unpredictable. Capable of anything."

"Exactly," I say. "He's unpredictable and likely to make mistakes. What better chance will you have to catch him than me? Surely with all the hunters you talk about, you could keep me safe."

Sly's eyes shift to Sebastian and the vampire frowns. "No. The hunters are fallible. People in their care get hurt. People who trust them. I won't let you die for this."

And then it all clicks into place. "You were one, weren't you? A hunter?"

Sebastian nods.

"And someone under your care was hurt? Died?"

He looks away.

I reach for his hand. "I'm not them. And I get to make my own decisions. You said so yourself. I always have a choice. And this is what I'm choosing. You have to trust me."

We lock eyes, and I can see he's still going to fight me on this, so I push harder.

"I'll do it without you if I have to." It's a hard thing for me to say, though it's still true. And part of me hopes he'll walk away and let me risk this alone. So he's safe. So my heart can break free of his. The more time we spend together, the deeper I fall into something that can never be, and the weight of that knowledge is threatening to break me.

"Stubborn woman," he mutters.

I just smile. "Does that mean you're in?"

"It means I'm not letting you do this alone."

Sly claps his hands together and grins. "Excellent. I do love a good bait and switch. Let us head to the drawing room to prepare, shall we?"

I'm anxious to leave the corpse of my best friend and breathe some fresh air, so I follow quickly and I don't look back. There's a part of my heart that's mourning for the person I thought she was. For the memories we shared. The time we had together. The friendship I will miss. But then I remember the things she said and did. I remember her smearing my blood on her body and laughing as I died, and bile rises in my throat that I ever thought her a friend.

It's a strange thing, to finally see the truth of someone and to then have every memory re-colored by this new reality. It's disjointing. But I don't have time to play with the past. First, I must stop a killer.

The plan we settle on is pretty straightforward. Sebastian will take me home and I will wait for Steven to come and try to kill me. Hunters will be stationed around my house and ready to pounce once he arrives, and we will all live happily ever after. Well, except Steven.

Sebastian looks perpetually worried.

I'm actually pretty okay with this plan. At least right now. I'm sure the crazy of it all will settle in eventually. I had toyed with the idea of going back to work, following my normal routine, etc, but I don't want to put my colleagues at risk. Presumably they aren't all psychopaths bent on mayhem and murder. I'm pretty sure only Molly holds that distinction.

Since Sebastian hasn't been to my house, he can't use a mirror, but, apparently, I can. Because when I look into one, I no longer see myself.

"You're officially a vampire now," he says. "How do you feel?"

I shrug. "Stronger. More attuned to my senses. But still mostly like me, just a powered-up version of my former self. I don't dislike it."

He nods. "There are some things you'll have to get used to."

"Right. Like finding blood sources. Can I use animals?" I'm not a vegetarian, so what's the harm in drinking my dinner rather than grilling it?

"You can, but you won't like it much. There are clubs that humans attend in order to offer themselves as blood donors. We can find one for you if you're interested. Especially in Vegas. There are a lot of vampires living there."

"Really? How interesting. And the sun? I assume that's a no-no?" It's an odd time to be asking questions, but I expect that he and I will part ways when this is over, so I need to learn all I can now.

"On this world, yes, the sun is harmful to you and can kill you with too much exposure. There is a world you can go to that would allow you to live in the sun, if you were ever interested. I think you'd like it."

That peaks my curiosity. "I think I would like to at least visit and see. I have nothing much holding me here other than my job. Does this world have books?" This is a serious question, obviously.

He chuckles. "Yes, and they are full of fantastical stories and ancient knowledge that would take you lifetimes to read."

My heart flutters at the thought. "Then it's a good thing I now have lifetimes!"

His smile is full of warmth as he takes my hand and instructs me to imagine the mirror I want to transport to. I think of the mirror in my bathroom at home and touch the shimmering glass before me.

Just like before, we are wrapped in magic and darkness and sucked through a portal that shakes up my insides and sends me spiraling into the cosmos before depositing us on my bathroom floor.

As I pull myself to a standing position, I notice my floor needs a proper mopping and my shower drain has bits of hair trapped. Everything here looks so mundane after where I've been.

And seeing Sebastian, this tall, gorgeous, vampire god standing in my bathroom is utterly absurd.

"I'll need to check all your exits and entrances," he says. "We don't want him getting in without us knowing."

I nod and show him around. It's a small place. One bedroom, one bathroom, a cozy living room and open kitchen with a two-person dining table. It's usually only me and sometimes Molly here, with the occasional short-term boyfriend I might bring home for dinner and a movie. Netflix and chill, I think the kids call it.

There are a few windows—which show the sun has already set for the night, a backdoor and a front door. He locks everything and towers over my living room, looking entirely out of place.

"Now what?" I ask. "Do you leave so I look like I'm alone?"

He shuffles on his feet. "That's the plan. But I don't like it."

"I know. But this isn't going to end the way it did last time for you. Trust me. I got this." I don't really got this, but it seems to be something he needs to hear. And I'll definitely give it the old college try, as they say. I feel reasonably optimistic of my odds of survival. That's something. "I'm getting stronger and stronger," I say, flexing my arm like that would prove anything.

He reluctantly grins at that. "Very well. I'll take my leave. But... well, when this is over, we need to talk."

I nod, afraid that if I speak, the raw emotions in my voice will betray me. I know what he needs to talk about, and I won't make it harder for him. But, in my heart, I worry that saying goodbye to Sebastian Kingston might be harder to survive than being eaten alive by evil vampires.

The house feels intolerably lonely once Sebastian leaves, even though I know he's not far away. In the quiet of the night, as I wait for a psychopathic vampire to kill me, I consider my life choices that have led me to this moment. If you'd asked me a few days ago if I regretted anything in my life, I would have said no. I've done all the things I set out to do by this point. I got my degrees. Traveled widely. Landed my dream job. What more could I ask for? But, as I look around, I realize I have kept everyone at a distance. And the only person I let close was a murderer. What does that say about me?

I head to the kitchen to make a pot of tea, hoping that will help pass the time as I continue to think through things. I may be losing Sebastian when this is over, but I can't let this be the end of love, of adventure, of romance. Something in me agreed to marry him that night. Something in me wanted more than a solitary existence defined primarily by my job as a librarian.

When the teakettle whistles, I pour a cup and bring it to my lips. The smell of hibiscus sends me back into my memories of that night as the cup falls from my hand and shatters to the ground.

I am with him. With Sebastian. We are dancing and seem high on life. "Is this how it always is?" I ask him.

"How what always is?" His eyes are alight with a joy I haven't seen since.

"When you turn someone."

He laughs. "So the stories say. To turn someone, you have to drain them completely of blood, infecting them with a poison in our teeth, then give them your blood to reanimate them. The process apparently creates a high in both people. But you're the first person I've turned, so this is all new to me."

I'm surprised to hear that. "Why me?" I ask as the music turns to a slow song and he pulls me into his arms. I feel at home against his chest, like all the pieces of my life have finally snapped together.

"I don't know," he says. "I saw something in you I couldn't let die."

"I'm glad. That you didn't let me die. I want to live." And I realize it's true. I want to live. I want to do all things. Love and be loved and travel with someone, sharing those memories of our adventures together. My parents died my first year of college. I had no siblings. No aunts or uncles. No grandparents. When they died, a part of my past died with them. They were the only ones who had known me as a child. And since then, I haven't let anyone else close enough to know me. Not even Molly, not really. Not until tonight.

And so I tell Sebastian everything. I share with him my whole life. And he shares with me. He tells me of the man who turned him. He, too, was on his death bed. A plague that had wiped out his village. But one man came to him and offered him a way to live forever, but at a cost. "He was a Prince on another world," Sebastian says. "An inventor who was always looking for ways to help people and often came to this world for ideas. He said his name was Ace, and that he could help me. I agreed, though I was so close to death I'm sure I didn't know what I was saying. But when he brought me to life, I understood. He taught me everything about being a vampire. We were close for many years. I spent some time in his world, and he came to mine. We haven't been in touch in awhile, but I think you would like him. I know he'd love you."

Somewhere in all that, in our bonding, we made it to the altar. Of course, now I know that he needed to do that to protect us from the council, but at the time it seemed spontaneous. It made sense. And in my heart, it still does. It's ridiculous to say I'll never find a love like him again. We've only known each other since yesterday, after all. But I cannot change the reality of what I feel. Of what I know to be true. I will never love anyone like I love him. But I will learn to live without that love, and find joy elsewhere.

I'm ripped out of my memories by a voice in my kitchen. "So here's the bitch who stole my brother from me."

Fear surges through my veins as I open my eyes and see the spitting image of the man who nearly sucked me dry and left me for dead. The Rendali brothers are twins. And this one hates me with a deep passion.

He will make me suffer. I can see it in his eyes. How did he get in? What happened to Sebastian?

As if reading my mind, he laughs. "Wondering where your rescue squad is? My boys ate them. But I saved my appetite for you. I'm going to enjoy draining the life from you."

I take a breath to slow my heart and look around for anything I can use as a weapon. I'm faster and stronger than I was before. I don't have to be a victim. My eyes land on a rooster shish kabob skewer I had pulled out for dinner the other night. It's vintage and was a gag gift at the library Christmas party two years ago, but I've grown fond of it. I'll have to be fast to make this work.

From lore, you kill a vampire by stabbing them in the heart with a wooden stake, which I'm lacking, through sun exposure, which I'm also lacking, or through beheading.

So... I guess I'm going with beheading.

Doing my best Xena Warrior Princess impersonation, I grab the skewer and rush towards Steven. His eyes widen in shock as I stab the skewer through his neck. Repeatedly.

I am covered in blood, screaming like a wild banshee, as I use the sharp end of my cocky skewer to sever what remains of his neck from his body.

This is how Sebastian finds me when he blows my door off its hinges with the force of his might. And it only takes him one twist of his strong hands to finish the job, pulling the man's head from his neck.

It's a gruesome, violent, and bloody scene, and I'm quite positive I'll have to burn the house to the ground to get out the bloodstains, but it's over. The monster is dead. Future women are safe. I've gotten my revenge.

And now I stand over the body, staring at my husband who is also covered in blood. This is it. This is when it all ends.

Except before I can say the speech I had planned, he pulls me into his arms and kisses me so deeply he steals all my words. His hands dig into my flesh, his lips probing mine, and I feel his need growing. This is just adrenaline, I tell myself, as he carries me to my bathroom and turns on the shower. As we both step in and...

As more memories resurface from that night.

Passion. Ecstasy. All the things I've ever read about and more, coming to life inside my body.

When we are both spent, and cleaned of all the blood, we exit the shower and I attempt to find him clothes that will fit his frame. He ends up in sweat pants that land just below his knees, and a pink "Readers Do it Standing Up" shirt that we sold as a fundraiser for the library during Romance Novels week. I find something cotton and comfortable to wear as well, because I'm not ready to say goodbye while naked.

Once we are both dressed, I slide the ring off my finger and hand it back to him.

"Thank you," I say sincerely. "For everything."

He frowns. "Is this what you really want? I thought... "

"I just, I know you had to marry me, but you don't have to stay married right? There's no rule about that?"

He cocks his head. "Do you think I only married you to follow the stupid council bylaws?"

It's my turn to cock my head. "Didn't you?"

"For a smart woman, you are a bit dense at times. You have stolen my heart and soul, if such things exist for a creature like me. I'm yours. Forever. If you'll have me."

I wait for the other shoe to drop. For him to tell me it's all a joke, but I can see the truth in his eyes, and my heart breaks open, flooding my eyes with tears of joy as I throw myself into his arms.

Sebastian calls someone to handle the mess in the house. We return to The Black Lotus since the hunters are still tracking down the rest of the Rendali brothers' crew, and my house is uninhabitable.

I ask him about the other hunters, and he said they got away. Steven's goons didn't 'eat them' as he promised. For that I was grateful.

That night we sleep long and deeply and when morning arrives with break-fast in bed, I feel my life turning into something entirely unexpected and new.

"What do we do now?" I ask.

"I'd say we should take a honeymoon," he says. "That would be the proper human thing to do."

I smile over my goblet of blood in agreement. "But where to go?"

He grins. "I fancy a visit to my creator, Prince Ace. What do you think? Want to see a whole new world?"

I can barely contain my enthusiasm. "I'm ready when you are!"

And so, our adventures begin. Oh, the libraries I will see. The books I will read. The lives I will live. And all with this man beside me.

THE END

ABOUT THE AUTHOR

Karpov Kinrade is the pen name for the husband and wife entertainment duo Lux and Dmytry Karpov-Kinrade. Together, they write award-winning, USAT bestselling books, make music, write screenplays and direct movies -- all the things.

They live in wine country with their three offspring who have crazy creative genius oozing out of them, one dog who thinks he's a cat and six cats who all think they rule the world (spoiler alert: they do).

Website: http://KarpovKinrade.com
Facebook: http://facebook.com/KarpovKinrade
Instagram: http://instagram.com/KarpovKinrade
Twitter: http://Twitter.com/KarpovKinrade

ALSO BY KARPOV KINRADE

For more in the Vampire Girl Universe, check out the following series and books:

Vampire Girl, the original series

Vampire Girl (Book 1)

Midnight Star (Book 2)

Silver Flame (Book 3)

Moonlight Prince (Book 4)

First Hunter (A new spin off series)

First Hunter (Book 1)

Unseen Lord (on preorder, Book 2)

Of Dreams and Dragons

SWAG

A LANDRY FAMILY SERIES SHORT STORY

ADRIANA LOCKE

A Landry Family Series Short Story featuring Lincoln Landry.

ONE

"Don't act like you aren't impressed." I toss the golf club into the back of the cart like hitting a hole in one is something I do every day. It isn't. It could be. I am Lincoln Landry, after all.

My three brothers scoff. They make their way across the green, each mumbling something under their breath.

"What?" I goad, breathing in a lungful of sweet, summer air. "I'm even impressed with myself for that one."

Ford shoots me a look. "I'm not acting when I say this," he says, climbing into the driver's seat, "but I'm not impressed."

"How was that excellent display of athleticism not impressive?" I pretend to swing a club in slow motion. "If I would've been swinging for real, that would've been a hole in one too."

"Shut up and get in the cart, Linc." Barrett laughs, smacking my shoulder as he walks by.

"Come on, Barrett. It was a Hole. In. One. How many times have you shot one of those?" I reconsider my angle. "Don't answer that. You were a politician. All you did was golf."

"It's more than you do these days," Graham grumbles as he takes the front passenger's seat and grabs a water bottle.

I climb in behind Ford. "And what's that supposed to mean?"

"Nothing. It means nothing," Graham replies.

"I'm just saying it wouldn't kill any of you to acknowledge my successes. I mean . . . how hard is it to get a little, 'Wow, great shot, Lincoln'?" I shrug. "Shouldn't be that complicated."

Ford twists in his seat and removes his sunglasses. "You do realize you shot your hole in one on a practice green at the Farm, right? Maybe if it had been a real course, we'd pat you on the back."

He has a point, but I'm not going to acknowledge it. Instead, I lift my water bottle out of the cup holder and take a sip. My brothers carry on chiding me, taking Ford's stupid point and running with it. I've always liked him the least.

"That's bullshit," I say after a particularly dumb comment from Ford. I point at him. "You ran a 5K last weekend and everyone went on and on about how great that was."

He doesn't bat an eyelash. "Um, I did it in under fifteen minutes. That *is* great."

"Not my point," I continue. "No one was pointing out that it wasn't a marathon. They took your achievement, however unimpressive it may have been," I say, ignoring his chuckle, "and celebrated it. If I recall correctly, my wife and I sent you flowers."

"And they were lovely," he teases. "Should I send you flowers for your hole in one today? Is that what this is about?"

Graham sighs. "Can we go now?"

"No," I say, getting comfortable. "When's the last time you ran a 5K, G?"

"Don't drag me into this. You two can go at it all you want, but can we do it on the way back to the house? I have a meeting in thirty minutes."

"It's Sunday." Barrett points out. "Take a day off, G."

Graham looks at our oldest brother. "It's about the property your wife wants to buy for the new house."

Barrett whips his head back to Ford. "Let's get on with it."

Ford hits the accelerator, and we're thrown backward in our seats. He takes a hard right turn that earns a slew of profanities from Barrett. Ford just laughs.

We rip across the freshly mowed grass at full speed. Across the field and down the little knoll, the sunlight ripples off the pond where my brothers, sisters, and I learned to swim.

"I'd say that shot was only about fifty yards," Ford notes, slowing the golf cart. "It wasn't far."

"I'd say less than that," Barrett chimes in.

"No one asked you." I scoff. "And that was way more than fifty yards."

Ford swerves the cart around a dip in the lawn and goes airborne for a split second. Graham sighs. We take a quick right around a jut of trees, and then the farmhouse comes into view.

The white exterior with black shutters looks like a picture from a history book. It isn't a farmhouse at all, really, but an old, plantation-style home that's been in the Landry family for decades. We celebrate everything here—holidays, birthdays, contract executions, and political wins. It's the epicenter of our family just outside of Savannah's city limits.

A smile twists my lips as I spy my wife's SUV pulled up in front of the house. I haven't seen her since before the sun came up this morning, and knowing she's just a centerfielder's throw away has my feet tapping against the floorboard.

"Problem?" Barrett asks, glancing at my foot.

"Nah. Just saw that Dani's here."

"You do live with her, right?" Graham asks, looking at me over his shoulder. "You see her every day, I'm assuming."

"Yeah, I see her every day. I had to leave early this morning and I think she'd been up most of the night with Ryan. I just want to check on her."

"For a second, I was afraid you were going to tell us she wised up and left your ass," Ford jokes. His head ducks forward, anticipating the half-punch I toss his way. Laughing, he rocks the golf cart back and forth. "Settle down back there."

"If you throw me out of this thing, I'll have Troy beat your ass," Barrett says, grabbing on to the railing beside him.

"Does that mean you're admitting you can't?" Ford asks.

"Hell, no! It just means I have people to do the dirty work for me."

"We know. You're a politician," I say with a snort.

"*Was* a politician. I'm retired. Living the easy life."

"That means you're old." I point out. "First step is retirement. Next step is needing a pill to—"

Ford cuts the wheels so sharply I almost fall out of the golf cart. It's a good thing, though, because I'm fairly certain Barrett was going to try to push me out of the other side.

"Sometimes I think you're all toddlers." Graham rolls his eyes. "For fuck's sake, Ford."

"What? Did that mess up your polo shirt?" Ford grins. "Relax a little, G. Here. I'll help." He jerks the wheel again—the other way this time—almost knocking Graham and Barrett onto the lawn. Unfortunately for Ford, our father is standing on the porch.

Our father and I have never been the best of friends. He's more of a stickler for the rules, whereas I like to think rules are meant to be broken. However, the look he gives Ford makes me envious. With nothing more than a dipped chin and set jaw aimed Ford's way, the golf cart slows, and I bow to our father's skills. I couldn't pull that off as a dad. I'm a sucker.

"Sorry, Dad," Ford shouts as we roll to a stop just below our dad. "There are some gopher holes out there, and I—"

"He's lying," I chime in. "He was trying to knock Barrett off. You should probably do something about that, Dad. Your all-American over there is trying to kill your golden boy."

"Someone jealous?" Ford asks.

"Me? Jealous of you? Delusions."

"Delusions are you thinking that hole in one was award worthy," Barrett laughs.

Graham trudges up the stairs and tosses Dad a look. "You're lucky they're all still alive."

We form a line and follow Graham toward the house. My heartbeat picks up, strumming wildly as I anticipate Dani just a few feet away. Then, like the asshole he is, my father halts my plans.

With a chuckle, he clamps down onto my shoulder. It's a veiled warning to stay put. "Let me know when dinner's ready, boys. I'm gonna talk to Linc for a minute."

"But . . ." I look at the door and then back to him.

"It'll just take a few minutes, Lincoln."

Fucking wonderful.

TWO

The door closes behind Barrett. It's just my father and I on the porch. The ferns my mother loves are evenly spaced on their hooks and sway with the breeze. I used to love sitting on the swing, a piece of candy I stole from one of my brothers in hand as I watched them go back and forth as a kid.

Today, though, it's mildly irritating. My wife is inside, and I haven't kissed her in maybe twelve hours. I had Ellie go check on her this afternoon. She took Ryan for a bit so Dani could get a nap. She thinks she has to do everything herself and hates asking for help, but her lack of taking care of herself is killing me.

Ryan is my world. A perfect mix of Danielle and me, there isn't a damn thing I wouldn't do for that kid. I'd fight a bull, swim with sharks, swallow fire. But Dani is what makes everything possible. She's my rock. My heart. My fucking soul.

Her ass isn't bad either.

I adjust my cock.

"What's up, Dad?" I ask, contemplating how quickly I can get him to say his piece and get out of here. He looks serious, so that isn't giving me the warm and fuzzies. These situations usually end with me being read a list of things I'm screwing up.

Sigh.

He moseys his way to the railing and leans against it as if we have all the time in the world. I drop onto the swing in the most nonchalant way possible. If he gets any sense at all I'm trying to rush him, he'll drag this out for hours.

"Well, Linc. I need your help."

Jaw. Hits. Floor. "Um, are you feeling okay?"

"Yes." His brows pull together. "Why?"

"You do realize I'm Lincoln, right? Your youngest son. Not Barrett, the former governor of Georgia. Not Ford, the American hero. Not Graham, the CEO of our lives."

"I realize who you are. The biggest pain-in-the-ass I have. I haven't lost my mind."

"Clearly, you have if you're asking me for help." I laugh. "You haven't ever asked me for help . . . except the time you needed tickets to the baseball championship. I think you even said 'please'."

"I—"

"I'm not complaining." I hold my hands in front of me, adding, "I've had a lot of free time and got out of a lot of boring political shit. So, I guess, thank you for never needing me." A series of memories rolls through my mind of college and various parties I went to. Get-togethers as a professional athlete. Drinks, laughs, women. While I wouldn't trade my life now for a lifetime of that again, I am quite fond of those memories. "Yes, thank you. I mean that."

Dad shoves off the railing and sits beside me. His hands clasp together as he rests his forearms on his knees in a move that reminds me exactly of Graham. As he stares off across the lawn, a ghost of a smile plays on his lips.

"We've had a lot of good times out here, haven't we?" he asks quietly. "I remember when you threw that pitch that busted Barrett in the eye. Remember that?"

"Yup," I say with a pop on the p. "In my defense, I warned him it was going to curve like a motherfucker. He didn't trust me."

Dad grins. "Remember when your sisters wanted to camp that Fourth of July? And Ford and I put up a little tent over there under that tree?" He points to a large maple near the side of the house. "Sienna was afraid her ice would melt, and Camilla needed to take lotion. I knew they'd never make it all night."

"And then Ford and I went out there in the middle of the night and scared the shit out of them?"

A slow chuckle ripples across the patio as Dad sits upright. "I hope Ryan is just like you."

"Oh, he is," I say. "He's cute as hell. Can already throw a ball really well even though he's still a baby. And you can't take him anywhere without women stopping to gawk. A chip off the old block."

Dad just shakes his head. "Let's see how that works out for you in ten years or so."

Suddenly, I get what he's saying. My hands scrub down my face as I envision calls from principals and busted glass from baseballs and girls showing up at the house while he has another one upstairs in his bedroom that his parents don't know about. Me.

I'm his parent.

Oh, shit.

I force a swallow. "I've been considering boarding school . . ."

Dad's laugh is loud. His chest rumbles as his hand smacks my thigh. "You're gonna be fine, Linc."

"I don't know."

"I do." He settles down and leans back in the swing. "Your mother and I have been doing a little estate planning."

"You aren't dying, are you?" The words come out of my mouth before I can catch them. "That was really rude if you are, but let's cut the crap, Dad."

"No, we aren't dying." He sighs. "We are getting older, though, and we thought it would be a good time to go over our things and make sure they're in order."

Leaning back, mirroring his pose, I shrug. "This really sounds like a conversation you should be having with Graham."

"Typically, it would be," he agrees. "But this is one I want to have with you."

"If you think you're cutting me out of the inheritance—"

"Lincoln, hush."

He shakes his head again. I think he's on the verge exasperation, but I don't give a shit. This conversation is weird, and I don't know where it's going. I look over my shoulder for Graham or Barrett, but no one is around.

I know my role in this family, and it isn't one that involves decisions or responsibility. I'm good with that. There's no need to mess it up now.

He takes a long, deep breath. "How would you feel if I were to make you the executor of my will?"

I had one beer this afternoon. I wasn't hit with a golf club. I got plenty of sleep last night, and I'm fairly certain Dani hasn't been poisoning me.

Yet, Dad's face isn't flinching. No one is jumping out of the bushes, pointing at me and laughing and yelling, "Gotcha!" So, what the fuck is this?

My stomach knots up as a lump settles at the base of my throat. "Um, I think I misheard you."

"No, you didn't."

"Okay." I can't help but wiggle in my seat like a child. "You want me to be the guy that makes sure your things are divided equally?"

"Yes."

"Why?" I balk. "Barrett's the oldest. Graham's the most responsible. Ford's the honorable one out of us," I reiterate. "Why would you want me to do that? Dani doesn't even let me mix Ryan's formula."

Amusement flickers across his face. "Do you remember when Camilla got a rabbit from the shelter when she was seven or eight? And then it got out of its cage in the middle of the night?"

"You all blamed me for that. I'm still a little salty now that I think about it."

Dad tries not to laugh. "But what did you do?"

"I rode my bike to the shelter and got her another one. I had to convince her it had reddish fur the day before and she just didn't realize it. That was a chore." I groan, remembering how I spent an entire summer day dealing with a bunny I didn't even like. My eyes flip back to my dad. "What's this have to do with your estate?"

"That's why I want you to be the executor."

"Because I got Cam a new bunny twenty years ago?"

"Yes."

Getting to my feet, I jab a finger his way. "You've lost your mind. It took longer than I thought it would, but here we are."

He stands as well and puts his hand on my shoulder. It's another warning not to move. To stay put. That I'm probably going to need to brace for whatever he's about to say. "Out of all my children, you and I are the most different."

"True. Very, very true."

"You don't have to say it like that."

"What do you expect? It's true. How much more different could we be?"

He considers this as he blows out a breath. Instead of directly addressing my question, he goes into storytelling mode. I settle in for the long haul and try to convince myself I don't hear Dani's laugh vaguely through the door.

"I got my first job as a twelve-year-old boy delivering newspapers to the neighborhood," he says. "I've worked every day since that day. Barrett, Graham, especially, and even Ford are just like I am."

"I know. You tell me all the time, which is why I don't understand why you didn't pick one of them. Are you punishing me? Is this some kind of way for you to get back at me for not wanting the vice president job at Landry Holdings?"

His arm goes over my shoulders like I've seen him to do my brothers a hundred times. It isn't really our thing, and it kind of feels a little awkward, but not bad.

"No, Lincoln. You're different from me, but that isn't a bad thing."

"Well, yeah. Obviously. Look at me."

He smacks my back before pulling away. "Don't get too cocky."

"Danielle calls it confidence."

"I believe your mother calls it arrogance, and hers is the opinion that matters at the end of the day."

I start to object, but his single crooked brow stops me. "As I was saying, your mother and I have been discussing the future and who should handle our affairs. Naturally, we considered Graham. He's the logical choice."

"Clearly."

"But Graham would divide everything up into six parts. He would kill himself over making sure everyone had their equal piece."

"Clearly. Which," I add quickly, "would make it five parts because he wouldn't need his when he keeled over from stress, and that does have its benefits."

He ignores that.

"Life isn't about being fair," Dad says, gazing over the lawn again. "It isn't about things or wealth or accumulating all kinds of shit that sits on a mantle. Do you understand what I'm saying?"

"Yeah. I mean . . . I could be playing in the majors right now if I wanted to bad enough. But I didn't want to give up being there for Ryan as he grew up or coming home to Danielle at night. There just isn't enough money in the world to make up for that."

"That's what I'm talking about," he says, nodding emphatically. "I hate to admit this, but seeing you with Ryan really shed some light on things for me. Barrett with Huxley, too, but that kid of yours . . ." He beams. "I should've spent more time with you playing catch and a few less hours at the office, Linc."

I try to swallow but can't. My throat is squeezed shut as I watch a man that could do anything in the entire universe look at me like a mortal.

When I look at my wife, I can tell what she's thinking by the look in her eyes. I've never had that happen with another person in the world. She doesn't have to speak, doesn't have to indicate what she's feeling or needs—I know. It's a conversation that doesn't need to be had aloud.

For the first time in my life, I'm having that same thing with my father. It's a moment I will never forget. Clearing my throat, I look away.

"You are my only child that understands what life's really about, Lincoln. You'd spend all day rolling around on the floor with Ryan."

"Or Danielle," I crack, needing some levity.

Dad laughs, tapping at his eyes with a handkerchief from his pocket. "Think about what I've said, all right?"

"Yeah." I clear my throat again, the lump not completely dissolved. "And Dad?"

"Yes, Son?"

"I'm glad you didn't play catch with me much. Your fastball is shit."

"Oh, Linc . . ."

His arm is around me again as we head into the house.

THREE

"Stop talking about me," I say as I step into the living room.

"Why would we be talking about you?" Ford asks. Ryan is propped up against him and is wearing a little camouflage outfit Ford's wife, Ellie, bought him last week.

Reaching down, I lift Ryan off Ford's lap, ignoring my brother's silent protest, and curl my son against my chest. He nuzzles into me, smelling of baby soap and his mama. The world could end right now and I wouldn't care.

I scan the room until I find Danielle. She's standing next to the sliding glass door that leads into the backyard. She's still a little rounder than she was before Ryan, her eyes a little darker. She's never been more perfect.

Her eyes meet mine, and despite the laughter from my mom and brothers' wives in the kitchen, Huxley's video game on the television, my father telling a story behind me that my brothers seem to love, all I can see is Dani.

Sometimes I watch her sleep and marvel that she chose me. She could have had any guy she wanted. Yet, she chose me—the goofy baseball player who was on his way out of the league with an injury. She saw past the jokes and failures and the way I drool in my sleep and agreed to marry me and have my babies.

My cock strains the fabric of my pants.

She comes toward me, her eyes never leaving mine. "Hello, Mr. Landry," she says softly, her arm going around my waist. A simple kiss is pressed to the top of Ryan's head. "How'd things go with your dad?"

"Really fucking weird," I whisper. "I'll tell you all about it later. We have things to do now."

She pulls away. "Like what?"

"Like get the hell out of here."

Her arms extend for Ryan, but I don't let go. This makes her giggle. "Camilla isn't even here yet, Linc. We can't leave."

"Yes, we can. It isn't my fault she and Dominic can't get out of bed long

367

enough to come to dinner."

"You're just jealous," she chides.

"Damn right I am. I want to be home in bed with you."

She leans closer so that her head is resting on my chest beside Ryan's and whispers, "What's this all about?"

"What's what all about?"

"You wanting to leave. You love it here with your family."

"*Our* family," I correct, not missing a moment to drive home the point that this is hers. Everything of mine is hers. That was why there was no prenup, no talk of splitting shit in the hypothetical event of our marriage coming to an end. If that happened, I'd be done. She could have it.

Her hands lock around my waist, her sweet perfume washing over me. "Our family," she repeats.

My fingers find the hem of her shirt and scoot beneath the soft fabric. My palm lays flat against the small of her back, the warmth of her skin heating mine.

As I glance across the room, my gaze finds my dad's. He's watching us. Public displays of affection aren't his favorite thing in the world, and I brace myself for his reaction. He surprises me by smiling. With a gentle nod, he turns back to my brothers.

"What are you thinking?" Dani asks.

That this is the way life is supposed to be. That I wouldn't change a damn thing. That I love you more every day and wouldn't be able to breathe without you.

Ford's hand thumps the back of my head as he walks by.

That Ford isn't getting shit from Dad's estate if he isn't careful.

"Oh, just that I'd like to be buried balls-deep inside you right now," I whisper into her ear.

She shifts from foot to foot, her breasts rubbing against my stomach. "Landry . . ."

"You were so hot this morning when I left," I tell her.

"I was in sweatpants and one of your old T-shirts cleaning up baby vomit. I'm sure that was so hot."

She looks at the floor, remnants of our recent conversations about her low self-esteem working their way through. I've tried to listen, to understand it, but when all I see when I look at her is complete fucking perfection, I can't understand. How can having a baby make her feel less pretty? Less desirable? If only she knew what she does to me.

"Look at me," I say, tipping her chin so she's doing just that. "What if I told you I've been half hard all day from seeing you like that? That I've rushed every damn meeting I've had and then irritated my brothers so they'd stop golfing and I could see you sooner."

Her cheeks flush a beautiful shade of pink. "I'd think you were lying."

"I've thought about you all day," I murmur. "And when I'm thinking of you, I'm not thinking of you in a dress or heels or fancy lingerie. I'm thinking of you with your hair all bundled on top of your head and wearing one of my old concert shirts."

"Really?"

"Yes, really," I say, bending and touching my lips to hers. Her mouth is soft, smooth, and inviting, which is all I really want—to be wanted and accepted by this woman. "I also think," I whisper against her lips, "of those big, round breasts and the way your ass bounces on my cock."

"Stop." She lets out a soft giggle.

"And the way your skin feels against mine when I'm touching you in every way fucking possible." I kiss her again. "No more T-shirts when we're together. I can't do it anymore."

"But Linc . . ."

"Those stretch marks you hate? I love." I bend closer, seeing as deep into her eyes as I can. "I love them."

"How can you?" she asks, looking at me with wide eyes.

"Because they're proof of how much you love me. That you carried my son. That you'd do that to yourself to give this to me," I tell her, glancing down at Ryan. "No more T-shirts, Dani. No more lights off and hiding yourself. You're so fucking gorgeous, babe."

Tears dot her eyes as she buries her face against my chest.

"I'm hard again," I groan.

Her hand moves down my abs and over the bulge in my pants. "Okay, I agree. It's fifteen after six. I say Cam's had enough time to get here."

"Atta girl," I chuckle. "You get the diaper bag and do your good-byes fast. I'll give Mom a kiss, Graham some hell, and we'll be off."

"Linc?"

I stop in my tracks. The look she's giving me almost has me getting off right here. "Yeah?"

She pulls me close, lifting up on her toes. Her breath hot against my ear as she says, "Thank you."

"For what?"

"For making me feel pretty."

"You have no idea how pretty I'm going to make you feel when we get home," I whisper back. "Now, get the diaper bag and go to the car so I can strip you naked and—"

Her giggle is soft as she smacks my behind. "Behave."

Graham is watching us from the other side of the room, Mallory at his side. He smirks. "I'm guessing our conversation will have to wait until tomorrow."

"You'd guess right. I have more . . . pressing . . . things to do. I'll be by your office first thing."

"I'll be expecting you around ten." He nods.

"Must be nice," Barrett chimes in. "Getting up on Linc Time."

"I get up way before then," I say, making my way toward the door. "I just don't do anything with any of you before then." Pausing at the threshold, I look back at Barrett. "Wanna meet me at seven at the park for a run?"

"I'll meet you," Ford laughs. "Seven, you say?"

"Oh, fuck you. No way in Hell I'm running with you."

My brothers laugh as I give everyone a final wave and blow Mom a kiss. Danielle is right behind me. We step onto the porch, but she stops as soon as the door is shut behind us.

"What's the matter?" I ask, searching her face.

"Nothing." She brushes a strand of hair out of her face. "I just . . . I love you,

369

Landry." She works the blanket up around Ryan's face. "You're the best, you know that?"

"Yes, I do. Now let's get out of here so I can prove it."

Her laugh trails behind her as she heads to the car. As I watch her go, I can't help but think Dad is right.

It isn't about how many women you ring up or how many stats you tally at work. It isn't about how good you look or what kind of car you drive or the people that associate your name with the word "valuable."

It's about eating takeout on the couch with a girl in sweatpants. It's about being in a relationship where you know she isn't going to watch your show without you. It's about making babies and cleaning up vomit and going grocery shopping on a Friday night instead of heading to the bar.

Dani opens the car door and bends forward, retrieving a pacifier from the floorboard. "I've been looking for this for a week," she says, taking Ryan from my arms. She buckles him in and kisses his forehead before turning back to me. "You ready?"

"The questions is: are you?"

She looks back at Ryan and then to me. "I want to ask you something."

"Okay."

She puts her arms around me, her lips curling at the corners. "I mean it."

"Okay," I say, kissing the tip of her nose.

"I know Ryan's still little and my emotions have been a little all over the place, but I kind of want to have another baby. Soon. I mean, not today but within the next year or so—"

My blood turns so hot I think I might pass out. "If you don't get in that car, woman . . ."

"Is that a yes?" Her question is dripping with sweetness.

"As if that's a real question. I . . . fuck it." Moving before she can sense it, I lift her up. Her legs go around my waist as I press her against the passenger's door of the car. My lips find hers, my tongue sliding between them.

Her hands slide into my hair as she moves her mouth against mine. The heat of her pussy is warm against my stomach, her swollen breasts pushed against my chest.

"I want to fuck you right here," I growl, but Ryan's cries ruin the moment. I pull back from the kiss and rest my forehead against Dani's. "Maybe we just practice for another baby for a while," I groan.

"Practice makes perfect."

"You're already perfect, pretty girl," I say, lowering her to her feet. "You driving or am I?"

"You just want to sit in the back with Ryan and play with him." She laughs because she knows she is right.

"So?"

"Go on," she says, rolling her eyes. "I'll drive."

I swipe the keys out of her hands. "Not a chance. You're too slow, and we have plans."

The sun begins to drop behind the tops of the trees. I jog around the front of the car but stop before getting in. Looking up at the sky and the wild pattern of purples and pinks, I think of all the things I hoped for in my life. None of them I got. Yet, somehow, it sure feels like I got everything.

ABOUT THE AUTHOR

USA Today and Amazon Top 10 Bestselling author Adriana Locke lives and breathes books. After years of slightly obsessive relationships with the flawed bad boys created by other authors, Adriana has created her own.

She resides in the Midwest with her husband, sons, and two dogs. She spends a large amount of time playing with her kids, drinking coffee, and cooking. You can find her outside if the weather's nice and there's always a piece of candy in her pocket.

For an email every time Adriana has a new release, sign up for an alert here: http://bit.ly/AmazonAlertAdriana or text the word adriana to 21000.

Facebook: http://www.facebook.com/authoradrianalocke
Instagram: http://www.instagram.com/authoradrianalocke
Goodreads: http://bit.ly/GRAdriana

ALSO BY ADRIANA LOCKE

The Exception Series

The Exception

The Connection, a novella

The Perception

The Landry Family Series

Sway

Swing

Switch

Swear

Swink

Sweet - coming Summer 2018

The Gibson Boys Series

Crank

Craft

Cross, a novella

Crave—coming Summer 2018

Standalone Novels

Sacrifice

Wherever It Leads

Written in the Scars

Battle of the Sexes

Lucky Number Eleven

12 Days Until Sunday—coming fall 2018

LOVE & HATE AT THE STALLION STATION

A DARK TEXAS NIGHTS SHORT STORY

LEX MARTIN

"Love and Hate at the Stallion Station" is a short story featuring Chase and Willow, characters related to the Dark Texas Night series.

LOVE & HATE AT THE STALLION STATION

A DARK TEXAS NIGHTS SHORT STORY

Chase

A bead of sweat rolls down my forehead, and I wipe it away with the back of my hand. It might be raining outside, but it's still humid as hell in the barn. I'm dying to knock off for the night, take a long shower so I feel human again, and toss back a cold beer, but these guys need to get tucked in.

I give Rowdy Good Time a scratch behind his ear.

"It's just rain, big guy." The sorrel stallion doesn't look convinced and stomps in his stall. "I promise, everything's okay." I speak in a soft voice, like I would to a child. I don't have any kids—thank God—but if I did, I'm guessing this is the way I'd sound. Nothing like I usually do when I have to bark out orders around here. But a nighttime routine in the middle of a Texas thunderstorm requires a gentle hand.

"Chin up. You'll see your girlfriend tomorrow."

It's probably sad that my horse has more going on in his love life than I do. Not that I've tried too hard up to this point, but as I get closer to my thirtieth birthday, the more significant this shit seems. Sure, I've dated but nothing serious. Sex with a willing, warm woman is easy enough to come by without any entanglements or drama.

Which is how I find myself alone, in a barn full of horses, on a Friday night.

My back pocket buzzes with another text. I pull it out and shake my head when I see the message from my cousin.

Ethan: You're really flying solo? Aww, the captain of the football team can't get a date?

Fucker. I laugh as I confirm that RSVP for his wedding later this summer. He

379

shouldn't be shocked I'm going alone.

It's not that I can't have a date. It's that I *don't want a date*. Not for a wedding. There's no one I'm serious enough about to tread those waters. Take a woman to a wedding and she starts imagining herself in that white dress and you at the altar.

No thanks.

Add in the way Ethan looks at his fiancée, Tori, and I want to gag a little.

The sound of tires squealing to a stop on my gravel drive out front makes me pause as I'm finishing up with the last horse. I step out of the stall into the center aisle in time to catch Willow Summers stomping through the barn looking fierce as fuck and just as fine as the first time I laid eyes on her in high school. Over the years, I've bumped into her around town, but she generally avoids me, so it's surprising to see her here.

"To what do I owe the pleasure of this delightful visit, Miss Summers?"

Her scowl deepens, and I chuckle. This woman could shrivel a lesser man's dick at ten paces with that glare. I don't fancy myself as someone who has crushes, but if I did, it'd be Willow. No one else has ever come close to fitting that bill except her.

"Don't you smile at me, you cocky bastard. You know full well why I'm here." Her long black hair looks wild about her shoulders. Droplets of rain glisten across her beautiful, albeit pissed, face.

For some reason, I've always had this effect on her. Like she's not sure if she wants to slap me or fuck me. Unfortunately, she's never given in to the impulse to get naked and horizontal with yours truly, but I'm pretty sure she's nearly slapped me a time or two in the fifteen years I've known her.

I allow myself a quick perusal of her petite frame.

A baby blue tank top that matches her hypnotic eyes. A billowy white skirt that teases me with glimpses of those luscious legs. A pair of scuffed cowboy boots.

I back away before all my blood heads south.

"Sorry, sweetheart. Haven't a clue." I tug off my baseball cap and reach for my T-shirt that's dangling off the back pocket of my Wranglers. After a quick swipe of the fabric across my forehead, neck, and chest, I can breathe again.

Something about this woman has always driven me crazy. Wish I could scratch that itch and get her out of my system once and for all, but she's never given me the time of day. I've never had any trouble getting my pick of females around here, but Willow's in a class of her own.

When she doesn't say anything, I turn back to her.

She stares up at me and blinks.

I don't miss the way her eyes take me in. The way they travel over my chest and shoulders. Down my abs.

She opens her mouth a few times before she says anything. "Can you please put on some clothes?"

I fight a smile. "Why? Afraid you can't control yourself around me? Is my virtue in danger?"

A laugh escapes me as she rolls her eyes, but I don't miss the heat rising in her cheeks. We've never lacked sexual chemistry. And I'd bet everything in my wallet that she'd have given into this long ago if I had a different last name.

She huffs. "You mean if you had any virtue left? I assumed you left that in Mr. Hillar's meadow our senior year."

My smile widens. "Had some fond memories there back in the day. Would've been fonder if some of them included you."

Her nostrils flare. "In your dreams."

"How'd you know?" She probably has no clue how many she's starred in. An image from the other night flashes in my mind. Of my fingers digging roughly into her thick locks. Of her moaning into my mouth. Grinding against my lap like she wanted me as much as I've always wanted her. "My favorite fantasy is the one where you're on top—"

"Would you stop?" With a wave of her hand, she cuts me off. "How can you be so flippant at a time like this?" She slaps a piece of paper onto my chest. Standing this close, I can smell the droplets of rain in her hair and something sweet. "You know how much my father's farm means to me. How could you do this?"

I grimace, my mind racing to understand what she's talking about. I'm so fucking confused. Even more so by the tears welling in her eyes. I've never seen this girl cry. Even when her mother passed last year, she was stoic. Probably for the sake of her dad, but still. Makes me want to give a good beatdown to whoever upset her.

My heart kicks against my ribs as I glance down at the letter, and that swell of anger grows when I see the letterhead of my father's attorney.

"Willow, I had nothing to do with this. I didn't know your farm was on Duke's radar." Duke Carter, my father, is a miserly bastard, which is why most of our family stopped talking to him years ago.

She snatches it out of my grasp. "Don't you fucking lie to me, Chase." Her lower lip trembles, and I decide right here and now to do everything I can to make this right.

I may have teased her from time to time when we were growing up, but only in dumb attempts to flirt. But this? Take her land? Harm her family? I'd never stoop so low.

I hold up my hands. "Swear to God, Lo. I'd never try to hurt you. You have to believe me."

I'm not sure when we became enemies. When she embraced this idea that we were on opposing sides. That I'd fight her for something as precious as her farm. She needs to know I'm not involved with this nonsense.

When that tear tumbles down, I can't help it anymore. I step closer and cup her cheek, rubbing gently across her soft skin with my thumb.

"Don't cry," I murmur. "It'll be okay."

Her breath catches, and her eyes widen as I stand toe to toe with her. In all of our interactions over the years, I don't think we've ever been this close. Close enough to feel the buzzing of electricity between our bodies.

I tower over her, and when she stares up at me, cheeks flushed, lips parted, looking so fucking beautiful, it makes me wonder why I didn't go after her years ago. Wonder why I let whatever weirdness that crept up between us stand.

"Lo, I promise I'll never let Duke foreclose on your farm." My voice is soft.

Calm. Barely above a whisper. "I know you've never liked me, but I'm not the prick you think I am, and I can tell you that I will always have your back."

I've never said anything truer. From the first day I met her, I've admired this woman. The way she always worked hard at school when I could barely get my shit together, lucky to skate by on my athletic abilities. The way she busted her ass on her father's farm when I was out joyriding with my friends. How she took care of her mother when she got sick, an experience I've never had, thankfully.

She takes a deep breath, but she doesn't step away. "We both know your father gets what he wants." It kills me to hear the defeat in her voice.

"Maybe. But I'm pretty sure I want this more than he wants your family's property." Her eyes search mine, and I hope she can read into what I'm saying right now. I give her my most charming smile. "Come on, Lo. Let me take you to dinner."

Which is the wrong thing to say.

"Is that what this is about?" She jerks out of my arms. "You want me to sleep with you to get your dad to back off?"

"What? No. Jesus." I scrub my face. "I mean, yeah, I've always wanted you, Willow. You must know that." She keeps walking backward. Fuck. "But that has nothing to do with Duke trying to foreclose on your farm. I'll stop him regardless of whether you let me take you out for a steak or not."

The barn door blows open behind us, and she shudders with the blast of wind. I jog over to shut it, and when I peer out across my property, the rain is coming down so hard, I can barely see her SUV ten feet away. When I finally get it closed, I'm drenched.

I'm laughing at how ridiculous this all is. Willow looks like she wants to murder me, but I'd give my left nut for her to believe me. I reach for my old T-shirt again and wipe the water off my face.

"Willow, how much do I love Shelby?" This whole town knows I'm obsessed with two things, my horses and my vintage 1967 Mustang.

Caught off guard by my question, she rolls her eyes. "Why are you asking me such a stupid question?"

I toss my T-shirt over a chair, and stalk closer, walking toward her until her back hits the stall. "Answer my question, doll."

She crosses her arms and tries to frown, but as she glances away, a smile tugs on her lips. "You love your car. Everyone ..."

"Everyone knows that, right?" She's nodding, looking at me like I'm a dumbass for asking her something so random. I grab her hand and place it on my bare chest, across my heart, where I know she can feel it hammering away. "I promise on my beloved Shelby that I will not let my father foreclose on your property regardless of whether you finally give into this crush you've had on me since high school and let me take you to dinner."

Her mouth falls open, and her eyes open wide. "I do *not* have a crush on you, you pompous jerk."

Propping my arm against the wall behind her, I smile as I dip my head toward hers. "Yes, you do. Stop fighting it." When I can feel her minty breath on my lips, I pause and wait for her to smack me or kick me in the balls, but she doesn't.

There's one thing I need to know, though, before I take the last step.

As I graze the back of her neck with my fingertips, I ask, "Do you believe me? About your father's farm? I need to know."

For some reason, it feels like the world stills its spinning. The rain beat down outside, and the horses shift in their stalls.

Her big blue eyes study me as she worries her bottom lip. Even though her wide pupils and flushed skin tell me she wants this thing between us as much as I do, I know she's putting her father's farm first here. It's one of the qualities I've always admired about her. She puts her family first. Always.

After a beat—the longest one of my life—she nods yes.

A shy smile surfaces on her beautiful face.

That's all I needed to know before my lips crash against hers

Willow

I'm wondering if I blacked out after my father told me about the foreclosure notice and I'm dreaming, because how else can I explain why Chase Carter has pinned me to a stall and is kissing the daylights out of me?

But that's what's happening right now. His big hand is in my hair, his thick thigh between my legs, and his wicked tongue hot against mine

And holy cow can this boy kiss.

Except he's not a boy anymore.

No, the cocksure quarterback and star athlete I knew in high school is all man. A man who's just admitted that he likes me. Something he never would've done in high school. Why would he when he had a bevy of hookups at his beck and call?

Tall and broad, with surfer good looks and charm, Chase was every girl's crush growing up. I was the new kid who never quite fit in, shuttling back and forth between my mother's house in Austin and my dad's farm every time they split up. Which was often. My parents were the talk of the town with their fiery blow ups and quiet reconciliations. So when Chase's friends made snarky comments about my parents for their on-again, off-again relationship, I assumed he thought those things too.

But now I'm wondering if I've been wrong about him all this time.

He reaches down to cup my ass, hoisting me higher so I can wrap my legs around his trim waist, his mouth opening on my neck and sucking so hard, I feel my pulse hammer between my thighs.

"Chase, if you give me a hickey, so help me, I'm gonna strangle you. I'm not your property. You can't mark me."

He chuckles and presses his forehead to my shoulder. "You mean I can't pee a circle around you and tell the guys that if they so much as look in your direction, I'll beat their asses?"

I shake my head, biting back a smile as he straightens.

It's been more than ten years since he played football, but he's somehow even more handsome than he was in high school. His thick, dirty blond hair hangs tousled over those devastating green eyes, and his once lean frame has filled out with muscle from working on his father's farm.

Before I lose my nerve, I run my hand through his hair, and he closes his eyes and leans into my touch. *God, I've always wanted to do this.*

His hair is damp from sweat and the thunderstorm that blasted him when the barn door blew open a little while ago, but it's soft and smells like him. Like sandalwood and sexy man.

"What am I going to do with you?" I ask myself. Because what *does* a woman do with the guy whose father is trying to foreclose on your family's property?

His gaze sobers and his eyebrows press together as if he's considering my question. With mischief in his eyes, he answers seriously, "Hopefully, take me home and make me your sex slave."

On a sigh, I run my finger down his stubbled jaw. "You're trouble, Chase, with a capital T. Always have been."

"Maybe," he tells me quietly before claiming my lips in another kiss. "But I'd like to be your kind of trouble."

My heart flutters. *Yes, I'm definitely still at my father's house. Probably suffering from a brain aneurysm.*

A loud snort startles me, and I turn to see one of his huge horses eyeing us through the slats in his stall.

Chase waves him off. "Nothing to see here, Blackjack. Move along."

With the moment broken, Chase lets me slide down his body until my feet hit the floor. After he steadies me, he straightens my skirt, and I'm touched by his thoughtfulness.

When he takes a step back, I can't deny I'm disappointed that he's stopped touching me, but I try to school my expression. No sense in setting myself up to get hurt. After all, every girl in this town knows that Chase is a "for now" kind of guy, not a "forever and ever" sort of man. He's just not the settling down type, and I can't imagine burdening him with my tears and my problems would change that.

His words rush back to me, giving me pause. *I've always wanted you, Willow. You must know that.*

How is this possible? Was I so overwhelmed by my parents' marriage drama that I missed Chase's interest? I know I was shy in high school, but how did I miss something this huge?

And judging by what Chase thrust between my legs a few minutes ago, huge is the right word to use.

My eyes bore into the ground. I'm confused, turned on, and feeling more awkward than I have since I was a teenager. It was easy to put up a front and run my mouth when I thought he was an asshole like his friends. But present me with a sweet, thoughtful Chase who says he's always liked me, and I can't form sentences.

Despite his previous admission, I'm still surprised when he threads his fingers through mine and walks me to the entrance of the barn, stopping to kiss my forehead.

He reaches for his T-shirt, all the while watching me as he slips it on and stretches it over his broad shoulders. "Wait for me? I just need to do a couple more things around here before I head out. But I'd like to take you to dinner if you don't have any plans."

When I agree and that heart-stopping smile breaks out on his face, I wonder if one of the worst days of my life has just turned into one of the best.

Willow

We run through the rain without umbrellas, dodging puddles the size of water buffalos, and hop into his truck. We're laughing and shivering from the sudden drop in temperature from the barn to the windy field where he's parked.

Water drips into his eyes, and he squints at me. "Guess I didn't think this through too well. Sorry I don't have anything to warm you up." He peers into his back seat and riffles around, but comes up empty-handed.

We're drenched, and I feel bad that we're probably destroying his expensive leather seats.

"Do you think anything's even open right now? It's getting late. Bet the diner closed early when the downpour started."

He sighs as he heads down the driveway. "You're probably right." Pausing, he turns to look at me. "Rain check or ... I could make us a pizza back at my place. If you promise not to strip me naked and have your way with me."

I snort and shake my head, trying my damnedest to ignore the electricity still zinging between us. "I could go for pizza." And the nakedness too, if I'm being honest.

A seriousness settles over his expression. "You know I'm teasing you, right? I'd never take advantage of you, Lo. You'll always be safe with me."

I'm not going to hold the past against him. His cocky persona in high school made it easy to judge him, but he's been nothing but sincere tonight.

This time, I reach for his hand and give it a squeeze. "I wouldn't be in this car if I didn't feel safe with you, Chase."

We stare at each other a beat before grins break out on our faces. I feel like a kid in a candy shop. Giddy and light. Like anything could happen tonight. *Oh Lord. What am I getting myself into?*

A few minutes later, we've reached his house on the other side of the property, and I'm momentarily struck by the stupidity of this decision.

"We won't ... we won't see your dad, right?"

I think his father lives in the main house, a sprawling complex on the other side of the compound, but I can't be sure.

Chase shakes his head, but then holds up a finger. "That reminds me." He digs out his phone, punches a few buttons, and then switches the call to the speaker on the truck, so I can hear it ringing.

A gruff voice answers. "You'd better be in jail right now to be calling me so late."

Chase sighs and taps on the steering wheel. "Sorry to disappoint you, Duke."

I freeze at the realization that he's called his father.

"Well, get on with it. I'm about to go to bed."

"I want you to cancel the foreclosure on the Summers property."

An unamused laugh rings through the vehicle. "Why the hell would I do that? Larry Summers is an ingrate. Late on his payments for as long as he's owned that farm. It's about time I got my hands on that property."

Chase frowns, sending me an apologetic glance. "You want me to compete next month, right?"

"What's this about? You know you can't bow out now."

"Do you want me to compete at the Western Nationals or not? If you do, I suggest you find it in yourself to give Mr. Summers an extension on his payments."

Duke's string of curses make me flinch, but Chase gives me a wink.

I'm so stunned, my mouth falls open.

Chase comes from a family of cutting horse breeders and is a champion rider himself, so I'm guessing that bailing on this event would be a big deal.

When his father continues to balk, Chase sighs. "If the money is really the problem, then I'll compete, but I'll be giving you my winnings when I get back from Colorado, and you can send me the deed to the property. I'm sure I can cover whatever balance remains."

"Don't be ridiculous. What will you do with that land?"

"I don't plan on doing anything with the land, but I will be giving the deed to his daughter, Willow."

The wind could blow me over right now, I'm so shocked.

When Duke's curses fill the car again, something about being "pussy-whipped" and "head up his ass," Chase cuts him off and hangs up.

Without another word, he pulls into his garage. I follow him up into the house, all the while dazed from that conversation. Did this man really save my father's farm? The one my dad slaved away over the years to keep afloat?

Words escape me, and all I can do is stand there.

A sense of relief passes over me. My dad isn't going to lose his house. And this man, who I've been entirely wrong about for a decade and a half, saved him.

My breath stalls as I process what just happened.

One by one, low lights flicker on, and I hover in the hallway as he tosses his keys in the entryway bowl.

His tidy bachelor pad is a spacious ranch with leather couches, a huge flat screen TV, and beige walls. It's orderly and well cared for, but not homey. There are no photos of family and friends. No cozy blankets for nights binging on Netflix. No trophies, though I know he must have dozens.

With a father like his, it's no wonder.

All of a sudden, I know what I want to say. What I need to say. "Chase, I'll pay you back. Every penny that you give my dad."

He turns to me, and after a moment, the corner of his mouth tilts up. "Sure. Whatever you want."

Did he really agree that easily? This is so overwhelming. "Please consider this a loan, one that I'll repay instead of my father."

With a sigh, he scrubs his face. "Lo, in case you missed this, I'm not hurting for money. I'll never miss the winnings from that competition. What do I need? Another car? A new PlayStation? More clothes?" He shrugs. "If I know my father, he's charged a criminal amount of interest on the money your dad borrowed. It's okay if you want to think of this as the universe's way of settling a wrong."

How did I ever think poorly of this man? My heart overflows with gratitude. I move closer to him and place my hand on his strong chest, my eyes filling with tears. "How can I thank you?" I swallow the fist-sized boulder in my throat. "This is the kindest thing anyone's ever done for my family."

Those green eyes rove over my face as he lifts my chin up. "There is one thing you could do."

"Name it." Chase could ask me to walk home naked in the rain, and right now I'd do it.

"Think you could make me some of those pumpkin muffins you always sell at the farmer's market?" He grins. "They're always sold out by the time I get there."

I choke and blink back my tears. "You want my muffins?"

"More than you know. I am *dying* to taste your muffins." We're both chuckling as he tugs my hair back and kisses me. Softly at first until he tugs me closer, and then I'm in the air and wrapping my legs around his waist. "But just so we're clear," he says between kisses, "I didn't make this deal with Duke in order to taste your muffins."

I nip his bottom lip. "How about we not talk about our parents when you have your tongue down my throat."

"Deal."

We move through the house, but I'm too busy kissing his neck and clinging to him like a needy koala bear to pay attention. A minute later, we're tumbling onto his king-sized bed and ripping each other's clothes off. His jeans. My skirt. His T-shirt. My tank. Until all I have on is a sheer bra and boy shorts and his taut body strains against his gray boxer briefs.

"Why Chase Carter, you look even better than my fantasies."

And he does. When I saw those abs in the barn, I knew I was a goner, but up close and personal?

Divine.

Not sure what's making me so bold. I feel buzzed like I've been drinking. But I'm buzzed on Chase.

Is this how every girl feels with him when they come here? Like they're special? Like they mean something to him? Thinking back to how he dated other women over the years smarts, and I can't deny the jealousy that shoots through me.

I shake my head, refusing to let anything stop me from enjoying tonight. I have no idea if this will go anywhere, if what's between us is more than just some intense attraction or blowing off steam, but I won't allow the past or thoughts of what happens tomorrow morning ruin my night.

He slides over me, all muscle and solid man, until we're pressed chest to chest, and holy crap, he feels amazing. Between gentle sucks and licks to my neck, he whispers, "You have no idea how many times I've thought about you, Willow, but I can say that being here with you is definitely better than the fantasy."

If his goal is to melt me into a puddle, mission accomplished.

I'm slammed with the realization that although I've known Chase for years, I don't really know him. Not like this.

His thick thighs slide between mine, and I moan and writhe against him.

I let my hands wander over his smooth back. Over those wide shoulders. Into his unruly hair.

When our mouths connect, that frenzied feeling intensifies, his slick tongue dueling against mine while he rocks into me, his steely length the perfect counterpoint to the beat hammering between my legs.

"I can feel how wet you are through our underwear." His gruff voice makes me shiver.

387

"That's because I'm about to combust." I pant. "Why did we wait so long to do this?" I help him unhook my bra, loving how he groans when he grazes my nipple with his teeth.

"No idea, but we're going to fuck each other silly to make up for lost time. Pencil me in from now to Christmas."

I gasp, then moan as his hand reaches into my panties and glides against my wet skin, my eyes nearly rolling back in my head as he presses one, then two thick fingers into me.

"Oh God." I arch my back, my whole body buzzing and tight and so close. "I'm gonna come."

"That's right, baby. Fuck my hand." He thrusts hard while gently circling my clit, and I fly apart, my whole body pulsing.

When he slides out of me a minute later, I'm immediately at a loss and reach for him as he rolls over. I don't want to break this connection.

His big arms wrap around me, and I try to quell my gasping breaths when I collapse on top of him.

"That was ..." Amazing? Life-altering? *With just his hand.* I don't have words.

"Hot as hell." He chuckles, and I grin against his neck that's slick with sweat and rain and smells so damn good, I have half a mind to bite him.

But there's something I want to do more.

Chase

My breath catches in my throat when Willow sits astride me and smiles. She's so fucking beautiful. Her black hair is tangled around her and those blue eyes twinkle back.

She's smart. Witty. Honest. My ideal woman, honestly. Most of my friends had boners for her growing up.

For me it's more, though.

I stare at her, feeling like a teenager with his first crush and not caring that I probably have my feelings stamped on my forehead. Yeah, I like this girl. Always have.

So when she leans down to kiss me and rolls her hips against mine, there's one thing I need to know before we do anything else.

"Lo, can I ask you something?" I plant my hands on her thighs to still her motion.

She nods slowly, clearly caught off guard that I'm throwing on the breaks.

"What was your beef with me in high school? Was it just that my dad was an asshole, so you assumed I was too?"

Sure, I was a cocky little shit, but isn't every hormonal guy at that age? I just want to make sure there wasn't anything else. That I didn't say or do something that really hurt her.

I'm half aware that dredging up old memories doesn't bode well for reaching that final act tonight, but I'm more interested in making sure we have a shot at more than a one-time hookup.

She pulls the sheet to her chest and looks away, so I tilt her chin toward me.

"It's okay, Lo. Whatever it is, just tell me. I wanna know."

A long, quiet moment stretches between us, and finally she sighs.

"Your friends were pretty vile to me in school. Called me trash and all kinds of ... other things. When the whole town knows your family's dirty laundry, I guess that's par for the course, but it came at a really bad time for me, and I thought you must've felt that way too since those guys always followed you around."

I hear what she's not saying. "You thought I felt that way? That maybe I instigated them bullying you?"

She nods slowly and tries to slide off me, but I shake my head and pull her closer.

Did I hear some of the rumors our friends said about her? I must've, but I never paid them any mind since they talked shit about everyone, even me. But I never let those assholes harass anyone when we hung out.

When she rattles off a few familiar names, I nod, this whole thing finally making sense.

"Every single one of those douchebags had a hard-on for you, Lo. Each one would've given their left nut to be with you." She frowns and starts to object, but I cut her off. "I'm not saying that excuses their behavior, because it sure as shit doesn't, but I'm guessing that's why they were dicks to you. Because they wanted you, and you knew they were idiots. And let me say I never had anything to do with them bullying you. I would've kicked their asses had I known."

I parted ways with those dumbasses back in college.

"Is that everything, baby? Is that why you hated me?"

Those big blue eyes shimmer in the darkness. "I didn't hate you." Her voice is thick with emotion.

"It's okay if you did. I would've too had I experienced all that." I rub her thighs, trying to soothe her. "I just want you to know I'm sorry all this shit went down, and I was right there at the middle of it, apparently, but was too wrapped up in my own life to stop those little pricks."

She's nodding when I hear a sniffle escape her, and even though she's sitting on top of me, she feels too far. I roll over and tuck her to my side, grateful that she wraps her arms around me and snuggles close.

Her breathing finally calms as I rub her back. Somehow, her lips find mine. She tastes sweet, and I can't get enough.

Her touch feels so good. Over my pecs. Through my hair. Down my abs. I let myself explore her too. Her perfectly round ass. Those long, smooth legs. Her mouth-watering breasts.

When she slides her thigh over mine and moans, my cock pulses against her.

But this is Lo. I don't want to go too fast and mess up any shot I have of something more with her.

Fuck me, I can't believe I'm gonna say this. "Babe, we don't have to do anything more tonight. If you don't want."

She grabs my face in her hands. "I want. And if you stop one more time for another heart-to-heart, I swear to you, I'll go postal."

I chuckle and tackle her to her back, making her squeal with laughter when I bite her neck. She tugs at my briefs, and we're a tangle of limbs as we shove off our underwear. And then she's reaching for me, cradling me between her gorgeous thighs, her wet heat searing my cock as I glide across her.

I'm in such a frenzy to get close I nearly go in bare. Whoa.

389

With a pained groan, I lean over her to snag a condom from my nightstand, nearly combusting when she wraps her hand around my dick to help me wrap it up.

"Hurry," she whimpers, guiding me back.

But I'm a big guy, and I want to make sure she's ready, so I dip my fingers into her and coat her plump little clit, rubbing small circles until her breasts heave. Until she's thrashing beneath me.

Leaning back on my knees, with this stunning woman spread out before me, I want to take it all in. Burn it into my memory. The way her hair is spread against my pillows. How her skin is flushed and glistening with sweat. The way she stares back at me with the kind of hunger that's clawing inside me too.

I fist my cock, feeding myself into her, inch by inch. I go slowly. Wedging myself in there. Watching every moment of our connection. Like this matters. Because it does. Everything about Willow fucking matters.

Watching her stretch around me nearly makes me come undone, and I have to take a breath because she's so tight, but I don't want to blow our first time together.

With one hand planted above her head and another massaging her swollen clit, I finally move my hips, thrusting deeper and making us both moan. The sounds of our bodies slapping together fills the room. I drive into her, rutting like an animal, but I don't think she minds. Her nails are digging into me, her hips lifting to meet mine, her teeth bearing down on my shoulder. Seeing her so turned on pushes me closer to the edge.

I've never felt such a feral desire for any woman before. Just Willow.

And when she comes? Screaming, *"Yes!"* her tight pussy fluttering around me and squeezing my cock so tightly I see the Holy Grail? I can't hold back any longer. I wrap my arms around her and hold her to me as I fuck up into her, deeper, harder, until the headboard knocks against the wall and I'm coming so fiercely, I think my dick might break off.

Instead of collapsing onto her, I roll to the side to keep from crushing her. But I can't let go of her, and she can't seem to let go of me.

Not sure how long we lie there in a sex stupor, quaking from the aftershocks, since we're still connected, but when I can finally peel open my eyes, and I find Lo's sleepy, sated gaze staring back up at me, I'm pretty sure I'm the world's luckiest man.

"You okay, baby?" I rub her back, and she gives me that smile that's always knocked me on my ass.

She clears her throat, and when she finally speaks, her voice is raspy. "For the record, I think that was worth the wait."

"Hell yes, it was." I kiss the top of her head. "But let's not wait another fifteen years to do it again."

"How 'bout next weekend?"

"I was thinking in about twenty minutes, but another hell yes to next weekend and the one after that."

We're laughing and joking, but there's one more thing I need to ask.

"Lo, whatcha doing in mid-July?"

When she shrugs because she probably doesn't have a clue since that's six weeks from now, I take the big step. Something I've never done before or imagined I'd do anytime soon. But I really hope to do with her.

"Wanna come to a wedding with me?"

Would you like to read more of Lex Martin's Dark Texas Nights series? Be sure to check out her new release, RECKLESS, a USA Today bestseller.

ABOUT RECKLESS:

For the record, I'm not going to hook up with my boss.

I'm a lot of things—a screwup, a basket case, a flunky. But when I take a nanny job to be near my pregnant sister, I swear to myself I'll walk the straight and narrow, which means I cannot fall for my insanely hot boss.

I don't want to be tempted by that rugged rancher. By his chiseled muscles or southern charm or the way he snuggles his kids at bedtime. Ethan Carter won't get the key to my heart, no matter how much I want him.

ABOUT THE AUTHOR

Lex Martin is the USA Today bestselling author of the Dark Texas Nights series, the Dearest series, and All About the D, books she hopes her readers love but her parents avoid. To stay up-to-date with her releases, subscribe to her newsletter or join her Facebook group, Lex Martin's Wildcats.

Website: http://www.lexmartinwrites.com/
Newsletter: http://bit.ly/2KmFyoG
Facebook Group: http://bit.ly/2dRXBGE
Instagram: http://bit.ly/2rJMwfN

GOING DOWN

A SPIRAL DOWN SHORT STORY

ALY MARTINEZ

Henry and Evan from The Spiral Down struggle to find a private spot for their cocky adventures. (MM Romance)

ONE

Henry

The rain was coming down in fat, cold drops. The kind that soaked you to the bone and sent a shiver down your spine. The weather had been shit since I'd woken that morning, but as I ran to my private plane—the cool November air whipping all around me and the most gorgeous man I'd ever seen at my side—I didn't let it bother me. With his hand securely locked on mine, his subtle smile aimed at me, and five full days of peace, quiet, and lovemaking ahead of us, I decided not to allow my anxiety to have any place on our upcoming flight.

Well, that was until we climbed on board and Evan exited the cockpit, informing us that we were going to have to switch planes due to a mechanical issue.

"Oh God! We're all going to die!" I yelled, my voice echoing around the lavish interior of my private plane.

"Jesus," Sam muttered, flashing a pair of wide eyes at his wife, Levee. She also happened to be my BFF for life, so our relationship trumped theirs. (What? That's totally true. It's written into the best friend bylaws. Look it up!)

"Henry, stop being such a diva," Levee said, gathering her daughter in her arms.

See? It was obvious she loved me the most.

Because she clearly hadn't heard me, I repeated, "We're all going to die!"

Levee took this news in stride. With a huff, she cradled baby Bridget against her chest and allowed Sam, who was weighted down with bags like some sort of pack mule, to guide them down the steps. She probably would have had a stronger reaction to deplaning if she'd taken her eyes off her daughter long enough to look in a mirror and see that her long brown curls currently looked

397

like she was wearing an electrified poodle on her head. Humidity was not her friend.

Bad hair aside, I was still losing my fucking mind.

And not a single person was surprised.

"Oh God," I cried, my heart slamming into my ribs as I folded over and put my head between my knees.

"Breathe," Evan urged, perching his muscular body on the leather armrest. "I promise it's going to be okay."

"That's what you said when we got on this plane," I argued before sucking in a painfully deep breath of air that, judging by the way my lungs burned, held no oxygen.

His deep baritone got soft. "And it *is* okay. Jackson sent over another plane. The crew is switching over all four hundred pounds of Levee's luggage now. We'll be wheels down in North Carolina before you know it. I've got a handle on this. I swear." His strong hand glided up and down my spine, which was something it did so often when we were together. Usually, I was naked and he was behind me when he did this, but him comforting me in the middle of a flight-induced panic attack wasn't exactly something new.

I'd become terrified of flying after my plane had been struck by lightening a few years earlier. It had been paralyzing at first, and as a touring musician, flying wasn't something that I could just avoid. It wasn't until I fell in love with Evan that I was able to even step foot onto an aircraft without a liter of gin coursing through my veins. He was an amazing pilot—a more amazing boyfriend—and I trusted him with my life. But with a broken wrist thanks to a not-so-friendly game of basketball with the kids at the youth program we sponsored, Evan's abilities in the air would be limited. A thought that had made me lose more sleep than I'd ever admit.

"Maybe we should just drive," I said, turning my head to catch his gaze without sitting up. "First your hand and now the plane? What's next? Dixon isn't ready for this."

His stark blue eyes danced with humor as he grinned down at me. "Babe."

That was it. That was all he said. And he'd said it in a condescending tone that transformed my fear into anger. He thought I was overreacting.

Okay, I probably was, but that didn't make the distress any less real.

"It's a valid concern!" I snapped entirely too roughly. "This trip has been shot to hell since I planned it."

His chin jerked to the side, and he arched an admonishing eyebrow. "You gonna bring that attitude down a notch?"

I folded my arms on my knees and rested my head on top of them, strategically avoiding eye contact as I sniped back, "Are you going to stop with the placating 'babe' shit? My attitude isn't going to matter much when we're both dead in a plane crash. Which is exactly what's going to happen if you force me into another plan with Dixon behind the controls."

His hand on my back froze, and a pang of guilt socked me in the gut.

It was a known fact that I could be a teensy-tiny bit of a dick when I was scared. But if there was ever a man who did not deserve to be on the receiving end of that anger, it was Evan Roth. He'd been good to me too many times when I didn't deserve it. When I'd wigged out after discovering he was bi-sexual, he hadn't let me go, not even when he should have. Back then, I should have been the one groveling at his feet, begging for him to take me back. But that wasn't Evan's style.

He was patient and tolerant.

Loving and kind.

Everything I didn't deserve.

He took care of me on a daily basis, and let's be honest, that wasn't the easiest of tasks. It could be said that I was a *smidge* high maintenance. But Evan didn't seem to think so.

He loved me unconditionally.

I closed my eyes and sucked in a sharp breath, trying to align the right words to form an apology. Before I could, though, he gently trailed the tips of his fingers up my neck.

"Mmm," I hummed. My body sagged, and my heart slowed as he threaded his fingers into the back of my hair.

Then, with a sudden tug, he yanked me up until my back hit the seat.

"Ow, ow, ow," I complained, swatting at his wrist, but he didn't release me.

Evan was known to do a little hair pulling in the bedroom.

And I was known to enjoy it *immensely.*

But he'd never touched me like this.

I couldn't decide if this was the beginning of some seriously hot foreplay, or if I'd finally found the right button to push to piss him off.

He forced my head back so that I was staring up into his darkening eyes. Looming over me, he brushed his nose against mine. "You think I'd ever let anything happen to you?"

My heart stopped, guilt washing over me.

He wasn't mad. Nor was he trying to get me naked.

He was hurt.

"I didn't—"

He gave my hair another sharp tug and lowered his mouth to mine. His plump lips, which were the beginning and end of every sexual fantasy I had, moved against mine as he asked, "You trust me?"

"Always," I breathed, my eyelids fluttering shut as I swayed toward him, desperate for his mouth.

He dodged me.

When I opened my eyes, I found him glaring at me expectantly.

Oh, I knew what my man wanted.

My lips tipped up into a ghost of a smile. "Always, *Evan.*"

"Fuck." He groaned, his eyes searching mine before he dipped down to bite my bottom lip. The nip was followed by a deep and reverent kiss. It was the perfect combination of brute masculinity and tender romance that had made me fall in love with him in the first place.

He released my hair and blew out a ragged breath. "I shouldn't have grabbed you like that."

I licked my lips seductively. "Yes, you should have. And perhaps you should do it again tonight . . . with slightly less clothing and a lot more lube."

He rolled his eyes, moved off the armrest, and dropped into a squat beside me. I took the moment to appreciate the way his powerful thighs strained against the denim of his jeans. My man was gorgeous beyond reason. I had no idea what I had ever done to deserve him. But he was mine. And I was his for as long as he would keep me.

Resting his casted hand on my thigh, he said, "You know I won't let anything happen to you in the air."

Sheepishly, I brushed the dark brown hair off his forehead. "I know."

"Then trust me to make the right decision here. Dixon is a good pilot. A pilot I trust. A pilot who has co-captained for me on every single flight you've taken this year. A pilot who is so fucking overqualified, he's only a co-captain because you pay him a captain's salary and give him approximately three hundred and five days off a year."

I peeked up at him, a smirk pulling at my lips and a modicum of anxiety ebbing from my system. Tracing circles he'd never feel over the plaster covering his palm, I continued with my hissy fit, just at a slightly lower decibel. "Dixon's first flight in command does not need to be one in which we have such precious cargo on board."

With two fingers under my chin, he tipped my head up. "And just to be clear here, this precious cargo we're talking about is you and not Levee's baby, right?"

"Obviously. Though, now that you mention it, we do have a baby on board."

He chuckled and shook his head. "North Carolina is a forty-hour drive from San Francisco. If that is what you want to do, I'll support it. Full disclosure: I'll probably rant, grumble, and have road rage for at least thirty-nine of those hours, but for the rest of the trip, I should be fine." He flashed me a brilliant white smile.

I swallowed hard. As much as I did enjoy making Cranky Evan uncranky, forty hours in the car was really going to cut into our mountain vacation getaway. It was rare when Sam, Levee, Evan, and I could all find time in our busy schedules to spend time together like the family we truly were. If I forced them all to drive, I had a feeling those times together were going to go from rare to extinct.

"Oh God." I groaned, knowing he was right.

Evan grinned in victory. "You gotta trust me, babe."

"No. What I need to do is get drunk."

He rose to his full height and offered me his good hand. "Come on, I'll clear out the mini bar and play bartender in the terminal."

The image of my man serving up drinks while wearing nothing but a bowtie popped into my head. His chiseled pecs and sculpted abs traveling down to the delicious V that drove me wild.

He pulled me to my feet, and I purposely stumbled forward, landing hard against his chest.

"Hey! Easy there, tiger. You already drunk?" he teased, steadying us both.

Trailing my finger across his chest, I inched my way around the planes small interior until I was standing behind him. At six two, Evan was a few inches taller than me. But when he was bent over a seat, his tight ass up in the air, that wasn't the size that mattered.

Pressing up on my toes, I nipped at his ear. "You know what sounds more relaxing than a drink?"

"Oh, fuck." He moaned as his head lulled to the side to allow me more access.

I laved my tongue up the side of his neck. "Yes. Exactly that."

"Henry," he murmured, reaching over his shoulder to palm the back of my head. "Baby. We can't."

I rolled my hips, my thickening cock seeking its way home. "Oh, but we can, *Evan*." I purred his name just the way he liked. "Last I checked, I own this plan, which means I'm bound by legal obligation to fuck you on every surface."

"I'm not sure that's a legal obligation." He arched his back, circling his ass against my length unfortunately still hidden beneath the denim.

We both groaned at the friction.

"You want to break out a magnifying glass to read the fine print or"—I glided a hand around his trim waist, popped the button on his jeans, and drove a hand inside—"do want to drop your pants and let me fuck you."

"Jesus, Henry." He moaned again as I started working his shaft. "Baby . . ." He leaned back against my chest. "We can't... Fuuuck." He slapped his good hand down on the leather seat beside us for balance. "Henry, wait. " It was safe to assume I did not *wait*. He had this nasty little habit of putting the brakes on sex, using some ridiculous excuses like, "The priest might see us," or, "The paparazzi is outside our window."

Using his casted hand, he grabbed my wrist. "Henry, stop. There's another plane going out soon, so we need to hurry up and move off the tarmac."

"Then I suggest you hurry up and get naked."

Suddenly, he turned in my arms, forcing my hand to slide out of his pants or risk injuring us both. I could deal with him only having one hand for the next few weeks, but if any harm came to the real Captain Roth, we were going to be in some serious trouble.

He palmed the side of my face, his blue eyes boring into mine as his unbelievably expert mouth tipped up at the corners. "Relax, babe."

I rolled my eyes. "That's what I was trying to do until someone, who shall remain nameless . . . cough *you* . . . decided to cock block me."

His lips came to mine in a deep and dizzying fashion.

I reached around and grabbed his ass—strictly for balance, of course. "Cock blocking hurts us both, ya know?"

Smiling, he opened his mouth, the tip of his tongue sneaking out like the welcoming committee. In the grand scheme of things, Evan and I hadn't been together long. Our time measured in months rather than decades. But morning, noon, and night, I took his mouth every chance he gave me, and each and every time, it set me ablaze.

I threaded my fingers into the dark hairs at the nape of his neck, slanting my head to take our kiss deeper. And he gave, because that what was Evan did. He was a real humanitarian if you asked me.

All too soon, his mouth was gone. "I know what you're trying to do. Sex as a distraction because you're freaking out about the flight. But you don't need worry. You know I won't let anything happen to you." He winked. "King Kong always takes care of his lady, remember?"

"Does that include a blow job in whatever empty room we can find?"

He started to shake his head, but I kissed him again, mumbling against his mouth, "Come on . . . say yes. It's a private airport. There's got to be a secluded little spot somewhere."

And even though Evan was slightly more reserved about when and where he cashed in the multitude of perks that came with being in love, he smiled and replied, "You offering or asking?"

TWO

Henry

W hen we got off the plane, I made a beeline into the airport searching for any space that my sexy-as-sin a lover could possibly construe as private. Places I'd come up with: Nofuckingwhere.

The bathroom was crazy nice but also crazy public so there wasn't a deadbolt on the door, just the keyed door handle. However, like a sexual terrorist, Evan refused to allow me to call a locksmith.

Then the single solitary office I could find was locked—again, no keys. I considered breaking the window and just paying to have it fixed later, but a shattered window seemed counterproductive to privacy. Also, destruction of federal property was likely frowned upon.

And for some damn reason, Evan shot down my suggestion of hanging up our shirts to make a curtain under the table that held the coffee and various accouterments. My man had no sense of adventure.

Eventually, I was forced to give up and face reality. I was going to die with blue balls.

I was standing by the window, staring out at the empty runway, when I felt Evan sidle up beside me.

"You still freaking out?" he asked, extending a no doubt expertly made gin and tonic in my direction.

"Well," I let out a deep breath as I took the drink from his hand, "my nerves are shot and my mind is spinning in a million directions, most of which end with me in a fiery grave. But, to answer your question, no, I am no longer freaking out. I have officially accepted my untimely demise and an afterlife in sexual purgatory."

He chuckled, throwing an arm around my shoulders and curling me into his front. "You are quite possibly the most dramatic man I have ever met."

403

Mumbling into his chest, I replied, "I've heard Styles is worse."

"Good to know. If you two ever end up on a tour together, I'll be sure to catch the Bubonic plague or something." He gave me a tight squeeze. "I hate it when you're scared. What can I do to help you through this?"

Guilt soured my stomach. "Stop being such a good guy, you're making me feel guilty."

"Then this is about to get a lot worse for you."

"Fantastic," I murmured, inching deeper into the curve of his muscular body, careful not to spill my drink.

His lips came to my ear, his smooth, clean-shaven jaw scrubbing with mine. "Do you remember the day we met?"

I smiled at the memory. "How could I forget, Maverick? I called you the Doogie Howser of pilots."

"Yeah, you did," he murmured, his voice thick with amusement . . . and something else.

I leaned away to try to get a read on him, but I was in no way ready for what I found.

He was smiling, but his eyes were sparkling with emotion, and his brows drawn together as though he were anxious.

It set me on edge immediately. "What's wrong?"

"Shhh." He kissed me chastely. "No talking. Just listen. Yeah?"

"Evan, I—"

"Shut it, Henry. You can be as dramatic as you'd like in just a few minutes."

I clamped my mouth shut.

He took the untouched drink from my hand and set it on the edge of the window.

"The day I met you, my life changed forever. And not because the paparazzi now know everything about me down to my shoe size, but because a gorgeous, sexy man entered my life and taught me what it means to feel loved. Before you, I wasn't sure where I belonged in the world. I was bouncing from one relationship to the next, trying to find that elusive happily ever after, all the while continuing to build my skillfully crafted walls. And then I met you. The cocky celebrity with more money than sense, who bull-dozed into my life, stripped me bare, and then showed me where I truly belonged." With shaking hands, he palmed either side of my face and kissed me.

Hard and promising.

Deep and lingering.

Raw and exposed.

Evan.

"Baby, I—"

"Shh. Let me finish."

I nodded, biting my bottom lip. The whole no talking thing wasn't my forte.

"Henry, you are a diva who would make Mariah proud. But beneath the dramatics and," he paused to smile, his cheeks pinking adorably as he whispered, "salacious sexual appetite, there's more to you than anyone could ever know. You have such a tender soul. And your heart? God, you have an amazing heart. When you love, it's utterly and completely consuming. As someone who has been lucky enough to be on the receiving end of that love, I can testify that it's the most beautiful feeling in the world."

Confused but undeniably touched, I glanced around the room to see who was watching us. I found Sam holding up his cell phone as though he were recording us, and Levee sitting in a chair, twin rivers rolling down her face and over her gigantic smile.

What? I mouthed to her.

She pursed her lips and jutted her chin back to Evan, mouthing back, *Pay attention.*

As if on cue, Evan went back to talking. "I didn't want to do this here. I was going to wait until we got to North Carolina. Take you somewhere special and romantic. But, baby, if you need a distraction to get on this flight, I don't want it to be a quickie or a bottle of gin. I want it to be my promise to love you for the rest of your life and my ring on your finger." Releasing me, he shoved his hand into the pocket of his jeans, retrieving a platinum band that was encrusted with diamonds.

My heart seized. "Oh my God—" I choked on the words as tears welled in my eyes. "What are you doing right now?" I sucked in a ragged breath and repeated, "What are you doing?"

"There is nothing in this world I don't want to give you, Henry. Body, heart, soul. Forever. You *are* my exception. You *are* my reason." His voice cracked as he dropped to a knee. "Now, tell me you'll be my husband."

I couldn't breathe. I couldn't speak. I couldn't see around the tears flooding my eyes.

But I didn't need to.

Who needed air when you had the most incredible man offering you forever?

Who needed words when every dream you'd ever had was suddenly coming true?

Who needed vision when . . . okay, I take back that last one. I absolutely needed to see his handsome face.

Dropping to my knees, I took his hands in mine and brought them to my mouth, kissing each and every one of his fingers. "I never thought I'd find you. All twenty-one years of my life—" Levee barked a laugh, and I paused to level her with a glare. She threw her hands up in surrender and then blew me a kiss. I turned my attention back to Evan. "As I was saying, I never thought I would find someone to embrace my madness the way you have. You deserve so much better than me, Evan Roth. So, so much better. But I am just selfish enough to keep you for the rest of my life. I would be beyond honored to be your husband. And to call you my own."

His gorgeous face lit and less than a second later, his mouth was on mine.

Cheers from Levee and Sam rang out in the room, followed by a loud cry from baby Bridget.

I'd spent so much of my life worrying about the spiral down.

Personally.

Professionally.

Literally from the inside of a plane.

But as he slid that ring on my trembling finger, I realized that there was nothing to fear.

Because, no matter what, Evan and I were going down together.

"I can't believe you just did that," I murmured between kisses. "You know what this means, right?"

He grinned, pulling me up with him as he stood. "That you're stuck with me for the rest of your life?"

I circled my arms around his neck. "Well that, and that you will literally do *anything* to avoid public sex."

He threw his head back and laughed, loud and long. I drank him in, knowing I'd never get enough.

When he finally sobered, he quirked an eyebrow and once again dug into his pocket, revealing yet another surprise.

My mouth went dry and my body came alive like a power grid.

A set of keys dangled off his finger.

"Oh, did I leave the part out where I found these?"

Ten minutes later . . .

"Fuck, baby," I cried out. My chest was pinned almost painfully to the bathroom door. Evan's rock hard body was behind me, his hips driving his length inside me.

All I could say was: God. Bless. Pocket-sized lube.

Discover more books by Aly Martinez at www.AlyMartinez.com
or sign up for her newsletter at http://bit.ly/AlyNewsletter
The Fall Up: http://bit.ly/TFUCocky
The Spiral Down: http://bit.ly/TSDCocky

ABOUT THE AUTHOR

Born and raised in Savannah, Georgia, USA TODAY bestselling author Aly Martinez currently living in South Carolina with her husband and four young children. She passes what little free time she has reading anything and everything she can get her hands on, preferably with a glass of wine at her side.

Website: http://www.alymartinez.com/
Newsletter: http://bit.ly/AlyNewsletter
Facebook: https://www.facebook.com/AuthorAlyMartinez/
Instagram: https://www.instagram.com/authoralymartinez/
Amazon: http://bit.ly/AlyMartinezAmazon

ALSO BY ALY MARTINEZ

Wrecked and Ruined Series
Changing Course
Stolen Course
Among The Echoes
Broken Course

On The Ropes Series
Fighting Silence
Fighting Shadows
Fighting Solitude

Standalones
The Fall Up
The Spiral Down

The Retrieval Duet
Retrieval
Transfer

The Darkest Sunrise Duet
The Darkest Sunrise
The Brightest Sunset

Guardian Protection Series
Singe
Thrive

COCKSURE CO-STAR

KAYTI MCGEE

He's cocky as hell. He's gorgeous as sin. I love his body and hate his guts--
heaven help me get through this movie with him as my co-star.

ONE

JAYA

I'm at least seventy percent certain the director of this movie is banging his assistant. They are the very definition of the chemistry everyone looks for when they cast co-stars.

In the immortal words of #teamjen, I'm very happy for them, and not at all jealous.

Just look at the way his gaze lingers on her. It's so heartwarming that it really doesn't matter that I can't remember the last time someone liked at me that way.

"I walked in on them banging earlier. She was calling him daddy. It was pretty hot," comes a voice in my ear. Daddy? Gross. I turn around to see who disagrees with me and there he is.

Huck Ivanson.

All six foot something, blonde haired, blue eyed, Emmy-winning Viking god Huck Ivanson.

Hot mess, tabloid fodder, arrogant Huck Ivanson.

The guy who, just last week, told a national gentleman's magazine that social media was ruining Hollywood by allowing untalented upstarts like Jaya Brazill to act.

I was *not* informed he was who I'm screen-testing with today.

Me, the aforementioned Jaya Brazill.

"That's how us untalented upstarts get jobs, you know," I tell that cocky jerk with the sweetest smile I can muster.

"In which case, kiddo," I bristle and he smiles even wider, "I'll be looking forward to hearing you call me daddy soon."

My jaw drops open and I take a step toward his broad chest.

"I would sooner choke." The smile never leaves my face, but I can feel my eyes narrow so he knows I'm not kidding. I will never, ever sleep with this cock-sure snob.

Even if he *is* even hotter in person.

"You might. I'm pretty proportional." He winks. *Winks.* As if I would ever even consider—

Oops. I looked. I didn't mean to look. But he mentioned it and I couldn't help myself. And now I can't look away, because I think he's actually enjoying this conversation, if you know what I mean.

Like, for all his badmouthing me, he seems pretty happy to see me just now.

I think he *is* proportional, and I am sort of choking already.

On my anger.

"Like what you see?" he asks me.

"I'm just curious. What's happening here?"

"Oh, I think you know what's happening. And what could happen as a result, in the bathroom down the hall after we nail this screen test." He moves even closer in, using his body to overwhelm my senses with all those muscles filling out his shirt, that cologne that smells like juniper and leather, the rumble in his throat that becomes a low chuckle at his own cleverness.

"Oh, you misunderstand me," I tell him, not backing down an inch. "I was wondering if you talked shit on me because you pretty clearly have a big crush? Or if you just get off on having women put you down, because I think you can pay people to do that and leave your colleagues out of it."

He blinks.

But it doesn't stop him for long.

"If you like to get paid for it... well, that's a new kink for me, but I've got lots of money, kiddo. Name your price."

That's one step too far for me.

"Asshole," I utter, and then I stand up on the tippiest of my tiptoes, haul off, and slap him as hard as I can across the face. Except that I'm pretty short, and he's pretty tall, so I mostly just smack the shit out of part of his chin.

As my heels clack back down on the ground, I remember where I am. Oh, *no,* I did *not* just slap one of Hollywood's biggest A-listers while trying to get cast opposite him in what would be my first ever feature film.

But oh yes, I did.

All this runs through my head in the split second before I pivot to face the director who is definitely screwing his assistant, the smile still glued on, perfectly matching Huck's.

He, the assistant, the casting director Corinne, and a few PA's are standing as frozen as my face.

Then they burst into applause.

"That was amazing!" says Corinne.

"The chemistry was *spot-on,*" says Daddy, as his assistant nods eagerly.

"I don't think we even need you two to run lines. We've got our leads! Welcome to *Miss Match,* you two. Our people will be in touch with your people."

My chest hasn't stopped heaving from my anger, and now I can't catch my breath because holy shit, I'm a fucking movie star. I have to call my roommate Kami. I have to call my mom. I have to go be alone and scream and jump up and down.

I have no idea what to do with myself, but Huck is stepping forward to shake everyone's hands and thank them and that seems like a pretty good meantime thing to be doing.

I'm perhaps a little overly effusive with Corinne and Daddy, but when Huck turns to me I have to let him know that this changes nothing.

"Congratulations, kiddo," he says.

"Fuck you," I tell him, my hand completely swallowed up by his proportionately large one as we shake.

"Bathroom down the hall?" he asks.

"Only this once."

TWO

HUCK

She was right, of course. I've been having inappropriate thoughts about Jaya Brazill since the first time I watched her webseries two years ago. It pissed me off how good she was, honestly.

Not that I was ever going to tell her that.

I worked my ass off to get the kind of classical theater training that Benedict Cumberbatch would envy, sometimes subsisting on three hours of sleep a night so I could work the night shift to afford just a few more lessons after classes were over for the day.

I can do eight different regional British accents to match any Shakespearean character you name, I can read Beowulf in Middle English, and all those assholes who say they "just want to direct"? Well, I actually won an award for one of my student films. Yeah, I know what the fuck I'm doing when it comes to acting.

Naturally, I'm known for being the sexy Viking god on *Northlanders*, where I spent six entire seasons brooding into the camera, flexing my muscles, and occasionally making a loud proclamation.

My IMBD is also populated with roles like Dumb Musclebound Car Racer, Yelling Muscley Roman General, Ripped Football Player With Heart of Gold (Who Dies).

To say I've been typecast is an understatement.

So, yeah, I'm more than a little pissed off that this hot little Midwesterner with zero acting pedigree can just show up in Los Angeles, bat her stupidly long lashes, and get rave reviews for her indie character roles.

My only solace is that I'm positive I'm worth at least eighty-three of her, financially.

And I want my chance in an indie character role. I even have a script. I wrote it myself, which is why no one will read it.

Who wants to read a script by Heroic Buff Cop in Disaster Movie? Answer: my mother is so far the only volunteer.

417

She thought it should be lightened up a little, though.

I tried to explain that it's difficult to lighten up a story about a widower struggling with depression. She suggested I rewrite it as a cozy mystery with a feline co-star.

She was right about one thing, which is that I do need to be seen as more than a gym rat. So, baby steps, here I am starring in a romantic comedy. Opposite a social media upstart who had the nerve to slap my chin.

I grab her hand and pull her into the bathroom before dragging the trashcan in front of the door as a makeshift lock.

"God, you're an idiot," she breathes, just before I grab her by the ass (it's luscious) and set her down on the sink. There really is something wrong with me for being this turned on by her hatred. It's not a normal thing for me. But for some reason, I don't want her to like me because I spend three hours a day working out and take my shirt off a lot onscreen.

I do, however, want her to maul my body as I make her come.

She's going to hate it.

I grab a handful of her dark hair and pull her head back as I nibble on her cherry-and-rose scented neck. She smells like the sweetest little kitten but hisses and arches her back like the hellcat I hoped she'd be when I was jerking off to her on my computer.

I start to pull back and she shoves my head back into her.

"Don't kiss me," she groans. Oh, I wasn't planning on it. This is not that kind of a hook-up.

Instead I double down on kissing and sucking a line up and down, from the sensitive spot just under her ear down to her clavicle and back up again. She's going to be marked up tomorrow, unable to pretend this didn't happen.

I bite down just out of spite.

She's going to remember this.

I'm so hard it's painful when she finally recovers her wits and starts ripping my shirt off. Buttons fly through the air. I help out by pulling it off, and her nails rake down my chest in response. She's not the only one who's going to wake up marked in the morning.

My cock is pressed up against her and she's rocking her hips. Even through our pants I can feel the heat of her and fuck, this is so good.

But this isn't how I want her. I pull her back down, rough, spin her around and lean her over the counter.

"You want me?" I groan, wanting to hear the way my name sounds in her mouth.

"No," she pants, and I freeze. Our eyes meet in the mirror. "I only want the proportional parts of you. Hurry up."

I'll take it.

"Pull your pants down," I tell her, unable to handle being trapped in my own khaki prison for even a second longer. By the way, the khakis were what the casting director, Corinne, told me to wear. Certainly not a choice I'd make for myself.

She shimmies her own dress slacks down as I make quick work of the button and zipper and then enjoy the show as she starts to slide her hands under each side of her thong. It's hot as fuck, and so is that ass I've only fantasized about before now, perfectly round and just a little bigger than her frame would suggest it ought to be. But it's taking too long, so I just rip it for her.

"Jesus!" Her reflected face looks shocked and pissed.

"Just me, but a common mistake."

"How about don't talk anymo—oh!" But I don't need to talk, because my dick is nestled in tight against her and ready whenever she is, which as she slides back against me and one small piece of me at a time is swallowed up, is right now.

This is exactly how I wanted her, wet and wanting and rough and dirty and she can't even see what I can see, where we join, how gorgeous it is to watch her pussy suck me in.

I let her go slow now, adjusting to me as she's slowly easing my thickness into her tight little channel, but she's taking my cock like a champ.

So I smack her ass.

She tightens around me, surprised, and that's when I grab her by the hips and start fucking her for all that I'm worth. You know, eighty-three million's worth. She's making little noises that are getting higher pitched and closer together like she might come, so I reach around and press my thumb to her clit, working tiny circles until I feel her clench hard as the orgasm hits.

It takes everything I have to hold mine back while she rides hers out—rides *me* out— but finally her spasms quieten and I pull out.

I use one hand to pull up her blouse and the other fists my cock as I start to spurt all over her back.

Just then, the fatal flaw in my bathroom plan becomes apparent.

The trash can I'd moved in front of the door? Well, the door opens *out*, so all it did was provide a place for my brand-new director to prop his elbows as he gazes at the sordid scene before him.

"I told you I was seventy percent sure they were banging," he remarks to his ever-present assistant.

"Huh. Gross."

THREE

JAYA

I really tried my damnedest to be prepared for everything about this movie. I read the book it's based on five times. (The script is literally nothing like it. St. Martin's can *not* have signed off on this shit.) I practiced my lines for hours a day. I even dyed my hair red to match my character, and I *never* let chemicals near my hair.

I was not even remotely prepared to face Huck Ivanson's smug face every day on set.

"Hey there, hellcat. Nice hickeys," he'd say. For the first entire week. Or, if someone else was around, something clever, like, "God, I'm so hungry I could eat Brazill."

I could do without it.

I could also do without the longing my body seems to have taken up feeling each time his large and proportional one gets anywhere near me.

The weird thing about movies is that you often shoot in reverse order. So, a couple months in, and suddenly, we're back at the beginning. We're trying to shoot the first kiss scene, and it's not going well.

My character, Candy, has taken a job at a kombucha bar where her sister Kaci is doing stand-up comedy. It's a terrible job, but she'd rather do that than work for Drake Jonathan as a matchmaker.

In that sense, I'm not really acting at all.

I'd actually rather brew fermented mushroom tea than work with Huck right about now. It's not that I'm ashamed I hooked up with him—he's hotter than hell—but since there is no way on earth I'll do it a second time, I'd prefer not to listen to his self-satisfied remarks about it.

"Cut!" the director calls for what feels like the hundredth time. "You're supposed to swoon at him, not stomp on his foot."

I didn't think he'd notice that.

But what was I supposed to do? Huck was whispering filthy things in my ear about what we could do in the bathroom in his trailer. I cannot abide that sort of cockamamie. This is my big break.

And that is *his* big... well. It's pushing up against my stomach as Huck promises the director we'll get this take for sure.

We will, too, if for no other reason than I'm ready to be alone for a while. Not to pull out my battery-operated meditation device. Nope. Just to have some peace, that's all.

"And... action," and the clapboard claps and I do what I *do* and forget that I'm standing on a soundstage filled with people staring at me from under lowered lashes and I just become Candy.

"Drake?" I ask, my voice quavering just the right amount to show my disbelief, and also my pleasure at seeing him in a pair of jeans.

Note: this is not acting, either.

"Yes, Candy. Yes. It's me," Huck says, the smirk on his face changing the dialogue from flat to self-aware.

"But why are you here? I turned you down," I-as-Candy remind him. That's when he presses his own reminder into my hip.

"Well, Candy, I want you to work for me. Find me a wife, and I'll make sure you never have to drink kombucha again." With those words, he leans down and pauses, waiting for my eyes to dilate when I smell that juniper and leather scent before he gently touches my lips with his. The tiniest bit. It's delicate.

This is a real departure from the arrogant way he claimed my mouth in the last ninety-nine takes.

I find myself being the one that parts my lips first, the one whose hand comes up to his face for just a second before dropping away again. I'm the one that deepens it, and I'm the one who doesn't hear the "cut!" and keeps on kissing him.

So for once, I can't even blame him for looking so cocky.

I invited it.

Once I hear (and I actually *do* hear it this time) "that's a wrap," I just go ahead and walk myself over to his trailer. We have another bathroom to christen.

I can't decide if I'm annoyed or accepting of the fact that giving me three orgasms might contribute to some of that attitude he's got. I guess that's probably why I agree to split a bottle of Cris with him.

I don't even like pricy bubbles. My roomie, Kami, would never have the audacity to show up with a bottle that could cover our Nissan payment for the month.

Then again, Kami isn't making Huck money as a makeup artist—yet—and if he wants to waste it, I can help.

By the time I head back to my own trailer, I'm tipsy, confused, sexed up, and weirded out.

None of that is a good reason why I choose to post a two hour video about Huck Ivanson, acting, Huck Ivanson, the differences between books and movies, Huck Ivanson, how much I love the kitty on set named Kitty, Huck Ivanson, and finally, shamefully, *worst of anything ever and at all,* whether Jaya Ivanson is a good name.

When Kami wakes me up at four in the morning to inquire what I've been thinking, I can only answer that I haven't.

And also that my only recourse is to fake my own death. Goodbye, cruel internet.

FOUR

HUCK

Internet videos are by far the stupidest things about the internet, which I do tend to be a pretty big fan of. Jaya's roommate, Kami Gold? I'm not ashamed to say I subscribe to her HerTube channel.

There's something really soothing about watching someone apply various thingamajigs to their face until it looks shiny and new.

But the problem with internet videos is that anyone on the internet can post them.

They don't even need their agent to sign off.

Although, I've met Jaya's agent at a few events. He's so senile, I'm not sure he understands how The Internet works, much less what a shitshow Ms. Brazill is stirring up right now.

Luckily, Corinne gets it.

So she's the one I call, after my first few attempts fail.

Someone else picks up.

"Hey, I need Corinne," I say, assuming its her husband or manager or whatever.

"Sir?" comes the answer.

"...yeah?" I eventually answer, concerned a paparazzi has compromised our casting agent's phone.

"It appears that Corinne has been eaten by a shark. If this is a professional call, I'd suggest you refer it to her agency," says the man I assume is a cop on the other end.

Oh.

Huh.

Well.

Corinne always *was* scared of sharks.

I suppose...

425

But no. This isn't the time. I choke back my sobs, and I tell Jaya's agent's answering machine, "This isn't over. Tell her it isn't over."

And it isn't. Not by a long shot.

If she wants to be Mrs. Ivanson, I can do that for her.

All she has to do is call me back.

ABOUT THE AUTHOR

Kayti McGee lives and loves in beautiful Kansas City, Missouri. Her interests include blood and guts and love and stuff. Also, wine. And your mom.

Website: http://kaytimcgee.com
Facebook: http://facebook.com/kaytimcgeeauthor

COCKBLOCKED

A CONSOLATION DUET SHORT STORY

CORINNE MICHAELS

Navy SEAL, protector, and full-time cockblocking father of his two teenagers is how Liam Dempsey describes his life. See what happens when his kids are grown up and start dating …

ONE

"You're going to behave, Liam. I don't care what you say, this is a big deal for any girl, and I swear to God that you will be on the couch if you screw this up for her." I point at him, but all he does is grumble.

"How are you so okay with this?"

"I'm not okay with this," I sigh and touch the side of his face. "I just have to be a grown up, like you will be."

He shakes his head. "This isn't fun."

"Nope, it definitely blows, but it's prom and part of the ritual."

It isn't easy watching my beautiful little girl grow up. I want to freeze time, make her stay the sweet child who said funny words forever. Time doesn't work that way, though.

Aarabelle is seventeen years old.

She's practically a woman.

"Prom is when kids have sex, Lee."

Here we go again. "I didn't have sex at prom," I inform him.

"Well, neither is Aarabelle, so at least we'll be two for two."

I'm not even going to ask how he plans to stop her if that's what she wants to do because that's a rabbit hole I'll never get out of.

"What's the plan, Athair?" Shane, our son, asks Liam as he walks in the living room.

Our kids both call him that because there was never a day that he wanted to be just "Liam" to Aara. Since his Irish roots are very deep, we use the Gaelic word for father. Liam never wanted to take Aaron's place as her father, but he *is* that in every sense of the word. He's here when it's hard. He cares for her when she's sick, helps with homework, and is her father. He's the constant in her life, and her relationship with him shows that.

Shane decided it was cool so he uses it too.

Boys.

431

These two are ridiculous. Absolutely out of their minds. Shane is fourteen, but almost two inches taller than his sister. He has dark brown hair and blue eyes like his father. The only thing he got from me is his IQ. Shane is a ladies man through and through. I can't think about you how many girls call his cell phone because if I did, it would make me want to scream and lock him inside a cage.

Liam had a long talk with him about girls, which I'm sure included a bunch of that's-my-boy type crap, but when it comes to Aara? Forget it.

That girl is lucky he doesn't have her stashed in an ivory tower somewhere.

"The plan is we teach the jackoff coming to take my daughter to prom how we roll around here."

"And how do we roll, babe?" I ask.

"SEAL style."

"Oh, Jesus," I mutter under my breath and leave the room.

I head upstairs, looking at the photos that line the wall. Time goes by so fast. I feel as though it was just yesterday that Liam and I fell in love. I remember how he made me smile when all I wanted was to cry, how he cared for me when I was enduring the loss of Aaron, and just how precious our love is.

I see the photo of Aarabelle from when she was just about two years old. In it, she's sitting on Liam's shoulders as they chase the geese at the park. Our wedding picture, taken at a moment when not even God himself could have convinced me that one day I would love him more. A picture from the day we brought Shane home from the hospital.

It's all there in little permanent memories.

Now we have teenagers who make me question my life choices.

"Mom," Aara calls from the bathroom.

"I'm here." I push through the door, and she turns to smile at me.

"Can you help me with this dress? I can't get the zipper up."

Aarabelle is truly beautiful. And I don't just think that because I'm her mother. She really is naturally gorgeous.

I'm sure the years of dance have helped with her figure, but the girl doesn't wear makeup and is still stunning. She got my blonde hair and Aaron's eyes. She's a perfect mix of her parents.

I slide the zipper up for her and then adjust the skirt. I don't know when dresses started to become two pieces, but she was adamant this is what she was wearing.

"All done," I say as I touch her shoulder. "You look gorgeous."

She smiles in the mirror. "I wish Dad could be here."

"I know."

There isn't much to say to comfort her. Sometimes things just don't work the way we want them to, and when it comes to Aaron, no truer words apply. Life is ever-changing, and she learned that at an early age.

"Did you talk to Athair?" she asks. "About being nice to Chase and not totally embarrassing me?"

Oh, I talked to him all right, but it didn't go the way she would've liked. He went on and on about punk teenagers and how it's his job and right as a father to scare them from his daughter.

"I did, but Aara, you know how he is . . ."

She sighs. "Yeah, protective and crazy."

"Pretty much."

"Can't you . . . I don't know . . . threaten to beat him or something?"

"I did, but he's not exactly known for listening to me."

Aarabelle groans. "Well, maybe he'll at least try not to embarrass me."

That's funny. There's not a chance in hell he's going to do that, but we can at least hope he doesn't scare her date off. "I wouldn't count on it, honey. This is the first time you're bringing your boyfriend around, I would expect loads of hell."

"I can't bring boys around here because I have my idiot brother and Athair!"

I wish I could completely sympathize with her, but it isn't something I'm complaining about either.

Now for the awkward conversation that must happen.

"Aara, can you sit?"

"Sure," she draws out.

"Listen, it's prom night, and I know that sometimes you get a little rowdy." I pause when her face scrunches.

Believe me, kid, I don't want to talk about this either.

"Mom," Aara puts her hand up, "if you're talking about sex, gross and no way because Chase is just a *friend*, for the millionth time. If you're worried about drinking, don't be. I'm not stupid."

"No, but you're a teenager."

She's a good girl by all counts. Aarabelle is honor roll, top in her class, and a very accomplished dancer.

Her life is ballet and nothing will stop her.

"I'm not having sex, Mom!"

"You damn well better not be," Liam bellows from behind me, making her cringe.

"Well, I'm not. He's a friend—again, not my boyfriend. You guys are so weird!"

"Whatever, Chase William Leighton has a clean driving record, is currently on the honor roll, and lives in Baylake Pines—I have his exact address here in case you're home late." Liam hold up a sheet of paper for emphasis. "His parents are Katy and Josh, and he has a younger sister."

"Oh, my God!" Aarabelle yells. "Are you insane? You had him investigated?"

She has no idea the lengths this man will go to ensure her safety. Liam gives me a look because he's taking the heat for this one. He wasn't the one who had Chase's information checked, it was me.

I trust Aarabelle, but working for a security company has its perks sometimes.

"Of course we did," he says unapologetically.

"I can't believe this."

"Believe it, princess. A father will do just about anything for his kids." Liam steps into the room and looks at her dress. "Where's the rest of it?" he asks, waving his hand up and down.

"At the store." The sarcasm is thick as she rolls her eyes at him.

"Funny, go back and get one that's not missing material."

"Dear God," I mutter to the ceiling.

"It's fine, Athair. It's a dress. All the girls have them just like this."

Liam rubs the bridge of his nose. "You look beautiful, princess. Truly. You also aren't leaving in that."

"Mom!" Aarabelle spins to face me as if expecting me to stick up for her. I told her he wouldn't approve of it, but she wouldn't budge.

Having kids is so much fun.

"Don't cry to her, I'm not letting you out of the house in half a dress. Your stomach is showing, Aarabelle!"

Hadn't I told her he would say that?

Yes. Yes I did.

Overprotective and Liam should be synonymous. She's his little girl that still climbs on his back, runs into his arms when he gets home from work, and wants him to teach her how to shoot.

He doesn't get that none of that is reality anymore.

"I'm not changing. This is more than my bikini I wear on the beach." Her lip trembles.

I see the tears threaten to form and step in. "You've helped raise her into a beautiful girl, you have to let her shine. She's wearing the dress, put your macho crap away and knock it off."

"She can shine wearing a sea bag."

"Liam." I sigh.

"Natalie."

I turn to Aarabelle. "Finish getting ready, and we'll meet you downstairs. You don't worry about him." Then I shove my husband out the door. When we're far enough away that I know she won't hear me, I shove his chest. "Really?"

"What?"

"Are you nuts?"

He raises his brow. "Only about you."

"Don't be cute, Liam."

"I can't help it."

He makes it so hard to stay mad at him. "She spent hours searching for the perfect dress. She needs you not to be a lunatic father for once and be the man I know you are."

Liam smirks and taps my nose. "You're giving me more credit than I deserve. I am a lunatic father, and that boy is going to shit himself when he comes here. Accept that, and we'll be much happier."

I really pray Aarabelle doesn't put Exlax in his brownies next time she bakes, but if she does, I won't blame her.

"What am I going to do with you?" I ask rhetorically.

"I can think of a few things . . ."

"I bet you can." I giggle as my hands glide up his strong arms.

"If I behave, will you be naughty later tonight?"

I'm bartering him sex for not acting like a dumbass. The things we do for our kids. Who am I kidding? This really only benefits me.

"I guess you'll have to see."

"Don't tease me, woman."

I sigh and press my lips to his. "I thought you liked a little teasing."

Liam pushes our bodies back so he has complete control. I feel him harden as he moves so he's at that perfect spot. "I think it's you that likes to be teased."

"Gross," Shane says as he gets to the top of the stairs. "Seriously, you guys are ridiculous."

Liam shrugs. "Cover your eyes then."

Shane shakes his head. "I need bleach and some kind of memory eraser."

"That can be arranged," Liam tosses back as I try to shove him away. "Where are you going?"

"Downstairs." I try to move, but it's pointless. He has me right where he wants me, and he's ten times stronger than I am.

The doorbell rings, and he groans. "I really have to be nice to this tool?"

"For Aara."

"Fine."

We trudge down the stairs with Liam grumbling about locking her in her room until she's thirty. When I open the door, I'm a little shocked to find that it isn't her date.

"Douchecanoe!" Mark yells as he steps inside. "I brought reinforcements."

Sure enough, in walks Jackson, Quinn, and Ben—the new guy. Ben is heading up the protection detail side of the company, and he might be the only person in the company who scares me a little. The guy is huge, and I don't know that he knows how to smile, except when he looks at Gretchen . . .

Which is definitely the reason that Liam had him come.

"What the hell are you clowns doing here?" I ask. "No one told you to be here."

"Liam invited us," Mark informs me.

"Well, this is me telling you to leave." I hold the door open and point outside.

There is no way this is going to go over well. If Aarabelle sees that her uncles came to join the party, she might lose it.

Mark laughs. "Not this time, Sparkles."

"Jackson?" I plead since he's the most reasonable of this lot.

"I have girls, this is par for the course," he says with a shrug. "I expect the same courtesy. This is what we do."

"Your funeral," I say. "Aara is not going to like this."

Jackson grins. "That's the point. We know what boys think, we were those boys, we want to hunt those boys down and beat them if they have those thoughts about our girls."

As if they didn't break hearts as adults. Please. I've had ringside seats to their circus for most of my life.

Right on cue, Aarabelle comes down the stairs. The look of horror on her face is almost comical. "No, no, no, no way! No! You have half the SEAL team here?"

"I protect my family," Liam explains as he pops the top off his beer.

"No one in the world has this much insanity in their family!" Aara screeches.

"I swear," I warn them all in a harsh whisper, "that if you ruin this day for my daughter, I will make each one of you pay for it . . . got me?"

They may be big bad former SEALs, but I'm not afraid of any of them. Plus, their wives will ensure it continues far past the rain I bring.

"We're just going to scare him a little," Quinn says. "This is the fun part of what we do."

"If she sheds one tear"—I point around the room—"dead."

"Isn't she cute when she gets all mama bear?" Liam says and I level him with a stare.

"You really shouldn't test me."

"Sweetheart, that's all I live for." He smirks and leans back.

There's no point in continuing the conversation. I know that he knows better than to really try his hand about this.

Satisfied that they won't do anything stupid, I head in the kitchen as the group of guys talk about sports and deployments. Aara comes in, typing on her phone.

"I'm going to meet him there," she says.

"Aara."

"No way am I going to let him show up here with them in the living room. Uncle Mark is going to . . . I don't even want to think about it."

"Your family just loves you. They protect what they care about." I try to explain their craziness.

"Yeah, well, they're nuts."

"Yeah, they are."

I push her phone down from her face and tilt her chin up. "I'm proud of you."

"Thanks, Mom."

"And you look beautiful."

She smiles. "I look like you did when you went to prom with Dad."

God that feels like forever ago, well, it was. I wore a deep plum-colored dress with my hair down, and Aarabelle is doing the same.

"Well, you look much prettier than I did."

"Your date is here!" One of the guys yells from the living room.

"Please help me," she gives me one last plea.

Oh, honey, if only I could.

We exit the kitchen, and I swear that I don't even know what alternate universe I just stepped into.

How long were we in there?

Clearly long enough for the guys to change into full gear and paint their faces as if they were on some mission in Afghanistan instead of shooting the shit in my living room.

"Liam Dempsey!" I yell as he hoists his gun over his shoulder. "Are you on drugs?"

"It's not loaded."

"Not the point!"

"I'm just introducing the kid to what it's going to be like to date my daughter." He grins through the face paint, and I could get lost in those blue eyes I'd know anywhere.

Then I remember I'm pissed at him.

"Come on in, son," Jackson's voice is booming as he pulls the boy inside.

Aarabelle marches through them, pushing their chests so she can get there. "Don't listen to any of them, Chase. They're all . . . dead to me."

The kid looks like he could shit himself. I sort of feel bad for him.

Shane comes running down the stairs to watch the shit show. "Hey, Chase." He grins. "Remember what we talked about . . . this isn't even half of it."

"You're so stupid." Aarabelle sneers at her brother. "Go away."

"You can say that to me, but what about Athair?"

Her face pales as Liam walks over, wipes his brow with his sleeve, smearing the paint. "So, you like my daughter?"

"Ye-yes, sir," Chase stutters.

"Do you think you're good enough to go out with her?" Mark steps in.

He looks over at the tallest of the men crowding my living room. "Yes, sir."

"So you think you're better than Aara?" Liam takes a step closer.

"No, no, sir. I just mean . . ."

Jackson clears his throat. "He just means that Aarabelle is good, but not as good as he is."

"I didn't say that," Chase tries to clarify.

"So, wait, you're good enough for her, but she isn't better than you?" Quinn asks as he slips a knife out of its sheath and acts as if he's cleaning his nail.

"I think Aarabelle is great," Chase tries.

"But not amazing?" Liam asks.

There are no right answers here. No matter what he says, they'll twist it.

"Mom!" Aara looks at me for help.

I'm always the one trying to keep these idiots out of trouble, but the mother in me is also enjoying this boy being aware that there are four very skilled men ready to protect her. It leads me to believe he will be on his best behavior.

"Chase," I smile warmly, "why don't we head outside for some pictures?"

She practically throws him out the door just to get away from the firing squad. When I get to the door, I turn and face them. "You guys are bad, but that was funny."

Liam steps forward, takes my face in his hands, and presses his lips to mine. "I'm having fun with this."

I roll my eyes. "It shows."

He kisses me again, surely getting green and black on my face.

"All right, let's line up for a photo!" Jackson says as I stand in the doorway laughing.

"You can't say it's not a good photo," Liam says as he leans against the door-frame with nothing but a towel on.

"It's ridiculous, but it's a good one."

Aarabelle endured another twenty minutes of her father and uncles giving her hell before she was finally able to get into the limo.

She sent both Liam and me a text with a photo from her phone.

It has her on one end, Chase on the other, and the idiots in the middle. It's really comical, but it's also a sad reality of her dating life. She'll always have these dopes in the middle of it if they have a say.

I put the phone on the table beside me and climb up onto my knees. "You know . . . I thought it was really sexy seeing you in your gear again."

He smirks and steps toward the bed. "How sexy?"

"On a scale of one to ten?" I bite my bottom lip and pretend to ponder. "An eight."

"Just an eight?" Liam asks as he reaches the bed.

"I think I know what would bring it to a ten . . ." I lean closer, pull his towel free, and then toss it across the bed. "That for starters."

"I like the way you think," he says and grabs my hips.

Liam tosses me down onto the bed and pulls my shorts off. "Am I getting warmer?"

I love when he's this way. His confidence that borders on cocky makes me thankful that he's mine—all mine.

"Definitely."

He kisses my stomach before moving lower. "Now?"

"Liam." I hiss his name when his tongue swipes across my clit.

"Am I at a ten now, sweetheart?"

I moan, unable to form words.

"Or are we at a nine?"

Why is he talking? "Don't stop," I beg.

"Yes, ma'am." He chuckles and then gets back to work.

My hands grip the pillow, pulling it over my face so when I scream I don't wake the neighbors. He circles my clit, making my legs shake as I climb higher. I'm hovering on the edge, sitting in that place where it's almost painful because I need to release. Liam knows exactly what he's doing, and I'm not complaining one bit.

I start to twist when it becomes too much, but his strong hands hold my legs down. He moves his tongue in lazy circles, keeping me on the edge, and it's as though I'm being ripped apart.

"Liam!" The muffled sound of my voice is desperate. "Please!"

"Take the pillow off your face, I want to hear every fucking noise tonight."

Aarabelle is at the after prom, and Shane is at a sleepover. For once, we don't have to worry about kids hearing us.

I do as he says and toss the pillow onto the floor. "Yes," I whimper as he circles my clit. "God, Liam!"

My head thrashes from side to side as pleasure overtakes me. I writhe beneath him, my pulse races, and I bite down on my lip.

I'm hanging on the edge, ready to go over, needing to release the pressure. Liam continues his slow assault, taking his time to bring me to the brink. "Yes. There. Oh. Jesus!" My fingers grip his hair as he sucks hard while flicking my clit, and I explode.

My orgasm rages on and on as he continues to pull every ounce of pleasure from my body.

Once he's satisfied, he climbs up so we're face to face.

My eyes open, and a blissed out smile tugs at my lips. He's perfect, and he's one of those men who look better the older he gets. I touch his strong jawline, which is covered in a beard long enough for me to run my fingers through it. His crystal blue eyes are filled with so much love that it takes my breath away.

I'm a very lucky woman.

"Why are you smiling?" he asks.

"Because you're mine."

He moves my hair off my face and smiles back. "Damn fucking right you are. Now, I'm going to make love to my wife and make her scream my name a few more times."

I move my fingers through his hair. "She would really like that."

Liam shifts as I part my legs, giving him the in that we are both craving.

He pushes forward, taking me, owning me, loving me the way that only he can.

Our eyes stay trained on one another. "You feel so good," he says before kissing me.

"You always feel good."

"I love you so much, sweetheart. So much."

"I love you more."

He starts to rock back and forth, giving me all the love in the world. When we're together, life makes sense. We've been lucky that he hasn't deployed in the last two years.

Liam is the other half to my soul, and being a SEAL's wife means I have to share him . . . and possibly lose him.

I never want to live in a world without him, and my eyes fill with tears before I can push the thoughts away.

He's here. He's alive and came home to me, just like he promised he'd do.

"Am I hurting you?" he asks quickly.

I shake my head and wipe the tears from my cheek. "No, baby, I'm just allowing myself to feel how much I love you."

"Fuck, Natalie." Liam groans as he moves faster, pushing so deep inside me that we're completely one.

I need more. I need all of him.

His fingers tangle in my hair, and he squeezes as he roars.

We lay like this for a few moments, breathing each other in, reveling in the moment.

He doesn't move for so long that I start to think that he fell asleep—inside me. I wait another minute, and he finally turns his head toward me.

"Hi." I smile.

"Hi."

I run my fingers up and down his spine. "You all right?"

"Oh, I'm very all right."

I shake my head at the playful tone. "Are you planning on getting up?"

He grunts. "I'm fine."

"Liam." I giggle as he tucks his face against the crook of my neck.

"What? It makes it easier for round two."

He's a mess. A beautiful mess. "Come on, babe. I need to get up."

Liam hoists himself up a little, his smile is lazy and beyond sexy. Everything about him makes me happy. He runs his thumb against my lips, touching each part of my face. "Each day I ask myself what in the world I did to deserve you."

"You were you," I reply as if it's the only answer in the world.

"And you were meant to be mine."

He presses his lips to mine, and once again, tears spring to my eyes. "Then I guess it's a pretty good thing we found each other, huh?"

Liam nods. "You've given me everything a man could ever want in his life."

My heart swells, and I brush my thumb across his cheek. "Yeah?"

"I have a son and a daughter who I would lie down my life for. A woman who loves me more than I deserve. You're the other half to my soul, Lee. You think I say this shit because I'm so sweet or whatever crap you tell Catherine and Charlie, but the truth is that I wouldn't be who I am without you."

"Why do you have to be so amazing all the time?"

Liam rolls off to the side, pulling me against his chest. "Because I love you, sweetheart. I know you're tough and you don't need anyone to take care of you, but I see the cracks."

My head sits on my hand while I look at the man I love with my whole heart. "You keep coming home to me, and I'll keep spackling."

"You're not the handiest person."

I laugh and slap his chest. "You shouldn't talk, Mr. Duct Tape, you're the one who taped your daughter's diaper and then tied the Christmas tree to the ceiling."

He shrugs. "You love me."

"That I do, I most definitely do."

"I love you. You know what else I love?" Liam asks.

There's mischief in his eyes, and I can only imagine what the hell is coming next. "Now I'm scared."

Liam pushes my hair out of my eyes with a wicked grin. "Chocolate."

"Oh, I can get with some chocolate!"

We climb out of bed and throw on some clothes. Once in the kitchen, I grab the bag of KitKats I keep hidden from Aarabelle and Shane.

"That's where you keep the stash?" He laughs as I'm climbing down from the chair I used to get in the top cabinet.

"Don't judge. I need my candy when you're gone."

"Come here," Liam says, holding a hand out to me. "I want to show you something."

"Okay," I say hesitantly.

Liam pulls me out of the kitchen, grabs the blanket off the back of the couch, and tugs me back toward the hallway.

"What are you doing?"

"Showing you what it's going to be like when the kids are out of the house. Sex in all the rooms. Starting with the dining room."

TWO

"Where is she?" Liam asks as he paces the hall as he pulls the beanie off his head.

"Calm down!"

"Don't tell me to calm down, that little cocksucker was supposed to have her home five minutes ago," he bellows.

Sometimes he's this calm, level-headed man that I love being around. Then, we have this madman who makes me crazy by being a complete freak show.

"Liam, sit down."

He goes to the window, pushes the blinds down, slips his beanie back on, and then grumbles again. "I can't. This little shit is probably—"

"Is, nothing," I finish. "They went to a movie across town, you and I know better than anything that traffic here is horrible."

My phone vibrates.

Aarabelle: There's an accident on Shore Drive. I'm trying. Please tell Athair we're coming and not to shoot anything or anyone.

Me: Okay. Just get here safely.

"See?" I hold my phone up. "She's on her way, but there's an accident."

He laughs. "Yeah, right. She was probably doing God knows what and lost track of time."

"Oh, so she acted like you as a teenager?"

Liam levels me with a stare. "Don't try to send me over the edge."

I'm pretty sure he jumped over the edge ten minutes before she left. Since the prom where Aarabelle was adamant they were just friends, she and Chase have grown very close. He's a good kid, though. He came to the house and asked Liam for permission to ask his daughter out.

441

Liam, of course, is a dick and made him sweat it out.

I bet he wishes he said no now.

But, seriously, Chase is a good kid.

"Where is your son?" I ask absently. It's been quiet the last hour in the garage where he was working on his bike.

"He's in the garage . . ."

"Go bother him. Maybe he needs some help while you wait."

Liam kisses my forehead and heads out the door.

I watch as he leaves, admiring the view of his ass. Sometimes, I can't help it. He's just too cute.

Instead of waiting in here, I walk out to the porch with my coffee cup and curl up on the wicker couch. I love sitting out here at night. I can hear the waves crashing against the shore. The salt air calms my soul, and it always makes me grateful I got to stay in this house.

"Are you fucking *crazy?*" I hear Liam's deep voice yell.

"Dad!"

"Don't you dare *Dad* me!"

"It isn't what it looks like!"

Oh, this can't be good. I place the cup down and jog around the front of the house to see what the yelling is about.

When I get to the garage door, I see Shane pulling his shirt on and a girl doing the same.

"Fucking hell, Shane!" I say with horror in my voice.

"I swear, we were—"

Liam slaps Shane in the back of the head. "Shut your mouth."

"But she—"

Another smack.

"I didn't give you permission to talk. I'm contemplating letting you breathe much longer," Liam says through gritted teeth.

"You should head home," I say to the girl, whose face is bright red as she refuses to look anywhere but at the ground.

Shane opens his mouth to say something and Liam steps closer, grabbing his neck. "Not a word."

Why is it the bigger they get the bigger my fears are? Can't we go back to diapers and duct tape? Anything other than condoms.

She scurries out just as headlights illuminate the driveway.

Great. Aarabelle is here now and is going to get the wrath of this fiasco.

"I'm sorry, I'm sorry," Aara says as she and Chase walk up the drive. "I swear, we weren't doing anything."

"No one! No. One. Other than me and your mother should be having sex in this house. No one. Do you understand?" Liam explodes, his eyes firmly locked on his son as Aara and Chase come to stand next to me. Clearly, my daughter doesn't think she is included in that edict, which tells me she isn't doing anything she shouldn't be.

Like an idiot, Shane laughs, which has both Aarabelle and I looking on in horror.

"What are you talking about?" she finally asks, drawing Liam's attention.

No. No. No. Aara. You should know better than to talk when Liam has that look on his face.

"Did you have sex? Is that why you were late?" Liam, still holding Shane's neck asks as he moves toward her.

"No! God! We were stuck in traffic!"

He turns to Chase. "I swear that if you were at some sleazy motel or steaming up the back seat, boy . . ."

Chase lifts his hands. "I swear, Mr. Dempsey, it was traffic."

"Liam." I step in.

"These kids are nuts, sweetheart! They're nuts! I catch one with his pants down and the other . . . well, I don't know what she did, but . . ."

Or maybe their father is the one who's nuts, but I decide to keep that one in. I think the hardest thing about parenting is the loss of control.

The older they get, the less control you have. It is just the way of life.

"Everything okay, Lee?" My elderly neighbor asks from the window.

"We're fine, Mrs. DeMatteo!"

I wave and really hope she doesn't have her hearing aids in.

"Sorry, Mrs. D," Liam yells.

"All right then, honey. I just heard the shouting." She blows him a kiss and then shuts the window.

I can't even with the women when it comes to him. He's like catnip to the opposite sex. I know he's beyond good-looking, but come on. It isn't like he's God's gift to women. I live with him. I know this to be true.

"Now that you've announced to our neighbors that we're the only ones allowed to have sex, would you like to take this inside?"

Liam releases a heavy sigh through his nose. "You"—he points to Chase —"you were to have her home on time. Did you do anything that I would want to kill you for? And don't lie because I'll know?"

"No, sir."

"You"—Liam points to Aarabelle—"get inside."

"Can I say good night to Chase?" she asks.

"Do you want me to show Chase where all his pressure points are located?"

"Good night, Aara!" Chase says as he climbs back in his car.

"See! He's smart." Liam looks at me. "Why did we get the dumb one?"

Oh, the come backs I have for this. "Because he's half yours . . ."

He grabs Shane by the back of the neck and marches forward. "Well, I'm about to slap the stupid out of him."

I don't know who he's trying to fool, he would never raise a hand to either of them, but Shane's eyes widen.

Our children have grown up with the knowledge that most of the men in their lives are trained in some pretty scary things. Liam's way to bond with Shane was to teach him a lot of them as well. They love to rough house, roll around, and see how many dead legs they can give each other before someone cries.

Sometimes I wonder if maybe he ate lead paint or something.

"Shane, go up to your room. Your dad and I will be up in bit to talk about this. Once we've calmed down enough not to hang you on the flagpole by your underwear."

443

"I'm sorry, Mom."

I close my eyes and nod. "Just go to your room and leave your phone on the counter on your way up."

He walks inside the house, and Liam wraps his arms around my waist.

"Tell me they weren't . . ." I beg.

"They weren't. I don't know if they planned to."

"Great."

"I know, they were on top of Robin," he grumbles.

His car. He's worried about his freaking car. "God forbid."

"What if they scratched her?"

Liam and his car need a moment. He's had this freaking thing since before we started dating. It's basically a museum in the garage. Every few days, he comes out here, talks to her—because the car is real to him—and tinkers with it.

"I'm sure Robin is just fine."

"If she isn't, he's going to pay."

I don't doubt that. "Don't you think you should be more concerned that he had a girl here and was missing clothing?"

"No." He scoffs. "I love that car."

"And you don't love your kids?"

"Not as much as Robin. I've had her longer, she's good to me, and doesn't give me half the headaches those two do."

We walk over to the porch and sit together. His arms wrap around me from behind while my head rests on his chest.

"Well, I'm not worried about her."

"Honestly, I'm concerned about everything. They're growing up so fast, and it feels like we're losing control."

I nod because I had been thinking the same thing moments ago. "They just think they know it all."

"How wrong they are . . ."

"No shit. We didn't learn how wrong we were until we were in our thirties."

Liam laughs lightly. "And even then, we're still figuring out we were dumb as fuck."

"This parenting gig sucks." I sigh.

"There's no one else I'd rather suck with, though."

I smile and look back at him. "Same here."

"Good thing you're really good at sucking." He laughs at his dirty joke.

"You know . . ." I sit up to get a better look at him. "You're able to turn anything back to sex. No wonder our son was in there on top of your car and doing whatever he was doing."

He shrugs. "He's a Dempsey. We're natural ladies men."

"Oh, for the love of . . ."

"You can trademark that line, baby."

"Sometimes I wonder what the hell I was thinking when I fell in love with you." It's a lie.

I know exactly what I was thinking—*here's a man who loves me in my most broken state. He's kind, loyal, protective, and wants to do the right thing, even if he has to walk away to save us all.*

Liam walked beside me during the most difficult part of my life. He was self-sacrificing at every turn.

My life could've gone a very different way if it weren't for him.

My heart might still be broken, but his unyielding love healed every last broken shard.

"You were thinking that I had the biggest—"

"Heart."

"Wrong body part, Lee."

I shrug. "This is why our son thinks the way he does . . . you."

"Please, like your eyes didn't go to my dick when I said that." He laughs.

"Whatever," I say as he pulls me back against his chest and I tilt my head so I can look up at him.

"I love you, Lee."

"I'm glad you do."

"Yeah?"

"Most of the time," I joke.

"Good."

I stare into Liam's blue eyes and smile. "I love you too, you know?"

"I do, but you gave me a defective child that we must return."

Ugh. The boy. The boy with raging hormones and the charm of his father.

"Listen, that kid is all you, so . . . good luck with him. I'm way too young to be a grandmother, so you need to scare the hell out of him or something."

"You'd be the prettiest grandma around."

He is *not* funny. "I'll handle Aarabelle being late. You handle Shane being an idiot."

He nods. "Fine, but let her know I'll be watching and remind her that I know how to hide a body."

Sad part is that he's not kidding. He really does know how to.

"And after that, we'll have some wine," I say, pushing myself to my feet.

"Deal, but you have to promise to be naked tonight."

I lean down, pressing a quick kiss to his lips. "Maybe, considering we are the only ones who are allowed to have sex in this house."

He kisses me this time. "Damn right, I'm about to cockblock these kids until they're thirty."

My head falls back as I laugh.

Only Liam can take the crazy and make it feel like it's going to be okay.

If you enjoyed Cockblocked, be sure to grab Consolation, and find out how Natalie and Liam found each other. Or you can grab Beloved (Book 1 in the Salvation Series) FREE for a limited time!

To read an EXCLUSIVE preview of my upcoming novel, sign up for my newsletter and you'll get a look at it before anyone else! Sign Up Here:
http://corinnemichaels.com/subscribe/

Or for Text Alerts: Text cmbooks to 77948

ABOUT THE AUTHOR

New York Times, USA Today, and Wall Street Journal Bestseller Corinne Michaels is the author of nine romance novels. She's an emotional, witty, sarcastic, and fun-loving mom of two beautiful children. Corinne is happily married to the man of her dreams and is a former Navy wife. She enjoys putting her characters through intense heartbreak and finding a way to heal them through their struggles. Her stories are chock full of emotion, humor, and unrelenting love.

———————

Newsletter Sign up: http://corinnemichaels.com/subscribe/
Facebook: https://www.facebook.com/CorinneMichaels
Twitter: https://twitter.com/AuthorCMichaels
Instagram: http://instagram.com/corinnemichaels
Bookbub: https://www.bookbub.com/authors/corinne-michaels

ALSO BY CORINNE MICHAELS

The Salvation Series

Beloved

Beholden

Consolation

Conviction

Defenseless

Indefinite (Coming 2019)

Return to Me Series

Say You'll Stay

Say You Want Me

Say I'm Yours

Say You Won't Let Go: A Return to Me/Masters and Mercenaries Novella

Standalone Novels

We Own Tonight

One Last Time

Not Until You (Coming 2018)

If I Only Knew (Coming 2018)

GETTING IT UP

LIV MORRIS

A Curse, a Cocky Bastard, and a Dick Doctor = A Hard Luck Outtake.

Copyright © 2018 Liv Morris

Editing: Word Nerd Editing

ONE

Cali

When I tell people what I do for a living, nine times out of ten, their first response is an inquisitive: *"Oh, really?"* Then they lean closer with a crooked smile and a slight eyebrow waggle, probably hoping I'll spill some sordid secret. Believe me, I have a story or two to tell, but according to the law, I can't utter a single word. Well…that's not one hundred percent true. I can give vague generalities, like the time I saw the world's smallest penis or the pecker that permanently pointed toward the man's hipbone.

However, one nine-inch tale will go with me to the grave. Brady Luck is a cocky, well-hung Chicago baseball player who claims he's having a hard time getting hard, but after seeing him "rise to the occasion," I know otherwise. Even without measuring, he sports the largest tool in the toolbox I've ever seen, and I've encountered hundreds.

I don't work on a porno set or a questionable street corner in stilettos. I'm a physician's assistant for a group of dick doctors—an illustrious PA who tends to trouser snakes of all shapes and sizes. The practice's slogan, *"you've seen one, you've seen them all,"* applies to the everyday care and maintenance of Chicago's weenies. That is, until Brady Luck strutted into our office a couple weeks ago with his package. Since then, my life has been turned upside down. Or is that inside out? Let's just say, considering my profession, it's been nuts.

The problem in Brady's pants—though I do believe it's more in his head; the top one versus the one below his belt—has created a dilemma for me as a woman and medical professional. I can't even discuss the situation with my best friend due to HIPAA laws, and I need to talk to someone. It's bewildering. I've never wanted to jump a man's bones while, at the same time, despising him with a fiery passion.

Maybe it's the passion part that confuses me, or the way he claims no one can get his penis to cooperate but me. *What a line!* I'm sure it's not his gorgeous blue eyes, lickable jawline, chiseled chest, sculpted forearms...and don't get me started on his tight tush that has me all disorientated. Hot guys like that stalk me every day...in my dreams.

Anyway, I want a day to regroup before going back to work tomorrow. Monday's are hard enough, so I'm declaring this Sunday a Self-care Day. I haven't had one of these in...well, like ever. First things first, I need to call my best friend in hopes she can join me for mimosas and shopping before taking a nice long nap.

"Cali, do you know what time it is?" Taylor mumbles into the phone after the fourth ring.

A quick glance at the clock on my nightstand says it's after ten, which shouldn't elicit such a sleepy response since she rises and shines with the sun.

"It's time to get up and go to brunch. Sound good? Maybe Magnolia's." I hear a raspy male voice in the background. She's not alone. Obviously. And talk about working fast. When I left her last night at the bar, she wasn't even talking to a guy, and that was after midnight.

"Actually, I'm...well, it's complicated," she says, then whispers something I can't quite make out, like she's pulled the phone away from her mouth and is speaking to the mystery man in her bed, or maybe she's in his. I rack my brain with guy possibilities, and not a single one comes to mind except the hot bartender who kept throwing free drinks our way.

"Okay. But you'd better call me later with all the details."

As my feet hit the floor next to my bed, a bolt of lightning illuminates the sky outside my bedroom window, followed by an exploding blast of thunder that makes me jump. Another streak of light flashes, and I count between it and the sound of thunder.

"One-Mississippi. Two..." The heavens clash before I get to the second Mississippi. The storm is right on top of me. "Guess I'm staying in today."

Why am I talking to myself like a crazy person? Two words. Brady Luck.

It seems logical to blame him. I've been "off" since the day I fell at his feet... or more like swooned until I hit the floor of a bar in his presence. I need to explain this incident in greater detail. I'm not a boy-crazy, weak-kneed type of woman. I usually learn a guy's flirting with me after Taylor kicks me in the chin to get my attention and raises her brows suggestively.

My woes began a few weeks ago when Taylor and I were at a local club here in Chicago. At the time, I was the head cheerleader for Brady Luck fangirls—at least in my head. Yeah, I had it bad for him. When Brady showed up later, along with his teammates, he spotted me in the crowd of batting eyelashes. Stunned he even noticed *me*, I slithered off the barstool in a swoony type of motion onto the floor. It was a proud moment for me. Actually, I wanted to die of humiliation.

After I assumed my position on my seat...with Brady's assistance, I watched him walk away with his friends. I thought it was my brief shining moment with my crush, until I walked into an exam room where a new patient was waiting inside. It was Brady under a fake name, but I'd know that lopsided grin and gorgeous face in a room as dark as midnight.

Long story short—or is it the short story that became long?—he was able to get his formerly limp equipment to work in my presence. And for some crazy reason, he thinks he can only get a hard on if I'm around him, or when hears my voice. So, guess who's been stalking me? He even followed me into the infant department at Nordstrom and proceeded to tell me how he wants a ton of kids. I think the entire department store heard my ovaries explode. I had to hightail it out of the place before we started making babies near the bibs and blankets.

Well, enough is enough. I don't want to be his erection booty call, so I've refused to see him as a patient anymore, even though he calls the office several times a day.

While stewing over my Luck issues, I pop a bottle of sparkling wine—aka cheap girl champagne—and pour half into a small pitcher with some fresh O.J. I'm skipping coffee this morning and going straight for the hard stuff. I throw a couple frozen waffles into the toaster—and voilà! Breakfast.

I prop my pillows against the headboard, making a comfortable nest for my brunch in bed, place the mimosa pitcher on my nightstand—I can refill my glass from the bed. *Win!* I snatch up the erotic book I started this past week from where it's laying on the floor. The story was getting to the good part last night. I thought the couple was finally going to give in to their forbidden desires, but then, sadly, I couldn't keep my eyes open any longer, and the book must've fallen from my hands.

I start reading the naughty novel, and finally, the professor tells his student to lock the door behind her as she enters his office. I bite my lip as he rises from his desk and tosses his jacket onto a leather chair. In just a couple strides, he encircles his arms around his startled and—*dammit!* My cell phone rings and an unknown number with a Chicago area code pops up.

Hitting "ignore," I wait for a voicemail, but nothing comes. I roll my eyes at the stupid interruption, drink what's left of my first mimosa, and refill the glass nearly to the top before reaching into my nightstand for my favorite self-care toy. My phone better not ring again. I plan on having both hands busy.

TWO

Brady

My teammates are sitting at tables in the hotel private dining room, stuffing their faces with breakfast fit for a king. *Me?* I'm trying to figure out why my life is shit. Even the smell of bacon doesn't hit me right. I've moved over to the wall of windows looking out over the Saint Louis skyline. Dark clouds threaten, and I really hope a storm gets our afternoon game called off. I've been playing like hell and letting my team down.

My entire body is strung tight, and my mind is a million miles away from the ballpark down the street. All I can think about is my dick and its inability to perform. Hell, it's never let me down before. I have one hope left: Cali Jones. She's the only woman my dick likes for some reason, and she's refusing to see me or take my calls.

My friend, who happens to be a Class A hacker, found her personal cell number, so I called her a few minutes ago. She didn't answer, and I didn't leave a message. I had no idea what to say anyway. I can't think straight. Maybe it's because I've never had to beg a woman for sex. Who knew getting laid was this tough?

I stuff my phone in my back pocket and rub my palms over my face. Someone places a firm hand on my shoulder, and I turn around. *Shit*. It's Coach. His levels me with a stony expression as he slowly shakes his head.

"Brady, what the hell's going on with you?" he asks with a heavy sigh. "You're acting like your puppy died."

"Well, you're close." I give him a bitter smile. I might as well play "Taps" over my dick.

"Listen, you ate anything yet?"

"Nah. I'm good." I brush off his question and stick my hands in my pockets.

"Like hell." He rubs the back of his neck and breaks eye contact with me for a beat. "Eat something and come up to my suite. We need to talk. See you in fifteen."

He lowers his head and walks out of the dining room. A few guys call out to him when he passes, but Coach ignores each one, and all eyes focus on me. I shrug my shoulders and flash my trademark cocky grin, but they look back at me with worried eyes. Smiles aren't going to be enough to calm the tension. I need to execute on the field. It's like they want me to tell them everything's going to be okay. If only I could.

Fuck.

I'm used to being the guy with all the answers—the player who lights up the scoreboard and jokes with everyone in the dugout. Chicks dig me. Guys want to be me. People don't know this other version of me: the one who's striking out at the plate and making rookie errors. I don't either.

My mind can't get past the last three hookups that ended with me as limp as a manicotti noodle. I blamed it on cold medicine each time and fled the scene with a cough and sneeze, but I doubt the girls were fooled.

After my failed attempt last night, I don't know where to turn…well, other than Cali. Even the sound of her voice works to get things up and rolling.

I stuff a donut into my mouth, grab a water bottle, and make my way to Coach's suite. I knock on his door and wait. For what, I have no clue, though I imagine it's a king-size grilling.

"Brady, come in." He opens the door, and I follow him toward the living room area. A brown couch and two matching chairs make it look inviting. I can't say the same for the glare on Coach's face. "Have a seat."

I sit in the middle of the couch. He stays standing.

"It's Sunday morning, so we're going to church right here. Have a little come-to-Jesus moment," Coach says, taking the chair across from me. "Enough of this *'nothing's wrong, everything's fine'* bullshit. Spill."

Coach leans back in the chair and places his elbows on the armrest. He brings his hands to his face and rests them under his chin. He might as well be wearing a priest's collar, because I see no way out of this confession.

"My spark is gone," I sigh.

"Well, you need to find it. Chase it down the street, wrestle it to the ground, and carry it home if you have to. Snap out of it, Brady."

"Believe me, it's not that simple."

"Something else is going on. You've turned into a powder keg. No one turns on a dime like this without a reason."

"How'd you get so smart?" I ask him.

"Years of dealing with knuckleheads like you." Coach laughs.

I take a deep breath before I begin. "My game's off because of this girl I hooked up with. She's a voodoo princess or some shit. Anyway, I slept with her one night…" I don't mention not having any memory of the actual fucking part. I just woke up with her in my bed. "She thought we were a thing or something. She became wild-eyed and crazy when I handed her a wad of money for a cab ride home. Before she left, she pulled a voodoo doll out of her bag and stuck a pin in its…" I point to my crotch. "And now…" my mouth goes dry, and I pause. This is even worse than the confessional booth.

"My mojo isn't just off in the batter's box. It's messed up in the sack. I can't get it up," I exhale the words like a weight's been lifted off my shoulders. "Well, except for this one chick."

I decide to leave out the fact that she's my dick doctor...or was. That's creepy.

"So, what's the deal with the girl? Not the psycho one."

"Her name's Cali Jones, and she doesn't want anything to do with me." My shoulders slump back into the couch. I feel like the biggest pussy. Maybe this happens to dudes with my condition. No wonder my game's all fucked up.

"This has to be a first," Coach huffs. "Brady Luck getting a no."

"Yeah. I've tried calling her. Putting on the Luck charm. Still, she refuses to speak to me."

I leave out the fact that I've been stalking her delicious ass all over Chicago. He doesn't need to know that.

"Got your phone with you?" he asks, and I nod my head.

"Pull up her number and give me your phone." Coach holds out his hand.

"You're going to call her *now*?" I swallow and blow out a quick breath.

"Is she a baseball fan?"

"I think so?"

"Let's hope she takes one for the team," he says with a bristling chuckle.

I hand my phone over to Coach. From what I've dealt with firsthand from Cali, I have a bad feeling about this, but what do I have to lose?

THREE

Cali

I'm on my third mimosa and the professor has pushed his student up against the wall. He grabs her ass, and on instinct, her long legs wrap around his waist. I check my peen replacement device on the bed next to me. I don't want the batteries to be low when it's time to take off...

As I refocus on the book and dive into the sex scene, my phone rings. A Chicago area code, but different than the last one. The fact that it could be someone from the office trying to reach me has me going against all the rules of self-care and answering the call.

"Hello?"

"Is this Cali Jones?" asks a man with a very deep voice. He seems older, more like my father's age. Bill collector? Publisher's Clearing House? Well, I'm about to find out.

"Who's this?" Yeah, I need details.

"This is Jimmy McDermott, coach of the Chicago—"

I stop him there. "Right. Like Coach McDermott is just going to call me out of the blue on a Sunday. Are you a friend of Brady's? If you are, I have some choice words for you to pass on to him."

"Actually, I am Brady's coach. Friend is taking it a little far," he laughs into the phone.

"Okay, say you are Coach McDermott, why would you be calling me?" I glance at the clock. The first pitch in Saint Louis is only four hours away. "You have a game today. One would think you'd be busy."

"It's Brady. He's a fucking mess. And I think you know why."

"Um, maybe?" Oh my God, what does the Coach know? I'm afraid to find out. I slide down my headboard and cover the bedspread over my face.

"Say you'll talk to him. Help him out." He pauses. "Help the team." Coach is a legend in Chicago, a hero of heroes, and we're coyly talking about Brady's erectile dysfunction. There's a good chance I'll die of embarrassment before this call is over. "The penchant is in reach for Chicago. We have a chance at breaking the curse."

"I'm not sure," I stutter in a whisper. This is a hairbrained idea.

"What can I do to sweeten the deal?" Coach asks, like we're negotiating a player's contract. "Box seats for the season? Free hotdogs and beer?"

"We're at the end of the season."

"Smart girl. I like that. How's this? Season tickets for you and a friend. All the food and drinks you want, plus playoff games, and, God willing, World Series seats. Just talk to the guy, please?"

"Okay, but there will no phone sex," I declare, because I have dignity...and I'm a virgin in that department.

A couple guys I've met from dating apps have sent me dick pics, but I see those up close and personal all day long, so the appeal is limited and not that impressive. Now, a dick pic of Brady would be in a class all its own. What did he say? *"I'm nine inches of fine."* The guy is *so* modest.

"He'll call you in five minutes," Coach says, his tone seeming lighter than when we first started talking. "Work for you?"

Panic sets in. I'm in my bed. My hair's a rat's nest of epic portions. Mascara flakes from last night dot my cheeks like freckles. Not to mention, I feel slightly drunk.

"Nothing like FaceTime or anything visual." Ground rules laid for a crazy plan. I shake my head. People are always calling me smart and sensible, but this is dumb and ridiculous.

"Of course. Anything you want."

As soon as we hang up, I scramble off my bed, comb through my hair, and brush my teeth. I consider applying some lip gloss, but realize he's not going to see a thing. What is it about hot, cocky boys that makes girls turn to mush? I return to my bed, nestle under the covers, and wait, glancing sadly at my discarded book and aim-to-please friend.

My phone lights up. *It's him.* I take a deep breath and silently tell myself to play it cool. After all, he's the one chasing me.

"Hello," I say in a steady voice, one that doesn't match my racing heart and sweaty hands.

"Cali," Brady rushes out. "Thanks for taking my call. Hell, I'm going nuts. You're a doctor. What do you think's happening to me?"

I have to admit, he sounds desperate and nothing like the cocky guy hunting me down at every turn.

"First off, I can't give you medical advice since our practice is no longer seeing you as a patient. Second, you didn't have this problem in the exam room. Are you faking it?"

"Hell no," he practically shouts. "I would never lie about something like this. Promise."

"I had to ask. I don't know if there's anything I can do for you, Brady." I could tell him it's all in his head, but from experience, that doesn't help.

"But there is," he declares with an intense passion.

"You're wrong if you think I'm going to tell you what I'm wearing or listen while you list off what you want to do to me."

"That's not going to happen. Coach said I needed to keep things on your terms. And I gotta say, just talking to you right now helps. A guy would have to be blind as a bat to miss that you're hot as hell. What I like most about you, Cali, is your sass. You don't take shit from anyone, including me."

I try not to let the fact that he thinks I'm hot affect me. Yet, I squirm in my bed and feel my face flush. I glance up at the mirror on the opposite wall and see a dopey smile on my face. I look like a girl whose crush just said he liked her. Before the entire Erection Gate, it would've been true. Maybe there's a small part of me, likely my lonely vajayjay, that crushes on him still.

"Thanks, Brady. I think."

"Talk to me. Like, what are you doing right now...well, besides talking to me?" He chuckles in a sweet, non-cocky way. Maybe he is willing to look at me as a real person, not just a quick fix for what ails him.

"I was reading." I glance at my book and battery-operated bean machine. What started out as a great day of self-care now seems sad to me. I really wish I had someone real in my bed.

"What's the book?" Brady asks. *Of course.*

"An erotic romance. I'm sure you've never heard of it."

"Oh, really?" he says with an abundance of enthusiasm. I'm pretty sure he's getting the right idea about my day. "Why don't you read a hot part to me?"

"Like a sex scene?" I bite my lip, considering the option. What would it hurt? I close my eyes and take a centering breath.

"Yeah. I'd like that, but only if you're okay with it," Brady says in a husky voice, and my pulse quickens.

"Okay." My response is weak and unsure. Can I really pull this off? Does it make me slide down Slut Street? I let out a heavy sigh, caving into reading him smut. "Let me put you on speaker phone."

"Thanks, Cali." He seems as happy as a kid in a candy shop mixed with a big side of relief.

I open the book and find the page where the scene sex begins, trying not to imagine what Brady will be doing while I read it.

I stand at Professor Black's open door. Glancing up from his desk, he motions for me to enter his office. I look down the dark hallway. It's afterhours and all the other teachers and staff are gone for the evening. We're alone for the first time, and my mind swirls with the possibilities...

"Holy shit. He's her professor. This is gonna be good," Brady says in a gleeful voice. I imagine him rubbing his hands together...or over something else.

"No interrupting please," I scold him.

"Gotcha," he says, and I swear I hear the sound of a zipper running through its teeth. I get a visual of him exposing those glorious nine inches, and shake my head in an attempt to clear my thoughts—as if that's possible.

"Are you sure, Professor Black?" I ask, still standing in the threshold.

"Be a good girl and do what I say," he commands while rising from his desk. He's so tall, dark, and forbidden. I've never wanted anyone like him, but does he want me too? His hooded eyes and heavy breaths tell me he does.

"Does she go into his office?" Brady asks.

Dammit.

"Hush," I whisper-yell at him.

"Sorry," he whispers back. I roll my eyes, wondering if he's going to interrupt after every sentence. He'll end up driving me mad.

"One more interruption and I quit reading. Three strikes and you're out. Got it?"

"Yep," he quips. "Promise."

"Yes, sir," I reply, no longer caring about the right or wrong of my decision.

"Lock the door," he instructs while tossing his tweed jacket with suede elbow patches onto a leather chair. He rolls up his sleeves as I reach behind me and turn the lock. As soon as it clicks, a shiver runs over my skin. This is going to happen.

Professor Black steps to me in two long strides, then pulls me into his arms. I meld to his body. Hard lines meet softness. He bends down and ravishes me with a kiss.

"You're as sweet as I thought," he mutters into my ear. His lips continue from my jaw to my throat. I lean my head back against the door, allowing him better access to the rest of me.

"More please," I moan.

Brady hasn't said a word, though each inhale and exhale he takes registers in my ear. I picture him with his hand around his penis, stroking it in a fast motion.

He places his large hands under my behind and lifts me up. I wrap my legs around his waist, feeling his erection pressing against my most secret place.

"May I touch you, Monica?" he asks.

"Yes please," I breathe.

Professor Black pushes me against the door and holds me in place as he snakes one hand under my skirt. He inches his fingers up my inner thigh, stopping at the edge of my lace panties. I hold my breath, waiting for his next move.

"Are you wet for me?" he asks in a raspy tone.

"Yes. Please, I need more."

He answers my pleas and moves my panties to the side. When his fingers enter me, I cry out from his touch. It feels divine.

"So wet and naughty," he pants.

Brady's breaths are coming out in short puffs too. In a moment of weakness, or complete and utter horniness, I grab my magic wand and switch it on. I place it

464

against my clit and my mouth drops open. I need a release so damn bad. It was on my to-do-list anyway. Let the rationalization begin…

"Only for you, Professor," I utter.

"I want you," he says between kisses. "All of you."

"Then take me." I wrap my legs tighter around him and unbuckle his belt. His button and zipper are next. Finally, I have him in my hands. He's hard and huge.

"I can't wait anymore." I give him a couple strokes and line him up to where I need him the most.

"Yes." His voice is ragged with need, just like mine.

He pushes his hips forward and enters me, filling me completely in one motion. I scream his name in ecstasy. All those times I sat in his class and dreamed of this moment could never compare to how it feels to finally have him inside me.

"I want to see your breasts—take them in my mouth and make you come on my cock."

He grips my blouse in one hand and yanks it to the side. Buttons fly around us, exposing my bra to his view. He pulls down the cups, freeing my breasts. A second later, my nipple is in his mouth. The sensation of him devouring my body brings me to the edge. I want to fall over, let go, but only with him.

"I'm close. So close," I mumble as he continues to make love to me.

"Come with me, baby," he commands. After a couple more strokes, I do.

"Oh. Oh, oh," I call out as waves of pleasure wash over me.

As soon as I come, I stop reading. It's also possible I moaned Brady's name. There's silence on the other end of the phone, and I wonder if he's still there.

"Brady?" I ask quietly. I'll be humiliated if he hung up on me.

"Cali," he sounds like he's catching his breath, "that was hot as fuck. Were your 'ohs' for real?"

"Yeah," I confess to my lapse in judgment. Seriously, what did I think would happen when I went all clit happy? I should've known better.

"They were beautiful and everything I needed to hear. You've got the Midas touch for me, babe. Thank you."

"You're welcome?" I mean, really, what do you say to a guy after he says thanks for…not giving him phone sex exactly, but still getting him off? I'm at a loss, but the leftover bliss makes it somewhat worth it.

"This afternoon, I'm hitting a homerun just for you. I'm going to blow you a kiss when I walk up to bat. Watch for it."

"I will."

After we hang up, I finish the book and get a little more mileage out of my pretend boyfriend before the game starts.

True to his word, when Brady steps up to the plate his first time at bat, he blows an air kiss into the wind. The announcers laugh. I swoon. But everyone cheers when he hits the ball out of the park.

Now, time for that nap…and nine-inch dreams.

What the full monty? Find Brady and Cali here: http://bit.ly/HardLuckBro

ACKNOWLEDGMENTS

Penny Reid and Fiona! Thanks for making this entire collection possible. You two amaze me. Hats off to all of the authors who put their WIPs on hold and contributed to this collection and for those who helped shout it from the mountain tops. Jenn Watson, you're a rock star and got the PR ball rolling in a split second. Thank you! Emma Hart is secretly a webmaster. It took a great team to pull off this cocky celebration. I'm thankful to have been a part of an anthology with such a worthy mission. Keeping our words FREE!

ABOUT THE AUTHOR

USA Today bestselling author, Liv Morris, resides on the concrete rock known as Manhattan with her first and hopefully last husband, because he's a keeper.

———

Facebook: http://www.facebook.com/livmorrisauthor
Instagram: https://www.instagram.com/livmorrisnyc/
VIP Newsletter: http://www.subscribepage.com/c6k0f5
Book + Main: http://bit.ly/LivBookMain
Pinterest: http://www.pinterest.com/LivMorrisBooks/

ALSO BY LIV MORRIS

Bossy Nights: Release date: June 22nd
I can't wait to bring you Barclay and Tessa's love story!
Goodreads: http://bit.ly/bossynights
LIVE Alert: http://bit.ly/BNalert

Hard Luck

Tough Luck

Felony Ever After

Adam's Apple

Adam's Fall

Marry Screw Kill

HER COCKY RUSSIAN

A KINKY MÉNAGE

RED PHOENIX

A sexy bonus chapter between two best friends (blood-brothers) and one lucky submissive from the popular series Brie's Submission.

HER COCKY RUSSIAN

A KINKY MÉNAGE

Brie was sunbathing on the beach, enjoying the warmth of the sun on her skin as she listened to the soothing sound of the waves roll in. She turned her head to the left and stared at Rytsar Durov. He was laid out on his back, eyes closed, soaking up the Californian sun. Her eyes slowly traveled from his muscular chest, and down to his tight swimsuit that effectively showed off his manly assets.

"I can feel your eyes on me, *radost moya*," Rytsar said with a smirk, his eyes still closed.

Brie giggled and turned her head to the right. Sir Thane Davis was lying on his stomach, his head resting against his folded arms. Unlike Rytsar, his eyes were open, and he was staring straight at her. The ravenous look in his gaze made her pussy wet.

Biting her bottom lip, Brie turned her head to look up at the bright blue sky. Sir and Rytsar had something planned for her—she could feel it in her bones.

The two experienced Doms kept her constantly on her toes.

She loved being challenged by these two and wondered if today might include Rytsar's favorite tool or bondage scene or even a dual flogging by both Masters. She shivered in delight at the thought.

Of course, there was always the chance it might be something new she'd never experienced before. Sir and Rytsar were wickedly creative, and they consistently came up with fresh ways to please and test her.

Patience had never been Brie's strong suit, so she snuck a peek at both men. Sir's intense gaze was still on her, and now Rytsar's was, too.

"Téa."

Brie felt the butterflies start. Sir only used his pet name for her when they were about to scene together. "Yes, Master?"

"Rytsar needs refreshment."

"*Da*, I do," the Russian growled, licking his lips seductively.

475

Brie smiled. "What would you like, Rytsar?"

"Chilled vodka...and you."

"I'll have the same," Sir stated.

Brie stood up, her heart racing as she bowed to Sir. "If it pleases you, Master."

She left both men on the beach, walking the short distance to Rytsar's house. Brie had a soft spot for his beach home. Rytsar had taken her to this place after he'd won her bid at the Submissive Training Center auction. At the time, she'd no idea he spoke English and could understand every word she said.

Rytsar had come from Russia to attend Brie's first auction, per Sir's request. The sexy Russian had wanted to play out the warrior fantasy she'd written in class. Brie hadn't known at the time that he was the world-renowned Dom who was famous for his creative flair. He took her simple fantasy and transformed it into a real-life experience.

Brie lived out every emotion, as well as the physical aspects, of the fantasy she had written. Rytsar had left her breathless and totally captivated by the end of that evening. She'd never forgotten that night or the passion he had inspired in her.

Brie thought back on it as she poured two generous shots of Rytsar's favorite vodka and put several pickles on a small glass plate for them. She picked them up and turned to rejoin the Doms but stopped short when she saw both men were standing there.

"Kneel," Sir commanded.

She gracefully lowered herself to the marble floor as she'd been taught and bowed her head in reverence, two glasses of vodka in one hand and the plate in the other.

Sir and Rytsar each took a glass and a pickle from her plate. Brie heard the clink of glasses as the two men silently toasted each other, low chuckles filling the room.

Oh, these two were experts at teasing her! Not knowing what they were planning had Brie wet with desire.

"We are retiring to the bedroom, *radost moya*," Rytsar explained using his Russian pet name for her, meaning 'my joy'.

Sir commanded, "Join us after you take a shot of vodka yourself, and undress."

Brie watched them leave and smiled to herself. Both Doms at the same time? A submissive's dream...

She dutifully poured herself the shot and threw it back before consuming a small, delightfully sour, pickle. The smooth vodka quickly warmed her inside, making Brie feel even friskier.

She then took off her bikini set, laying it on the counter, before approaching Rytsar's closed bedroom door. Brie was surprised to find the door shut and knocked softly. "Master?"

"You may enter, *téa*."

She unconsciously held her breath as she opened the door and walked inside. Letting out her breath slowly, Brie stared at both men standing beside each other in all their naked glory.

Brie loved Sir's masculine body. He was tall, with a head of dark hair and that

476

sexy five o'clock shadow that outlined his chiseled jaw. Dark hair covered his toned chest and framed his impressive shaft, which was the most handsome cock she'd ever seen.

Rytsar was Sir's perfect counterpart. Equally tall, he had no hair on his head. No, the Russian was sexy bald, with a strong jaw and riveting blue eyes. His broad chest and ripped abs complemented the large dragon tattoo on his left shoulder.

"Do you remember the gift I purchased for you, but we never had the chance to use, *radost moya?*"

Rytsar was an extremely generous man and Brie was embarrassed to find herself at a loss. She looked to Sir for help, but he only smiled at her.

"I am sorry, Rytsar," she admitted, blushing intensely. "I do not."

Both men stepped sideways, revealing the sex machine set on the floor behind them.

Brie squeaked in surprised delight, remembering the extravagant gift Rytsar had surprised her with. It was known for giving women multiple orgasms because of the dual stimulation of its vibration and rotation. The machine itself looked similar to a leather saddle that a woman could "ride" and was completely customizable.

For today's session, Rytsar had attached a large, chocolate brown phallus to the machine she would straddle. The cock was realistic looking and intimidating in its girth.

"You want me to ride that?"

"*Da,*" Rytsar said with a wicked grin.

Although the size of the shaft had her feeling trembly and weak-kneed, she very much wanted to try it.

"Come, téa," Sir said, holding his hand out to her.

Brie walked forward and grasped his hand for support. She noticed that the cock had already been prepared for her and was liberally coated with lubricant. She gave a nervous giggle as she settled above it and slowly descended onto the huge head of the cock. Biting her lip, Brie forced her muscles to relax to encourage the invasion of the giant phallus.

"That's it," Rytsar growled lustfully as the dark shaft slowly disappeared into her pussy. Brie knelt on the floor, straddling the machine with the shaft deep inside her. This position gave her the ability to grind against the cock as if it were real.

Rytsar held up the controls. "Now for the fun."

He turned on the power. The machine buzzed loudly, and Brie felt the vibration go from her pussy all the way deep inside. She closed her eyes and began grinding against the toy, enjoying the unique stimulation it was creating.

That's when the Russian sadist turned the power up. Her eyes popped open as her entire body was rocked by the intense vibration. "Oh, my God!"

Sir took the controls from Rytsar and stared at her hungrily as he turned the other dial. Brie's eyes widened as the cock began rotating in a circle—the huge shaft rubbing against her G-spot in slow, rhythmic motions.

Rytsar chuckled lustfully. "Now she understands the power behind the stallion."

Brie held her breath when her body suddenly tensed, readying for an orgasm. "Permission to come," she begged, knowing she could not prevent it.

"That is the plan, téa," Sir answered smoothly. "Come for your Master."

Brie felt tremendous relief because the intensity of the machine-created climax was building with each rotation as her entire body shook from the vibration.

She closed her eyes and let the sensation take over…

Both men groaned when she threw her head back, screaming in passion as her body shuddered in the throes of a powerful orgasm.

Thankfully, Sir turned off the machine afterward, giving her sensitive clit time to recover.

She sat there looking up at both men, breathing hard and smiling like a little kid. "That was freakin' amazing!"

"Good," Sir said, leaning down to cup her chin before kissing her. "We plan to make you come repeatedly with it."

Brie's heart skipped a beat. She knew from experience that multiple orgasms could prove just as challenging as orgasm denial. However, she was up for the challenge.

Rytsar positioned himself on her left and Sir on her right, their shafts hard and ready for her oral skills—a talent she had acquired during her course at the Submissive Training Center.

Sir turned the machine back on and commanded, "Open."

Brie grasped his cock and kept her eyes on him as she took his shaft into her mouth. Sir moved her hair to the side and held it there, so he could watch. She took his shaft as deeply as she could without choking, then pulled back, trying again.

"That's it, téa…"

Brie swallowed, allowing the head of his shaft to travel slowly down her throat. She took him deeper and deeper until her lips touched the very base of his shaft. Once there, she began rocking gently back and forth, letting her throat caress his cock with its tight constriction.

The movement of her mouth, in unison with the rhythmic stimulation of her G-spot from the wicked cock inside her, caused an orgasm so intense she had to stop deep-throating him when she came.

Brie grinned up at Sir and apologized afterward.

Rytsar was turned on watching her and demanded in a gruff voice, "I want that mouth."

Brie turned her lips toward the Russian.

"Take him down your throat while you stroke my cock," Sir ordered.

Brie took several deep breaths before opening her mouth and taking Rytsar between her lips. Rytsar fisted her hair, guiding her movements while he slowly thrust his cock into her mouth as she relaxed her throat.

Brie managed to keep stroking Sir's cock with her hand, despite the added distraction of the machine's intense stimulation. Rytsar went excruciatingly slow as he forced his shaft down her throat. The Russian watched her hungrily as he let go of her hair and she pulled back to catch her breath.

She licked and nibbled the sides of his cock before encasing the head of his shaft again. Both men watched in rapt attention as her lips slowly moved from the head of his cock down to its base as she took his entire shaft in her throat.

Rytsar roared in pleasure, fisting her hair again as he began fucking her mouth. Brie willingly becoming his vessel of pleasure.

The fact was, the feel of his cock pumping her mouth complemented the movement of the cock inside her, and she came again, moaning against his shaft as she climaxed.

He forced her to hold still, then commanded her to stop, scolding her for almost taking him over the edge. Brie loved hearing that she'd been able to bring Rytsar that close to losing control.

Brie turned her attention back on Sir, keeping her hand on Rytsar's cock so she could pleasure him while sucking her Master. The low, guttural sound of Sir's pleasure when she took him back into her mouth made Brie gush, covering the sexy machine with her excitement.

Sir pulled out, then pushed his cock slowly back into her mouth, running his fingers through her hair. "My good girl…"

Sir's praise seemed to have a physical effect on her, because she instantly came again.

Rytsar smirked. "It seems *radost moya* enjoys the stallion. We could switch out the cock for a more challenging double penetration attachment, *moy droog*."

Sir looked down at Brie hungrily, shaking his head. "No, I prefer doing DP the old-fashioned way, old friend."

Brie only nodded, Sir's cock still in her mouth.

"Agreed, comrade," Rytsar growled. "But I need more sucking from those lips before we release her from the stallion."

"I will play with her body while téa pleases you."

Brie dutifully returned her attention to Rytsar.

Sir knelt beside her and whispered in her ear, "I enjoy watching while I explore your body."

Brie closed her eyes, concentrating on her Master's touch as she pleasured Rytsar with her mouth.

Sir caressed and tugged on her nipples, ordering in a seductive voice, "Grind on the machine for me."

Brie moaned around Rytsar's cock as she pressed her wet pussy against the vibrating machine, forcing the phallus even deeper inside her. Chills ran through Brie as her body tensed for another climax—but when this one hit, it didn't seem to end.

When Brie finally pulled back from Rytsar's cock to take a breath, Sir grabbed her breasts in both hands and descended on a nipple, sucking hard as she continued to grind against the machine.

She cried out in blissful pleasure, the multiple points of stimulation driving her absolutely crazy. "Oh, my God! I…can't…stop coming."

Both men chuckled, enjoying her heightened state of arousal.

"Look at me, *radost moya*," Rytsar commanded.

Brie gazed up at him with tears in her eyes—it felt so good.

"Do you like my cocky gift?"

She nodded, coming again as he asked.

Sir turned off the machine, but Brie's whole body continued to buzz from the vibration. He helped her disengage from the machine and Rytsar picked up her weakened body, carrying her to the bathroom to clean Brie in preparation for their next scene.

Brie was already flying high from her ride on the machine and squeaked when he touched her clit in the process of cleaning her.

"Are we sensitive?" he asked with a wicked grin.

Knowing Rytsar was a sadist, Brie was reluctant to tell him the truth, but knew better than to deny it. "Yes, Rytsar."

He raised an eyebrow as he fingered her pussy. "Oh hell...your pussy is burning hot, *radost moya*. I must fuck it now!" he declared, carrying her back into the bedroom where Sir was waiting for them on the oversized bed.

Rytsar set her down on the bed and joined her. He lay on his back and pulled her onto him. Brie straddled Rytsar like she had the machine. Rubbing her pussy over his cock, she could still feel the ghostly echo of its vibration as she coated Rytsar's hard shaft with her excitement.

When he could take no more, the Russian guided his cock into her, grunting as he thrust. "Oh, fuck, you're hot!" He grabbed the back of her head, kissing her forcefully on the lips as he thrust deeper into her.

Sir changed positions, moving behind Brie. "Your ass calls to your Master, téa."

Brie felt butterflies start when Sir began caressing her buttocks. Soon, the cold chill of lubricant followed as Sir slowly inserted his lubricated finger into her ass to help relax her inner muscles for the double penetration.

Brie then heard the sexy slick sound of Sir lubricating his shaft. Wiping his hands, Sir tossed the hand towel to the floor and grabbed her hips. "Let me inside..."

Brie's pussy contracted with desire, squeezing Rytsar's shaft when Sir pressed the head of his cock against her taut opening. He slowly forced his rigid cock into her ass, causing her to cry out when he breached her opening and sank inside.

Sir threw his head back and groaned. "God, I love the feel of you."

Brie rocked against his cock, wanting this—*needing* to be penetrated by both the men.

She whimpered when she felt Rytsar's teeth on her neck, giving her a sensual bite as Sir rolled his hips against her, forcing his cock deeper.

"Damn...Brie *is* extremely hot," Sir growled, reaching around to play with her nipples, helping her body to relax and take him even deeper. A tingling chill coursed through her body when she finally took the fullness of both cocks.

Rytsar sought out her lips, ravaging her mouth as she was claimed by both men.

Brie's pussy could not resist the pressure of two cocks moving inside her, and she felt the telltale signs of an intense climax building.

"I'm about to come again," she whispered.

Rytsar let out a low growl. "I'm going to pump my seed deep into your pussy when you do."

Brie whimpered, her orgasm building to dangerous levels.

Sir responded by smacking her on the ass. The sexy sound of it echoed throughout the room, turning her on even more.

Rytsar groaned as he thrust his hips upward, forcing his cock all the way into her and gripped her ass. "Are you ready to be thoroughly fucked?"

Brie bit her lip and nodded.

The Russian pulled her down so that her torso lay on his chest while Sir repositioned himself behind her for deeper penetration. Brie screamed the first time they each gave her a full stroke in tandem. It was almost too much, but Sir commanded huskily, "Give into it, téa."

Sir ramped up, coordinating his thrusts with Rytsar's, as they released their passion on her body. Soft mews escaped Brie's lips as the exquisite sensations they were generating took control—each thrust bringing her a symphony of pleasure.

Rytsar growled hoarsely, "Come for my cock, *radost moya*."

With her pussy stretched unnaturally tight by the two men, the pulsing sensation when her orgasm took hold was far more intense—her senses heightened by the rush of it.

Both men cried out as they followed her orgasm with their own, pumping her hard as they each came.

Pure submissive bliss…

Sir pulled out afterward and lay beside her while Brie continued to rest her cheek on Rytsar's chest, listening to his rapidly beating heart. Brie was enjoying being still, floating in the unique subspace their dual penetration had evoked.

Sir's lusty groan, coupled with a slap on the ass, caused her pussy to start pulsing and she milked Rytsar's spent shaft with a last orgasm. Afterward, Sir pulled her to him and kissed her.

Wrapping his arms around her, he nuzzled her neck, holding Brie captive in his embrace. "I love you."

Her heart fluttered whenever he said those words.

"This Russian loves you, too, *radost moya*," Rytsar stated, gazing at her with those intense blue eyes. "And I am about to show you how much…"

He got up from the bed and Brie watched as Rytsar opened his toy chest and went through it. He meticulously laid out each item one after another in a neat row on his dresser—a set of nipple clamps, a pair of cuffs, a bejeweled butt plug, spreader bar, and his wicked cat o' nines.

Brie stared at the array of tools, her heart beating faster.

Sir leaned over and nibbled her ear. "Téa, are you ready for our next round?"

Oh, yes…please.

1-click the First Box Set for FREE
Brie's Submission (Books 1-3)
https://goo.gl/EY3bho

ABOUT THE AUTHOR

USA Today Bestselling Author - Red Phoenix is an award-winning romance author (and submissive in real life) who gained popularity with her series, Brie's Submission.

When she is not writing, you can find her on Facebook, Twitter, or Instagram interacting with fans. "I heart my fans!" ~Red

Goodreads: https://www.goodreads.com/author/show/5557309.Red_Phoenix
Facebook: http://www.facebook.com/redphoenix69/
Twitter: http://twitter.com/redphoenix69
Instagram: https://www.instagram.com/redphoenixauthor/
Newsletter: http://RedPhoenixAuthor.com/newsletter-signup

ALSO BY RED PHOENIX

Over Two Million readers have enjoyed Red's stories!

Brie's Submission Series:
https://redphoenixauthor.com/reds-books/brie-series/

Teach Me #1

Love Me #2

Catch Me #3

Try Me #4

Protect Me #5

Hold Me #6

Surprise Me #7

Trust Me #8

Claim Me #9

Enchant Me #10

A Cowboy's Heart #11

Breathe with Me #12

Her Russian Knight #13

Under His Protection #14

Her Russian Returns #15

In Sir's Arms #16

Bound by Love #17

Also part of the Submissive Training Center world:
Safe Haven (Captain's Duet, #1) Slated for 6/12/18
Destined to Dominate (Captain's Duet, #2) Late Summer 2018

CONFESSIONS OF A COCKBLOCKED WINGMAN

DAISY PRESCOTT

A short story starring the cockiest Wingman, Tom Donnely.

CONFESSIONS OF A COCKBLOCKED WINGMAN

First of all, you should know that when people call me cocky, I always take it as a compliment. Sure, sometimes they add asshole or prick as an insult, but that's okay, I probably earned it. Pretty confident even my beautiful wife has called me cocky dozens of times and a few of those times were in anger, not awe.

Such is life.

With great abundance comes great responsibility.

And I have more than my fair share when it comes to looks, talent, and luck.

Sure, call me cocky. Call me a reformed man whore. Hell, I still happily answer to Tom Cat.

But don't think for one minute, not even a second, that I'm not one hundred percent loyal and completely in love with my wife.

Hailey is my beginning and my end. As long as she'll have me, I'm hers. I want to be old and crotchety with her.

Cocky or not, I'm not stupid enough not to realize when the love of my life is mad at me.

Banish might be too strong a word, but when she gave me "the look" and told me there was nothing to eat in the house, I knew I'd be better off hunting and gathering dinner than sticking around. And I'm smart enough to bring the baby with me to give Hailey a break.

Shaw happily chirps away in his car seat behind me in Hailey's new Highlander while I pull into a parking spot and pull out my phone. I have no idea what Hailey wants to eat and won't risk grabbing something she hates. While I wait for her to respond, I strap on the baby carrier and secure my six-month-old son against my chest, facing out so he can see the world.

I didn't bring the cart cozy thing Hailey uses and there's no telling what germs are coating the seat and handles. Better to avoid cross-contamination. You never know when there's a stomach virus lurking around.

"You're staying strapped in today, buddy." I rub his head. His pale blond hair curls at the ends. There's zero doubt he's mine. And if there were, his tendency to flirt with every woman he sees would erase any speck of uncertainty. Little dude has his dad's charms.

My phone vibrates and pings with Hailey's list. I laugh when I see the mix of salty junk food, chocolate, and random staples like cereal and milk. I know we have a half gallon of milk and four boxes of her favorite cereals at home. With my thumbs hovering over the screen, another message comes through. She's also placed an order from Sal's Pizza for me to pick up on the way home.

Figures.

On our way into the store, a few women I don't recognize smile and wave at Shaw. Their eyes light up when they see him, some deep, primal desire brightens their smiles.

Babies are irresistible to a lot of women. The scent of baby wash alone can flip a switch inside a woman. I don't think I ever realized the full extent of this power before watching women react to Shaw.

I should've been more prepared. After all, Hailey and I reconnected at my sister's baby shower. The power of tiny humans was at work on me even if I hadn't realized it then.

Even sleep deprived and feeling like I'm doing things wrong with Shaw half the time, I really want Hailey pregnant again. We aren't using anything to prevent it, but we're not exactly trying either. Hell, we barely have sex these days, choosing sleep above almost anything else. Need to change that. I miss my wife.

"Hi there, good lookin'. Aren't you a dream boat?" a woman who appears to be my mom's age makes a beeline for us, hands outstretched and fingers wiggling. In the past, my ego would take the compliment, flash her a grin and put a smile on her face. But her smile isn't for me. Nope. She's focused solely on Shaw.

Not taking any chances, I grab a cart and keep it between her and us.

Shaw laughs and claps his hands, his tiny feet swinging and kicking way too close to my groin.

One of our would-be attackers sighs. "Nothing cuter than a man with a baby. And the cheeks on both of you. I don't know which I want to pinch more."

She must be friends with the local gossip brigade. They're more perverted than most men I know.

Weaving my way through the aisles, I dodge more women with the same gleam in their eyes. I can feel the weight of their staring.

One lady sneaks up in a side ambush, her hand brushing my arm before she tickles Shaw's sock-covered foot. "I love a man with dimples."

I don't know which one of us she's complimenting.

Happy for the attention, Shaw bounces and jiggles against my chest, waving his arms and giggling.

"You aren't helping," I whisper near his head when the tickling woman walks away. "It isn't my face that's at risk of being pinched."

After a woman in a Whidbey sweatshirt rubs a peach against her cheek while eyeing us, I decide to get out of the produce section.

I curse Hailey for requesting breakfast sausage after running into Connie, who makes a comment about girth when she sees me holding a roll of Jimmy Dean.

At that point, I resolve we need to start ordering our groceries online.

Even though ice cream isn't on the list, I decide to buy a couple of pints, knowing we can never have enough.

"Well, if this isn't the most ridiculous, asinine thing I ever thought I'd see. Tom Donnely parading around like a kangaroo." Olaf's voice surprises me from behind.

With three pints of ice cream tucked in the crook of my arm, I close the freezer door and face him. Shaw claps his chubby hands and gurgles at the cranky bartender from the Dog House. He must like the old man's beard.

It isn't like I've been playing pool on Thursdays with my baby. I'm sure Shaw would have a good time hanging out with the guys, but I think Olaf's head might separate from his body and float away if we brought our kids into his bar. John's son, Mac, is the same age as Shaw and we've started a bet on when the two of them will first get in trouble together. John's wife Diane and Hailey joke if they're going to turn out anything like their fathers, we should put the money into a fund for bail money because we'll need the compound interest.

"Hey, Olaf." Using a falsetto, I wave Shaw's arm.

"I've seen everything now," Olaf grumbles. "Next thing I know you'll be asking me to turn the bar into a romper room."

I chuckle because I called that. "Might help your business if you were more family friendly instead of snarling at everyone."

"You sound like Dan, getting in my business and telling me what to do. Bunch of cocky assholes."

I cover Shaw's ears in mock outrage. "Language in front of the baby."

Olaf's grumbling provokes my laughter, which annoys him more. "If that kid's first word is profanity, you only have yourself to blame."

Shaw finds this funny and giggles, flailing his arms and reaching out to touch Olaf.

With a grunt, the man gives in and sticks out his finger for Shaw to wrap his chubby fist around. Not even he is immune to the charms of my son.

A fraction of a smile cracks through his typical scowl. "Damn kids."

"They're tiny but powerful, right?" I let Shaw hold my finger in his other hand.

"Pure innocence. If only they could stay that way." He pulls his finger away and straightens his back.

I forget he has two grown sons who live off the island. From what I hear, they don't have the best relationships. I can't imagine how much that sucks. The Donnelys are a close-knit family, too close at times, but I wouldn't change it.

We say goodbye to Olaf and check out without a single pinch or grope from Sandy the cashier.

After picking up the pizza at Sal's, I swing by Fellowship of the Bean to grab a coffee on the way home.

"Do you need a babysitter on Saturday afternoon?" Standing inside of the drive-up coffee hut, Jonah nervously strokes his dark beard.

"You volunteering to take my kid?" I eye him with suspicion. Despite being business partners with Erik Kelso and being Ashley's brother, he's a good man. A little weird, keeps to himself and is the last of the bachelors in our original group, but reasonable all the same. "The only people who want to hang out with a baby besides us and other people with babies are his grandparents and aunts. Since you don't fall into any of those categories, what's the deal? You need a reminder to keep your dick wrapped?"

His hand pauses near his mouth and a low chuckle gets muffled behind it.

"Busted. Offering to babysit sounded better than asking if I can borrow Shaw for a couple of hours." He busies himself with making my coffee, dumping out the old espresso grounds before grinding fresh beans.

"He isn't a chainsaw or a truck. What do you need a baby for?" I lean my arm on the open window of our SUV and watch him work.

Jonah focuses on the process of making an Americano like it's the first time he's ever done it and not the millionth.

"Did you ask John to babysit Mac? Being his second, he's more chill about the kid."

His lip curls up slightly. "Thought I'd start with you."

"Why me?" Pieces of the puzzle click into place. "This have anything to do with a woman?"

"Maybe. I figured if anyone would understand, it would be you. Because, well, you know..." The sound of sputtering steam cuts off the rest of his words.

I wait for him to finish before speaking. "Man, even I didn't use my sisters' kids to pick up women."

"A new low?" he asks with a sheepish smile.

"It's fucking brilliant, devious as hell. I'm jealous I never used this trick when I was single. Who's the woman? Anyone I know?" Hailey isn't going to approve of this plan at all, but I'm curious enough to hear him out.

"I don't think you know her. She's new to the island. No family here." He won't meet my eyes.

"How is Shaw going to help?"

"I'm not sure he will, but he might give me the air of responsibility I'm apparently lacking in a certain woman's eyes."

"Sure you don't want to start with taking Nameless on a walk instead? He's adorable, too. There still might be shit involved, but easier to deal with."

He puts a lid on my coffee. "You're probably right."

"When's Ashley due? Can't this wait until your niece or nephew is born? Doting uncle is a good look for you." I accept my cup of coffee and try to hand him a five.

He waves off my cash. "Newborns are scary. The way you can see their pulse through the gap in their skull freaks me the hell out."

I nod in agreement. "Totally get that. Let me ask Hailey if she has plans. I can't promise she'll agree, but I'll give it a shot. No taking him to bars or to a club in Seattle. Olaf's forbidden all babies from the Dog House under threat of a lifetime ban on their parents. Not sure if he means his life or ours, but let's not push it"

"You know Dan and I are in talks with Olaf about taking over after a buyout? About time he retired, but he's too stubborn to admit it." Jonah finally smiles, leaning on the small counter next to the window. His sleeves of tattoos are on full display beneath the short sleeves of his T-shirt. He's a borderline hipster but still good people.

"Makes sense. Sal's practically runs itself, and Erik seems surprisingly capable of running the coffee business. Better two locals than someone from the city. Let me know if you want another business partner. I could be interested." John too, but I don't mention it to Jonah. For all the money we've spent on beers, we should already be Olaf's silent partners. Shifting back into drive, I tell him I'll let him know about Saturday.

———

On the short drive home, Shaw falls asleep in his car seat. It's early for his afternoon nap, but I'm not going to complain.

I carry him inside the house and up to his room, settling him into his crib. Briefly, his eyes flutter open before he finds his blanket and snuggles himself back to sleep.

After making sure the baby monitor is on, I close the door behind me. Only then do I realize there's no music or television noise coming from downstairs.

"Hailey?" I call softly as I walk down the hall to our room.

She's tucked under a blanket on top of our bed, completely crashed out. Our dog lifts his head and blinks at me with sleepy eyes. I click my tongue, and he jumps off the bed. Not wanting to wake her, I pull shut the door and head downstairs.

Nameless follows and then takes off outside, bounding off the front porch to chase a squirrel into the woods surrounding the house. He'll come back when he's ready, so I don't bother calling for him.

Back in the kitchen, I put the ice cream in the freezer and turn on the oven to keep the pizza warm. I open a beer and flip on the television in the living room. Mariners are playing and I find the game. Two innings later, they're up seven to zero when Hailey pads downstairs. Her dark hair is a mess and she has an imprint of pillow wrinkles on her cheek.

"How long have you been home?" she asks, crawling onto my lap and resting her head on my chest.

"Long enough for the Mariners to start winning." I run my hands down her back before slipping my fingers beneath the waistband of her sweats, touching warm, soft skin as I cup the round curves of her ass. We don't have a ton of time, but maybe we have enough to fool around. "You aren't wearing underwear."

"You make it sound sexy when it's only laziness. If I weren't nursing, I wouldn't be wearing a bra either. And I'm pretty sure I've worn these sweats for the past three days, even with the muddy paw prints on the thigh from where Nameless jumped up on me. I've never been less hot in my life. Except that time when we both had the stomach flu." She squirms and sits upright, pressing

493

herself against my growing hard-on. "How can you be turned on by this hot mess?"

"It's not your hair or makeup or what clothes you wear that makes you hot. It's you, every gorgeous inch of you."

"Take off your pants." Her voice is commanding as she grinds against me. "Now."

"When was the last time you showered?" I tease her, reaching for my fly.

"Thomas Clifford." Admonishing me with my full name, she rises onto her knees and pulls at the knot holding her pants closed. "You can be funny or you can get laid."

"Are you saying I can't do both?" I take her words as a dare. "I accept your challenge."

On the baby monitor, Shaw grunts and stirs.

She grimaces and sticks out her tongue at me. "We don't have time for your antics. The baby could wake up any minute and cockblock us."

"Little bastard." Grinning up at her, I pull her shirt over her head.

"He is your son." Fabric muffles her voice, but I hear her clearly.

Once topless, she leans forward to kiss me as I flip the clasp on her bra. I brush my tongue against hers and moan when her hand cups me through my jeans. One touch from her and I'm throbbing. It's been two weeks since we had sex and that was a quickie in the shower before work. I miss my wife. A petty part of me hates sharing her time and attention with anyone. Then I feel guilty because I'm jealous of my own kid. But I'm never going to admit that aloud.

Instead of focusing on what's changed and what I'm missing, I focus on this moment and challenge myself to see how quickly I can make her come.

With my mindset, I lift her and off me, setting her feet on the floor before standing in front of her. I drop my jeans and boxers, loving the way her eyes widen when she stares at my body. I swear my cock swells with pride under her attention.

Shaw fusses, and we both freeze again, waiting for him to do more, but he quiets. Our time is running out.

"This isn't going to be slow. You okay with that?" I ask, already knowing the answer.

Nodding, she licks her lips. "Fast and hard works for me."

Unable to resist, I kiss her deeply and then drag my teeth over her bottom lip. "God, I love you. Turn around."

"I love you, especially when you're bossy," she says over her shoulder, bracing her hands on the end of the couch. Her full, plump ass lifts in the air, teasing me. She loves it in this position.

I find her as ready as I am, easily slipping a finger inside her. Without wasting time, I guide myself to her opening and thrust inside. We groan simultaneously. I pull out and slide back in to my base. A few more thrusts and I'm right on the edge. But this isn't about me getting off in a few strokes. Locating her clit, I press my thumb in a tight circle, matching the rhythm of my cock sliding against her g-spot.

From upstairs, a few grumpy baby squawks crackle over the monitor.

"Damn, hurry. Please. I'm so close." Hailey's hand rests over mine to encourage me.

No pressure. It's like making love with a ticking bomb winding down the seconds to explosion.

Shaw quiets, and I refocus on Hailey's orgasm. Soon I feel the telltale tightening of her inner walls around me, and I know she's nearly there. Bending over her, I squeeze her nipple with my other hand and whisper near her ear, "I can feel you squeezing my cock, and it's so fucking hot to be inside you when you come."

That does it. With a soft moan, she bucks and arches and then stills as her orgasm pulses through her.

A low moan of my own rumbles in my chest. Unable to hold off another second, I push deep and then grind into her as I explode.

Panting, I stay inside her for a moment, relishing the feel of her after our dry spell. Another screech from Shaw causes me to straighten up and I slip out of her, shuddering at the contrast of cool air after her heat.

"I needed that." Hailey sweeps her hair out of her face. She glows with pleasure. "I think that was a new record for us."

Glancing over at the kitchen clock, I estimate we've been naked for all of seven minutes. "Someday we'll have more time. Then I'll ravish you until you can't walk. Sound good?"

Her lashes flutter as she closes her eyes. "Promise?"

Shaw yells in his room, his patience gone.

I tug on my boxers and kiss Hailey a quick peck. "I'll get him."

"I'll make a salad to go with the pizza."

Upstairs, I find a pair of sweats before I rescue Shaw from his crib and change his diaper.

"Thanks for being a good wingman and napping this afternoon like a champ." With a kiss to his head, I lift him off the changing table. "You don't know what a wingman is, but someday you and Mac will figure it out. He'll always have your back, and you'll have his."

He smiles at me.

"Let's go see Mom."

Hailey's in the kitchen, chopping a pepper. The pizza sits on the counter next to a giant bowl of salad. I love that she thinks I'm going to eat lettuce when I bought a bag of garlic knots.

I settle Shaw into his high chair first, and then step around my wife. "I saw Jonah today at the coffee hut. He offered to babysit for us next weekend."

"Why?" she pauses her chopping. "That's strange."

"You like Jonah. We've known him forever. It isn't like I'm handing our kid over to a stranger." As a precaution, I remove the chef's knife from her hand for the next part. I never lie to Hailey. "He asked if he could borrow Shaw for a few hours. Sounds like a win-win situation for us."

"Wait, you want to loan our baby to Jonah? Why?" Hailey's voice levels up to a near screech.

"Think of it as babysitting. We can have a couple of hours on a Saturday afternoon all to ourselves. To do whatever we want."

She frowns at me. "Stop waggling your eyebrows at me. You look like a horny cartoon dog when you do that."

"Sorry if the thought of hours alone with my wife excites me. We could spend the entire time naked."

"Or we could nap."

"We could do both. Multi-task. And we won't be cockblocked by a baby monitor." I kiss her neck. "Maybe we can even create a sibling for him."

She sweeps the chopped pepper into the salad. "Aren't you worried it's too soon? We can barely manage with one baby, what are we doing to do with two?"

"Be exhausted but happy?" I step behind her and wrap my arms around her waist, resting them below her navel. "Come on, we did so well on the first one."

Humming, she continues stirring the onions.

"Hailey?" I nuzzle her neck with my nose.

"I'm late," she whispers, staring into the bowl.

"Late?" I ask because there are a lot of things she could be late for and I need clarification before I let myself react.

"I'm pretty sure I'm pregnant. Again."

Happiness and pride swell inside my chest. "Really? Are you serious?"

"Didn't you pay attention to the shopping list?" she laughs.

"I thought you had PMS, not cravings." I'm in shock. "We're having another baby?"

"We are." Her smile is hesitant as her eyes fill with tears.

"Please don't cry. This is the best news. Here I've been thinking about knocking you up again and I've already done it." I want to give my sperm a million high-fives.

"You're so proud of yourself." Wiping her eyes, her laughter reappears. "If only you could carry this one."

I would if I could. I'd do anything to ease her discomfort and pain, but there's no way I could handle birthing a baby. Not a chance in hell.

"We both know you're stronger than I could ever be." I kiss away her tears and then press my lips against hers. "I love you. I love Shaw, and I'm going to love our daughter."

I feel her lips curl into a smile. "I love how sure you are."

Tilting my head so I can stare into her eyes, I reassure her. "Girl, boy, or twins, I'll love them because they're ours."

Her pupils dilate as she widens her eyes in shock. "Twins?"

"We've got this. Look at Shaw. We're amazing parents."

Our son bangs his fists on the tray of his chair, letting out a loud fart.

Hailey smothers her giggles. "I'm not sure the world can handle more Donnely men."

She's probably right. So much awesome in one family isn't fair.

We fill our plates and sit at the table near Shaw. After a few moments of silent eating, I ask, "What about Jonah?"

"I'm going to need more information." She bites into her crust.

"All I know is it involves a woman."

Her brows lift with surprise. "Does this have anything to do with June?"

"As in this month?" I ask, once again confused. "It's for next Saturday."

"No, the woman who owns the yarn shop next to the Dog House. She made a blanket for Shaw?"

Doesn't ring a bell.

Hailey sighs. "I love how oblivious you are to other women."

"What can I say? You've domesticated the tomcat in me. I'm working on my dad bod and everything."

"Let's not get too carried away." She leans over the corner of the table and kisses away the smirk on my mouth. "I like you cocky."

Find out about Shaw's adventure with Jonah in The Last Wingmen, releasing October 2018.

ABOUT THE AUTHOR

Writer, traveler, gardener, taco lover, friend of sloths, and USA Today Bestselling Author of romantic comedies.

———————

Mailing list: http://smarturl.it/daisysignup
Facebook: https://www.facebook.com/daisyprescottauthorpage
Twitter: https://twitter.com/Daisy_Prescott
Instagram: https://www.instagram.com/daisyprescott/
Bookbub: https://www.bookbub.com/authors/daisy-prescott
Pinterest: https://www.pinterest.com/daisyprescott/
Daisyland Facebook Group:
https://www.facebook.com/groups/1416649935215295/

ALSO BY DAISY PRESCOTT

Wingmen:

Ready to Fall

Confessions of a Reformed Tom Cat

Better Love

Small Town Scandal

Wingmen Babypalooza: A Christmas Babies Novella

The Last Wingman (Coming Fall 2018)

Love with Altitude:

Next to You

Crazy Over You

Wild for You

Up to You (Releases 6/12/18)

Modern Love Stories:

We Were Here

Geoducks Are for Lovers

Wanderlust

A Series Crossover Short Story Collection:

Love, Laughter and a Happily Ever After

Bewitched:

Bewitched

Spellbound

Enchanted

Charmed

A COCKY CORRUPTION ENGAGEMENT

A CIVIL CORRUPTION BONUS SCENE

JESSICA PRINCE

What happens when a big, bad security guy falls for the girl with a smart mouth? A whole lot of fun.

A COCKY CORRUPTION ENGAGEMENT

A CIVIL CORRUPTION BONUS SCENE

Ian

Jesus fucking Christ, this was my Hell.

"What if we made a trail of flower petals—"

Fuck me. I tuned Tate's voice out before I had an aneurism. This wasn't what I wanted. I never should have let these damn girls know I planned on proposing to Corrine. If I'd just gone with my gut and did my thing without telling Tate, Gwen, and Gina I wouldn't be standing here right now with them trying to hijack my proposal.

"I'm not trailin' fucking flower petals around my house," I grunted, staring daggers at them. "No flowers, no string quartet, no skywriter. For fuck's sake, just stop giving me suggestions. I know what I'm doing, and she's gonna love it."

Gwen scowled and slammed her hands on her hips. "Someone's cocky"

Crossing my arms over my chest, I hitched the corner of my mouth up in a smirk. "It's not bein' cocky when it's true. I know my girl and she's not into all this hearts and flowers shit."

"Maybe not," she continued to argue, "But there are exceptions. And getting engaged is one of them. *All* girls want that hearts and flowers shit when the guy they love is planning to ask her to marry him."

"Not Corrie."

"Yes, Corrie!" she snapped back. "She's only been my best friend fore*ver*. I think I know what I'm talking about."

Normally I adored Gwen. She was good people, and I'd been through enough and seen enough when I was in the service to know the good from the bad when I saw it. Gwen was salt of the earth. Even if my gut didn't tell me so, the way she was with her and Garrett's adorable little girl Liddy was all the proof I needed. That little girl wanted for nothing, but wasn't spoiled rotten. She had a

505

heart even bigger than her mother's, which was saying a lot. But right now, I kinda wanted to sew her lips shut just so I didn't have to hear her talk anymore.

"And I'm the one who's been screwin' her. No offense, babe, but significant other trumps BFF every time. That's just the way it is. Men and women shared more with the person they were in love with than even their closest friends."

She knew I was right, and by the look on her face she wasn't happy to have to admit it. "Fine," she mumbled with a pout. "No flower petals. So what are you gonna do, then?"

"Don't you worry about that. I've got it all figured out. I just need you to do me a favor tomorrow."

Gwen smirked conspiratorially. "Whatever you need, I'm totally on it."

I was counting on it.

Corrine

"Gwen, babe. No offense, because you know I love you with all my heart, but if you drag me into one more freaking bridal boutique, I'm going to murder the hell out of you."

"Don't be such a Debby Downer. Bernie's watching Liddy for the day, and I'm getting married!" She'd shouted *I'm getting married* approximately 1,249 time in the past four hour, and while I was stoked out of my freaking mind for her, we'd hit up five boutiques before lunch, and she hadn't found *anything* she liked.

Don't get me wrong, I was always down for a shopping spree there hadn't been a single thing I could buy for myself in any of the shops we'd visited without looking like a psycho, not my idea of fun.

"Just one more," she pleaded, clasping her hands in front of her. "I promise. This'll be the last one. Then we'll go grab something to eat."

"And have drinks," I demanded. "Lots and lots of drinks."

Grabbing my hand, she dragged me down the block. I knew the instant we stepped through the doors that this was going to be a complete and utter waist of time for her. For me, on the other hand..."

"Seriously, Gwennie? This place totally isn't your scene." But it was absolutely mine. The moment we crossed the threshold I felt like I'd stepped into a store that catered solely to my special brand of quirky awesomeness. "Omigod!" I gasped, rushing to one of the rack sand slapping at the hangers. I sucked in a huge, dramatic gasp at what I saw. "Feathers!" I squealed with uncontrollable glee. "Look, Gwen! This has feathers!" Another gasp. "*And fringe!* Holy shit! I've totally died and gone to Heaven. If the day ever comes when Sam and Dean Winchester profession their undying love for me and request sister-wives type deal I'm totally rockin' a dress with feathers and fringe!"

"Just a couple things wrong with that scenario, honey," she said on a giggle. "First of all, they're fictional characters."

"Spoilsport," I grumbled, running my fingers along the delicate beading along the bodice. The gown was the palest of pinks, trumpet mermaid cut with a sweetheart neckline and a full skirt and train made of layer upon layer of feather and fringe. It was the most stunning thing I'd ever seen, and it would be mine. Oh yes… it *would* be mine.

"Secondly, you remember Ian? You boyfriend? That big mountain of a man who could pop a watermelon like a freaking balloon just by squeezing it in his hand? I'm not thinking he'd be all too thrilled with you marrying anyone but him."

My chest heaved with a heavy sigh, and grumbled, "Yeah, I guess you're right. Stupid sexy Ian, making me love him when the Winchesters could just be waiting in the wings."

"Good afternoon, ladies," a shop worker greeted in an overly shipper voice. "Is there anything I can help you find today?"

Shouldering me out of the way, Gwen grabbed the dress I'd been caressing and shoved it into my chest. "Yeah, can you show her to a dressing room? She needs to try the on."

"Whoa! Wait, hold on." I dig my heels in as she tried to shove me away. "No, no, no. No way. Isn't that, like, bad luck or something? And we're supposed to be here for you, not me."

"Oh, that's just a stupid old wives tale. It's not bad luck, and this dress is absolutely, totally you. You have to try it on."

I caved almost instantly, practically skipping toward the dressing area the sales clerk led me to. Closing myself in, I stripped out of my clothes and stepped into the incredible gown. Zipping up and getting everything tucked where it needed to be was much harder than I expected. But the end result was *so freaking worth it.*

"Holy shit," I breathed as I stared at my reflection in the mirror.

"What? What is it?" Gwen called from the other side of the door. "Is it too tight?"

"I. Look. Amazing!" I shouted. "I'm never taking this off. Like, ever. I'm sleeping in this thing, Gwen. And not only because I can't get myself out of it, which I can't, but whatever."

"Well get your pretty but out here so I can see!"

The second I stepped out Gwen's mouth dropped open and her eyes brimmed with tears. And I knew for certain that I was spending the rest of my life in this dress.

"Told you that shop would be a bust."

Gwen had walked out of the last empty handed. She'd decided to call it quits for the day, and we'd gone to my favorite little café for lunch. In all the years I'd lived in Seattle I had no idea this place existed until Ian brought me. Their quiche melted in my mouth, and I damn near spontaneously orgasmed when I tried their chocolate soufflé. This place was my Heaven, and I made a point to eat here as often as I could.

The kindhearted swung by to refill our mimosas for the third time. Gwen sucked half of hers back and licked her lips. "I wouldn't say it was a complete bust. I might not have found anything, but at least you did, so it was good for something."

I snorted into the raspberry torte I'd ordered for dessert and spoke through a full mouth. "Yeah, because that matters. I'm not the one getting married babe. What do I need a wedding dress for?"

"You never know," she replied, smiling a manic, frightening Cameron Diaz smile.

Sitting my fork down, I stared across the table and asked, "What's the deal with you, huh? You're acting weird."

"I'm not acting weird!" she chirped. Gwen wasn't a chirper

"Are too. You've been like a freaking ray of sunshine all day long. You're never in this good a mood. Usually you spend the first half of the time we spend together coming up with elaborate ways to murder Garrett and get away with it."

"Can you blame me?" she asked in defense. "I mean, you've met the guy. He can be a pain in the ass." She wasn't wrong about t hat. Before the two of them had gone and fallen madly in love, they'd spent three years at each other's throats. I might have been teasing about her wanting to kill him *now*, but back then I used to worry I'd get a call from the cops wanting to know if I could provide her with an alibi. "Who better to bitch about him to but my best friend?"

"Whatever," I muttered, rolling my eyes as the smartest waitress in the world refilled my glass again. "No of that changes the fact you're being weird, whether you're willing to admit it or not."

"I'm not being weird! I'm just in a good mood. Can't I be in a good mood for ten flipping minutes without you accusing me of being up to something?"

My forehead wrinkled in confusion. "What the hell are you talking about? I never said you were up to something. I just said you were acting strange."

Gwen's eyes bugged out at the same time her face went pale.

"Wait... *are* you up to something?"

"No! I have to pee. I'll be right back." She shot from her chair and sprinted toward the restrooms at the back of the restaurant.

Not being weird my ass.

I was just about to pull my phone from my purse and text Tate and Gina to find out what was up, when the chair across from me squeaked across the floor.

"Ian?" I asked when I looked up to see my boyfriend had taken Gwen's chair. "What are you doing here? I thought you said you had stuff to do today."

Ian

I had to admit, for someone who was usually so confident, I was pretty fucking nervous right then.

That picture Gwen sent me an hour ago hadn't done jack to calm my nerves. Corrine's beauty took my breath away most days. But when I'd seen her in that dress I'd nearly had a heart attack. It should have looked ridiculous, pale pink with goddamn feathers and fringe... but she looked like an angel in it. I could imagine her walking down the aisle toward me in that dress. It was my girl in everyway... absolutely perfect.

The waitress I'd made an accomplice to my little plan came sauntering up with a beaming grin and two thumbs up. "She's on her fourth mimosa, but I remember her from being in here before, and her tolerance is surprisingly high, so I don't think you have anything to worry about."

That was the understatement of the year. My girl could drink an Irishman under the table and walk away in four-inch heels without so much as tripping. That was only part of the reason she was so goddamn perfect for me. Another part was that attitude of hers. Most people saw me instantly coward. With my height and build I could pretty much intimidate anyone. But not Corrine. She never batted an eye. If I so much as raised my voice she'd dress me down worse than any CO I'd come across and my Southern Momma combined.

If anything, the damn woman scared *me*.

She was fierce and loyal and tender hearted, and she was funny as hell. Nobody could make me laugh the way she did. She soften my hard edges. She was my other half, and being with her made me a better person.

"Thanks," I muttered, wiping my shaky palm along my brow. Christ, I was sweating like a whore in church. What was taking Gwen so damn long?

Just when I was starting to think I was going to have to go out there and crash their little party she cam rushing down the hall looking more than just a little frantic.

"It's showtime!" she cried. "Now, just a heads up, she might be a little suspicious right now, so you might not want to leave her waiting too long."

"*What*?" I barked in a way that made everyone around up nearly jump out of their skin. Oh, another person who wasn't scared of me? Gwen. Yeah, her and Corrine were definitely cut from the same blunt, sharp-tongued cloth.

"It wasn't my fault!" she cried, throwing her hands wide. "I'm too excited, okay? I might have been acting a little... off."

"Fuck me," I ranked a hand through my hair in agitation. "I knew I shouldn't have told you I was doin' this."

"I'm sorry! Just... hurry. Before she calls and hounds Tate and Gina into spilling the beans."

All of a sudden I felt like I was going to be sick. I'd been to some seriously dark places and seen the worst of humanity, but none of that scared the shit out of me as much as this. I was beginning to doubt myself. What if I wasn't enough for her? What if I didn't deserve her. And worst of all, what if she said no?"

"Shit. I... Maybe I should wait."

"Ian." Gwen placed a calming hand on my arm. "Are you starting to have second thoughts?"

Yeah. No. Maybe. Christ," I grunted, squeezing my eyes closed and rubbing at my forehead. "I don't know. What if... What if she says no?"

For some reason that made her smile like a Cheshire cat. "You're scared she'll say no?"

I wasn't just scared. I was fucking terrified. "I know you said she'd say yes, but what if you're wrong?"

"Oh, sweetie." She moved in and wrapped her arms around my waist, squeezing as tight as she could before pulling away and looking up at me. "You know how you said men and women share more with the person they were in love with than even their closest friends? Well, when it comes to the people they love, best friends don't hold back. And she's gone for you, honey. Absolutely crazy, stupid, over the moon gone for you in a way I've never seen her with another man. So I swear to you, she'll say yes."

And just like that, I didn't just feel better, I felt like I could concur the goddamn world.

"Now go get your girl."

I didn't have t be told twice.

Coming around the corner and into the main dining area, I spotted Corrine rummaging around in her purse, and pulled out the chair Gwen had vacated just a little while ago, and sat down.

"Ian?" she asked, confusion in her big beautiful eyes. "What are you doing here? I thought you said you had stuff to do today."

"I do."

Her forehead puckered in confusion. "What the hell is everyone's deal today?" she asked, looking around the room like the answers would pop out of thin air. "First Gwen's acting like she woke up farting roses this morning, and now you're being all mysterious and stuff. Will someone tell me what's going on before I lose my mind?"

Reaching into my pocket, I pulled out the black velvet ring box and rested both my hands on the table. Corrine gasped and clasped her hands over her mouth as soon as I flipped it open.

"I love you, baby," I started, saying the very first words that popped into my head. "I didn't realize something was missing from my life until I met you." My hand shook as I set the ring box aside and took hold of hers.

"Oh my god, honey—"

"I never gave much thought to my future. I was just fine living day by day. But then I met you and started wanting things I never even considered."

"

"Now I wake up every single morning and turn over to see my future sleeping beside me."

"Ian, I—"

"You're my better half, baby, and I can't imagine not having you in my life. I didn't think marriage was in the cards for me—"

"Oh my god! Ian!"

"What?"

She lifted her hands to my lips and peppered my knuckles with kisses. "I love you too, more than you could even imagine. But if you don't get to the end of this speech so I can say yes and have you slide that *stunning* ring on my finger, I'm gonna choke you, so help me god. And that would put a real freaking damper on the celebratory blowjob I'm planning to give you in the bathroom right after."

Honestly, I didn't expect anything less from my Corrie. She knew what she wanted, and when it was sitting right in front of her she'd reach out an grab it with both hands.

A smile stretched across my cheeks as I pulled the ring from the box and took hold of her left hand. "Marry me baby. Make me the happiest fuckin' man in the universe and marry me."

Tears shimmered in her eyes as a wobbly smile tipped her lips up. "I didn't hear a question in there."

"That's because I wasn't asking," I stated. "I just told you I can't live without you, and I meant it. You can either say yes, or I'll cuff you to my bed until you see reason."

Her head fell back in a burst of laughter. "That whole cuffing me to the bed thing sounds a little fun. Not much of an incentive to get me to say yes."

Leaning closer, I lowered my voice so only she could hear. "Say yes and I'll use the cuffs in a much more fun way. You have my word."

Those tears broke free and slide down her cheeks as she said the one word that made me the happiest I'd been in my entire life.

"Yes."

"Really?"

"Yes. Yes! I'll marry you!"

I slid the ring on her finger and shot out of the chair. Circling the table, I pulled her into my arms and kissed the air from her lungs. When we finally broke apart she was panting and grinning like the cat that ate the canary.

"I'm heading to the ladies room. Wait two minutes and meet me in there."

Oh yeah. She was absolutely fucking *perfect* for me.

ABOUT THE AUTHOR

Jessica is a wife and mother, a self proclaimed caffeine addict, connoisseur of inexpensive wine, and the worst driver in the state of Texas. When she's not nose deep in her next manuscript, or binging on sit-coms, you can usually find her with her kindle in hand.

FACEBOOK: http://www.facebook.com/authorjessicaprince
INSTAGRAM: http://www.instagram.com/jessprince_writes
TWITTER: http://www.twitter.com/JessPrince2013
JESSICA'S PRINCESSES READER GROUP: http://bit.ly/JPsPrincesses

ALSO BY JESSICA PRINCE

THE PICKING UP THE PIECES SERIES:

Picking up the Pieces

Rising from the Ashes

Pushing the Boundaries

Worth the Wait

THE COLORS NOVELS:

Scattered Colors

Shrinking Violet

Love Hate Relationship

Wildflower

THE LOCKLAINE BOYS (a LOVE HATE RELATIONSHIP spinoff):

Fire & Ice

Opposites Attract

Almost Perfect

THE PEMBROOKE SERIES (a WILDFLOWER spinoff):

Sweet Sunshine

Coming Full Circle

A Broken Soul

CIVIL CORRUPTION SERIES:

Corrupt

Defile

Consume: coming July 9 (http://bit.ly/GRConsume)

GIRL TALK SERIES:

Seducing Lola

Tempting Sophia

Enticing Daphne

Charming Fiona

FIGHT OR FLIGHT

MEGHAN QUINN

Fight or Flight is a brief intro into the fighter pilot world I'll be bringing you into this coming June. (June 21st to be exact). The story is contemporary, military romance and revolves around the two main characters Colby and Rory, with a HUGE twist. Get ready for flight suits, fighter jets, and one epic romance.

Please note, this story is raw and unedited

FIGHT OR FLIGHT

STRYDER

"Get your ass down, cadet! Are you listening to me? I said ass down."

Grunting out another push up, I listen to the berating of a fellow cadet next to me who is tired, winded, and ready to quit, I can see it in his eyes, I can hear it in his grunts, in the pained "yes, sirs" he continues to deliver over and over again.

Thirty-five.

Thirty-Six.

Thirty-Seven.

I push my body to it's limits, never letting up, never giving in, never letting the screaming or mental abuse get to me, because I'm used to it. Coming from a long lineage of fighter pilots in my family, I've been trained for this moment, I've been prepared and broken down to be able to face this moment head on without even batting an eyelash.

Forty.

Forty-one.

Forty-two.

Up and down, up and down. A sharp pain ricochets through my chest, echoing down my arms but I continue, I don't stop. I don't need to, I know I can continue to go on, to push past the pain.

"Get up. Now!"

Hopping up, I stand to attention, legs together, feet forming a forty-five-degree angle, arms stiffly at my sides, head forward. My abs are burning, my shoulders on fire, and my chest aches, not wanting to be lifted right now, but I hold formation.

I've been through worse.

"About face."

Twisting in a one-hundred and eighty-degree angle, I turn with my fellow cadets, facing the west, the picturesque Colorado Rocky Mountains a backdrop for our training, for the Air Force Academy's basic military training.

I've grown up staring at these mountains, memorizing each peak, the sway of the rocks, the bald spots, and the lay of the terrain. To me, they remind me of a home I never wanted to be a part of, a family I wished I could trade in. To the cadets who are from out of town, who are staring at these mountains for the first time, they're awe-inspiring, giving them a surge of pride to be a part of something. But to me, they are a dull reminder of the expectations waiting for me back home.

"Fall out and return to your tents."

Releasing the tension in our backs, we all relax and head back to our designated sleeping areas.

What a fucking day.

Marching.

Obstacle course.

Team building.

It's all the kind of stuff my fellow cadets came here for.

Integrity first. Service before self. Excellence in all we do. The words we live by. They were drilled into us over and over again as we were shuffled off the shuttle bus that brought us up to BMT. They were spoken to us as we fell into line, picking up our gear, getting our heads shaved, passing through immunizations, and now as we battle it out at Jack's Valley encampment for physical and mental strength.

We're day five into our eighteen days at camp and I can see the toll it's taken on everyone so far from the slump in their bodies, the limping in their legs, the weary look in their expressions.

I might be sore, I might be tired, but I know how to push past it. I know what it takes to be on top, to be the best, because my dad didn't let me be any other way.

Countless hours in the gym, out in the backyard, pouring down rain, carrying a rucksack on my shoulders, holding a gun above my head, jogging in place while my dad stood in front of me, umbrella shielding himself from the rain, drilling into me, over and over again until I was nothing but a puddle of a man on the floor.

This is nothing compared to that. I could go another five hours before even considering to ask for a break.

Popping through my tent door, I head toward my sleeping bag and sit down just as Colby, my friend, takes a seat next to me.

Colby Brooks. I met him during intake, he was the only other guy in our group that I didn't see true fear in his eyes. He was conditioned to know the proper way to talk to our commanding officers, his shoulders were stiff and upright like mine, and when a cadre approached him to scream at him about something, he stood there, in perfect from, not even blinking an eye.

I saw a piece of him inside of me and I knew we were going to be friends.

"Tired?" He asks, taking his boots off, making sure to stuff his shoelaces inside.

"Nah." I shake my head and lean back, taking in the sorry bunch of mother fuckers who are kissing the ground, begging to take a nap. "You?"

"A little sore, but not tired."

After the first few nights in the tent spending some time with Colby, I've come to find out becoming a fighter pilot has been his dream since he was ten. The reason why he's so conditioned to the lifestyle is because he taught himself, spending countless hours learning the moves, reading up on what it takes to be in the Air Force and to be accepted into the academy. He's a wealth of knowledge, born and raised to be a part of the Blue Line.

Leaning over so only Colby can really hear me, I say, "Did you see Johnson split his pants when hopping over one of the obstacles."

A small smile peaks past Colby's lips as he nods. "Right up the crack, gave some of the girls in the squadron a show."

I chuckle quietly next to him. "It's the little things, man. That made my goddamn day."

"Sure as hell didn't make Johnson's day. Spent the rest of the day with split pants, having to slink through water and mud."

I shake my head. "The sorry mother fucker."

Coming up to us, hobbling like an idiot, our friend Hardie takes a seat and leans all the way back on the ground, draping his arm over his eyes. "Fuck me."

Colby and I exchange glances. "Dude, not a good thing to say," Colby replies.

"Definitely don't say it in the showers," I add.

Hardie strips his cap off his head and tosses it at my chest. I catch the mud-soaked hat just as Hardie says, "I didn't mean it literally, assholes." He eyes the both of us and groans. "How the hell are you two still able to sit up after what we went through today?"

"It's called training," I answer for the both of us.

Hardie shakes his head. "You know what everyone is saying about you?"

"Me?" I point to my chest.

"Yeah, you?"

I look to the side, lips thin and pressed together, trying to come up with an answer. "Hmm, that I'm a triple threat; handsome, strong, and ready as fuck?"

"Pretty close, they're all saying you're a cocky mother fucker."

As I should be. Besides Colby, I'm the only cadet in my class that came to intake not only prepared for the physical work, but I came with nothing to lose. This won't make or break me, at least that's what I keep telling myself, convincing myself over and over again.

I don't need this, they need me.

I come from a lineage of fighter pilots, its in my blood.

The sky is where I belong, flying through the clouds, protecting my country.

I might be cocky, but I have a reason to be.

"Sounds about right." I thumb toward Colby. "What about this guy over here. What's everyone saying about him? Manly with a feminine voice?"

"Fuck off." Colby punches me in the arm and shakes his head. He doesn't have a feminine voice but it's fun to fuck around with him, especially since he's so quiet all the time.

Hardie props himself up on his elbow and says, "They think he's one of those guys you don't fuck with or he'll snap and go on a punching rampage."

We're supposed to stay quiet during this time, never really drawing any kind of attention, but I can't help it, I let out a deep laugh. A punching rampage, yup, I could easily see that.

Whereas I'm more outgoing, Colby is reserved, doesn't talk much, observes more than anything, always taking in every scenario, it's like he doesn't know how to turn the military in him on and off. There's times where you can relax and just be a human again but Colby doesn't seem to have that trait.

"I'm not going to snap," Colby says tersely.

Chuckling, I pat him on the back. "Try saying that next time without the foam forming in the corner of your mouth."

He rolls his eyes and turns away from us.

"Oh great, you've upset him," I chastise Hardie. "Now I'm going to have to spend the rest of my night talking to his back instead of his pretty face."

"You're fucking ridiculous," Colby says with a shake of his head.

"See," I point to Colby's back while talking to Hardie. "All night long."

We spend the next hour getting washed up and eating our meals while some try to nurse their wobbly legs. Some of the guys still pass their hands over their heads, trying to get used to the haircuts we've been forced to have, some guys try to grab a wink of sleep before we're barged in on and asked to get ready for another bout of marching.

Staring up at the green tent with a patched-up hole, hands behind my head, I say to Colby who's only inches away, "What made you want to be a fighter pilot?"

Without even having to think about it, Colby answers, "My grandpa. He was one and told me all about his glory days up in the sky. I knew that's what I wanted to do, to follow in his footsteps."

It's not the first time Colby has mentioned his grandpa, it seems like he's played a huge part in Colby's life.

"What about you?" he asks.

"It's what I'm supposed to do," I answer, knowing the real reason that rests closely behind the truth I just announced. It's not one I've shared with anyone, one that I've kept close to my heart since the moment I realized it. I've kept the real reason on lock down in fear my dad would find out.

"You said your dad was a pilot?"

I nod. "For twenty years." And my brothers are pilots, uncles, my grandpa was a pilot. It isn't an option in the Sheppard household of what you want to do with your life, it's an obligation you have to fulfill.

"Is he retired now?"

"Yup."

And that's the end of that conversation. Silence falls between us, the subtle sounds of some of our fellow cadets sleeping ring through the air as well as the shifting of sleeping bags.

Basic military training, it's only the beginning of this life-long journey, what lies in front of me is a world I never thought I wanted, but one I'm ready to be a part of.

"Stryder Sheppard." Standing in my dress blues, I pivot toward my cadre, arms swaying to the perfect height, my march on point, my father standing a few feet away, watching . . . analyzing.

Two of my commanding cadets flank each side of me and present me with my cadet boards, signifying my entrance into the cadet wing. I made it through basic and now I'm entering as a fourth year into the academy, a rigorous class schedule ahead of me.

I stare ahead at my dad, in his dress blues, looking prestigious with all his chest candy decorating his uniform. For a retired airman, he still is in shape, could hold a candle to any of the cadets on this field, and I hate that. I wish he was out of shape, I wish he was a contradiction to everything he represents, but that wouldn't be Tyler Sheppard, no, he's precise and polished with everything he does and says . . . at least he is when he's not behind closed doors. Always putting on a show, that's his game.

"Congratulations." I shake hands with both my fellow cadets and then go to the end of the line, watching closely as Colby receives his cadet boards as well, pride beaming from him as his shoulders are set high, a lightness to the dark scowl he usually wears.

This is his first step into the academy he's worked his ass off to get into. There is no doubt in my mind that this is a moment he won't ever forget.

After the ceremonies, I briskly walk over to my father where he holds out his hand to me. Knowing it's all for show, I take it in mine and give it a firm shake.

There is no smile, there is no pride coming from him, just an expectation. I can check off one of the boxes in the long list of to-dos he's laid out for me.

Leaning in, quietly he says, "Don't fuck this up."

Ahh, words of wisdom.

No congratulations, no job well done, not even a how are you doing?

Just a terse don't fuck this up.

I'm not surprised.

I answer back with a shake of his hand. "Yes, sir."

He nods and then spins on his heel, leaving me behind while others who were lucky enough to have their family members attend, take pictures and beam about how much stronger their kids look.

Shaking off the lackluster moment with my father, I turn to find Colby talking to a man in a wheel chair, a nurse next to him. I study the interaction for a few seconds before making the connection. That must be Colby's grandfather.

And fuck, the old guy looks damn proud of his grandson.

I want to be jealous, but knowing Colby's past, fighting through basic with him, I just nod my head and smile. Colby deserves this moment with his grandfather.

COLBY

"By golly, look at you." He tugs on Darlene's arm—his nurse—and says, "Do you see my boy, look at those shoulders in that uniform. He's a real looker, isn't he?"

"Gramps," I chuckle, "Be cool."

He leans forward. "Bet all the lady cadets have their eye on you." He winks obnoxiously.

"Christ." I drag my hand over my face.

"Oh come on, I can't rib my grandson on his day of acceptance into the cadet wing?"

"No, you can." I look around. "Just keep your voice down."

A hearty laugh comes out of my grandpa as well as a brisk and sharp cough. Over the last year it seems like he's aged ten years. Not even letting it get to the point of a fight, my grandpa sold his house and put himself into a senior living center. When I asked him if he was okay with that, he said why wouldn't he be okay with being doted on all day.

Growing serious, Gramps says, "You look good, Colby, proud."

"I am." I take in a deep breath, laughter and comradery surrounding me. This is what I wanted when I first decided to join the Air Force, I wanted a place where I could belong and so far, I've never felt more a part of something in my entire life. I feel fulfilled and fucking excited for what's to come. I can't wait to dive into classes, to take my first trip in the glider, to try out for the Wings of Blue, the parachuting team at the academy. I'm bound and determined to soak up every last moment while I'm here, preparing myself to get into flight school so one day, I can fly a fighter jet.

When I glance around, I see Stryder looking off into the distance. I noticed his dad was here and I watched their interaction which probably lasted no more than a few seconds. Stryder wasn't lying when he spoke of his dad in such a negative light. Just from the brief snapshot I caught of them, I could see the tension between the two, the hatred Stryder has for his own father, there was no hiding it.

Hating that Stryder is all alone, I call him over. "Stryder, over here." I nod with my head.

He spots me and jogs over, making it in a few steps.

Lending out his hand to my grandpa, he says, "You must be the infamous Gramps."

Gramps takes Stryder's hand in his and nods. "At your service."

"It's nice to meet you, sir. I've heard nothing but amazing things about you."

"That's right you have." He winks at me and then let's Stryder's hand go, giving him a once over. "You know, you might give my son a run for his money when it comes to the ladies."

Laughing, Stryder squeezes my grandpa's shoulder and says, "Sir, with all do respect, your grandson doesn't hold a candle to me in the looks department."

Gramps looks me up and down and then Stryder. Shaking his head, he leans toward me and says, "I'm afraid he might have you there, son."

Stryder's head falls back as he holds his stomach and laughs. Over these last few weeks, I've been able to gauge Stryder for the type of guy he is, always putting on a show, always laughing and joking around, but under all of the easy-going façade, his heart is a hardened stone. His ambition is low, his will to work automatic, and mainly he's just going through the motions with no real passion behind his movements. The only time I see a hint of willingness to put an effort in is when we're talking about flying and our dreams to become fighter pilots. That's when I see it, the same kind of passion I possess.

"I think I like your grandpa, he's a good man." Once again, Stryder shakes his hand and then says, "I think I'm going to head up to the dorms. It was nice meeting you . . . Gramps."

Gramps nods his head and says, "It was a pleasure meeting you, Stryder." Pointing his finger he says, "Watch my grandson's six, work hard, and make sure this guy has some fun on occasion."

Stryder walks backwards when he says, "I can try, Gramps, but I make no promises. Catch you in the dorms." He waves his hand and takes off.

Gramps still has his eyes on Stryder when he says, "That boy is hurting, I just hope it isn't for long." Letting out a long breath, he turns to me and grips my arm, bringing me down to eye level. Grabbing my cheek, he looks me in the eyes and says, "This is the beginning, Colby, the first stepping stone to your dream. Don't lose focus but also don't forget to have fun and if you meet a girl who rocks your world, let her."

I chuckle, my Gramps the ever romantic. "No distractions, Gramps."

"Sometimes you can afford them." He winks and then hands his phone over to Darlene. "Would you mind taking a picture?"

"Of course not."

I stand next to my grandpa, chest puffed, his arm around my waist, my hand on his shoulder and I smile, knowing fully well this picture is going to be shown all around the senior community when he gets home.

I say my good byes and watch as my grandpa is wheeled off the field, happier than I think I've ever seen him.

If you meet a girl who rocks your world, let her.

I shake my head and chuckle. Never going to happen. I have one goal and one goal alone, I'm going to become a fighter pilot and nothing and no one is going to stop me from reaching that goal.

To be continued . . .

THE UPSIDE OF FALLING is a contemporary, military romance releasing June 21st, that will pick up during Colby's final year at the academy and his life after. This emotionally charged book full of heart-stopping romance will be the first book in a duet. **THE DOWNSIDE OF LOVE** will be releasing two weeks later on July 5th and will feature one hell of a TWIST you will never see coming.

To be the first to know when the books release, sign up here:
https://www.subscribepage.com/n5t3e9

Want to hang out with me? Be a part of weekly giveaways?
Join my reader group here:
https://www.facebook.com/groups/280485535469847

ABOUT THE AUTHOR

Author, wife, adoptive mother, and peanut butter lover. Will dance for laughs, won't eat anything spicy because you asked, but will squeeze boobs in replace of a hug. Grew up in Southern California, lived in New York, and now resides in Colorado with my wife, our son, two dogs, three cats, and my multiple book boyfriends. Loves love, anything romantic, and will die if I ever meet Tom Hanks. Yay, books!

Website: https://authormeghanquinn.com/
Facebook Group: https://www.facebook.com/groups/280485535469847/

BEARD AND HEN

PENNY REID

Cletus and Jenn's story continues.

PART 1

RICHARD BADCOCK AND THE SERENITY OF GOOD LAYERS

Jennifer

There's no faking quality.

A thing was either high quality or it wasn't.

And I was convinced Mr. Richard Badcock's organic, free range eggs were the highest quality anywhere in Green Valley, east Tennessee. Perhaps the whole of Tennessee. Maybe the southeast USA. For that matter, quite possibly in the entire universe.

They were the platinum-diamond-Nobel Prize of eggs. Some were narrow, some were wide; some had sage green shells, robin blue, tawny brown, or snow white; some were even speckled. But all his eggs contained firm whites and the most gorgeous orangey yolks, brighter than orange sherbet—*don't get me started on the yolks!*—that I'd ever seen in all my years of baking.

I didn't take to broadcasting this much, mostly because folks already thought I was a little off, but I didn't think anything I made tasted as good if I didn't use Richard's eggs. My creations lacked a richness, a texture, one I could only achieve with Badcock eggs, and that was fact.

Which was why I was currently up to my eyeballs in despair.

"What do you mean you don't have any eggs?" I looked behind Mr. Richard Badcock, searching his huge gated lawn and fancy hen house in the distance.

It had gables, eves, a white gutter, and even an actual picket fence.

My gazed shifted back to the man, moved over this new Mr. Badcock who had never been anything but kind to me in the past. I had no idea why he was behaving this way, but I couldn't spare a thought to that. I was too much occupied by the great egg-dearth of the decade.

"Just what I said, Ms. Sylvester. I'm plum out of eggs." His voice was firm, hard, and—if I wasn't mistaken—laced with distrust. "But if you want some fresh chicken, we just butchered last—"

"I can't put a chicken thigh in a custard, Richard!" I wailed, unashamed in my anguish, my teeth chattering in the early-January cold snap. "It's not a gelatin. Fat and meat and bones won't do me any good."

Mr. Richard Badcock sighed, his eyebrows tenting on his forehead in an arrangement of both compassion—*finally*—and helplessness. "I am very sorry, Ms. Sylvester. If I had some eggs, I'd give them to you."

"I'm sorry too, but this doesn't make any sense. You must have a hundred chickens back there, and—"

"We have sixty-one chickens." He sniffed, looking down his nose at me, once again hostile. "Unlike some folks, we believe our hens need space, autonomy, greens, and serenity to be good layers."

Good lord, now I'd offended his serene egg-laying chickens.

"Of course, Mr. Badcock." I tried to make my tone conciliatory. "And I can't tell you how much I just love—and I do mean *love*—those eggs. Which is why, please pardon my outburst, I am feeling a great deal of desolation at the prospect of baking without your superior product."

His shoulders relaxed, apparently mollified, and he quit peering at me, instead sighing for maybe the tenth time since I showed up. "Ms. Sylvester, there ain't nothing I can do. I *am* sorry. But we had two unexpected—and very large—orders late last night. I'm cleaned out for at least two weeks, and—"

"Two weeks?" I clutched my chest and shrieked, completely beside myself.

He sighed again, taking off his hat and wiping his brow with the back of his flannel covered forearm, saying nothing. His old brown eyes moved over me with a look that seemed speculative, and I got the sense he was having himself an internal debate.

Meanwhile, I was going to cry.

I could feel it. The twinge in my nose, the sting behind my eyes, the tremor of my chin. But I couldn't go two weeks without Badcock eggs. I couldn't. Folks would remark. They'd *notice*. We'd be asked if we'd changed our recipes, and not for the better. Once, I'd gone three days without the eggs and the church choir near pitched a fit about my coconut custard pie.

"It's *fine*." Mrs. Seymore—the pastor's wife—had said to my momma. "But what I don't understand is, why didn't Jenn make it? We specifically asked for Jennifer's coconut custard pie."

My momma had hemmed and hawed and, in the end, she'd lied. She told them an under-baker had made it, and had eventually given it to them for free.

The thing about the church choir was, it didn't take much to get them to sing, *if you know what I mean*. In fact, one might even say they were *gleeful* about spreading unhappy news.

Therefore, once I did have the eggs, I made coconut custard tarts with shaved coconut and dropped them off—in person—to the Saturday choir practice.

All had been forgiven and my praises were sung once more.

But . . . two weeks? With the church picnic coming up?

Lord have mercy.

I swallowed my panic and nodded for no reason. "Well," I croaked when I found my voice, "I guess . . . I guess . . ."

Mr. Badcock made a clicking sound with his tongue. "Fine, fine. How about this?" He sounded reluctant, and for some reason, the reluctance gave my heart hope. "I have four dozen eggs up at the homestead."

"Oh Mr. Badcock, I would—"

"Now settle down." He lifted is hands, even the one holding the hat. "I'll give them to you, for double the price."

I swallowed again, because that was a tough pill to swallow. *Double the price?* His eggs were already ten dollars a dozen. Part of me wanted to argue. I told that part to hush: serene eggs didn't grow on trees.

"O-okay." I tried—and failed—to smile.

"And from now on," he continued, "the Donner Bakery needs to pre-order their eggs three months in advance, with a-uh . . . fifty percent down payment. That's right, fifty percent." He nodded as though agreeing with himself.

I found myself momentarily at a loss for words, not because these were unfair terms, but because Mr. Badcock had never expressed any interest in pre-orders or pre-payments prior to right this minute.

And it took me less than a second to respond, "But, of course. Absolutely, Mr. Badcock. In fact, I'll be happy to place our order for the entire year right now."

He blinked at me. "You would?"

"Yes. I most certainly would. I don't want anyone's eggs but yours."

He blinked some more, standing straighter. "You wouldn't?" His voice cracked.

"No." On a whim, I reached forward and held his hand. He looked between my face and our joined fingers as I spoke from the heart, "Mr. Badcock, your eggs are. . . well, they're magical. And I guess I should have told you prior to now, but all other eggs in comparison might as well be applesauce."

Applesauce being the low-fat, vegan replacement for eggs in baking recipes. In other words, a sad and inferior imitation.

"Oh," he was blinking faster now, and a bit of color touched his cheeks. "My goodness. I don't—I mean, I don't know what to say. This is all very unexpected."

I released his hand, stepping away as he watched me retreat. "Just, thank you. Thank you for your eggs. Thank you for taking the time to raise those chickens right."

"You're welcome, Ms. Sylvester." He sounded a bit breathless, a bit dazed, but also proud.

As he should be.

"Anyway," I laughed lightly. "Look at me, getting all emotional. Again, I'm sorry for my outburst. Should I send a check over? With the deposit for this year? Or how do you want to handle that?"

"Uh . . ." He glanced at the ground, looking like he was frantically trying to find his wits. "I guess, uh, a check is fine."

"Glorious!" I clapped my hands together. "I'll send my momma over on her way home from the hotel."

Now he stiffened and his face blanched. "Your—your momma?"

"Yes." I tried to give him a reassuring smile. It was no secret in Green Valley that my momma was as well respected as she was feared, especially with the local business owners.

"Mrs. Donner-Sylvester?" His voice cracked again and he pulled at his open shirt collar like it was too tight.

"It's just Ms. Donner now," I reminded quietly.

"Oh, yes. That's right." Mr. Badcock pushed his fingers through his sweaty hair, frowning as he glanced down at his clothes. "What time would she be by?"

"About nine, I suspect. As long as that's not too late or disagreeable to you." Glancing at my watch, I saw it was now half-past three. This egg-encounter had taken much longer than I'd expected. I needed to get those four dozen eggs back to the bakery and in the fridge soon. Three new orders had come in—all for custard—and the way I made it, the mixture needed to rest overnight.

Plus, I didn't want to be late for the jam session.

Oh no, I certainly do not want to be late for that.

"Well, alright then." Mr. Badcock, seeming both overwhelmed and resigned by the turn of events, motioned me forward. "Let's go up to the house and get you those eggs."

I followed dutifully, happy to have avoided a disaster.

At least, for now.

PART 2

CHOKING THE CHICKEN

Cletus

W hy must people always talk?
        "What's wrong?" Drew leaned toward me as folks closest to our make-shift stage swarmed around my brother Billy, chattering good-naturedly and getting on my last nerve with their vociferous compliments.

Mind, the compliments didn't ruffle my feathers, it was the talking and ensuing racket that had my back up.

If folks could've communicated their praise via some other means—perhaps via a silent handshake and shared stare of admiration, or a hand-written note, or a mime routine, or an interpretive dance—I wouldn't have cared. Mylar balloons with tidy messages were an underutilized resource, for example.

A silence ordinance: that's what we needed. A day where folks would be forced to keep their voice boxes on the shelf or else pay a fine. I made a mental note to discuss it with the mayor, he'd always been pragmatic about new revenue streams.

"Cletus?" Drew was still looking at me, one eyebrow lifted higher than the other.

We'd just finished the last stanza of 'Orange Blossom Special.' I surmised my friend's unbalanced brow and question was in response to the frown affixed to my features.

I should have been pleased.

I was not pleased.

Drew was on guitar, I was on banjo, Grady was on fiddle, and I'd talked my brother Billy into singing–a rare achievement as Billy hardly ever agreed to lend his pipes to our Friday night improvising at the Green Valley jam session.

But Jenn was late.

Correction, she wasn't just late, she was late *as usual* on a night she'd promised to be early.

"It's time to take a break" I didn't look at my watch again, I'd already looked at it ten times. "I need to make a call."

Drew's stare turned probing. Abruptly, his expression cleared, and then he smirked a little, in that very Drew-like way of his. Which is to say, his mouth barely moved.

"Ah. I see." Drew nodded, returning his attention to his instrument and plucked out a C followed by a G. "Where's Jenn, Cletus?"

A person walked between Drew and I, side stepping and almost knocking my banjo with his knee in his eagerness to reach my brother Billy. Drew lifted the neck of his guitar to keep it safe, tracking the lumbering moron with his eyes.

Usually I'd take notice, add this person to my list of affronters as, *One who does not respect the sanctity of the banjo.* But I didn't, because I was fixating.

Billy had finished the song with flourish, which earned him happy gasp from the audience. They'd begun their applause before the strings had ceased vibrating. Several of the spectators had even come to their feet to whoop and holler their appreciation. I wasn't surprised. My brother had a stellar voice, I mean cosmically good.

He should've been a musician. Or, he could've been one of those Ph.D. engineer fellas with a mohawk on the TV, telling folks how rockets work. If he hadn't had his leg broken in high school, he also could've been a pro-football player.

But no.

Now he was the vice president in charge of everything at Payton Mills in the middle of Appalachia. *And he's probably going to be a state senator, next. And after that, a congressman.*

Good lord.

My expression of displeasure intensified.

I was officially fixating on my misaligned hopes for my brother, determined to be irritated with his course in life since I couldn't be content with my present circumstances.

She better not be working.

I swear, if that dragon-lady mother of hers was keeping her late at the bakery yet again, I would . . .

I would . . .

I won't do a thing.

Damnit.

I took a deep breath, scowling at the bright red theater chair in the front row. Next to it was a wooden chair that my youngest brother, Roscoe, would've called *mid-century modern*, or something hoity-toity like that.

"Where's Jenn?" Drew repeated the question, apparently convinced the lumbering disrupter was no longer a threat, his attention coming back to me.

"I don't know, Drew." I didn't precisely snap at my friend, it was more of a nip than a bite.

He ignored my hostility, strumming out a chord. "She working late again?"

"Apparently." I said under my breath, It wasn't my place to say anything to Diane Donner-Sylvester (soon to be ex-Sylvester) on behalf of her daughter. It was up to Jenn to stand up to her mother, set and enforce boundaries. Jenn needed to be the one to call the shots. I knew that.

But I didn't have to like it.

Maybe once we get married. . .

A knot of unease twisted in my stomach, adding a heaping helping of restlessness on top of my frustration.

Over Thanksgiving, we'd—

Well, I'd—

Damnit.

The truth was, we'd discussed marriage. I'd asked her while we'd been informal. She'd said yes. That was that. If or when she needed help planning the wedding, I surmised she would ask me.

But now it was January, and she hadn't deigned to mention the wedding, or marriage. And when she introduced me, I was a boyfriend.

Boy. Friend.

Now I ask, would anyone who'd met me ever use either of those words as a descriptor? Can you imagine? Good lord.

Then again, in her defense, marriage wasn't the only thing on her mind as of late. Jenn's busiest season was between Thanksgiving and New Year's, and on top of that, her momma was going through a tough time, seeing as how Diane Donner-Sylvester's soon-to-be ex-husband—and Jennifer's daddy—Kip Sylvester was a real pain in the ass.

I'd hardly seen her for going on six weeks. When I did see her, it was either a Winston family affair where we had no privacy, or me showing up after work at the Donner Bakery. We'd fooled around a little—a *very* little—but mostly, Jenn had been exhausted.

Thus, I did my duty as her betrothed and administered foot rubs and back rubs, completed her grocery shopping, and maintained her homestead, plus car maintenance and absolutely no expectations.

That's right. No expectations. Merely a heckvalot of hopes. Unfulfilled hopes meant I may have been frustrated by the lack of Jenn's time and attention, but I wasn't allowing myself to dwell on it. I looked to the future, to a time when Jenn's momma was less dependent, and folks hadn't yet cheated on their New Year's diets with baked goods.

In the meantime, Jenn's porch had received two new coats of lacquer, her shutters had all been cleaned, repainted, and rehung, I'd installed two ceiling fans in anticipation of the summer, and I'd replaced her garbage disposal.

But now, the time was night. New Year's was last week. I'd gathered all my hopes, stacked them in a pile, and stapled them to today's date on the calendar. Tonight was the night, our night. Finally. She was supposed to leave work on time.

Sitting as straight as my spine would allow, I craned my neck, lifting my chin and peering at the back row of the room, specifically the seats closest to the door. My attention flicked through the faces there. Mr. Roger Gangersworth was wearing unsurprising overalls; Posey Lamont was wearing a bright pink shirt heavy with unfortunate plastic beading in the shape of a rainbow, except it was a calamitous arrangement of RYOGBVI instead of ROYGBIV; and Mrs. Scotia

Simmons wore a sour expression indicative of a woman who'd lived a self-centered existence and was thusly dissatisfied with everything and everyone.

But there was no Jennifer.

I needed to get away from the crowd and their talking.

"Go on with the set if you want, I'm making that call and I can jump back in when I'm done." Standing, I placed my banjo in its case and then leaned it against the back corner, away from the threat of any future lumbering morons.

"Fine. Once Billy's fan club clears out, we'll get started again." Drew sounded unperturbed at the loss of my superior banjo skills, which meant he must've sensed the call was important. "Tell Jenn I say hi."

I grunted once, in both acknowledgement and aggravation. Great. Now I had to remember to say *hi* to Jenn from Drew on the off-chance she picked up her phone when I called. And if she didn't pick up, I'd have to remember to say *hi* the next time I happened to see her.

Why did people do that? Send salutations through other people? I am not the post office, nor am I a candygram. Why not send a text message if one is so eager to impart a greeting? Why did I have to be a "hi" messenger? Another reason why a silence ordinance was needed. If today had been a no-talking day, the chances of Drew writing me a note, pointedly asking me to "say hi" to Jenn, would have dropped *my* chances of being an unwilling messenger precipitously.

Talking, I was beginning to suspect, was the root of all evil. The ease of it in particular was an issue.

Talk it out. Talk it over. Talk it through.

Useless.

If more folks thought it out, thought it over, and thought it through instead of talking, then the world would be less cluttered with opinions and assholes.

Navigating the room easily, I made a point to give Posey Lamont a wide berth, careful to keep my beard far away from her beaded shirt. The last thing I needed was a beard-tangle with an ignorant representation of the visible light spectrum.

Once free of the labyrinth, I strolled down the hall of the Green Valley community center, aiming for the front door and the parking lot beyond. It was cold, even for January, and the lot would likely be empty. My head down to avoid eye contact with passers-by and hangers-on, I typed in my password and navigated to Jenn's number.

I was just bringing the phone to my ear when I heard a woman shout, "Cletus!"

I halted, only because the woman sounded like Jenn, and twisted toward the voice, anticipation filling my lungs before I could quell the instinct.

And there she was.

Well, more precisely, there was a version of her. She wore a blonde wig on her head, a yellow dress on her person with a brown collar and trim, and pearls around her neck.

Frustration grabbed a shovel and dug a deeper well within me.

Jenn rushed to close the distance between us while I stood stock still, her expression a mixture of guilt and hope, a bakery box clutched to her chest. My eyes moved from the bakery box to her shoes and I sighed quietly.

She jogged to me in high heels.

She must've just left work.

As an aside, jogging in high heels really should be added to the Olympics as a sport, but I digress.

When Jenn was about five feet away, her smile—looking forced—widened unnaturally and she said, "Hey, there you are."

"Here I am." I stuffed my hands in my pants pockets.

She stopped abruptly about two feet away, unable to come closer without moving the Donner Bakery box to one side, and that would have been awkward. It was a big box, both a literal barrier as well as a figurative representation of what separated us.

A second ticked by. She said nothing. Maybe because I was glaring at the box. I didn't want to be the first to speak; I was too persnickety to be trusted. But then I remembered Drew's request, and I relented.

"Drew says hi," I said.

There. That's done. Message conveyed.

"Oh." The word was airy, like she was out of breath. If I'd just jogged a hallway in high heels, I would've been out of breath, too.

Another second ticked by, then another, and that deep well of frustration began to rise, reaching my esophagus and higher, flooding my chest with suffocating disappointment.

Damn it.

I felt her shift closer and the movement drew my attention to her sweet face and gorgeous eyes.

"Please don't be mad." The hope in her features had been entirely eclipsed by guilt. "I am so sorry. I would have been on time, but Mr. Badcock sold all my eggs to somebody. And then he was treating me like I was a person of suspicion, like he couldn't trust me. Truth be told, he was downright hostile."

What's this? Hostile?

Stepping around the box, I came to her side, my hand automatically lifting to her back. "What did he say to you?"

Note to self, Richard Badcock, add to list: Maim for mistreatment of my Jenn.

"Nothing harsh." She quickly shook her head, holding my gaze and allowing me to steer us down the hall, away from the entrance. "But I did have to convince him to sell me eggs again, and then he'd only sell me eggs with an advance and a deposit. And then, once that was settled, it turns out he did have a few dozen in his house, which he eventually gave me. But trekking up the hill and back down again took longer than I'd planned."

I stopped in front of the door leading to the stage area of the old cafeteria and pulled out a key to unlock it, listening intently to her egg-tale while keeping an eye out for any passer-bys or hangers-on. I didn't need folks following us or asking me about how it was that I possessed a key.

"So, when I got back to the bakery," she went on, her words dripping with fatigue, "momma was in tears, 'cause my daddy had just called. You know, he wants half the hotel and the bakery, so he was threatening her with that again."

I grimaced. I was aware of Kip Sylvester's reprehensible behavior: he'd popped up again this last week after being mostly gone for just about a month, making all kinds of threats.

"When she stopped crying, there was still the custard to make, and only four dozen eggs. After some fretting and discussing the issue with Momma, I decided it was best to go to the store and pick up a few dozen eggs there—since Blair Tanner had already left, I was the only one to do it—and use half Badcock eggs and half store bought to get the most out of the Badcock four dozen. I'll need them later this week."

"Did you make the custard?" I ushered her forward and shut the door to the backstage area, tired on her behalf. We were enveloped in dark, which meant she couldn't see at all, and I—like all my siblings—could see tolerably well.

"Yes. I made the custard, it's sitting in the fridge. Used the last of my vanilla; I'll need to order more. I just hope no one realizes about the eggs," she finished with an agitated exhale, allowing me to lead her through the darkness.

I took the infernal bakery box, set it on a nearby crate, and then brought her near a corner, placing her back against the wall. This particular corner was scarcely illuminated by a sliver of light coming in through the stage curtains.

The cafeteria was just beyond the curtains, and the loud buzzing of town gossip and chatter from earlier in the evening was now a low murmur of scant conversation. Apparently, most folks had moved to on to the music rooms, likely because all the coleslaw had been eaten. As long as we whispered, we wouldn't be overheard or noticed.

"Is everything settled? With Mr. Badcock?" I studied her expression, noting the groves of worry on her forehead and the way she was twisting her fingers.

"I think so. Momma is going to drive out there tonight and drop off a deposit check, try to smooth things over with him."

"That was your idea?" I questioned, already knowing the answer.

It was a great idea, so of course it was Jenn's idea. Mrs. Diane Donner-Sylvester, Jenn's dragon-lady mother, was one of the most powerful business persons in the region. A visit from Diane was a big deal indeed. As well, Diane clearly needed a distraction from her divorce woes.

"Yes." She whispered, her eyes searching for mine, but seemingly unable to settle on the right spot—my face must've been wholly in shadow. "We're putting in an order for the entire year."

"That's good." I nodded, but part of her story troubled me.

Why would Mr. Richard Badcock treat Jenn with even an ounce of hostility? It didn't make any sense. Folks who knew Jenn—or of Jenn—considered her harmless, or less than harmless. A novelty, a local celebrity of no real substance or consequence, which was also how they saw me (minus the celebrity part).

I knew better: she'd revealed her genius to me last fall while proving to be the most brilliant opponent I'd ever faced, by far. She'd bested me.

Consequently, having no choice in the matter, I'd promptly fallen in love with her. *Obviously.*

But back to Dick Mal-Rooster and his antagonism.

"Did he give a reason for his poor temper?" I asked, studying her.

The question seemed to agitate her, and she huffed, stepping forward and reaching out blindly. "Cletus, can we talk about that later? Where are you?"

My mental processes shifted gears and abruptly, the flood of disappointment from the deep well of frustration rose to my throat. I swallowed, stepping away from her searching hands as I stuffed mine back in my pockets.

"Jenn—"

"I am so, so sorry, Cletus. I know I promised I'd be here on time, and I wasn't, and for that I'm sorry." She found me, her hands grabbing the front of my shirt. Her warm palms slid over my chest, up to my shoulders, her arms twisting around my neck.

I braced myself for the feel of her body, but I was unprepared for the reality of it. Soft and warm and impatient, Jenn pressed herself to me in a way that felt at once eager and content. Her lips brushed lightly over my neck. I tensed. Her hot tongue coming out to lick a path to my ear had me jumping, every inch of me aware of every inch of her.

"I've missed you," she whispered, a note of vulnerability in the words, her breath scorching as it spilled over my skin, a counterpoint to the disappointment still burning my chest. "Have you missed me?"

I was at once inebriated by her actions and incredulous of them.

"You know I have," I answered gruffly, keeping my hands in my pockets for both our benefits.

Likely, she didn't want our first time together in over six weeks—and our second time together *ever*—to be me ripping off her underwear and taking her against the backstage wall of the Green Valley community center. Rationally, I knew this to be true.

Irrationally however, I wanted to rip off her underwear and take her against the backstage wall of the Green Valley community center. I wanted to tear open the buttons of her dress and feast on her body, the smooth silk of her skin, while I filled her and claimed her and satiated myself with what would surely be an unrefined display of possessiveness.

Jennifer pressed herself more fully against me, one arm still hooked around my neck, a hand sliding dangerously lower, from my shoulder to my chest and stomach. I caught her fingers before she could slip them between us and cup me over my pants. Or inside my pants.

"Not a good idea." My body shook, a surge of covetous mindlessness threatening to overtake my good intentions.

"It's been *weeks*," she complained between biting kisses on my neck, bringing my hand to her breast, pressing it there. "Don't you want me?"

I choked on my incredulity. If she didn't know how much I wanted her, then I'd been doing something very wrong.

"You're asking me foolish questions," I ground out, catching both her hands and holding them hostage between us to force her to back away a step. "And you're not foolish."

I needed a minute.

"Then what's the problem?" She pressed forward. Jenn didn't fight my hold, but she did feel restless beneath my fingers. "Why aren't you kissing me back? Why do you keep stuffing your hands in your pockets? Why won't you touch me?"

Lost of words, I settled on whispering the truth, "I'd like nothing more than rip off your underwear and—"

"No need, I'm not wearing underwear." Jenn bent her head and placed a kiss on my knuckles.

Meanwhile, I needed. . . another minute.

What?

"What?" Equal measures of astonishment and lust drove away any of my remaining good intentions, leaving me only with lust.

"I took them off in the car." Her tongue licked the juncture between my index and middle fingers. "I know I've been working a lot and, God Cletus, I just want you so—oh!"

Unceremoniously, I backed her against the wall, tossing away her hands and clamoring for the hem of her skirt. Sliding my fingers up her legs as I lifted her dress, I groaned when I discovered no material at her hip or bottom. Since I already had a handful of her, I squeezed, resisting the urge to fall to my knees and take a bite of her perfect backside.

I'd wanted us to have privacy. I'd wanted to unwrap her. I'd wanted to take my time. I'd wanted conversation and kisses—many kisses—and a lot more light sources. Sunlight, lamps, spotlights, I wanted to see every part of her.

I pressed my forehead against the cold wall, unable to resist touching her, slipping my middle finger into that hot, silky place.

Her breath hitched, her arms once again wrapping around my neck as her hips rolled forward into my hand. "Please, please."

Damn, but I missed her. Her skin was heaven, her fragrance paradise, and I couldn't get enough. I was breathing heavy, wanting her all around me, in my lungs. I couldn't think. I just wanted.

I took her mouth with mine, no preamble or gentle invasion, but a full-fledged frenzy. She moaned, a sound I took as encouragement.

Jenn's nails scratched down my shirt, her fingers shaking as they found my belt, tugging and pulling frantically while I nipped and licked and kissed her jaw and neck, stopping at her breast to place a wet, biting kiss at the center, all the while working her with my fingers.

Her hands faltered as I devoured her collarbone and neck, preparing to lower to my knees, lift her skirt completely, take a bite out of that ass, and then spread her wide for my tongue and mouth and pleasure.

But then, her phone rang; Reba McEntire's, 'I'm a Survivor;' that was her mother's ring tone. The woman had recently programmed it into Jenn's phone.

She squeaked, fumbling for the device. Her face briefly illuminated just before quickly rejecting the call.

"Don't stop." She reached for my belt again, this time deftly undoing it, the button of my pants, and my zipper while I stoked her.

Her phone buzzed. Then it chimed. Then it buzzed and chimed two more times. Then it rang, again Reba.

Cursing, Jenn pulled the phone from her pocket and once again her face illuminated, murderous rage in her eyes. Her finger moved to the power-off button. She blinked, hesitating. Her eyes widened, her body stiffened, and she gasped.

"Cletus!"

Something about her tone, like she was horrified, and maybe a little afraid, cut though the heavy haze of lust inertia, and my hands stilled. Shaking myself, it took me a few moments to realize she was showing me the phone screen, and another few to bring the content of the text messages into focus.

Momma: *Jennifer Anne Sylvester, pick up your phone. If you're with that man of yours, I need his help too. Please.*

Momma: *ALL THE CHICKENS AND ROOSTERS ARE DEAD! PICK UP YUR DAMN PHONE!*

Momma: *I'm calling you in a second, pick up the phone. Mr. Badcock's chickens are dead. All of them. I got here and he's running around, deranged, yelling about his dead chickens! I called the police and they're on their way. Please, please, please pick up the phone!*

At some point, I must've taken the phone from Jenn and stepped away, because I glanced up upon reading the messages for the third time, finding the phone in my hand and Jenn fixing her skirt.

"This is nuts." Her big eyes searched mine imploringly. "Who could have done this?"

I shook my head, having not yet managed to fully shift brain gears. My gaze dropped to the wet patch on the front of her dress, where I'd had my mouth seconds prior, and my erection throbbed.

So we're . . . not having sex?

"Why? Why would they do it?" She took her phone back, her tone bewildered, distracted, and distraught.

She was distraught because of the dead chickens, like any normal person would be.

I was distraught also, but my distress had nothing to do with farm animals.

"We have to go." Jenn grabbed my hand and began walking blindly toward the direction of the hall door. "This is crazy. Poor Mr. Badcock. And those poor chickens." A sound of mournful distress escaped her throat. "This is terrible."

It was terrible.

And I was going to hell.

Because all I could think was, *Talk about a cock block.*

-end-

Dear Reader,

These two parts are the very raw, unedited beginnings of Jenn and Cletus's first book ('Engagement and Espionage') in their cozy mystery series (Handcrafted Mysteries) coming in 2019. These chapters were written specifically for this anthology and are in no way final. But I hope you enjoyed the peek into my raw work, before I get a chance to read and re-read, draft and re-draft, edit and re-edit. HUGE thank you to Author Camilla Monk (of the awesome Spotless series, http://camillamonk.com/) for giving this story a quick edit. You are a magical unicorn of stellar proportions.

Wishing you all the best, Penny Reid

The Winston saga continues with Dr. Strange Beard, releasing July 9, 2018.
Pre-order here: http://pennyreid.ninja/books/dr-strange-beard/

ABOUT THE AUTHOR

Penny Reid lives in Seattle, Washington with her husband, three kids, and an inordinate amount of yarn. She used to spend her days writing federal grant proposals as a biomedical researcher, but now she just writes books.

Come find Penny-
Mailing list signup: http://pennyreid.ninja/newsletter/ (get exclusive stories, sneak peeks, and pictures of cats knitting hats)
Facebook: http://www.facebook.com/PennyReidWriter
Instagram: https://www.instagram.com/reidromance/
Goodreads: http://www.goodreads.com/ReidRomance
Email: pennreid@gmail.com ...hey, you! Email me ;-)
Blog: http://pennyreid.ninja
Twitter: https://twitter.com/ReidRomance
Ravelry: http://www.ravelry.com/people/ReidRomance (if you crochet or knit...!)

ALSO BY PENNY REID

Knitting in the City Series
(Contemporary Romantic Comedy)
Neanderthal Seeks Human: A Smart Romance (#1)
Neanderthal Marries Human: A Smarter Romance (#1.5)
Friends without Benefits: An Unrequited Romance (#2)
Love Hacked: A Reluctant Romance (#3)
Beauty and the Mustache: A Philosophical Romance (#4)
Ninja at First Sight (#4.75)
Happily Ever Ninja: A Married Romance (#5)
Dating-ish: A Humanoid Romance (#6)
Marriage of Inconvenience: (#7)

Winston Brothers Series
(Contemporary Romantic Comedy, spinoff of *Beauty and the Mustache*)
Truth or Beard (#1)
Grin and Beard It (#2)
Beard Science (#3)
Beard in Mind (#4)
Dr. Strange Beard (#5, coming 2018)
Beard with Me (#5.5)
Beard Necessities (#6)

Hypothesis Series
(New Adult Romantic Comedy)
Elements of Chemistry: ATTRACTION, HEAT, and CAPTURE (#1)
Laws of Physics: MOTION, SPACE, and TIME (#2)
Fundamentals of Biology: STRUCTURE, EVOLUTION, and GROWTH (#3)

COCKY CAPO

CD REISS

Antonio, Theresa, Jonathan, and Monica meet in Napoli, and it's utterly insane.

COCKY CAPO

NAPOLI - ITALIA

THERESA

From the minute I met Antonio, I thought I knew him. I didn't always know how he'd react, or what exactly he'd do, but I always knew why. To me, that was enough. Reactions are a mixed bag of circumstances and upbringing. The measure of a man was in his motivations. He was motivated by love and responsibility.

I was wrong about his measure. There was more to it than that, and I didn't realize it until I saw him in Italy.

He breathed more deeply. Held me more tightly. Laughed more naturally. On the veranda, with the olive groves behind him and the morning breeze tousling his hair, he fit into the landscape like a puzzle piece. He belonged there.

"What's bothering you, Contessa?"

"Nothing." I shrugged. I didn't want to break the spell of his perfection.

He put his cappuccino cup down empty. "Don't make me fuck it out of you."

The prospect was tempting, but I was already sore from the morning's activities.

"I don't think I've ever seen you so happy."

One beautiful black eyebrow arched slightly higher.

"I'm relieved to be home," he said. "Give me a few days to smell the garbage."

The orchard had been abandoned for years. Antonio had to open the rusted chain on the front gate with bolt cutters. I drove the Aston Martin down the cracked drive and he followed on foot, a pillar of perfection against the overgrown landscape in the rearview mirrors.

When I stopped the car he jogged to catch up, opening the door for me and offering his hand to help me out. He kissed my hand before clasping it tightly.

"*Benvenuto Casa Spinelli.*" He waved his arm at the boarded up villa. "The home of my ruined heart."

"Stop. Your heart is fine and it's beautiful here."

"My heart is fine because of you, and you make everything beautiful." He put his arm around me. Ivy had overtaken the cracked walls of the stone manor all the way to the second floor, and the front steps were broken. "I go first. It might not be safe."

"Hush. I'm going with you every step."

"*Come vuoi tu,*" he said, scooping me up in his arms with such speed I yelped in surprise. I put my arms around his neck and he carried me up the broken stairs. The weather was perfect Mediterranean spring, with soft clouds drawn over the clear blue sky, and the sweet smell of blossoming olives in the air. My hand had a mind of its own, stroking the black scruff on his cheek, up to his forehead, tracing the straight scar to his ear.

He slid me back onto my feet at the front door. It was thick wood, carved with a border of olive branches. A metal hinge had been screwed on over the brass doorknob. Antonio took the bolt cutters from his back waistband and cut the padlock as if it was a piece of cardboard. It fell to the ground with a solid *thunk*.

"Are you ready?" he asked with his hand on the brass knob.

"I'm ready."

He turned and pushed, but the door didn't budge. I laughed. He stepped back and assessed the door before laughing with me.

"Thwarted," I said. "Can you pick the lock?"

"I don't have tools." He pointed to a chair with a busted wicker seat. "Stand over there. I'll knock it down."

"Hang on," I said. "In this entire house, there's no side door?"

He smirked and picked up the bolt cutters. "Always the sensible one."

I took the hand he offered and we walked around the veranda to the side. That door was boarded completely.

"I have a crowbar in the car," he said. "But we check the back first, no?"

"See? You can be sensible too."

He put his arm around me and we walked to the back. As we turned the corner, the orchard opened before us. The trees were planted in orderly rows starting about fifty feet from the house, but the ground beneath them was overgrown with bushes and grass. The back garden was rutted, broken, with tables and chairs cracked and overturned. All except one.

It was a white plastic picnic chair set up next to a tree stump. I broke away from Antonio and walked down wooden steps. The stump had darkened grease spots on the top surface.

"Someone's been eating here," I said. I could feel Antonio's senses tingling as he scanned the area for more signs of life.

"You should go back to the car." His voice had dropped to a whisper, and he pointed to a trodden path of grass that began near the house and extended to the orchard.

"These stains could be years old," I said softly. My skin tingled with anticipation. I didn't want to go to the car. "And it's someone eating. Not someone shooting."

Everything jumped out at me now. The plywood plank next to the back door, not nailed against the frame. The baskets piled by it didn't have any growth. The water spigot dripped into a half-empty bucket. Three tomato plants hidden in the grass were caged.

"I'll take you back to the car." He reached for my arm, but I dodged him.

"Stay back!" I said as I hopped up the back steps.

"Theresa!" he barked, getting behind a tree.

I turned the knob, threw the door open and ducked behind the wall.

Nothing. No gunshots. No voices. Just the birds and the rustling of leaves in the breeze. Antonio hopped over the fence around the back veranda and joined me.

"You're impossible," he whispered.

"I'm only hiding here to appease you." When I looked back at him, I saw real worry for the first time since we touched the ground. "I ran your empire while you were in prison, Antonio. It's fine. I can feel it."

He stared at me—into me—for a moment, as if reminding himself why he married me in the first place.

"I go first," he said.

"*Come vuoi tu.*"

As he came around me to get close to the door, he said, "Your accent, Contessa."

Then he was gone, around the corner and into the house. Something made a scuffing noise and water splashed. Antonio cursed.

"Antonio?"

"It's nothing."

I went inside. With the windows boarded and the sun rising over the front of the house, the kitchen was poorly lit. Antonio stood by a table covered in stones, surrounded by tall buckets full of water.

My eyes adjusted and I saw the table wasn't covered in stones, but olives on a tray. The buckets were full of liquid.

"Olives brining," I said.

"*Si.*" A female voice came from somewhere, paired with the loud *clack* of a rifle being cocked. Antonio held his hand toward me to signal that I should stay still, as if I hadn't frozen in place already.

"*Who's there?*" Antonio asked in Italian. "*We won't hurt you.*"

"No, you won't." The English was halting and thick with an Italian accent. The voice was young, clear, confident.

Another voice uttered a few sentences from the cabinet below the sink, which was ajar. Female and tiny, it belonged to a child. I didn't understand a word.

But Antonio laughed.

"*Basta, Simona.*" A boy came through the doorway with his rifle pointed at us. He was about twelve years old, with shoulder-length dirty brown hair down and one blue eye open so he could aim.

"*Where did you get this?*" Antonio asked, drawing his finger from the side of his mouth and along his cheek. I put together their conversation based on the little Italian I knew and their gestures.

"Where did you get yours?" The kid jerked the gun to indicate Antonio's forehead.

"Bullet."

"I won't miss."

Antonio shrugged.

"Shoot them!" Simona cried from under the sink. I couldn't tell how old she was or what she looked like, but I could tell she was scared.

Slowly, I crouched to the ground.

"What you doing?" the kid demanded in English. I kept crouching, putting my hand on the floor, then my hip.

"Contessa. Stop," Antonio hissed. I ignored him, lying on the dirty floor, my legs on either side of a brining bucket, and spread my arms out.

"Senora! I will shoot you!"

The minute he moved the rifle to aim it at me, Antonio would take it. If the kid kept it on Antonio, we were okay. If he moved it, we were also okay.

"I'm dead." I closed my arms and lolled my tongue out.

Silence.

I opened one eye. At that level, I could see Simona in the crack of light through the ajar cabinet door. She was about six. She wore a pink T-shirt with a crown on it. Her hair was black and her eyes were as blue as the boy's.

She giggled. *"You're not dead."*

"Hush. I'm dead."

I closed my eye and stuck my tongue out again.

The cabinet door squeaked. Rustling. The creak of floorboards.

"Simona!" The boy scolded.

A light pressure on my forehead, then the tug of fingers through my hair. The soft notes of a little girl humming a sweet song.

Then, the *clack* and *thump* of a scuffle above us.

I didn't need to look to know Antonio had the gun.

I didn't move. Simona kept stroking my hair and humming as if she and I, and Antonio and the boy, were locked in two separate worlds.

The boy's name was Nevio. His eyes constantly darted around as if looking for a hidden army. He sat in the white plastic chair with his legs spread so he could spring forward if necessary. A greasy lock of hair fell in front of one eye, and he jerked his head to move it. He was a cocky little bastard with a heart full of well-earned rage.

Antonio didn't bother keeping the gun on him. He'd unloaded it and slung it over his shoulder.

They barked at each other in Italian so quickly I couldn't keep up. I sat on the broken back steps and watched Simona pluck the stems from a bucket of olives. I reached a hand in the bucket and she froze. I took an olive, pinched the stem off and put it on the porch rail, next to hers.

554

She relaxed and pointed to it. "Quindici." She started at the first. "Uno. Due. Tre. Quattro..." and on to fifteen. Quindici. I clapped.

"*Bene! Allora.*" I put another olive at the end. "*Sedici.*"

"*Se-DI-ci.*" She corrected my pronunciation, of course, and produced another olive. "*Diciassette.*" Seventeen. I wasn't even going to try it.

Behind me, the conversation between Antonio and Nevio had gotten gentler. Less barking. I turned to see if they were biting.

Nevio was telling a story. Antonio leaned on a barrel with his arms crossed, nodding and adding the occasional, "*Si, si.*"

I wondered why he wasn't worried someone else was going to show up with more than a rifle.

"Simona," I said. "*Where's your mother?*"

The girl didn't look at me. Didn't answer with a word or a gesture. She just hummed, plucking stems off olives, making a new row on the edge of the railing without counting.

She was humming the same tune she did when she'd stroked my hair.

"Put me the fuck down!" I beat Antonio's back, elbowed the back of his head and aimed at his face when I kicked, but he held me over his shoulder and walked me the length of the estate's driveway like the caveman he was.

"*Basta*, woman!"

I looked up, leveraging my hands on his back, and looked at the house. One of the upstairs windows didn't have plywood over it. The shower curtain that covered it moved. I waved. The kids were watching.

"This is a great example you're setting."

He opened the passenger side of the car. "Obedience is also an example," he said, dropping me to my feet.

"We can't leave." I pushed his chest. "They're all alone." His felony black eyes were unreadable, but the tightness of his mouth told a story of inner conflict.

"They've been alone for a year. Now get in the car."

"Why?" I asked.

"I don't want to scare them. Now please. Get in the fucking car."

With a last glance to the upper floor, I sat in the car and he shut the door. In the seconds it would take him to walk around to his side, I could get out. I could run back to them and...

And what?

Cook them dinner?

Hug that little girl and listen to her hum?

He was in the car before I could come up with a productive plan, and we were off.

"What the hell is going on?" I growled. He didn't reply. He just drove slowly past the gate and got out, leaning in before he walked away.

"Do not get out of this car, Contessa, or I swear to you..."

"What?" I snapped.

He walked away without telling me.

555

In the passenger rearview, I watched him close the gate and wrap the chain again. He put the padlock on an uncut link, tossing the broken segment into the brush.

He got back in the car and rested his hand on the gearshift. He'd spoken to Nevio for a long time while I'd sat by the girl I assumed was his sister. They were obviously squatting and obviously alone. She'd broken my heart in her little pink shirt with the crown. She'd started to trust me, and taken me around the house where I saw their fire pit with the charred bones of a small animal piled to the side. Cucumbers growing along the side of a fence. A naked Barbie doll she named *Principessa*.

I didn't need Antonio to tell me any of what I already knew, but there was more to these two squatters than met the eye.

I also knew my husband. He'd earned my trust.

"What's going on?" I put my hand on top of his.

"We drive," he said, putting the car into gear. "Then we talk."

I could live with that. I had no choice.

I thought he was going to take me back to the city, but we only went deeper into the guts of the countryside. He was driving for the sake of driving, thinking and processing in the presence of his wife. On a winding two lane road bordered by trees, he swung the car onto the shoulder and slammed to a stop. He put the car into park and held up a finger.

"I have something to say."

"Go on."

"That's my grandfather's house and I'm responsible for what's in it."

That was heartening.

"I'm responsible for what happens inside it, past, present, and future."

Also heartening.

"We call the welfare agency when we get back."

Why wasn't that heartening?

"Are you nervous?" my sister-in-law asked. She bounced her one-year-old daughter on her knee. Gabrielle had been born with the Drazen trademark ginger hair, but it was changing to her mother's rich brown.

"About?" I could have been nervous about a hundred things. The waiter helped me stall by taking our plates. My husband and my brother Jonathan had taken to the patio to smoke. We could see them through the French doors overlooking the harbor, and Monica watched Jonathan like a hawk. He had a transplanted heart, and neither she nor his doctors wanted him near cigarette smoke. Not such an easy proposition in southern Europe.

"He's upwind," I said. "Here." I held my arms out for Gabrielle. "In case you want to dive through the window."

She passed the baby over. "He's so cocky about that heart." She slid the board book Gabrielle was looking at over to me, but the baby twisted in my arms and rested her head on my shoulder. "He thinks he's freaking invincible."

The baby breathed wetly against my neck, and I laid my hand on her back.

Her scent and the way she felt in my arms was so sweet I couldn't imagine ever standing up.

"Maybe you're the one who's nervous," I said.

"About Jonathan? I'm always nervous. But anyway..." She swirled her wine and took a sip. "I was asking about meeting his family."

Antonio's estranged mother and sister lived in the city, and once his father died, he negotiated a way back into Italy and planned a meeting with them. We arranged for the honeymoon we never had, crossing my brother's family for a couple of days while Monica was on tour.

"I'm not nervous, no. I was yesterday but this afternoon..." I hesitated, rocking the sleeping baby. "We went to his father's abandoned orchard."

"Oh? Olives?"

"Yes."

And children.

"Well, you guys are experts at that now."

Antonio and I owned an olive orchard in Temecula, and she thought I was nervous about that. I wasn't. Maybe it was that misunderstanding. Maybe it was the baby sleeping on my shoulder, or the comforting sight of my sister-in-law in a strange place. Maybe it was all the violence I'd seen and done contrasting with the gentleness of the surroundings. Maybe I'd been holding back tears for hours and they were ripe. But my face scrunched and my sinuses tingled, forcing out a sob.

"Jesus, Theresa." She pulled my napkin from my lap and handed it to me. "What happened?"

I could barely speak through the tears, but I finally got it out.

"There were children."

JONATHAN

"How do you like it?" Antonio asked, releasing a plume of smoke toward the sea. Antonio stood by the railing, upwind, mindful of my transplanted heart.

"It's like Los Angeles twenty years ago," I said. "Same weather. Smells like shit."

"But the people are better."

"Truth." I tipped my wine to him and sipped. One glass was all I was supposed to drink, and I savored every drop.

I could get used to southern Italy, except the cigarettes. Every time we walked down the street, someone was smoking. And every time, like goddamn clockwork, Monica pulled me away like a mother hen.

I counted the times. Twelve times yesterday got her twelve swats with my belt last night. My guess? She did it because she liked the punishment.

I glanced through the restaurant's patio doors. She was watching me. Five times I checked, five times she was watching me and not the baby. That would be five strokes with my hand plus seven with the belt for pulling me away from smoke during the day. She handed the baby to my sister, but she'd still get swatted if she didn't keep her concern to herself.

I loved my wife's concern more than I loved punishing her for it.

A waitress brought espresso and Sambuca with curls of lemon peel on the rim.

With the last drag, Antonio stamped the cigarette out and sat across from me. He spoke in Italian, but a little more slowly than normal. I was capable of speaking a few languages, but my fluency wasn't always as good as a native.

"Your daughter is beautiful," he said, rubbing the lemon on the edge of his cup and dropping it in the saucer. "She's losing the red hair."

"If we're lucky she'll look like her mother." He dropped a bit of Sambuca in his cup.

"Salud to that." He tilted the cup toward me.

"Maybe you'll have a bunch of redheads."

He shook his head. "She didn't tell you?"

"I don't know what I don't know, brother."

"No kids." He tipped his espresso down, finishing in one gulp.

I was surprised. Theresa had always wanted children. I couldn't believe she'd marry a man who didn't.

"I'm not supposed to ask why."

"Why not?"

"It's rude."

"Fucking Americans."

"Well, we're in Italy, so I'm asking. Why won't you let her have kids?"

I tried not to sound angry, but maybe I did.

"Me?" He tented his fingers over his chest. "It's not *me*."

"Then?" I prepared my espresso. "What did you do?"

"Now I know why Americans don't ask." He crossed his legs and leaned deep in his chair. "You're pushy."

"That's why we rule the world."

A shot of a laugh escaped his lungs.

"*Mio Dio.* Asshole. I should blow smoke at your face just to watch your wife take you out of here by your ear." He fingered his Zippo as he looked over the railing to the sea, but didn't light a cigarette. "It was the accident."

The accident.

My sister had fallen off a second story veranda with an infamous mob boss. Antonio had taken the blame for the boss's death, but when mafia soldiers started secretly paying tribute to her in the hospital, we all suspected Theresa had done the deed.

Antonio put Sambuca in his espresso cup and drained it.

"She can't have children," he said. "A shard of hip bone punctured her..." he paused, pointing to his own stomach. "You know."

"Uterus?"

"Fucking Americans. Yes. They took it out." He poured more Sambuca. Between the sugar and the alcohol content, he was going to pickle his brain. I hailed the waitress.

"Can you get this guy an aperitif?"

"*Limoncello,*" he cut in. "And Pellegrino for the American."

When the waitress was gone I leaned forward, putting my elbows on my knees.

"You could—"

"*Basta*. I don't want to adopt. No surrogates. It's children as God intended or nothing. I give my life to my Theresa. That's the end of it. Let's talk about *calcio* or something normal."

I leaned back and glanced through the window into the restaurant. Monica wasn't watching me. She and Theresa were talking closely, with real seriousness to their posture. Theresa wiped her eyes. Turning back to Antonio, I was glad he didn't see his wife's tears, and changed the subject so he wouldn't react.

"You inherited a house," I said.

"Went today. Roof leaks. Foundation's cracked."

"I can take a look at it. I build things for a living, in case you didn't know."

"I don't know. I'd sell it but…"

He waved his hand to dismiss the conversation.

"But it's home?"

He shook his head and smiled, looking back at me as if I'd said something particularly incisive. "Fucking Americans."

***

Gabby was sleeping across the hotel hall with her nanny.

I was naked from the waist up.

My wife was naked with a belt in her teeth, bent over the footboard with her wrists tied to the rails and her ankles tied to the bed's legs. She had a pillow under her abdomen so the bar didn't dig into her. The only discomfort she should feel should come from me.

The red patches on her ass were hot to the touch. She'd taken the swats from my hand like a champ, and when I slid my fingers into her seam she was soaking wet.

"Now," I said. "You pulled me away from cigarette smoke seven times and reminded me to take my meds an hour before I was supposed to. That's eight."

She looked around and grunted an objection. The belt in her teeth was wet with spit. I took it out.

"That's totally not fair! There was a time change from Prague."

"Nine, then."

She rolled her eyes at me. I never punished her for that because it didn't bother me. But she was getting used to pain, and nine would barely make a dent in her defenses.

"You know what?" I said, tapping her red bottom gently with the loop of the belt. "Let's make it an even dozen. Count."

I brought the belt down on the soft, raw skin of her ass. When she buckled, my balls throbbed.

"One," she said.

Damn, she was perfect. She fit right into my life. I hit her in the back of the thighs.

"Two." She was trying to sound bored, but a hot pink mark rose where the belt had been.

"Oh, Goddess, you're such a brat." Across the ass, where her cunt was blossoming, I tried to hurt her free of boredom.

"Three." Clenched teeth. Another across the same spot. "Four," she grunted. I stroked her ass, feeling the rising swells of skin, then slid two fingers deep inside her.

"Italy agrees with you."

"Yes, Sir."

"Eight more."

She counted three strokes as they came in fast succession, yelping "seven."

"Why was my sister crying?"

She paused for too long, so I gave her one on the back of her thighs.

"Eight. There were two kids squatting in Antonio's dad's place. She was sad."

Coupled with the conversation I'd had with Antonio, I could imagine she was. I could get the rest of the story later.

Swat.

"Nine." Her tone was almost relieved, as if she'd arrived at a destination.

Swat.

"Ten."

"These next two are coming hard, Goddess."

"Okay."

I never knew if she forgot out of brattiness or if she was so deep in subspace she had limited syllables.

"Okay, what?" I touched her sore, friction-heated skin and she jumped.

"Okay, Sir."

Pulling her cheek away, I inspected the tight pucker of her ass.

"Three more. A baker's dozen."

I brought the belt down and she counted to thirteen.

Leaning close to her, I kissed a tear from her cheek.

"You are absolutely perfect."

She smiled and mouthed, "so are you."

"Do you want to use your safeword?"

"No, thank you."

"I'm going to take your ass. Are you ready?"

"Yes."

I put the belt by her lips. "Open."

She opened her mouth and clamped onto the leather.

Behind her, I ran my fingers over her cunt, gathering moisture to spread over her ass, tucking a finger inside to stretch her.

I wet my cock on her seam, and she groaned when I pushed in for a single stroke. I pinched her clit between thumb and crooked finger.

"You ready?"

She nodded.

Slowly, gently, I pressed my cock to her anus, watching it give for me. Changing from a peck on the cheek to a gaping, open mouth. I knew her. I knew how slow to go. I knew how to minimize the pain and maximize the pleasure. How she liked her clit touched, how powerful her orgasms were when I was in her ass, and how it pulsed around me when she came.

I left everything inside her.

"Jesus Christ," I said into her back. "This never gets old."

She made a *mm* sound, and I took the belt from her teeth. "Hang on."

I untied her. She was like jelly in my arms. Droopy in subspace. I laid her on her stomach and kissed her everywhere before rooting around in my bag for lotion.

"How are you doing?" I asked, soothing her welted skin.

"Thank you." She spoke in barely a whisper.

We didn't say more for awhile. After I'd taken care of her body, I tucked her under the covers and joined her there, cradling her head on my shoulder.

"Thank you for being there for my sister," I said. When she looked at me quizzically, I continued. "You tore your eyes away from me long enough to take care of her."

"She's upset."

"Antonio told me about the kids on his father's farm," I said. "Did you know she couldn't have any?"

"Yeah."

"How come I didn't know?"

"You've had other things on your mind." She stroked the scar in the center of my chest.

"What did she say they were going to do?"

"They called the Italian equivalent of child protective services, but...welcome to Italy. No answer. It's a holiday weekend in August and no one's around."

Antonio had told me the same. I was just testing to see if my sister had the same story.

"I think they're staying until after the weekend to sort it out."

Her phone buzzed three times against the night table, then two times, then three.

"Shit," I said, watching Monica sit up. "What did we bring a nanny for?"

"So you could fuck me in peace," she replied, standing in all her naked glory. "Not so she could do our job."

"You should stay." I threw the covers off me. "I'll go."

Monica was already getting on her pants.

"No. I'll go." She wiggled into her shirt. "You went last time."

She crawled onto the bed and kissed me. I put my palms on her cheeks to keep her close.

"See you in the morning, Goddess."

"See you then, my king."

We kissed again, then she left to take care of Gabby.

———

THERESA

A lock of hair fell over his forehead, swaying with the rhythm. I had one leg over his shoulder, one arm around his neck, his knees using the plush of the mattress as leverage as he drove into me so hard his body rubbed my clit.

"Deeper," I cried, clutching the hair on his chest. "Fuck me so deep."

"Take it. Take it all."

He found another millimeter and I rubbed against him, exploding, arching away as he pulled me into him. He took my hair in his fist and pulled my face into his so I could see him come inside me, all gritted teeth and power, not just coming but conquering.

Then our joints and bones melted into each other, and he settled behind me with his chest to my back, fitting together in a matched pattern.

"I love you, Capo," I said when I finally had the breath to speak. "*Ti amo, ti amo.*"

"Your accent, Contessa..."

I laughed and tried to wiggle away, but he held me.

"I'm sorry," he whispered. "Today. I'm sorry I pulled you away from the house."

"It's all right. I understand." I didn't need to ask him any questions, I just needed to give him space to speak. He rolled onto his back and I tucked my head in the crook of his arm.

"They were the caretaker's children," he said.

"Ah."

"Fuck." He rubbed his eyes and drew his hand down his face. "Their parents hid them in the basement." Hard swallow. "They only heard the gunshots. Nevio almost suffocated Simona trying to keep her quiet. Made her unconscious. He thought he killed her."

"How old were they?"

"She was five. He was eleven." He turned his head to look me in the eye. "A year ago."

It was my turn to create the long pause. I didn't know what to be sad about. The fact that they'd been on their own for a year, or the fact that their parents were assassinated when Antonio and I were married.

My husband saved me a response. "They were in the front yard. The parents. I don't even know their names. The children dragged them into the orchard and buried them. It took a week, he said. They were so little."

"And they were too scared to leave."

"*Si.* I need a cigarette."

He tried to get up but I pushed him down.

"Capo," I said. "No. Don't run away. Talk to me."

He dropped back down, surrendering for once.

"It was the Carlonis. Donna Maria's son, Luca. What they did? Payment for marrying you. Revenge for rejecting their daughter. I will not let that go."

I turned and straddled him, pushing his shoulders to the mattress. Physically, I couldn't hold him down. He was stronger and more vicious than I'd ever be, but the fact that he hadn't already left me in the hotel so he could run off and shoot Luca Carloni told me he wasn't past sense.

"No vengeance."

"It's not revenge. It's justice."

"It's a cycle."

"This will hang over us for the rest of our lives," I said. "Is that what you want?"

"If you do what I know you're thinking, we're going to spend the rest of our lives looking over our shoulders. No, Antonio. No. I won't. Not until they come for us, and they won't."

"Those kids—"

"Are alive. And if you kill Luca Carloni? You're putting them right in the middle of a pattern that almost ruined your life. Is that what you want? To fuck them up too?"

He cupped my face in his hands. "I can't let it go."

"Don't let it go, but don't kill. Please." I took his wrist and kissed his palm, speaking into it like a prayer. "No more."

I laid on top of him, feeling his heart beat against mine. I thought I'd convinced him. But I'd have to win this battle over and over. Revenge was a habit only death could break.

"I have to go talk to some people," he said.

"Antonio. No."

He pushed me off him and stood by the bed.

"If I don't, and we get through to the agency...they're corrupt. It's all corrupt. The kids will be targets. That what you want?"

"Of course not."

"Then trust me." He plucked his clothes out of his bag. Clean clothes, as if he had to dress for the following day.

"Oh, like hell."

"After everything, you can't believe me?"

I kneeled straight on the bed, legs apart not to offer myself, but to stand my ground.

"I believe you now, but once you get around those people—"

"I'm not so weak." Hotel key. Wallet. Switchblade. He couldn't get a gun on the plane, thank God.

"You'd better be back here in time to see Nella and your mother, and without blood on your hands." I sounded hysterical. I'd run a criminal enterprise for a year and a half, and I was acting like a powerless mafia wife. That wouldn't do. I wouldn't kneel, and I wouldn't agree with his decisions out of deference.

"They know I'm here, and they are not evolved. They still live in vengeance. If they know the children are there they may come for them."

"They may not."

He stood over me fully dressed and put his thumb on my chin.

"There will be no blood on my hands," he said, stepping back to button his jacket with hands already stained red with violence.

I stood between him and the door with my arms crossed under my breasts.

"That means you don't dirty someone else either. Not for money or favors. Do you hear?" That was my capo voice. That was the voice I used with his foot soldiers. It didn't threaten consequences. It promised them. "I can't stop you from leaving, and I won't."

He got close to me. He didn't try to go around me to the door, but gazed down at me and waited for me to move.

"I trust you," I said.

"Besides your love, your trust is the most valuable thing I have."

"Then don't break it, or you'll break both."

He nodded in understanding, then jerked his chin over my shoulder, indicating the door.

I opened it, standing behind it so I wouldn't expose my naked body to the hallway.

"Be safe, Antonio."

"I am safe. You stay here. Don't leave this room."

He leaned on the jamb and lightly pressed his lips to mine. He didn't linger. He didn't make more of the kiss than he had to.

This wasn't a final goodbye.

I closed the door and got dressed.

MONICA

Theresa drove our rental. Even in the middle of the night, she knew where she was going. She spoke enough Italian to read road signs and—bottom line—I wasn't confident staying to the left.

Also, she was just too badass to be driven around.

My hands were shaking too hard to drive anyway. Jonathan would kill me if he found out I'd lied to him, and by "kill me" I meant "be very, justifiably too angry to punish me the way I liked."

"We'll be back before he even notices you were gone," she said, turning onto a side road. The groceries in the back seat shifted. Gabby's nanny, Martha had picked them up after we'd gotten out of dinner and kept them in the room across the hall.

"He sleeps like, nil," I said. "So we have to be quick."

"We will." The dashboard lights made the contours of her face bluish green, blackening the red of her hair. She looked so much like Jonathan I couldn't help but love her.

"Was Antonio sleeping when you left?"

She let out a sardonic laugh. "Fucking men."

"Wait, was he awake? Does he know?"

"No. He went off to see some friends."

She glanced at me sharply, then back to the dark road.

"Friends? Okay."

She didn't say more, so I didn't ask. Theresa's life was left to the imagination. In the years I'd known her, she'd focused on running the Temecula olive orchard, while I focused on Jonathan's transplant and my career. But the family whispered, about Antonio's business and Theresa's acuity in running them. I never got to the bottom of what the business was, exactly.

We came to a gate, and she stopped.

"Shit," she muttered.

The gate was open, and a metal chain hung on a rung with a padlock on the end.

"What?"

"Antonio locked that today."

564

She twisted around to see behind her, and backed the car up, pulling off the road and stopping behind a copse of trees. The engine cut and we were in the dark.

"So," I said, "What do we do?"

"You stay here."

"Okay? Why?"

"Because. Trust me."

She switched the dome light to *off* and got out, closing the door before it beeped. She opened the back door and collected the bags.

"Dude," I said. "You're taking the groceries?"

"I don't have a gun. If I bring this I look like a harmless little woman delivering food to children."

Martha had gotten very ambitious at the market, and Theresa didn't have enough arms for all the bags. She struggled, leaving an entire tube of salami and a flat of pepper plants behind. She closed the door, walking toward the road in the moonlight.

I looked back at the food and plants she'd left, then at her.

If she could play the helpless woman, worse, if she *needed* to, I could play as well.

I caught up to her at the open gate. She didn't acknowledge my presence for a few steps.

"Plants?" she said. "Literally?"

"I told Martha they were growing tomatoes. She figured they had land. Teach a man to fish, et cetera."

"She's a keeper."

Up ahead, an old stone house loomed. It was dark and empty. Theresa got off the main drive and moved around the side. My heart was pounding so hard it hurt. If something happened to me, Jonathan was going to kill me for real.

"I don't see another car," I said.

"They hid it."

"Just like we did?"

She stopped behind shoulder-high brush and dropped her bags.

"That's why you're staying back while I go in. Put that stuff down."

I laid the salami tube and the flat of pepper plants on the ground.

"Look," I said. "I know you're like some kind of badass or something, but—"

"Monica." Exasperated, she picked up the salami and left the rest. "Don't make me sorry I brought you." She walked toward the house, head up, eyes everywhere.

Fuck that. I could be badass too. As long as I came out alive Jonathan would forgive me.

I picked up a canvas bag full of cans and followed her.

"If you're going to come," she said without looking at me, "stay behind and watch my back."

I could do that. I looped the bag's handles around my fist and let her get ahead. The crickets thrummed at a deeper pitch in southern Italy, and the birds made a cacophony of noise I hadn't heard before. I checked behind, to the sides, everywhere. We were clear. A bug slapped against my shoulder and I jumped.

"*Shh!*" If a shush could be a shout, Theresa made it. She waved me over to a dark corner on the side of the house and pointed to the back. "Light."

She was right. A warm, yellow glow filtered through the interior to the backyard. We waited. Or, more accurately, Theresa waited. I would have just strolled on back there with my cans of beans.

The light shifted and swung to the left. A flashlight. Voices. The squeal of a little girl. Theresa sucked a breath when she heard it.

The girl laughed.

Theresa exhaled, but still, she didn't move.

"If we sneak back there it looks like we're up to something."

"You have no idea who it is," she growled.

"Shit or get off the pot," I growled back.

"Fine." She strode to the center of the side drive and walked to the back of the house. I followed, head high as if we belonged there.

He came out of the bushes—a shadow bum rushing Theresa with his arms out, trying to get at her waist. I didn't take a second to think. My nerves were code red, and my muscles had a mind of their own. I swung the bag before he reached her, smacking him across the side of the head so hard he was flung back four feet.

"Antonio!" Theresa cried as she ran to him.

My heart sank. I dropped the bag.

"I'm sorry!"

Antonio shook the bees out of his head while Theresa and I helped him up.

"Nice shot, goddess."

I let Antonio go when I heard footsteps and Jonathan's voice behind me.

"What the—" I didn't finish. A little girl was at my feet, punching my leg and screaming in Italian.

"Ow!"

A boy picked her up and took her away, not to save me, but to protect her.

Standing in a circle: Antonio with his hand on his head, Theresa cooing at him, Jonathan looking at me as if he didn't know what to think, and two children huddling defensively, we were frozen in time.

It was late and I was in a mood.

"We have more groceries in the car. Little help, please?"

ANTONIO

Jonathan and I had brought tools and materials to fix the roof and the pipes. They'd brought food. For over a year, the kids had eaten fine by themselves but the women brought food and fucking toothbrushes. I thought this was the thing that bothered me. After I let Nevio know my sister-in-law was safe and we put everything away together, I was too tired to defend my position.

566

Jonathan and Monica went home at three in the morning. I found my wife on the worn, dusty couch in the candle light with Simona's head on her lap. Nevio slept on a cushioned chair, curled into a ball, drooling as he hugged his rifle.

"This is a scene from an opera," I said, pulling a dining room chair from the corner. I planted it across from Theresa. An ornate wooden coffee table was between us. "Except for the olives." I pointed to the rows of olives on the broken glass of the coffee table.

"I think counting soothes her."

"*Si, si.*"

"What should we do, Antonio?"

I rested my elbows on my knees.

"Tell each other where we're going, first of all."

She smiled and looked down at the girl whose hair she stroked.

"I was so relieved you hadn't gone to the Carlonis that it didn't even occur to me to be mad." She looked back up at me. "I guess it occurred to you."

"I was going to throw you over my shoulder and put you in the car."

"That didn't go well."

"It did not."

"How's your head, by the way?"

"Fine. *Bene.*"

We sat in silence. Nevio turned onto his back, draping his legs over the arm of the chair and gently snoring.

"What should we do?" she asked again. "We can't leave them here. They witnessed a crime, and you said yourself that putting them in social services, or whatever you have here would expose them."

"We can't take them back."

"Can't we?"

It was the first time she spoke aloud what I knew she'd been thinking since that afternoon. Possibly, she hadn't been able to speak the words in her own mind. Or she was waiting for me to hear it first.

"They've been through enough," I said. "Taking them out of the country to a place where they don't know the language? Look how they live. Did this one," he jerked his head toward Nevio, "ever say he wanted TV or video games? No. He's more mature than most adults in America and he'll be held back in school." I sat back in the chair, imagining how hard it would be to move them. Not just the change of language, but the change in culture and expectation. "And who are we to these kids?" I asked. "We landed in their place like a conquering army, bearing gifts like diplomats. I own the land and the house, of course, but not to them. To them, this is their world."

"You're a sensitive man," she said.

"Don't try and handle me."

"Well, you are."

"Just say it, wife. Speak your wishes."

She took a single, deep breath that filled her chest, driving it up and out. With Simona in her lap, I realized those gorgeous tits would never be used to feed a baby.

"What if..." she paused for another breath. "What if we stayed for awhile?"

"Awhile?" I crossed ankle over knee, settling in. She knew we had responsi-

567

bilities in California better than anyone.

"We could fix up the house around them. And you can actually do what you said you were going to do."

"Which is?"

"Talk to someone. But this time, you talk to them about leaving the children alone. You tell them they're under your protection, and if they're hurt in any way…"

She trailed off.

"Threats only work if you intend to carry them out, Contessa."

"It would be hard for me not to carry them out, Capo."

She was a woman of frightening depth, capable of angelic kindness and unspeakable savagery. She'd kept me honest for a long time, now it was up to me to return the favor.

"I'll save you from yourself, then."

She caught herself mid-breath.

"Is that a yes?"

"If we stay here and rebuild this house and our lives around children you don't know…will it make you happy?"

"To take care of them?"

"Will that make you happy?" I repeated.

"Yes." Her voice cracked. I held my palms up in surrender.

"Then what else can we do?"

She blinked, and candlelit tears fell down her cheeks.

"Antonio." One word. No more.

"Why are you crying?"

"I don't know."

I got up and kneeled at her feet, reaching over Simona to wipe my wife's tears away.

"It's going to be really hard," she said.

"I inherited the house and everything in it. A bad roof. Cracked foundation. Two resourceful children. I have to take care of it. All of it."

"Can your mother and sister come?"

"You don't even know them."

"It's such a big house even…" She had to stop herself to catch her breath. I didn't have a handkerchief or anything, so I sat next to her and wiped her sobs away with my sleeve. "…even…even with children in it."

She broke down completely before I could object. Which, I had to admit, was fine.

I wasn't going to deny her the family she'd always wanted.

I wasn't going to deny her anything.

ABOUT THE AUTHOR

CD Reiss is a New York Times bestselling author. She still has to chop wood and carry water, which was buried in the fine print. Her lawyer is working it out with God but in the eantime, if you call and she doesn't pick up she's at the well hauling buckets.

Born in New York City, she moved to Hollywood, California to get her master's degree in screenwriting from USC. In case you want to know, that went nowhere but it did give her a big enough ego to write novels.

She's frequently referred to as the Shakespeare of Smut which is flattering but hasn't ever gotten her out of chopping that cord of wood.

If you meet her in person, you should call her Christine.

If you loved the Drazens, you'll love the Edge Series. Four intense, sexy books and a free prequel, all releasing in the three month window.
Get them here: https://cdreiss.com/books/edge/

If I'm new to you and you want more kinky, hot sex with a touch of darkness and off-the-charts intensity, start with Submission:
https://cdreiss.com/books/submission-series/

Text--> cdreiss to 77948 to get a notification whenever I have a new release!

Website: https://cdreiss.com/
Facebook https://www.facebook.com/CDReiss.writer/
Book and Main Biteshttps://bookandmainbites.com/cdreiss
Instagram: https://www.instagram.com/cdreiss/

THE COLOR OF LOVE

JULIE A. RICHMAN

First meeting in summer camp as teens, cocky NYC doctor and sexy southern belle push each other's boundaries of love and acceptance, as they discover the true color of love.

AUTHOR'S NOTE (PLEASE READ)

Hello Readers:

Thank you for purchasing *Cocktales* and supporting the author community.

Following is the first four chapters of *The Color of Love*, a new work set for release in late 2018.

This book is a saga that spans a fifteen-year period. The reason I'm mentioning this is because the beginning of *The Color of Love* is set when the H/h, Bray and Misty, first meet as teens in summer camp. Please note that **this is not a YA book**, although in the first four chapters, you will only see them as teens. **The majority of the completed book will take place during their adult years.**
  Soooo . . . enjoy getting started (a little early) on my upcoming release.

Stay Cocky and keep reading!

Peace & Love,
  Julie A. Richman

The sky is blue
The lake is blue
We're gonna turn the white team blue
What's the color of Color War?
Blue, Blue, Blue

~ Chant of the Blue Team
Color War
Camp Tonkawa
Summer of 2000

THAT SUMMER...

ONE

BRAY

The first time I laid eyes on Misty Davis, I realized just how white I wasn't. It was not merely the peachy glow of her sun-kissed skin or the natural highlights in her long blonde hair, it was something else. Something I couldn't quite put my finger on.

She was a new camper at Camp Tonkawa, and this girl was impossible not to notice. I'd been catching glimpses of her over these first few days of camp and now she was starting to invade my thoughts. Not a typical thing for me. I'd already learned two things about her. Her name was Misty she was from somewhere in the South.

Overhearing her talking to some fellow campers, I was totally amused by her slow Southern drawl. It was the only accent like it in the entire camp, which was all kids from the Northeast.

I wondered what this new girl was doing here in Maine. These clearly were not her stomping grounds. It was not only her speech and the way she accented her words, saying SEE-ment instead of cement or JEW-lie instead of July, it was what I'd observed of her mannerisms and the way she carried herself, that made her stand out. I'd never met another fifteen-year-old girl who possessed such natural grace. That was, unless, as I'd also witnessed over the past few days, she was on any kind of playing field. It didn't matter if it was a soccer field, baseball diamond, or an archery range, the girl was a fierce competitor, kicking ass and taking no prisoners. She became so focused only on the win that her femininity transformed into an almost feral ferocity.

I was finally seeing her up close for the first time when our groups were in a co-ed Tug-of-War match. Positioned three back from the center knot, she was the second girl in the formation on the opposing team. Our eyes met before the ref even called for us to start, and they remained locked until my team took hers down and her entire line did a face plant into the sandy pit.

When she got up, anger flashed in her expressive blue eyes and stayed there as she dusted the sand from her shirt. I couldn't help but smile at her, which unfortunately went unreturned, stinging my ego more than anything.

Over the next few hours, our groups kept crossing paths and I could feel her eyes on me, observing as if I were a new species that needed examination. I decided that she needed a closer look.

The girls from her bunk were all friends of mine from years past. A few had been former make-out partners, who'd been instrumental in helping me perfect the art of French kissing. And one had been more to me.

Sauntering over to their lunch table in the dining hall a few hours later, I was warmly welcomed with squishy hugs from her bunkmates.

"Bray!" Several girls greeted me in a simultaneous chorus.

I had a girl in each arm when Misty looked up from her salad. *A salad?* Almost everyone else at the table had been chowing down on burgers and dogs, but not Misty. What made her choice even more odd was that she was picking through the lettuce and removing anything that was yellow.

She was eyeing me as if she were seeing a new species, and maybe for her, I was. To everyone else at Camp Tonkawa, I was just Bray Hamilton, fifth-year camper, New York City boy, Dalton student, son of a prominent cardiac surgeon father and a socialite mother, who was the daughter of the infamous finance scion Richard Morgan van der Heyden III.

With her friends still hanging on my limbs like Christmas ornaments, I needed to build that bridge between us. It began with a smile. "Hi. I'm Bray."

She nodded and gave me a small, shy smile that slammed my heart like a fastball finding its way home into the worn webbing of a catcher's mitt.

"Nice to meet you, Bray. I'm Misty."

Those words, the way she pronounced my name, dragging it out into nearly two syllables, had m

y head swimming.

And although the aquatic center had always been a second home to me, in this instance, I knew I was drowning.

TWO

MISTY

H is skin was the color of Kraft caramels, those little squares that they keep in bins at Kroger's. Mother would always swipe my hand when I'd sneak them out, but if I were really lucky, I'd pop one into my mouth, let it melt for a moment, and give the flavor a chance to spread across my tongue before chewing it.

Just looking at him had me tasting that sweetness on my tongue. His sweetness. And I felt uncomfortable.

He had held my gaze throughout the whole Tug-of-War, and I could see his eyes were pale, and from a distance they had looked green, and I just wanted to see them close-up. When he had smiled at one of his teammates, laughing at something the other guy had said, I had stopped breathing. Even from a distance, that smile, with his beautiful even white teeth and deep dimples, was mesmerizing. I had known I needed to get a closer look. I'd never seen a boy so beautiful and exotic-looking or had felt so physically drawn to someone.

Later, as my bunkmates and I walked to the dining hall after our defeat, they were all abuzz about a boy named Bray.

"He's gotten so tall and more handsome, if that's even possible," Ashley said before sighing. Literally.

"I know, and did you see his chest and arm muscles? He's been spending some serious time in the gym." Becca turned to Ashley. "And that smile just slays me. You're right, he's handsome. He isn't cute, he's already handsome."

I just had to know. It had to be that same guy.

"Who are y'all talking about?" I asked, feeling like more of an outsider than I already was with this group of girls who'd summered together for years.

"Bray Hamilton," Ashley informed me as if I should know.

"I don't know who that is." I let her know as we climbed the last hill to the dining hall.

"Misty, he was a few back on the other side—tall, dark-skinned, black hair, and the most gorgeous smile in the world."

Pretending I hadn't noticed, I just shrugged and shook my head.

"I'll point him out in the dining hall. He is so hot, and the crazy thing is that he's really a nice guy, too. Most handsome guys are total douchecanoes, but Bray is such a good guy."

"I wonder if he has a girlfriend back home." This time, it was Charlotte who spoke. The leggy Connecticut beauty flung her mane of silky mahogany hair over her shoulder, training her pale blue eyes on me as she added, "I know his cousins in Darien."

There was something in her tone that made me feel as if she were staking claim on him. Inwardly, I laughed. She had just played her hand, showing me that she saw me as the biggest competition in the bunk for this guy Bray's attention. All it had done was intrigue me more.

Corn belongs on a cob. Or in my Gran's Thanksgiving casserole. Or on a plate glistening in melted butter. The only other acceptable place for corn was as part of succotash. Period. It had no business being in a salad. But there it was.

I guess I shouldn't have been surprised since corn had been served with fried chicken and mashed potatoes at last night's dinner. This was repurposed corn, which made it that much more unacceptable in my salad. While I was picking it out, I decided that the vinegary banana peppers needed to go, too. It was a process, and I was close to completing it when Ashley and Becca suddenly jumped up from the table, their voices becoming high-pitched shrieks.

Close up, his eyes were even more arresting than I'd suspected from a distance, drawing me in and daring me to look away. I didn't dare. Totally entranced, I'd never seen eyes that were as pale and translucent as this boy's. Green—a true green—rimmed with long, ebony lashes, and all I could think was that peridots, my birthstone, looked beautiful set against the creamy caramel of his skin.

His bold gaze made me feel shy and insecure, two feelings that were generally alien to me. Yet, I still couldn't help but smile. The boy was beautiful, and his eyes were radiating an inner warmth that I definitely was not used to. I did not expect to be dazzled by the smile he returned.

"Hi. I'm Bray."

And I knew what all the fuss was about.

"Nice to meet you, Bray. I'm Misty." My accent was thick, and the corners of his mouth rose even more, giving me the impression that he got a kick out of it.

"I'm guessing you aren't from Brooklyn, Misty," he quipped.

"No. I'm from Jackson. Jackson, Mississippi." I felt the need to qualify.

He just nodded, ignoring the way Ashley and Becca were all over him. His eyes held mine until Charlotte stepped between us, her tall frame blocking my view of Bray.

Our moment was gone. But I was pretty sure we had *a moment*

THREE

BRAY

We were three weeks into the first four-week session of the summer, and I had yet to spend a moment alone with the elusive Misty Davis. Every time I thought we would have some private time, one of her bunkmates or mine would insert themselves, sometimes literally between us. To say I was frustrated would be an understatement.

My plan was to change that at tonight's campfire. Campfire nights happened every other Saturday and from Thursday on, you could feel the testosterone in the bunk rising and raging with the hope of copping a feel or, if you were really lucky, a hand job from a hand that wasn't your own. Not that I was angling for one from Misty, not yet at least. I just wanted a chance to talk to her at the cookout and maybe grab some alone time during the campfire.

The night began with a cookout with the girls' groups. When they arrived, the girls' looked like a parade sponsored by Juicy Couture as they sported an overwhelming number of T-shirts, announcing via some slogan, just how juicy they each were. *A message to the guys*, I wondered. Charlotte stood out from the crowd in a short tropical print sundress that accentuated her long, colt-like legs, which had turned golden brown in the few short weeks we'd been in camp.

Trying not to be conspicuous, I made the most of my peripheral vision as I searched for Misty. I should have known that I didn't need to be on the lookout, that I would just feel her arrival. And I did. But when she appeared, it was anything but a side-glance that I was giving her. Nope, I was watching her openly and appreciatively, admiring her soft white cotton, off-the-shoulder shirt, and frayed denim shorts. Where Charlotte's long legs should have affected me and didn't, the curve of Misty's tanned shoulders did for me in spades. It was the first time I'd ever wanted to kiss a girl slowly from her shoulders to her neck. Turning around for a moment of privacy, I had to adjust myself and take a deep breath.

I needed to get her alone.

Ashley, Becca, and Charlotte joined me and my two closest buds, Tyler and Jake, at a picnic table for dinner. Not surprisingly, Charlotte took the spot on the bench next to me.

"Misty," I called out to her before raising my hand and motioning for her to join us.

As she slowly made her way over with her plate in hand, a look of confusion created a crease between her pale eyes. "Oh, there's no room for me here."

"Well, we'll make some." I jumped up from my spot on the edge of the bench. "Hey, can you guys squish a little?" I asked Charlotte and Becca. "Thanks."

Instead of sitting next to Charlotte, I slid my plate to the very end of the table and took Misty's from her, placing it on the worn wood planks between my and Charlotte's dinners. I waited for Misty to sit first and then I slid onto the bench next to her. We were so close that our thighs and shoulders were touching and there may not have been any other spot in the entire universe beyond where our bodies merged. I pressed my leg against hers a little, needing to send a message . . . to let her know. She had to know.

Misty didn't press back, but I watched her lips twitch, the corners raising slightly. And she didn't pull her leg away.

She knew.

Now all I had to endure was the endless wait until nightfall for the campfire to begin. Campers had been eying one another for weeks waiting for this night. And I was no different.

I was intrigued by this aloof girl who wasn't tripping over her bunkmates to get close to me. My fear was that Charlotte may have led Misty to believe that there was something going on between us. But there wasn't.

That was long over.

FOUR

MISTY

As we warmed by the campfire, the last rays of rose-tinged light touched the pine tops before fading to inky blue and eventually to black. With the darkness, couples enjoyed a newfound freedom, wandering off on paths into the woods or down to the lake's sandy shore. I was becoming more anxious as Bray's arm, which was barely brushing against mine, was the only thing I could think about. Consciously focusing on my breathing, which had become shallow and labored, I tried to quell my excitement, hopeful anticipation, and above all, fear. I was afraid. Not of Bray, but of my attraction to him and the confusion that came along with it.

I jumped when his shoulder nudged against mine, and he smiled as he leaned over and whispered, "Wanna go for a walk?"

"Sure." Standing and brushing the dirt from the back of my shorts, I suddenly felt extremely self-conscious. I was so attracted to this boy that when he looked at me, the need to touch him was almost overwhelming.

Under that, though, I felt guilt, and I didn't know quite why. I knew that my parents would disapprove of him, so maybe that was why.

As I turned to walk away with him, I didn't miss Charlotte's pointed glare. She was clearly not happy with Bray's interest in me, and I could only imagine how she was going to take that out on me later.

"So, what are you doing all the way up here in Maine, Misty?" We found an outcropping of boulders and climbed to the top, sitting with our legs dangling over.

"I wanted to come somewhere different. Somewhere that didn't look like home." I shrugged before adding, "Somewhere not so darn hot in summer. So, I looked for camps in Maine and Minnesota."

"Are you just partial to M states?" He laughed.

It took me a moment to understand what he was talking about, that he was joking with me, and then, as if I were on some kind of seven-second delay, I laughed with him. "I hadn't even realized that."

"Well, you chose well. What do you think of it up here?"

"It's beautiful." Why was I so tongue-tied with him? I wanted to be engaging and quick and funny, but I couldn't even form a complete sentence.

"And?"

"And the nights are so beautiful and cool. Down south, the summer is sweltering. You always feel like you need a shower, even right after you've taken one." I was talking fast, trying to get as much out as I could before my brain shut down again. "I love how it stays light so late up here and then there are more stars than I've ever seen. I thought we had a lot in Mississippi, but it's nothing like here. I don't ever think I'd get tired of looking at the night sky up here."

"I know what you mean. Even after five years, I'm blown away every night. We don't see many stars where I'm from, so for me, this is like being in a planetarium every night."

Sitting back on the boulder, we both gazed up into the darkened sky, quietly enjoying the arch of stars above us.

"Do you find people different up here?" Bray broke the silence.

I was surprised by how intuitive he was. "Yes, everyone up here says what they think for the most part. I'm not used to the bluntness," I confessed.

"Blunt as in offensive or refreshing?" He smiled.

I didn't answer for a moment because I was transfixed by his smile and his dimples. Could this guy be any cuter?

And then as if snapping out of a fog, I shook my head. "No. It isn't offensive at all. Just different." I needed time to pull myself together, so I threw the conversation back to him. "So, tell me about you. I know nothing about you, except that you are Mr. Popularity around here." I bumped my shoulder against his and was met by some unyielding muscle.

He smiled again, and I had the urge to run the tip of my finger down the groove of his dimple.

"Well, I'm from New York City. Born there. Live there. Go to school there."

"What school do you go to?" I asked. I needed to know the details about him. He was not like anyone I'd ever encountered in my social circle in Jackson, which were the children of my parents' friends, so their social circle was mine, next gen. I had never been given my own choice of friends or activities or camps until this summer. For the first time, I had gotten to choose who I wanted to be close to, and that person was Bray.

"Dalton."

I nodded. "I've heard of that." It wasn't a lie, either.

"We have a few famous alums. Chevy Chase went there." He smiled.

"Brothers and sisters?"

"No. Just me."

They got it perfect the first time.

"Are your parents originally from New York?" I couldn't imagine what it would be like to live in such a big city.

"My mom is from Connecticut. She's a van der Heyden." He laughed. "Actually, she's a disowned van der Heyden."

"Oh no, what did she do to get disowned?" I was enjoying the sparkle in his eyes, and I could tell he loved this story about his obviously rebellious mother.

"She married my father," he said, matter-of-factly, picking up a small pebble from our boulder-seat and tossing it into the air a few times before he threw it into the darkness.

"And her family disowned her?" This was going to be juicy.

He nodded. "Well, you've gotta understand the family history. Like I said, my mom is a van der Heyden. They came here from Holland back when New York was New Amsterdam, like in the 1650s with the Dutch West Indies Trading Company. They were fur traders. So, she's old money, a debutante, Miss Porter's, the whole bit."

"Okay." I was taking it in, and I could totally picture his mother.

"And my dad, well, my dad is a cardiac surgeon. He's department director at New York-Presbyterian Hospital, which if you are going to have a heart problem in New York, that is where you want the ambulance to take you."

"I'll remember that." I laughed. "I don't really understand, though. Why did your mom got disowned for marrying a cardiac surgeon?"

Smiling, Bray shook his head and then looked me straight in the eye before he spoke. "My mom got disowned for marrying an African-American cardiac surgeon."

Ah. I got it. Dutch society blue blood on one side and African-American on the other. I could just envision the scandal that might have caused. Amongst my parents set in Jackson, it would have been more than just grist for the gossip mill. All of society would have shunned the poor woman, and she would have forever been talked about in whispers.

"Wow, her family just abandoned her?" I felt terrible for his mother.

"No. Not everyone. Just my grandfather, who is a well-known racist and bigot and keeps everyone in line by threatening to cut them out of the will. My grandmother and my uncle, my mom's brother, never severed ties. But the old man cut her out of a serious inheritance."

"That's crazy, but really cool that she walked away from it for love." My heart was swooning. It was like abdicating a throne or something.

"Yeah, well, my dad makes enough that it isn't like she was plunged into poverty."

"Have you ever met your grandfather?" I couldn't imagine a life without my grandparents in it.

"Nope. Never."

"Well that's his loss." I was indignant. How could he not want to meet his own grandson just because he was biracial?

He was staring straight ahead, and I had a feeling the hurt went deeper than I could ever imagine or than he would ever admit.

"That's what my mom says. She also says that my never having met him is no great loss."

"And you? What do you think?" I reached out and slipped my hand in his.

Turning to look me in the eyes, he tightened his fingers around my hand and shook his head. "I don't know if it's just curiosity or if I just want to have the chance to tell him that I'm just as good as his other grandchildren."

"What a jerk." It was out of my mouth before I could stop it.

Bray burst into laughter. "My, my, Misty Davis. That is the last thing I expected out of your sweet Southern mouth."

I was glad he couldn't see the heat rise in my face, because I was sure I was beet red. Still, I was mad as hell. What kind of grandparent refused to meet their own grandchild? And in that moment, my stomach knotted because I knew both my grandparents, and my parents, would react the same way. They would totally pass judgment without ever getting to know him. I suddenly felt sick.

"What about your grandmother?" I asked.

"I've met my grandmother. We see her a few times a year. And my uncle and his family are around all the time. So, I do know my cousins from that side of the family. It's just the old man."

"Jerk," I repeated to make Bray laugh.

And he did, throwing in a shoulder bump for good measure.

"What about your dad's family? Where is he from?" I wondered if it would be as juicy as the disowned heiress.

"My dad . . ." He turned to me and smiled. "My dad is from Harlem."

Bray's reaction told me I had not done a good job of keeping a poker face. His green eyes widened in surprise, and then I was gifted with another flash of his dimples.

"You're picturing the mean streets. My dad at twelve, flipping open a switch-blade, fighting for his life. Oh, Mississippi Misty—" He paused as if in deep thought and then raised an eyebrow at me. "Hmm, I think I'll shorten that to Miss-Mis. So, Miss-Mis, Harlem is actually really cool. A lot of the blocks are brownstones that are very nice. Pretty much looks like where I live on the Upper East Side. People think it's the slum, and it has quite the reputation, but it's actually just another neighborhood. I mean, yeah, there are rough areas, but there are some really beautiful ones, too. My grandma still lives there."

"Are you close to her?"

"She's my girl." The pride and love in his voice was unmistakable.

"It sounds like someone's been spoiled by his grammy."

"Oh, no doubt. She was a single mom, raising two kids. Always worked two jobs. Her thing was to make sure my dad and my aunt got a good education."

"She sounds like a smart lady and your dad definitely did well in school."

"Yeah, he's something of a Brainiac and definitely has that God complex that doctors have." Bray paused, the look on his face told me he was taking a moment to formulate what he was about to say next. "So, Miss-Mis, let me ask you something. Have you met many people like me before?"

His bluntness took me aback. The elephant had been led to the center of the room.

"Like you, meaning . . ."

"Parents of different races," he clarified.

My first inclination was to deny it and tell him that he was just like the people I knew back home, but somehow, I knew he'd see right through me.

"My school and my neighborhood are mostly . . ." I had no idea how to address this in a way that didn't make me come across as uppity and sheltered.

"White?"

Wanting more than anything to look away, I forced myself to look directly into his eyes, and nodded.

Squeezing my hand, he admitted, "So are mine. But I think it might be less of a big deal in New York City than in Jackson, Mississippi." Pausing for a moment, he added, "Or Connecticut."

"Jerk." I knew that would make him laugh.

"Are you going to keep surprising me with that sassy Southern mouth?"

I responded with a playful shrug.

After that, we sat in silence for a long time, my hand still nestled in his. I wondered what was going through his head and hoped he didn't think I was too different. If I were to tell Mother and Daddy that I'd met the son of a wealthy socialite and a cardiac surgeon, they would love that. I just feared what their response would be if they learned his father was African-American. But I already knew the answer to that.

I think Bray did as well.

Silently, I cursed the differences in our lives because I knew for sure that Bray Hamilton and I had much more in common than not, and at the top of that list was our deep attraction to one another.

Bray took my hand in his and then wrapped his other arm around my waist to help steady me as we made our way down from the boulder. I felt his body against mine for the briefest of moments, and I craved more. I needed to feel him again. It wasn't a want. It was a need. I *needed* more moments.

"How tall are you?" I asked once my feet were back on the ground and I found myself looking up at him.

"I'm about five eleven." He linked our hands back together and turned toward the trail that would lead us back to the campfire.

We walked along the path in silence for a few minutes before Bray began to speak again. "I really love that shirt, Misty."

I could feel the heat rising from my bare shoulders to my cheeks, glad the night air was cool enough to chill them down and provide camouflage in the darkness. I certainly wasn't going to admit that I wore this shirt, probably the only sexy thing in my entire wardrobe, in hopes that he would notice me. Mission accomplished. I was playing with fire. And it was exciting. And scary.

"Thank you," I responded to his compliment. "I'm glad you like it."

"Like it? Miss-Mis, it's driving me crazy."

"My shoulders are driving you crazy?" I laughed.

Suddenly, he stopped and tugged my hand until we were off the path and I was pressed against him. I held my breath as I let my body feel his muscular frame.

This is it. He's going to kiss me.

But Bray Hamilton took me by surprise when his lips ended up on my bare right shoulder, sending a shiver down my spine.

"I've been dying to do that all night," he admitted.

I've been dying for you to kiss me all night.

I wanted to tell him that, but it was too forward.

His head dipped down again, and this time, his lips landed in the crook of my neck. "I've been dying to do that, too."

My breath caught in the base of my throat because what he had just done to me was more exciting than anything I'd read in a book or seen in a movie.

How did he know to do these things?

"We'd better get back before they send a search party for us." I didn't know why that came out of my mouth. Fear that maybe I might do more with Bray than I'd ever done before? Inexperience? A kiss to my shoulder and one to my neck caused much more than butterflies. I was feeling a raw heat, and I wasn't quite sure what to do about it.

"As you wish, Miss-Mis." When we started walking again, he grabbed my hand, and I let him, but a few steps before we hit the clearing, I pulled free of his hold.

That action had the muscle in his jaw twitching, in anger or disappointment, I didn't know. He had read my gesture as I didn't want people to know I was with him, when in fact it was only partially that. I didn't care about everyone, only my bunkmates. I was attempting to minimize being ostracized more than I already was, because girls can be mean and competitive. Especially when the boy they like, likes you.

My heart hurt knowing I had made Bray feel he was anything less than the most intriguing and incredible guy I'd ever met. But I had. And those words "less than" were chiseling the edges of my heart. The reality was that he was more than . . . more than any guy I had ever met. And the evening ended without me telling him that or letting him know how I felt.

"Isn't Bray the best kisser." We were all sitting on our beds and Becca looked directly at me when she said it. It wasn't a question. It was to let me know I wasn't special and that she'd kissed him.

Only, she didn't know that I hadn't actually done anything with him.

"Of course he's the best kisser, after all, I was the one who taught him how to do it." Charlotte brushed her long mane, making eye contact with me in the mirror.

"That's not all you taught him," Ashley chimed in, letting me know it was one against three and that she and Becca were all too willing to do Charlotte's bidding.

Turning from the mirror, Charlotte tipped her head to the side and smirked, "Understatement."

This tall cool glass of Evian from Connecticut was expecting me to fight back like a Northerner, and that was not going to happen.

Bray had chosen me tonight, and Charlotte was going to have a summer filled with watching him pursue me hard, not the other way around. The meaner she got, or the more people she got to gang up against me, the more she would hurt herself, and I wouldn't have to do a damn thing.

Clearly, she didn't understand that.

Whatever was going to happen between me and Bray was going to happen. We were captivated by one another. And as they babbled on about summer's past with him, I sat cross-legged on my bed brushing my hair, effectively tuning them out as I replaced their noise with a soundtrack of my own, filling my head.

My mind's eye was wrapped up in a tale, a summer love, playing out on the sports fields and the trails, around campfires in the night, a North-South West Side Story.

Drifting off to sleep that night, I envisioned the sky from earlier in the night and hoped that Bray's and my stars weren't crossed.

More to come . . .
Want to be the first to know when the rest of Bray and Misty's story is coming out . . .

To preorder The Color of Love: http://bit.ly/2Ko9oJw

To add to your TBR :
Goodreads: http://bit.ly/2G5R1qb

ABOUT THE AUTHOR

A native New Yorker living deep in the heart of Texas, Julie is obsessed with reality TV, the existence of past lives, and Bruce Springsteen. And she misses the ocean. Big time.

Website: http://www.juliearichman.com/
Newsletter : http://bit.ly/JulieARichmanNewsletter
Facebook: https://www.facebook.com/AuthorJulieARichman/
Instagram: https://www.instagram.com/authorjuliearichman/
Twitter : https://twitter.com/JulieARichman

ALSO BY JULIE A. RICHMAN

Searching for Moore

Moore to Lose

Moore than Forever

Needing Moore Series

Bad Son Rising

Henry's End

Slave to Love

The Do-Over

Love on the Edge of Time

Moore than a Feeling

The Color of Love

ALIGNED

A SHORT RETELLING OF THE BEGINNING
OF THE INFIDELITY SERIES

ALEATHA ROMIG

A fun, alternative look at the beginning of the bestselling Infidelity series—not about cheating.

Get firsthand insight into Lennox "Nox" Demetri's inner thoughts as he and Alexandria "Charli" Collins begin the "...sexy suspense saga that will leave you hot, bothered, and begging for more." ~ *Redbook magazine*

And for lovers of the Infidelity series, don't miss the bonus chapter guaranteed to make you remember all the reasons you fell in love with this cocky hero.

ALIGNED

A short retelling of the beginning of the INFIDELITY series
Series Copyright © 2017 Romig Works, LLC
Published by Romig Works, LLC

2017 Edition

Editing: Lisa Aurello

ONE

LENNOX

"Another drink, Mr. Demetri?" the bartender asked as he cleaned a small glass tumbler, wiping the rim with a white cloth.

Standing with my elbow on the makeshift bar, I contemplated his offer. The dinner was over, and as I surveyed the large ballroom, my gaze came to rest on the round table near the front of the room with two empty chairs.

One was mine.

My chair.

My seat.

Where my ass was supposed to be.

The woman seated next to my empty chair smiled politely, talking to our table companions as her eyes flickered about the room, no doubt trying to locate her date for the evening.

That was the problem.

I didn't want to be here with her or consider her a date, escort, companion, or any other appropriate descriptor.

To me, she was no more than a person to occupy the seat next to mine, an accessory for my evening, as significant as a pocket square or diamond cuff links. She was a woman from my company, someone who worked in public relations. I barely knew her, and for some reason, that made this entire scenario more unsettling.

Then again, I had no desire to get to know her. It wasn't her work or drive that made her undesirable. She was a valuable employee, and I appreciated anyone who had a strong work ethic. It wasn't her personality or appearance. She was pleasant enough to be around and not bad on the eyes. Even though blondes had never been my thing, I knew a beautiful woman when I saw one. Perhaps, it's the Italian in me, but brunettes were the ones who caught my eye.

The reason I wasn't interested was that I wasn't in that place—that place in my head or heart to allow anyone to get close. Not again. Maybe never. Those stars had once aligned. Physics told me that it wouldn't happen again.

That was the problem. I suppose I was concerned that the woman in the seat next to where I should be seated wanted more. I could capitalize on that, take her to her home, stay and get my needs met, not giving a fuck about hers.

It's not that I'd never done that. It's that she worked with me. For me. I'd see her again. Using her and walking away would make me no better than my father. I wasn't a good man, but I sure as hell was better than him. Granted, the bar wasn't set that high, but I needed to start somewhere.

Mindlessly I rotated the gold band on the fourth finger of my left hand. Truth be told, I was a confident businessman who possessed very few—if any—nervous habits. Rotating my wedding ring wasn't so much as a nervous habit as it was a routine, a comfort, a reminder of a time when life was better, a time when stars aligned, a time when I had fucks to give—in all meanings of the word.

"Lennox," Deloris Witt said as she came to a stop, standing beside me.

Before acknowledging the woman whom I employed, I nodded to the bartender. "Make it a double."

"You need to be in your seat for the presentation. After all, this room is filled because of your donation, the donation made by Demetri Enterprises. They need to see a face with the name."

"Silvia should be the face." I was less angry about Silvia's inability to attend this benefit than I was bothered. When it came to Silvia Demetri, our relationship had its ebbs and flows. Right now, I was here because she asked me to do this and I agreed.

It might be worthwhile to note that I'm not always an asshole.

I looked to Mrs. Witt. "*I* know, Deloris, *you* could be that face." The deep green of her dress caught my attention as I scanned her up and down. It wasn't often that I gave Deloris Witt's gender much consideration. It didn't matter to me whether she was a man or a woman. What mattered was that she got the job done—handled my affairs with the utmost diplomacy and discretion.

Her lips pursed. "I work for Demetri. I'm not Demetri. That's you."

I shook my head as I looked down and noticed the way her dress reached all the way to the tops of her shoes. "You look very nice. Are those high heels?" I felt the way my cheek quirked with amusement. "I didn't even know you owned high heels."

"There's a lot about me that you don't know."

"Well, that seems unfair. After all, you know all about me."

"I do. I know you should be going to your seat, and you should probably leave the rest of the drink here."

There weren't many people in the world who spoke to me the way Deloris did. As I gave that more thought, I narrowed the field. *No one* spoke to me the way that Deloris did. She was old enough to be my mother—if she gave birth at fourteen. And yes, that could be possible, but it wasn't.

Deloris wasn't my mother. She was the closest thing I had to a conscience. And given her line of work, past and present, it meant that my conscience was less like Jiminy Cricket and more like Penelope on that crime show.

"I don't appreciate that you suggested...*insisted*," I corrected, "that I bring Millie."

Deloris's voice lowered. "We needed someone at your side. It's not like she's an Infidelity employee."

My jaw clenched at the mention of that company. I despised everything about it.

"She's a colleague," Deloris went on. "That's all. She's simply here so you're not sitting alone, you're not being photographed alone, and you're not alone. She knows that this is merely for publicity. That's what she does. Besides, it's about time to get your face out more and squash the rumors of the brooding, workaholic hermit."

I laughed as I swirled the remaining whiskey. The aromatic scent of oak with a hint of mint filled my senses, reminding me how good it tasted. "Why? Brooding, workaholic hermit sounds like an accurate description."

Glancing at the custom tuxedo I was wearing, I looked up to Deloris and winked. "Oh, and don't forget devilishly handsome, especially tonight in this monkey suit."

For the first time since she came to find me, she grinned. "Yes, Mr. Demetri, you're handsome. But you know what? It's okay to enjoy life a little too."

"I do. I enjoy working. I enjoy building Demetri Enterprises."

"What about your philanthropic work?"

My head wobbled indecisively upon my shoulders. "It's more Silvia's thing. She cares and all that shit. Give back. Pay it forward. Make the world a better place. My ship sailed on that one, but I get it."

"And she couldn't be here, so you are." The ceiling lights dimmed as the area around the podium grew brighter. "That's your cue," Deloris said.

"I hate this."

"No, you don't," she said as she reached for my not-yet-empty glass, taking it from my grasp and placing it on the bar. "Go."

"Mrs. Witt, we need to discuss the boundaries of your job. I believe you're bordering on insubordination."

She smiled. "Yes, tomorrow we'll have that discussion."

I narrowed my gaze. "If you're still employed."

Instead of answering, she waved her hand—an upside-down queen's wave—shooing me toward the table we both shared.

Straightening my shoulders and adjusting my tie with Deloris a step behind me, we walked into the sea of tables, dodging chairs as murmurs grew quieter and a woman in a long black gown approached the microphone. Without thinking, I reached for my left hand. The smooth band spun as I gave it a twist.

If only.

Millie's gaze met mine as I reached our table and tugged my chair. Once I was seated, she leaned closer. "I was afraid you left."

My body involuntarily stiffened and jaw clenched as sweet perfume replaced the scent of whiskey. The way her hair grazed my cheek caused the small hairs on the back of my neck to stand to attention. I noticed Mrs. Witt's stare as she sat at the other side of the table. Forcing myself to remain seated, I feigned a smile. "And miss this presentation? I wouldn't think of it."

Millie reached for my hand, my left hand. As her fingers grazed my skin, she looked down at the golden band. "Lennox, I know...I'm—"

Pulling my hand away, I shook my head and turned my gaze to the front of the room. The woman in the long black dress had begun to speak.

"...tonight. As you all know, were it not for the generosity of Demetri Enterprises..."

TWO

LENNOX

The shrill noise shattered my restless sleep, the ringing of my phone propelling me from slumber to reality. My heart thundered with that first microsecond of uncertainty. Blinking away the remnants of sleep, the red numbers of my clock came into view: 4:56.

What the fuck?

Taking a deep breath, I pushed myself up to sitting and wiped my hand over my face as my pulse steadied. A day's worth of beard overgrowth abraded my palm before I raked back my hair and reached for the phone. I had little to fear with an early-morning call. Barring disaster, Demetri Enterprises was solid. Sadly, but honestly, there wasn't anything or anyone else who warranted my concern.

That being the case, the incessant ringing wouldn't disturb anyone else. I was the only one in my bed, my bedroom, and my apartment.

Since my alarm was set for four minutes into the future, the loss of four fucking minutes of sleep shouldn't make me angry. And yet, somehow knowing —even without looking—who was responsible for the loss of slumber sent kerosene through my veins.

The last way I wanted to start my day was with a phone call from him.

It wasn't like he was interrupting his sleep. No, it was five hours later in London. Hell, he was probably eyeing his liquor cabinet and making lunch plans.

"What do you want?" I said, after confirming my suspicions with the name that flashed on the screen. I didn't even try to disguise my irritation as I stood with the phone at my ear, my morning wood quickly losing its rigid form. Despite the quelling erection, my cock was in full view. Whether alone or not, I never was one to sleep in...well, anything.

"The day's half over," my father's voice boomed. "I'd assumed my son would at least be awake."

"The day's half over in London. I'm in New York. What do you want?"

603

Oren Demetri was many things: irritating as hell, a pain in my ass, the CEO and founder of Demetri Enterprises, and also, unfortunately, my father.

What he wasn't was a waster of words.

"Things are heating up in California. We need Senator Carroll on our side; we need to know we have the votes."

I shook my head as I paced, putting the proverbial pieces of his puzzle together. That was the way it was with Oren. No niceties, no casual discussion of life. None of that Andy Griffith father-and-son shit. He jumped to the point. "That isn't news. We're all gearing up for the Senate Finance Committee next fall."

"Exactly."

"I've recently had a couple of calls with Carroll."

"Think bigger, son. Calls aren't enough. I'll be in New York tomorrow, and then I'll go on to California and deal with this myself. I thought that you might want to know."

My head spun. I'd been working this deal for over a year. I was the one who knew the ins and outs. Sure, I'd told my dad what he needed to know, but I didn't want or need him coming in like the proverbial knight on the fucking white horse, thinking he was saving a deal that I'd already secured. His presence wouldn't be as a knight; his going to California would be more like a bull in a fucking china shop, leaving nothing but destruction and devastation in his wake.

When I failed to respond immediately, Oren went on. "This takes precedence over other matters and it seems as though if I want it done right—"

I shook my head as I pushed through the raspy tone of my thwarted sleep and made my opinion of his plans known. "No."

"No?"

"Yes. No. You're not storming into Carroll's office and browbeating him when we're as close as we are. I have this covered."

"If you had it covered, you'd know that Senator Carroll won't be in Sacramento at his office this week or in DC. He'll be in San Diego."

"What fucking difference does that make?"

"It makes a difference because he's meeting with heads of some of the big tobacco companies down there. It's a summit of sorts. It's why Demetri Enterprises needs to move. We can't allow them to get their sticky fingers involved. You've primed the pump. I'll go make our position clear."

"No. Our position is clear. The position of Demetri Enterprises is clear." Holding the phone with my right hand, I spun my gold band on my left. The smooth circle provided a small bit of comfort as I worked to contain the bubbling displeasure brought on by this five-fucking-o'clock-in-the-morning tirade.

"It's already settled," Oren said.

"What is settled?" I asked.

"I'll be in New York tomorrow, probably by the sound of things, before you even wake. And then I'll head west. I have reservations in Del Mar."

"Del Mar? You're not crashing the senator's hotel? Why not find out what suite he's in and book the room next door. I know, you could get one of those rooms with the connecting doors. That way you could advise him of our stand while he's taking a shit."

"Lennox, that attitude is exactly why I need to be the one to do this."

"I'm assuming the reservations were made by the company?"

"Yes."

"When do the reservations start in Del Mar?"

"Tomorrow. Time's on my side heading west."

I could think of fifty different reasons not to get on a company plane myself and fly to Del Mar, California, but they all paled in comparison to my desire to keep this deal on track—the track that I planned. It was working.

The future in legalized marijuana was a whole new world—a recently discovered planet. The possibilities were limitless, and I wasn't planning on Demetri coming in second to Big Tobacco or any other industry. I was the man for this job, not the old washed-up has-been bellowing on the other end of this call.

"I won't be here when you arrive in New York," I said matter-of-factly.

"I think you should pry yourself out of bed, and we should spend a few hours—"

"I'll be the one in Del Mar," I interrupted. "I'll take Deloris with me, she has family out there..." That wasn't the only reason for her to accompany me. She was a magician when it came to learning information. By the time we arrived in Southern California, she'd have all the information on Senator Carroll's summit and know exactly who and what we were up against. "...and take your reservations." Before he could reply, I asked the question whose answer I was relatively confident of. "Presidential suite, I presume?"

Like my father, I enjoyed the comforts that our hard work could provide. The Del Mar resort was one of my top ten places to stay when in So Cal for business. The isolation of the resort and the beauty of the view from the presidential suite were enough to entice me to change my schedule and take a few days to solidify Senator Carroll's position and assure us the votes needed for the upcoming Senate committee.

Besides, I would still be able to carry on my work from there. Minus meeting with people here in New York, much of what I did was done via computer and telephone. The presidential suite had a nice office with a view of the communal pool. When I took the time to watch, some of the guests could be downright entertaining.

"Dad?" I asked again. "Presidential suite or were you planning on saving the company a few dollars and reserved a downgrade?"

"I'm still coming to New York."

A smile crept over my lips. *And I won't be here.* I wanted to say that. Instead, I went on with my plan. "Not necessary, Dad. I don't know how long I'll be in Del Mar."

"I booked the suite for a week. I wasn't sure how long it would take."

My smile grew...until it faded.

Was he giving in too easily?

Or maybe it was that he was old and tired and traveling from London to San Diego was more than he wanted to do once he gave it some thought.

"Then it's settled," I declared. "I'm going. You can stay in London and do whatever it is you do."

"Don't screw this up, son. A cocky attitude isn't what works best in business."

"Bye, Dad."

Disconnecting the call, I decided it was a good thing that I knew my own strengths because getting support or encouragement from my father was never going to be my go-to for confidence.

I could do this. I could get this deal secured. I knew it. My father called it cocky. I called it confident. After all, I was the one who'd met with the senator in the past. I was the one who came up with the idea of getting Demetri Enterprises in on the ground floor of legalized cannabis.

Shaking my head, I laughed as I realized my nakedness.

Yeah, Dad, I am cocky.

Even though my morning erection was no longer at full mast, putting on shorts, socks, and running shoes before hitting the treadmill was a good idea.

First, I sent a quick text to Deloris Witt:

"ARRANGE TRANSPORTATION. WE'RE HEADED TO DEL MAR TONIGHT. MY SUITE IS BOOKED BUT WILL NEED TONIGHT ADDED TO THE RESERVATION. BOOK ANOTHER SUITE FOR YOU. I'M SURE YOU'LL TAKE CARE OF EVERYTHING."

The last sentence was purposely ambiguous. There was more to my travel than securing a company plane and a hotel room. There would be people, people I rarely saw. Just knowing they were there was enough. I had other things to concern myself with. Deloris would take care of everything else.

She replied immediately:

"IT WILL BE DONE BEFORE YOU GET TO THE OFFICE."

A few minutes later, as I turned on the treadmill, my wrist buzzed with an incoming message.

"PLANE WILL BE READY BY 3PM."

There were a few appointments to rearrange, but it was doable. I was headed to Del Mar.

THREE

ALEXANDRIA

I lifted my chin to the salty sea breeze, allowing my long auburn hair to float around my face as the Southern California sun warmed my cheeks. The large-brimmed hat in my grasp would soon save me from the dangers hidden within the warm rays.

However, at that moment, I didn't care.

I was on vacation—a much-needed and well-earned vacation—with my best friend. Our future was full of change, but that was yet to come. This was now, and presently my eyes were closed as my skin absorbed the seductive warmth.

"There are a couple of chairs," Chelsea said excitedly as we made our way around the large pool.

Taking in the scene, I was surprised by how many people were already poolside at this early hour. Following her lead, I moved toward the two available lounge chairs not far from the pool's edge. "Perfect."

"Yes, we can see everything from here." She nudged my side as we got closer. "And, boy, is there a lot to see." Her eyebrows danced, peeking out from behind her sunglasses.

"Chels, you go ahead and look. I'm enjoying my time with you and my Kindle. Do you have any idea how many books I've been dying to read? And there isn't one textbook or required reading among them." I patted my beach bag. "This baby is full."

"I didn't know you could really fill a Kindle."

I pursed my lips as they quirked into a grin. "Not literally, babe."

Smoothing her beach towel over the chair, she giggled and lowered her voice. "None of that matters. Remember what you said yesterday?"

As I stretched my legs out on my towel-covered chair, secured my floppy hat, and took in the beautiful scene around me, I thought about Chelsea's question. I did remember what I'd said yesterday. Yesterday I'd declared that for this week I was no longer Alexandria. I was no longer Alex. For this one week, I would forget my past and not think about my future. For one week I would be Charli with an *i* and no last name.

To facilitate that even further, I booked this week at the Del Mar Resort under Chelsea's name. I'd secured the funds, and no one besides my attorneys knew where we were. It was a week to reinvent myself. A week to live as I've never lived before. A week to enjoy just me and my best friend.

"What's your name," my friend asked.

I grinned as I turned her way. "You know, we've been best friends for years. It seems we should be past the introduction phase."

Chelsea swung her legs my direction. "No, I mean it. Tell me your name."

Pulling my Kindle from my beach bag, I mumbled, "Charli."

"No way, girl. Louder."

"Charli."

"Louder," she said, practically shouting the demand.

"Stop it. People will stare."

"Let them stare. I don't care. You don't care about them. You're Charli with an *i*."

I shook my head. "You're one crazy-assed lady sometimes."

She nonchalantly hitched her shoulder. "That's why you love me. I make life fun."

There was no questioning her statement. Chelsea not only made her own life fun, but she made life fun for everyone around her. She was nothing like the girls I'd known in Savannah. Meeting as roommates our first year at Stanford was the best thing that ever happened. No matter what life's ups and downs entailed, she was there. She was the sister I never had. "I do love you." Raising my voice, I proclaimed, "And I'm Charli."

"With an *i*."

"Yes, with an *i*."

"Hey," Chelsea said, her gaze going to the handsome man in khaki shorts with a tray bearing frozen concoctions. The customary navy resort jacket was replaced with a collared shirt in the same color with the Del Mar emblem on the chest. No doubt, more comfortable to wear in the sunshine. "We should get drinks."

"We just had breakfast."

"And your point is...?"

She raised her hand as he came our way.

"Ladies, may I help you?"

"Yes," Chelsea said excitedly, "I think I'll have a—"

"A strawberry-mango slushy," I interrupted. "No alcohol."

My friend turned my way. Even with her sunglasses, I could see the question in her expression.

"Babe, you do what you want. I want to enjoy myself and remember it."

"Fine," she said, turning back to the waiter. "I'll have the same. But don't go far. It won't be our last order."

The man smiled politely as he took our room information and walked away.

Time passed as the sun grew warmer, my slushy turned to liquid, and the large pool area became more crowded. With my mind on the story on my Kindle, I was lost in the words when Chelsea nudged my side.

"Hey, you're not listening."

"What?"

"Do you see those two good-looking guys over there? They keep looking our direction." When I started to turn, she said, "Don't look."

"How can I see them if I don't look?"

"Okay, just a quick look."

I turned. As I did, it was hard if not impossible not to see. This resort was filled with fine specimens of male and female patrons. After all, the resort catered to the elite. Those people spent a lot of time and money making sure their outer selves were perfection. I knew too well that when it came to pretty people, that perfection didn't always translate to their inner selves.

In the direction that Chelsea had tilted her head were two men about our age staring directly at us. Everything inside me wanted to turn back to the story on my Kindle, and then I remembered my one-week mission. I lowered my sunglasses and returned their attention. The one with a surfer's body and blond hair did the same. His closed-lip grin was cocky and confident.

Before I could do more than smile, he and his friend were up and moving our direction. "Shit," I said. "They're coming our way."

"I said look, not invite him over."

It was too late.

FOUR

LENNOX

I paced back and forth in the office of the presidential suite. Deloris went above and beyond. The information she obtained was now on my computer. I knew who was attending Senator Carroll's summit and most of the important information regarding their companies and bids. Hell, I even knew arbitrary information.

It was my first full day in California, and I'd already arranged a meeting for later in the afternoon with the senator. I planned to feel things out in person before jumping to conclusions, before deciding on my course of action for the rest of the week.

This was why I was better at this than my father. I wouldn't barge into the senator's plans; instead, I would make my presence known in a confident and assertive way, reminding him of the agreements we'd already made and the plans we had for the future finance committee.

The reason for my pacing was that I had a couple of hours to kill before our meeting. The flight, lack of my own bed, and inability to exercise this morning had me feeling itchy and on edge, as if I were ready to jump out of my own skin. Of course, the resort had an exercise facility, but I rarely did communal activities. I preferred my own treadmill in my own apartment with just me and the morning news getting me up to date on the foreign markets.

Now that time had passed. I'd updated myself with coffee and my computer screen. It wasn't enough. There was even the possibility that the coffee was adding to my jumpiness. To make matters worse, the resort was filling my private pool. I wasn't sure why in the fuck they didn't have it already filled. Deloris said it had something to do with extending the reservation. They weren't expecting a Demetri here until today.

The large pool through the window and stories below caught my attention. I needed to blow off steam. I could either try the exercise room or throw on some swim trunks and do a few laps. Even though most of the chairs seemed filled, the water was relatively empty. That was the way with places like this. The people were merely decorations, not living breathing beings. The exception was the hot tub. That was filled with laughing, talking people. I didn't want the hot tub—I didn't want people. I wanted to push myself. I could accomplish that with a series of laps, clear my mind, and prepare myself for my afternoon meeting.

Leaving the office, I made my way to the suite's balcony to check on the pool's filling progress. Beyond the railings, the ocean glittered all the way to the horizon. The view from this suite was stunning at all times of day; however, I particularly loved the sunsets in Del Mar.

I exhaled, finding the private pool still half empty. Maybe it was half full? I had too much shit on my mind to figure out what my initial perception said about my current mental well-being.

"Deloris, I'm headed down to the pool to swim laps," I said a few minutes later, as I passed through the living area wearing my trunks and flip-flops.

"You're going to the pool?" she asked. "The one with people?"

"Yes."

"Who are you?"

"I'm someone who is about to lose my shit. I'm anxious to see the senator and with the names and information you provided, I want to rush the meeting. Swimming will...it will..." I searched for the right word.

Deloris nodded. "Go. You have time. Maybe it will help put things in focus."

Focus, as if a swim could align the magnitude of my thoughts.

The doors of the elevator closed as I was whisked down to the ground floor. The private elevator was another reason I liked this resort.

"Mr. Demetri," the doorman guarding the private hallway to the isolated elevator said. "Sir, I'm Fredrick. If you need anything, please don't hesitate to ask."

"Thank you, Fredrick. I'd like water in my pool. Other than that, everything is as accommodating as usual."

"Sir, we are very sorry. There was evidently a mix-up on your arrival. We promise to have it filled by this afternoon. May I secure you a chair at the large pool?"

"That won't be necessary. I only plan to swim and return."

He nodded. "If you change your mind, it will be immediately arranged."

Thoughts of the resort's dedication to service replaced my annoyance over the pool situation. It was as I was mulling the names over in my mind—the names that Deloris had discovered—that *she* caught my attention.

For only a moment, my steps stuttered.

This wasn't me.

I didn't notice women, not in a way that knocked me off my feet while simultaneously, rerouting my circulation. And yet, as I stood in the Southern California sunshine, surrounded by more people than I cared for, I saw only one. At the far end of the pool, with a large floppy hat and a figure that beckoned me closer, a cosmic explosion erupted.

I stood unmoving as the stars shifted.

At the other end of the pool was one of the only women to ever take my breath away.

Perhaps she is a mirage?

Kicking off my sandals, I dove into the pool, allowing the cool water to return my blood supply to where it belonged, especially when surrounded by strangers. I pushed against the water, stroke after stroke, lifting my head for air as I somersaulted and swam the other direction—away from her.

It didn't help. Even under the water, even behind my closed eyes, I saw her.

Reading and smiling, as if the words she saw gave her happiness. With each stroke, I became filled with an overwhelming need, the need to be the one who did that—to provide her happiness, relief, and reason to smile. The feeling was overpowering in a way I hadn't experienced since...my thumb went to the gold band. In the cool water it rotated easier than usual, almost too easily.

Ten lengths back and forth and I stood in the shallow end. The water came to below my waist as I took in the view, now different than earlier. Where before she'd been reading, now she was talking with the woman by her side. I was about to swim another lap when I noticed two men approaching them.

It shouldn't upset me. I didn't have any right to step in, and yet, I recognized the men.

Men or man was a generous description. They were really only boys. They worked this resort and I knew that. They didn't work *at* this resort. They worked it.

I wasn't sure what kind of a deal they had with the management. Maybe the young men cut the supervision in on their earnings. Maybe the resort personnel turned a blind eye or perhaps refused to see what was under their noses. I didn't care. The two blonds now standing near her and her friend were familiar because from my view high above, I'd watched as they conned women out of money, drinks, food, and God knows what else.

It wasn't a conscious decision, yet before I knew it, I was at the end of the pool near her chair.

In the time it took me to swim the length, her friend had gone and one of the blonds was in the chair beside her. My muscles flexed as I pulled myself from the water.

His voice was flirtatious and filled with suggestion. Another step closer to his chair and I could hear him better. It took almost more self-restraint than I possessed to keep my hands at my side. I imagined lifting the little shit from the chair and throwing him into the pool where I'd just been.

"...we're being secretive," he said. "My guess is there's a boyfriend..." He glanced at her hand. "...no ring. So it can't be a fiancé. But there's someone back wherever home is."

"Guess again." Her voice was a melody flowing through the air, breaking the sameness of my mundane monotone world.

"You're an aspiring actress, and this is the week before you do a big shoot."

She laughed. "Two strikes. One more and you're—"

"Out," I said, unable to remain silent any longer. With the sun to my back, my shadow loomed over their legs as the muscles in my neck tightened and my hands balled into fists at my sides. There was something about seeing her with this con artist that brought out a primal response.

No longer was I thinking about the senator or my meeting. Rescuing this beauty was my only thought. That's not true. Causing bodily harm to Mike or Max or whatever the hell he was calling himself today was also in my thoughts.

When they didn't speak, I repeated, "You're out."

"Excuse me?" the little shit asked. "Who the hell are you?"

She didn't speak. Instead, the beauty in the hat and bikini lowered her sunglasses, revealing the most stunning golden eyes. Peering up at me, they sparkled with the reflections of the sun, surf, and glistening pool.

Each second her gaze lingered on me, mine did the same on her.

There was a buzz of electricity that I'd forgotten. Cosmic alignment. A magnetic pull that I couldn't back away from if I'd tried. My feet were rooted to the concrete as my jaw clenched.

I no longer cared about the little shit beside her. I couldn't even think about him as I unashamedly scanned from her dark auburn hair and floppy hat, along her sexy, toned body barely concealed by the material of her bathing suit, and all the way to her brightly painted toes. The longer I stared, the more intense the connection.

She felt it too. I knew it. Not only in my heart but by the way her skin peppered with goose bumps. My cheeks rose as my attention went to the way her nipples pebbled beneath the thin material.

Fuck. I needed to see under that material.

How do you miss a feeling when you forgot it existed?

I wasn't sure. It had been too long since I'd felt like this. The energy was potent to the point of overpowering. I turned back to the blond shit and lowered the tone of my voice. It came out decisive, protective, and arrogant.

"I'm her husband. That person you mentioned..." I paused to let my words sink in, "is me and I'm not somewhere else. I'm here. Leave my wife alone or I'll have you thrown out."

My stare zeroed in on the boy until he shook his head, lifted his hands in surrender, and wisely stood. I was easily six inches taller than him, probably outweighed him by thirty pounds, and none of that mentioned my time as an MMA champion. It would be nothing to send him squirming into the pool.

That wasn't my objective. I simply wanted him gone.

"Bye, Charli with an *i*," he said. But before he walked away, he added, "Maybe you should wear your rings?"

His words prompted me to scan her fingers. He was right. She was without a ring. I couldn't refrain from adding to her scolding, "Yes, *Charli*, don't tell me you've misplaced them again."

Her gaze never left mine as her lips quirked upward to a grin. "No. I'm most certain they're right where I left them."

I hope you enjoyed this alternative POV to the beginning of Betrayal, book one of the Infidelity series (not about cheating).

If this was your first experience with Lennox Demetri and Alexandria Collins and, after this small taste, you'd like to learn more about this sexy, cocky hero and strong, intelligent heroine, please give Betrayal a chance. It's the first book of the completed six-book Infidelity series and is free on all sales platforms: https://www.aleatharomig.com/betrayal-free

*For those of you who have met Lennox and Alex and have enjoyed the Infidelity series... I have **one more chapter** for you.*

Warning: if you haven't read the Infidelity series, the bonus chapter contains spoilers.

Enjoy!

And turn the page.

BONUS CHAPTER

Nox: (You've been warned)

Years into the future

My footsteps echoed up the stairs. Reaching the top, I stilled, not wanting to wake anyone at this late hour. Step by step, I continued until I reached the large double doors to our bedroom suite. I imagined Charli asleep in our bed, her beautiful hair fanned over her pillow, her pert lips parted as she breathed.

My dick hardened as I pictured her beneath the blankets, her sexy body unclothed, nothing to stop my touch as I pulled her warmth close.

I shook my head. That fantasy most certainly wouldn't be the reality. Not with our two children sleeping down the hall, the same two children who had strict orders not to disturb Mom and Dad while we slept.

The same two who managed at least one middle-of-the-night emergency every other night.

Of course, emergencies for a six-and-a-half-year-old beautiful girl and her nearly three-year-old rambunctious brother weren't exactly the kind of emergencies that in my head warranted the opening of our bedroom door or the leaping into our bed. Yet on each occasion, in their minds, their reasons were valid.

Unquenchable thirst.

Ravenous hunger.

You'd think we starved the poor children.

A noise.

A monster under the bed.

The list could go on and on.

The moral of that story was that my beautiful wife no longer slept in the nude nor did I. My lips quirked upward as I reached for the door handle. I was all right with that, unwrapping her was equally as fun and built the anticipation.

The darkened suite was bathed in the moon's blue glint as the sphere hung low over the Long Island Sound and cast eerie shadows over the familiar surroundings. Turning to the bed, I found it empty. Even the covers were undisturbed.

My pulse quickened.

It was after midnight. I'd gotten home as soon as I could from the meetings on the West Coast. My Charli was great about keeping me informed of her whereabouts. So too was her necklace. She should be here.

Where was she?

Last week she'd taken the children to Savannah for some annual party her mother threw. It was funny to think about the way my wife now enjoyed her childhood home, something that came about after we met.

One night, she explained it to me.

"I want Angi and Dominic to love Montague Manor. Someday they will be the ones who decide what happens with it. I don't want it to be a monstrous, unfriendly castle. I want them to think of it as a home."

"Their grandparents' home," I said.

Charli smiled. "As weird as that still is, yes. And also where their momma grew up."

"If it makes you happy..."

"It does," she said. "And you don't know how much I like that."

Looking around our house in Rye where we now lived and called home, I did know.

I wasn't able to go with my family to that party, though they flew on our bat plane.

Although I refused to be the workaholic my father was while I was young, there was still work that needed to be done. There were still Demetri Enterprises and Montague Corporation. Charli and I knew the pressures. She worked part time in Demetri Enterprises' legal department. After all that she and her mother had been through, learning the ins and outs of corporate law became her passion.

My wife was as smart as they came and nothing stood in her way.

However, I was thankful that practicing law wasn't her only passion. And as I scanned our darkened suite, I wondered about another, the passion I'd planned on showing her upon my arrival home.

The drapes covering the glass doors leading to our balcony rustled in the autumn breeze as a shadow outside caught my attention.

Going to the open door, I peered out. Standing at the railing in a long satin robe was my wife. Her beautiful hair wasn't fanned over her pillow, but blowing back, clearing her gorgeous face as she watched the lights play across the dark waters of the sound.

"Princess?"

Charli jumped as she spun my direction. "Oh my God, Nox, you scared me."

In merely one stride, I was before her, my hands upon her arms as I pulled her petite frame close to mine. "What are you doing out here? It's late."

She nodded against my chest as we melded together. Like two pieces of an interlocking puzzle, we were strong on our own, but together we were invincible. "I was waiting for you. Isaac said you wouldn't be too late."

I grinned. "I told you the same thing."

She peered upward as her golden eyes shone with amusement. "And I believed you. I just like confirmation from Isaac or Deloris."

Lifting her chin, I brushed my lips over hers. The small moan as she snuggled closer returned the blood to my cock. Wrapping my arms around her small waist, I pulled her closer.

"Nox?"

"Princess, I've missed you."

Her small hand found its way to the front of my trousers and rubbed my growing erection. "I didn't notice."

My head fell backward with a laugh. "Then I'm losing my touch."

"No way," she purred. "I've missed you, too."

Reaching for her hand, I tugged her inside our room. The late September night air held a hint of the impending season change, leaving her hand chilled in my grasp. "How about we go check on the kids," I asked, "and then we come back here and I show you how much I missed you?"

Charli nodded. "I like that. Just please don't wake them."

"No way. I have plans for our bed that include two, not four."

I slipped off my shoes and wiggled my sock-covered toes, peering at her with a grin and a wink. "We can be sneaky."

"I like sneaky," she said. "Like Batman."

"I think that would be stealthy."

Together we made our way first to Dominic's room. At nearly three years of age, he resembled something of a starfish as he slept, arms and legs pointing all different directions. His little head was covered with dark hair, reminding me of myself as a child. And as if life hadn't thrown us enough obstacles, he seemed to have a bit of my defiant attitude. When he's older, some may call it cocky.

It was hard to argue that Charli and I were in for some rough waters as opinions clashed. Luckily, right now our disagreements were over things like screen time and snacks. My father was quick to remind us that we had no idea what we were in for, but he would enjoy watching every minute of it.

I ran my palm over my son's hair. When he barely noticed, I leaned down and gave him a kiss. My senses were filled with the scent of baby shampoo and lotion. It was something Jane had done for Charli when she was young, and now my wife insisted on nightly baths with head-to-toe lotion. It had gone on for all of their lives. At this point, it was almost as if the children couldn't sleep without it.

Closing Dominic's door, we moved farther down the hall to Angelina's room. Her lilac walls glowed by the light of her nightlight. I stifled a giggle as Charli began to move Angi's menagerie of stuffed animals until she uncovered our daughter. I wasn't sure how our little girl slept with all of those friends in her bed. However, from experience, I could attest that if even one were missing, the entire household was on alert until the search-and-rescue mission was complete.

No one slept until the wayward animal was found and safely returned to her bed.

The image I'd had of Charli was there before us, shrunk to pint-sized form, as we stood above Angi's bed. Long auburn curls fanned over her pillow and her small mouth was drawn to a bow as she slept. Again, I ran my hand over her hair and leaned down to give her a kiss.

"Daddy?" she said, rolling toward us.

"Yes, princess. I'm home."

"Good. I love you."

"I love you, too. Go back to sleep."

"All right."

Charli and I stood for a moment in complete quiet, both undoubtedly saying silent prayers that our daughter would do as she was told and go back to sleep. When she remained still, Charli and I made our way back to the hallway. As soon as I closed the door, Charli shook her head and leaned against my chest.

"I guarantee she won't remember that in the morning. If she were really awake, that would not have gone as well."

I puffed my chest. "Even in her sleep she loves her daddy."

Charli reached for my hand. "Now, Mr. Demetri, come with me. It's my turn to love her daddy."

My smile grew as we made our way down the hall and back to our room.

Taking off my jacket and throwing it to a chair, I said, "Beautiful, I know it's late, but could I convince you to wait up for me while I take a quick shower?"

Charli leaned against the wall and crossed her arms over her breasts. Her gaze sparkled as she watched me undress. "I think my answer is no."

I stopped in motion as I removed my shirt over my shoulders. "No?"

She nodded with a grin. "No."

"You won't stay awake?"

She reached for the sash of her robe, untying the tether and releasing the satin, revealing that underneath she was as I had imagined—every inch of my wife, my princess, at my disposal. "I won't wait." She stepped forward, allowing the white robe to float to the floor as she reached for my belt. Her hand stilled on the buckle—the one with a silver swirl—as she looked up at me. "I've always been partial to this belt."

Fuck!

"Princess, you're playing with fire."

"After all these years, haven't you noticed? I like to be burnt."

Minutes later, mist filled the air within the shower as warm spray peppered our skin. As the water flattened her hair and covered mine, I took her in my arms, pulling her close. She was as stunning as the day we met. "Have I told you that on the day I first saw you in Del Mar, it was as if the stars had aligned?"

Her smile grew. "You have. And I felt the same way. Like the world—no, the universe—wouldn't be right if we weren't together."

"I never knew I could love someone again. You're my whole world. I hate leaving you and the kids for work."

Charli shook her head. "I understand. I'm pretty busy here, and I'm all right with that." She took a step back. "Are you?"

"Am I all right with your being here with the kids and working in legal? Of course. I'm all right with your doing whatever makes you happy. I would just like to be the one doing it with you."

"And you are." She reached for my hand and placed it on her flat stomach. "I wasn't sure how to tell you..."

My eyes widened as I fell to my knees on the floor of our shower. After peppering her stomach with soft kisses, I looked up. "You're...?"

She nodded as her eyes grew glassy. "We're."

I tugged her toward me, caressing and kissing. It was as her head fell backward that I stood. "You're absolutely sure?"

"I am. I went to the doctor today."

"I love you."

She wrapped her arms around my waist. "I love you, too."

My grin quirked upward. "Maybe we should keep trying? I mean, I want to be confident."

"Oh, Nox. I'm good with continuing to try, but lack of confidence has never been your problem."

Some call it cocky.

As my wife and I became one in the warm shower and again in our large bed, I didn't care what it was called. I was home with my family, the moon shining outside, and the stars perfectly aligned.

If you haven't read the Infidelity *series, I promise you many twists and turns in this six-book saga before reaching this point. Don't miss the "...sexy suspense saga that will leave you hot, bothered, and begging for more." ~ Redbook magazine.*

https://www.aleatharomig.com/infidelity-series

ABOUT THE AUTHOR

Aleatha Romig is a New York Times, Wall Street Journal, and USA Today best-selling author who lives in Indiana, USA. She grew up in Mishawaka, graduated from Indiana University, and is currently living south of Indianapolis. Aleatha has raised three children with her high school sweetheart and husband of over thirty years. Before she became a full-time author, she worked days as a dental hygienist and spent her nights writing. Now, when she's not imagining mind-blowing twists and turns, she likes to spend her time a with her family and friends. Her other pastimes include reading and creating heroes/anti-heroes who haunt your dreams!

Aleatha released her first novel, CONSEQUENCES, in August of 2011. CONSEQUENCES became a bestselling series with five novels and two companions released from 2011 through 2015. The compelling and epic story of Anthony and Claire Rawlings has graced more than half a million e-readers. Aleatha released the first of her series TALES FROM THE DARK SIDE, INSIDIOUS, in the fall of 2014. These stand-alone thrillers continue Aleatha's twisted style with an increase in heat.

In the fall of 2015, Aleatha moved headfirst into the world of dark romantic suspense saga with the release of BETRAYAL, the first of her five-novel INFIDELITY series that has taken the reading world by storm. She also began her traditional publishing career with Thomas and Mercer. Her books INTO THE LIGHT and AWAY FROM THE DARK were published through this mystery/thriller publisher in 2016.

In the spring of 2017, Aleatha released her first stand-alone, fun, and sexy romantic comedy PLUS ONE, followed by ONE NIGHT, A SECRET ONE, and ANOTHER ONE.

Aleatha is a "Published Author's Network" member of the Romance Writers of America and PEN America. She is represented by Kevan Lyon of Marsal Lyon Literary Agency.

Facebook: https://www.facebook.com/AleathaRomig
Amazon: http:// amazon.com/author/aleatharomig
BookBub: https://www.bookbub.com/authors/aleatha-romig
Goodreads: http://www.goodreads.com/author/show/5131072.Aleatha_Romig
Instagram: http://instagram.com/aleatharomig
Twitter: https://twitter.com/AleathaRomig

ALSO BY ALEATHA ROMIG

ALEATHA'S LIGHTER ONES

Stand-alone "lighter" romances

PLUS ONE

A SECRET ONE

ONE NIGHT

INFIDELITY SERIES:

BETRAYAL

Book #1

(October 2015)

CUNNING

Book #2

(January 2016)

DECEPTION

Book #3

(May 2016)

ENTRAPMENT

Book #4

(September 2016)

FIDELITY

Book #5

(January 2017)

RESPECT:

A stand-alone Infidelity novel

(January 2018)

DUPLICITY

(Completely unrelated to book #1)

Release TBA

THE VAULT

Sexy, fun stand-alone novellas showcasing the hot and steamy side of Aleatha.

UNCONVENTIONAL

(January 2018)

(Originally appeared in THE VAULT anthology)

UNEXPECTED

(Coming August of 2018)

ALL: A GRIP & BRIS STORY

KENNEDY RYAN

Dear Reader:
If you have not read the GRIP Series—*FLOW, GRIP & STILL*—this story contains spoilers.

Please consider starting the series for FREE with *FLOW*.

Grip, a prominent musician and social activist, and his manager-wife Bristol, navigate the life that's all they ever wanted, and more than they bargained for.

ONE

GRIP

I hate waking up to an empty bed.
Scratch that.

I hate waking up without my wife. I draw that distinction because there was a time when I loved stretching from one corner of a California king to the other. After growing up in tiny, cramped spaces—which were sometimes shared with various family members, depending on their "situation" at the time—when I had my own space, my own bed, I luxuriated in it. But it only took sleeping with Bristol once to make any bed she's not in feel just . . . empty.

It isn't even light outside yet. Shadows cloak our bedroom. I press the little light on the cheap ass watch Bristol won for me so many years ago. This thing has been to the shop a lot, but it's still ticking enough to show me it's four in the morning. I've only been asleep two hours after a long night at the studio.

With the drapes drawn, barely a sliver of moonlight penetrates the darkness. I caress the rumpled, still-warm spot where Bristol should be and stare up at the ceiling. What my eyes can't see, my memory paints on the dark canvas overhead. A Ferris wheel with us at the top sharing our first kiss, Bristol's short, sweet breaths and urgent hands intoxicating me. I see Bristol, gorgeous against a back-drop of scarlet sand in the Dubai desert. Bristol under a night sky spilling snowflakes like secrets, and me on my knees, asking her—shit, begging her—to marry me. I see her standing in a mountaintop chapel with majestic, white-capped peaks outdone by the devotion shining from her eyes as I lay my heart at her feet, verse by verse in the vows I wrote for her. I see her weeping, broken, devastated on the hardest day of our lives. And I see her joy-lit face when she gave birth to our children

Our life together is panoramic, stretched wide in ugliness and pain, vast in love and passion. I wouldn't trade one minute of it and I savor every day we have together. Not everyone gets to spend this life with their soul mate. Some walk all their days with half a heart, with the ache of something missing. I know what that feels like, and I hope to never feel it again.

Despite the exhaustion weighing me down, I swing my legs over the side of the bed, scrubbing a weary hand over my face. Not bothering to grab sweatpants, I walk from our bedroom and down the hall in my briefs. First stop is Nina's room. Our little girl sleeps like a log. She zips all over this house with boundless energy, a two-year-old tornado, leaving a trail of toys, soiled clothes, and hair bows in her wake. Every night it's a fight to get her to bed. Once she's asleep, though, not a peep.

Her nightlight illuminates the plump curve of her cheeks and the soft cloud of dark, curly hair fanned out on her pillow. I draw a sharp breath through the emotion tightening my chest. What I had with Bristol was all-encompassing before, but having Nina added another dimension to our love, to our lives, that I couldn't have conceived before my daughter. Words are my creative currency, but this feeling defies words, goes beyond the scope of what I can articulate. It didn't exist until this little girl did. It was born with her. Family has always been important to me, but this is another level. The people under this roof are my whole world. Not the Grammys or the fame or the money—none of it counts for shit without them.

I'm still smiling about my daughter's out-like-a-light state when I pad down the hall to find Bristol. She's in the nursery feeding our five-month-old son Martin. I hope I never get used to this, to the way my heart contracts when I see her breastfeeding. Or cooking dinner. Doing Nina's hair. Brushing her teeth. Putting on makeup. Practicing yoga poses. Bristol doesn't have to be doing anything monumental to make my heart stop. Just the fact that she's in my life, the center of my world, makes me count my blessings.

She looks up from her seat in the glider and smiles at me as I lean one shoulder against the doorframe.

"Hi," she says, her voice and eyes warm and soft. I smile back but don't speak. I just take her in. She recently cut her hair to just above her shoulders, and it halos around her face in dark waves and coppery streaks. Martin has fallen asleep at her breast, idly suckling every few seconds even though he isn't awake to enjoy it.

But I'm enjoying it.

Bris wore one of my shirts to bed, which she does on purpose because she knows how damn sexy I think it is. The buttons open to her navel, and one panel of the shirt covers her left side, but the other falls away to bare her right shoulder and breast where Martin's lucky little mouth wraps around a nipple.

"Hi," I finally reply, my voice a little hoarse and my dick stiff in my briefs.

"I tried to stay awake," she whispers. "But I was too tired. How'd the recording session go?"

"Not great." I push out a frustrated breath. "Everything feels forced."

I walk deeper into the room until I reach them, bending to take Martin from her, careful not to wake him. Her nipple, distended, shiny and wet, pops from his mouth. I lean down to her ear, sucking the lobe between my lips.

"Grip." Bristol's breath stutters and her eyes drift closed.

Holding Martin to my chest, I trail kisses over her jaw and down to her collarbone.

"Go wait for me," I say, my voice low and lust-rough. "I got him."

She stands and quickly leaves the room while I lay my son in his crib.

He squirms and twists as soon as his little body hits the mattress.

"Missed you today, handsome boy," I say softly, pushing thick curls off his round face.

His eyes, dark like mine where Nina's are gray like Bristol's, snap open. I catch a curse, hoping he goes right back to sleep so I can go fuck his mother. Our gazes lock in the lamplight for a few seconds before his long lashes flutter, his head lolls to the side, and he falls back asleep.

Who would believe such a little person would require so much work? So much vigilance? Bristol is back in the office for half days, but the rest of the time she's here with Nina and Martin. I'm here when I can be, and a nanny, whom Bristol vetted like the FBI, helps for a few hours a week. Sarah, Bristol's assistant, is at our house all the time working. Bris is constantly in Zoom meetings and on teleconference calls. She works harder than ever.

I help, of course, but I'm preparing for the next album and a tour. I've been more absent than I like to be. On the surface, everything is working, but there's a restlessness I've been trying to ignore so I can go through the motions of managing this complicated life of ours. I miss my time with Bris. I need more of her. If I sound like a whiny, needy wuss, I don't really care. If there is one thing I'm in tune with, it's my most base needs. And there is nothing more essential, more fundamental to my happiness, than my wife.

When I make it to our bedroom, I'm still considering her heavy workload, the time she devotes to our kids, and most of all—most selfishly of all—how little time I've had with her since Martin was born.

Those thoughts fly away on a horny breeze when I see Bristol naked in Lotus pose in the middle of our bed. Her breasts are bigger. Ass is fuller. She's always been slim, and still is, but there's a ripeness to her body after Martin that is sexy as fuck. She keeps trying to Pilate it away and yoga it off, but I love it.

"Did Martin wake up?" she asks.

Our bedside lamps casts light over the supple lines of her body, showing me the wide, sensual curve of her mouth. The thick, rosy lips exposed between her legs. The delicately muscled plane of her stomach. The small scar from the C-section she had with our first child.

"He's asleep, yeah." I stand at the side of the bed and brush my thumb under her eyes, evidence of just how hard she's been working and how little rest she's getting. "Which is what you need to do."

I should let her sleep. Guilt reaches every part of me . . . except my dick, which obstinately remains erect, undaunted and unsoftened by guilt.

"What I need to do," she says, eyes locked with mine while her hand latches on to the pole poking through my briefs, "is take care of my husband."

I haul air through my nostrils and expel it harshly through my mouth at her touch. I train my eyes above tit level because, if I look any lower, I'll be all over her, all up in her, ramming from behind, from the side, from any angle I can get it.

Don't look down. Don't look down.

I mentally repeat the mantra like I'm walking a tightrope.

"I'm all right, babe." I lie through gritted teeth. "Really. Get some sleep."

Disappointment flashes across her pretty features, quickly followed by determination. She leans back on one elbow and spreads her legs, slipping a hand between them.

"You go on to sleep, Grip," she says, dropping her head back and moaning. "I'm just gonna come at least once before I turn in."

Motherfucker.

Literally.

Without acknowledging her dirty trick, I grab behind her knees and drag her to the edge of the bed. Her husky laugh floats around us in the dimly lit room.

"Changed your mind?" Her eyelids fall to half-mast over smoky gray eyes.

"You changed it for me," I reply, tipping one side of my mouth. "Touching my pussy."

"*Your* pussy?" A lift of her brows challenges my possessiveness.

I shrug and drop to my knees, putting my face on level with the pussy in question.

"You be the judge," I say before lowering my head, widening her thighs with a press of my hands, then spreading her lips with my fingers and burying my tongue in her wetness.

We both groan.

There is nothing like this pussy. I run my nose along the slick slit before swiping my tongue through her juices.

"Oh, good Lord," Bristol breathes, rolling her hips into my greedy mouth. "Fuck, yes, Grip. Don't stop."

To quote GRiZMATiK . . . as we proceed.

Two fingers plunge inside, and I suck on her clit. She bucks against my face and loops her long legs over my shoulders, digging her heels into my back. I tug until her ass hangs just off the bed and she's supported by the grip I have on her thighs. I devour her, table manners discarded. Grunting, slurping. She comes once, and I want seconds.

"Grip, stop!" She gasps. "I can't take . . . please."

"Whose pussy is it, Bris?" I ask, biting one plump lip and then the other.

Silence. Stubborn woman makes this so much damn fun.

I apply my mouth with more enthusiasm, and then run my thumb through the wetness before plunging it into her ass to the knuckle.

"Ahhhhhh! Shit!"

Her scream pierces the quiet. With my thumb working her ass like a job, I reach up to cover her mouth.

"Whose pussy, Bris?" I demand, my tongue darting into one hole and my thumb fucking the other.

"Y-yours," she mumbles under my hand, the word breath-starved and choppy. "It's your pussy."

I plunge my thumb in deeper until my palm touches her ass, and she bucks wildly, her hand gripping the back of my neck and holding me in place while she thrusts against my lips. Once the tremors racking her body die to twitches and her moans settle into tiny whimpers, I carefully lift her, taking her place on the edge of the bed and turning her to spread her thighs over mine. She snuggles into my neck, the scent of her skin and shampoo mingling with the sweet muskiness covering my face and coating her thighs.

"Holy shit," she says, her deep-throated chuckle rumbling into the curve of my neck and shoulder. "I can't think straight. Did you suck my brain out when you were down there?"

"Focus. I think you mentioned something about taking care of your husband." It's my turn to lean back on one elbow. I gesture to the briefs I'm still wearing and the obviously eager erection straining to get out and in.

"It's all coming back to me." She shoots me a mischievous glance from under long, curly lashes.

"If it 'comes' any louder, you'll wake the neighbors *and* the kids," I warn her, my grin smug. "And the way I feel right now, Martin will just have to cry until Daddy's done."

"Ah, speaking of Martin," she says, her smile and the look in her eyes devolving into something baser.

My dick gets even harder. She grins. She knows. She leans up and cups her breasts, her thumbs stroking the fat nipples.

"You can taste. It's just us, Grip."

She caresses her breasts in hypnotic circles, and I'm mesmerized by how the nipples peak and harden. I grip her back, my fingers meeting on her spine, and I pull her breasts to my face. They're slightly damp when I pull one into my mouth and suck so hard that she draws a sharp breath above me, but I don't stop. I find a rhythm, my mouth and tongue and teeth cooperating to get what I want. When a few drops of her milk hit my tongue, it drives us both into a frenzy.

"That is so fucking hot," she gasps, scrambling to get my briefs down and off before she scoots as close as possible on my lap, the smooth skin of her thighs dragging over the rougher skin of mine.

She holds my cock in her hand, fisting it tight, pushing up and down, her thumb caressing the head.

"Don't play with it, babe," I say abruptly. "Take it."

I need to feel her tight and wet and hot around me. Beyond the horniness— *which let the record show, is at an all-time high*—I need that connection. The one we've forged through years, through pain, through unimagined highs and heart-crushing lows. So much in our lives is changing, but this never does. This scorching slide of her flesh on mine, of her taking me in so tightly, is a sweet chokehold on my cock that makes me hiss. I would know this pussy in the dark. I could be blind and half-dead, and you couldn't fool me with another woman. Just this one. This fit. This perfect friction. The grooves of our souls fit as tightly as our bodies do.

Her forehead drops to mine, panting breaths misting my lips while she rides me, her arms hooked behind my neck. The pace grows more frantic as I thrust up aggressively, meeting her pussy halfway. I grab her ass cheeks, spreading them and taking over the rhythm so I can slam her body down onto mine over and over, deliberately. We're grunting, rutting animals mindlessly taking our pleasure by force. Our guttural sounds bounce off the walls. Bristol's head tips back and then down, tears sliding over her cheeks and onto her bouncing breasts. I lean forward, lapping at the mixture of her milk and her tears before sucking her nipple hard. Biting her breast hard.

"Grip!" Bristol comes like a rocket, flattening her hand against my chest for support.

The sound of her coming undone, the contraction of her body squeezing every ounce of pleasure from me, sends me over the edge. I swallow my shout, having just enough presence of mind not to wake the kids. It doesn't matter if I own Bristol's pussy. This woman owns my heart. She's got my mind, my will, my soul, my emotions—all of it on lock. Happily trapped in the palm of her hand.

She's still trembling against me when I pick her up and lay her against the pillows. Now that we fucked the edge off, there is room for other things. Like exhaustion. She's already half asleep.

"Love you," she murmurs, turning onto her side and tucking her pillow between her head and her shoulder.

I *was* exhausted, but now I'm wound up, unable to sleep. Mind-blowing sex opens the floodgates. Everything pours into my mind at once. Possible fixes for the song that wasn't working tonight in the studio. The memory of my kids up the hall, snug and secure in their beds, and almost too beautiful for words. The sounds of Bristol coming, her whispers fueled by pleasure.

The shadows under her eyes.

As much as it feels like the planet shakes when we make love . . . that the very foundations of the earth shift, tectonic plates sliding to make a whole new world, it isn't. Those dark circles under her eyes remind me that the things I was concerned about before we made love still need to be addressed.

First light filters in through tiny cracks where the drapes aren't completely drawn tight. I hook a leg over Bristol's hip and an arm around her waist, possessively anchoring her back to my front.

Tomorrow.

I'll ask about the shadows under her eyes and work and the kids, and the question I asked her once before and have to ask her again.

Did she mean it when she said she would follow me anywhere?

TWO

BRISTOL

I don't think my boobs will ever be the same.

Seriously. Why are they so big? I alternate between fear that they will never return to their original size and dread that they will deflate and hang low and be saggy balloons with nipples. I was still breastfeeding Nina when I found out I was pregnant with Martin. Back-to-back babies meant very little recovery time for the rack.

And I know for a fact my feet will never return to pre-baby proportions. A half size up, and I can't wear any of my Louboutins. Also, I am not above re-vagination if things start feeling loose down there. I need a tight-fit fuck. Though given the size of Grip's cock, I don't think that will be a problem anytime soon.

Damn, he fucked me into a coma last night.

Not complaining. I can attest to the fact that a good slumber fuck is waaaaaaay better than melatonin. With all that I have going on, you'd think sleep would come easily, but mine has been sporadic. No rest for the weary.

Or the busy.

I can't seem to turn my brain off even when my body is ready to tap out. Between feeding Martin in the middle of the night, trying to keep up with the warp speed of Prodigy's expansion and growth, and keeping Nina's little adventurous self *alive*, I'm half-zombie. I'm just really good at covering it. Lots of concealer. Lots of yoga. Lots of juicing.

What's LA without juicing?

I'm doing everything I can to keep all the balls in the air, and I think it's working. Sure, I'm exhausted and smell faintly bovine most of the time, but the kids are healthy, happy, and spend more time with me than anyone else, which is important to me. My clients are all flourishing, climbing and succeeding. Prodigy is a force. I set up the New York office before Martin was born, but I really wanted to be in LA for the birth, surrounded by my family. Now the New

York office needs some TLC, so it may be time to head back. I have to talk with Grip about camping out on the East Coast for a while, and I'm dreading it. I'm thinking, though, if the kids and I stay in New York when he goes on tour in a few weeks, it should be fine.

I'm feeling especially good today. Frieda, our nanny, came early because I have a meeting this morning. So she has the kids for a few hours. After Martin's first feeding, a nice long shower has me relaxed. I'm wearing my favorite knee-length cardigan, and I actually fit into a pair of pre-Martin jeans. The sex last night has my blood singing hallelujah as it flows through my veins. I didn't realize it has been over a week since we had sex. That's a long time for Grip.

Hell, I guess it's a long time for me, too.

I tiptoe through our bedroom, trying to be quiet and keep the room dark so Grip can sleep. Between working on the new album, and prepping for the tour, he's been stretched as thin as I have.

I walk into our closet to study the shelves of shoes, half of which I'm not sure I can wear anymore. I'm considering a pair of Gucci stilettos when Grip walks in.

"Morning," I say over my shoulder with a smile. "I hope I didn't wake you."

"Nah." He sits on the tufted ottoman in the middle of the closet, running a hand over the back of his neck. "I wanted to talk before the day gets away from us."

"Talk?" My hand freezes over three pairs of red pumps. I turn to face him, temporarily distracted by the stacks of muscles flexing in his stomach and rippling under the taut skin of his chest. A thin, silky trail of hair bisects his abs and arrows down to the drawstring of his sleep pants. I can see the morning wood-ish outline of his dick. My mouth waters. When was the last time I gave Grip head? I can't remember.

Oh, God, I can't remember.

"Bris?"

"Huh?" I jerk my eyes from his crotch to find one thick brow quirked over amused dark eyes.

"You know you can get it," Grip drawls, leaning forward to grasp my wrist and pull me down to his lap. He cups my jaw with one big hand and takes my mouth as a willing hostage. Our tongues twist, and I taste toothpaste and his natural addictive flavor. His hands wander beneath my tank top, and he finds my nipple, squeezing gently.

"Baby, I have to go," I mutter against his lips and then move to stand.

"No." He spans my waist and firmly pulls me back down. "We need to talk."

"We can." I drop a kiss onto his lips and get up, grabbing the Gucci heels and wiggling one foot in. "Later. Gotta go."

"Where are you going?" He frowns. "I thought you weren't in the office until this afternoon."

"Yeah, I had to flip my schedule for this meeting. A producer for that big new period piece wants to cast Kai."

"Is there nudity?" A grin lights his handsome face. "Because you know Rhys is not about that life."

"There is a little nekkid." I lean one hand against the wall and balance to put on the other shoe. "And Rhyson will have to grow the fuck up and get over it."

638

"What's that mean?" His grin drops.

"It means this is a great opportunity for Kai, one she wants to take. She shouldn't let his outdated caveman hang-ups stop her."

"Last I checked," Grip says, "that isn't how they run their marriage."

"You're right. I'm sure he'll manage to convince her it isn't right for *them* and she'll turn it down." I roll my eyes and walk back toward our bedroom. "I hope not. That's why I'm going to this meeting. To salvage any of the offer we can and see what compromises can be made."

"Maybe we have some compromises of our own to make," Grip says softly from behind me.

I stop and turn, one hand on my hip and head cocked to the side.

"Now what's *that* mean?" I demand.

He sketches a quick frown and shakes his head.

"We can talk about it tonight," he says. "I don't want to make you late."

"Is everything . . ." I search for the right word. "Okay?"

Are we okay?

We've known each other more than fifteen years, and half that time we weren't even close to okay. I was scared to risk loving him for a long time. I never want to be *not okay* with him again. We had amazing sex last night, but I know with our schedules, we haven't been nearly as close as we're used to.

"It's fine, Bris. I just . . ." He licks his lips and blows out a quick breath before meeting my eyes. "I miss you."

My heart slams to a stop. I know this man like I know my own skin. Something's not right. I take a few steps back inside the closet until I'm standing in front of him. I step between his legs, forcing the muscled thighs to widen and bracket me. I slip one hand behind his neck and the other cups his jaw, tilting his head up until our gazes lock.

"Tell me," I whisper, searching his eyes for the answer he hasn't offered yet.

"I thought you had a meeting." His hands slide up my thighs and he squeezes my ass.

"Five minutes. I can give you five minutes."

He nods but gently pushes me away before standing and heading toward our bedroom.

"We need more than that," he says. "I'll wait."

"No. Tell me." I'm nipping at his heels, and grab his elbow, turning him back to face me. "Baby, what is it?"

"It's what I said." He reaches up and spears his fingers into the hair brushing my shoulders. "I miss you."

"But I'm right—"

"Don't say you're right here," he interrupts sharply. "You know that isn't what I mean, Bris."

"Sex?" I ask, a frown knitting my brows. "Is this because we went a week without having sex?"

"That's just a symptom." He caresses my cheekbone with his thumb. "This is not what I signed up for, babe, and I'm not gonna tolerate it."

"Not tolerating what?"

"Half measures. Glimpses of you. Snatches of time. Weekly fucks. That is not who we are, and I won't settle for it."

"It's a *season,*" I say gently. "Everyone has kids and a job and commitments that pull them in different directions for certain seasons."

"We don't have to. I love our kids. I'd give my left nut and my whole life for them. You know that, but they aren't the reason I married *you.*"

"But, Grip—"

"And I love my career. Love performing and doing all the things I get to do, the things you help make happen for me, but I don't want those things more than I want you."

"I get that, but—"

"If we aren't first, nothing else feels right, and I want to adjust things before they ever feel wrong."

"Agreed." I finally get a word in. "After the tour—"

"No, before the tour," he cuts in softly. "On the tour."

I tip my head back to study the implacable lines of his face.

"What do you mean *on* the tour?" I ask. "I was thinking I would work from New York while you're away. So what do you mean *on the tour?*"

His beautifully sculpted mouth tightens and turns down at the corners.

"I want you and the kids to come on tour with me."

My eyes widen and a frown pulls my eyebrows low.

"Babe, there's so much going on. I can't possibly drop everything to trot off after you around the world."

"I'm not asking you to drop everything," he says, his voice taut with irritation. "And I sure as hell would never ask you to *trot,* but you have to admit we've been seeing less of each other."

"I've got shit to do, Grip."

"So do I, Bris, but none of it is more important than this." He presses my hand to his heart, which thuds the rhythm of his love and devotion against my palm. "More important than us."

"Of course not." I step closer, resting my forehead against his chin. "Of course not, but we have responsibilities. We can't just—"

His thumb lifts my chin so we're staring at each other.

"We can do whatever the fuck we want to do," he says decisively.

He dips his head and seals his lips over mine, invading my mouth with powerful strokes of his tongue until my knees go weak and my bones melt. By the time he's done, only his wide hands holding my hips and my fingers clinging to his shoulders keep me standing.

He bends to leave kisses on my neck. I tilt my head back so he can lick me, bite me, whatever he sees fit to do. His lips brush my ear with feather-soft words.

"I pulled out of the campus tour," he whispers, sending a shockwave over me.

I jerk back, peering up into his face. He and Dr. Hammond, his former professor, have continued the *Contagious* campus tours, raising awareness and money for community jail funds and legal representation for the wrongly accused. It's vital work that I know gives Grip a sense of purpose like nothing else does.

"No." I shake my head. "It's important. You have to do it."

"It is important," he agrees. "And I will do it. Later."

"This is just a season, Grip."

"Exactly. For this season, I can't do the tours. Not and grind in the studio for this record and prepare for this tour and be the father I need to be." His dark eyes caress my face. "Be the husband I need to be, which of everything, is my most important role. We only get this life together, Bris, and I don't accept that there's a season where you and I aren't as close as we can possibly be. There can be a season where I'm less active in the issues that I care about. There can be a season where I don't record as much or where I don't tour. But there will *not* be a season where we miss each other."

A dark chuckle vibrates from his chest to mine before he adds, "Or only have sex once a week."

I swallow, emotion scalding my throat. There are so many things I'd have to adjust to take our family on tour with Grip. So many responsibilities I'd have to delegate. So many opportunities I might miss.

"Just think about it." Grip drops a kiss onto my lips and swats my butt lightly. "Don't be late. Go get Kai that movie."

I'd forgotten all about the meeting.

"Okay, yeah." I step back, slanting a glance up at him. "Tell me we're okay, Grip. I can't—"

I look down at the floor and shake my head, unable to wrap my mind or heart around us being on the outs.

"We're okay," he reassures me. "Hey, look at me."

When I do, I see the open honesty in his face.

"We're okay, but I'm gonna make sure we stay that way. I don't want to drift, Bris. This business breaks marriages. You know that. I'm protecting us. I've pulled out of the campus tour. I'll do whatever it takes."

I nod, stepping away to grab my purse and my iPad from the bedside table where I left them.

"Frieda's here for the kids," I toss over my shoulder.

"Oh, I'll send her home."

"Send her home?" I stop and turn. "I thought you had a meeting this morning?"

"I told them I'd call in." He shrugs and offers a rueful grin. "I've been gone too much."

I nod, wondering if maybe I've been gone too much, too.

THREE

BRISTOL

"Your brother's gonna kill you." Kai laughs when we reach our cars in the parking lot. "He loves me too much, and we have sex a lot, so I'm safe. But you? You, he's gonna kill."

I chuckle, clicking my car unlocked and propping my hip against the hood.

"Hey, you just scored a role in one of the biggest movies of the year," I say. "Rhyson will be proud and happy for you."

Fingers crossed.

"He will be." Kai nods, her dark hair blowing across her face. "You got them down to partial nudity, which is more of a concession than I expected."

"Well, the director really wants you for this role." A cynical grin tweaks my lips. "And he doesn't want to alienate one of the most powerful men in this town, your husband."

Kai smiles and rolls her eyes.

"Well, Rhyson will be happy for me," she says. "That's part of loving someone, right? Wanting to see their dreams realized. I want everything for him, and he wants everything for me, as long as there is no full-frontal involved."

It occurs to me that Rhyson and Kai are two high-powered entertainers making their family and their careers work. Maybe she has some insight.

"Kai, can I ask your advice on something?"

She looks at me curiously. I'm not really one to seek advice from people. I'm usually barking orders and telling everyone else what they should do. Know-it-all is a prominent strand in my DNA.

"Sure," she says, an eager note in her voice. "What's up?"

"You had a hit album and were doing Broadway shows, and Rhyson had so much going on with his career. Did you ever feel like you were . . . I don't know. Missing each other?"

Her eyes narrow at the corners, but her lips twitch.

"Yeah. I thought I had it all under control. The baby was taken care of. I never missed a rehearsal. Knew my lines cold. Executed all my numbers flaw-lessly." A husky laugh shakes her shoulders. "But, apparently, I didn't have *Rhyson* under control. We had, what we in the South like to call, a come to Jesus meeting."

"Yeah, I think Grip and I just had one of those this morning," I say wryly. "He wants us, the kids and me, to go on tour with him."

"Wow." Surprise widens her dark eyes. "That would be hard for you, huh?"

"Very." I sigh and run my hand through my hair. "I was going to focus on the New York office while he was on tour. I knew we were missing each other, but I just thought it was a season. I just don't want to let anyone down, especially not Grip."

"You're helping run one of the fastest-growing record labels in the country and managing some of the biggest stars on the scene," Kai says gently. "You have a two-year-old and an infant who's still breastfeeding and not quite sleeping through the night. Cut yourself some slack."

After I had Nina, I had so much to do at Prodigy that I threw myself into work. Then I got pregnant with Martin and ran myself ragged preparing for maternity leave. I cut leave short to get back and make up for lost time.

"Yeah, you're right." I smile weakly. "I just thought everything was running smoothly. For Grip to feel that we're drifting . . ."

I link my fingers in front of me and shake my head helplessly.

"Bris, we're married to brilliant men. They're possessive, intense, demand-ing. They want *everything*."

"Yeah, I'm aware."

Kai's smile is wistful.

"But they give everything, too," she says. "There isn't anything Rhyson wouldn't do for me. Nothing he wouldn't give up for me. Loving him, living with him, is like standing in a storm sometimes, but I wouldn't have it any other way. Our guys are rare. I hit the lottery when I met your brother, and I don't mean because of his money. I wouldn't trade him for all the movie roles in Hollywood. I'm a lucky woman."

Her phone rings from her purse, and she reaches for it, but holds our stare.

"And so are you," she finishes, glancing at the screen. "Speak of the devil."

"Rhyson?" I ask with a smile, because he's probably waiting at home with a ruler to measure how much skin they're allowed to show in this movie.

"You guessed it." She puts the phone to her ear and grins. "Hey, you."

"I'm gonna go," I whisper, leaning over to kiss her cheek.

She nods and waves.

"Yeah, we insisted on the no nipple clause you wanted," she says, rolling her eyes at me.

Demanding. Intense. Possessive.

That's Grip, but Kai's right. I wouldn't have him any other way. I have big decisions ahead of me. I can't lose him, but I can't lose myself either. I don't want to resent him down the road because I feel like I missed out on something. I *do* have two young children. I *am* running a booming record label.

And I *can't* remember the last time I gave Grip a blow job.

That's kind of my thing. I'm really good at it.

But I also can't remember the last time we watched television together or discussed politics or something he's written. I'm driving home and combing my thoughts for those missed moments when the phone rings.

"Mrs. O'Malley," I say, using the car's phone connection so I can remain focused on the road. "How are you?"

It's been months since I spoke with the woman who sold us our place in New York, but I'm always glad to hear from her.

"I'm not . . ." Her voice breaks. "Bristol, I'm sorry to bother you, but I need to get into the apartment."

I frown and get off on the exit that takes me home.

"What's wrong?" I ask. "You sound upset."

"There's a letter," she says, tears soaking the words. "From Patrick."

My heart stumbles in my chest at the name of her husband who lost a prolonged battle with Alzheimer's a few months ago.

"Where?" I ask, feeling her urgency reach me across the phone and across the country. "What letter?"

"The home he lived in at the end, the staff found some of his things that had been left in another room. Before he . . ."

She breaks off again and her small sob tears at my heart.

"Go on, Mrs. O'Malley, please."

"At the end, he lost speech and wasn't even connected to this world, but he must have had a flash of memory before he died," she continues with difficulty. "He wrote a note telling me there was one letter I never found. We used to leave letters for each other all over the house, and there's one I never found."

"We've done significant renovations, Mrs. O'Malley." I rack my brain for anything we could have unwittingly discarded. "I haven't seen anything. I'm not sure if it would still be there."

"Is the tree still in the greenhouse?" she asks, hope pinned to every word. "On the roof?"

"Yes! We haven't touched the tree."

"Good," she breathes. "When I was working on a difficult design, I would go out there to plant flowers. Dig around until things made sense. There was a bed of roses at the base of that tree."

"There still is," I assure her.

"He buried it there," she says tearfully. "It may only say don't forget the wine for dinner. I don't care. Any word from him, anything. I'll take anyth—"

Her words are lost in tears. I allow her space, not knowing where to begin comforting her. I've only had a few years married to Grip and I would be inconsolable if he died. She and Patrick were married fifty years.

"I'll call and let building security know you're coming," I say after a few moments. "They have all our codes on file and can get you in."

"Thank you, Bristol," she whispers. "Give Grip and the kids my love."

Grip and the kids.

"I sure will," I promise with a tearful smile.

FOUR

GRIP

I hear the garage door open and close, followed by the chime of the security system when someone enters the house.

Bristol's home.

I glance at my watch, noting how late it is. She's been gone all day. Other than a text telling me she had something come up, I haven't heard a thing from her. After our conversation this morning, that doesn't bode well.

I pull the cover over Nina's narrow shoulders before turning out the "big light" as she calls it. I poke my head into the nursery to make sure Martin is still asleep. He'll be up for a feeding in a few hours.

A few hours. With my wife, who I hope didn't bring any work home. I canceled tonight's studio session so we could have some time together. I don't want to come off as the guy who expects his wife to set aside her ambitions to follow me. It isn't that. It's just not the right time for us to be apart. And if we can arrange it so she and the kids can come with me . . .

Of course, we can. I have lots of money and so does Bris. Prodigy is her brother's label. If there was ever a recipe for flexibility, we've got it. It's a matter of priority. I know what my priorities are. Will ours align?

When I enter the kitchen, she's transferring food from take-out containers to plates. She looks up with a wary smile when I enter.

"Hey," she says softly, pulling silverware from the drawer. "Did you get my text that I was picking up dinner?"

"Yeah, sorry I forgot to reply. I was giving Nina her bath."

She sets the plates onto the marble countertop and perches on one of the bistro stools, nodding to the seat beside her.

"Sit? Eat?" she asks and pulls out a bottle of wine, pouring herself a glass. "Wine?"

I don't answer but I take the other stool and pick up a fork. I don't realize how hungry I am until I have my first bite.

"Hmmm." I chew the succulent chicken and the fresh vegetables. "That new place up the street?"

"Yup." She takes a sip of wine and says, almost defensively. "Just a little wine won't hurt. It's been a long day. I have some milk I pumped if Martin wakes up."

"It's fine, Bris." I take a sip of my wine and shrug. "I trust you to have it all worked out."

Her smile comes after a few seconds of silence, and then she resumes eating. I don't know what this silence is about. After spending all day with Martin and Nina, I'm so bone tired I don't have much to say. I don't know how Bris does so much for them and still manages to be a boss at work. Every time I step into her shoes, even if it's only for a little while, I gain respect for how amazing she is.

"Mrs. O'Malley called today," she says when we're done with our food.

"Yeah?" I bend an inquiring look on her. "What's up?"

We make our way to the living room while she tells me about this letter Patrick buried in the garden. Possibly the last thing he ever wrote to his wife before he lost his grasp on reality and time.

"God, Grip, if you could have heard her," Bristol says, sinking into the over-stuffed cushions of the sectional and tipping her head back to stare up at the ceiling. "She was crying, and she sounded so . . . lost. So lonely."

"Well, it hasn't even been a year since he passed." I settle beside her, deciding to ignore any awkwardness and squeezing in as close as I can. "They were together fifty years. I can't imagine."

I'll never forget Mrs. O'Malley calling to tell me her husband had died. She sounded lost and lonely that day, too. I guess it takes time. I glance at my beautiful wife, eyes closed and long lashes fanning over the shadows under her eyes that bother me so much. I wouldn't ever recover if I lost Bristol. Not really. I could probably pick myself up and go on. But "going on" is not the same as what I have now, which is *living*. Absorbing every experience with her at my side. Understanding that everything is sweeter, richer, brighter when she's with me. Even so, maybe I pushed her too far when I asked to bring the family on tour.

"We'll come," she says softly, eyes still closed.

"Huh?" My head swings around to study her delicate profile and stubborn jaw. "Come where?"

She turns her head and meets my eyes. Her hand covers the few inches separating us and tangles our fingers.

"On tour," she says, biting her lip and smiling. "The kids and I will come on tour with you."

"Seriously?" I bark a surprised laugh. "What . . . for real?"

"Yes, for real." She scoots a little closer and drops her head to my shoulder. "That's where I was all day. Sarah and I had an emergency meeting to see how we can make it work. What we need to do and shift and adjust."

"Can you?" I rub my cheek into the silkiness of her hair. "Make it work, I mean?"

"I think we can." She nods and angles her head so our eyes meet. "We will because we have to."

"*Have* to?" I lean forward to rest my elbows on my knees and look back at her still pressed into the cushions. "Babe, if I pressured you—"

"Of course, you pressured me," she says with a laugh. "You pressured me for years to be with you. You pressured me to move to New York when you went to NYU. You pressure me every time you think you know what's right for us."

Put like that, I sound like a domineering prick.

"And you know what?" She leans forward to rest her elbows on her knees, mirroring my posture so our lips are mere inches and a breath apart. "You're right."

"I am?" I can't resist. I close the space and kiss her, reaching up to gather her hair into my fist while I trace her lips, slip inside and suck her tongue.

"Hmmmm." She moans into our kiss. "You are."

She slides off the couch to the floor and scoots between my knees. Her fingers nimbly undo my belt buckle and unfasten my jeans, brushing my cock as she goes.

Okay. I'm intrigued.

"Mrs. O'Malley's call persuaded me, and a conversation I had with Kai today helped, too," she says huskily, her eyes blazing into mine. "But you know what really convinced me we aren't spending enough time together?"

In an economy of words, I lift my brows since obviously her question is rhetorical and the sooner she tells me, the sooner we'll fuck.

"I couldn't remember the last time I sucked your dick."

Said dick goes steely in my pants.

"That *is* a sad state of affairs," I agree, helping her out by shucking my jeans and briefs off and spreading my legs to make it easy for her to reach my dick.

"I'm about to rectify that," she says, lowering her head and taking me into the hot wet heaven of her mouth.

"Damn it," I hiss, my hand palming her head and shoving my fingers through her hair. "You give good head, Bris."

"Hmmmm," she hums, sending a vibration from one head to the other until I think my brain may explode from pleasure.

I sit up and take control, holding her still and thrusting in, fucking her face until I'm just shy of coming in her mouth. Oh, no. I have better plans for this load. I pull out, swiping my thumb across her swollen shiny lips and joining her on the floor.

"What are you doing?" she asks breathlessly.

It's my turn to undress her, shimmying her jeans down along with her thong. Disposing of her tank top and cardigan.

I bend her over and suck the curve of one round cheek into my mouth, working it until I know it's marked.

"Jesus, this ass, Bristol," I say against the reddened skin. "I love your body so much. I love you so much."

"I know, baby," she breathes out.

I turn her so her elbows are on the couch and settle behind her to take long swipes of her pussy with my tongue.

"Oh, my God, Grip." She clenches and a shudder rocks her body. "Again."

I love it when she thinks she can tell me what to do. I widen her legs and take to her pussy again, licking and biting and sucking until her juices run down the inside of her thighs. That's what I wanted. I sit up on my knees, running my cock through her wetness and dipping my thumb in, smearing it on her asshole. She knows what that means.

649

"Yes," she pants, reaching back to spread her cheeks, "In the ass, Grip."

We've come so far.

"You want it in the ass, Bris?" I ease my thumb in her ass and pass my other hand over her breasts, pinching her nipples. "I've only got two hands here. Division of labor. Can you touch your clit for me?"

"Yes," she chokes, reaching between her legs to touch herself.

"Finger it for me, Bris."

Her breath is ragged, and I hear the wet sounds of her finger passing through the creaminess between her legs.

"That's my girl." I line my dick, shiny with her juices, up with the hole I've owned so many times now. I plunge in and almost blow it at the first stroke. I stop and hold, giving myself time to pull it together.

"Grip, move. Fuck me." Bris grabs a cheek in each hand, spreading her ass for me, thrusting back. "I need it hard."

I think that's the only way I can give it at this point. I grab her hip and thrust forward again and again, over and over until I'm lost in a fury of pounding and grunting. I pull her up so her back is to my chest and keep working her ass and pinching her nipples. Bristol's fingers stroke frantically over her clit, and she keeps thrusting back to meet every aggressive stroke. Her moans dissolve into sobs and she shakes with an orgasm as I empty myself inside her, burying my face in her hair to muffle a roar.

We stay like that for a few seconds. On our knees. One of my hands cupping her breast, the other wrapped around her hip. My dick in her ass. I refuse to move. This is Nirvana. Not just anal sex and the blow job.

Though, let's be honest. It gets no better than that.

Our scents mingle in the air. Deep breaths heave our chests. I press my palm over her heart, feeling the hammer of it. This is peace. My wife in my arms. My kids asleep upstairs. I'll have them with me on a tour I was dreading because I hated the thought of leaving them.

"Thank you, Bris," I whisper into her neck.

"It was my pleasure," she chuckles, turning to face me and frame my face between her hands. "And it had been too long."

"Not the blow job." I meet her raised eyebrows head on. "Okay, yeah that, but before that. You bringing the kids on tour with me. Thank you for that."

The striking lines of her face relax.

"Mrs. O'Malley was desperate for even a crumb from her husband now that he's gone," she says, looking into my eyes, showing me her love. "I have you. I have our kids. I have this life with you, and you're right. There shouldn't be a season when we miss each other. I'll make it work."

"*We'll* make it work," I correct gently, brushing the hair back from her face. "I don't expect you to make all the sacrifices. I just expect us both to want it more than anything. To want each other more than everything else."

I grimace at the demand of my words, at the mandate of my heart. I don't know how to halfway want Bristol. How to halfway love her. I need to have everything and all the time. I have only one gear when it comes her.

All.

But that's what I want to give her, too.

All.

She smiles up at me, face flushed, her hair a disorderly halo from my fingers and fists. In her eyes, I see it all. Our past and our future. I see us looking down from the top of the world, painfully young with reckless hearts. That was the start of us. Sometimes you don't know you're at the beginning when it's happening. And even though Patrick had been sick for so long, the last time she saw him, Mrs. O'Malley had no idea that it was the end. That's why we relish every moment. That's why, even though I may seem selfish or chauvinistic or whatever someone looking in from the outside might call it, I will fight for every second I can get with this woman.

I believe in all the things cynics despise. First kisses on Ferris wheels. Soul mates and once-in-a lifetime loves. I believe in fifty years and forever. I'm sure Neruda has a poem, a line, that would fit this moment perfectly, but I can't think of it. I can't think beyond the woman in front of me, and the word "still" tattooed on her ring finger and mine. I only hear the vows poured in cement over my heart.

I said the words that day in a church on a snowcapped mountain, and I'll say them every day for the rest of our lives.

Always.

Evermore.

Even after.

Still.

And today, I add another word. The one that encircles and seals everything else.

All.

ABOUT THE AUTHOR

Kennedy Ryan is a Southern girl gone Southern California. A Top 40 Amazon Bestseller, Kennedy writes romance about remarkable women who thrive even in tough times, the love they find, and the men who cherish them. She is a wife and a mother to an extraordinary son. She has always leveraged her journalism background to write for charity and non-profit organizations, but enjoys writing to raise Autism awareness most. Kennedy's writings have appeared in Modern Mom Magazine, Chicken Soup for the Soul, USA Today and many others. The founder and executive director of a foundation serving Georgia families living with Autism, Kennedy has appeared on Headline News, Montel Williams, NPR and other media outlets as a voice for families living with autism.

Website: http://kennedyryanwrites.com/
Mailing List: http://bit.ly/KennedyMailingList
Release Txt: https://clk2.me/mgFv
Amazon: http://bit.ly/KennedyRyanBooks
Instagram: http://Instagram.com/kennedyryan1/
BookBub: http://bit.ly/KRBookBub
FB Group: http://bit.ly/KennedyFBGroup
Book+Main: http://bookandmainbites.com/kennedyryan
Facebook: http://facebook.com/KennedyRyanAuthor/

SHORT STORY WITH MAL AND ANNE FROM THE STAGE DIVE SERIES

KYLIE SCOTT

Once upon a time, Mal decided to go play with Anne at the book shop.

SHORT STORY WITH MAL AND ANNE
FROM THE STAGE DIVE SERIES

"I'll be taking all of these, thank you, ma'am."

The redheaded fox behind the counter sized up my stack of books, a pen tapping against her pretty pink lips. "That's a lot of books."

"I don't like to do things by halves. Not my style."

"Mm."

"Read much yourself?" I asked, setting an elbow on the counter and leaning in. Just getting comfortable. Also, it gave me a great line of sight for checking out the curves beneath her staid black dress. Very nice. Then again, everything about her was.

With a cute little line between her brows, the babe looked at our surroundings. "I work in a bookstore."

"Right. Sure."

"There seems to be a theme going on here." She inspected my selection. "*The Kama Sutra. The Joy of Sex. Sex: How to do Everything. The Good Vibrations Guide to Sex. Guide to Getting It On. The Complete Idiot's Guide to Amazing Sex.* Did you just empty out our sex section?"

I grinned. "Yeah."

"In need of some help in certain areas, huh?"

"No!" I scowled. Why the nerve of her. "Absolutely not. I'll have you know, Miss, that I am very much experienced in the carnal secrets and delights of the bedroom. And various other rooms of the house, as required."

She delicately wrinkled her nose.

"I am," I insisted.

"Whatever you say, Sir."

"Why, I'll have you know a number of young ladies have informed me I should pen a book on the subject. One even insisted that I owed it to the world to do so."

She frowned at my collection. "So you're surveying the existing literature to see what's already out there?"

"Exactly!" I nodded, pleased that she'd seen straightaway what was going on. "Great minds think alike, and it's possible some of my less outrageous inventions might already have been stumbled upon by some sex aficionado from an earlier age. Unlikely, but possible."

She seemed to hiccup in response, as if clamping down on a cough.

I detected a hint of skepticism. "Indeed, the fact is…"

This time, her brows rose. Waiting.

"I'm too much for most women." I puffed out my chest with pride. All of those hours spent sweating my ass off in the gym ought to be good for something. "It's sad really. A burden of mine."

"Are you talking about size?"

I nodded. It was the plain God's honest truth.

"Ego, or…" She jerked her chin in the direction of my crotch.

"Are you calling me arrogant?"

"I don't recall mentioning *that* word exactly."

I tilted my head. "Perhaps you think I'm lying?"

"Perhaps I'm not thinking anything about you at all."

"Impossible." I scoffed, flinging back my long blonde hair. Such golden waves of awesomeness combined with rugged good looks. Oh, she could pretend otherwise, but I know she got off on it care of the dilation of her pupils. Women loved me. Some dudes too. When you were this hot, it just couldn't be helped. "Who could ignore all of this goodness?"

She just blinked.

I countered by batting my eyelashes at her. Some say my eyes are my best feature. Cerulean blue. Like a pristine lagoon in the Pacific or something like that. I don't know. It usually worked, but this chick was being difficult.

"Did you just bat your eyelashes at me?" she asked, curious.

"No." I flexed a bicep. Thank fuck it'd been warm enough to wear a t-shirt. The cooler months in Portland made it hard to show off my wondrous body. And seriously, why go to all of the afore mentioned trouble (gym, sweating, pain, etcetera) if not to share it. Why, it'd just be selfish to keep this all to myself.

She squinted. "Why is your arm doing that? Do you have a tic? You know, they probably have medication for that. There's a chemist down–"

"I don't have a tic. I'm just very muscular."

"Right," she soothed. "Okay. Got it."

Thank God the shop was empty. The woman was shredding me. And to think I'd been so sure this redhead in particular would fall for my wiles. No, that was quitter's talk. Sooner or later, with her full enthusiastic consent of course, she would be mine. Probably. I mean…given my track record, the odds were quite good. People had always said that my self-belief was one of my defining attributes. I could not allow her to shake my faith in my delectability. Not happening.

"So, you live around here?" I asked, giving her my best teasing hint of a smile.

Her brows descended. They were so expressive. "Are you coming onto me?"

"What? No."

"This is outrageous. I'm at work, sir!"

"And I respect that totally. You look very authoritative standing behind that counter. Like a hot naughty librarian." I grinned again. Only if anything, she looked even more pissed. "Wait, no…ma'am. I mean, like a wizard of words, sharing her bookish knowledge with the world. Yeah. That."

On a scale of appeased, she rated maybe a five-percent, at best. Shit.

"Why I think that helping people find literature is a wonderful calling," I continued. "Spreading wisdom far and wide, helping people to expand their minds. I respect you for it big time."

In lieu of answering, she started tallying up my purchase. Her long sensual fingers stabbing at the buttons as she added up the figures. Such violent motions made her breasts jiggle beneath her dress in a thoroughly beguiling manner. Had the girl not worn a bra? I bet she hadn't. How awesome.

"You're ogling me," my lovely one sniped. "Stop it, please. You're making me feel uncomfortable."

"Like in a hot and flushed, turned on kind of way?"

Her mouth formed a perfect o.

"Will you at least tell me your name?"

Her pert nose rose high up in the air. "No."

"Oh come on. I'll tell you mine. It's–"

"Sir, I do not care to know your name."

"That's so hot how you call me 'Sir.' Do you do that in the bedroom too?"

She gasped.

"Sorry. Just curious." I tried to look apologetic. But honestly, it wasn't an emotion I ascribed to in general.

Eyes wide, she just stared. "Why, I've never met such an ill-behaved rogue in my entire life. You, sir, are cocky. That's what you are. And I mean it as no compliment."

I got in closer. "Did you just say you wanted to see my cock?"

"I bet it's as small and insignificant as your manners."

"Is that a yes?"

"No," she hissed. Then she suddenly seemed to change her mind, her pretty face returning to stern. So hot. "Actually, yes. If only to witness firsthand on behalf of all womankind how inadequate you truly are."

"Excellent!" I rubbed my hands together. This was exactly how I'd imagined her falling into my arms demanding sexual pleasure. Well, mostly it was.

The woman tapped her foot loudly. "I'm waiting."

I inspected our surroundings. It was your usual hipster bookshop. Beyond the large plate glass windows, a steady stream of people passed by. Normal for this hour of the day in the Pearl District of Portland. Not exactly the place to whip your dick out unless you wanted the police to come calling.

"I can hardly just get it out right here."

"Why not?"

"Well, if you must know, my penis is not only unusually large and beautiful. But I'm sort of famous." I shrugged. "A rock star, actually. Thought you might have recognized me by now, but obviously not."

She yawned.

"If I get my dick out right here, we'll have a riot on our hands."

"I doubt it."

"Doubt away, but it's still the truth." Hands on hips, I faced her down. "I'm sorry, miss. For your and my safety, along with the well-being of all the books in this fine establishment, we're going to have to take this into the back room."

With a toss of her shiny red hair, she nodded. "Fine. Whatever."

"Glad you're being sensible about this."

The woman strode out from behind the counter, crossing the shop floor, and flicking the lock on the door. Now we were getting somewhere. It was hard to keep the smirk off my face. I looked really good smirking. "Sure you don't want to tell me your name?"

"Nope and I don't need to know yours either. This way..."

I followed her out back to a storage room, mesmerized by the sway of her curvy ass beneath the skirt of her dress. She really was my perfect woman. If only she'd admit it. Though there was a certain delight to be had in a woman playing hard to get. So long as she enjoyed herself too.

"I don't expect this to take long," she said, facing me with arms crossed in the crowded little room. Shelves lined the walls, full to overflowing with various tomes and shit. "Oh, wait, I didn't think to bring a microscope. Am I even going to be able to see it unaided?"

"Haha, madam."

She smirked. It's quite possible she looked even better smirking than I did. Dammit.

"Try not to faint or anything," I said, tearing open the buttons of my jeans. "It's a bitch to catch swooning women with your pants around your ankles."

The girl couldn't have looked more bored. "I'll do my best to hold it together."

"You say that now, but many have been overwhelmed by the sight of my naked genitals. Why, it happens so often I've basically been declared a hazard to heterosexual women everywhere."

"Do you always talk like this?"

In answer, I pushed down my black boxer briefs, baring my splendor to the world. Or to her at least. And there hung my dick in all its glory. "See, I even did some trimming for you."

"That was considerate." The corner of her lips crept up. "Stay in character. This won't work if you don't stay in character."

"I'm staying in character, you stay in character."

She giggled, then straightened her shoulders, taking a deep breath. "Oh. My. God."

"Right? My dick's amazing, isn't it?" I happy sighed. "Told you, but no...you wouldn't believe me."

"I can't believe you'd show a complete stranger your goods."

"Hey now, you act like I get it out for just anyone and that's not true. You're special to me. Whoever you are."

"This is so shocking. I'm shocked."

"But in a good way, right?" I asked.

"It's so..."

My heart was beating harder. It wasn't easy staying cool when she stared at me like that. Already I was half hard, my cock hardening and lengthening. My balls felt heavy, ready. I licked my lips. "It's so what?"

"Thick and ropey and meaty," she said in a breathy voice, gaze still glued to me. "What turgid magnificence."

"Sure, sure. I've used those words often myself."

Now she turned coy, twirling a strand of hair around her finger. "Can I touch it? Please?"

"You've been pretty mean to me. All this disbelief combined with the harsh vibes, I honestly don't know if you deserve it."

At this she snorted.

"Pumpkin, stay in character," I hissed. "How are you going to win a sex Oscar if you can't stay in character?"

She bit back a smile and tossed her hair around once more. Some of it sort of whipped her in the eye which had to sting a little. But she carried on like a trooper. "How was I to know all of your aggressive male cockiness actually hid the cock of a god?"

"Ooh, good line," I said. "Anyway...I've shown you mine so now you have to show me yours. Obviously. Lift that skirt, lady."

Her hands covered the general area of her downstairs pink bits, her eyes wide with fake shock. "You want to see my pussy?"

"I demand to see your pussy."

"Oh, no! But–"

"Just drop the panties."

An actual real live blush hit her cheeks. "I can't do that."

"Why not?"

"Well, you see, I'm not wearing any." Timid like, she looked away. "I forgot to put them on this morning. It was a total accident. I was just in such a rush that I plain forgot."

"That is *so* awesome." I swallowed hard, shuffling over to her. Pants around the ankles issues. With my dick sticking straight out, it wasn't exactly easy getting to my knees. People think you can just wander around doing whatever with a hard-on, but I'm here to tell you, the whole swollen groin thing can really be tricky to manoeuvre. My bare knees hit the cool dusty concrete floor and I tsked. "You really need to sweep out here. This is bordering on unhygienic. Not that I care."

"I'll tell Reece later."

"Good work." I cleared my throat. "I won't tell you again, Miss. Get that skirt up and widen your stance. Show me."

"Why, whatever are you going to do down there?" she asked, slowly, teasingly lifting up the dress.

"Stuff. Important stuff. Never you mind."

"You know, that's not very sexy. Shouldn't you be more poetic or something if you're a rock star? Are you sure you're not just a roadie?"

I barely held in my laughter that time. "Hey, now. Roadies need love too."

"Fine. I guess since I'm here already..."

Didn't matter how many times I'd seen her, the thrill never dulled. Her body, her voice, her mind, turned me on like no fucking other. She leaned back against a shelf of books, couldn't have been comfortable. Ever so gradually, she exposed herself to me. Long bare legs, the curves of her thighs, and yes!

"Very nice," I growled, wrapping my hand around her thigh. Already, wetness lingered on those juicy lips. The musky sweet scent of her went straight to my head. I leaned in, lapping at her with my tongue, humming with pleasure. "For the record though, I really am a hugely important internationally renowned rock star. I have fan clubs and everything."

"Mm-hmm."

I licked her again. "It's true."

"Sure. Whatever." She shifted one foot out, giving me more room to play. "Eat my pussy."

"So demanding. Next time, let's pretend I'm your sex slave. Subject to your every whim."

"Sounds good." Her fingers threaded into my hair, pulling just a little. Lighting me up even more. Lust tugged hard low in my gut. I breathed on her swollen sensitive flesh, nudging her mound with the tip of my nose, licking now and then. Her tummy trembled, her breath caught. "Stop messing around, Mal. I can't keep the shop closed all day."

Calm as can be, I slid a finger into her. Fuck. She was so hot and wet inside. My day dreams and sleeping dreams and every other kind of dream come true. First I pumped one finger into her, then two. And the noises coming out of her throat were so fucking sweet. "Is that really what you're thinking about right now, the shop?"

"No."

"Good girl."

Then I ate her like it was my job. Because it was job. My life rocked like that. If you didn't get girl juice all over your hands and at least half your face when you gave head, then frankly, you weren't doing it right. Nobody likes someone who half asses a job. So rude. I licked and sucked and generally made a meal of her. Then fingers hooked, I rubbed against her sweet spot, aiming to get her off hard and fast. Her legs shook and she came with a cry, eyelids slammed shut.

Now my aching dick pointed straight at the ceiling. There was no time to lose. Before she could come all the way down, I got to my feet and lifted her. Like we'd done it a million times before, which we probably had, she wrapped her arms and legs around me. I slammed my dick up into her, fucking her hard. Just how she liked it. Sure as hell just how I liked it. After tremors had her pussy fluttering faintly around me. It felt amazing. My balls swung with each thrust, slapping against her hot body.

"This is going to be quick," I panted. "But I'll make it up to you later."

She just groaned in my ear.

Lungs labouring, heart hammering, I fucked her. Shelves rattled and banged back against the wall, a couple of books fell onto the floor with a thud. My hands sat on her ass and back, trying to protect her from the worst of it. But Anne didn't mind a little rough and this had, after all, been her choice of location. At her workplace. Dirty girl. I tried to think of something else apart from the heat and tightness of her body. How good it felt being inside of her again. But with my cock slamming into paradise and my balls drawn up tight, it couldn't be helped. I came hard, pouring myself into her, giving her everything.

My head shot off into outer space, sailing out amongst the stars. My body nothing but light. No one but her did this for me. To me. My wife's hands slid over my back, all loving and soothing. Slowly I caught my breath.

"Another exceptional sexual performance," I muttered. "I'd give me eleven out of ten as per usual. You weren't bad either."

"Thanks," she laughed. "Happy almost third wedding anniversary, Mal."

"Right back at you, Pumpkin."

She made her happy noise, holding onto me tighter.

"I've been thinking," I said.

"What?"

That's when some asshole banged on the storage room door. "Anne? Are you in there?"

Carefully, I set her down, smoothing a few sweaty strands of hair back from her face. "I'm here. Just a minute."

"That was fun," I whispered. "But there's something I wanted to talk to you about."

"Is Mal in there too?" Reece the asshole asked through the door.

"No," I said, pulling up my pants. "Fuck off please, and don't come back later."

"Mal," my wife chided. "Sorry, Reece, we'll be out in a minute. We just had to, um, discuss something."

"Christ's sake, you guys. You can't have sex at the shop. That's what you're doing, isn't it? Don't lie to me. That is not okay. It really isn't." The idiot finally stomped away. And it had to be stomping because I could hear it through the door.

Anne smoothed down her dress, taking a deep breath. Then she smiled at me. Man I loved that smile. "What did you want to talk about? It'll have to be fast."

"Yeah. Okay. So I was thinking, we should make a baby."

She froze.

"I mean, it seems a crime for us to be this good looking and not pass it on."

"Are you serious?"

I nodded. "I mean...if you still want to?"

The slow smile spreading across her face was even more beautiful than the one before. Holy shit the woman levelled me. Truth be told, I'd give her all the babies she wanted. The thought of her carrying our child, of being parents...it was scary, but exciting.

"When do you want to start trying?" she asked, eyes glossy.

"Whenever you're ready is good with me."

"Wow." She wiped away a tear. Jesus I hated it when she cried. Though I guess these were happy tears, so not as bad. Her cheeks were still pink, her mouth swollen from kissing. The most beautiful girl in the world. "Pretty cool anniversary present."

I frowned. "Huh? Fuck no. Got you diamonds at home."

She laughed. "Of course you do. My rock star."

"World famous, incredibly important, rich, and handsome, rock star," I corrected. "You know, I was checking last night and my Instagram account has way more followers than Davie. He must be so bitter about it. Bet it's just killing him inside, poor sap."

"Oh really?"

"Well, five more followers."

"Holy cow, yeah, you're burying him."

"Right? Though Jimmy unfollowed me again, the prick. He thinks it's funny or something."

She laughed, winding her arms around my neck. I pulled her in tight, sitting my cheek atop her head. We fit just right. We always have.

"Mine," she said.

And I could only agree.

ABOUT THE AUTHOR

New York Times Bestselling Romance Author

Website: http://www.kyliescott.com
Facebook: https://www.facebook.com/kyliescottwriter
Instagram: https://www.instagram.com/kylie_scott_books/
Twitter: https://twitter.com/KylieScottbooks

ALSO BY KYLIE SCOTT

Lick

Play

Lead

Deep

Strong

Dirty

Twist

Chaser

Trust

Flesh

Skin

Flesh Series Shorts

Coming Up Next...

It Seemed Like A Good Idea At The Time

UNTIL THE
COCK CROWS

SIERRA SIMONE

Reverend Dr. Mark Trade is too young, too handsome and too cocky...and Corabel Dennis is not impressed. Until that is, she learns that they share the same dirty secret...

UNTIL THE COCK CROWS

Reverend Dr. Mark Trade wasted no time in pissing me off.

There was, of course, the scowls whenever he passed by my desk and I didn't appear to be working hard enough for him. There was the swagger when he walked to the pulpit—the same swagger that had all the teenage girls fluttering their eyelashes at him, like this was an Austen novel and he was the handsome young clergyman just come to town. And most damningly, there was the high-handed way he wanted to change things. They weren't always *bad* ideas; some of the changes I'd been suggesting myself for the three years I'd been working in the Thrive United Methodist Church office. It was just the way he wanted to do them, as if he merely wanted to snap his fingers and have his will be done.

Like God. And I only liked my men godlike in bed.

"Cocky," Edith the organist had muttered to me one day after a meeting. "I've seen preachers like him before. Too young, too handsome, and too damned cocky."

It didn't help that his cockiness—that *swagger*—wasn't entirely unearned. He already had his ordination and his PhD at age thirty, a host of diplomas and certificates on his wall, and his sermons were...well...they were really fucking good. He didn't perform his sermons like a southern televangelist because he didn't have to; he could command a room of hundreds with his deep, slightly husky voice; he could captivate an audience with his brilliant, insightful thinking.

And he *was* handsome. Dangerously so, with dark eyebrows slashing over clear blue eyes and a straight bladed nose with the tiniest crook at the bridge. There was a mouth lush enough to belong in a cologne ad, fair skin with a hint of suntan, and a shock of silky brown hair just long enough to brush over his forehead sometimes, causing him to flick at it with an annoyed hand, as if

671

offended that his hair had the audacity to pull his concentration out of whatever deep and powerful thought he was having at the moment.

But still. The reason I was a Methodist at all was because I'd needed to find a denomination with less men obsessed with power. Like I said—I have a place for powerful men (my bed), but once the sun rises, I'm back to wrinkling my nose at any man who so much as *thinks* about birth control policy within a fifty-foot radius of me.

And the good Reverend Dr. Mark Trade was not in my bed, he was my boss. And alleged spiritual leader. Sigh.

So I was not in the best frame of mind when two months after he'd started, he sent me an email. A terse, one-line email at the end of the day when I was the last one in the office, right before I was about to pack up my bag and head home.

Corabel—

See me in my office.

—Rev. Dr. Mark Trade

The fucking nerve…

My desk was in the staff room—I was the communications director and wedding coordinator for the church—and was possibly a whole two-minute walk from his own office on the other side of the sanctuary. He could have come and seen me right now! He could have called my office phone! He could have at least pretended I had better things to do than to be at his beck and call!

Righteous indignation burned through me, and I considered—really considered—not going. Simply pretending I hadn't seen the email, finishing up for the day and then going home to my cat and my frozen entrée and my usual roster of British gardening shows.

Then a second email came in.

I mean it, Corabel.

Something else burned through me, so fast it was gone before I could catch hold of it. But it left contrails through my lower belly, tingled at the tips of my breasts, and a small shiver worked its way up from the base of my spine.

No! *No.* This was dumb. I was not one of those front-row teenage girls hoping the preacher man would take her flirting seriously, and I was not the kind of employee to be barked at like a dog. I was going to go to his office, *fine*, but I was going to go there to give him hell and that was it. If he wanted to bitch at me about the church bulletins needing more room for sermon notes or for the email newsletters needing better open rates, he could do it another day. *After* he'd scheduled a meeting with me.

I stormed down the hall to his office, not bothering to knock on the door before letting myself inside.

He was sitting at his desk, the usual sprawl of bibles, books, and papers in front of him, looking academic and stern in a thin sweater over a button-down shirt. He looked up at my sudden entrance, his expression mildly displeased. "It's polite to knock," he said.

Oh, that motherfucker.

"It's also polite," I seethed, "not to demand my presence like you're entitled to it."

My irritation had the simultaneous effect of both amusing and disappointing him. His eyes flashed with something hot as his jaw worked. But instead of scowling and lecturing me even more, he said nothing at all, getting to his feet and coming around his desk.

I couldn't help it, my breath caught a little at the sight of him unfolding into a tower of wide shoulders and lean hips, of a firm, masculine body that even his sweater couldn't entirely conceal. And the way he *moved*—with that kind of purpose and intensity—it made my heart race and my mouth go dry, arousal pushing up alongside the anger and making me dizzy. I suddenly thought about how the Reverend Doctor would be in bed, if he would push my head down and test my cunt with bored fingers. If he would make me crawl naked to him on the hardest floor he had, every light on, cold satisfaction gleaming in his eyes. If those broad shoulders and muscled arms were strong enough to take my weight as he fucked me against bookshelves full of lectionaries and tomes of Wesleyan theology.

I shivered.

"Close the door," he said.

"I'd rather not," I said, my voice still shaky with my earlier anger and now also shaky with something else. It wasn't discomfort exactly—I was confident he wouldn't hurt me, and even more confident that I could hold my own if we fought—but it was some kind of apprehension. I was nervous to be alone with him not because I thought he was dangerous, but because I suddenly realized that I might be just as dangerous.

He stopped walking toward me and raised a dark brow. "You'd rather not," he repeated, and it reminded me of something, *something*, but I didn't know what. I only knew that the déjà vu was so forceful it made me dizzy. "Alright then. We'll have this conversation with the door open."

"Fine," I said, reaching down for my anger again, "and firstly, we need to talk about how peremptory you're being with me. I'm not your secretary and I'm definitely not your servant. I do communications, I do weddings, I don't do your bidding. Is that clear?"

To my immense frustration, a small smile tilted his mouth upward, and the effect was to make him unbearably handsome. "Preemptory," he echoed. "Well, then."

I had to resist the overwhelming urge to stamp a foot on the ground. "Are you listening? You can't just summon me here, and you especially can't treat me like you hate me for two months and then expect me to be cheerful when you order me around."

At that, his smile fell and his brows pulled together. "I don't act like I hate you."

"Fine, like you dislike me," I said, waving a hand to show that I didn't care about the semantics.

"I only have deep respect and fascination where you're concerned," he corrected, taking another step forward. "No hate. No disdain. The more I learn about you, the more I want to know."

Uncertainty drizzled through my thoughts. "You can't feel that way. You don't know a thing about me."

This brought the smile back to his mouth, and how had I never noticed how unsafe that smile was before? Arrogant, yes, attractive, fine—but the way he smiled at me brought to mind the way a wolf might smile at a lost, innocent doe.

Except I wasn't a doe and I certainly wasn't innocent. I made a noise at his smile and turned to leave—I was going to go and damn the consequences—but he stopped me with a single sentence.

"I saw you at Persepolis last night."

Panic, cold and meanly jagged, dragged through my entire body, shredding my composure and sending my thoughts flying in all directions like woodchips from a log being split.

Persepolis.

He saw me.

Oh God, how much did he see?

Is he going to tell other people?

Is he going to find a way to convince the church to fire me?

I stopped and turned back.

"Would you like to shut the door now?" he asked.

Yes. Yes, I would.

I shut the door and then leaned against it, eyeing him warily.

"I know lots of things about you, Corabel Dennis," he continued. "I know that you could be making three times what you earn anywhere else, but that you choose to work here. I know that you haven't had a boyfriend or girlfriend since I've met you and that you prefer to walk around the grounds on your lunch break instead of eating in the staff room. I know that you use the word *peremptory* in a sentence." He took another step forward, close enough now that I could see the individual arcs of his sooty eyelashes. "And I know that last night you let a man strip you bare on a stage and give you pleasure while a crowd of people watched. While I watched."

My heart pounded in my chest like it was fighting to get free. Because I finally realized the source of my déjà vu earlier, the reason for my earlier responsiveness and arousal.

He's exactly the kind of man I like in bed.

Godlike.

Dominant.

Fuck.

I grabbed for self-control, lifted my chin. "I hope I don't have to explain to you that you don't have a right to anything—to any part of me—just because you saw me at a sex club. Just because I like certain *consensual* games in my free time does not make me easy or a whore."

The word *whore* earned me a severe look. "That was never my assumption, nor is it necessarily what I wanted to talk about."

"Okay, good," I said, his reply leaving me fumbling a bit. I'd expected condemnation or entitlement to my body, and he'd displayed neither, which was of course a relief. But also a bit unsettling—because what else could he want with me? My earlier worry resurfaced, and I blurted, "And you better not use this to try to get me fired, because you were at the club too, and don't think I won't tell—"

He silenced me with the press of his warm, blunt fingertips to my lips, not pressing hard enough to actually stop me from speaking, simply using the surprise of his touch and the stern glare of those blue eyes to rob me of my words.

"You really think the worst of me, don't you?" he said, his arrogant displeasure now sounding more like frustration. "You honestly think it's more likely that I would judge you as a Jezebel or make a pass at you or try to fire you, than..." he trailed off, his gaze dropping to where his fingers still pressed against my lips.

"Than what?" I whispered from under his fingers, and his eyes snapped up to mine.

"Than if I wanted to ask..." His voice turned shy and red dusted the tops of his perfect cheekbones. "If you would like to play together sometime."

Of all the ways this conversation could have gone, of all the things he could have said, this never would have occurred to me, this respectful request that was made almost *sweetly*.

My lips parted under his touch in pure shock. "You want to play with me?"

"Of course I do," he said. "Ever since I came here I wanted to ask you for a date, but I also wanted..." His fingers fell from my mouth and began to trace along the column of my neck. I knew what he was imagining, because I was imagining it too. Collars, ropes. Maybe even a little playful choking.

I flushed so much at the thought that I could feel the burning in my toes.

He continued. "I didn't think it would be ethical for me to date a staff member anyway, but especially a vanilla one...it would be courting trouble."

"But now you know I'm not vanilla."

"And I don't think I can hold myself back from courting trouble. If you'll let me, Corabel."

I searched his face, finding only honesty and unfiltered longing there. His fingers had started trembling where they touched my neck, except I was trembling so much underneath him that it was impossible to tell who was the more affected.

Did I want this cocky, *peremptory* man in my bed? Did I want him playing games with me, did I want to call him Sir, did I want to trust him with the deepest and most unruly parts of my mind?

The answers came before I could even really consider the questions.

Yes and yes and yes and yes.

God, who didn't sometimes dream of a partner like that? Unbearably good-looking, unbearably confident, their only apparent weakness how much they wanted you?

Because wanting me was a weakness of his, I could see. In two months, I'd never seen him flounder for speech, never seen him blush, never heard him say anything in a voice that wasn't precise and clipped and controlled. But with me, he almost seemed boyish. Uncertain. It made me flush even more—out of flattery and feminine pride, of course, but also out of happiness. Just plain, uncomplicated happiness. It made me happy to know that he wanted me. It made me realize that I wanted him back—and *had* wanted him for quite some time.

Tale as old as time, Corabel. Girl meets boy, girl thinks she hates boy, girl actually wants boy to use her as a footstool before he fucks her senseless.

Go figure.

"I'm not a masochist," I finally said, wanting to say *yes, yes, go ahead and fuck me right now on top of your unfinished sermon* instead but also wanting him to know all the facts.

"Luckily for us both then, I'm not a sadist," he replied. "What else?"

"Nothing illegal, no edgeplay until we know each other better, and no one at the church can know about us."

"Done. Do you want to make sex a part of play?"

Oh God, yes, my pussy wanted to scream on my behalf. I managed to keep myself from nodding a thousand times in rapid succession. "I would like to do that, yes. With you. Very much."

My obvious fluster seemed to please him, a bit more arrogance creeping back into his expression. "And birth control and disease prevention? I'm happy to wear condoms."

"I'm on birth control," I said, thanking Jesus and all His angels that I was a Methodist nowadays, and Methodists generally didn't fuss about such things. "And I'm clean. If you are as well, I can go without the condoms."

He nodded. "I'm clean. And your safeword?"

"Cherubim."

"Not seraphim?" he teased, and I thought it might be the first time I'd ever heard him make a joke, even a bad one.

"They come first in the hymn. Seemed right."

That netted me a big smile, which faded fast into a look of intense concentration. "I want to touch you again," he said in a low voice. "Right now."

"Yes."

He reached past me to lock the closed door, and then he leaned down enough to press his forehead to mine. "Oh Corabel," he breathed, his hands coming up to cradle my face. "When? When can we start?"

I should have said another time, another place. My apartment in a couple days. Or Persepolis next week. But I couldn't. My body already glowed with heat at his nearness, the seam between my legs already felt heavy and swollen and slick. And *I*—whatever thing made up Corabel Dennis independent of her body, whether it was her mind or her heart—craved him even more. He was intelligent and strong and possibly the slightest bit cruel, and everything inside me wanted to tangle with him. To fight him and fuck him and best him and be bested by him.

"Now," I managed, my throat dry with wanting him. "We can start now—"

I didn't even have a chance to finish before his mouth crashed down against my own, before his warm hands were on my waist, on my ass, pulling me up against him so that my legs went around his hips and his hands supported me under my thighs with the casual ease of a strong male. And then his hips pressed into me, wedging a stout and lengthy erection against my cunt. I'd worn a skirt today—a skirt now hiked up around my upper thighs—and so the only thing separating his surging cock from my opening was a thin lace thong and his slacks.

I moaned.

A large hand clapped over my mouth, and another blue glare seared right through my soul. "You'll be heard, Corabel," the reverend said quietly. "If you want to stop or to wait, that's one thing. But if you want to play right now, if you need a Sir's hands on you before you can think straight, then I suggest silence. Got it?"

He lifted his hand but I was already nodding like the good little girl I could be in these situations. "Yes, Sir," I whispered. "I'll be quiet. Just please don't stop."

Please don't ever stop. When was the last time I'd been this turned on? This lit up, this excited? When was the last time the Dom I'd chosen for the hour or for the night actually elicited my genuine respect? When was the last time he'd been a man worth getting to my knees for?

Too long.

Maybe there hadn't even been a real last time. Not compared to this.

My whispered plea was all he needed to hear, apparently, and with abrupt and deliberate roughness, I found myself bent over his desk, my face on his sermon notes, my skirt up over my ass as his hands shaped the curves there with palpable appreciation.

"Fuck, you're a treasure," he said, squeezing and cupping me. When he turned to reach for something on his desk, I felt the fabric-covered bar of his cock brush against me, and I tried to push against it, wanting it, wanting him.

He made a noise at that—all arrogant amusement—and then I felt what he'd gotten from his desk against my hip. Scissors.

They kissed cold sensation all along my ass until they found the line of my thong and bit into the lace. Soon my pussy was bare and the scissors were on the table next to my face, and then he squatted behind me.

His thumbs ran parallel lines up my folds once or twice, making me shiver with anticipation, and then he spread my cheeks apart with his palms while his thumbs parted my secret place open for his viewing.

"So wet," the reverend *tsk*ed. "Has it been too long? Too long since this little pussy was satisfied?"

I nodded against the papers under my face, my skin prickling with shame and delight—which to me are the same thing, at least when fucking is involved. "Please," I moaned. It was agony to be held open and gazed at and not touched; it was agony to feel the heat of this prideful man behind me and not be made his. My entire body keened for it, for him, for him to take all the desire and all the dislike and all the destiny between us, and turn it into something sweaty and real.

And to be honest, I needed to come *already*, even though we hadn't even gotten close to the kind of sex where coming was an option, but still. It felt like if I didn't come, I'd die.

Even rough, uncaring fingers would get me off at this point.

Even the edge of the desk, if he'd let me rub against it, which I doubted. The Reverend Doctor Mark Trade did not seem like the kind of man who allowed those kinds of liberties from his submissives.

His fingers moved, testing me, sampling the wet and gauging how slick it had made me.

"You need fucked," he decided aloud. "Badly."

"Yes, *please*," I said in a voice maybe a bit more irritated than it should have been, because the next thing I knew he was bent all the way over me, one hand fisted in my hair and the other covering my mouth.

"I'm not a sadist...*necessarily*," he growled low in my ear. "But don't think just because I won't take a crop to your ass that I won't gag that pretty mouth. That I won't tie you to this desk and devote the next three hours to wringing some respect out of you. Got it?"

Oh *God*. Even just his low threats in my ear were enough to make my belly curl in a needy ache. I wanted to be good for him, but also holy fuck, those punishments sounded so hot—a classic submissive's dilemma.

But I behaved—for now.

"I got it. Sir."

A noise of approval, and then I was hauled up onto the desk on my back, no care whatsoever given to the papers and books underneath me, and then Mark crawled over me with glittering eyes.

"Next time," he promised. "Next time, we'll play for real. I want you in my ropes...you'll look so pretty there, Corabel, all tied up and waiting for your Sir. Or perhaps I'll tease this pretty pussy until you're crying to come."

"Yes," I sighed up at him. "Yes to all those things."

He traced my jaw with possessive fingers and then reached down to his zipper. "What else do you like, fiery girl? What else do you want to do?"

My cheeks heated bright red, but if there was any time to be honest, it was flat on my back on the preacher's desk while he slowly unzipped himself. "S-servitude," I managed to say.

His hand paused its work. "Servitude," he repeated, tilting his head, as if he thought he'd misheard me. Which was fair, given that I'd snapped at him earlier about not being his servant. But sometimes the best kinks are the most contradictory.

My cheeks went from red to the deepest, hottest crimson, and humiliation crawled all over my skin. "You know," I whispered. "Domestic stuff. Tending to you. You using me like furniture or a servant or..."

His own eyes fluttered closed, as if my words had a nearly painful effect on him. "Yes," he said in a strained voice. "Yes, I do know."

Do you like it? I was desperate to ask. *Do you get off on it?* Some men and women didn't—for some it was too abstract, and for others, it wasn't abstract enough. Nothing will make you confront your shame and anger like being told to bake a cake naked or to balance a glass of wine on your back while your Dom or Domme reads from a book in a comfortable chair next to you.

Nothing felt more forbidden, nothing felt more juicy and wrong than to be treated like that. To make myself a vessel of someone else's least important needs.

I loved it. And God, how I wanted Mark to love it, I wanted it to be his kink as much as it was mine.

"Would you like it?" I finally gathered up the courage to ask. "If I came over and served you for the night? Cooked or cleaned or even just held things for you while you read or worked?"

He shuddered above me, opening his eyes to reveal troubled pools of blue lust. "Yes," he ground out. "Yes, I would like that. Fuck, Corabel, I'd—I'd do anything for that."

The answering smile on my fast was too big and too fast to stop, and he bent low with a growl, biting at the smile and then kissing it right off my face. His

678

hand went back between us, and then he pulled out his cock for real this time. The head of it—hot, blunt, hard—fell against my thigh and then moved up, nudging right against the place that would squeeze him so very tightly if only he dared to take it.

He dared.

He was big enough that he had to force it a little, each inch spreading me so wide that I thought I might break in half. And when I squirmed underneath him, the real Dom came out at last, his legs easily pinning mine and his hand capturing both my wrists to secure above my head. His other hand came down and pressed my face to the side, baring my throat for his nips and my ear for his filthy, intoxicating words.

"I can't wait to play with you," he breathed, his hips moving in slow, grinding thrusts that left me seeing stars. "I'll have you on your knees for my cock. I'll have you on all fours scrubbing my floor with your cunt exposed and waiting. I'll cuff your ankle to my desk and keep you like a pet while I work."

"Yes," I moaned from under his hand. I wanted it, I wanted it all, and I wanted it with *him*.

"And only when you've been so very good and so very helpful will you earn this," he said, emphasizing his words with a sharp thrust. My toes curled in response. "Only then will I see that you get what you need."

"And what do I need?" I goaded breathlessly. Partly because it still riled me to have him so cocksure and bossy even as he impaled me with his heavy cock... and partly because it aroused me beyond belief to have this cocksure and bossy man fucking me into his desk like a sailor on his first night of shore leave.

I expected him to say something filthy. I expected him to scold me or shove his fingers in my mouth for my impertinence.

Instead, his hand moved to take hold of my chin and turned my face up to his. "You need someone," he said simply, his breath warm on my lips. "You're not happy alone. You're not happy rotating anonymous partners at a club. You hate that you want more, that you want something as cliché as a lover, and the more you hate it, the more you fight it. But it never stops being true."

I closed my eyes for minute, not able to handle his steady gaze and his words at the same time.

"Am I wrong, Corabel?" he asked gently.

"No," I whispered, my eyes still closed. "You're not wrong."

I'd forgotten this part too. That kink wasn't just about clubs or concepts that gave you frissons of sinful, dirty delight. It was about trusting another human to see the inside of you and give you what you need. It was about doing the same for them.

Mark leaned down and bit lightly at my jaw. "Then let me be your someone and give you what you need."

I opened my eyes. "And what do you need?" I asked.

"To be *your* someone," he said without hesitation or shame. "I've needed it since the moment I met you."

There were no more words after that. He collared my throat with his hand, his body huge and heavy and still clothed over mine, and clearly Mark had never heard that a gentleman should take his weight on his hands, because he made sure that I felt all the weight and strength of him, made sure that all of his effort went into grinding and stroking and stretching me rather than holding himself up. He buried himself deep enough that his tip kissed places in my belly, and he angled himself so that every stroke rubbed my clit. The tensing muscles of his arms and thighs pressed against me; even through our clothes, I could feel the steel flex and bunch of his abdomen as his body moved to couple with mine.

For a preacher, he sure fucked like a god.

I felt it in my thighs first, a slow tightening clench that spread to my belly, cradling the singing sensation in my cunt between them. And I was going to ask for permission, I really was, but Mark felt it too, giving the corner of my mouth a kiss. "You may," he said, without me having to ask.

And then I came.

Everything seemed to ball together and then fly outwards, seizing ripples of delicious feeling, the contractions so strong that Mark's pace faltered and he stilled over me, muttering to himself. And it felt like he was everywhere as I came—I was full of him and under him and being held by him, and it was just *him*. Him, him, him, this cocky preacher I thought I hated.

He claimed my mouth in a torrid kiss as my climax drifted into stillness, and our eyes locked in a heat of blue need as he gave a final push and then filled me with his release, throbbing and pumping until I was full of him and he was empty of everything except satisfaction.

"Corabel," he murmured as his orgasm left him. "Good God. Corabel."

He gave me a final kiss and then climbed off his desk, leaving me limp and dazed and...well, grateful. It wasn't just the sex—which was the best I'd had...*ever*—it was the connection. It was that he'd respectfully and almost shyly asked if I wanted to play with him, it was that he listened to me, it was that he wanted the same things. It was that he'd wanted me and wanted to be my someone.

He came back to the desk with a box of tissues and helped me clean up, only tending to himself after he was satisfied that I was comfortable and clean.

"You know I'm not 24/7, right?" I asked him.

He glanced at me. "I might have guessed," he said dryly.

"Okay, good. I only like kink in bed, and just because I like playing with domestic servitude does *not* mean I want to be a model preacher's wife and teach Sunday school and bake brownies and—"

He helped me to sitting and then kissed me to shut me up.

"I like you as you are, fiery girl," he said after he pulled away, leaving me breathless and bit stunned. "I don't want you any other way. Even if it means you argue with me at every single staff meeting. Even if it means you give me that look every time I walk by you."

I sputtered, "You're the one with a *look*! You scowl every time you walk past my desk!"

He laughed, and the sound was so foreign that it surprised the indignation right out of me. "I'm not scowling at *you*," he explained, his face still smiling and relaxed. "Scowling at myself. You see, it's not good for a preacher to get hard every time he walks past a certain church employee..."

Oh. *Oh.*

I blushed, thinking about all those scowls and what I now knew they meant. "I see."

He laughed again. "I bet you do." He took my hand and guided it down to his penis, which was already hardening again.

I licked my lips. "I don't have any plans tonight. You could always take me back to your place and make sure I really see."

The swagger was back as he grabbed his car keys, pulled his office blinds open to make sure the parking lot was empty, and then swung me easily over his shoulder.

I squealed, but I was laughing too, and the Reverend Doctor Mark Trade swaggered all the way out to his car with me as his captive, and I stayed his captive long, long, long into the night.

Until dawn, actually. Until the cock crowed.

ABOUT THE AUTHOR

Sierra Simone is a USA Today Bestselling former librarian (who spent too much time reading romance novels at the information desk.) She lives with her husband and family in Kansas City.

Website: http://thesierrasimone.com/
Facebook: http://sierrasim.one/facebookpage
Instagram: http://sierrasim.one/insta
Spotify: http://sierrasim.one/spotify

ALSO BY SIERRA SIMONE

Misadventures:

Misadventures with a Professor (Coming November 2018)

The American Queen Trilogy:

American Queen

American Prince

American King

The Priest Series:

Priest

Midnight Mass: A Priest Novella

Sinner

Co-Written with Laurelin Paige

Porn Star

Hot Cop

The Markham Hall Series:

The Awakening of Ivy Leavold

The Education of Ivy Leavold

The Punishment of Ivy Leavold

The Reclaiming of Ivy Leavold

The London Lovers:

The Seduction of Molly O'Flaherty

The Persuasion of Molly O'Flaherty

The Wedding of Molly O'Flaherty

CHOCOLATE AND COCKUP

(A CHOCOLATE LOVERS BONUS SCENE)

TARA SIVEC

Bonus scene from Tara Sivec's Chocolate Lovers series. The crazy gang is back and they're wreaking havoc on a retirement community!

CHOCOLATE AND COCKUP

"HOLY SHIT, COCKSUCKING MOTHERFUCKER!"

My body jolts and my heart starts racing when the scream from the padded lounge chair next to mine interrupts the beautiful, peaceful morning. Taking a few deep, calming breaths, I turn my head and glare at the man sitting next to me.

"Dammit, Drew. You made me mess up my crocheting. Can we keep the noise level down to at least a three? Right now, you're at *toddler throwing a hissy fit* level. People are staring."

Drew gapes at me with wide eyes and an even wider dropped-open mouth as I attempt to fix the stitch I just botched when he scared the hell out of me.

"What the hell, shit stick, you woke me up from my nap," my best friend Liz complains from her chair on the other side of Drew.

Liz leans forward and rubs the sleep out of her eyes before giving Drew the same annoyed glare I did.

"How am I gonna stay awake for bingo tonight without my mid-morning nap? Virginia Albright has won three weeks in a row. This was my week, asshole. The grand prize was a bus trip to the casino. You suck."

Drew just continues to blink rapidly at both of us, before he gets his own bodily jolt when our friend Jim pops up from the other side of Liz.

And when I say 'pops up', I mean that sarcastically. Jim has a bad back. He basically just slowly lurches forward with a loud groan.

"What's going on? What happened? Where are we?" Jim mutters, looking around in confusion.

"We're at the retirement community, out by the pool, sweetie. Go back to sleep. I'll wake you up when it's time for your blood pressure medication," Liz tells her husband.

Jim lets out another groan as he lays back down in his chair, crosses his arms over his chest and goes back to sleep.

689

"Where's Jenny?! Where the hell is my wife?! JENNNNNNNNY!" Drew suddenly shouts.

Liz reaches over the arm of her chair and smacks him in the arm, then points a few feet away to a grassy area next to the pool, where Jenny is lying on her back, rocking from side-to-side as she stares up at the clouds.

"She's fine. She's frolicking in the grass," Liz tells him.

"Uh, I don't think she's frolicking. I believe she's fallen, and she can't get up. Liz, go help her up. You know she'll just lay there all damn day without asking anyone for help," I sigh.

"Why the hell do I have to help her up? I helped her up last time. It's your turn."

"Fuck off, and go help her up before she gets a sunburn," I argue.

After lifting her arthritic finger in the air and flipping me off, Liz gets out of her chair with a moan as we all hear a few of her bones creak and pop with the effort it takes for her to move.

"You're alive," Drew whispers in astonishment, looking around at all of us, including my husband, Carter, who is still peacefully snoring in the chair next to mine.

He better thank me later for telling him to turn down the volume on his hearing aid before he settled in for his nap. He gets to continue enjoying the quiet morning while I have to deal with whatever shit show is about to happen with Drew.

"Uh, yes. I'm alive. What the hell is wrong with you?" I mutter, shaking my head in annoyance when I realize I'm going to have to undo this entire row of stitches to fix the mess I made of the scarf I was crocheting for Carter.

"I had a dream. A bad dream. An awful dream. We were all dead. You, me, Jenny, Liz, Jim, and Carter. Holy fuck, it was so real. You and Carter died in your sleep on your 75th wedding anniversary after a celebratory game of Metamucil pong. Liz and Jim kicked the bucket on their 78th wedding anniversary from heart attacks when they tested out an entire new shipment of vibrators. Jenny died in the parking lot of the emergency room, next to our personalized parking space, when she slipped on a sheet of ice trying to dislodge a whisk from her vagina and hit her head, which caused her to swallow the ball from the ball gag my arthritic fingers were unable to remove, and she choked to death. I died from a heart attack overexerting myself giving her CPR."

When Drew finally finishes rambling, I roll my eyes at him as I set my knitting down in my lap. I'd like to say that the things coming out of my friend's mouth surprise me, but they don't. At all. Over the years, he's said plenty of insane things and honestly, this dream he had, while ridiculous, sounds exactly like the way each of us could potential die someday.

Hello. My name is Claire Ellis, and I hate old people.

God, that sounds awful, but I'm allowed to say it because I'm one of those old people. I like myself just fine; it's *other* old people who get on my last damn nerve. Like Drew. And everyone else we live with in the lovely retirement community of Park Summit in Coral Springs, Florida.

"It was just a dream, Drew," I remind him as he continues to breathe so hard and fast that I'm afraid he might have a panic attack.

"How the fuck are you so calm?! WE WERE ALL DEAD! Six feet under.

Gone. Vanished. Never to walk this earth again. Never to have sex again..." he trails off, pressing his hand against his chest. "Oh, God. No more sex. This is it. I'm having a heart attack. The dream was false. I won't die hovering over my wife while she chokes on a ball gag. I'm gonna die surrounded by old people knitting, playing shuffleboard, taking naps, and every other boring, old people shit everyone around here does!"

"Drew, we're in our seventies. We live in a retirement community. This is what retirement looks like. Quiet and peaceful," I remind him, glancing around at the beautiful scenery that surrounds us.

When Drew needed hip replacement surgery a few years ago after he and his wife Jenny went a little overboard with trying out things in the Kama Sutra book, he found out his doctor had moved down here to Coral Springs. Naturally, Drew followed him for the surgery. After the hip replacement, his doctor set him up in the rehabilitation area of Park Summit. We all came down to visit him and immediately fell in love with the place.

My best friend Liz and I started a business back when we were in our twenties called *Seduction and Snacks*, which is a combination sex toy store and bakery. Our friend Jenny was hired on to handle marketing and promotions for us. After decades of working our asses off, opening up franchises of *Seduction and Snacks* all over the United States, and then eventually handing the bulk of the business over to our kids when they became adults, visiting Drew at Park Summit made us realize it was time to slow down, trust our kids to take care of the business, and just relax. The six of us moved here permanently three months after we visited Drew, and we've been here ever since.

Park Summit has everything you could ever need. We each have our own two-bedroom condo, and they offer a library, fitness center, beauty salon and spa, fun activities, beautifully landscaped grounds with a swimming pool and Jacuzzi, and even nursing care. It's like living full time at a tropical resort.

"I don't understand. How are we in our seventies already? Weren't we just in our fifties like, three years ago?" Drew asks in confusion.

"Don't try to math, Drew. No one gets math," Jim pipes up from his chair, with his eyes still closed. "Can you stop yammering now? I've got a Jazzercise class in the pool in an hour, and I need my rest."

"Baby! I think it's time for your bottled water medicine!" Jenny announces, her hand clinging to Liz's elbow as they amble over to us, and Liz helps her sit down in the chair she vacated.

"For the last time, Jenny, it's his *water pill*. It's not the same as drinking bottled water," Liz complains with a sigh.

"Jesus. JESUS!" Drew shouts, throwing his arms up in the air in frustration. "Will you look at us? What the fuck happened to us? We used to get drunk and make poor decisions. We used to get drunk and get kicked out of public places. We used to play dinner roll baseball. We used to wear awesome shirts that said things like *Hello, my name is Slutbag McFuckstick*. We used to go to BronyCon."

"*You* used to go to BronyCon. We just pointed and laughed at you for being ridiculous," Liz laughs. "And might I remind you, you're currently wearing a hat that says *I ain't dead yet, motherfuckers*."

Drew reaches up and touches the brim of his hat.

"This *is* a pretty awesome hat, if I do say so myself. But it's a fucking fishing hat. It has fishing lures on it, Liz. I am wearing an old person's fishing hat and I HATE FISHING. Fishing is for old people."

"We *are* old people," Carter says with a sigh as he adjusts the volume on his hearing aid and sits up in his chair. "Is it three o'clock yet? They're serving strawberry Jell-O and meatloaf at dinner."

"JESUS CHRIST!" Drew yells, forcing all of us to give apologetic looks to the handful of people in the pool who stop what they're doing to stare at us. "Are you guys even hearing yourselves right now? Crocheting, casino trips, bingo, mid-morning naps, Jazzercise, dinner at fucking three o'clock in the afternoon, where all they serve is soft, mushy food so our dentures don't fall out."

"But...strawberry Jell-O is delicious," my husband mumbles.

"The point is, I get it. We're getting up there in age. But why the hell are we acting like it? This is not who we are. We are not these people. We are people who fuck shit up. We're all just sitting around waiting to die," Drew complains.

"He's right, you know," Jenny nods. "Sure, we moved out here to Florida to relax, but that doesn't mean we can't still have fun. Our kids are all grown up; they're living their own lives and having fun doing it, and they've spooked us."

"Christ, Jenny. They didn't spook us. It's *ghosted*. They *ghosted* us. And they didn't ghost us. They visit all the time, call practically every day, and they're busy running our *Seduction and Snacks* empire," Liz reminds her.

"Whatever. I'm just saying, we need to live a little. Remember what it was like to have fun. *Real* fun. Not old people fun."

I really, really wanted to take a nap before dinner, but the things Jenny and Drew are saying are kind of making me a little sad. What *has* happened to us? We moved to Florida and suddenly we're not fun anymore? What the hell is that about? We started a company that sells sex toys, for God's sake. Our business is all about fun. When the six of us hung out back in the day, we had so much fun we almost got arrested. We had so much fun it resulted in a few of us going to the emergency room. Drew's right. We *are* just sitting around, waiting to die. And like his stupid fishing hat says, we ain't dead yet, mother-fuckers.

"I could handle a little fun," Jim suddenly states.

"I do have a brand new medical marijuana card for my bursitis I haven't put to good use yet," Liz muses.

"If we're fucking shit up, can we still stop by the kitchen and get Jell-O before we get started?" Carter questions.

"Before we start making plans, Drew needs to take his stool softener," Jenny announces to the group, leaning over the arm of her chair and grabbing her purse from the ground.

She sets it in her lap and digs around inside until she finds the blue, plastic, seven-day pill box, pulling it out and popping open the lid for today.

"I got you new ones since the old ones were huge and way too hard for you to swallow," Jenny informs Drew.

"THAT'S WHAT SHE SAID!" he shouts as he takes the little brown square from her fingers.

"You'll like these ones better, baby. They're chocolate chews!"

Drew holds the piece of medical chocolate in front of his face and studies it for a few minutes, before his eyes light up and he gets a devious look on his face.

"Claire, sweetie, honey, woman who my best friend knocked up at a frat party in college...do you and or Liz by any chance have a few boxes of sex toys sitting around in a closet at your condo?" Drew asks before popping the chocolate chew in his mouth.

"Why in the hell would we have *boxes* of sex toys? We don't run the company anymore, remember? All the free samples and excess product goes to our kids now. I have my own personal stash in my nightstand drawer, same with Liz," I tell him.

"Eeew, I don't want anything from your own personal stash with your old lady vagina juices on them," Drew shudders.

"I have a box of butt plugs, two boxes of bullets, a half a box of strap-ons, four small boxes of nubby finger vibrators, and three boxes of g-spot touch finger vibes," Jenny announces proudly.

"I knew there was a reason I married you," Drew tells her, leaning over his chair to give her a kiss.

Drew pulls back from Jenny and points at Liz.

"Go put that medical marijuana card to good use and get us some awesome shit."

"I can do that. I just have to check with Kevin and see if one of the golf carts are available," Liz replies.

Kevin is a wonderful young man that works as the activities director for Park Summit. He not only schedules all sorts of things to do for the people who live here, but he also handles the schedule for the fleet of golf carts the retirement community owns that residents are free to use if we need to make a quick trip to the store or want to get away and go somewhere else for dinner.

"No golf cart!" Drew yells. "Jesus Christ, we're trying to *not* be old. Only old people drive golf carts to the fucking marijuana dispensary. Take an Uber. Or a taxi. For shit's sake, don't tool up in there in a God damn golf cart. You people are a disgrace."

Drew then turns to me and gives me a chin lift.

"Think you can whip up some baked goods for us when Liz gets back?"

It's been a while since I've been in a kitchen, and I have to say, I really miss it. I was responsible for the "snacks" part of *Seduction and Snacks,* and my recipes are world famous now.

"You're damn right I can," I tell him with a smile.

"Perfect. Carter, Jim, and I will handle everything else."

"What exactly does *everything else* entail?" Carter asks.

"Duh. Inviting people to our rave, dumbass," Drew says with a roll of his eyes.

"Do people still rave? Is this still a thing? I feel like this is not going to end well," Liz says.

"When has anything we've ever done not ended well?" Drew asks.

We all start to open our mouths and he immediately holds his hands up in the air.

"Never mind. Don't answer that. This won't be like any of those other times, I swear. We're going to show all these other old ass people what it's like to have fun again. Get your crotchety, wrinkled old asses moving, and we'll meet back here in three hours."

We all push ourselves up from our chairs and as everyone else disperses, Carter slips his hand into mine and pulls me up against him.

"If we die today, I hope you know how much I love you," he tells me with a smile, leaning down and kissing the tip of my nose.

Even after all these years together, this man still gives me butterflies.

"We're not going to die today. Didn't you hear Drew's prophecy? We're not dying for a good twenty more years after an intense game of Metamucil pong," I remind him.

"STOP MAKING OUT IN PUBLIC BEFORE I PUKE, FUCKERS! LET'S GO! TIME'S A WASTING! WE'VE GOT SHIT TO FUCK UP AND POOR CHOICES TO MAKE!" Drew shouts from over by the door that leads into the main section of condos.

"Scratch that. We're probably going to die today," I mutter as Carter and I pull apart and make our way over to the building.

"Oh, my. There are a lot of...all I see is...there are so many..."

"It's okay, Kevin. You can say it," Liz states, patting poor Kevin on the back as he stares around the party room at the retirement facility in a state of shock. "Here a cock, there a cock, everywhere a cock-cock."

I can't help it, I let out a giggle when Liz says *cock-cock.* It feels good to giggle. It makes me feel young. It makes me feel like I can do anything.

As soon as I remember how legs work.

"Why does every gentleman in this room have...a problem in his pants?" Kevin asks in the nicest way possible as Mr. Schumacher walks by and gives us a wave.

None of us wave back. Our eyes all immediately drop down to the giant tent in his pants that is sticking out, loud and proud.

"Okay, the good news is, I threw away what was left of the chocolate chews. The bad news is, there were only three left out of the hundred I made," Drew explains, rushing over to us as fast as his old bones will allow, wearing a t-shirt that says *I fucked your grandmother last night.*

"Chocolate chews? Do I even want to ask what you put in those chocolate chews?" Kevin asks. "When I told you guys you could throw a small get-together today, I didn't expect...whatever this is."

"DON'T YOU JUDGE ME, KEVIN!" Drew shouts. "I was trying to liven this boring place up! Put a little excitement back into everyone's lives so it wasn't just about napping and early bird dinners!"

"Don't yell at Kevin," Jim scolds Drew. "Not all heroes wear capes. Kevin is a saint for being here with us every day, taking on the task of organizing fun activities, and making sure Mrs. Swanson doesn't drive another golf cart into the lake. Corralling us old people isn't easy. He's doing the Lord's work. You got too cocky with this party, Drew. It happens to the best of us."

"Please, will someone just explain why every man in this room has a giant bulge sticking out of the front of his pants?!" Kevin pleads, quickly wiping the panicked look off his face when another elderly gentleman that I recognize from bingo night walks by and smiles at him. "Lovely day we're having, isn't it, Mr. Jasper?"

"Best day I've had since my prostate surgery five years ago, Kevin!" Mr. Jasper announces, pointing down at his boner proudly. "Has anyone seen my wife? I need her to take care of this."

Kevin lets out a nervous laugh and points over to the buffet table filled with all of the cupcakes, brownies, cookies, and cakes I threw together earlier, where Mrs. Jasper is currently filling up a plate.

As soon as Mr. Jasper walks away, Drew lets out a sigh.

"Jenny crushes up my Viagra and puts it into delicious things because I have trouble swallowing pills. I saw those stool softening chocolate chews this morning, did a little pill crushing and mushing the powder into chocolate chews when I got back to our condo, and came up with Chocolate and Cockup. I guess I didn't think this plan through very well," he explains.

"Heh, heh, you can't swallow," I giggle.

"I HAVE A SENSITIVE ESOPHOGUS, CLAIRE!" Drew complains loudly.

"So, basically, all the men in this room are going to have massive erections while shitting their brains out. That should be fun," Carter deadpans.

All of this just makes me giggle even harder, which makes Liz look at me quizzically.

"What the hell is wrong with you? Why are you so giggly?"

I try to smother my giggling by pressing my hand against my mouth, but I can't contain it. Everything is so funny right now. Men are just wandering around the room with huge hard-ons. They're standing in small circles, talking about their golf game, with huge hard-ons. They're drinking punch and getting jiggy with it, *with huge hard-ons.*

"Oh, my Jesus. You ate the pot brownies, didn't you?" Liz suddenly asks. "You were supposed to just *make* them, not eat them. How many?"

I shrug my shoulders and look up at her sheepishly from my chair.

"I dunno. A few. Also, I don't think I need my shoulders anymore."

"For fuck's sake. Didn't you learn your lesson when we were in our twenties and you licked the wall of *Seduction and Snacks?* You never eat more than one. NEVER! At your age, you should only eat a bite. And don't even tell me you thought it wasn't working, so you kept eating them. THAT'S EXACTLY HOW IT WORKS! Not high, not high, not high, oh, my God, I'm dying. You're a grandmother! What would your grandchildren think right now?" Liz asks me with a shake of her head.

"My grandchildren would think I'm the shit!" I tell her. "My doctor told me months ago that my blood glucose level was getting close to the diabetes territory. Do you have any idea how long it's been since I've had real sugar? So, I licked the spoon when I made the brownies. And then I licked the beaters. And then the bowl. And I had to taste-test the actual batter with a few spoonfuls before that. And who the hell makes brownies and doesn't try a few when they're warm and gooey from the oven? Also, I think I might be paralyzed from the neck down."

Liz continues to shake her head at me, but she has to admit. This party has been a blast. We're listening to loud music, and it's not just the theme music from game shows on TV, and it's not loud because half of the people in this room can't hear it. It's loud because we're having *fun*. People are dancing. People are laughing. People are sneaking off to have sex all over this retirement community because the men overdosed on Drew's Chocolate and Cockup. Mrs. Anderson ate three cupcakes and is telling everyone who will listen what a big penis Mr. Anderson had, complete with holding her hands in the air at least a foot apart. This wouldn't be all that strange under normal circumstances, I guess, but Mr. Anderson died twenty years ago. Ever since I met her, all she does is cry whenever she mentions him. And now she's smiling and laughing and making dick jokes. No one in this room is acting like they're just sitting around waiting to die. They're *living*.

With huge cocks and medical marijuana highs.

"Are you gonna shut our rave down, Kevin? It was just getting good," Drew complains with a *harrumph*, crossing his arms in front of him.

"No, I'm not shutting things down. But I am going to start handing out water to everyone, get the nurse in here to take some blood pressure readings, and make sure no one else eats any brownies," Kevin informs us.

"Or cupcakes, or cookies, or cakes," I add.

"You put it in *everything*?!" Kevin asks.

"Liz got some good shit. A *lot* of good shit," I shrug, with the shoulders I realize I actually *do* still need.

Kevin mutters under his breath and then scurries off to save the day and make sure no one around here dies, just like always.

"He's a good man, that Kevin. Someone should nominate him for president," Jim states.

"You guys! Why are you all sitting over here in the corner? You're missing all the fun!" Jenny says us as she joins us, waiving a large pink vibrator in her hand. "The vibrator races are just about to start over by the refreshment table."

"NOOOOOOOOOOOOOOOOOOO!" we all scream at the top of our lungs as Liz reaches over and snatches the vibrator out of her hand.

"Will you guys calm down?" Drew huffs, wrapping his arm around Jenny's shoulders. "I'm sure Jenny isn't conducting *those* kind of vibrator races this time, are you honey?"

Back in our younger days, we attended a charity function where Jenny entered a vibrator race contest. You were supposed to pick your weapon of choice, set it down on a homemade racetrack next to a bunch of other contestants, turn it on, and then whosever vibrator made it down the track first, won. Our dear Jenny thought vibrator race meant you had to stick the thing down your pants and whoever *finished* first, won.

That's definitely something none of us wanted to witness back when we were in our twenties. Seeing that shit *now*, in a room filled with elderly people, would definitely kill everyone, and then Kevin's life would be ruined.

"You guys have such little faith in me," Jenny says with a shake of her head, pulling out from under Drew's arm. "We're doing the vibrator races the way they are supposed to be conducted. By putting them in your mouth and whoever gives the best blow job, wins!"

Jenny turns and makes her way back over to the refreshment table while we all stare after her.

"So, it looks like a lot more of our neighbors will be getting dentures today after they chip all their teeth," Jim muses, pushing himself up from his chair and turning to hold out his hand to Liz. "Let's go, my love. It will be fun. I'm sure there will be lots of blood. You like blood and pain when it's happening to other people."

With a sigh, Liz grabs his hand and laces her fingers through his.

"If someone whips out their dentures and I get hit with them, I will murder you in your sleep," she warns him as Jim gives her a kiss on the cheek.

They amble over to the now growing crowd around the refreshment table, listening to Jenny give instructions. When they're gone, Drew turns to Carter and me.

"Thank you guys for your help today. It really means a lot to me that you would do all of this. I just...it means a lot. We've been friends for a long time. Jesus, over fifty years. I know sometimes I can be over the top, but I just wanted us to have fun. I just wanted a day where we could remember what it was like to be young again," he tells us with a smile.

"Awww, buddy, look at you being all sweet and emotional in your old age. It's the stool softener, isn't it? A good daily poop just puts you in a better mood," Carter laughs, giving him a pat on the back.

"I HAVE A BOGGY PROSTATE, AND IT GIVES ME CONSTIPATION!" Drew shouts, punching my husband in the arm before turning and walking over to the vibrator races that have just begun, going by the shouting and screaming we hear on the other side of the room.

Once he's gone and it's just Carter and me left, my husband grabs both of my hands and gently pulls me up from my chair, wrapping his arms around my waist. I press my hands against his chest and look up at him with a smile, knowing that even with age, a few wrinkles, and a full head of salt and pepper hair, he's still the handsomest man in the room, and I'm lucky that he still puts up with me after all these years.

"I have a surprise for you," Carter says with a mischievous smile, removing one of his arms from around me to reach into the front pocket of his pants.

He fishes around for a second and then pulls his hand out, holding it palm up in between us.

"Oh, my God. Is that a Chocolate and Cockup?" I ask with a laugh when I see the little chocolate chew sitting in the middle of his hand.

"I confiscated one right before Drew threw what was left away. So, what do you think, Mrs. Ellis? Wanna go sneak off somewhere and have some crazy, young people sex for a few hours?" he asks with a wag of his eyebrows.

"I love you so much. And I would like nothing more than to go find somewhere quiet and have some crazy, young people sex with you."

I take the chocolate chew out of his hand, stare at it for a few seconds, and then toss it over my shoulder.

"Damn, now I won't have an uncontrollable boner for the next three hours," Carter complains with a laugh.

Clutching the front of his shirt into my fists, I pull his face down closer to mine.

"The Viagra was mushed up into a stool softener, remember? You also won't have uncontrollable shitting for the next three hours," I remind him.

"Yeah, that doesn't sound very enjoyable," Carter nods.

Tipping my chin up, I give him a quick kiss on the lips before pulling back to look into his eyes.

"Baby, I would love to have crazy, young people sex with you, but we are no longer crazy young people," I remind him.

"We did successfully throw a rave today, and you got stoned out of your mind. I may or may not have taken a picture of you staring at the wall with a little drool coming out of the corner of your mouth and sent it to the grand-kids," he informs me.

"And, what did they say?"

"They said their grandma is the shit," he says with a smile and a shrug.

"Damn right she is! So, how about we just go back to our condo, take a nice, long nap, then I'll take out my dentures and give you a blow job during Wheel of Fortune?" I suggest.

"Can I eat strawberry Jell-O, while watching Wheel of Fortune, while you give me a blow job?"

"Yes, yes you can."

"We're not crazy young people anymore," Carter says with a shake of his head.

"No, we are not."

"I'm okay with that. Wheel of Fortune Jell-O blow jobs are more my speed anyway."

Pulling away from each other, my husband takes my hand and we make our way through the room, pausing to glance over at all of our friends who are still watching the vibrator race. Jim and Liz break away from the cheering, screaming group first and meet us over by the door.

"This was a fun day, but I need a nap," Jim says with a sigh.

"Claire, I think I'm skipping bingo tonight. I'm exhausted and my knees are killing me," Liz adds.

"Yeah, we were just heading upstairs to take a nap too. Those pot brownies are wearing off and the arthritis in my hip is bothering me," I tell her.

"Are you guys leaving the party already?" Jenny complains with a pout as her and Drew join us. "We still have three more rounds of vibrator races before we crown a winner, and Drew sent Mr. Sampson out to go steal a few golf carts. We're gonna sneak out after curfew and go to a strip club! This party was such a huge hit, that every said we should make it an anally thing."

"I don't think that means what you think it means," Liz sighs.

"Anally. Every year. Duh," Jenny scoffs.

"Maybe next time, sweetie," I tell her with a smile before Liz starts losing her shit. "This was a good day, wasn't it?"

Everyone nods and murmurs their approval, while also rubbing their backs and wincing a little bit in pain.

"Are we getting too old for this shit?" Jim asks.

We all take another look around the room at all the smiling, happy old people and shake our heads, replying in unison.

"Never!"

"Anally it is then!" Jim says with a laugh. "We'll have an entire year to rest up and prepare for the next boner marijuana rave."

Good lord, we're all so ridiculous. But at least we're not boring.
Or too cocky for our own good.

The End

Check out Tara's newest comedy series, The Naughty Princess Club:
http://tarasivec.com/series/the-naughty-princess-club/

ABOUT THE AUTHOR

Tara Sivec is a USA Today best-selling author, wife, mother, chauffeur, maid, short-order cook, baby-sitter, and sarcasm expert. She lives in Ohio with her husband and two children, and looks forward to the day when they all three of them become adults and move out.

Website: http://tarasivec.com/
Twitter: https://twitter.com/TaraSivec
Instagram: https://www.instagram.com/authortarasivec/
Facebook: https://www.facebook.com/TaraSivec.authorpage/
Newsletter: http://ow.ly/acjS30cheLd

ALSO BY TARA SIVEC

Romantic Comedy

The Chocolate Lovers Series:

Seduction and Snacks (Chocolate Lovers #1)

Futures and Frosting (Chocolate Lovers #2)

Troubles and Treats (Chocolate Lovers #3)

The Chocoholics Series:

Love and Lists (Chocoholics #1)

Passion and Ponies (Chocoholics #2)

Tattoos and TaTas (Chocoholics #2.5)

Baking and Babies (Chocoholics #3)

The Holidays:

The Stocking Was Hung (The Holidays #1)

Cupid Has a Heart-On (The Holidays #2)

The Firework Exploded (The Holidays #3)

The Bunny is Coming (The Holidays #4)

The Naughty Princess Club:

At the Stroke of Midnight (The Naughty Princess Club #1)

In Bed with the Beast (The Naughty Princess Club #2)

Kiss the Girl (The Naughty Princess Club #3)

Romantic Suspense

The Playing With Fire Series:

A Beautiful Lie (Playing With Fire #1)

Because of You (Playing With Fire #2)

Worn Me Down (Playing With Fire #3)

Closer to the Edge (Playing With Fire #4)

Romantic Suspense/Erotica

The Ignite Series

Burned (Ignite Series #1)

Branded (Ignite Series #2)

New Adult Drama

Watch Over Me

Contemporary Romance:

Fisher's Light

Worth the Trip

The Story of Us

Wish You Were Mine

Romantic Comedy/Mystery

Jed Had to Die

The Fool Me Once Series:

Shame on You (Fool Me Once #1)

Shame on Me (Fool Me Once #2)

Shame on Him (Fool Me Once #3)

Psychological Thriller

Bury Me

THE GOLDEN SOMBRERO

A BALLS IN PLAY NOVELLA

BY KATE STEWART

The boys are gearing up for another world series and have suddenly become superstitious. The girls are just fine with it, until the new routine includes abstinence.

Golden Sombrero - In baseball, a golden sombrero is a player's inglorious feat of striking out four times in a single game.

ALICE

I looked over to Rafe and licked the salt off the side of my margarita glass. His eyes flared before his subtle, but all-knowing smirk appeared. Cocky bastard! He might have won the battle before dinner by effectively ignoring the naked tease I did for him before I got dressed, but I was determined to win the war.

Erica and I exchanged a conspiratorial glance across the table as the guys rattled on about strategy. Our husbands—two of the sexiest and most talented players in baseball—were gearing up to take the field tomorrow in an attempt to win the last game in the world series. Well, it will be the last game of the season if they continue their winning streak and the second series win for them both.

Erica and I were confident it was in the bag, but because they didn't get past the playoffs last year, Ren and Rafe were in a different state.

They were nervous . . . and suddenly so superstitious that they'd decided sex with their wives was off the table until the series was taken. It was an old superstition of Ren's from high school that Erica told me about at lunch yesterday when I couldn't figure out what had gotten into my husband. Rafe always rose to the occasion, literally, when I made any sort of pass at him. He'd never turned me down for sex and was usually the one to initiate it, but for the past week, he'd done everything to avoid it.

Erica and I decided that we were going to put that bullshit, half-baked notion that abstinence enhanced performance to rest tonight.

The four of us decided to have an early dinner and spend a quiet night at home. We still had the home field advantage, which meant tomorrow's game was the last Denver would host. Our ballers had no intention of packing any bags, so when the guys were done obsessing at dinner, they would both go home and tear up the carpet alone in an attempt to psych themselves up for the game.

Despite the amazing fit of baseball pants and the showcase of athleticism on the field, baseball was all about numbers, statistics, and a hell of a lot of preparation. My husband, Rafe "The Bullet" Hembrey was currently and inarguably the best pitcher in the league. Erica's husband, Ren "Tin Man" Makavoy, was his catcher and go-to strategist. The only thing missing was Andy, a mentor for both Rafe and Ren who had to fly home due to the impending birth of his daughter. I knew if we didn't have our all-stars out at this Mexican restaurant, they would no doubt have Andy on facetime, contractions or no contractions. It was the nature of the baseball beast.

All three men lived by the family-first philosophy, but end season was the one and only time we let that rule slide, especially when the series was on the line. Our boys ran with it, trying their best to maintain their badassery without giving away that their emotions and nerves were the true rulers of the day. They were as nervous as school girls on prom night. Our job was to take their shit with a grain of salt and do whatever we could to be supportive. Neither of us minded doing our jobs until they pulled the no "O" card.

It was one thing to withhold sex with your spouse out of a long-running superstition, but it was another thing entirely to withhold all sex because you got an inkling. Erica and I weren't a couple of horny teenagers. We were mothers and wives who deserved the same amount of consideration. It had been a long season for *all* of us, not just the two men ranting over fajitas.

"Rafe, honey, eat something," I said, softly leaning his way so he got a money shot of my cleavage. Both men's eyes darted down briefly out of man instinct and then quickly away. Erica winked to let me know she took no offense. They were boobs. And both men were boob men, which was why we'd both worn tight-fitting dresses and push-up bras that had our girls held up high and exposed just enough for any healthy man within a small radius to take notice. Basically, our tits were on the table in offering along with the fajitas.

There was zero room for shame when we had goals. In the name of seduction, I wore my long blonde hair down—just the way Rafe liked it—and painted my lips in crimson, which should have jogged up some healthy sexual memories.

Rafe surveyed my tabletop tits.

"Stop it. Those are my tits, and everyone is looking."

"Sorry." I shrugged. "I think they're confused as to who their owner is at the moment. They just wanted a little attention."

He moved in, his voice dropping to a heated whisper. "Tomorrow night, I'll give them all the attention they want," he promised, eyeing the two breast friends on my chest as if they had turned on him. "And I believe I've made it abundantly fucking clear who they belong to."

"Oh?" I said, a little smile playing on my lips. I could feel the tension between us and reveled in the little victory of seeing him squirm when I ran my tongue across my lower lip.

"Stop that too," he ground out between clenched teeth.

"Are you getting hard?" I asked in a breathy whisper. "Because I think I saw a private dining room back there for parties. We can start in there with my lips and then . . ."

There was a small amount of commotion on the other side of the table, and we both looked over to see Erica looking guilty while Ren fumed.

"Everything okay over there?" I asked amused.

"Perfect," Erica said, doing a horrible job of hiding her shit-eating grin. We were up to no good and it felt great.

Rafe darted his eyes between the two of us. "What's going on?"

"What do you mean?" I asked, feigning innocence. If he wasn't going to come out with a confession, I wasn't about to either.

Ren's brows rose as he looked between his wife and me. "Are you two boycotting our cockblock?"

Ren was amused as we remained mute; Rafe was not. I had a feeling I was in for more of a fight.

"What are you talking about?" Erica asked innocently.

Ren leaned in. "You know damn well what I'm talking about. This morning, you cooked breakfast naked."

"I was hot," she said before she took a scoop of guacamole.

"You were hot, huh?" He chuckled. "But you still wore your Uggs?"

Erica shrugged.

"Okay, if that's how you want to play it," Ren whispered with a sly grin.

"You aren't making it past midnight, Cinderella," she whispered back, loud enough for us all to hear. Ren rubbed his hands together with glee. Her challenge was accepted.

"Oh, it's on, baby, but my bedtime is nine," he warned playfully as she shook her head at his nonsense. "I think you can manage to seduce me by then?"

Erica's hand disappeared from view. "I really have no clue what you're talking about," she murmured as she leaned toward him. A second later, he jerked in surprise, leaving no doubt where her hand had wandered. I burst out laughing as a string of curses erupted from him.

Erica grinned at me, and I grinned back.

Club wives were a force of nature in our own right. In all my years with my husband, I'd never used sex as a weapon or a strategy. During the season, I spent every minute I could with him, intimate or not, and I always looked forward to the offseason. It usually started with a sex fest of epic proportions, and while I knew my patience was about to pay off, I had a point to make. He didn't get to use our sex life as a bargaining chip with the baseball gods.

We all sized each other up, silent resolution in our minds.

It. Was. On.

We all knew the stakes. It was a power play.

A power play that my husband was not at all happy about. I could see it in his posture. It was the longest we'd gone being in the same house without getting intimate. He was as ready as ever to raise the white flag. I was his weakness, and the wife in me rejoiced over him still having such a softness for me. My libido liked it too. Rafe pensively studied me as if he was trying to decide if I was a friend or the enemy.

"What's eating you, Hembrey?" Ren asked smugly from across the table. "You afraid she'll get the best of you?" He was toying with him as if Ren didn't have a thing in the world to worry about himself. Cocky was not in his favor. In fact, cocky was about to get his ass handed to him.

"I'm good," Rafe muttered with false confidence. "You should worry about yourself."

"Oh, I think I can handle it," he said, taking a sip of his water. The men were stone sober, which was going to make it harder for us, not that alcohol was a tool, but for me, it was a miracle worker when it came to freeing my inhibitions and conquering my gag reflex. Unfortunately, I hadn't had a drop. When Rafe ordered my usual Margarita, I'd asked the waitress to nix the tequila on the sly. It was a strategic move on my part to throw him off while keeping him on his toes. The lower the drink in my glass got, the more worried Rafe looked.

I kept my laugh to myself as I sucked the rest of the sweet and sour concoction down, making an exaggerated amount of noise.

"That's enough, Mrs. Hembrey. We should probably get back to Clover," Rafe said as he took my glass from me before gesturing to the waitress for the check.

"She's with her grandmother for the night," I said with a hiccup.

Rafe visibly paled. "Oh?"

"Yeah, I told Dutch to keep her, I thought I'd give you a massage before bed."

Ren cleared his throat and Rafe met his eyes. "I've seen your balls man, and I'm truly sorry for what you weren't blessed with, but now would be a time to *Grinch* them up and make them three sizes bigger."

"Fuck yourself," Rafe spat back. "I can handle my woman."

Ren didn't miss a beat. "No, you can't."

"Thank you," I said, taking it as a compliment before I turned to my husband with a wink. "Shall we, Bullet?"

Rafe's scorn-filled gaze met mine and he slapped his Amex on the table the minute the check was set down.

"Rafe, let's talk a minute," Ren said, as I winked at Erica who was biting her cheeks to keep from laughing. The night was still young and no matter what shenanigans we had planned, it was still early enough for us to have our fun and for the boys to get enough rest for game day. Ren and Rafe took off to the bar and began what appeared to be a heated conversation as Erica and I sat lingering at the table giving them little waives when they both looked back at us.

"Looks like more strategy," Erica cooed, blowing a kiss at Ren.

"They're afraid. We've already got them," I assured as Rafe turned around caging Ren in, his back to us.

It. Was. So. On.

RAFE

What a fucking disaster. I didn't have a chance in hell. Not only did I want to fuck the hell out of my wife but also she was determined to seduce me before the night was over. Truth be known, I was already there. Between her ruby-red lips, long platinum locks, and the dress that she looked poured into, my balls were aching and my cock had been at midnight for the last two hours. As ridiculous as it was, I'd agreed with Ren to keep sex out of the equation and focus on training. I was still pitching solid, but I knew my years in the majors were numbered. Every pitch mattered, and the countdown began as soon as the ink dried on my new contract. Someone would come along in a few years and take my place, but I had made it my mission to make that glove hard to fill. I just wasn't sure doing so at the expense of my sex life was all that worth it. I'd seen her hurt the last few times I'd rejected her. I hated doing it, but I didn't know how she would feel about my and Ren's attempt to keep focused and the ridiculous lengths we were going to. We were pro ball players, and sure, it wasn't our first rodeo, but I wanted it just as much as I did my first pitch in the majors.

Facts were facts.

Fact One: Fasting was a sign of faith.

Fact Two: Fasting on pussy, well that was the ultimate sacrifice for ball.

And I was seconds away from committing a sacrilegious act.

My wife was true proof that God existed.

She gave me a pensive smile while we walked to her Land Rover. Even after years of marriage, I still loved her fiercely, and my attraction to her hadn't waned a single fucking second. Nothing in the world would feel better than pushing into her and sliding home. My cock ached at the thought as I subtly adjusted myself in the seat before I started the SUV. The last thing I wanted to do was alert her to the fact my dick was turning purple. She had every bit of my attention, including earlier when I pretended not to notice the sway of her hips as she toweled off after her shower. She was freshly shaved, bare, and I knew she was wet. She was prepped for me and the only thing that kept me from walking over to her and taking it was the stupid ass pledge.

I could just give in, but she had thrown down the gauntlet and challenged me. I wasn't some macho asshole who couldn't handle eating a little crow. I'd swallowed a lot of shit during our relationship for the sake of keeping the peace. But Alice was dangerous when she was set on something. And I didn't mean that in the naughty, dangerously sexy sense. She was downright dangerous if not disastrous in break-out-the-fucking-headgear-and-knee-pads-before-you-bend over-and-kiss-your-ass-goodbye kind of way.

Inside the Rover, the battle had begun. Alice had kicked off her heels and propped her feet on the dash, her perfect, pink painted toes sparkling in the fading sunlight. Her dress rode up her thighs, showcasing her lengthy, toned legs. She worked hard on her body—for herself, for our daughter, for me—and I'd never failed to show it my appreciation, until this past week.

It was never a question of what mattered the most to me. Ball took a back seat to my family. It was her and our baby girl, Clover, who was my other good-luck charm. It would always be them. Four seasons in the majors had only proven I was right to choose her and a lucky son of a bitch because she chose me back. My wife was a bad ass. A pilot, club wife, and mother, who was damn good at all her jobs.

"I love you," she said simply as I pulled the belt over my shoulder. I paused briefly as she leaned over, the look in her eyes sincere, raw, and vulnerable, a deadly combination for me.

"Alice." I prayed and protested at the same time. "Come on, baby, show some mercy."

"Forget about all that for a second," she whispered sweetly before she crawled onto my lap and wrapped her arms around my neck. "I'm so proud of you," she murmured between us. "I think you are amazing, Rafe Hembrey."

My heart bottomed out as I was reminded of the time she confessed her affection for me in front of a table of ballplayers. That might have been the moment I realized I loved her. She was so bold then, and not much had changed. I grew rock hard beneath her, but she showed the mercy I had begged for and ignored it. She was sincere with her temporary truce.

"I've been thinking about our life a lot lately, all the things we've done. I wake up and thank God every day that I'm yours. There are so many things we have left to do. And I really want to give you a son."

Everything inside me exhaled as she leaned in and took my lips.

"I love you too, baby. I want him too."

"We can practice tonight." She panted as she broke away from my kiss. "I'll hold back from swallowing."

"Jesus, Alice." I grunted as she started a slow grind on my lap, her truce flying out the window.

"I need you," she hummed the words, tugging my bottom lip between hers before she let go. "God, can you imagine how amazing it will feel if you pull that zipper down right now?"

"That's it," I said, lifting her easily and depositing her onto her seat. She looked wildly beautiful, her skin flushed with need for me. All I had to do was get her home and feed her some of her favorite ice cream. A full stomach always knocked her out. I'd make it up to her. I'd given Ren my word.

"That was a dirty move, Alice. I need to keep sharp," I stated in resignation. "It's just business, baby, don't take it personally."

"Fine, I'll keep my hands all to myself." She reclined her seat back, a wicked gleam full of intent in her eyes.

"Don't you dare," I warned.

"Just like old times," she cooed, trailing her hand from her knee to mid-thigh before it slipped under her dress.

My dick jumped as I started the engine, but the noise wasn't even close to loud enough to drown out the tiny moan and then a whimper that came from her lips. She arched her back as I backed the truck up at warp speed and parked in another space when I heard another moan. I couldn't help my lust-induced haze at her display. Her movements were subtle, her hand well hidden, but it was the look in her eyes as she watched me, touching herself, that had me on a tightrope.

"Rafe, please. I need you."

She was pulling out the big guns. "Oh, fuck, don't do that."

"Then you do it," she challenged tossing her head back with another low moan.

Fucking disaster.

Surveying the parking lot and seeing the coast was clear I called her bluff and pulled her dress back to see no panties, and not only that, she was halfway to bringing herself to the brink.

I might have given Ren my word that I wouldn't do the deed, but that didn't mean I couldn't help her out.

"Rafe," she whimpered as her eyes implored mine.

"Jesus baby, if I do this, will you let it go?"

Unable to wait for her answer I gripped the back of her head and caught her next moan on my tongue. Her whole body trembled in my hold as I kissed her deep and slapped her hand away, replacing her fingers with my own.

"Fuck, you are so beautiful," I murmured as she rode my fingers and clutched the back of my head while I took a sound bite of her exposed cleavage.

"I'm going to come," she moaned out weakly before her body started to shudder under my touch, her core squeezing my fingers. I was so hard up, I was grinding against the console halfway into her seat and rubbing my shit raw as her breath caught. "I'm about to . . . wait, Rafe, it just isn't fair."

She reached between us and stilled my hand. I was so eager to see her come, her words were like a tide of iceberg water.

"What are you doing?" I asked as she straightened herself in the seat.

"I'll wait for you," she assured. "I want to wait for you."

"What?" I pulled back. "You were about to come."

"I was sooo close but I want to wait. Get me home and finish me off?"

"Stop this shit." I was trying to pull her dress back up as she tried to keep it down. "Damn it, woman, let me have it," I said, making an effort to get back to where I was, seconds away from blowing my load in my jeans. "I'll take one for the team."

"Not much of a team without you."

Pissed, my dick spoke on my behalf. "That was your one and only shot, Mrs. Hembrey. Don't come begging when you get yourself all worked up later."

Her answering smile had an underlying hostility behind it that told me that, as soon as this game was over, I'd be paying for that comment.

"Let's go home," she whispered, her tone a decibel away from an order.

"Okay." I straightened in my seat and re-buckled my belt when the idea occurred to me. "I need to stop at Home Depot first." She looked at the clock on the dash while I hid my smirk.

Some men hated the mundane things like keeping up with the grass or fixing up the house. Not me, I lived for the days I could have Clover ride the mower with me or being there to reach something Alice needed from the top shelf. It was the little things that kept me grounded. Last year, I spent my off days building Clover's playhouse. I was a shitty carpenter, but you wouldn't know it by the look on my daughter's face when she saw the purple eyesore in our backyard.

"We need to get back, I think I left a candle burning. Can Home Depot wait?"

Damn it! We both knew she hadn't left a damn thing burning but the candle trumped any excuse I could have come up with to stall her. And she knew it too. All I could think about was her tight wet pussy and my fingers. If I caught a whiff of her scent on them, I was fucking done. I opened the console and found some hand wipes and snatched one. We had fifteen miles to home and then I was a free man. I could hide out in my man cave watching game stream to prep for tomorrow and Alice couldn't argue about it. It was an unspoken agreement that we had toward the end of the season. I was all business and she was compliant.

She frowned at me when I tossed the towel in the small trash bag she kept up front. I kissed her cheek. "Tomorrow, baby. I'll make it up to you; I promise."

I took her answering silence as confirmation.

Feeling home free, I tapped my fingers to a song playing on the radio. I hummed along as game day thoughts began to circulate. I was getting back on track just as my wife spoke up.

"I was thinking we could try anal tonight."

ALICE

"Rafe!" I screeched as he swerved back into our lane after narrowly missing a Prius. He hastily pulled over to the side of the road, a string of curses coming from his mouth.

"Was there something in the street? What happened?"

He took a few calming breaths before he turned to me, his eyes narrowed. "What happened?" he boomed, his voice making me jump. Apparently, those breaths hadn't helped. "*You* happened. Anal? What in the *hell* are you doing, trying to get us killed?"

"I didn't do anything." I couldn't help it, I finally let a little anger seep through. "I was just—"

"Cut it out, Alice. I mean it. Tomorrow is important to me, I can't deal with this right now." His words were clipped.

"*Deal* with this? Or did you mean deal with *me*? I wasn't trying to make you *deal* with anything."

"Newsflash, Mrs. Hembrey, the last time you had a bright bedroom idea you broke my nose."

It was true, we'd been going at it doggy style like a bunch of crazed porn stars and reenacting the video when the unthinkable happened. "The website said I shared to video on my newsfeed! I was freaking out!"

"Yeah, I had two black eyes and a broken nose opening week because of it."

"Well, it was an April fool's joke and one I didn't mastermind. I still wonder how many orgasms they ruined. And that was totally not my fault."

"This is the series, Alice. I can't just push repeat. So, I'm sorry, but you're going to have to put your grand plans on the back burner for one more day."

I bit my lip to keep my explosion inside. The man was missing the point—not that I was even sure I wanted to make it anymore. I didn't want us at odds right before one of the biggest game days of his career. At the same time, with

717

all the effort I'd put into the night, not being able to take advantage of it all made me want to break his nose the old-fashioned way.

I decided to take the high road.

"I'm sorry."

He expelled a frustrated breath. "I am too. Let's just go home, okay?"

I nodded, turning to face the window to keep from letting him see my hurt. My emotions were volleying. I'd been hormonal for months and I finally knew the reason. I already had his son . . . or daughter growing inside me. But I hoped it was a boy. I was going to tell him after I seduced him and we had a night of no-holds-barred, clothes-ripping sex before our next chapter began.

Plus, what better time to tell him than before he won his second series?

I pushed the anger down as he got us home. In the garage, he sat idle as I gripped the handle to get out.

I glanced his way and saw a distant look in his eyes as a sweet smile budded on his lips. "Remember that time you got pissed at me and tried to walk home?"

I nodded.

"That was the night I knew I was in love with you. I was thinking about it earlier tonight. I loved you because you were bold, mouthy, and had zero fear when it came to taking chances."

A part of me softened at his attempt to make peace, but the resentful part of me was too angry to do anything more than give him a small smile. The night he was referring to he couldn't keep his hands off me, which was stark contrast to where we were in that moment.

"It was a good night."

His expression softened and he slipped his hand around mine. "I'm sorry, I shouldn't have blown up on you." He chuckled. "God, Alice, anal?"

"Let's just forget it."

"How long are you going to be mad at me?"

I scoffed and slid from the car.

"That long, huh?" He muttered behind me as we made our way to the garage door.

I turned on him suddenly bumping into his chest and he stilled us both.

"Stay here, okay? Just wait a minute before you come in."

He frowned down at me. "Why?"

"Because I'm asking nicely."

"Nope," he said, letting out a loud breath. "I thought we agreed to table this."

"Listen, you arrogant ass. I'm long past worrying about your cock, okay? Trust me, I'm *far* from in the mood at this point. But I did something in there I don't want you to see. So just give me a minute!"

He raised his hands in defeat. "Fine."

I turned and rushed through the door to start cleaning up the mess I made before we left. Rafe had waited twenty minutes in the garage for me while I set everything up. I was just about to hit the kitchen counter when I heard him speak up behind me.

"What's all of this?"

"You said you'd wait."

"I lied," he said, his eyes roaming over the counter full of supplies. "What's going on here?"

"Nothing," I said, sweeping an arm over the sauce bar I set up and tossing it into a trash bag. I was so looking forward to giving a caramel blow job.

Rafe picked up the bottle and smiled. I snatched it out of his hand, but he just took the bag from me and started rummaging through it.

"And what was this for?" He lifted the spikey cover band and stretched it with his index and pointer finger.

"It's a tickler. One of the wives had a kink party a few weeks ago, and I got a few things."

He raised a brow as he started pulling things out of the bag. "A few things?"

"Fine, I bought one of *everything*," I said in a huff. "Lots of couples use toys."

"And what were you planning on doing with this?" He pressed the button on the slim green dildo with an alien head handle, and it began to vibrate.

"It's an anal probe."

"Oh," he said, as he studied it closely.

"And I was going to use it on you," I added.

His eyes widened.

"I've been googling and—"

"That's never a good thing." His chuckle didn't let up as he studied the toy.

"Oh, you can just go to hell." I snatched the dildo and bag from his hand , but before I could retreat, I was caught by the wrist and brought back to his chest. "What's going on, Alice?"

"Nothing, I just thought we could have some fun tonight."

"You were serious back there about . . ."

"You will never know," I said "I just wanted to experiment a little, it's healthy."

He pushed out another breath. "Alice, I didn't know you went to all this trouble. I really am sorry."

"I know," I said softly. "It's fine. I'm going to take a bath and go to bed."

Rafe looked at the clock. "It's only seven."

"Yeah, but I'm sure you have some things to do, right?"

He shook his head as his eyes did a quick perusal. "You look so beautiful. Did I tell you that?"

"You did," I said, hating the sound of my voice. It was full of disappointment.

He frowned. "Tell me how to make it up to you?"

"It's over, you win," I said, giving him a mustered wink. Inside my heart broke a little.

"Hey," he said, moving to stand in front of me as I tried to leave him there. He was so tall I had to crane my neck to look up at him. I felt stupid and childish with my bag full of toys and my tantrum. There was absolutely nothing wrong with our life, sexually or otherwise. I didn't know what I was looking for, but it damn sure wasn't to guilt my husband the night before one of the biggest games of his career.

"It was a stupid idea."

"Baby you know I want you every day, right?"

"I know. Rafe, nothing's wrong, I just thought we could have some fun, and instead I pissed you off."

He smirked. "You always piss me off."

I could hear the grandfather clock tick in the hall. Our house was eerily silent without Clover there. For a brief moment, I wondered what our life would be like when our children were grown and the noise was gone. I had to check myself. We would be fine. Of course we would be fine.

He studied my face for a few seconds. "I'm a fucking dick. I should have never agreed to that bullshit. At the very least, I should have talked to you about it first. I'm sorry."

He slid one strap of my dress down and placed an open-mouthed kiss on my shoulder. I sighed into him, pulling him closer. "I've been hard for hours, baby, please put me out of my misery."

"Really?" I said, pulling out of his reach, my eyes searching his. "I don't want a pity fuck."

He took the bag and emptied it onto the island behind me. "Well, I do. Forgive me?"

"Rafe, I feel stupid."

"Today I've imagined you in a hundred different scenarios before you came screaming my name. I'm about to test out half. Let's get you naked."

"Rafe, if you don't want—"

He ripped my dress away from my chest before he bent to take a nipple in his mouth. His groan sent an electric current straight to my clit.

"Rafe," I moaned, as he went straight to the other nipple while he lifted me to sit on the island. Seconds later, I was spread wide, my feet planted on the large marble top while I writhed below him. He slowly dipped his finger inside me and watched it go in and out before his chocolate stare drifted like fire, licking every inch of bared skin before his eyes met mine.

"You're sticky wet." He groaned as he pushed another finger inside and I grappled to hold onto the edge of the counter behind me. I loved it when he stared at my naked flesh like it was the eighth wonder of the world or some mystery he couldn't solve and didn't want to. "So tight, so fucking sweet."

He bent slowly as he fucked me with his fingers, and out tongues met in a fiery kiss. I was soaked by the time he pulled away and audibly aroused. Eagerly, I sat up to free his massive erection and he pressed me back down with his palm. I loved the contrast of his tan skin on my porcelain complexion and the power he held with that act alone.

"Do you want my tongue or my cock?"

"Both," I answered hoarsely. He reached behind me and grabbed the caramel lube and squeezed the bottle so that only a small amount fell onto my clit before he took a taste from his finger. His thick digits were still tearing into me, and he twisted them as he studied my face for a reaction.

"I'm going to come," I warned.

He bent over me, his whisper gravel. "Hands, tongue, cock, repeat."

"Rafe—" I started matching the thrust of his fingers.

And then there was a sensation I'd never felt in all our years together.

"Rafe is that your—"

"I hope you were serious," he whispered, his eyes lighting fire in a way I'd never seen. "Because I want this." His thumb circled my forbidden, and he pressed just hard enough to have me gasping.

"It's yours," I said softly. "All of me, always." Just as I said it, he pressed his thumb fully into my ass. It felt piercing at first, then foreign, and then incredible with the added movement of his skilled fingers in my core. I saw stars. "Oh, god, oh god." Rafe leaned forward, demanding my eyes and my every reaction as I came in a rush. His fingers never slowing as I lay lax on the counter. I felt it then, the rush between my legs.

"Wait . . . what is that?"

Rafe looked equally surprised. "Damn, baby."

"What? What?"

Rafe looked satisfied and giddy at the same time. "You little freak."

I looked down to see I was soaked, and not just soaked, leaking. "Is this normal?"

"For freaks like you. Shhh," he said leaning down to take my mouth in another explosive kiss. When he pulled away, he gave me one of his rare smiles that let me know he was impressed by me. It seemed we both had just tapped into something unknown. And if that last orgasm was any indication of what was to come, I would fly the freak flag proudly.

"I'm such a lucky son of a bitch," he said sweetly. He kissed a hot trail down my chest before he dove between my legs and licked me from ass to clit in one swipe. I looked down at him as he pushed my thighs apart, spreading me wider before he pressed his tongue into me. My eyes rolled back as he took his time licking leisurely a while he palmed my ass. As soon as I was relaxed, Rafe pressed another finger into my backside. That time it went in far easier, and I gasped in surprise.

"I fucking love being able to touch you this way," he said before he closed his plump lips around my clit and pressed them together *hard*. I detonated as he got more adventurous with his finger, pumping it in and out of me as I shuddered and came.

Barely recovered, I moved to touch him and hadn't realized he had already rid himself of his jeans and briefs, the fat head of his beautiful cock gleaming with precum. He wasted no time once he lined himself up and pushed into me with purpose. My whole body jerked at the feeling while we both exploded in sensation.

"Fuck, Alice, *fuck!*" He roared, as he pistoned his hips, slamming into me, his chest flexing under his T-shirt. I gripped his collar and tugged. "Off, Rafe, take it off," I said, my heart knocking in my chest and threatening to break free. He was ravenous, his body flexing as he threw every piece of himself into his fucking. I could see the build in him as he pressed in harder. I wanted the night to be memorable, so I began to voice my thoughts, which only spurred him on.

"You're so hard, baby, fuck me. I've been dreaming about this cock all week. Get it, Rafe."

He pressed in harder with each word I spoke, fucking animalistic, and his eyes turned to pools of black as he pinched my nipples between his fingers and sped up.

Thinking quickly, I grabbed the small bottle of liquid next to my head on the counter and popped the top thrusting it toward Rafe's nose. Confused, he looked down at me as he kept a madman's pace, hammering me into the island.

"Fuck, baby, I'm about to go."

"Inhale this right when you're about to come," I said in offering. And when you come, do it all over me."

"You want that?" he asked, a hint of shock in his voice as his eyes flared.

"Yes. *Please.*"

"Jesus, Alice, so fucking dirty," he grunted, his orgasm within reach. He pulled out, his cock fisted in hand as I thrust the bottle toward him. He grabbed it with his free hand and inhaled deeply, pumping himself with the other. It took only a few seconds before confusion took over his features and then his eyes crossed. His dick went from rock hard to a noodle in his hand before he passed out and disappeared from my line of sight, taking half of the counter's contents with him.

I'd done it. I'd finally killed my husband.

I heard the crash as he went down.

"Rafe! Oh my God, Rafe!"

He was on all fours next to the trashcan, which had toppled over upon impact, while the smiling alien dildo vibrated next to him. In seconds, I was down on the kitchen floor, calling his name. Agonizing moments passed before I heard his answering groan.

"Rafe, are you okay?"

He came to a minute later as I tried my best not to laugh. I'd never seen anything like it. One second, he was fucking me like a God, his cock the hardest it had ever been, the next he was *assed*-out on the floor. I studied the bottle as he sat up against the cabinets and glared at me. "What in the hell was that?"

Scrambling for words, I let them all out in a rush. "It's called poppers. It's supposed to enhance your orgasm. She said it was safe!"

He snatched the bottle out of my hand and gave me the nasty side-eye as a nervous laugh I had absolutely no control over escaped me.

"This fucking shit is toxic. Look, it says 'harmful if inhaled'. What the hell were you thinking?"

I took the bottle away. "This doesn't make sense, Amy said she and Rhett use it all the time."

"Well, that explains a lot about Rhett," he snapped, moving to stand. "Damn it, woman, are you trying to kill me?"

"Rafe, I'm so sorry." My laughter chose that moment to break through the terror I felt just seconds earlier. I was hysterical as he glared at me.

"I really am so sorry," I said, my apology shit due to the fact that I couldn't stop laughing. Rafe stormed off, his beautiful ass the last thing I saw as he tore out of the kitchen. Once I'd pulled myself together and cleaned up the mess I didn't want to have to explain to his grandmother or our daughter in the morning, I found Rafe in his study, watching highlight reels. He was livid as he sat in his recliner, and I was sure his ego was bruised. I wasn't about to try to make it up to him sexually. I was one strikeout away from pulling off a golden sombrero. I would just have to suck it up and admit to Erica when it came to seducing my husband, I was nothing short of a disaster.

"I know you're mad, just remember that I thought it was going to make you feel good. I would never intentionally hurt you or try to sabotage your game, and you know it."

Silence. *Shit.*

"For what it's worth, I'm sorry," I said with a wobbling chin. "I'm going to take a bath and go to bed." My voice cracked, and a second later the dark eyes I loved so much scoured me before they drifted back to the television.

I turned on my heel and spent the better part of ten minutes counting my blessings. There was absolutely nothing wrong with the way things were. So what if my plans had gone awry. I would make it up to him. And after he won the series tomorrow, I would tell him he had a son or daughter to look forward to. I didn't have it in me to screw that part of the night up.

And though it made me a bit of an asshole, I couldn't help the giggle that escaped when I thought of the expression on Rafe's face when he smelled the bottle. After another laughing fit, I sank into the lukewarm tub. I was surprised when the water jostled a few minutes later. I opened my eyes to see Rafe had joined me in the bath and was pouring water over his dark locks and sweeping the hair away from his head. He looked so sexy, dark and wet. I had to resist the urge to lunge for him. I loved that looking at him still made me feel that way.

"You forgive me?"

He gave me a weary look. "I'm trying."

A tiny laugh escaped my lips, and he narrowed his eyes before a hint of a smile appeared on his. A few seconds later we were both laughing hysterically.

When some of our hilarity had subsided, Rafe playfully pushed some water my way. "God woman, you're a walking hazard."

"I know," I said, coughing out the rest of my giggle as I tilted my face toward the heavens. "Someone has to be looking out for us, you think?"

"It would appear that way with all the shit we've managed to escape. Do you know what that shit was?" Rafe asked.

"She said it was poppers," I said with a shrug.

"Babe . . . that was fucking *huff* liquid."

"What?"

"Yes. Google it. I'm surprised you didn't."

"Oh. God. Rafe! Do you think it will do any long-term damage?"

"No," he said as if the idea were absurd.

"I swear I didn't know."

"I know."

"That was a blonde moment for sure. Jesus. I'm smarter than that. I think I was just excited when I got all that stuff. I feel terrible. I could have really hurt you."

He pulled my foot onto his chest. "With that face, body, and sexual imagination, babe, you're the most dangerous woman alive."

"You should divorce me now and cut your losses," I said before rubbing my hands over my face. "I had that crap in the house with Clover."

He pulled my hands away. "Don't ever say divorce again. There is *no end* to us. Ever. Don't use that word. Got it? It was a mistake and not a big deal. There isn't a damn thing either one of us can do that we can't get through."

"I know."

"I love you, you crazy, crazy woman."

"I know."

"No end, Alice."

I nodded. "Got it."

"Good. Let's just try to enjoy the rest of our night, okay?"

"Okay. And you better take a shower before the game tomorrow, Bullet, you don't want to hit the field smelling like a pansy," I said, blowing some lavender-scented bubbles out of my hand in his direction.

"This is nice, I needed this," Rafe said, as we massaged each other's feet. He held mine on his chest while I had to practically turn around in the tub to get my hands on his.

"Your feet are huge."

He gave me a sultry smile. "You know what they say about big feet. I can back up that theory."

"Well, you blessed our innocent little girl with your huge feet. She'll be made fun of."

"The *hell* she will. I'll beat that bully's ass," Rafe interjected looking pissed.

"Jeesh. She starts kindergarten next year, you intend to beat all the babies that mess with yours?"

"Hell yes I will, I'll push those little booger munchers down when the parents aren't looking."

"You're terrible," I scorned. "And your daughter told me today I needed a 'tude justice.'"

Rafe's laugh echoed through the bathroom. "An attitude adjustment, huh?"

"Yeah, I turned the cartoons off for naptime."

"Mean," he said, taking her side. He always did. It was the only time we argued.

"God, I hope we don't have another girl," I said, giving up on his feet and settling on his calves. "This one better be a boy."

"This one?" Rafe's hands stilled on my foot and gave me a pointed look.

"I'm pregnant." His jaw dropped, and I grinned while his eyes watered. "I was going to tell you after we experimented, but, well, that went to hell in a handbasket. You're a daddy, again."

Before I knew what was happening I was in his arms, wrapped so tight I couldn't breathe.

"Rafe," I choked out as he squeezed me harder.

"Damn, Alice," he croaked before he pulled away. The look on his face was priceless. "You kept that from me all day!"

"I know, I'm sorry, but I wanted to make it special."

"Baby, we're in a bathtub filled with lavender and have the house to ourselves, I would say this is special." He grew hard beneath me, and I sighed. "Maybe after your game tomorrow we can get Dutch to watch her one more night and—oh, oh God," I moaned as Rafe took a nipple into his mouth and began to push inside me. I looked down to see the raw desire etched all over his features. Apparently, telling Rafe he was going to be a daddy was all the aphrodisiac I needed.

"This is amazing. I love you."

"I love you too," I whispered, the moment bittersweet.

"Alice, tell me what's wrong," he asked studying my face as he pumped slowly inside me.

"Nothing, Rafe, ah," I whimpered as he pushed his hips up burying himself. I was impaled, and my clit pulsed as it rubbed along the edge of him.

"Tell me," he insisted as he thrust up, hooked his arms through mine, and then pulled my shoulders down hard with his hands. I damn near came with his next thrust he was so deep. "I try not to press you when you're pissed, because, for one, you can't speak well for yourself when you are. But you're hiding something."

"I'm not hiding, ah, ah—" He had reached around and was pressing a finger against my backside. My eyes grew. "Rafe, I don't know if I can handle that tonight."

"And I don't care about that, I'm about to make you feel so fucking good."

"God," I whispered as I gripped his damp hair and pulled it between my fingers.

"I promise to make it good," Rafe said biting my lip, "but not until you tell me what's wrong. And don't say nothing again. This is me. Talk to me."

"It's just," I said, my jaw shaking at the feel of him, "I just wanted to have one more night of the freaky before we go through it all again, ya know? Before the late nights, the puke, and the . . . poo." I didn't mention the libido killers in our immediate future that consisted of leaky boobs, stretchmarks, uncontrollable gas and the inevitable hemorrhoid flare up.

"We can have all the freaky you want," he said, as he pressed his thumb against my clit while his probing finger slipped inside "Look at me."

"I'm looking," I said longingly. "It's just that you were so careful when I was pregnant with Clover. And while I love you more for it, I don't want this to change. I know it's selfish."

"It's not selfish. I was paranoid last time. This time it'll be different, I promise. And I think we need some time alone. She's almost five and we haven't done anything without her since she was born.

"Rafe," I whimpered.

"If you want to come, you need to agree," he warned.

"You know I can't leave her."

"You won't be *leaving* her. You'll be taking a break, there's the difference. You haven't been able to take your clients overseas because of your rule to be home at night." I swiveled my hips to match his thrusts. "Fuck, Alice, ride it just like that." He closed his eyes briefly as he picked up the pace, punishing me with his cock and his finger. "Didn't you say you had a client who wants to go to Greece next month?"

He pushed up again, and this time, we both moaned.

"Alice?"

"Yes, Rafe, yes."

"That's good enough," he whispered as he thrust up gripping my hips so that we were locked. I came undone.

"God, I'm coming," I barely got the words out before I was swept away. Rafe swallowed my screams with his kiss as I thrashed around in the tub, my heart hammering as I sank into him. Seconds later, my head was gripped as he unraveled beneath me, his release lasting a small eternity.

"Fuck, that felt incredible," he croaked, as I lay against his chest. Breathless and spent I could only reply with a *mmm* noise.

I wasn't sure how much time had passed before he pulled us to stand.

"How far along are you?"

"Almost eight weeks."

"We're going to Greece."

I smiled against his chest as he wrapped us in a towel and began drying us off. "You can't just decide we're going to Greece."

"I believe I just did."

"So damn cocky. You're like the spokesman for cocky."

"It's only right for a man with so much cock . . . y to give." His smile took my breath away. When he deposited me onto our bed, I reached for him only to come up empty.

"Where are you going?"

He was gloriously naked as I admired the planes of muscle that led down to thick thighs and the beautiful dick between that was pointed directly at me.

"I'm going to get more of that arsenal of yours from downstairs. I want to test out those nipple clamps."

"Oh," I said with a smile. "Time to get dirty?"

"Fucking filthy," he promised.

"Rafe?" I asked kneeling on the bed.

"Yeah, baby?" He moved to stand in front of me, proud of his growing progress below. I reached out to stroke him, and his eyes closed with a hiss.

"I want it hard."

"I think I can handle that," he grunted, thrusting gently into my hand.

"What about Ren and your pact?"

A burst of breath left him as I sped up my fist. "I think he's probably dealing with his own mess right now. And I really don't give a shit."

"You know the game tomorrow is yours, right?"

"I hope so."

"Will you believe me instead?"

"I'll try," he said, pushing the soft-skinned steel in my hand.

"Ren's going to be a daddy too."

He paused his hips. "No shit?"

"We're due within three weeks of each other."

"So, all of this today wasn't only about the sex?"

"Yes and no. Technically, it's all about the sex you already had. But mostly it's because I missed you."

He leaned in and brushed his lips against mine. "I missed you too. I'll always be here, risking my life with you while you try to seduce me."

"Har, har," I said, gripping him tight in my hold.

Worry creased his brow as I got more aggressive with my hand. "Please be gentle."

"You just relax, sir. Right now, it's *all* about your cock . . . y," I informed him as my eyes slid down to his ready, fat dick. Leaning in, I darted my tongue against the opening of his tip before I let him go and gave him a sound smack on the ass. "Don't forget the tickler."

In preparation for the sex to come, I threw every throw pillow we had onto the floor and broke out my newly purchased rubber sheets while my inner freak rejoiced.

I was just about to shoot off a text to check on our daughter when my phone beeped with an incoming message.

Erica: The ego has landed. 🌎
Me: The noodle has been cooked.
Erica: ?? LOL WHAT?!
Me: Long story. Actually, it's short story. I'll tell you later. Don't use the poppers!
Erica: 10-4 good buddy.

The next day, my husband won his second world series.
That night, we used the alien probe.
Two weeks, later we flew to Greece.
Seven months later, I gave birth to our son.

NO END

Want more Alice and Rafe? Start the Balls in Play series with *Anything but Minor*.

Learn more: www.katestewartwrites.com

ABOUT THE AUTHOR

A Texas native, Kate Stewart lives in North Carolina with her husband, Nick, and her naughty beagle, Sadie. She pens messy, sexy, angst-filled contemporary romance as well as romantic comedy and erotic suspense because it's what she loves as a reader. Kate is a lover of all things '80s and '90s, especially John Hughes films and rap. She dabbles a little in photography, can knit a simple stitch scarf for necessity, and on occasion, does very well at whisky.

Let's stay in touch!
Facebook: https://www.facebook.com/authorkatestewart
Newsletter: http://www.katestewartwrites.com/contact-me.html
Twitter: https://twitter.com/authorklstewart
Instagram: https://www.instagram.com/authorkatestewart/
Book Group: https://www.facebook.com/groups/793483714004942/
Spotify: https://open.spotify.com/user/authorkatestewart

Sign up for the newsletter now and get a free eBook from Kate's Library!

http://www.katestewartwrites.com/contact-me.html

ALSO BY KATE STEWART

Room 212

Never Me

Loving the White Liar

The Fall

The Mind

The Heart

The Brave Line

Drive

The Real

Romantic Comedy

Anything but Minor

Major Love

Sweeping the Series

Erotic Suspense

Sexual Awakenings

Excess

Predator and Prey

COCKY ALPHA

LEIA STONE

A bitchy witch, who hates a cocky alpha werewolf, gets conned into going on a date with him.

ONE

Tatiana

Dax Cohen was the bane of my existence. That smart-mouthed asshole came into my shop every new moon, and it took everything in me not to throw a penis shrinking spell right at his crotch. He was the cockiest alpha male I'd ever met, and that was saying a lot for a witch who ran a supernatural spell shop. I'd met them all, been hit on by them all, but Dax Cohen really grinded my gears. He stood at over six foot six and looked as if he was chiseled from stone by the Goddess herself. He was a living, breathing Adonis... and he knew it. He'd slept with half the witches in my coven, and if rumors were true, he had a thing for red heads. I grinned, twirling a lock of my glossy long red hair. Tonight when he came in for his shifting potion, I was going to make him beg for it. Payback for that prank he'd played on me last week. Sold me what he said was a werewolf's tooth when in reality, it was a kitten's. My entire spell exploded in my face.

"You're stirring that too quickly," my high priestess admonished me. I nodded to Rowena. She was a good coven leader, and I enjoyed working underneath her.

I slowed my stirring and called out to her. "Must we supply the wolves with this potion for the rest of our lives? Surely our ancestors put an expiration date on the contract?"

Rowena's lips curled into a grin. "They did not, and you know that—it was your own mother who signed the deal with him after all. The wolves did us a favor many years ago and it's our duty to repay them."

Easy for her to say—she wasn't the one making the potion every month. *Cat Tails And Other Magical Things* was handed down to me by my parents. It had been in our family for generations. And the spell that kept a werewolf from shifting on the full moon and pillaging the town in a blood thirst, rested with me and me alone. I'd only moved here to Rock Springs, Wyoming when my mother died, to carry on my magical lineage and all that jazz. Before her, my grandmother owned the shop, and I had a handful of memories coming here as a child.

Rowena trailed a finger across my cheek. "Where you feel anger, I sense passion," she said and then grabbed her purse and left the shop for the night.

I raised an eyebrow. Rowena was full of random Yoda-like sayings like that. My eyes flicked outside, and I noticed the sun was just about to set.

Sigh.

Dax would walk in any minute and would attempt to charm me. I would tell him to shove his charm up his ass and then up-charge him ten percent, and he would leave in a huff. Typical new moon night.

The man had been trying to sleep with me for two years. Poor guy couldn't take a 'no.' I was just pouring the contents of the spell into the copper jar, when a sharp pain sliced into my chest. Dropping the jar onto the counter top, I stumbled backwards.

No.

"Rowena!" I shouted, as I gasped for breath. The searing pain did not abate, and I knew then that my high priestess had sustained a mortal wound.

Tears trailed down my cheeks as I reached shakily for my wand. Whatever killed her was close by, as she'd only just left my shop. The pain ripping through my chest had turned to a warm tingle as my coven leader's magic left her body and filtered into me. I gasped as the purple mist fell from the ceiling and coated my skin, making me feel like I was holding onto a live wire. As second-in-command of the coven, it was my rightful place to inherit her magical linage in the event of her death. I just hadn't expected it for another decade or so.

I stumbled forward, wand outstretched, ready to avenge my coven leader, when a flash of muscle and black hair dashed through my doorway.

Dax Cohen, covered in blood, had fallen through the entrance of my shop. His forearms were glowing with protection symbols. *Rowena's magic.*

His abdomen was leaking blood and upon further inspection, I noticed a gash. It looked deep, and he held the wound with one of his massive hands. At his heel was his pet dog, a Cocker Spaniel aptly named Cocker. Why the alpha of the most powerful pack in the Northwest had a tiny adorable dog, I would never know, but he took him everywhere. That mutt was like a child to him, and he whined and jumped up on Dax's leg as the werewolf fell onto me, resting his two hundred pound weight on my small frame.

"What happened? Rowena!" I rasped. I was still in shock, complete disbelief, but the power that flowed through my veins did not lie. My priestess had ascended, she was with the Goddess now.

Dax breathed in slowly, wincing at the pain. "Nyx."

That one word flushed complete terror through my veins. With one flick of my wand, my shop door slammed shut and the lights outside turned off, two more flicks and I'd thrown up enough magical wards to keep the entire town out. It wouldn't keep Nyx away but it would buy me some time.

Nyx... it wasn't possible. The most vile witch I'd ever learned about as a child who'd been put into a five hundred year sleep by my own mother, had awoken?

I dragged the big ass werewolf behind the counter to my back room and lowered him onto the couch in my office. Cocker leapt up onto his legs and whined while pawing at his jeans.

I rubbed the mutt's head, infusing his aura with a calming spell, and his whine died off as he lay on the alpha's lap and rested.

Peeling back Dax's hand from the wound he was staunching, a spurt of crimson gushed out into the room. I tore open his shirt to get a better look at the wound and the dark magic imbedded in it.

"You trying to kill me woman?" He growled as his wound continued to leak blood all over my clean floor.

I thought about that. I could let him bleed out right here and be done with making his potion every month. The contract only said I had to make it for him, not his pack.

"Tatiana!" he scolded me, and I rolled my eyes. Pointing my wand at his stomach, I uttered half a dozen healing spells and he finally sighed in relief.

"Tell me what happened," I demanded.

He grimaced, sitting up to rub behind Cocker's ear. "I was coming to the shop to get the potion when I felt... a darkness."

My brow furrowed. Yeah, if Nyx had been resurrected, darkness would follow everywhere she went.

He continued, "I turned the corner and saw Rowena on her knees, black tendrils of magic around her throat. Standing before her was... Nyx. In the flesh."

I frowned. "That can't be! She's supposed to sleep another hundred years at least!"

He shrugged as the wound on his stomach stitched itself before my eyes. Werewolf healing. I only needed to remove the black magic, and his body did its thing. I tried and failed not to notice the way his heavily defined muscles looked enticing.

"It was Nyx alright," he confirmed. He was old enough to know, so I'd have to take his word as I'd never met her in the flesh, thank God.

"And how did you survive the blackest witch to ever live?" I raised one eyebrow at him.

He reached out and fingered a lock of my red hair, giving me a cocky grin. "Oh, I don't know. Maybe she didn't want to kill something so beautiful."

I rolled my eyes.

He sat up, slowly putting Cocker on the ground. He was in my personal space and not backing down, just staring at me with dark green eyes, threaded through with bolts of orange.

"You need to stop her or she'll pillage the whole town, killing your entire coven in revenge," he stated.

I exhaled, feeling the tension build in my shoulders. "I know that." I growled.

If someone had resurrected Nyx early, she would be fueled by vengeance. It was my coven that put her into the night sleep in the first place, led by my mother with Rowena as her second. With Dax's pack having helped... That was over a hundred years ago, before I was even alive, but they'd done us a great favor by helping, which was why we owed them the moon sleep tea every month. With Rowena dead, I was sure we couldn't do it alone. I had the power of a high priestess now but not the training. I was only two years into my education as a high priestess's second hand. Something most witches did for a good fifty years before they took on the title. But I wasn't going to tell him that. The last thing I wanted was to look weak in front of an alpha.

"Dax Cohen, Alpha of the Moon Called pack, if your werewolves help us, then I, High Priestess of the Lightwood coven will owe you a debt. Name your price."

My hand lit up with blue magic as I held it out to him. He would name his price, such as moon sleep tea until the end of time, and we could shake. Then that would be it. Magically sealed forever.

A sly grin crept over his face, and I should have called it off the moment I saw those dimples form in his cheeks. "I pledge Moon Called Pack to help in this deed if you Tatiana Ravenwood will go on a date with me when it's done. Dinner, movie *and* a nightcap, at my place."

"A powerful witch offers you any favor you can think of, and you want a date?" He couldn't be that stupid.

"Yes," he said without hesitation.

He was that stupid. I rolled my eyes and extended my hand further. "Deal."
Cocky idiot.

We shook on it, and magic zipped up my arm and tingled along my elbow. It was law now. If we survived this, I was going on a date with Dax Cohen. I could only hope he would die on the quest so I wouldn't be put through such an atrocity.

TWO

Dax

Tatiana Ravenwood was the most uptight woman I'd ever met, and she hated me. Absolute hatred. So, naturally I wanted to sleep with her. Not just sleep with her, I wanted to take her out and show her I wasn't the cocky asshole she'd somehow believed I was. I wanted to, needed to, change her opinion about me. Maybe it was the alpha in me, brother wolf's need to control everything. I wanted to control the way she thought about me. I wanted her to beg me to kiss her. I wanted what I couldn't have. That red head would be *mine*.

"Are you coming?" she snapped, annoyed, as we exited her shop.

I reached down and pet the spot between Cocker's eyes. *'I'll be back for you later,'* I told him.

'No. Cocker go with.' He growled.

I chuckled. My thirty-five pound dog wanted to take on Nyx, the darkest witch I'd ever met. *'Not safe buddy. Stay here.'* I gave him a little shove and shut the door, locking him inside. He'd be okay in there as long as he didn't eat any of Tatiana's weird witch shit. That woman had threatened me with so many potions in the years I'd known her, and I had no doubt she could make my dick fall off and render me impotent for life. God knows what Cocker would find in there.

'Don't eat anything in there.' I told him through the door.

He ignored me. He was mad. I'd have to bring him a double cheeseburger later to make up for it.

When I turned around, I nearly slammed into Tatiana. She was watching me with wide, green curious eyes. "Did you just speak into his mind?"

I flinched. "How can you tell?" That was one of my secrets. I didn't tell many people I could speak to the mind of any animal.

She reached past me and locked the shop door, leaving the scent of vanilla and sage in her wake. "One of my new gifts as high priestess I guess. I dunno, I *saw* it," she answered, seeming flustered.

She glanced ahead on the sidewalk. Rowena lay on her side, dead, black bands of magic tightened around her neck giving her a pale, ghoulish look.

Tatiana choked on a sob as she stared at her fallen high priestess.

Shit. I wasn't sure what to do. If I tried to comfort her by patting her back or something, she might rip off my hand.

Instead I ran my fingers through my hair. "Ah, I'm sorry about Rowena. She was a good witch. I knew her a long time."

Tatiana nodded. "Thanks." Then she pulled out her wand and I stepped back a pace. I was peaceful with the witches but I didn't like their magic. It was unpredictable and made my hackles pull up.

She flung her wand towards Rowena's body and muttered a few words. Suddenly, like an invisible blanket had fallen over the witch. She was gone.

"I'll deal with that later," she said.

I was going to comment, ask her what the plan was, when I felt them. Lines of power coming at me like a flashlight searching in the dark. *My pack.*

Two black SUVs turned the corner and pulled up next to us.

"What's the emergency?" Brayden, my second-in-command, asked. I'd asked him to bring all of my dominants and meet me at the witch shop. I didn't want to say what it was about over the phone.

"Nyx has awoken early, and we need to shove her back into her grave before all hell breaks loose," I stated.

Brayden didn't cow, but lines of worry crossed his face. He was old enough to remember the days when Nyx ran rampant across North America, conjuring demons and making my life a living hell.

The back seat window of the SUV rolled down, and Nick Pichette looked Tatiana up and down like she was a piece of meat. "We're partnering with the witches?" he asked seductively.

'Look at her again and I'll kill you.' I told him, infusing alpha power into my command. He lowered his head then and rolled up the window. Nick was a little, twenty-year-old punk who needed to learn his place with women. He would not be doing that with Tatiana. She was *mine.* If he weren't so dominant and such a good fighter I wouldn't have allowed him to come.

Brayden grinned, he knew I'd just bitch-slapped Nick. "Do you know who woke her?" my second asked Tatiana respectfully, keeping his eyes above her neckline where they belonged. For a woman who claimed to not like getting hit on, she sure liked to wear cleavage popping shirts and tight jeans a lot.

Tatiana sighed, and it puffed out her already plump lips. "No one but a very, very powerful witch could have awoken Nyx early."

My head reeled in her direction. "What are you saying?"

She put up her hands. "I'm saying someone in my coven probably woke her. Someone you've slept with I'm sure," she added rolling her eyes.

Ouch. "Hey, I've only slept with like, three people from your coven and I'm over a hundred years old so that's one every thirty years or so." I defended myself.

She laughed wildly. "Don't make me add them up in front of your boys."

Fear gripped me. Jane, Willow and Frannie. That's it. Oh wait, Mariah. Four, only four and I didn't just sleep with them, I dated them. I was a goddamn grown man—I could do what I wanted!

"Adrianna," she started to list and I'd totally forgotten about the New Years eve bash of 1993.

I put my hands out to stop her. "Okay, we get it. You think I'm a man-whore. Let's just catch Nyx already, because I have a hot date tonight." I smiled smugly.

She stepped off the curb and opened the back door, shooing Nick in order to scoot him over. "Take me to the cemetery," she asked Brayden.

"Is that where she is?" I questioned her rationale. For all I knew, she'd muttered some tracker spell on Nyx.

Tatiana glared at me as I opened the door, making Brayden sit shotgun so I could drive.

"Witch magic works similar to pack magic. She killed Rowena so the coven magic fell to me, if she kills me, the coven magic falls to her as third in line."

The very thought of Nyx trying to hurt Tatiana had my inner wolf rattling my skin like a cage, threating to break free. And the thought of Nyx ruling the Lightwood coven was beyond sickening.

"So she's after you?" I asked, looking at her through the rearview mirror.

She nodded curtly. God, she fucking hated me.

I was an alpha. I needed to know the detailed plan. What didn't she understand about that? "So we're leading her to the cemetery, where she'll try to kill you and we'll hopefully put her back in her grave?" I asked her.

Tatiana clapped, looking around at my boys in the car. "He's a genius," she told the car.

My hands tightened on the steering wheel until my knuckles were white. Shoving my foot onto the gas, I took off.

Tonight might be the worst date of my life but I was determined to make this woman fall for me sometime this decade, and she was getting a spanking for that comment.

THREE

Tatiana

Dax was getting on my very last nerve with all of his questions. Acting like he cared what happened to me or my coven. He was the self-centered, hired muscle and he needed to act like it. I had enough on my mind with my life at stake I didn't want to have to dodge his advances while I was at it. He'd literally been hitting on me since the day I moved here from North Carolina two years ago. On top of all this Nyx drama, I had to figure out which of my coven mates betrayed us and resurrected her, no doubt in a bid to become her second.

When Dax pulled the SUV up to the cemetery, I saw that my coven was here, standing in a circle, looking up to the new moon for guidance. I'd have to tell them about Rowena, I'd have to appoint a second but I didn't want to do that until I knew who'd betrayed us. My best friend Lydia was the only one I truly trusted but her lineage was not powerful enough to make second. She'd weaken the coven.

"Can you have your wolves surround the place?" I asked the alpha.

He nodded, and without a word his boys exited the car in unison and started stripping naked, shifting forms. Trading their lean chiseled human forms for their wolves. I never understood the werewolf male obsession, I was more of a vampire girl myself, maybe even a human before I'd date a were.

I popped open the car door and got out, then I reached down to gather my wand and a few other items, and when I looked up, Dax was standing right in front of me, shirtless, in low slung jeans and no underwear that I could see. Desire flushed through me, and I scolded my body for betraying my feelings.

"Would you like me in human form or wolf?" he asked in a husky voice.

His eyes were glowing orange and I knew that meant his wolf was close to the surface.

I cleared my throat. "Wolf. I'll need all the teeth I can get."

With that, he grinned and in one swift motion dropped his pants.

I swallowed hard, and it took every ounce of self-control I had not to look down at the dangling appendage I could see in my periphery. I hated Dax Cohen with every fiber of my being, but I'd always wondered what he looked like naked. Before I had to wrestle with the situation any longer, he started to shift, and I side-stepped him and began to walk to my coven. It took me a moment to catch my breath after seeing him naked like that. Cocky asshole or not he was nice to look at, even though I would never admit that out loud.

My coven was looking at me with worried eyes. They stood over Nyx's churned up grave with a hundred questions, I'm sure. I had to play this smart, otherwise I was going to lose my head. Literally. Pulling out my wand, I traced a few protection spells up my arms, powerful ones similar to the kind Rowena had traced onto Dax. When I got within earshot of my coven, I wasted no time getting right to the point.

"Nyx has been resurrected, and Rowena has ascended," I told my kin.

Their faces fell into shock and confusion, some were openly crying, holding onto each other as they simultaneously mourned our high priestess and dealt with the news of Nyx's resurrection. Seraphina Pluckhart however, was not carrying a worried look. She looked... nervous.

Gotcha.

"One of our own has betrayed us and conjured her. I'm sure of it." I stated as Seraphina slowly pulled her wand from her pocket.

Bitch was going to burn for what she did to our beloved Rowena.

I went to step towards her, when a darkness descended onto the cemetery. A heavy blanket of despair fell over me, and I found myself fighting the dark magic best I could. My breathing was labored, and dark thoughts, blood, death and despair flashed through my mind. Thousands of cockroaches flooded the grounds of the cemetery, and I had to fight the urge to run.

Nyx had arrived.

Lydia was bound to me, as soul sisters and conjure partners. All I needed was to trace a quick message for her on my arm and then the same one would appear on hers. Wiccan text.

Kill Seraphina. I sent her.

Seraphina forgotten, I spun to see a big grey wolf at my back.

Dax.

Behind him, a black fog was spanning out into the cemetery carrying misery and fear with it.

"Tell your pack to shield their minds," I told the wolf.

I didn't know much about wolf magic but I knew they had some sort of mind control, or Dax did and he could protect their minds. I hoped so at least, otherwise we were screwed. Nyx could make a weak human take their own life in seconds. She was a master of mind control.

That's when all hell broke loose, the sound of Seraphina and Lydia fighting behind me had started, but I kept my eyes forward. Gliding over the hill was Nyx in all her glory, the king of the local vampire court at her side with a dozen of his cronies.

Shit.

I take back what I said before. I hate vampires *and* werewolves. From now on, I will only date humans.

Dax's low growl beside me reminded me he was here with me, and I was suddenly grateful for his pack's presence. I was going to make him earn this date.

"Ladies!" I shouted. "Whoever kills the most vampires becomes my new second." I told my coven.

Mariah, a powerful witch and good contender for second, burst forward, flinging injury spells left and right.

Good girl.

The rest of my coven advanced, stalking slowly, building up large spells with their wands, and I saw a few of Dax's wolves come up behind the vampires on the other side of the hill. Of course she went to the vampires—it would be her only chance at beating us. I was convinced the reason Rowena was killed so easily by her was because she was caught of guard with no protection spells. For some godforsaken reason she chose to throw protection spells at Dax and not save herself.

I sighed. Time to put this bitch back in her grave. I was a little nervous, if I was being honest, I had the power of a high priestess sure but not the confidence. I knew Nyx couldn't be killed. it was an impossibility but she could be put into a sleep. For that I would need a shitload of magic, my own blood blinding the spell and a sacrifice.

Sacrifice. Shit!

The cockroaches were skittering across my feet now, and I could feel the dark magic trying to press in on me. Trying to suck away my happiness and make me get lost in the dark thoughts that were floating through my mind. The longer Nyx stayed awake and the more people she killed, the more powerful she became. I needed to end this tonight because by tomorrow she might be too powerful for me to wrestle back into the sleep.

I remembered something then.

"Hey, can you talk to all animals or just your dog?" I asked Dax who was stuck to my side, his fur brushing against my leg.

He looked up at me... and said nothing, because he was a wolf. Right.

"Can you call an animal over so I can sacrifice it for a spell?" I asked him. If he said no, I'd have to pray one of these cockroaches counted but I wasn't sure they were real, probably an illusion spell.

He looked conflicted for a second but then he nodded.

I was just about to pet his head or something to affirm he was a 'good boy' when a spell from Nyx slammed into my chest, throwing me backward.

Pain exploded inside of my stomach but ebbed directly after, as my protection spells kicked in.

"You didn't earn your title you know that, right?" Nyx's raspy, 100 pack a day smoker voice filtered over to me from a few feet away. "You only got it because mommy and grandma were powerful witches."

Good. Let her think that.

I dug my nails into my palms letting the blood drip onto the earth.

Then I started to murmur an ancient spell in Aramaic, it wasn't in any spell books, it was passed down from my gran to me through word of mouth and it made the earth my ally. When I finished it I slammed my palm onto the ground, feeding the earth my blood.

Nyx was slowly stalking toward me, her raven black hair hung limply at her sides, clods of dirt still in it. She was taller than I thought she'd be, nearly six feet and clouds of black magic followed behind her like messengers of death. My eyes flicked briefly to Dax who had the king of the vampires neck in his mouth. It took longer than I expected for my spell to work, but when it did, the ground shook violently and Nyx was thrown off her feet unprepared.

I shot up then, flinging my wand at her, throwing spell after spell to weaken her power. They crashed against her invisible shields as she countered my spells. Then just as quickly and out of thin air, a sword appeared in her left hand.

Damn, weapons-conjuring was some dark magical shit.

I didn't have that ability but I did know how to conceal them. One tap to my bracelet from my wand and it transformed from the everyday piece of jewelry to a twelve inch dagger with a poisoned blade.

Nyx grinned looking from my dagger to her sword. "Mines bigger," she said.

She whipped out then, with one of her black tendrils of magic that floated about her, and it slammed into my neck, curling around it and shattering my protection charms.

Shit. I thought my protection wards would hold, but this magic was powerful. Nyx must have been resting in hell for the past hundred years because she'd learned some shit while she was gone. I sliced my sword through the black tendril in vain but nothing happened. My blade passed through it like it was air and yet it felt like a very real, tangible thing was choking me. I couldn't breathe. My eyes darted around to see the chaos before me and affirm that no one would be helping me. Everyone was locked in their own battle.

I kicked off my shoe then and sank my foot into the earth, still in control of my previous spell. It was hard to be concurred with mother earth at your whim. A tree root sprang out of the ground then, wrapping around Nyx's abdomen and dragging her to the earth. The black tendril around my throat fell away when she'd smashed into the soil, and I gasped for air, grinning.

Hah! Gotcha bitch.

Stepping forward, I raised my dagger, ready to end this, when something moved in my peripheral.

I saw Seraphina too late. Her fist holding a large rock, she cracked me over the side of the head, and then everything went black.

FOUR

Dax

I'd just ripped out the vampire king's throat when I saw a blonde witch come up behind Tatiana and knock her out with a rock.

A howl rocked my chest as I launched off of the ground and ran past Nyx who was hacking away at a tree root, so that I could intercept the blonde. I leapt and sailed through the air landing over Tatiana's fallen body. Looking up at the blonde witch, I growled. She held the bloodied rock in her hand but looked unsure now that she was faced with going through me. She didn't seem to have her wand, so I knew she wouldn't be a problem, I'd take her head clean off in seconds. Tatiana's body moved underneath me then and I glanced down to see her eyes opening.

With a groan, her arm burst out from under my body and she slammed blondie with a spell that made her eyes go cross-eyed. She dropped to the ground right there, the rock falling from her grasp.

That was effective.

Tatianna moaned and I stepped away from her, my eyes on Nyx. Those fucking black magical bands were reaching this way, and I wasn't sure if I had any power to rival them.

"Enough!" Tatiana shouted beside me, flinging her wand and an insanely bright light shot out of it, like she was harnessing the sun. It spread across the now dark graveyard and chased the black magic away. Nyx shrieked and held her ears. One by one the other witches in the coven made their way to stand in a circle around Nyx, wands outstretched all with a beautiful bright light coming from them. Nyx was hissing, and pacing the circle unable to break free. The ground was littered with skittering cockroaches and dead vampires.

"My sacrifice?" Tatiana asked me.

Oh yeah. I'd called a rooster from the nearest farm to come over and he was waiting by an adjacent tree.

I felt really bad about luring him to his death but I figured it was the only way to get Nyx back into her sleeping grave, otherwise Tatiana wouldn't have asked. One rooster for the good of humanity seemed like an okay sacrifice to make.

I pulled on his mind and the big red roosted walked out from behind the tree and strutted over to where we were.

Tatiana, still holding her wand before her, looked down at the cock.

A wonky grin lit up her face, and I couldn't help but think of how awesome it was that after two years I'd finally gotten her to go out on a date with me. Never mind the fact that it was somewhat forced.

She picked the rooster up by the neck and muttered an apology before breaking his neck quickly in her hands.

Damn woman.

Then Tatiana sliced her palm cleanly pouring her blood over the dead rooster.

"Nyx Blackwood! I bind you to the earth to sleep for a thousand years!" she shouted and thunder cracked overhead. "May you only be awoken by me and me alone," she shouted and the wind picked up, carrying leaves and the smell of rain with it.

My wolf shivered, and I stepped back a pace. I didn't like all this magical shit. It smelled weird and it was too unpredictable for my taste.

Nyx ran at Tatiana then, teeth barred and sword out but the redhead threw her dagger from where she stood and it sank into the dark witch's chest with a thunk. The moment it slammed into her chest, the cockroaches and black bands of magic disappeared and Nyx fell backward, eyes open.

Tatiana flicked her wand then and tendrils of white light wrapped Nyx like a cocoon. The other witches followed suit, and then Nyx was floating a few feet above the ground, her head hanging limp as they lowered her into a deep grave. The earth shook a few times as they dropped her in, as if she was protesting taking such an evil thing into her dirt. But in the end Nyx was buried 6 feet under with a dagger in her chest and a promise to sleep for a thousand years.

When it was all done, I shifted, covering my junk with my hands. Tatiana turned around, for the first time, letting her eyes run slowly down my body.

"Thanks for your help," she said stiffly. Dried blood was caked at the side of her temple.

I nodded. "You're welcome. Would you like my pack doctor to look at your head?"

She waved her hand. "I'll be fine. I have a lot to deal with here since Seraphina got away. How about you pick me up tomorrow at seven?"

Shock ripped through me. I wasn't going to have to beg?

"Seven is fine," I responded.

"I'll see you then," she said a little less sternly than she normally spoke to me. Like maybe she didn't hate me anymore. Only disliked me a little.

I nodded in return and started to walk away, knowing without a shadow of a doubt she was looking at my ass.

FIVE

Tatiana

We were lucky no one died last night. Although Lydia was on strict bedrest from our coven healer, everyone had made it through. Seraphina was missing and I knew that was going to come bite me in the ass later but for now I tried to just deal with the present. Rowena had been laid to rest this morning in the family plot on my mother's land, and I was now preparing to go out on a date with Dax Cohen. I couldn't stop thinking of the way he stood over my unconscious body, protecting me until I woke up. Why would he do that? Was it in the realm of possibility that I could have judged the local alpha wrong.

"You're NOT wearing that," Lydia said from her place in the bed as I finished my makeup in the mirror.

I looked down at my black t-shirt and tight jeans tucked into ankle boots. "Why not?" I asked.

Lydia rolled her eyes, her short, black, cropped hair moving as she shook her head.

"Because you look like you're going bowling with your mom not out on a date with the hottest werewolf in town."

I sighed. Lydia loved werewolves—they were the only thing she dated. I was shocked to hear she hadn't slept with Dax.

"This is a fake date," I told her. "He wants to win this for his ego, and I'm being forced. I'm not wearing a dress for a fake date."

Lydia rolled her eyes. "You have issues," was all she said.

The doorbell rang then, and I slid off of the stool I'd been doing my makeup in front of.

"See ya soon," I told Lydia casually.

"Feel free to sleep over!" she called out after me and I rolled my eyes.

Swinging my front door open, I was taken aback by the clean cut man before me. He was holding flowers. Pink peonies. My favorite.

"Good evening Tatiana." He extended the flowers.

"Ah, thank you. Good evening," I responded flustered.

I hadn't expected this to be a sincere, dressed in a suit holding flowers kind of date. He looked down at my t-shirt and jeans. "You look beautiful."

"Thanks," I responded. Maybe I should just sleep with him so that he could get over it already and realize he was only after the chase.

Nah. I respected myself too much to have a one night stand with the man whore. I set the flowers on my coffee table and we made our way outside. The full moon was two weeks away, and they had to drink the tea for a full ten days before.

I reached into my purse and pulled out the copper jar with his tea in it. "Here, I forgot to give you this." I handed it to him. He stopped and took it from me, brushing against my fingers as he did.

As we reached his SUV, he opened the door for me but stopped me before going in. Reaching into his pants pocket he pulled out a black tie. "I'm sorry but I have to blindfold you, otherwise this won't be a surprise."

I raised one eyebrow. "Blindfold me to drive me to the burger shack?" I asked with one hand on my hip. This was a small town, and there were only a handful of places he could be taking me. He unfolded the blindfold and placed it over my eyes. I could feel his breath on my lips, smell him, and desire spiked through me fresh and hot.

Traitorous body.

He lifted me into the car and buckled me in, grazing my stomach with his hand as he did. This date was a horrible idea. What was I thinking agreeing to this? Dinner, movie, nightcap and then home. That was it. No funny business and no falling for this fake romantic crap.

He started the car and then we were moving. I didn't like being blindfolded, I didn't like not having control. "So, did your pack end up healing okay?" I made light conversation.

"Yes, thank you for asking. We now have a major problem with to local vampire coven that needs to be worked out though," he stated.

I sighed. "Yeah and Seraphina got away."

"Shall I make us a meeting with the new king? See if we can draw up a peace treaty before there is retaliation?"

Working together? Well, I was high priestess now, and Rowena worked closely with Dax often on these types of matters.

I nodded. "That would be fine."

We crossed a bridge. I could hear the tread under the tires and my brows drew together.

"Where are you taking me?"

I could hear the smile in his voice. "A special place."

Okay...

I was trying to play nice but I really wanted to rip this tie off and just see where we were going. Yet, his pack risked their lives helping us yesterday, and the only thing he'd requested was this one date, so I'd let him have his fun. For now.

The car slowed and then pulled to a stop. He put it in park.

"I'll be right back to get you," he said, and the door opened then shut quickly.

This was getting a little ridiculous—alphas and their need for control. I couldn't see!

The door opened, and then his strong hands were unbuckling me and helping me out of the car. I tilted my head to the side to listen for any clues, the sound of a live band or a crowded bar. When I heard nothing but birds chirping, I frowned.

"Alright. We're here," he said, and I detected a hint of nervousness in his voice.

I felt his hands reach around the back of my head and then he untied my blind fold. When he pulled it away, I had to blink a few times to be sure of what I was seeing.

Hundreds and hundreds of tea lights covered the lush green grass of island park, where a blanket and picnic basket had been set up.

Island park was literally an island smooshed between the two banks of the green river where it split, leaving a lush, beautiful oasis in the middle. It was my most favorite place to go, my grandmother had taken me every time I'd visited when I was younger, to teach me about nature.

"I..." I was speechless. I'd been expecting a loud bar, an action movie and then a move to get in my pants.

Dax was grinning ear to ear, and it was hard not to notice how handsome he was. "Rowena told me that your grandmother would often take you here, and that it was a special place to you. I thought it might be a nice spot for dinner."

I just stared at him as if he'd sprouted two heads. "You asked Rowena about me?" My brain was short circuiting, I didn't know what to think. How could I function if Dax weren't this big cocky asshole?

He grinned again. "Often." He took my hand and stepped in front of me. "Look, I know I have a reputation but that's because I'm really old and this town is too small for privacy. I promise you only fifty percent of what you've heard is probably true."

I raised an eyebrow.

"Okay, sixty-five. *Max*. The point is, I want you to take this date seriously because I'm serious about getting to know you. I've felt a connection with you since the first day you showed up in town and not just the physical kind." His cheeks were a bit red and he looked... nervous.

Whoa. He'd just laid his feelings out in the open, bare and raw and... submissive-like. It was the sexiest damn thing he'd ever done. Without overthinking things like I normally did, I popped up on my toes and wrapped my arms around his neck, running my hands through his thick hair and pressing my lips to his. The second our lips touched, heat traveled south of my navel and pleasure exploded inside of me. I didn't realize until this moment how badly I'd been wanting to do this. His hands reached around to cup my butt, and he hoisted me up so that I could wrap my legs around his waist. My lips parted to let his tongue inside my mouth, and he gave a husky growl. When I pulled back, he was smiling.

"Does this mean I get a second date?" he asked, eyes pinned on my swollen lips.

I unhooked my legs from his waist and shrugged. "We'll see." I said with a smirk.

He chuckled.

"Challenge accepted, Tatiana."

DAX

Mine.

THE END

ABOUT THE AUTHOR

Leia Stone is the USA Today bestselling author of the Matefinder series which is optioned for film. She writes urban fantasy and paranormal romance with sassy kick-butt heroines and irresistible love interests.

You can see more of Leia Stone's books here on amazon:
https://www.amazon.com/kindle-dbs/entity/author/B00KBXMBDA

And follow her on Facebook. https://www.facebook.com/leia.stone/

Pre-order Leia's next new series, Dream Wars: Rising Book 1. Kit Steele protects billionaires from aliens while they sleep. But her new client might be able to end the Dream War, if she can keep him alive long enough.
https://amzn.to/2rOWInp

TRISTAN & ANNA: A BACHELORS OF THE RIDGE SHORT STORY

KARLA SORENSEN

In this exclusive short story, Tristan and Anna prepare to say "I do".

ONE

THE NIGHT BEFORE

Anna

Maybe most brides would have a hard time sleeping the night before their wedding, but not me. From the moment I crawled under the soft sheets in our big bed, the one that Tristan and I had shared for the last eleven months, my eyes drifted shut, and I fell instantly into the kind of slumber reserved for people truly at peace with their life.

Before I went to bed, Tristan had told me he'd be right behind me, even though I knew he wouldn't stay the night.

My future husband was a stickler for tradition. No surprises there.

Which is why it didn't surprise me when I was pulled from my deep, contended, at-peace-with-my-life slumber by the feel of his large hand coasting up my back, sweeping across my spine. My lungs filled slowly with a deep breath and I stretched on a happy sigh.

"What time is it?" I mumbled as I tried to pry my eyes open.

"Just after eleven," he whispered against the top of my head as he curled himself around me.

All around me was the smell of him, the sweet protective cage off his big body. Something I'd never tire of, something that never failed to warm me completely.

"I didn't mean to wake you," he said.

"Liar." I turned so that I could face him, and in the stretch of bright moonlight coming through the window of our bedroom, I could see the tiny smile on his face. I cupped the side of his cheek, felt the soft bristle of beard that he'd been growing for the last couple months. "What's going on in that head of yours?"

Tristan took a deep breath, his deeply brown, bottomless eyes searching my face in the dark. "Nothing that doesn't go through my head every time I look at you."

I couldn't stop my smile. Happiness like this didn't seem sustainable, but in the last year, he'd proven me so, so wrong, my big, quiet man.

"Tell me."

He leaned forward to place a soft kiss on my waiting lips, slid his tongue against mine before pulling back. His massive arm wrapped around my back so that I was flush against his chest, which happened to be my favorite place in the entire world.

"Don't you want to wait until my vows tomorrow?"

"No chance you'd tell me those tonight, huh?" I asked uselessly. For a solid month, I'd seen him scribbling in his notebook, erasing and starting over with a thoughtful look on his face. Every time I asked him if he needed help, he'd just give me a steady look with barely curved lips as he shook his head.

"What do you think?" he answered.

I huffed into the bare skin over his heart, but I softened my faux annoyance by dropping a kiss over the steadily pounding rhythm. If I thought too hard, too long about him, the kind of man he was, the way he loved me, I'd burst into tears.

Some days, it felt like too much, like I'd been slipped into some dream that I'd never be able to reconcile as reality.

My eyes pricked hotly, and I buried my nose against his chest.

"What are you thinking in that head of *yours*?" he asked. His hand moved up and down in a steady, never faltering pattern and I relaxed even further. When I didn't answer, he hooked his hand over my shoulder and pulled me onto my back, so he could see my face. "Are you stressed about tomorrow?"

I shook my head and ran my hand over his forearm, up over the rounded curve of his shoulder. "No, Rory, Brooke, and Julia pretty much took care of everything. Did you see the tree?"

He nodded. "Looks good."

"Good? It looks like a fairy tale."

Backyard weddings, especially in the backyard of the bride and groom, weren't for the faint of heart. There was no escaping something to be done, something to be set up, last minute details to be taken care of. But between my friends, my sister-in-law, and my mother, who'd taken up wedding planning with the precision of a five-star general, there was very little for me to worry about.

Tristan's hand coasted around my waist in a slow track, and my skin began to hum in response. Maybe I should've been sleeping, maybe he should've been too, but it was impossible for him to touch me without this happening. Without the slow, inevitable build, the buzz in my blood that made me want to purr happily.

But his hand stopped over my stomach and stayed there. Fingers spread wide over my skin, only slightly rounded. I laid mine over the top of his and tangled our fingers together.

"Feel anything yet?" he asked in a hushed whisper, like he was afraid to wake eleven-week-old baby Whitfield.

I smiled. He asked me this at least three times a day, from the moment we saw the positive pregnancy test.

"Not yet."

"I still think it's a boy."

My smile grew and I shifted to face him. This was the other thing he said at least three times a day. "That's because having a girl terrifies you."

He pressed his palm even further into my skin, like he could pick up sound waves from the baby, feel it's tiny heartbeat, learn something new that all our books, all the websites we'd read couldn't tell him. "Of course, it terrifies me," he said grumpily. "She'll look like you, and then I'll have another Anna in the world to yank my heart out of my chest. How could I ever let her out of my sight?"

I laughed, only stopping when he kissed me again. I wound my arms around his neck and hitched my thigh up around his waist to deepen it. Tomorrow, he'd be my husband.

My husband.

Into his thick, long hair, which was unbound, I dug my fingers and held onto the curve of his head. Ever since we found out I was pregnant, Tristan had treated me so gently, so carefully, and tonight, that wasn't what I wanted. I knew tomorrow night, when we crawled back in bed as Mr. and Mrs. Whitfield, I'd be exhausted to my core from dancing and laughing and being with all the people who loved us so much, who were so happy for us, but tonight, we had every-thing laid out before us like the sun was just starting to rise.

Tristan's breathing picked up as he rocked his hips into mine, and a groan came from deep within his broad chest when I sucked his tongue into my mouth.

"I don't want you to hold back tonight," I whispered against his lips. "Make love to me, Tristan, and tomorrow when I walk down that aisle to you, you'll know that I can still feel where you were on my body."

"God, Anna," he said gruffly, rolling us so he was fully stretched out on top of me. He propped his full weight on his forearms, which caged around my head. So large that he blotted out the light of the moon, Tristan stared down at me like he couldn't believe that I was there. Like he couldn't believe that I was his, or that he was mine.

I wiggled my hips under him and he grinned widely when he got the hint.

Clothes. Off. Now.

He kneeled between my split legs and used his big hands to ease my sleep shorts down my legs, followed by the sensible cotton underwear. Tomorrow night would be for lace and silk, tonight was still the reality before the rest of our lives began.

Careful of my sensitive breasts, already fuller than they'd ever been, he dipped his head and licked a wide circle around my flesh.

"You taste so good," he whispered.

I was already aching, shaking, trembling with need, and he'd barely touched me. Barely done anything.

Pregnancy was the best thing ever.

Tristan's hand wound through my hair and tangled through the strands. "Will this be down for me tomorrow?" he asked gruffly. "I love seeing it down your back. Love seeing it and knowing that I get to be the one to mess it up later."

"Yes," I moaned, biting the side of his neck where I could feel the thrum of his pulse.

Tristan pushed off his boxer briefs and slid back in place on top of me, and my hands ran greedily over the ribbons of muscle under his hot skin as he moved. "Will you be my wife tomorrow?"

"Yes. *Yes.*"

He lined up and paused there, staring into my eyes as I shifted restlessly. "Forever. This is forever, Anna."

Then he thrust, hard.

I cried out and held on.

It felt so good. He was so deep. He was everywhere. How I'd ever lived without him in my life felt impossible to conceive, unreasonable now that I knew what it was like.

To be loved so fully.

To be cherished beyond reason.

To be respected for every tiny thing that made up who I was.

"Tristan," I moaned as he moved faster, held my tighter, hands dug into my skin.

"You are everything," he rasped. "Everything."

Sweat gathered at my temples, and along his spine under my fingers as he pressed his forehead tight to mine.

"I love you," I said against his lips, and he captured the words with his mouth on mine, moving with a ferocity that took my breath away. The kiss was sloppy and endless, until I cried out his name, and he yelled mine into the darkness of our room.

I wrapped my arms tight around him as he tried to catch his breath, his head buried against my neck.

"You don't have to leave tonight," I told him in between pants.

Tristan lifted his head. "It's tradition. I can't see the bride the day of the wedding." He glanced at the clock. "Which means I need to be out of here in about fifteen minutes."

I pouted, which made him laugh under his breath.

"But," I pleaded, nuzzling my nose against his, "we can break a little tradition like this one. No one will know."

I didn't want to say it out loud, because I knew it bugged him when I did, but this wasn't my first wedding. I'd done the big ball gown with the perfect bouquet of roses, walked down the aisle to a man I knew I shouldn't have married. Following an arbitrary tradition seemed … well … arbitrary at this point.

To him, and to me, the fact that this was my second marriage, and my second wedding, wasn't a point we dwelled on at all during the planning. A casual, backyard wedding would have suited us just fine even if it was my first. Getting married under the tree where he asked me to marry him was exactly what I would have chosen, no matter how many times I'd done this, no matter if I'd never done it before.

Tristan exhaled heavily and rolled to his side so he could see my face. His hand swept away the mess of hair covering my face. There was such tenderness in the gesture that I felt a lump grow larger and larger in my throat.

"I'll know," he said after a while. His voice was so low and steady, and I knew there was no budging him. It was one of the things I loved most about Tristan. It was why he loved me for so long, even though there'd been very little hope. Because he just knew. He knew that I was it for him, even if it took six years for me to see the same thing. Be able to do anything about it. Be free to be with him. "And when you walk down that aisle toward me, my Anna, I'll see you in that beautiful dress that I've never seen and feel so damn lucky that I'm the man you're walking toward. There have been a thousand moments that I've waited for with you, and we've had almost all of them by now. But this one," his hand slid over the tiny, undetectable bump under my skin, "and watching you hold our child for the first time, are the next on my list that I'm most looking forward to. I want to give that moment the respect it deserves."

Well, damn it.

I sniffled, and he wiped away the single tear that fell in an awkward trail down the edge of my nose.

"Okay," I said in a watery voice.

"Okay."

"Are you leaving now?"

He nodded, dropped a kiss on my lips. "I'll see you tomorrow."

The overwhelming reality that was him and me crested in a staggering wave. It was something I'd never get used to. Never wanted to get used to. "I love you."

"I love you too." He kissed my forehead, gently touched my stomach before leaning down to kiss that too, and then he was gone.

In the silence after his departure, I waited for the sound of the guest room door to close, and I knew he'd be out of the house before dawn. Curling into a ball, I inhaled his scent off the sheets and sighed happily.

The room was lit by the bright, full moon, and I stared at the pristine white bag hanging from the hook on the bathroom door. Inside of it was my dress— flawless, uninterrupted ivory fabric with tiny straps and a simple design that banded around my waist, cut low over my modest chest, even lower down my back.

The skirt was flowy and full, perfect for a spring backyard wedding. Also, perfect to accommodate a slightly widening waistline, a secret that Tristan and I had decided to keep to ourselves for now. Not because we didn't want to celebrate with our families, but because there was a sweetness in having this time be just about the two of us.

I pulled myself out of bed to go clean up in the bathroom, and when I was done, because I couldn't resist, I lowered the zipper on the garment bag by just a few inches, merely to remind myself that tomorrow, I'd walk down a flower-lined aisle wearing that beautiful dress, that at the end of it would be Tristan.

With a tired smile on my face, I crawled back into our big, empty bed and wished he was there to wrap me in his arms.

My hand gently rubbed my stomach and I stared down at it, still trying to reconcile that this was my life.

"Baby," I whispered. "You and I won the lottery. Someday you'll know that like I know it, but until you do, we'll just love you."

I took a moment and closed my eyes, imagined a little boy that had my eyes,

Tristan's smile, the one he showed so rarely. Imagined a girl with my black hair and his brown eyes. I didn't care what we had, we'd already decided we wanted to be surprised. That we wouldn't pick a name until he or she made their grand entrance.

How they looked, who they took after, and whatever they turned out to be, they'd be perfect.

And with my eyes closed, sleep again came easily, because I knew what would happen after the sun broke open in the sky.

TWO

THE DAY OF

Tristan

U p until thirty seconds ago, everything had been perfect.

Up until thirty seconds ago, I was so happy that I almost felt embarrassed. My smiles were easy, my laughter was given freely to almost anyone who approached me among those gathered in our backyard.

The sun was bright and warm, only a few puffy white clouds breaking up the sky. There was just enough of a breeze pushing through the branches of the aspen trees along the back of our property that I could hear the leaves through the happy chatter.

And the sprawling branches of the tree where Anna and I would get married looked like something out of a fairy tale, just as she'd said. White lights dripped down like strips of sunlight, were wound around the branches and the trunk so that even when the sun went down, the whole area would be lit.

It was impossible to believe that our yard had been transformed into something so magical.

Then again, it was also impossible to believe that my brother Michael just walked up to me with a chicken under his arm and a nervous look on his face.

"Why are you carrying Petunia?" I asked.

"She has a *name*?"

I crossed my arms over my chest. "Of course, she has a name. They all do. Anna likes to talk to them when she pulls the eggs out."

He swallowed. "Just hear me out."

My eyebrows lifted slowly.

Behind him, my three-year-old niece Piper poked her head out and gave me a wide-eyed look that roughly translated to *uh-oh*.

"What happened?" I asked when he didn't speak.

"I was showing the kids the chicken coop."

763

"Okay."

"The rooster is *big*," Piper said in a dramatic whisper.

I made sure I was smiling when I looked down at her. "He is, kiddo. His name is Wentworth."

She blinked.

Michael cleared his throat, not interested in the Jane Austen hero that Anna named our rooster after.

"So, uhh, Wentworth or whatever the hell his name is, came charging at me and I got a little freaked out." He licked his lips and shifted Petunia under his arm. Her brown speckled feathers looked out of place against the navy blue of Michael's suit, which matched mine. He was the only person standing up for me, and Rory, Anna's sister-in-law would be the only person standing up for her. Or maybe I'd have an empty spot next to me depending on what was about to come out of his mouth next.

"And..." I said slowly.

He sucked in a quick breath. "And I thought he was going to like, eat my children or something, so I picked them up because they were screaming and scaring the chickens and that damn cock was flapping his wings and I wasn't really paying attention, and Piper got her foot stuck in my jacket pocket."

I narrowed my eyes. Piper blinked again.

"I sorry, Uncle Tristan," she whispered.

Michael's eyes pinched shut. "It's not your fault, sweet pea. It's daddy's fault."

She nodded solemnly and then ducked behind his legs again. Petunia clucked unhappily.

"What *happened?*"

"Petunia ate Anna's ring," he blurted.

"What?" I yelled.

He cringed. Then I cringed, because a couple guests looked over at us. Slowly, I inhaled, imagining the pristine gold circle that we'd picked to curve around her vintage engagement ring.

I pointed at the chicken. "That chicken ate her ring."

"Yes," he said quietly.

"Michael," I warned. I didn't even know what I was warning him about, but it felt like something I needed to do.

His face was turning a sickly shade of green.

"I ... I think it got caught on the edge of Piper's shoe, and when I pulled it out of my pocket, it fell on the ground. I didn't notice the ring was down there until Petunia got this *crazy* look in her beady little eyes. What kind of chicken eats jewelry? You got some psycho birds here, brother. Rooster attacking my children, a ring-eating chicken," he muttered. "Why couldn't you guys just get a dog like normal people?"

I pinched the bridge of my nose. In about fifteen minutes, the guests would take their seats, and I'd take my place next to the minister underneath the tree, where I'd wait for the love of my life to walk to me.

And her ring was inside Petunia the chicken.

"Why is Michael holding a chicken?" my friend, and soon to be brother-in-law Garrett asked as he walked up to us. Behind him were our friends Cole and Dylan.

I gestured at my brother. "Please, Michael, feel free to explain."

In tandem, all three guys turned to Michael, who got even greener. Piper stuck her head out again.

"The chicken eated the ring," she cried with a big smile on her face.

Dylan's mouth popped open. Cole tipped his head back and muttered something under his breath. Garrett's head swung between me, Michael and the chicken.

He pointed. "It's in there? My sister's wedding ring is in there?"

I nodded slowly.

"In the *chicken*?" he clarified.

Michael squared his shoulders. "Tell Tristan to keep his stupid rooster under control and maybe this wouldn't have happened."

Garrett burst out laughing. Dylan fought a smile. Michael looked like he was going to pass out, but probably because I was giving him a glare so potent that his balls probably shriveled up. Cole put a consoling hand on my shoulder.

He took charge. "Okay, this is what we're going to do. Michael, go put the chicken in the smaller coop by herself. That way when she shits, you get to be the lucky guy to sift through it. Tristan, you go take a walk for a couple minutes and get your head right again. Garrett," he pointed, "shut up, this isn't helping."

Garrett held up his hands but did as Cole said. Michael gave me one last look over his shoulder before heading back to the chicken coops I'd built a few months ago when Anna said she thought she might like to have some.

Oh, how I regretted that now.

Dylan slugged me on the shoulder. "It'll be fine, don't worry."

I nodded. "Thanks."

"Good luck." He went to find his seat next to his wife Kat, who was waiting with a happy smile on her face. She waved at me, and I lifted a hand in return.

Garrett gave me a back-thumping hug. "Sorry I laughed."

"I expect nothing less from you," I told him with utmost sincerity.

He grinned and wandered toward the lines of chairs facing the tree.

Cole gave me a serious look. "You okay?"

I took a deep breath and nodded. "I will be. I know it's just a piece of jewelry. It's replaceable, but..." I shrugged helplessly. "I wanted everything to be perfect."

"No reason it still can't be," he said. He looked around at the yard full of people who loved me and Anna, who wanted nothing but happiness for us. "This looks like as perfect a day as I can imagine for you two. Ring or no ring."

He nodded and walked away, leaving me alone for what seemed like the first time all day. Making sure I had time, I glanced at my watch before I walked beyond the chairs and past the tree so I could take a couple minutes to just breathe.

This wasn't what I wanted to be thinking about less than ten minutes before I needed to take my spot.

I wanted to be thinking about Anna.

I wanted to be thinking about what she'd look like.

I wanted to be thinking about the sheer enormity of the fact that tonight, when I pulled her into my arms, she'd be my wife.

My wife.

The woman I'd loved for so long, so impossibly, hopelessly long, was going to be my wife. And I was going to be her husband.

For some reason, it surprised me that those labels might make it feel so different. But it did. Writing my vows to her had been far more difficult than I'd ever imagined. How was I supposed to put into words what I wanted to promise Anna? How was I supposed to sum it up into a few lines, said out loud in front of a hundred people, when she was the only one who needed to hear them?

If I could've gotten away with two lines, I knew what I'd say.

Whatever may come, Anna, I will be there. That is my vow to you.

But that wasn't enough. It felt like I'd never be able to articulate my love for her properly. She often said the same thing to me. We were so equally yoked in how we felt.

I leaned back against the tree and took a deep breath, practicing the words in my head for the thousandth time.

Nothing in my life is clearer than you.

You are my vow. My love for you will never wane, will never waver, will never dim.

Every moment that I draw breath, I will support you, respect you, fight for you and for the things that matter to us.

Whatever may come, Anna, I will be there. It's a promise that I'll never break, will never go back on, will never regret.

I love you, and I choose you, today and every day.

The ring didn't matter.

I took a long breath and knew that she'd feel the same way.

Carefully, I leaned down and plucked three of the longest strands of grass I could find. My fingers were steady as I wound them together in a tight braid and wrapped the edges in an impossibly tight knot.

The minister poked his head around the edge of the tree and gave me a kind smile. "Are you ready?"

My chest expanded on a deep, steadying inhale and I nodded. I followed him around the tree and carefully tucked the grass ring into the pocket of my navy suit, then straightened the burgundy tie that Anna had chosen.

Feeling generous and far more centered, I gave Michael a rueful smile and he returned it as he joined me.

From beyond the line of chairs filled with smiling people, I saw Rory start her slow walk down the aisle. She grinned at me, then winked at Garrett where he was sitting next to his and Anna's mother, Kathleen, in the front row.

Kathleen was already dabbing at her eyes.

My heart was seconds away from exploding in my chest from the complete, mind-numbing torture of waiting to see her. I had to force myself to breathe evenly, and my fingers started tingling when the minister motioned for the guests to rise from their seats.

This is it, this is it, this is it, I chanted silently.

My head lifted and there she was.

Any air I'd had filling my lungs was gone. Poof.

She'd taken it.

Her lips spread into a wide smile and my vision blurred instantly, the press of tears hot and insistent, but I breathed slowly as she started in my direction.

She was holding flowers and wearing a dress in ivory, something I'd pay attention to later, but all I could see was her face.

Her perfect, smiling face, tears spilling unchecked down her cheeks.

I sniffed as one of my own fell.

Her hair was down, and my heart was hers, and the moment was perfect.

No, the ring didn't matter.

Anna stopped to hug and kiss her mom, who was weeping audibly. It registered finally that about half the guests were already crying.

She took her place in front of me, mouthing, *I love you.*

I love you too, I mouthed back.

"Dearly beloved," the minister started, and with those two words, our forever began.

The End

ABOUT THE AUTHOR

Karla Sorensen is a wife, mother, writer and life-long hater of folding laundry. She lives with her husband, two sons and big, shaggy rescue dog in Michigan.

Website: http://www.karlasorensen.com/
Facebook: http://www.facebook.com/karlasorensenbooks
Instagram: http://www.instagram.com/karla_sorensen

ALSO BY KARLA SORENSEN

The *Three Little Words* series

By Your Side

Light Me Up

Tell Them Lies

The *Bachelors of the Ridge* series

Dylan

Garrett

Cole

Michael

Tristan

Standalone

Hooked (cowritten with Whitney Barbetti)

The Bombshell Effect (Coming on June 14, 2018)

COCKY MAFIA

RACHEL VAN DYKEN

Chase Abandonato loses his cockiness as his wife goes into labor reminding him of everything he's lost...

EXTRA EPILOGUE EULOGY

Chase

I gasped awake, sweat dripped down my chest as I reached across the bed. Empty, it was empty. And it happened, faster than I could imagine, the pain, the agony, the thought that maybe it was a combination of the worst nightmare of my life followed by my greatest dream.

"Chase!" Luc yelled my name.

It jolted me out of my pity party though my adrenaline was still pumping loud as my brain told me lies that my heart wanted to burn to the ground.

Not good enough.

She'll leave too.

I squeezed my eyes shut and ran in the general direction of her voice, she was in the bathroom, holding her very swollen belly. Fear gripped every part of my body until black spots appeared in my line of vision.

Fear had always been my friend because I'd never recognized it for what it was, because I'd never truly experienced its truth until I was forced to relinquish control to the universe, to a God who would send me to Hell given the chance, to a darkness that was ready to welcome me with every stolen breath.

Fear was putting my trust in the untrustworthy — it was watching my wife nurture a soul I didn't deserve — it was praying that the ones I forced to leave this earth wouldn't be counted against me — against my offspring.

Because it was what I deserved.

But them.

Never them.

"What's wrong?" I appeared calm, but my heart was slamming so hard against my chest you'd think it was trying to break through my skin. "Is it the baby?"

Luc wiped a tear, "Uh I think? I don't know, maybe it's just my imagination but, I keep getting weird contractions, like stretching across my stomach."

I was fucking out of my element for once in my life.

I squeezed my eyes shut and tried to think, then opened them when I heard her sniffle again and wrap her arms around her middle in the protective stance I knew she wasn't even aware she was doing. God she was going to be an incredible mom.

Singing our baby lullabies and making chocolate chip cookies while I slit people's throats.

I gave my head a shake. "Do you want me to call Sergio?"

She chewed her bottom lip.

"You're hesitating, you're not sure, I'm making the call—"

"—but," She grabbed my arm. "What if it's a false alarm."

I pulled her into my embrace and kissed her forehead. "Then I'll rub your feet until you fall asleep."

"You've gone soft you know," She winked.

I didn't laugh.

I was too freaked out.

I stared into her trusting gaze. Unbelievable that she'd look to me out of all the people on the planet. My fears weren't unfounded, I didn't deserve her —but that didn't mean I wasn't going to do everything in my power to keep her.

"Our secret." I finally whispered as she wrapped her arms around me as best she could. I rolled my eyes and picked her up like she weighed nothing, she'd gained weight but if you looked at her from behind you'd think she was this tiny little waif, almost like the baby was stealing every ounce of water and fat her body possessed in order to sustain itself. I asked if it was normal at least once a week, and then the doctor would say something like, she's gained fifty pounds, I think she's going to be okay.

I didn't see it.

All I saw was beauty.

My baby.

Both of them.

Shit, I wouldn't survive this again.

And she wanted kids, plural, not singular.

My heart sped up a little faster as I deposited her on our bed and made a quick phone call to Sergio.

"Not again" He yawned, "Could you at least keep your midnight killing sprees to once a week? People need to sleep! I'm people by the way and swear on Tex's life if you're just worried about the baby because you heard hiccups I'm changing my number."

I growled into the phone.

He sighed. "Fine, what's going on?"

"Contractions," I hissed, "She says they're different than before and she's embarrassed to go all the way to the hospital and have it be—"

"—I'll be there in five."

Thank God he lived down the street.

"Thanks, man." Yup, still felt weird to say thank you but there I was, ready to slit my own wrists just so he could make a house call.

Things change.

They have no choice but to change, I just didn't realize how much I'd be a part of the change. I still battled, I battled like hell with the demons in my head and the love that tried to surge into my heart.

And I knew without a doubt if I was on my own.

If I didn't have her.

I wouldn't have made it another day.

Possibly another ten minutes.

I ended the conversation and went downstairs to open the door right when Vic rounded the corner and handed me a newspaper then started making coffee.

I groaned, took the newspaper and then checked the time. It was six in the morning, too early for me, but right on time for the vampire who refused to leave our family's side like we actually wanted him around when we had more important things to do.

He grabbed a bagel.

I watched with amusement as he pulled one out, the entire hole was cut out like it needed to make room for something. I snorted into my coffee, completely out of character for me when he continued to stare at it like he'd purchased defects from the grocery store.

"What the hell?" He looked over at me. "Do I even want to know?"

"I'd probably throw that one away." I nodded seriously, "Then again maybe you're into that sort of thing, I try not to judge."

"I miss grumpy Chase." He tossed the bagel into the toaster completely against my advice.

"Yeah well," I sighed, "He's still in there so I'd watch your back."

"Trust me, I know, you could smell the bleach from ten miles away."

I just shrugged. "I protect what's mine."

"But is it completely necessary to dissolve their bodies with acid?" He wondered aloud.

"Necessary? No." I sighed. "But it's a fucking joy hearing them scream."

"Monster." He seemed amused.

"Thank you." I smiled and then walked to the door, opening it just as Sergio was about to knock.

He scowled. "Stop being creepy."

"Are those joggers?" I pointed down at his black and white Adidas pants with my coffee cup.

He glared like he was seconds away from putting a bullet through my chest. "I was in bed you jackass, and Val was naked, as in no clothing on her perfect body so if your wife isn't actually in labor I'm taking one of your thumbs just to remind you that I'm still scary as fuck."

"Noted." I gulped knowing he would do it, but he'd have to actually get through me first, and I'd been doing all the fighting lately while his fighting took place online.

Sergio stepped in the contemporary one level house we'd moved into a few months back. It was a stark contrast to what I'd been living in.

Everything reminded me of life.

From the white marble floors to the high ceilings and wood beams to the indoor garden that I surprised Luc with so she always had herbs to cook with.

I inwardly smiled as Sergio looked his fill and then headed down the hall toward the master suite.

The same one that had a connecting plunge pool, jacuzzi, and floor to ceiling windows that pulled back to give Luc access to the backyard.

She never asked for any of it.

I could have moved her into a one-bedroom shithole, and she would have found something beautiful about it.

But I wanted to give her it all.

She cried for two hours when she saw our master bedroom. I was in agony thinking she was upset when she was just so thankful that when her tears ran dry, she jumped me so hard and fast I nearly got a concussion from the marble floor.

"Luc," Sergio smiled brightly down at her.

She had that effect on people.

And pregnancy only made her more... beautiful, caring, just... good. Fuck she was so good.

Her hair was longer trailing down past her shoulders in healthy waves as she sat up and puffed out air between her teeth. "I'm so sorry Sergio, I'm probably being ridiculous."

"Never apologize." He cupped her face like she was an angel as if he hadn't just threatened me downstairs, then again, she had that calming effect on everyone including Nixon who seemed more pissed off than normal now that the De Langes were refusing to cooperate. The man was ready to raise Hell, and I was more than happy to oblige him.

"Where does it hurt?" Sergio asked, she explained the contractions, he started timing them and then gave me a weird look.

"What?" My heart thudded to a stop. "What's wrong?"

"Well, I think she's in labor, but... she must have a really strong pain tolerance because those contractions are extremely close together." He felt her stomach. "I need to see how far she's dilated."

"Like hell you will!" I roared.

"Chase," Luc gripped my arm with her hand, tears in her eyes. "Please?"

I pulled out my gun pointed it at Sergio's head and said through clenched teeth. "You look, then you touch only as long as you need to touch, anything suspicious and I shoot off your right ear, got it?"

"Not my left?" He rolled his eyes as Luc tried kicking off her shorts.

I gently leaned down and helped her pull the silk past her ankles and then put the blanket over her body and did the same with her lacy underwear. I really shouldn't be getting turned on, but my body was more than ready to help that baby come out by any means necessary.

She winked at me while I tried to keep myself in control of every sexual instinct I had when it came to her smooth skin.

"All right," Sergio was all business as he lifted the blanket, "I need you to pull your knees up a bit to your chest, yup just like that," He ducked his head, and I literally saw his blood on my hands, wanted to end his life while I waited. He reached. She moved and hissed out a harsh breath.

His expression went from calm to something I couldn't really identify.

"Chase," he said in a low voice. "The hospital, her doctor, it's a thirty-minute drive in early morning traffic."

"I know this. Why are you telling me this?"

He eyed me and then her. "She's dilated to a nine."

"Really?" She perked up like she was proud of herself while I was ready to slam my face and his through a wall. "See I really am mafia."

I gave her a pleading look and then waited for Sergio's next words.

"I'll deliver her."

Yeah, knew it was coming.

"Her?" I repeated. "It could be a he?"

"You're right, but I keep praying God curses you with a girl who drives you insane and tries to sneak out on her sixteenth birthday, he owes me one so fingers crossed."

"As long as the baby's healthy," Luc said in a dreamy voice while I made a mental calculation of all the things that could go wrong.

"Grab one of the med boxes." Sergio quickly stood and went over to the bathroom to wash his hands.

I grabbed a med box from the closet and propped her up on a few pillows. "Are you okay? Do you need anything right now?"

Luc's eyes filled with tears. "Do you remember our wedding?"

I sighed touching my forehead to hers as Sergio grabbed the box and moved around the room, I heard the sound of metal supplies, the ripping open of packaging that I knew he'd use to make an IV for her, all the things I didn't want to happen were happening. And I had no control over it.

"Of course I do," I whispered, trying to keep the fear out of my voice even though I knew she could see it in my eyes. I was supposed to be strong. But it was a lie. She was my strength, and now she was going to be in pain and there was nothing I could do to stop it.

I gripped her hand so tight she winced, then relented. "It was perfect."

"You cried."

Sergio snickered.

I gave him the finger with my free hand and then kissed her forehead. "I thought you looked like an angel, and I was ninety-nine percent sure you were going to run the other direction when you saw the devil at the end of the aisle."

"I second that," Sergio whispered under his breath.

I ignored him. "I couldn't believe that you kept walking, all I could focus on was the silk fabric wrapping around your legs with each step, kissing your skin, the plunging neckline of your dress," I touched the middle of her chest with my finger and drew it down the front of her tank top. "The way your smile lit up the church," I swallowed, then touched her stomach. "And the fact that our little baby was already making an appearance. I didn't think you could get more beautiful. Clearly, I was wrong." I kissed her belly.

Tears streamed down her face. "Chase..."

"Yeah?"

"I'm glad I married the monster — I love him so much more than I could ever love the prince...."

"The story's backward."

"It's exactly how it's supposed to be." She wrapped one arm around my neck while Sergio grabbed the other and told her to hold still as he put in an IV.

He worked fast.

"I didn't mean to step on your dress." I kept trying to distract her, "But it was so long, and then all I could think about was getting you out of it."

"Which you did in the bathroom before the rehearsal dinner." She pointed out.

Sergio coughed.

I just grinned and said, "Twice."

Her laugh was like music to my ears.

"Oh, and before I forget, Vic found the bagels."

She paled and then burst out laughing. "You mean the bagel bagels?"

"I think he ate one." I wiped a tear from her eye.

"Chase!"

"What? When you're hungry, you're hungry," I pressed a kiss to her neck. "Am I right?"

"Never eating a fucking bagel again," Sergio said under his breath and then Luc nearly came off the bed as she gripped my hand, and tears streamed down her cheeks.

"That was a big one," Sergio said casually.

"You think!" I roared at him, gripping her hand while she tightly gripped mine right back.

"I see a head."

I wanted to look.

I really wanted to look.

I wanted to see life.

I'd already seen so much death in my years on this earth. I didn't mean to release her hand. She nodded to me though, and it was all I needed to squat down by Sergio.

The baby's head was crowning.

I was used to blood, gore. I expected the same.

Not this.

Just not this perfection.

"All right," Sergio looked up at her. "I need you to push once you feel the tightening of the contraction again okay?"

"Got it." She nodded and then. "I'm pushing."

"We know," I whispered as baby's head popped through, the crying was immediate.

"Two more pushes and this is going to be the easiest labor I've ever seen," Sergio said encouragingly.

She pushed again.

And again.

And then suddenly I was moving Sergio out of the way, gently of course, and holding the baby, my baby girl.

I laughed.

Sergio joined in as he took the baby from me wrapped her up in a towel then handed me scissors, I cut the cord, she had lungs on her, shit did she have lungs on her.

Sergio handed her to Luc she burst into tears immediately.

I couldn't stop smiling.

It was probably the first time I'd smiled longer than ten minutes since Mil's death, the first time I literally wasn't sure I would ever be able to wipe the smile from my face.

It felt damn good.

"Life." I croaked.

"Life." She repeated. "She's so beautiful."

She had inky black hair and a wail fit for a queen. Perfect.

"What are you guys going to name her?" Sergio was still working on Luc, cleaning up and because I read all the manuals I could I knew what came next as she kissed our girl one more time and handed her over to me.

"Violet." I whispered, "We said Violet for a girl."

Sergio pressed down on Luc's stomach as the rest of the embryonic sac came out along with enough fluid to make a lesser man pale.

Luc winced and then said through clenched teeth. "Violet Emiliana Abandonato."

Stunned, I just stared at her.

Luc, with tears streaming down her cheeks, looked over at me and smiled. "I can't hate the woman who gave me you. And you shouldn't hate the woman that gave you this."

And just like that, the final piece of my hatred dissipated as I looked down at my daughter and for the first time in a year whispered a thank you, and a prayer for my dead wife.

Maybe, just maybe, there was room for her in Heaven after all.

And I could have sworn in that moment I heard her laugh

Not one of mocking.

One of pure, joy.

And the first tear fell from my eyes onto my daughter's ruddy cheeks.

And I knew…

I knew.

I would protect this love, this very real love, with my life.

And I would kill endless people to keep it safe.

"I love you Violet."

Chase

My hands shook as I held my baby girl in my arms. It had been six weeks of pure hell, of being so paranoid of something happening to my child, my wife, that I decided it was in everyone's best interest for me to stay awake and watch everyone in my house sleep. Gun in hand, cocked, ready to go.

I had a hard time eating and my eyes burned.

The floor creaked near the door.

I held up my gun and pointed it just as Sergio walked in, hands in the air. "It's just me."

I lowered my gun and wiped my face with my left hand. "What the hell do you want?"

"I'm doing great thanks for asking." He crossed his arms and leaned against the door. "You need a break."

"Don't tell me what I need." I rasped.

"Fuck you're even more miserable to be around, and you have every reason in the world to be happy," Sergio muttered and looked into the crib and smiled. "You're lucky she looks like Luc."

"Did you need something?"

"Me? Not at all I just drove my ass all the way over here to make small talk." He grinned. "I'm here to babysit."

I shot to my feet. "Bullshit."

"I shit you not." He winked. "Val and I decided to give you guys a date night in. And before you start listing off all the reasons why you can't — let me just remind you that you have a very pretty wife who's been put through hell this last year... she was willing to die for you — the least you can do is stop with the paranoia and live for her."

I hated it when Sergio lectured me.

I also hated it when he was right. Which was usually ninety-nine percent of the time.

I hung my head. "I really don't feel comfortable with—"

"—Ready!" Luc was standing in the doorway wearing the tightest black dress I'd ever seen — it barely covered her ass, and I suddenly thanked God that she was breastfeeding because there was nothing decent about the way her breasts poured out of that thing.

"You have a bit of drool," Sergio pointed to his chin.

I flipped him off and stood. "You look..." I didn't have words. "Beautiful."

Luc's cheeks went bright pink as she sucked in her bottom lip and took a step toward me. "Thanks for agreeing to do this, Chase."

"Agreeing," I repeated then looked behind her to Sergio who was staring up at the ceiling. Bastard. "Why don't I just go get dressed then?" I was still in my jeans and a t-shirt I hadn't washed for days because I was so freaked out over leaving Luc and Violet defenseless.

Luc grabbed my hand.

I started to sweat when she tugged me out of the room.

Sergio put his hand on my shoulder as I walked past him. "It's going to be fine... Val's like a baby whisperer and I'll shoot anyone who walks into the room or breaks in through the window, ya?"

"Shoot first ask questions later."

"Always." He pulled out his Glock and turned off the safety then went to where I was sitting and started rocking back and forth. Huh, either the best babysitter on the planet or the creepiest.

Is that what I looked like? Just staring at the crib with my gun in my right hand, and my cell in my left ready to call in for reinforcements? He looked so out of place I almost laughed.

Val swept by me. "I brought books!"

"She's six weeks old." I pointed out.

She sniffed the air. "You smell. Go shower and change and—" She made a face. "Maybe do something about your hair."

Luc snorted.

"What's wrong with my hair?"

"The proper question is what's right with it." She winked and then dropped all the books on the table next to the crib and reached in to grab Violet who'd just started to fuss. "Who's a pretty, pretty, mafia princess!"

Violet giggled and looked so fucking beautiful at six weeks that I decided then and there that she was never leaving the house, and I would track down every last guy who asked to date her and shoot him in the dick.

"Hey," Luc squeezed my hand. "Stop dreaming about killing her future boyfriends."

"I'm not—"

"—Chase..." She pulled me in for a hug. "I know this is hard for you... it's hard for both of us... it's scary when you think that something so defenseless relies solely on you for life — but it's also beautiful. You need to relax. I love that you care, I love that you're forcing me to sleep in and taking care of her so I can heal, but right now, I need you. I need my grumpy husband. And I need you to put down your gun for at least five minutes so you can shower. I cooked."

I perked up. "You cooked?"

She pressed a kiss to my cheek. "Think of it as foreplay."

"Cooking's how you got pregnant... I kept walking in on you with that wooden spoon...."

She backed me up against the wall and rubbed her body against mine. My cock sprang to life so fast I had to clench my teeth and hold onto her shoulders to make sure I didn't lift that tight dress and decide to get naked in the hallway, mere feet from everyone.

"Wow, you feel..." Luc wrapped her arms around me and stood on her tiptoes then covered my mouth with her lips sliding her tongue into my mouth with slow strokes. "Good." She finished. "Hey here's a thought..."

"I'm not sure my brains functioning past that dress right now..." I fisted it in my right hand and jerked her against me, grabbing her ass with my left and picking her up. "This needs to come off before I rip it."

"Yes." She breathed as she slid down my body.

I moaned when she sauntered ahead down the hall and into our bedroom. She kicked off her high heels as I shut the door behind me.

And then she was facing me hands on hips, breasts sensitive, heavy. I took a step toward her, but she held up her finger. "Weapons off please."

"What about this one," I pointed at my cock.

"Do you have a permit?"

I smirked. "Cute."

"Hey, I'm just saying I don't want anything to go off and ruin the moment."

"If you don't take off your fucking dress I'm going to go off and ruin the moment..."

"Crude."

"Also true." I set my gun on the table, pulled two small knives from my back pocket and then peeled my shirt over my head. "Your turn."

"Oh, so now we're taking turns?"

"It's polite and I'm trying to set a good example for Violet."

"Nothing about you carrying a gun around and murdering people is a good example."

"Really?" I deadpanned. "Because the way I see it, I'm showing her not to take any shit from anyone and kill people who do. Nothing wrong with that."

Luc gaped. "You're kidding right?"

I shrugged and motioned for her to turn around.

The zipper was long, too long. Why the hell did dresses need long zippers? Why weren't there buttons or snaps like on track pants? Someone needed to invent that, so men like me didn't have to torture ourselves with the sound of a dress slowly zipping down a woman's back.

It just reminded me that clothes were in the way.

I zipped down to her ass then pulled the dress down over her hips letting it fall to her ankles and her tall black heels.

She turned in my arms and jerked me toward her with my jeans. I bit back a curse the friction was almost my undoing. Her eyes locked on mine as she slowly unbuttoned and another damn zipper.

I always imagined how I would die.

Assumed it would be looking down the barrel of a gun.

Not, death by zipper.

Death by waiting. Why the hell wasn't I doing this four weeks ago?

The minute I knew she could?

"Sergio and Val are fine with Serena," Luc whispered across my lips, her hands already tugging my jeans down.

Our foreheads touched. "Let's leave Sergio out of it since we're both half naked and I'm seconds away from burying my cock inside you, yeah?"

She gripped me with her hand and squeezed. "Yeah."

"Damn it." I slammed my mouth against hers as we stumbled back toward the bed. I hovered over her as she wrapped her legs around me. "I swear the fifth time we do this tonight I'll go slower but rounds one through four—" I slid my tongue past her lips then retreated. "Not gonna happen." She gripped my shoulders and whispered. "Good."

I thrust into her as her scream died across my lips. This, this woman was the reason I was alive... the reason I wasn't sucked into an oblivion of darkness and death.

I rolled my hips and closed my eyes as she clawed at my back and then found my mouth deepening the kiss while I moved inside her.

This woman.

Was my everything.

"Chase—"

She matched my rhythm. I knew it would be over too soon.

Six weeks.

Never again.

"I love you," I whispered as she clenched around me her nails digging into my skin my teeth grazing her neck as waves of pleasure pulsed between our bodies.

"I love you too." She locked eyes with me.

I clenched my teeth and chased my release as she clamped down her thighs and pulled me in.

And minutes later when we were both lying there staring up at the ceiling. It wasn't the sound of her screams or my ability to make her orgasm, but her light snore that brought joy to my face.

The perfect life.

I had it.

And I would die protecting what was mine.

ABOUT THE AUTHOR

Rachel Van Dyken is the New York Times, Wall Street Journal, and USA Today Bestselling author of regency and contemporary romances. When she's not writing you can find her drinking coffee at Starbucks and plotting her next book while watching The Bachelor.

She keeps her home in Idaho with her Husband, adorable son, and two snoring boxers! She loves to hear from readers!

Want to be kept up to date on new releases? Text MAFIA to 66866!

You can connect with her on Facebook www.facebook.com/rachelvandyken or join her fan group Rachel's New Rockin Readers.

Website: http://www.rachelvandykenauthor.com
@RachVD

CODE OF CONDUCT

APRIL WHITE

The first chapters of book one of the Smartypants Romance series set in the world of Quinn Sullivan's Cypher Security Systems: Shane Matthews is a PI who destroys cheaters, and Gabriel Eze is the Cypher agent whose client is in her sights. Shane's secrets become Gabriel's mission, and yet somehow, she just can't stay away...

ONE

SHANE

"If you think they're cheating, they probably are. Or you are, and you're just trying to wipe your conscience."

– SHANE MATTHEWS, P.I.

I intimidate people. It's one of my superpowers.

I learned the benefits of intimidation early. A five foot, nine inch-tall, thirteen-year-old California girl with the finely-tuned battle instincts of a dedicated RPG gamer can wield a well-timed glare like a weapon. Now in my late twenties and six-one, I had confidence, athletic ability, and superior survival skills to add to my arsenal of intimidating glares.

I also had a pretty badass array of prosthetic legs with cool functions and Swiss Army-type gadgets at my disposal. But most of my clients didn't even realize they got Black Widow with an Iron Man leg when they hired me. And the morons of dubious judgement who prowled the streets and bedrooms of Chicago certainly had no idea who was coming for them.

My other superpower was less "kick your ass" and more "drain your bank account and ruin your life," but it was dangerous enough to add a little extra steel to my spine, which also helped disguise the limp that no amount of carefully-weighted titanium could erase.

The limp and the height were the reason I'd arrived early to the little, out of the way Northshore restaurant for my date with Chicago business mogul, Dane Quimby.

I say "date" because that's what he thought it was. To me it was a job with a high probability of being mostly unpleasant, but served with a side dish of smug satisfaction.

I use the Black Widow analogy because of my Iron Man leg, but I grew up on a steady diet of Charlie's Angels reruns. Even though I'd been compared to

Jaclyn Smith, the "glamorous" P.I., I was way more Kate Jackson, the "athletic" one. My own P.I. license had taken six thousand hours and a test to earn, and as far as I was concerned, the fact that it was only legal in California where I'd lived until last year was just a technicality. To get a license in Illinois required a twenty hour training course and forty hours of firearms training, neither of which I'd done. I wasn't a fan of guns, and didn't really want my fingerprints on file with the State of Illinois, because … reasons.

So, here I was, waiting for a married guy to buy me dinner before he tried to get into my jeans. They happened to be my favorite skinny jeans, with enough lycra to make sitting possible without blood-flow constriction, and they were tucked into my super-favorite tall riding boots. The boots were flat and therefore comfortable. They also did a great job of hiding my prosthetic lower leg from Judgy McJudgersons and their stale notions of "handicaps." Someone would have to get me naked to know I was a below-the-knee amputee, and no one but my dog ever saw me naked.

Dane chose the location for our "date," which was notable for its lack of pretension and, indeed, any redeeming quality whatsoever beyond a curvy wait-ress and a cheap menu. I had nothing but respect for large-busted women, since I could only imagine the back pain and underwire bras they endured. I was just as happy with the two-dimes-and-a-piece of tape version of lingerie which kept my nipples from becoming a distraction that diminished my powers of intim-idation.

The waitress greeted Dane with an enthusiastic kiss on the cheek when he came in, and I smirked at the difference between his internet dating profile picture and the truth of him.

My date for the evening was vertically challenged, sporting blond from a bottle, and had the athletic build of a man who did his treadmill miles with the Nasdaq scrolling under his news, and the smile of a shark who negotiated deals for a living.

His eyes found me with just the slightest double-take, and I he took stock of all my visible body parts as he approached the table.

"Sophie?" He asked, wearing his version of a rakish grin. I didn't bother to point out the bit of something green stuck in his teeth. Sophie wasn't my real name, of course, because I am too paranoid to use verifiable information on the internet.

I held my hand out to shake his. "Hello Dane, It's nice to finally meet you." Dane was obviously not paranoid enough, or just exceptionally cocky, as it actu-ally was his real name. His wife hired me to discover if he'd been cheating on her, and it only took three internet searches and fifteen minutes to determine that he was on four internet dating sites and was practically a platinum card user of Tinder.

He sat down across from me and shook his head with a chuckle. "You look exactly like your picture. I guess that means everything else in your profile is true?"

It had taken me twenty minutes to hack into the website and data-mine his search histories, and another ten to build a profile to match his wish list. "Yes, I really am a tantric yoga instructor. Doesn't everyone tell the truth online?" I said vapidly.

He winked. "I can't really talk about my time in Special Forces, so I guess you could say my profile is true-ish."

It had taken thirty minutes of background checks using mostly public databases to determine he'd been drummed out of the military for misconduct his first year. "Oh wow. Were you, like, a spy or something?"

He chuckled. "You're from California, aren't you?"

You mean my best Valley Girl imitation didn't give it away? "I basically grew up on the beach." Actually, I grew up backpacking in the Sierras, but I let him keep the mental image of me in a bikini.

"I always thought I should live in Cali," he said. "I'd work out on the strand like those guys in Venice Beach, and be friends with movie stars."

The effort not to laugh out loud was costing me. "I've seen those guys in Venice. You'd fit right in," I said with a smile. My first job as an insurance investigator was in Venice and I had to navigate the gangbangers and homeless guys every day. Also, no one in California *ever* calls it Cali.

He held up a finger and did the "I'll have what she's having" thing to order a drink like mine. I smirked at the waitress's raised eyebrow. Wouldn't he be surprised when he got sparkling water with lime instead of the vodka tonic he thought I had?

"You must wonder what attracted me to you," Dane said with a knowing smile.

Actually, I was mentally calculating my billable hours and hoping to be done here in less than thirty minutes because ... round numbers. "You read my mind," I said with a low, breathy voice. To my own ears I sounded asthmatic, but experience had taught me that horny guys dig breathless women.

Dane set his cell phone on the table next to him, screen up, so I'd see how very important he was when he got all those calls and texts he was expecting.

"Your profile says you're looking for uncomplicated with a side of kinky," Dane said, leaning forward to trace the path of ice sweat down the side of my glass. Ew. His meaningful glance was all *imagine me doing this to you*, and I barely suppressed a shudder as I forced a languid smile.

"I guess that's one way to interpret my profile," I said. *The other way is to actually read the words, dumbass, which said I like simple pleasures and I'm open to trying new things.* I pushed my drink away because he'd touched it and now his cooties swirled above it like poop molecules in a public bathroom, but which Dane took as an invitation to share because he was presumptuous like that. He slid his hand down the outside of the sweaty glass with a suggestive wink. This guy had *all* the moves.

"So, tell me about tantric yoga." His hand fisted up and down the glass before he took a big gulp. To his credit, he hid his shock at the bubbly lime-water well, but I shot the waitress a grateful smile when she set the fresh drink down in front of me.

"Are you ready to order?" she asked. Dane was about to answer, but I quickly interrupted.

"Could I have a minute?"

"Sure, take your time," said Tiffani, with an "i" dotted by a smiley face sticker. She walked away with the self-assured hip-sway of a woman who knows her own appeal.

I turned my gaze back to Dane and answered his question with a slow, seductive smile. "Imagine the possibilities of a person who can hold her leg behind her head." I conveniently didn't mention that I wouldn't actually be wearing the leg that I'd be holding behind my head. I pictured my peg leg prosthetic resting on my shoulder like a wooden bat. Of course I had a peg leg prosthetic, because who wouldn't?

Dane thought my low chuckle was for him, and I could just imagine the mental images with which he was torturing himself. And because the thought of giving him even a moment of pleasure was approximately as appealing as sucking all the snot out of a dog's nose, I changed the subject.

"Tell me about yourself, Dane. What do you do? I mean now that you're out of Special Forces, there must be something you do besides work out."

He actually preened. "Oh, you know, I dabble in web development, mostly for social media."

This guy was awesome! What he really did, according to my background check and an hour's worth of research on his company, was sold digital ad space. It explained his confidence in the ex-Special Forces cover, because if you could sell the promise of eyeballs – not the actual eyeballs themselves, mind you, just the possibility that x-amount of people *might* look at your thing for the two seconds it takes to scroll past it – you could probably sell birth control to your grandmother.

"You must be really good at computers," I purred. Actually, I was trying not to giggle, and had to drop my voice to keep from choking.

"Oh yeah, baby. I'm the best."

Seriously, how had this guy ever gotten laid? *Ever?*

"Are you on Tinder?" I thought about batting my eyelashes, but decided it was too much, and I'd probably blink out a contact lens anyway.

"Of course I am. Aren't you?"

Of course he was. I shook my head and bit my bottom lip. I'd practiced the move in a mirror once and thought it made me look dim, but apparently dim was like catnip to men who lied to get laid. I looked at his phone. "Can I see your profile? I've been trying to decide if I want to join."

His grin went wide and he quickly unlocked his phone for me. "Sure," he said, as he scooted closer and showed me the app. "You get in like this, and see, here's my profile."

"That's a great picture," I said. "You look super fit." *And about a decade younger than in real life.*

"I know, right? I get a lot of matches with that pic."

"Do you mind if I scroll around for a minute, just to look?" I asked sweetly.

He waved his hand at me. "Go ahead. Just don't swipe right on any ugly chicks." *Dude, really?* Just for that I'd be swiping right on the biggest, most redneck, *Deliverance*-looking guy I could find.

Tiffani approached the table again. "What can I get you, Dane?"

I silently blessed her for her timing, and after my left-swipe on Junior No-Teeth, I navigated to Dane's notes app and about a second later, air-dropped the whole file to my own phone. He had three banking apps in his office folder, and I clicked on one randomly. The account name was ADDATA, which was his business, so I switched to the next one. Dane was ordering something off-menu with a whole bunch of substitutions, so I took a minute to look back through his notes.

I had been counting on Dane's arrogance and stupidity, and the simple statistics of probability, and neither one disappointed. The notes app from his phone included a page of account information and passwords, which listed, among other vital things, his social security number (who doesn't remember their own social?) and all his banking passwords. It took only a few more seconds to find Dane's private bank account – the one which his wife suspected paid for his "entertainment" – and another minute to transfer half the money into an account she'd already set up in her name. The wife had wanted to take it all, but I convinced her that a cornered dog was likely to bite, and she'd have a better chance of getting the house if she left him some operating cash.

"Hey," Dane said suddenly. I cursed myself for jumping, then pasted a smile on my face. "Since you have my phone, you should just put your number in my contacts."

"Oh, sure. Do you want me to put it under my first, or my last name?" I was pretty sure the answer would be neither, and he confirmed my suspicions.

"Just leave it open to that page and I'll add your name."

I typed in the number to my favorite bankruptcy specialist as he finished up his elaborate and high-maintenance order with Tiffani, and then slid the phone across the table to him.

Tiffani stood patiently, waiting for me to order. "I just need another minute. Go ahead and put his order in, okay?"

She shrugged charmingly. "Sure, I'll get his appetizer started."

"So, what do you think about Tinder?" Dane asked with a slow wink.

I bit my lip again, and realized I'd chewed off all my lip balm in my attempts to appear unthreatening. Dry lips were my kryptonite, so I re-applied, and took enough time with it to seem like a tease. "I've heard it can be hacked, and that makes me nervous. You seem pretty confident about putting your information online, though."

He shrugged. "Oh yeah, my company has the best private security money can buy. No one can touch me without setting off alarms all over the place."

I was about to ask about such mythical security, but just then Dane's phone rang. I almost reached for it automatically, but held the movement down to a flinch. I did check the screen though, and saw *Cypher Security Systems* flash as he picked it up.

"Speak of the devil," he said with a grin. "It's the security guys at work. It'll just take a minute." He answered the phone with a deep voice. "This is Dane," he said importantly.

I looked up at Tiffani and said quietly, "I don't think I can eat anything, thanks." I'd heard about Cypher Security Systems, and they actually were pretty mythical. They were the kind of company banks used to check for hacking vulnerabilities. I didn't think Dane's business was big enough to need that kind of protection.

Someone spoke briefly, and Dane answered. "At the Northside Grill, why?"

My gut clenched in a way that usually signaled lactose intolerance or an attack of the flu. I didn't like any association between Dane Quimby and Cypher Security Systems, much less one that placed me in Dane's proximity.

I stood up to pull a twenty out of my back pocket, and Dane's eyes widened as they followed me up and up and up. He scowled, and covered the phone again. "Where are you going?"

I nodded toward the phone in his hand. "You're busy, and I have to prep for a colonoscopy tomorrow."

He made a face and spoke into the phone again. "Hang on," he snarled. Then he covered the mouthpiece again. "When can I see you?"

I brightened. "Why don't I find you on Tinder and we can look for men to share."

He frowned. "To share? But I'm not gay."

I put on my saddest face. "You're not? Oh, that's too bad, because I am."

Before he could untangle that ridiculous parting shot, I handed Tiffani the twenty as I headed for the door. "Thanks Tiffani," I said brightly. "Keep the change."

"What happened to your leg?" she asked. "You okay?"

She must have seen my limp, and she looked sweetly concerned. Dane was still on his phone, and I could hear his voice rising angrily in the background. "What do you mean, you'll be right here? Why?"

"Oh yeah, it's nothing. Just a shark bite," I said with a quick glance back at Dane before I stepped outside.

I'd taken about five steps down the sidewalk when a big black SUV barreled around the corner and drove past me to screech to a stop in front of the restaurant. The passenger shot out of his seat and stalked into the building so fast I barely caught a glimpse of a good suit, dark sunglasses, and neck tattoos. The driver was still in his seat, and I could see his eyes on me in the side view mirror.

Something in those eyes locked my knees in place and forbade my legs to move.

Then the driver opened the car door, and was out on the sidewalk facing me before I could exhale.

I hadn't even registered the driver's appearance and I was already cataloguing my options. Bond? Bond Girl? Or Bond Villain? I knew I looked good tonight, and I could charm my way out of most situations, so Bond Girl was on the table. I'd worn a special knife holster on the titanium shaft of my prosthetic leg, invisible inside my boot, which gave me Bond powers of attack and defense. But I'd just emptied Dane's private cootchie fund of two hundred and fifty thousand dollars, and transferred it to his wife as payment for fifteen years of services rendered. So maybe I was actually a Bond villain instead.

But then I took a breath and actually *looked* at the man on the sidewalk in front of me.

He wasn't much taller or older than me, which made him about six two or three, and put him in his early thirties. He wore a sharp black suit tailored to make his shoulder-to-hip ratio look like an inverted triangle, and made me think quarterback instead of linebacker. He stood like a cop and dressed like a CEO, which made me think private security – and that made me think that somehow, Cypher Security was on to me.

An aura of power radiated from the Man in Black like wavy heat above a desert road. It didn't help my temperature that the guy's Idris Elba smolder threatened to set my skin and various articles of clothing on fire. For one insanity-filled moment I imagined casually walking over and introducing myself.

I must have flinched, because his hand twitched toward a holster he wasn't actually wearing. Then reality intruded on the fantasy. I was a Caucasian female alone in a predominantly Puerto Rican neighborhood in Logan Square, having just committed something akin to a felony, albeit justly deserved, standing in front of a guy who probably used to be in some form of law enforcement.

And perhaps because I must have truly gone insane, I smiled at him. It was pure reflex, like the sigh at a spectacular sunset, or the grin at a child's laughter, and was as if the pale green eyes, dark skin, and powerful build of the man in front of me composed my picture of male perfection, and my smile was the acknowledgement of having beheld it in person. He very nearly took a step toward me, then seemed to come to his senses and halted in place. It was at this point that I compounded my idiocy by accidentally waving to him as I turned to hurry away down the street.

Who waves at the guy who could probably bust her ass ten ways from Tuesday?

Finally, cold logic, survival skills, and James Bond took over control of my hands. I powered down my phone, took out the battery, and tucked both into my back pockets as I walked. I also ducked down an alley and circled back on myself twice. I never carried a purse if I could help it – my phone, keys, a credit card, my L card, lip balm, and two twenties were all I ever had on me, and even squeezing my not-insubstantial hips into skinny jeans had left room enough for those.

I half expected squealing tires and slamming doors to find me before I got to the L, but remarkably, I made it to my train unimpeded. My heart still pounded uncomfortably in my chest as I dropped into a seat, and it annoyed me that I had reacted so strongly. Was it because the Cheater McCheaterson I'd just relieved of a quarter mil had connections to Cypher Security, or was it the Man in Black who had made my stomach clench in a way that was decidedly *not* like lactose intolerance or the flu? I was almost grateful for the two young hoods who sat down across from me and leered suggestively.

Seriously boys? That's all you've got? I front-loaded disdain into my pointed glare until they got up and slid down the train, leaving me alone with my slamming heart.

I'd just hijacked Dane Quimby's phone and moved half his money into his wife's account.

How long until someone connected the dots between my "date" with Dane and the missing money?

I absently rubbed the skin above my leg socket and let my head fall back against the window of the train. I might have even tapped my head against the glass a couple of times to drown out the whooshing sound of impending doom that filled my ears.

TWO

GABRIEL

"You have to be smarter than them, talk softer, smile bigger, and let all the words roll off your back. It'll be hard, son, but someday you'll find someone who wants to see your light, and when you do, you're going to shine."

– FELICITY EKE

W ho the hell was that?
   I took another step forward, but she was already walking away – fast, like she had a place to be. She had a slight hitch in her step and I almost got back in the car to offer her a ride, but that was madness from an overactive protective gene I seemed to have inherited along with a penchant for self-destructive behavior. It didn't matter how nice the suit was, a black man in an SUV did not offer a ride to a beautiful white girl he didn't know, not even when the man in question had a British accent and an Oxford education. At a minimum, she'd call the police, and I did not need to explain my misguided chivalrous instincts to Chicago's finest tonight.

"You alright, man? Why'd you stay outside?" O'Malley asked, as he stepped out of the restaurant. Dan O'Malley had the Boston accent and tattoos of a thug, and the generosity of a gentleman. He'd been showing me the ropes at Cypher since I came onboard, and he was one of those people who made the new bloke feel welcome without doing anything particular to show it.

His voice broke the spell I was under and I tore my eyes away from the excellent view disappearing around the corner. "I'm fine. Thought I'd give you first impressions. What's your opinion of Quimby?"

"Well, Quinn's been phasing out private clients, and this one's definitely on the block. Alex is taking a look at the numbers, but my gut says the guy's a mess. His company's hemorrhaging stockholders like rats from a sinking ship, and guys who cheat on their wives lie like shag rugs. The liability's too high for us to keep untrustworthy clients."

"How do we know he cheats?" I hadn't read the client file yet, and wondered if fidelity was part of their profiles.

O'Malley gestured inside the restaurant. "The waitress said he brings a different woman in about once a week. Last one just left, actually."

I tried to shrug off the unaccountable feeling of disappointment at the thought that the lovely bird with the spectacular rear-view had already been claimed.

"The account breech that called us here is going to complicate things, since he's still technically our client, but hopefully we can sort that out soon enough. Come on, you should meet him, get a feel for what he's made of."

I followed O'Malley inside the hole-in-the-wall, and wondered how any man, much less a married one, thought he could shag a girl after a date here. The waitress was in her early twenties, and had the pouty bottom lip that made me think she practiced it in a mirror. The bloke I assumed was Quimby sat at a table in the corner, scrolling manically through his phone. He was probably about my age, and handsome enough to make up for being short in a tall man's world. His date had looked like she was over six feet tall, and this bloke didn't seem like he had the confidence to pull that off. A mystery to ponder some other time, perhaps.

We approached the table and Quimby looked up with a wide-eyed expression that had shades of panic in it. His quick glance dismissed me and landed on O'Malley.

"It's gone!" he squeaked. His voice sounded as though someone had his stones in a vice.

O'Malley didn't say a word, just arched in eyebrow and waited. A good tactic, and one I used often with squealers. I wondered idly if he'd ever been with the police.

Right on cue, Quimby answered the unasked question. "My money! It's gone!"

The waitress looked over at us from the salt shakers she was refilling and I gave her an easy smile. She looked away quickly and went back into the kitchen.

"Calm down, Mr. Quimby," said O'Malley as he pulled out his phone. "Why don't you tell Mr. Eze the details while I get our tech person on the line." O'Malley pronounced my name with the proper "Azay" inflection that told me he had a good ear for language or music.

Quimby continued talking to him as thought I wasn't in the room. "I have an account at National. It's been emptied."

"How much is missing, Mr. Quimby?" I asked.

He looked startled at my accent, then glared and spoke to O'Malley again. "I had a half a million dollars in that account!"

O'Malley turned his back and walked away a few steps to speak on the phone. I knew he was doing it on purpose, and it seemed to infuriate Quimby.

"So, five hundred thousand is missing?" My voice was deep, and I usually spoke softly enough that people had to lean closer to hear me – a useful tool for gathering information about everything from personal hygiene (unfortunately) to lipstick or blood splatter on a collar.

Quimby glared at me. "Who are you?"

"Gabriel Eze with Cypher Security."

"I don't know you. I'm going to wait until he's off the phone so I don't have to repeat myself."

I shrugged. "Suit yourself."

I adopted an at-ease posture and studied the table Quimby had shared with ... someone. I had no proof it was the lovely bird, but she was who I pictured sitting across from him. A barely-touched glass of sparkling water with a wedge of lime sat in a small puddle of ice-sweat on the table. She'd had at least one sip, but the sides of the glass were wet enough to make fingerprints unusable. She wore some sort of lip balm rather than lipstick, which, for some reason, made me think of pretty young girls and athletes instead of mistresses.

The chair had been pushed quite a way back from the table, as though a tall person had been seated there. I studied the chair-back and saw a few strands of long brown hair caught in a crack in the wood. Again, totally circumstantial – the hair could have been there for months – but the bird outside was a brunette, with thick hair she'd worn down past her shoulders. I pictured it up in a sloppy ponytail, or long and loose, spread across a pillow, and I shook myself sharply and concentrated on Quimby again.

Why him? Why would she choose him? Unless ...

"May I see your phone, Mr. Quimby?" I asked just as O'Malley returned to the table.

"I'm not giving you my phone!" He spat.

"Give him the damn phone, Quimby, we have to talk." O'Malley sounded tired and disgusted. No mean feat for a man I'd only ever seen behave in a completely professional manner.

The tone startled Quimby, and he shoved the phone across the table at me, sliding it through puddles left behind from wet glasses. I didn't pick it up. Like hell was I going to wipe the water off on the tailored suit.

The phone was unlocked and on the home screen, so I navigated to the call icon. The screen opened to a blank contact, containing a phone number and no name. I memorized the number and then searched the recent call list. There were three missed calls from "home," then about twenty minutes later, O'Malley's phone call. So, the wife calls multiple times before the mistress gets here? I took a screenshot of his call list, airdropped it to myself, and then navigated back to the home screen and slid the phone back across the table.

O'Malley was just barely keeping his temper in check, as evidenced by the jaw muscle flexing with every clench of his teeth. "Exactly how much is left in the account that you claim no one knew about?"

Quimby's voice was back up to squeaking levels. "Two hundred-fifty thousand dollars."

I started chuckling as I dialed the number I'd memorized from his contact list. "Half," I said under my breath.

"You think it's funny to have a quarter million stolen from an account I worked damn hard to fill, Easy?" Quimby squeaked angrily. Calling me Easy rather than correctly pronouncing Eze with long "a" sounds was exactly the cheap shot I expected of him. I also noted that he said fill, not earn, but I ignored him as the ringing phone in my ear was picked up by an answering machine.

"You've reached the Divorce and Bankruptcy Specialists of the greater Chicago area. Please leave a message after the beep."

My chuckle turned into full on laughter as I jerked my head at O'Malley, indicating we should leave.

"We'll be in touch, Quimby," he said, to the cocky bastard as he followed me out of the restaurant.

"What's so funny?" O'Malley asked as I climbed behind the wheel of the SUV.

"It was the wife, and she must have used the girlfriend to do it."

I had yet to figure out what Dan O'Malley thought of my work for Cypher Systems during the month I'd been employed there, but for the first time I got the sense that he might be impressed.

"Well, good for her," he said as I pulled away from the curb. "Serves him right for cheating."

ABOUT THE AUTHOR

APRIL WHITE has been a film producer, private investigator, bouncer, teacher and screenwriter. She has climbed in the Himalayas, lived on a gold mine in the Yukon, and survived a shipwreck. She and her husband live in Southern California with their two sons, dog, various chickens, and a lifetime collection of books. Marking Time, book one of her five-book time travel fantasy series, is the 2016 Library Journal Award winner, and her other works include historical mystery and contemporary romance.

Website: https://www.aprilwhitebooks.com/

ALSO BY APRIL WHITE

The Immortal Descendants series

Marking Time

Tempting Fate

Changing Nature

Waging War

Cheating Death

The Baker Street series

An Urchin of Means

Forthcoming for Smartypants Romance

Code of Conduct

ACKNOWLEDGMENTS

Thank you to all the authors who dropped everything and miraculously found the time to write original content for this anthology (in less than a week).

Thank you to Jenn and Sarah at SocialButterfly PR, who probably wanted to murder the organizer of this anthology more than once...

Thank you to Avery Flynn at RWA for liaising with us! And thank you to Cristin Harber for making the introduction and being gracious.

Thank you to all the authors, bloggers, and readers who helped spread the word!!

Thank you to Ashley Williams with AW Editing for donating your time/talents editing many of these stories, Janice Owens for her mad proofreading skillz, C.D. Reiss for designing the cover, Emma Hart for the logos and website design, Fiona Fischer for formatting and herding cats, and Lex Martin for pulling together the print-materials for promotion.

83987538R00455

Made in the USA
Middletown, DE
16 August 2018